The Suragi Tree

The Suragi Tree

Prabhaker Acharya

MapinLit

AN IMPRINT OF
MAPIN PUBLISHING

First published in India in 2006 by
MapinLit
An Imprint of
Mapin Publishing

Mapin Publishing Pvt. Ltd.
31 Somnath Road, Usmanpura
Ahmedabad 380013 India
T: 91-79-2755 1833 / 2755 1793
F: 2755 0955
E: mapin@mapinpub.com
www.mapinpub.com

ISBN: 81-88204-40-4 (Mapin)
ISBN: 1-890206-48-2 (Grantha)

Design by Janki Sutaria / Mapin Design Studio
Printed in India

Preface

I wouldn't have written this novel if Harish, my nephew, hadn't given me, for my sixtieth birthday, a Home Publishing System; and if I hadn't used up all the ink in a fortnight, writing letters and taking several print-outs of a circular; and then found that the ink tank for the machine was not available anywhere in Bombay.

The machine was something I enjoyed writing on. It had no hard disc, but one could use a floppy and save what one wrote, for future printing. So I bought a floppy disk. But as you don't write letters for 'future printing,' I decided to write a story.

Some eighteen years earlier, when I was staying at Borivli, I had had a serious attack of chicken pox. It was an awful experience, much worse than what I have described in the last part of this novel. I was alone, and the friend I was then staying with used to leave the house early in the morning and come back late at night. A friend who came to see me on the first day of fever warned me not to take any allopathic medicine; so I took no medicine, not even paracetamol to control the fever. As the fever rose, and my head started buzzing with words I could not make sense of, I got worried that I was losing control of my thoughts. So I tried to write stories—in my head, not on paper —in an effort to regain control of my thought-flow. I completed half a dozen of them. I have described this phenomenon in the novel, and also given the outline of two of the stories I wrote. The others remain in my mind, faded, and I have no desire to recollect and put them on paper.

But one of the stories, which I tried to write during my long incarceration after the fever came down, kept on troubling me. It was about my chicken pox experience—good material for a story—but somehow it did not work. The experience, I realized, needed something else to set it off.

I found that 'something else' some years later, when I went down to Koteshwar. Two of my cousins there had cut down a suragi tree. They had to cut it themselves because their workers refused to do the job—because they believed that a Yakshi, a deity whom they worshipped, lived in the tree. As chicken pox and smallpox were associated with certain female deities, I felt that I had found the incident that could react with my chicken pox experience and produce a symbolic story of crime and punishment, of sin and expiation.

What I planned to write was a light-hearted story with symbolic overtones, a story that hovers between fantasy and realism; like one of Forster's stories.

But once I started writing I discovered that I had taken on more than I had bargained for. The story threatened to grow much longer than I expected. As I was sitting one morning trying to trim and pare what I had written the previous evening, Suhas walked in. Suhas—Professor Suhas Gole—was a friend from my M.A. days who stayed in a flat above mine, and used to come down every day to look at what I was writing. He shook his head and said, "What you have on hand, I think, is a novel, not a short story. Why are you snipping at its roots, trying to convert your tree into a bonsai? Why not just let it grow?"

Suhas knew that I did not like bonsai. I think there is something cruel in turning a potentially large tree into a dwarf that would fit into your pot. So I let my story grow, though I was not sure I had the stamina to write a long novel.

After completing the first nine chapters, I shifted to Koteshwar, my village. I missed Suhas. Writing is a form of self-expression, yes, but it is also communication. You try to reach out to people through your writing. But the trouble with writing is that though it can be a more thorough exploration of one's inner being than talking, it is a bit lonesome. When you write a story, or a poem, or an essay, this is not much of a problem, for at the end of a week or a fortnight or a month, your work is ready. You can get it published, or at least show it to people. Or forget it. But to go on writing for months together, your work still locked up in you, is tough. Novel writing is a very lonely activity.

I sent Suhas the first two volumes of my manuscript as soon as they were ready. But the third volume never reached him. Santan Rodrigues, a former student of mine, was very keen to read the novel. I sent him the third volume and asked him to collect the first two from Suhas. He was to give the entire manuscript back to Suhas after reading it. Santan changed his residence then, the third volume got misplaced and could not be traced for nearly three months. By the time he found it, Suhas was in the ICU of a hospital. He died before Santan could go to see him.

To me it was a shattering blow. He was the first reader of my novel, someone whose literary judgment I trusted. He was a gifted, infinitely talented person: painter, sculptor, sportsman, and a brilliant teacher of both English language and literature. But he left nothing much behind, because he did not want to. Even for his sculptures he deliberately chose a medium that would not last—gum tape! Those Assyrian and Egyptian chariots, and a host of other things he sculpted—using nothing but gum tape except for pins for the axles of wheels—were beautiful. "How long will they last?" I asked him once, and he said, "Six months perhaps. I don't want to be burdened with my old works, you know. I just want to keep on making things with my hands."

Suhas died a couple of days after I signed the agreement for the publication of this novel. Then I lost two more of my friends. Murari—Dr Murari Ballal, economist, environmentalist, social activist and author—was a remarkable person. He had a congenital cardiac problem—a hole in the heart—and could not keep pace with even the slowest of walkers. ("I am living on borrowed time," he used to say.) But he had trekked everywhere in the country including the Himalayas, and there is not a single reserve forest in South Kanara he had not walked through. It was in his house at Ambalpady that I had read, to a small audience, excerpts from my novel when it was still incomplete. He persuaded me to shift to Ambalpady, near Udupi, to the house next to his. I did so in May. Two months later he met with a small accident while riding on the pillion of his friend's bike—he was on his way to distribute invitations to a function where his latest book was to be released. He walked to the hospital himself, got admitted and then went into a coma, from which he did not recover.

Murari was a wonderful host. 'Manasa', his house where several celebrities—writers, filmmakers, artists, musicians and thinkers—have stayed, now stands deserted. To go to the market I have to pass through its garden. Some days ago I noticed a sapling in its north-east corner, obviously planted after Murari asked me to shift to Ambalpady. It is growing well, and there is enough space for it to grow up into a large tree. Only the other day I realized that it was a tree that had become quite rare in our district now: the suragi.

The last bereavement was the demise of Shama Futehally, novelist, short-story writer, poet; and one of the warmest of people I have known. I had met her in poetry reading sessions in Bombay years ago. When my novel was accepted for publication by a Delhi publisher, but the agreement, which I was to receive 'immediately', did not come, I remembered that Shama was in Delhi. I sent a copy of the manuscript to her—it was called *Suragi Flowers* then— asking her to read it first, and if she liked it, to suggest what I should do.

Shama was shifting house, and it took some days for her to open the manuscript. Then I got this email:

Dear Prof. Acharya, I am only writing to say that today I cast aside all worries about carpenters and plumbers and took to my room with Suragi Flowers. I have only read about a hundred pages, but I cannot prevent myself from writing to you to tell you what this afternoon has been like. How I have entered your world in Nampalli, and gone to the habba and been bored in the classroom—people say the same thing happens when you read R K Narayan, but Narayan reduces everything to a toy-world. This world is life-size, and it is so very real, it makes me feel that every sentence I have ever written has an extra, unnecessary, artificial layer to it which needs to be peeled off. I rang up my friend…and I read out to her the passage about recovering from an illness and watching the new green world… How easily that could have been a too poetic passage—beautiful, but too poetic—but just the use of the words 'stacked' for the clouds, and the words 'listening with my whole skin' turn it into something one has lived—something remarkable and ordinary at the same time. I have put the book away now because I don't want it to end too soon. I don't want to have to leave this world which takes me back to my own childhood afternoons during the monsoon. Those afternoons were not particularly joyful, perhaps, but in retrospect one does realise, as the clichés tell you, that what one was living then was happiness. I will do everything I can for the book once I have read it all—I can't skip—but I have some fear that it may be too real and true and unpretentious to become fashionable in today's literary establishment. That is something from which many of us have suffered. But then no doubt there will be many many readers who feel as I do, and who are grateful for this gift, and finally that is what one writes for.

That was generous praise, over-generous perhaps, but I needed it then. I was, at that point of time, so dispirited by the delays, and the long-drawn-out battle with the editor about cuts and deletions, that I was seriously thinking of giving up writing altogether.

Shama talked to the publishers, and then felt that I should contact others too. She contacted a couple of them herself and then suggested that I should send the manuscript to Mapin. She was very ill then, but that did not come in the way of her efforts to get the novel published. I don't think I have ever come across a more generous and warm person—someone who got so involved with other people's problems that she had no time to worry about her own.

Suhas, Murari and Shama. They were the ones to whom I wanted to give the first three copies of my novel, when published. Now that they are no more, all that I can do is to dedicate it to their memory.

Prabhaker Acharya

To the memory of

Suhas Y. Gole, Murari Ballal and Shama Futehally Chowdhury.

Contents

PART I

A Knock on the Door

ℒ

What we call the beginning is often the end
And to make an end is to make the beginning.
The end is where we start from.

T.S. Eliot

Deivas and Devatas

❧

I admit that the knowledge I flaunt is often shallow. I can hold forth, quite impressively, on a variety of subjects but there is no depth in my knowledge. Perhaps I am not really interested in many of the subjects I talk on. What interests me is the talk itself, the act of communication, the flow and clash of ideas.

So I found myself talking, one evening, to Mr. Fahme, an officer of the Iranian Consulate, on something I knew very little about—Hinduism as an evolved religion. That was way back in the early seventies when the Shah ruled over Iran, and hordes of Iranian students came to Bombay for higher studies, and spent their time chasing girls or playing soccer; and officials of the Iranian Consulate moved about in air-conditioned cars, and gave parties where good scotch flowed like water.

The party was at the house of another officer of the Iranian Consulate. There were a dozen people around, including four Indians, three of us college teachers. The Iranians, apart from the two Vice Consuls and their wives, were all doing some study or research at the University—which perhaps explained the choice of the Indian guests. I was sitting with Mr. Fahme in a corner. People came and joined us, said a few words and then moved away. Ms. Shums, a tall graceful woman with graying hair, who was trying to wheedle a Ph.D. in history from the University of Bombay after failing to do so in Bonn and Paris, joined us for a while. She glanced at Hasan, Fahme's younger brother, who was chatting with a very pretty Indian girl, and sighed. "Nice couple," she said, "but you know marriage with a Hindu will not be recognized in Iran? Because Hinduism is not a revealed religion, it's only an evolved one; and you have no Holy Book."

"That's not quite right," I said. "Hinduism is an evolved religion, yes, but it's also a revealed religion; a religion that has evolved through Revelations. We *have* our holy books, Ms. Shums. The *Vedas*, for example, among the oldest books in the world. Composed long before writing was invented, they are called *apaurusheya*—not created by man—because they are believed to have come directly from God. Then there is the *Bhagavad-Gita*, a book all Hindus swear by."

Then the talk veered to monotheism and so on, and Ms. Shums got up and joined another group. And I found myself talking to Mr. Fahme on the way Hinduism had grown and evolved over the millenia, and its absorption of primitive pantheism.

I told him about deities and spirits that lived in stones and trees, and were worshipped by the common people. Hinduism, when it started spreading, did not try to sweep aside these existing pantheistic beliefs and practices like Christianity did centuries later. At the core of Hinduism, I told Fahme, was the conviction that there were more ways than one of worshipping God. Devotion of all kind was valuable and nature-worship could be a way of worshipping the God of Nature. So Hinduism accepted pantheism, with the proviso that the pantheistic deities were subservient to God.

Some of these spirits were benevolent and kind, some aggressive and easily provoked. I told Fahme about Kalkutika, one of the most irascible among the spirits of our district, who harassed those who angered him a great deal. I narrated a story I had heard in my childhood, of one Mr. Soans, the 'Drill Master' of the school in my father's school days. He was a Christian but like many converts he found it easier to give up his Hinduism than his primitive pantheism. There was a Kalkutika stone in his backyard which was worshipped by many of his neighbours and, it was suspected, by him too. The Church could not tolerate this and pressurized him to throw that stone away. That very evening, and for the next two, his house was stoned, human excreta thrown into his kitchen, and no one could see who were throwing them. He brought some of his students to guard his house but they ran away the moment the rain of stones started. The troubles stopped only after he reinstated Kalkutika, with due ceremonies, in his backyard.

"But that is bad," said Mr. Fahme, looking quite shocked, "that's evil. How can any religion tolerate such evil?"

"Are we all good, Mr. Fahme?" I asked, quite sharply, and was myself surprised by the needless asperity of my tone. "We are good at times and bad at other times," I said, "some of us are tolerant and kind, some vindictive and cruel. But God created us all and gave us our place in the scheme of things. Why should we think that He did not create other beings, capable of both good and evil like us, invisible to us but with their own place in the scheme of things?"

"But...I'm so sorry, please excuse me," said Mr. Fahme, his Persian politeness becoming a little painful, "but how can we call these beings deities, and worship them?"

"Deities and worship are mere words," I said. "They can be misleading because they can mean different things in different cultural contexts. In Kannada for example..."

I talked about the different words we used in Kannada for different deities. The word *'devaru'* with the respectful suffix 'ru'—like the use of capital G in English—meant God, and *devatas* were the gods. We had a host of these devatas, I said, who were like the Greek or Roman gods: Indra, the king of gods, like the Greek god Zeus, and so on. The local deities were called *deivas*. They were worshipped, not with Vedic hymns and prayers like God or the gods, but with votive offerings of coconuts, cocks and goats. Some of them could be aggressive and violent, even vindictive, when roused, but they were not evil. The evil spirits were called *devvas* and they were never worshipped.

"So the problem, Mr. Fahme," I said, "is only a linguistic one. There are different kinds of deities and different kinds of worship. The villager who 'worships' a deiva does not feel the way you or I feel when we worship God. It's a different kind of relationship altogether. A much more intimate one because the deivas don't reside in a distant heaven or in the sanctum sanctorum of a temple. They live in trees and stones, close to people, and can be approached when people are in trouble."

I then spoke of *darshana*, the fascinating ritual in which the deivas manifested themselves and spoke to their worshippers. It was an eerie ritual that gave us, the children, gooseflesh. The pulsating music of drums and pipes was simply hypnotic. As the *patri*, the medium through whom the deivas spoke to men, was putting on his ceremonial dress—a tight-fitting pair of red trousers with hundreds of tiny brass bells—the pipes would whine in an agony of ecstasy that sent shivers down our spine. As two men held and helped him to put the dress on, he swayed and shook in tune with the music, which rose to a crescendo as he donned the sacred brass anklets, a sign that the deiva had finally taken possession of him.

The dialogue between the deiva and the people was dramatic, and at times comic. The deity listened to people's complaints, responding with loud throaty 'hoon's', at regular intervals, the sound, a sign of patient listening, finally rising to a bull-like bellow indicating that *he* now wanted to speak. But though people were deferential, they were never intimidated, except of course when they had done some wrong. You might, for example, hear someone say, "Look, I gave you a cock last year, but one of my bullocks died, and our cow, which used to yield good milk and was docile, now kicks if her udder is touched. What kind of a deiva are you?"

When there were disputes or thefts, the villagers often complained to the deivas rather than to the police and got justice on the spot. "I know who has stolen your hen," the deiva would say threateningly, "he has already cooked and eaten it. Let him pay you five rupees for the chicken and place one rupee at my feet as fine; or else the chicken will turn into poison and he will die vomitting blood." Few people could digest chicken after such a threat.

"This pantheism," I said, "meets and satisfies some of the deep-felt social and psychological needs of the people. The deivas act as links between man and nature. The villager who believes in them does not feel that he is all alone in an indifferent or hostile world. He is surrounded by spirits, and can turn to them for help or guidance."

"You seem to have read and thought a lot on this subject," said Mr. Fahme, and before I could protest, added, rather hesitantly, "But two questions, please: do you really believe in these—deivas? Do they really exist? And— doesn't this belief in deivas come into conflict with the belief in One God?"

"The second question is easily answered," I said. "No, it doesn't. These deivas are subservient to God. If they have any power, it's only because God has permitted them to have that power. Even the illiterate deiva worshippers are convinced of that. The first question is difficult to answer. You know, Mr. Fahme, some of these spirits are quite fascinating. There is a *suragi*—a lush green flowering tree—behind our house in our village. People believe that there is a *Yakshi*—a dryad-like spirt—living in that tree. When I was a kid I used to go and sit under that tree and read for hours. And I had this funny feeling that there was some Presence in that tree—someone—or something— that liked my sitting there quietly and reading. As if the tree had a soul. But if someone had asked me then the question you asked, I would have said, what nonsense, I don't believe in any deivas—I was awfully anti-superstitious then. I am not so sure today. Belief is a funny thing. You think you believe in something, but suddenly you find that your belief has no strength. You think you don't believe, that it's all irrational, and then you find, in the deep recesses of your mind, seeds of that belief sown God knows when."

We had left the party, and I was in Mr. Fahme's car when I said this. He dropped me at my bus stop. As I got out of the car I said, "Do the deivas exist? I don't know. Perhaps I should say, yes, they exist, because people believe in them."

Amma and Mariamma

❧

Good scotch, they say, does not give you a hangover. Not true. I woke up the next morning with a splitting headache, which worsened as I thought of my previous evening's performance. What right had I to bore poor Mr. Fahme all through the evening? When the other guests were enjoying themselves with the usual light-hearted party banter, what stupidity made me go on and on, on a subject which was of no interest to those Iranians and of very little interest to myself? A real gasbag, that was what I was.

I wondered about that perversity, that quirk in my nature, which made me, so often, expose my ignorance and shallowness by talking on things I knew very little about. Hinduism and Pantheism! God, there were at least a dozen subjects I could have talked more intelligently on. And yet there I was, making a fool of myself...

I realize now that I did not understand the situation fully then. You don't really understand your own mind. You might know, at best, what is on display but you have no clear idea of what you have stocked in its dark cellars, or carelessly dropped in its remote corners. Quite a bit of one's knowledge comes incidentally, unsought, through random readings, by hearing what one did not listen to and seeing what one did not look for, by merely living one's life with a mind open to impressions and experiences. When you talk about things you haven't thought much about, and feel an excitement disproportionate to your known interest in the subject, you are perhaps on a voyage of discovery: an exploration of the cobwebbed corners of your mind where these bits of knowledge lie, waiting to be picked up; an exploration of what you did not know you knew.

I was not aware of this then, nor when I started this narration two days ago. For writing too is a voyage of discovery, a more thorough exploration than talking; but less enjoyable, because it is like bouncing a tennis ball on a wall rather than playing with an opponent across the net.

On that bleak morning of headache and regret I wondered how I had managed to say so much on a subject I knew so little about. Where did those ideas come from? Then I realized, with surprise, that many of the things I said had come from arguments I used to have twenty years earlier, at the ripe age of twelve, with someone for whose knowledge and intelligence I had little respect: my mother.

We used to have regular arguments then. I was a precocious youngster full of reforming zeal and my mother a die-hard unthinking traditionalist. I recollected, with amazing clarity, the argument I had with her on the day the *pujari*—the priest—of the Mariamma temple came to our house, ostensibly to invite us to the temple's annual festival but mainly to collect our donation. My mother's contribution, in the form of coconuts and cash, was generous, and the pujari, belonging to the bangle-seller community, went away contented. But I was furious. Why did we contribute to such festivals? Didn't she know that they sacrificed cocks and goats to Mariamma? Weren't we against animal sacrifice?

"We have to donate because we belong to the village," said Amma. "It is Mariamma who guards this village, protects it from plague and smallpox. She was here long before we came. We can't tell her, now that we Brahmins have come, she has to become a vegetarian."

"But you always say that bloodshed is bad, killing any creature is a sin. Can't you see that the money you gave can be used to buy animals for sacrifice?"

"Mariamma guards our village," Amma said, with an evident effort not to lose her temper. "If you are threatened and want someone to guard you, do you ask that person whether he eats chicken or meat? Do you refuse to pay him because he might buy chicken and meat with your money?"

My mother's logic was crazy but effective. She could always silence her opponents with it, and by the time they realized its fallacy the argument would be over.

But I was still upset. "You are superstitious," I said. "Mariamma might be the village guardian, but what about the argument you had with father yesterday? What about Kalkutika and the Yakshi who are supposed to be there right at the centre of the land father bought a year ago? We can't use that land, turn it into an orchard or a garden, when these deivas are there. So he wanted to shift that Kalkutika stone to a corner and cut down that suragi tree, but you wouldn't agree. Why? They are not our village guardians!"

"I had to argue with the father yesterday," said mother in exasperation, "and today with the son. Kalkutika and Yakshi were there, in that stone and that tree, long before your father bought that land or built this house. How can we throw them out now?"

"But they are not even good deivas," I said, "specially Kalkutika. You have told me such horrid stories about his mischief. How can we allow such deivas to be worshipped?"

"Don't talk nonsense," said Amma with asperity, partly because my little brother was crying in his cradle inside, and also because she was worried about Kalkutika's likely reaction to my remark. "Are we all good? Are we always good? God created us as we are, and He created the deivas too. They have their passions as we have ours, though they have no bodies. They are not evil, they are good to those who are good to them."

"You talk as if they really exist. But they don't exist. They can't be seen, and they are not mentioned in the scriptures. How do you know they exist?"

"They exist, because people believe in them," mother said.

Sitting in my room at Dadar with a splitting headache, twenty years later, I tried hard to recollect that argument and compare it with my previous evening's rambling talk. I was quite surprised by what I discovered. I had often caught myself, in the past, arguing vehemently, taking diametrically opposite stands; arguing *for* something one day and then, a few days later, arguing against it with someone who strongly advocated it, even using some of the arguments of my earlier opponent which I had myself convincingly demolished. Perhaps I hated strongly held opinions and thought, like Yeats, that "opinions are accursed". But with Fahme I had used not only my mother's arguments—which I had never accepted—but her very words, and in one place, even her tone. Do we always speak for ourselves or do we, sometimes, merely watch as others speak through us?

Kalkutika

About that argument father had with mother: It was too brief perhaps to be called an argument, because father had learnt, through experience, the futility of arguing with her. The moment she opposed him he would walk off, calling her a stupid woman; but as he never did anything she objected to, after such a walkout, one can call it a rather graceless accepting of defeat.

My father had a passion for land. As the only doctor in the village his income must have been considerable. But he never kept his savings in any bank. He used it all to buy land. People knew of this weakness of his, and so if anyone had a piece of land to sell he would first come to my father.

That was how my father bought that bit of land from Ramanna, who owed him some money because his wife and ten kids were perennially ailing. The land was lying unused and Ramanna thought of selling it off to clear his debts and to have some extra cash. We came to know later that someone had told him that his family's continual ailments were due to Kalkutika's anger and he should either offer the deity due worship or get rid of that land. He promptly sold it to my father.

If that piece of land were anywhere else, out of sight, father would not have bothered about it. But as it was just behind our backyard, he thought of growing some coconut, mango and jackfruit trees there. So we built a fence round it but it did not last. Two days later we found the fence broken at one place, and when that breach was patched up, a gap appeared at another place. And always, within a couple of days, a faint trodden path would appear from the gap in the fence to the Kalkutika stone. Our Kalkutika had suddenly become popular after the fence was put up.

My mother was the first one to guess who was behind this. She said that it must be Krishnayya Settigara's doing. But as she was invariably suspicious of everyone father was fond of, it took some time for him to concede that she might be right.

Krishnayya was one of my father's 'friends'. A village doctor, like the village deiva, is a lonely being. He has few friends because people are usually shy and diffident with him. But not Krishnayya. A brash, good-looking man, always dressed in immaculate white, he looked healthy but suffered from

21

venereal diseases. Vain of his clean dapper image, he must have hated the need to expose his rottenness to father. His show of friendship was perhaps a necessary pretence, so that he could visit the dispensary as a friend and sneak in for an injection—"Your bum is a regular pin-cushion," I had heard father say to him once—but he must have hated father, something father could not understand.

There was also another reason for his dislike perhaps: jealousy. He had a greed for land, a kind of covetous lust, quite different from my father's love. But he was a hard bargainer and so people always approached my father first if they had any land to sell.

Perhaps it was Krishnayya who convinced Ramanna that his children's ailments were all due to Kalkutika's ire. He must have thought that he would get that piece of land, which was adjacent to his paddy field, cheap. He did not expect that my father would buy it. So disappointed and upset, Krishnayya decided to wake up the sleeping Kalkutika.

There must have been a time when every large stone or tree in our villages harboured deivas. But as people's faith declined, many of them passed into oblivion and became 'sleeping' deities, only occasionally remembered by men whose ancestors had worshipped them. But the *jagrita*—wakeful—deivas demanded and received sacrifices and worship.

Mother came to know, from Lacchhi, our maid servant, who was her hotline to village gossip, about Krishnayya's method of waking up Kalkutika: spreading rumours about the deiva's powers. He dinned into people's ears stories of how Ramanna had suffered because he neglected the deity. His neighbour Venkappa, with whom he had had a quarrel, fell down from his bicycle and fractured his leg. Krishnayya said that it was because of his appeal to Kalkutika. "I said to the deiva, this man says that I am after his wife; don't I have a better looking wife of my own? If I still get the itch, can't I afford to go to a good-looking courtesan? Is his wife the only woman in the world? So I asked for justice and see what happened."

All this talk worked, for some months at least. Many people started visiting the two deities and left all kinds of votive offerings. I saw the suragi tree often daubed with vermilion and turmeric. I was surprised to find even Venkappa, early one morning, dragging his plastered leg along the thorny path to the Kalkutika stone. Obviously he was on his way to see the deiva, to present *his* version of the quarrel.

The outcome of all this was that the land remained unfenced and wild. People's interest in the two deivas soon waned, but so also had my father's desire for an orchard.

Homecoming

By the time I was fourteen I had stopped arguing with mother. I changed a lot during those two years. I grew nearly a foot taller, and looked down, literally, on my semi-literate mother. I had no time or inclination to argue with her as I spent practically all my spare time reading. I have been fond of reading all my life but during my adolescence it became an all-consuming passion. Even my daydreams were mostly of books. I dreamt that I had won a prize of one thousand rupees, a princely sum then, all to be used on buying books; and spent days making elaborate lists of all the books I wanted to buy.

I read every book in Kannada I could lay hands on: fiction, poetry, drama, biographies, reminiscences and what not. Both my appetite for books and my speed, particularly while reading novels, were prodigious; there were very few books I needed more than a day to read. As I invariably returned the book I borrowed from the village or the school library the very next day, the men in charge there grumbled that I borrowed books only to show I was a great reader. Our science teacher, therefore, decided that we must have a speed test of my reading.

The test was held on a Sunday. Some of my teacher's friends, who came to the school quite regularly on Sundays to listen to the radio, the only one in the village, run on a dry battery—those were days when we had no electricity in our villages and the transistor had not yet arrived—were also present. I was given a large novel I had not read. I was a bit nervous, very self-conscious, and the novel given was a rambling narrative difficult to concentrate on. For the first half an hour I could read only fifteen pages and thought I was in disgrace. Then it happened. I forgot where I was, forgot my teacher and his friends, and when they woke me up ninety minutes later, I had read nearly two hundred pages.

"How do you manage it?" asked Mr. Mayya, our teacher. "Even to look at all those words on a page, you'll need more time than the twenty-four seconds you took when you were reading with full concentration. What exactly happens when you are reading?"

"I don't know," I said, "maybe I don't look at each word separately; maybe I look at entire lines, or several lines at a time." I thought for a moment and said, "I begin reading, and then I forget I am reading. It's as if a gate opens and I enter the novel."

That was in fact what happened when I read novels. I found myself inside the novel, in a world which was different from ours; where I was more at ease, more at home, because I could understand everything that went on there. In that world I was like God—omniscient, omnipresent. Unseen myself, like God, I could see everything. I could not change anything, of course, but I did not want to change anything, though my heart bled at the misery and rejoiced at the happiness I encountered.

I have wondered, since then, whether the analogy that struck me then holds some profound truth the fourteen-year-old could not fully apprehend. Is God the greatest novel reader ever? Is this phenomenal world a cosmic novel? Is novel-reading an imaginative enactment, in a microcosmic way, of God watching over this world? Does this explain why we feel at times, while reading novels, a peculiar sense of power?

I have never been able to accept a God totally indifferent to human misery; nor can I believe that He would come down and set things right whenever we cry to Him for help. I think of Him as the Great Novel Reader, One who watches the events of this world with pity and concern but does not want to intervene.

"What about skipping?" said Mr. Mayya; "Do you skip or do you read everything?"

"I don't know," I said. "I suppose I skip a bit, but not consciously. Perhaps it's a bit like walking through a fair looking at the shops and stalls. We slow down when a stall interests us, move away quickly when it doesn't."

Mr. Mayya nodded. "That's a good comparison," he said.

I thought for a moment, and said, "No, it's not a good comparison." I had, even in those days, an irresistible impulse to contradict, even if it meant contradicting myself. "Those shops and stalls, they are just there. They are not in any way connected. If you like one you can spend a lot of time there without worrying about the next stall. The world of the novel is not like that."

"I understand," said Mr. Mayya. "There's no linear progression, like we have in the events or scenes of a novel. So we don't feel, in a fair, the kind of curiosity that drives us on in a novel."

"That's right, sir," I said, relieved that he put it much better than I could have. Then I added, "Perhaps I skip a lot when I read a novel the third or fourth time."

"Third or fourth time?" asked Ahmed, sounding quite surprised. He was a tall debonair chap who had worked as an untrained teacher in our school for a few months and then joined the Indian Railways as a clerk. Whenever he came on leave to the village he spent his afternoons in the school. The boys, who were jealous of him, said that he came to look at the girls, because school was one of the only two places—the other was the temple—where one could have a good look at the elusive girls of upper caste families.

"How many times do you read a novel?" he asked. "Why should you read a novel again when you already know the story?"

"The story is not the only thing," I said. I found it difficult to explain why I loved to read some novels again and again. "I have read *Marali Mannige* a dozen times or more. I have sometimes borrowed it from the library even when a novel I hadn't read was available there. I don't know why. May be it's like..." I hazarded an analogy again because analogies help you to evade clear-cut explanations. "Like how you come here, whenever you come down from Bangalore. You don't go seeking a place you haven't seen before. You come here because you like the place, feel at home here. Re-reading a novel is a bit like that—like going to a place you have visited before, and loved visiting."

"That is a good comparison," Ahmed said, echoing Mr. Mayya.

I did not contradict him. I must have myself thought, then, that it was a fairly good comparison. I realized that it was an inadequate analogy much later. Four decades later.

That was when I visited our village a couple of months ago, after a gap of fourteen years. I was fifty-eight, with only two years left for retirement. What would I do after that in this city where life was so hectic that the elderly were pushed aside, like flotsam and jetsam rotting on the placid river edges, and left watching with bewilderment and consternation the swirling stream, of which they were once a part, rushing past. I had to go home if only to see if it was home still.

Home. I thought of Frost's lines—how many times I had quoted them!— *Home is the place where, when you have to go there, / They have to take you in.* But who were *they*? My parents were both dead, and my brother, whom I had petted and played with, was only ten when I left for Bombay. Not likely that he would remember the bond that was there between us in his childhood. Our ancestral home at Nampalli was no longer ours, and the house built by my father at Kantheshwar had become a hospital. In my despair I recollected and found some solace in that other definition of home in Frost's poem: *Something you somehow haven't to deserve.*

I went by air because I thought I would not be able to stand the rigours of the twenty-four hour bus journey. My brother, that little baby in the cradle I referred to earlier, now a prosperous doctor, had sent his car to the airport. But the journey was far from comfortable. I was tired and restless, and when I reached Kantheshwar, found my brother's bungalow unbearably hot. I could not rest or relax. So in the afternoon, after my brother and his wife—a gynaecologist—left for the hospital, I decided to go out for a stroll.

I found myself walking towards the school and its playground after a lapse of more than twenty years. Why hadn't I gone there for so long? I loved the place in my school days and it had remained my favourite haunt for some years after I left school. But once there was a break, something grew between me and the place, a kind of estrangement, perhaps bred on the fear that I would find the place so altered that the changes would break my heart.

When I reached the school ground the sun had just set. The school and the ground were bathed in that bright golden incandescent twilight that lasts, alas, for only a few minutes. They had whitewashed the school building and it looked brand new. The playground looked the same as in my school days, only smoother and more even. The place hurt me not because it had changed as I feared, but because it hadn't.

Right at the centre of the ground stood the old banyan tree, standing sentinel for over a century now. The roots from the branches hung in clumps, like matted hair, at the same height as they did in my school days, their urge to reach the earth still unfulfilled. Some of the roots ended in claws, each finger tapering into a soft, worm-like, flesh-coloured tendril, which we used to break and eat. I ate one and found the slightly bitter astringent taste quite unpleasant.

I walked absent-mindedly towards the portico at the centre of the school building where I used to meet my friends in the evenings. When I looked up my heart skipped a beat, because I thought I saw, sitting on the portico, in the fast-fading twilight, my friends, risen from the past. The same animated discussions, the same wild gesticulations; even the faces of one or two looked familiar. Must be sons, or grandsons, of my friends.

But they did not greet me noisily as my friends would have. They ignored me totally. One or two of them looked at me, but with unseeing eyes. It was as if I did not exist. I had a strange uneasy feeling that I was dead and was roaming those old haunts of mine as a ghost.

On the way back I stopped for a while near the badminton court where a furious game of ball badminton was in progress. I could hardly see the yellow woollen ball in the gathering darkness but those ten young men seemed to have no difficulty in sighting it. They smashed and retrieved and smashed again, with amazing accuracy, with a small group of onlookers encouraging them vociferously. But neither the players nor the onlookers took any notice of me.

I knew it was stupid of me to be hurt by that neglect, but I was. I remembered vividly how I had played on that very court, egged on by noisy encouragement from onlookers and teammates, forty years ago. A great desire rose in me to tell those boys that I had once played the game well and captained my school team; was passionately attached to the game and had honed my skills with hours of patient practice. I wanted to tell them about a deceptive serve I had developed, with vicious side-spin and top-spin, with which I could, with no discernible change in action, make the ball skim the net and dip suddenly in front of my opponent, or go above his head just beyond his reach and then dip behind him. But there was no way I could reach out to those brash youngsters walled in by their youth. Perhaps the old banyan tree, thwarted in its efforts to reach for the earth, with its tentacle-like hanging roots left hopelessly clawing the air, could understand my frustration and bitterness.

On my way back to my brother's house, in the dimly lit street, I said to myself: this was perhaps what ghosts felt: angry and upset because they were totally ignored and alienated. Haunting the world they once belonged to but unable to communicate with anyone, they perhaps struck at people because they desperately wanted to make their presence felt.

When I reached my brother's house I found my ten-year-old nephew sitting in the hall, deeply immersed in a book. He made me think, for a moment, with nostalgia, of my own childhood. He lifted his head from the book, looked at me with unseeing eyes, and went back to his reading.

At the dining table we were all mostly silent. My brother said something but it took a full minute for me to realize that he had spoken to me.

"Did you say something?" I asked him.

"Ah, yes," he said, "where did you go this evening?"

"To the school ground," I said.

"I see," he said, and laughed. "So that's where you lost your tongue."

I tried to laugh but succeeded only in producing a grimace. The school ground was the place where children usually lost their things: pencils, pens, playthings and even money. One often found these children there in the evenings, forlorn figures in the gathering darkness, looking for what they had lost.

I felt tired and feverish but knew I would not be able to sleep for some time. So I went to my brother's room to look for something to read. There I found an old copy of *Marali Mannige*. I opened the book and found, on the flyleaf, my name: 'N. Sudhakara Rao'; and below that the date: '21st July 1953'.

"Moni," I called, and my brother, alerted by the urgency in my tone, came hurriedly in. "Where did you get this book from?" I asked him.

He took the book from my hand and looked at it. "Ah," he said, "Do you remember Ramakrishna Karanth? Did you know him personally?"

"Yes; he was in my class in college," I said. Moni looked genuinely surprised. "But he looked much older, at least twenty years older, than you," he said.

Karanth *was* older, maybe by ten years. He was intelligent, knowledgeable and articulate, but just could not write an examination paper well. So he failed in every class at least once, and by the time we reached college I had caught up with him.

"He died some years ago," Moni said. "Cancer. He was in the Manipal Hospital. After they did everything they could, they sent him home—to die. He was in excruciating pain and there was nothing we could do about it. They wanted to admit him in our hospital, but…" Moni suddenly sounded tired; "You know how it is in a village, Anna. Every death is regarded as a black mark against the hospital. Even when the patient is terminally ill. Ours was a fairly new hospital then and I couldn't take the risk. And then, a death in a small hospital affects the morale of the other patients.

"So I had to go to their house to see what I could do to ease his pain. Not much, I am afraid. On the last day it was terrible. I couldn't stay in that room for long, and so came out and sat in the hall. His wife was sitting there, like a statue. I didn't know what to say to her. So I started rummaging among the books in the shelf and found this book, with your name on the flyleaf. I said to her, more to make conversation than anything else, that it was your book. She just said, 'take it'."

21st July 1953. So that was the day I bought a copy of my favourite novel, *Marali Mannige*. I have a bad memory for dates but I remembered every little detail of that purchase. I had come back from home to Udupi, the town where I went to college, feeling rich because I had with me forty rupees, to be spent over the next four weeks. I went to the bookshop to browse, my favourite pastime, thinking that I might perhaps buy an American Pocket Book which cost one rupee eight annas then. But I found there a new edition of *Marali Mannige*, priced rupees five. I knew I might have to skip a few meals later in the month if I bought it but could not resist the temptation. For two days I carried my precious possession wherever I went. I did not read it. I dipped into it occasionally, savouring well-remembered scenes, but kept the pleasure of a full reading for the weekend.

But then the book disappeared, leaving me heart-broken. I asked everyone I knew if he had taken it, except, I think, Karanth, who never read any novels anyway. I don't know why he took it. Perhaps he wanted to teach me a lesson. He could not, I think, understand how anyone could be stupid enough to waste five rupees on a mere novel.

I thought of him, and the picture that appeared before me was that of a handsome, healthy, well-built man in his mid-twenties. I just could not visualize him as a sick invalid. I sighed, opened *Marali Mannige* and started reading.

The ivory gates of the novel opened almost at once, as though they had waited for me all those years. And I was again in that world of golden sands, swaying coconut palms and the sapphire sea; the world of Rama Aithal, his wife Parothi and his widowed sister Sarasothi. I did not read the book the way I had taught myself to read in recent years, but uncritically, as I used to in my childhood. I was no longer afraid of being sentimental. I cried unashamedly at the death of Parothi like I had when I first read the novel at the age of eleven. It was not that the novel merely opened the gates of a world I had visited before and loved visiting. It also opened, at least for that moment, the clogged springs of my feelings and gave me back my emotional youth.

I closed the book to wipe my eyes, and my glasses. From the dark forgotten depths of my mind, like a whale in the deep seas, rose the memory of that day in school when Mr. Mayya had given me that speed test.

"No, no, Ahmed," I said, "wherever you are, if you are still alive; that was not a good comparison. That was an inadequate one, a bad one."

What precisely was wrong with the comparison was something I had to explore. That terrible feeling of alienation I had experienced during the day in the school ground had clearly something to do with time and mutability. That much I was certain of. I was also vaguely aware that the feeling of elation I felt while reading *Marali Mannige*, that too had some connection with time.

I started reading the novel again and gave myself up to the flow of the story. Time flowed, years passed, Rama Aithal grew old and mellowed. His son Laccha, petted and pampered by everyone, grew from a loveable affectionate toddler to a selfish pleasure-seeking lout. His marriage to Nagaveni was a brief interlude of happiness, but it passed quickly, and he slipped into his old evil ways again. Time passed, Rama Aithal died of old age and a broken heart, the long-suffering Sarasothi died too, and Nagaveni, deserted by her husband, struggled on heroically to bring up her little son Rama, named after his grandfather. Time and mutability ruled the novel but they were tamed and made pleasant. Encapsulated in a timeless work of art, the temporal events became timeless, the ephemeral permanent. Passage of time became cyclical, like the passing of seasons, and even decay and death became the precursors of birth and growth. I was deeply moved.

At half past two someone knocked on the door. I opened the door, and he was there, my father. "It's past two, Babu," he said; "Enough of reading, now. Go to bed."

"Yes, Appa," I said obediently, closed the door, put off the light and went to bed.

A few minutes later, when I was on the edge of sleep, I suddenly got up with a start, goose pimples all over my body.

My father at the door? Twenty years after his death?

What door had he knocked on, O God, what door had I opened?

PART II
Nampalli

৯৯

We shall not cease from exploration
And the end of all our exploring
Will be to arrive where we started
And know the place for the first time.

T.S. Eliot

The Matha

I called Kantheshwar a village. If I were writing in Kannada I would have called it a *pethe*, a market town. It was a fairly large village even in those days. In the afternoons people came there from the surrounding villages to shop, to eat *dosas* in any of the three tiny restaurants, or just gawk and wander up and down the main road. Young men from the villages—particularly those who had seen cities or towns—felt that they could find relief from their enforced rusticity only by visiting the pethe every afternoon, even though it meant walking three or four miles in the hot sun and then back again in the evenings to their villages through dark woods and snake-infested fields; all for the pleasure of walking up and down the narrow dusty road, hanging around dingy shops, and, when a rickety bus came roaring and rattling, gratefully inhale the clouds of red dust raised by it. You could make a reasonably accurate assessment of the business done by a shop by looking at the bunch of young men collected in front of it: the more the crowd, the less the business. Busy shopkeepers found the loiterers a nuisance, but to those who merely sat in their shops swatting flies they were a welcome diversion.

But we shifted to Kantheshwar only when I was eleven. My infancy and childhood were spent in a quiet hamlet, Nampalli, about two miles from Kantheshwar. Nampalli, the place I belong to, the place that has given the initial 'N' in my name. In Bombay I am often asked what that initial 'N' in my name, N. Sudhakara Rao, stands for. I tell them that it's the name of my village. That is our practice in the south: a man is identified by the village he comes from. It is a bond that remains, even after one has left one's village.

Apart from our house, the largest in the hamlet, Nampalli had just eight Brahmin houses. The number of houses has remained the same over the years but there are fewer people staying in them now. Almost all the men from here work in restaurants and hotels in different towns and cities. Earlier they worked as cooks, waiters and as hotel boys, and left their wives and children at Nampalli. Now they have become prosperous and own hotels and chains of restaurants in cities like Bangalore, Mysore and Hyderabad. They stay with their families in those cities, and only old men and women who don't want to leave Nampalli, and a few poor relations, are left behind.

But till I started going to school at the age of six, even those eight houses were out of bounds for me. My world was limited to our house and its front and back yards.

The house was large enough for that. It was in fact built as a *matha*, a religious institution, late in the fourteenth century. Our Matha belonged to the Maadhwa sect, founded by Madhwacharya, who propounded the *dwaita* philosophy to counter the teachings of Shankaracharya. Shankaracharya, a transcendentalist, believed, like Plato, that the phenomenal world was unreal, a mere illusion. The seeker of truth, he said, must lift this painted veil and look beyond. He would then see the oneness of things, and realize that the distinction between *Jeevatma*, the individual soul, and *Paramatma*, the Supreme Soul, was an illusion. Such a realized soul would be able to say, with conviction: *Aham Brahmasmi*, I am God. This is *adwaita*, the philosophy of monism or non-dualism.

Madhwacharya could not accept that. An immanentist, he believed that the phenomenal world was impermanent but real. A profound love for all things created by God, and for the Creator, marked his teachings. He felt that we should constantly express our gratitude to God through devotion and worship, and it was only through them that salvation could be achieved. If one could say Aham Brahmasmi, the natural springs of devotion would dry up and worship would become meaningless: whom would you worship if you believe that you are yourself God?

So he propounded his dwaita philosophy, the philosophy of dualism, and founded the Maadhwa sect. He spent his life spreading his teachings to different parts of the country, and when he died in 1317, he left behind a well-knit team of teachers, headed by eight celibate Swamis, all chosen and initiated by him. Several mathas were built by these Swamis, and their successors, in the course of the next couple of centuries. Nampalli Matha was one of them.

Nampalli Matha must have lasted as a matha for two or three centuries. The seven *vrindavanas* in front of the building indicate that. A vrindavana is an altar-like structure built with red laterite stones over the mortal remains of a Swami of the Maadhwa sect. The sacred *tulsi* plant is grown on top; it grows well even if there is inadequate soil provided because the stone used for the structure is soft and porous, and absorbs and retains water. One of my earliest memories is of women of our family going round these vrindavanas every evening—*pradakshina* we called it—crooning sacred songs, and of how I used to tag along. We loved the vrindavanas. This surprises me now when I think about it, though at that time I was not even aware that there was anything strange in our attitude. Village people in India are invariably scared of the dead and of burial and cremation grounds. And yet no one was ever scared of these vrindavanas. In fact they were a source of courage and comfort. I remember how in my childhood, late in the evenings, when the elders were busy in the kitchen or elsewhere and I was frightened by the darkness congealing and thickening in the nooks and corners of that vast house, I often used to step out of the door, and sit, very quiet, on the verandah, looking at those sacred mouldering memorials, feeling comforted and protected.

The vrindavanas show that seven Swamis had lived and died in the Matha. Some must have died elsewhere, because the Swamis often lived at Udupi, where all the eight Mathas had their main branches. They also travelled extensively, spreading their Guru's teachings. So Nampalli Matha must have remained a matha for about three centuries.

Then came the day when the reigning Swami of the Matha felt that it was not practicable to have his headquarters at a secluded hamlet like Nampalli. So it was shifted to a place closer to Udupi, and a young married man—a householder—closely related to the then Swami, was brought to Nampalli with his family. He was installed there as a priest and manager, to perform the daily worship and to take care of the Matha's properties. That householder was my ancestor.

I don't think that the man felt that Nampalli was in the middle of nowhere. Most households then were more or less self-sufficient and consumed only what they produced. Rice they grew, and after it was harvested, black-grams, green-grams and other kinds of grams, which required less water. The cowshed was an important part of the house. Cows provided milk for the family and manure for the fields, and the fields provided hay and the husks of grams, to be stored as fodder through the year. Nothing was sold and very little was bought. There were hardly any cash transactions. Workers were paid in kind—rough brown rice was specially prepared to be given to them as payment because they did not like the white rice Brahmins ate—and the tenants too paid their dues in kind.

There were advantages in being in charge of a house that was once a Matha with extensive properties. The Matha owned practically all the land—fields as well as forests—and had let them out to tenants who regarded the Matha, and whoever resided there, as their landlord. Some land was kept for the Matha. The harvesting of this land was done free and so also the repairing of the roof once a year, because the tenants felt that it was their duty to offer a couple of days' free service to the Matha. These practices were still there in my childhood, in the 1940s. I remember vividly the excitement in the air as scores of men descended on our house, early in the morning, a few days before the onset of monsoon, and like monkeys ascended the roof, and set right, in a matters of hours, all the tiles broken or displaced by monkeys (real ones) in the course of the year.

The family prospered and grew. It became a large joint family after a couple of generations, and then, after another generation or two, separated into three or four families, each with its own kitchen and store-room, but sharing the rest of the house without much problems. The house was large enough to accommodate them all.

The House of the Matha

So Nampalli Matha became a house. The villagers began to call it 'the house of the Matha'. When they heard me, for example, screaming every evening just before supper, they would say with awe, "Listen, the boy from the house of the Matha is screaming."

I had terrific lungpower then and was quite a spoilt brat. As I was the only boy in the house—the other kids were all girls—I was pampered by everyone, and particularly by my grandmother. My mother's attempts at setting this right made matters worse. Every evening I found that what was being cooked for supper was something I disliked. I don't know whether mother deliberately cooked what I did not like, or whether I, contrary child that I was, was determined to dislike whatever she was going to cook. My screams would begin as soon as I discovered what was cooking and would continue till my grandmother, giving up her evening prayers, would enter the kitchen saying, "All right Babu, I'll cook what you want." Sometimes mother herself agreed to prepare what I wanted. But she deliberately made it too salty or tasteless, and I, tired after all the screaming, had no energy left to protest and ate the stuff quietly.

Doddappayya—the word means 'big father'—my father's elder brother, a very quiet man who never lost his temper or raised his voice, once saw me eating *sasami* mother had prepared after a bitter battle; and he realized, from the martyred expression on my face, that there was something wrong.

"Saraswati," he said to my mother, "May I have a little of that sasami?"

Mother coloured a bit and said, "I have prepared very little, just enough for him."

"Do you mind if I have a little of your sasami, Babu?" he asked me. "You can have it, Doddappayya," I said, "You can have as much as you want."

Mother served him a little of the stuff and he ate it. It was terribly salty, and we all knew that he hated anything salty. He had in fact been told by father not to eat much salt. But he quietly ate the sasami, asked for more and finished it off. Then he drank three glasses of water.

As I went out to wash my hands I heard him say, though he said it quietly enough, "Obstinacy is bad in a child but worse in a grown-up. A child will outgrow it, but what hope is there for us grown-ups?"

"But he has to be taught his lesson," mother grumbled, "Everyone is spoiling him."

There were not many people living in that large house in my childhood. Till the 1920s the population of our family had gone on increasing. Then the inevitable decline began. This was caused by two things: our increasing distance from the family that controlled the Matha, and the increasing population that made the income from the land inadequate. That ancestor of ours, who first came as a priest and manager when the Matha became a house, was the elder brother of the Swami. Then with passing generations we became the first cousins, the second cousins and so on, till we finally became only distant relations. So gradually all the administrative powers were taken away from our family and we had to depend solely on the yield from the land we had in our possession. Younger members of the family saw no future at Nampalli and migrated to towns and cities. Only two branches of the family stayed on.

The two branches that shared the *pooja* and the properties were Chikkajjayya's and ours. Chikkajjayya—small grandpa—was the only male member of his branch staying at Nampalli. His son had gone to Bangalore as a hotel boy and then opened a small restaurant there. Though he had no head for business, the restaurant prospered during the Second World War because it was close to the Cantonment, and the officers and soldiers who frequented it gave generous tips, and did not bother to collect the change after paying the bill. But he was not happy. He considered selling food degrading because food was to be given free to all one's guests. He was happy only after he sold his restaurant for a throwaway price, spent most of that money giving lavish feasts, and became a pauper.

The three daughters of Chikkajjayya lived with him. They were of course all married, but their marriages had ended on different kinds of rocks. The eldest one was a widow with two daughters: Lakshmi who was three years my senior, and Aditi, eighteen months her junior. Varijamma, Chikkajjayya's second daughter, was only eight when she got married. They did not know, when the marriage was arranged, that the groom was mentally deranged. He was so frightened by all the noisy festivities, and specially by the firecrackers, that he ran away the same night and was never found again. The third, Gangamma, was given in marriage to a rich man. But after she gave birth to a daughter her husband was told by some astrologer that he would get no sons from her. And so he married again. He did not throw his first wife out, and was in fact surprised and upset when she decided to go with her daughter and stay at her father's place. As he had enough money to support half a dozen wives, her decision surprised everyone, including, perhaps, Gangamma herself. She was one of the most timid persons I have come across. So timid and indecisive that I have sometimes wondered whether that one uncharacteristic act of defiance had drained her of all courage thereafter.

Lakshmi, Aditi and Gangamma's daughter Savitri were my childhood companions. I was the only boy in that large house but the girls, who were all older than me, took care of me and tolerated my tantrums. I did not much care for their girlie games like Channe Mane, games that required infinite patience and nimbleness of fingers. They must have found me a nuisance during those games as I slowed them down and also broke the rules. So when I wanted to join in their games I often found them saying, "No Babu. We are tired of playing. Tell us a story instead." That was one invitation I could never say no to.

I try to recollect what the three girls looked like then but I cannot see them, just as I cannot see myself as a child. They become a part of the dark interior of that old, large house; it is evening, and I see them as faint shadows for a moment; then they disappear in the thickening darkness, and a vague fear and an equally vague sense of loss come to me from the past. This troubled me for a time till I realized that what I had succeeded in recollecting was not something symbolic but a real experience, the actual *feel* of what must have happened every evening during those days. After doing their pradakshinas of the vrindavanas in the evening the girls used to come in and do pradakshinas of the temple at the centre of the inner courtyard; and I used to follow them, round the long corridors, getting a little frightened as I could not see them in the congealing darkness. But real experiences, when they come to us through the sieve of memory, can act as symbols. We can explore them and see in them patterns of meaning that are often too slippery for words. Perhaps if we merely recount these experiences without trying to interpret them, and if our choice of experiences and their arrangement are right, maybe we can then arrive at something close to reality. Wasn't it Yeats who said that man may not know truth but can embody it?

The three girls went to school for the greater part of the day. Even when they came back they were not always free to play with me. Being girls they were expected to do some small household chores, like cleaning rice. Then in the evening they had an important chore which they relished: to gather flowers from the trees and plants outside the house—*parijata, nanjibattalu, bagul*—and weave them into garlands for the daily pooja and also for their long plaits. It was then that they wanted me to tell them stories.

They sat with their hands busy with the flowers, wide eyed with wonder at my inexhaustible supply of stories. As they wove the flowers into garlands, I wove stories from elements I had gathered from stories I had heard from my grandmother, uncle and others. All through the day I used to dream up these stories, and unburdening myself in the evening to such a receptive audience was the greatest pleasure of my life.

On some nights we sat in the courtyard after supper and the story-telling sessions continued. In a house where the only sources of light were tiny oil lamps, the wide courtyard open to the sky was the least murky spot even under starlight, and it became a bright sea of milk under a full moon. On darker nights I sometimes brought ghosts and goblins into my story, mainly to frighten Aditi, but the stories would grow so scary that I often got more frightened than the others. Then we clung to each other, till we heard Varijamma's voice from the dark verandah saying, "Stupid children! Why do you tell such scary stories at night, Babu? You'll wet your bed tonight, I'm sure."

I am not quite sure why I told those ghost stories. The ghosts entered the stories invariably as afterthoughts. Either Savitri or Aditi would suddenly plead, in the middle of a story, "Please, Babu, don't bring in any ghosts tonight," and that would be a signal for a ghost to knock at the door of the story. I got a thrill out of frightening them and perhaps they got a thrill out of being frightened. It was all fun, including that clinging together in fright. We were very young—I was five and Lakshmi, the oldest among us, just eight—no doubt it was all quite innocent. No one bothered about us, not even my rather suspicious mother.

No one except Varijamma. She was always around when we were together, particularly at night, watching us from some dark corner of the house. We knew about it, and were in fact happy that she was always around. It is only now that I realize that she was spying on us, fearing, or perhaps hoping, that there was something sexual in what we did; if there was—some innocent kind of infant sexuality—who could understand it better than Varijamma, the child bride whose married life ended on the day it began, when she was just eight?

Telling Stories

The first person to tell me stories was my grandmother. She was the one who fed me and my two sisters our first semi-solid food, when we were six or seven months old. *Manni* it was called, made of arrowroot, milk and jaggery. Grandmother would sit on the ground with her legs stretched out, keep the child on her legs, hold its tiny fists gently in her left hand and feed it with a spoon—after checking up whether the manni was of the right thickness and warmth—all the while telling it snatches of stories. I cannot recollect Sita, just two years my junior, being fed like this, but I was often a very interested spectator when Savita, four years younger than me, was fed. It looked as if the baby was really listening to the story. She in fact refused to open her mouth whenever grandmother stopped her story. "Look," I used to say, "look at the way she keeps her mouth shut. She won't open it till you start the story again." And when grandmother started her story and the baby opened her mouth, I used to squeal with delight.

But grandmother was sceptical whether Sita or Savita really listened to her stories. "They just wanted to hear my voice," she said, "they wanted someone to talk to them when they were eating. They wanted to be sure that it was not just the spoon that was feeding them." Then she added, "But you were different. You did listen to the stories even when you were just seven or eight months old."

"How can you be sure of that?"

"Oh, one knows," grandmother said. "A good story-teller always knows when one's story is not listened to."

I had to agree that that was true. Lakshmi's mind sometimes wandered when I was telling my stories, and I immediately knew it.

"If there was something wrong with the story, if it became incoherent, you used to protest," said grandmother. "How did I do that?" I asked in surprise.

"You wouldn't swallow the manni," she said. "You blew through it. Whenever I saw those bubbles I knew. They were bubbles of protest." Then she added, "Even before you started eating manni, when I carried you in my arms, I used to tell you stories. And you listened. You are like Abhimanyu, Babu. May God give you long life."

I felt quite flattered. Abhimanyu was the boy hero from the *Mahabharata* whom I admired most. He was the son of the great archer Arjuna, and his mother was Subhadra, Krishna's sister.

Krishna had once gone to see his favourite sister when she was pregnant. Arjuna was not at home, so to while away the time he began to tell her about *Chakravyooha*, the military formation most difficult to penetrate. As Subhadra was not interested in military strategies, she soon fell asleep. But Krishna realized that someone else was listening to his narration with great interest: it was Abhimanyu, the child in Subhadra's womb.

Krishna stopped the story straight away. He had already described how to enter the Chakravyooha but he did not want the child to know how to come out of it.

During the Mahabharata war, the Pandavas had a problem. Their enemies, the Kauravas, had formed the Chakravyooha, and Arjuna, the only Pandava warrior who knew how to penetrate it, was away. All the Pandavas who tried to break through the vyooha failed, except little Abhimanyu. He broke through the formation but his uncles and others, even the mighty Bhima, could not follow him. So he found himself isolated and outnumbered, and though he fought bravely, was finally killed.

To me that was one of the most heroic and tragic chapters in the whole of *Mahabharata*. The episode did not raise any questions in my mind when I was young. A child responds to a story with his whole being, not with his mind alone. I gloried in Abhimanyu's valour and cried at the tragedy. The doubts and questions about the injustice of it all came much later. Why did Krishna hold back that all-important bit of information about how to get out of Chakravyooha from Abhimanyu, his own nephew? Didn't he, the omniscient incarnation of Vishnu, know that this would lead to the boy's death? Wasn't he on the side of the Pandavas?

When I began to ask these questions, my grandmother was no longer my main provider of stories. It was my uncle who had answers to these questions, though they did not fully satisfy me then. Abhimanyu, he said, was such a heroic figure that had he reached full manhood he would have become the most powerful man in the universe; so powerful that he could have stopped Kaliyuga from capturing the world. He talked to me about the Wheel of Time, Kalachakra, and how one *yuga* or era followed another in a predestined order. Satyayuga was the yuga of truth and goodness, followed by Tretayuga when some evil entered the world. There was deeper penetration of evil in Dwapara so that even the good were not left untainted. The Mahabharata war was fought at the end of Dwapara—at the turn of the yuga—and there was such evil unleashed that even the Pandavas could not escape from it. The war paved the way for Kaliyuga, the era of unmitigated evil. A man like Abhimanyu—had he lived to be a man—could have stopped it but that would have meant stopping the Wheel of Time, which was unthinkable. Kaliyuga had to come, and corrupt the world, so that it could be destroyed, and a New World created in its place, and a new era of truth and goodness could dawn. So Abhimanyu had to die—he was too good for the age.

My grandmother called me Abhimanyu simply because of that hero's embryonic eavesdropping, not because she saw anything heroic in me. She wished me a long life in the same breath because of Abhimanyu's early death.

After a couple of months of manni, children were fed rice, the staple food of our place. If the child had no teeth the rice was overcooked and mashed; otherwise it was always rice mixed with curds, with enough milk added to reduce the sourness to the minimum and a little salt added for taste. Children, not very eager to eat this wholesome stuff, dawdled, so the elders often hand-fed them even when they were old enough to feed themselves. I forced my grandmother to feed me till I was five, mainly for the sake of the stories I could exact from her. I taxed her story-telling skills to the limit, I believe: three stories a day, for nearly four years. Not even Scheherazade had a tougher task.

The stories were mostly about animals: tigers and jackals and cobras. Animals and human beings often interacted. In some stories they could talk to each other, in some they could not. The cobra often had magical powers, and could take on a human form. There were also stories of adventurous young lads on perilous missions, helped and guided by wise old women living in lonely cottages. I have often wondered at the presence of these old women—grandmothers called Adugoolajji—in most of these stories. They were there, I think, because the stories were grandmother's stories; not just told by grandmothers but created by them. While listening to these stories and while dreaming about them later, I always saw myself as the young lad and my grandmother as the wise Adugoolajji.

I was the only boy in that large house, and when my three cousins were away, the only child. Sita was just a baby, and though she could walk and even run about, with five women around she was always air borne. She was so light that people did not even notice they were carrying her. Gangamma, who made 108 pradakshinas of the inner temple every Tuesday to pray for the welfare of her husband whom she had left, once carried her all the way—more than two miles, surely—and then said, "God, she is so light, this child! She perches like a moth on your arm and you don't even realize you have been carrying her." Even when she was occasionally grounded, Sita would be in the kitchen holding on to mother's saree, which she needed because she had a perpetually running nose; whereas I raided the kitchen only when I felt like eating those salty or sweet delicacies grandmother specialized in preparing and kept in soot-covered tins on a shelf.

I roamed that large sprawling house alone, often holding a stick aloft, muttering to myself. I was in a world of my own, a world of imagination which I could seal off, after entering, from inside. From within that glass-bubble of a world I could perceive what happened outside, but I would not let those perceptions penetrate the bubble and impinge on my private world of imagination. When Varijamma giggled and said, "Look at this boy, he's going mad! Look at the way he holds that stick and talks to himself," I heard it, but heard it as if her voice came from another world. I laughed to myself because what Varijamma in her ignorance called a stick was in fact a mighty sword with which I was going to cleave a huge rock blocking the entrance to a cave, in which a pretty princess was held captive. Then it became a magic wand I had procured by tricking two stupid demons, who were quarrelling over it and wanted me to mediate; I had asked them to give it to me and show me how it worked. I had used the stick against them then, by chanting the mantra they had foolishly taught me: *Ya—ra—la—va—sa—ha—loo / Beat the demons black and blue,* and the stick had chased them out of sight and saved our village.

A dog barked outside. The stick slipped in my hand and I held it at the centre now, because it had become a bow, the one with which Ekalavya practised archery, all by himself, keeping the great teacher Dronacharya's image in front of him. When a dog's barking disturbed his concentration, he had sent a shower of arrows at that sound—because he knew *Shabda vedhi,* the art of shooting at a sound without looking—with such skill that the arrows got lodged in the dog's mouth without hurting it. Dronacharya, who had come to the forest with his students, was amazed by this feat, while Arjuna, who prided himself as the greatest archer in the making, was jealous. To appease Arjuna, his favourite student, Dronacharya had asked Ekalavya to give him his right thumb as *guru dakshina,* a gift for the teacher, and the boy had chopped it off right there. A terrific story, I thought, but I didn't want to live on without my right thumb, so the stick became the bow of Abhimanyu, the boy hero who died fighting the might of Kauravas alone. I began to prance about and dance as I had seen Abhimanyu do in the Yakshagana play; and outside the bubble I could hear Varijamma's giggles turning into hysteria: *This boy, surely he is going mad; he'll go crazy, and then he'll run away on his wedding day...*

My head was full of stories. Stories told by grandmother mingled with those I heard from my uncle, and with ghost stories Gangamma sometimes narrated. Mingled, mutated, and multiplied; and I had an insatiable urge to narrate them to people. I don't know when I started *telling* stories. Soon after I learnt to speak, I guess. Varijamma still mimics how, as a child of two, I used to force people to listen to my stories: "Thum, thum," I used to say, "Lithen thu my tholy." When I went to see her last she could not recognize me for some time—she was past eighty, and her eyesight was weak—but when she finally did, her face creased with the broadest of smiles. Covering her mouth with the end of her saree, because she had lost most of her teeth and was sensitive about it—a gesture of virgin coyness which I found touching—she said, "Thum, thum, Babu, lithen thu my tholy." "Ah, Varijamma," I said, "You have lost your teeth and started lisping." She laughed so heartily then that she forgot to cover her mouth. My heart warmed to this woman, for whom I had only contempt in my childhood. She was silly and hysterical; she was a gossip and was nosy. But she had a heart, and a memory where I still lived as a child.

I discovered, quite early, that a fertile imagination played a more important role than a good memory even in the re-telling of stories. Perhaps I learnt it from my grandmother who could alter a story anytime she wanted to, or invent a whole new series of incidents to transform an old story and thus silence me when I complained that I had heard the story before. My uncle's way of telling a story was different. To him every detail of the story was sacrosanct and unalterable. It was not that he depended solely on his memory. The way he could vivify those details and bring them to life showed that he had genuine creative imagination. But he held the great sages who wrote the *Puranas* and the poets who wrote the classics in such reverence that he just could not dream of changing what they had written. I remember how once, while telling me the story of Dandin's *Dashakumara Charitam*, he suddenly felt unsure of some details; "Babu, wait a little, I'll just look it up in the book," he said, but once he opened that work he got so deeply immersed in it that he completely forgot me; and I walked away after waiting for some time, amused by the absurdity of his devotion to insignificant details.

Uncle had studied Sanskrit at Udupi. He took up literature—the other options were astrology and philosophy—and got the title of *Sahitya*

Shiromani, the Crest-jewel of Literature. When he was ten or eleven, he attracted the attention of the Swami of our Matha, who hinted to grandfather that he might adopt him as the next Swami. My grandmother was very enthusiastic because that would have made our family rich and powerful. But this was just before the birth of my father, and grandfather did not want his only son to become an ascetic. The Swami was under pressure from his sister to choose her son and that was what he finally did.

Shiromani was then considered the equivalent of a Bachelor's degree and uncle got the job of a teacher in the High School at Chandapur. He got married, but his wife died in childbirth two years later. The child, a girl, survived for a couple of years and then died of cirrhosis of the liver, a common ailment among children then, caused perhaps by the accumulation of copper in the liver due to the use of copper vessels. The twin tragedy changed his life. Perhaps he was always selfless but the double bereavement burnt out whatever egoism was still there in him. He showered his love on his younger brother and helped him to become a doctor. And when I arrived, I found a fountain of love awaiting me.

What made uncle's love so special was that it was totally devoid of any egoism. He rarely used the word 'my'. He always introduced me as "Krishna's son", or "Doctor's son," never as "*my* nephew." This was not just a way of speaking. This was how he felt, and thought. He was a wonderful example of that quality of non-attachment which Hinduism values so highly. But disinterestedness does not mean indifference. Love freed from egoism is not only purer and healthier, it is also stronger, for it is the ego which clogs the springs of love. Uncle loved with all his heart but demanded nothing in return.

My relationship with my mother was ambivalent. We irritated each other and had frequent quarrels. I thought she did not love me as much as she loved my two sisters or my little brother who came later. If she did not, it was with some reason. My arrival—the birth of a male heir—was an event which our family, and specially my grandmother, had waited for, for a long time, after it became clear that uncle was not going to marry again. Grandmother, who had brought up four children of her own and nine grandchildren—children of her two daughters—felt that I was too precious an object to be left in the charge of her inexperienced daughter-in-law. So she took charge of me the moment I was born and my mother was relegated to the position of a mere wet nurse. So mother bore a grudge, curiously not against grandmother, but against me. The illogicality of it used to trouble me earlier but I now realize that all grudges are basically illogical—because they are emotional, not rational, responses to situations. My mother felt aggrieved that she could not have her first child all to herself. But she could not blame grandmother who was helping her out by taking care of her child. So she blamed me.

Even physically I was closer to my uncle in my childhood than to my parents. My father used to come back from Kantheshwar late at night. After his supper he used to go and rest in the upstairs room on the other side of the outer courtyard, the airiest and quietest room in the house. My mother could join him only after ten, after finishing her chores in the kitchen, and by that time all the children would be asleep—I in uncle's bed. To carry or drag me across that large outer courtyard and then up the steep staircase, simultaneously carrying a glass of milk for father, was beyond my mother's strength. So I was allowed to sleep on in uncle's bed, whereas my lighter and more docile sisters, when they arrived, were carried upstairs and slept with my parents.

Uncle used to sit cross-legged on the ground in front of our temple for about an hour every evening, reading the scriptures and the *Puranas*. The ritual is called *Parayana*. When I was seven or eight months old and had just learnt to crawl, I used to crawl to him and scramble on to his lap when he was reading. That was where I used to fall asleep, to the rhythmic chanting of Sanskrit *slokas*. "You came to me like the Lord in His different *avataras*," uncle told me some years later, his eyes becoming misty. "Like Matsya, the fish, at first, swimming on the ground; then as Koorma, the slow moving tortoise; then you learnt to move fast on all fours, and came as Varaha, the wild boar. And I thought, Lord, your response to my Parayana—can it be so immediate? Am I blessed even as I am reading?"

It is amazing how closely the order of the ten avataras of Vishnu follows the process of evolution. At first, when the whole world is flooded, the Lord comes as a fish; then He comes as a tortoise that holds up the Meru, the largest mountain in the universe, as it is used to churn the primordial ocean. He next descends as Varaha, the wild boar that lifts the world up with his tusks when it sinks into chaos. Then He takes the form of Narasimha, with the body of a man and the head of a lion, to destroy a Rakshasa king who had obtained a boon that he could not be killed by a man or beast or god. His next avatara is that of Vamana the dwarfish boy. The progression is from fish to amphibian, then to a beast, and then to one who is half beast and half man, and then to a dwarf. God takes the human form after this, but even here there is progression in the weapons He wields: Parashurama wields a battle-axe, Rama bow and arrows, Krishna a gyrating wheel, the *chakra*. Buddha, who comes next, preaches non-violence, but when that era ends the Lord will come as Kalki, the destroyer, and that will be Doomsday. The theory of evolution might hurt Christian sensibilities but a Hindu would take it in his stride.

I felt both flattered and embarrassed by what uncle said, and the way he said it. So to tease him I said, "What about Narasimha?" That made him smile, because Narasimha was his name. "Oh who can ever forget your Narasimha avatara?" he said.

He must be right, because those who heard me narrate the story of Prahlada and Narasimha to a large audience, including the Swami of our Matha, when I was just five, still remember it. Someone had told the Swami that I was a good storyteller. The Swami, a plump youngish man, was on one of his rare visits to Nampalli. He was reclining on the platform in that airy upstairs room where my parents used to sleep—my father was very upset that he had to give it up—being fanned by two boys and yet perspiring profusely. Clearly he was bored and any diversion was welcome. So he looked at me with his beady eyes and said, "Yes, boy, what story will you tell us?"

"What story do you want?" I asked him and that surprised everyone. It amused him too. He looked round, shaking a little in mirth, and then his eyes rested on my uncle. His whole body shook when he said, "Tell us the story of Narasimha."

I did not like him at all. I saw that he was laughing at uncle and that upset me. Somehow the way he laughed—with no sound but his whole body quivering—made his laughter more offensive. The indignation I felt at that must have added to the effectiveness of my story-telling.

I was pretty good at dramatizing. I turned the story into a kind of one-man theatre and acted out the story. I became Prahlada, who pleaded with his father to worship Lord Vishnu and give up his evil ways; then I became his father, the Rakshasa king Hiranyakashyipu, who treated his son with cruelty. Then finally I became Narasimha, the angriest and most terrifying of God's incarnations. The Swami, taken aback by the fury he saw, placed before me the plate of fruits—plantains and oranges—some devotee had brought for him. I tore into the fruits the way Narasimha tore into the entrails of the Rakshasa king. It was, they all agreed, a memorable performance.

I was carried away from there in triumph and grandmother, worried by the large number of envious and evil eyes I must have been the target of, placed a plate full of live coals in front of me and dropped some dried gum on to it. The pellets crackled and burnt, producing an enormous amount of pungent smoke, which made me cough and grandmother exclaim, "Good God! I have never seen so much of evil eyes before. May God protect this child!" She wanted to repeat the ritual but I ran away coughing.

That night I developed high fever. I was bed-ridden for three months, and was close to death several times. I vaguely remember waking up once and finding myself not on my uncle's bed but in his lap, with my grandmother, mother and others sitting around crying, father walking up and down, and uncle deep in prayer. Even my non-believing father had lost hope in the efficacy of his medicine and placed me in the protection of his brother's love and prayer. They did not fail. I survived.

I fell ill near the end of May, and in June the schools reopened. I was to join school that year but by the time I recovered, towards the end of August, it was too late.

After the Fever

During that long period of sickness I was indoors all the time. It was like I was asleep. The waking hours were like dreams. And then the fever left. I woke up one morning at dawn, feeling weak but light and fresh, after a good night's sleep. It had rained all through the night, and there is no sound more soothing and soporific than that of steady rain on a tiled roof. I woke to the sound of Gangamma churning butter in Chikkajjayya's kitchen, quietly singing to herself. She was too timid and self-conscious to sing well in front of others, but while churning butter she sang with feeling and without inhibitions, her voice rising and falling to the rhythm of churning. The song, an age-old one about Krishna's childhood—of *gopis*, the milkmaids of Nanda Gokula, churning butter, and little Krishna, the divine child, angering and delighting them by stealing it—gushed like a spring, joyous and spontaneous:

> *In the morning, while the gopis*
> *Were busy churning butter,*
> *Little Krishna in his cradle*
> *Called out to his mother…*

I listened, spellbound, for some time, to the sound of vigourous churning drowning the song, and then the song rising like newly churned butter over the gurgling buttermilk. Then I got up and slowly walked to the open door. Fascinated by the colourful scene the open doorway framed, I stepped out and sat on the verandah.

I had fallen ill in May when the earth was parched dry. Now, after two months of heavy rain, what I saw was a sea of green—fresh green grass everywhere and the dappled paddy fields, with different hues of green, rippling under the morning breeze. The rains had stopped, the eastern sky was clear except for fluffy gray-and-white clouds stacked on the horizon, and when the sun broke through them, the drenched grass glistened and the rain drops on the tiny leaves of the gooseberry tree turned to pearls; and little streams, produced by the night's heavy downpour, ran friskily over pebbles, bending and submerging the grass, their dimpled surface reflecting light and glittering like glass. Snatches of

Gangamma's song came drifting from inside, and I felt that I heard it not just with my ears but my whole skin. I sat entranced, shivering in delight, goose pimples all over my body, till Varijamma came out and dragged me inside, saying, "Look at the child, he's shivering with cold, he'll catch the fever again."

I forgot this experience totally, till I was made to recollect it nearly fifty years later. After an accident in Bombay, with the generous doses of analgesics and antibiotics impairing my digestive system, I went to a hospital of naturopathy near Bangalore to recoup; where, among other treatments, we were made to practise Yoganidra for thirty-five minutes every evening. We were made to lie down in the Shavasana position while a recorded voice instructed us how to achieve total relaxation. Then we were told to recollect the unhappiest moment of our lives, and after we had faced that, to recollect the happiest. I found the first task easy. They came crowding in, those old sorrows, and the only problem was to decide which of them was the saddest. But when it came to recollecting the happiest moment, a moment of unsullied joy, I was at a loss. I tried several but had to reject them all, because there was always something wrong, something missing. I found that the presence of some anxiety, some feverish excitement, spoilt even the happiest of moments. This exercise took me—on the first two days—very close to despair. Was I made only for unhappiness? Had I lived for so long and not known one moment of unalloyed happiness? Then on the third day, after the turmoil and churning of two days, rose the memory of that morning and of that moment of sheer joy— rose and floated, like butter churned by the gopis for little Krishna to steal.

I can only guess why the recollection of that moment was so precious. Perhaps because it showed that complete happiness was possible to a human being. The moment of happiness was brief, but somehow that did not matter. I understood, after so many years, why I had not protested when Varijamma dragged me inside. For I had gained, in that brief moment, something which I could forget but not lose.

After my long illness, and after all the care he took of me, uncle's attachment to me should have grown stronger. It did not seem to. I found him withdrawn and cold. A child knows when his love is spurned. I threw tantrums and made life difficult for him. He bore it all with patience but remained sad and remote.

Years later, after we shifted to Kantheshwar and I met him only occasionally, I asked him the question: Why did I feel that he loved me less after my illness? Did I imagine it or was he really trying to distance himself from me? Did he feel, after nursing me for three months, that he was tired of it all, and taking care of a child was a burden he could not shoulder any more?

"I can tell you now," he said, "because now you'll understand. Yes, I tried, tried very hard, to draw away. Not because your love was a burden, or I did not care, but because I was scared. As I sat in front of the temple with you unconscious in my lap, praying for your recovery, I suddenly remembered: this was precisely how I had sat and prayed, fifteen years earlier, with my daughter in my lap. I was horrified when I realized that my prayer was, word for word, the same: *Don't take away this child, O Lord, this is all I am left with.* God hadn't listened to my prayer then. What if he did not, again? Maybe there was a curse on my love. So I prayed, *This child is not mine, O Lord, I have no claim on it, and I shall never have any. Spare its life, don't punish it for my sins.*"

≈

My recovery took a long time. Perhaps I was in no hurry to recover. My schooling was delayed by a year. I "lost a year" according to mother, who asked my uncle to talk to the headmaster of the primary school at Kone to let me join school that year itself. But uncle felt that I was too weak to walk to school, and father agreed with him.

"But he will lose one year," said Amma.

"How does one lose a year," said uncle. He did not pose this as a question; he was brooding, talking to himself rather than to mother. "We do lose years, we lose them anyhow. We lose them when we don't do anything, we lose them when we are busy doing things. Perhaps we lose them fast—they just slip away—when we are too busy and too involved with our work."

Mother could not argue because she did not understand what he was talking about.

How do I remember this conversation which took place when I was only five years old? Because Amma would not let me forget it. She was a great one for arguments but could never draw uncle into one. The moment a talk threatened to turn into an argument he would withdraw into his shell, and use that brooding philosophic tone of his which effectively silenced mother. This always upset her; arguments she did not win, or have the last word in, troubled her and she could not get them out of her mind. Years later, when I was sixteen or seventeen, we had an argument, or the beginning of one, and I had wriggled out of it by using the strategy I had perhaps unconsciously learnt from uncle. My mother flew into a rage. "You are like your uncle," she rasped. "When you can't argue you talk in riddles. You talk nonsense."

51

"When did uncle do that?" I asked, angry and upset by her remark on uncle, which I thought was uncalled for. My anger was partly due to a feeling of guilt; I had not seen him for nearly two months. I was studying at Udupi then and came home only during the weekends, and somehow could not find the time to go to Nampalli, where he lived alone—alone in that large house which was built for a hundred people. There was also a vague feeling, at the back of my mind, that it was mother's fault that he could not be persuaded to come and stay with us at Kantheshwar.

Mother told me then about the aborted argument. Twelve years had elapsed since then, but she quoted uncle word for word, and even mimicked his tone. "Tell me," she said angrily, "You, your uncle's great disciple, tell me how we lose years when we are busy doing our work."

She stood at the door of the kitchen with a ladle in hand. Her hair was dishevelled and I noticed, for the first time, that her raven-black hair had started turning gray. The kitchen was filled with smoke and the struggle to kindle a fire with damp faggots had turned her eyes red. It surprised me, this anger of hers, at something that had happened twelve years earlier.

I wrinkled my nose and said, "I can smell something burning."

She went back into the kitchen. When she re-emerged from the smoke, the ladle in her hand dripping curry, she looked even more threatening. "Answer my question now," she said.

I wrinkled my nose again and said, "I think I can smell the milk boiling over."

She turned to go back, then stopped suddenly. "Don't bluff," she said. "The milk is not going to boil over for another minute. Why can't you answer my question?"

I looked at her and said, "How long have you been working like this in the kitchen, Amma? Ever since you got married, at the age of fourteen?"

"What has that got to do with my question?" she asked angrily. But she could not help answering my question. "Much earlier than that," she said; "I was ten when Amma died, and I had to take charge of the kitchen and cook for my father and younger brother."

"Since you were ten? How many years in all does that make?"

Her response was uncharacteristic. She did not shout at me for asking irrelevant questions. There was a lost look on her face and I could see her fingers moving: she was counting. "Twenty-five…no, twenty-six years," she said.

"Twenty-six years?" I said. "For twenty-six years you have been slogging in the kitchen, cooking for people who notice what they eat only when something goes wrong—like when there is no salt, or too much salt, in the curry. Twenty-six years of worrying about the curry getting burnt or the milk boiling over. Where are those years, Amma..."

I looked at her and stopped short, for I saw on her face something I had never seen there before—a look of despair.

Then we both heard it—the hissing sound of milk boiling over and putting the fire out.

The School at Kone

❧

The year was not lost completely, however. Even Amma had to admit that. A few months after my recovery it was discovered that I could do something that Lakshmi, after a year and a half of schooling, could not, and Savitri and Aditi could do only falteringly: I could read.

I was sitting, one afternoon, with my face buried in Lakshmi's school textbook—which I had quietly taken from her bag—when my father came home for lunch. I was so immersed in the book that I did not look up when he walked in.

He threw the toffee he had brought at my feet and said, "What's my boy doing?"

"I'm reading," I said.

"But I can't hear you reading anything," he said. "I don't even see your lips moving."

"I am reading silently."

Father laughed aloud. He turned to uncle, who was reading a Sanskrit book, and said, "Look at this nephew of yours. He has his head in the clouds always. When will he come down to earth? Look at him, pretending he's reading silently."

"He always does that," said Lakshmi, complaining. If my father and uncle were not there she would have snatched the book away. "He always takes my book. I try to keep my book clean and nice, but he handles it so roughly."

"Your book is clean because you don't read it," I said, "and you don't read because you don't know how to."

"This is how he teases me," Lakshmi said, whimpering. "He doesn't let me read in peace. He laughs at me and says I make mistakes." Tears started coursing down her fat cheeks and she added, "Ask Aditi or Savitri how much he teases me when I am reading."

Savitri agreed that I did laugh at them but only when they made mistakes while reading. "But how does he know that?" said father. "He can't read; he doesn't even know his alphabet."

It was true that mother's efforts to teach me the alphabet had come to nothing. Her method was the age old one of writing the letters on a slate and asking the child to go over them with a slate pencil several times, till the letters grew in girth. I did that once or twice and then was fed up. The next time she asked me to do it, I broke the slate pencil, took a small piece and used it lengthwise so that the letters got the necessary girth with only one attempt.

"I think he does know how to read," said Aditi, but Lakshmi did not agree. "He is a parrot, Mawa. He knows all the lessons by heart, because he listens when we read. He waits for us to make mistakes and that makes us nervous."

"What are you reading, Babu?" asked uncle, who was quietly listening. I told him what I was reading. It was the seventeenth lesson in the book and was about an old woman who lived in an isolated village with a rooster. The whole village woke up in the mornings when her cock crowed and that made her feel she was very important. She felt that the villagers did not respect her enough, and to teach them a lesson she hid herself in the jungle with her cock. The entire village, she thought, would sleep on forever.

"But he can't read that," said Lakshmi. "None of us can, because the teacher hasn't taught us the lesson. He is bluffing again."

"Will you read the lesson aloud, Babu," asked uncle, and I began to do so, a bit hesitantly at first because I was not sure whether I knew how to read. All that I knew was that the book spoke to me. Then I warmed up and read on, because I liked the story. When I looked up at the end and found Lakshmi's mouth open in astonishment, I burst out laughing. "Close your mouth, fatso," I said, "or a fly will enter it."

There was such widespread excitement at my performance that my ragging of Lakshmi went unnoticed. How, and when, did I learn to read? I could not, myself, answer that question. All that I knew was that I used to pore over the book with a great deal of fascinated curiosity and then gradually the words began to have meanings and the book began to speak to me.

I think I learnt to read easily because to me it was all play, and not work. My cousins tried to piece the letters together to form words. I wasn't interested in the letters, though I could recognize most of them. I wanted to get at the words, because words had meaning, stood for *things* and told stories. Quite often it was the words that told me what some of the letters were, not the other way round.

The day after the discovery I got four books, the first such gifts I received. Father brought from Kantheshwar the First and Second Standard Kannada textbooks, and uncle, from Chandapur, two thin storybooks, *Thata Pata Haniappa* and *Henu Sattu Kage Badavayitu*. I read the books again and again till I knew everything in them by heart.

By the time I joined school, in June, I had read quite a bit. There weren't many children's books in Kannada then, but I read whatever I could get hold of, and I read with a fair degree of fluency.

I said that my recovery was slow. Perhaps I was reluctant to get well because I dreaded going to school. Everyone, except my father, made some contribution to increase my dread. Even my uncle added to my fear by telling me about the ingenious punishments *his* teacher used to mete out to his students, and *his* teacher happened to be the father of the headmaster I was going to study under! Lakshmi and others told me stories—and they were horror stories—of this man walking about the school with a cane in hand, tall and slim and ramrod straight, looking like a cane himself. He was my uncle's student but I feared that he wouldn't remember that when he was incensed.

They all wanted, I think, to instill some fear in me. 'Fear' was a good word then, and a child who feared no one was thought to be in imminent danger of falling into evil ways. Some of them perhaps wanted to get even with me. *You are acting like this now, wait till you go to school, and Mr. Holla the headmaster catches hold of you.* How often did I hear that remark, from almost everyone in the house, except uncle and father.

The monsoon broke a week before the schools were to reopen. It rained heavily for four or five days, with occasional thunder and lightning. I prayed that the rains would continue so that I could have a few more days of freedom. Thousands of children must have prayed with me but Indra, the god of rains, did not listen to us. There was only a light drizzle on the day the school reopened. My uncle came with us to get me admitted to the First Standard. Ours was a long procession because there were eleven of us—four boys and two girls from the other houses of the hamlet, the three girls from our house, myself, and my uncle bringing up the rear—all walking in single file because we had to walk on the narrow rims of raised earth that separated the paddy fields.

I wanted to talk to my uncle desperately, but could not. One had to shout to be heard above the pattering of rain on our palm-leaf umbrellas, and the need to walk in single file made it impossible to say anything close to his ear. I wanted to know whether he had caned Mr. Holla when he was his student. I wanted him to tell Mr. Holla, "Look, I didn't punish you when you were my student, so don't cane my nephew now."

We reached school, Aditi and others went to their classes, Mr. Holla received my uncle with great respect; and I was sent to one of the noisiest rooms I had ever been in. There was no teacher in the class. Half the students were crying and the other half shouting themselves hoarse. I found a boy climbing a bench and jumping down. I followed his example and soon there were five or six of us jumping about. I decided that the bench was too low, and climbed on the teacher's chair and from there scrambled on to the table. I was standing there ready to jump, when I saw that the whole class had suddenly become silent. Even the crying kids had stopped their whimpering. I turned and saw, at the door, Mr. Holla, tall and thin and ramrod straight, brandishing a cane.

I panicked and burst out crying. On the way to school I had felt a strong urge to pee but was too anxious and nervous to realize how pressing the need was. Now the panic button was pressed and the floodgates opened. Standing there on the table, in full view of the class, I flowed, tears streaming down my cheeks and water from my shorts.

I don't know who put me down from the table and took me to the Third Standard, where I was made to sit between Lakshmi and Aditi. There I sat, all through the morning session, ignored by the class teacher but not by the students.

On the way back from school I was asked by the other kids from our hamlet what exactly had happened. I don't know what I told them, but the women of the hamlet were saying to one another in the evening: "Do you know what the boy from the house of the Matha did today in school? He stood on the table and peed at the headmaster!"

At home I was the laughing stock. By evening I had had enough. I firmly said to mother, "I don't mind being a cowherd or whatever, but I am not going to school again."

It took all uncle's persuasive powers to make me change my mind but I still refused to go to the class from where I had made such an ignominious exit. Uncle had to accompany me to the school again, to ask the headmaster to allow me to sit in the Third Standard with my cousins for a few days till I got used to school.

The headmaster readily agreed. So I began to sit in the Third Standard, between Lakshmi and Aditi. The class teacher ignored me and never asked me any questions. So I had an easy time and could sit there in the class and dream, or when I felt like it, listen to what the teacher said; whereas the other students were under constant pressure. They had to answer a barrage of questions and when they could not answer them, they were made to stand up on the benches and sometimes even caned. Months passed, but there was no talk of my going back to First Standard.

Then one day there was panic in the school. News had come that the Inspector would visit the school the next day. Those were days when teachers did not have the kind of job security they have now, and the School Inspector was a dreaded figure. The students were asked to go home early so that they could wash their shorts and shirts and come spick and span to school the next day.

In all that hustle and bustle it was forgotten that I belonged to the First Standard, not to the Third. So when the Inspector, a smiling young man, came to our class, I was sitting at my usual place between Lakshmi and Aditi.

I don't think I have ever seen a man so frightened as our class teacher was on that day. He was a tall thin man and we could almost hear his bones rattling. The fear he so plainly showed spread in the class. So when the Inspector started throwing questions at the class, there was no one with courage enough to raise his or her hand.

After two or three questions went unanswered, the smile began to fade from the Inspector's face and the teacher started trembling like the patri in a darshana. I was the only one left untouched by the fear that enveloped the whole class, a fear that was almost palpable. So when the fourth question, a simple one, was asked, I raised my hand.

The next few minutes were plain crazy. Every time a question was asked, my hand shot up. They were mostly simple questions, and there were perhaps five or six students—including Aditi—who could have answered them, but they had all lost their nerves. Every time I answered a question, I looked at our teacher's face and saw there, writ large, relief, disbelief and awe. He just could not believe that I could answer all those questions. In fact I did not myself know that I could; apparently, when I was dreaming my time away in the class I had one of my ears open to what was being taught.

The Inspector next wanted to see how we read aloud. His patience by then was beginning to wear thin, and whenever a student mispronounced or stumbled at a word, he promptly said, "Next." When Lakshmi's turn came, she was allowed to mumble through only half a line.

I was next. I knew I could read well but the teacher did not. He cleared his throat and made an effort to speak—perhaps he wanted to say that I was from the First Standard and did not know how to read—but the words got stuck in his throat. The Inspector looked at him; then turned to me and smiled encouragingly. I began to read.

I read, not just with fluency but with a near-perfect accent; something I had picked up as I grew up on my uncle's lap, listening to his enunciation of

Sanskrit, the mother of all Indian languages. The Inspector forgot to say "Next," and I continued till the bell rang. The expression on the teacher's face was not much different from the one I had seen on Lakshmi's face when I read aloud the seventeenth lesson of her Second Standard book.

If what I have written sounds conceited, I can only say that conceit or pride is the last thing I feel when I think of that bright little boy. What I feel is humility, and a sense of waste. I see very little in common between that child and myself. And if that child were to see the man he fathered, I'm afraid he would be quite disappointed. Old Wordsworth would have understood what went wrong: there was a breach, a loss of continuity, a severance of roots; a failure to ensure that one's days were bound each to each with natural piety. When did that happen and how—that is what I must explore.

That evening both the headmaster and the Class Teacher visited our house. Mr. Dhanya, the Class Teacher, bowed down to my uncle, and said, "Your nephew saved my job today. How well he read! And I did not even know he could read. We must thank you—for where else could he have learnt that pure accent but from you?"

Uncle was quite embarrassed. So he changed the topic and said, "Sudhakar has got used to the school now. When do you want to send him back to the First Standard?"

"Oh, no, no," said the headmaster, lifting his hands to his ears in that typical Indian gesture of protest; "if he is not fit to be in the Third Standard, who is? He will stay in the Third. No question of sending him down."

When they were about to leave, Mr. Dhanya said, with folded hands, "I am afraid I ignored your nephew all these days. I made no efforts to teach him. Here onwards I shall make amends. I shall pay special attention to his education."

I was quite pleased with that remark. It was only gradually that I realized what a terrible mess I had got myself into. I lost my freedom to dream in the class, and to pick up things as they came to me. The teacher directed most of his questions at me and expected me to answer all of them. I felt harassed and lost all interest in studies. Though I somehow managed to scrape through the exams and get promoted, I think I learned very little in the three years I spent in that school. In my final year—in the Fifth Standard—the headmaster was himself our class teacher. In my 'Progress Report', which he wanted me to show to my uncle, he wrote down the well-known Kannada proverb:

With the passage of time, the royal horse became a donkey.

Mangoes and Monkeys

❧

But those three years were not entirely wasted. I read a lot, as my uncle kept me well provided with books from his school library. School-going had widened my world and I now spent a lot of time playing with the boys of the neighbouring houses, who, having lived a less sheltered life, had fascinating things to teach me about the facts of life. We played all kinds of games. When the fields lay fallow after the harvest we played, on the rough ground, our own version of hockey, with a wooden ball and sticks we had ourselves cut and fashioned from the trees in the woods behind our hamlet; and cricket with bats made from the stems of coconut fronds. In the rainy season we often sat huddled together, eating *happalas* roasted for us by Ranga's, or Raju's, or Mahabala's mother, as I held them spellbound with stories from whatever book I was reading then.

In February the five large mango trees in the hamlet had clusters of little unripe mangoes. We soon finished off the ones in the lower branches with our fusillade of stones but most of those in the upper branches survived and ripened, to fall with a muffled thud on the soft ground below in the month of May. We often spent the hot, windy afternoons in the shades of those trees, waiting for the mangoes to fall. On windy nights we heard those soft thuds even in our dreams and those who could get up early, before sunrise, and scour the ground under the trees often struck it rich.

The girls were better at this than the boys. In our house, with Lakshmi, Aditi and Savitri all being habitual early birds, I stood no chance at all. Lakshmi, who loved mangoes, usually got up first when it was still dark. She then woke up either Savitri or Aditi. She had once gone alone, before daybreak, to look for mangoes but had come back screaming, when she saw a cowled spectral figure rising from the ground under the mango tree. The mystery was solved after sunrise when we went to investigate and found, at the exact spot where Lakshmi had seen the spectre rising from the ground, an unusually large chunk of human excreta. "Ayyayyo," said Varijamma, the leader of our investigating team, "it was no ghost, it was some poor man answering nature's call. Thank God, Lakshmi, you came here when he was still at it. Had you come a little later, you might have mistaken the thing for a mango!" And oh, how we laughed. It was not much of a joke, perhaps, but laughter can become uncontrollable when it comes after a fright. Even Lakshmi giggled nervously, though the joke was on her.

I started teasing Laksmi, calling excreta 'Lakshmi's mangoes'. This went on for some days till Amma heard me using that phrase once. She did not know what had happened. She was sweeping the floor then, but turned red when she heard that phrase and lashed at my legs with the broom in her hand. I let out a yell of pain and anger, for a broom, made of sticks gathered from coconut fronds, could really sting. "What are you beating me for?" I cried, "What have I done?"

"You have become vulgar and foul-mouthed," she said; "You are learning things from your friends, aren't you? I'll stop you from going there to play"

I understood what she meant when we were bathing in the tank a few days later. Aditi, who was scared of the water snakes in the tank, was the first to leave. Savitri could swim like a fish and was floating around. I was near the edge, thrashing about and trying to learn to swim, too scared to venture into the deep. Lakshmi was near me, lazing about, with the water up to her chin. She had never made the least effort to learn to swim but she loved to lie in water—like a water buffalo.

I floundered in my effort to swim and swallowed some water. The water was quite dirty. During the rainy season the tank used to be full and the water a clean bottle-green colour but in the height of summer it was a dirty moss green, and we had to descend thirteen or fourteen steps to reach it. I felt sick after swallowing that water and said to Lakshmi, "I am tired, let's go home."

"Let us," she said, and got up. Her blouse, thin and frayed, was clinging to her body. And I realized why mother was angry at my use of the words, Lakshmi's mangoes.

She saw what I was looking at, blushed and dropped back into the water. "You go home first," she said querulously; "I'll come with Savitri."

I went home quietly, feeling troubled and queasy. I hadn't seen them before, those little unripe mangoes. Where did they come from, suddenly? I thought I had seen, under the wet dress, even the dark little mango stems.

A few days later I saw Lakshmi sitting alone on the verandah of the outer courtyard with her hair dishevelled, looking sad and forlorn. I was sneaking towards her to frighten her with a loud 'boo', but it was I who was frightened by Varijamma's scream. "Don't, Babu," she screeched, "Don't touch her, don't go near her!"

"Why not?" I asked, quite startled by her vehemence; "What's wrong with her?"

Varijamma hesitated, and then said: "A crow has touched her, that is what is wrong. So don't you go near her for three days."

"O God," I said, "Is it the same crow that touches you and Amma and Kamalamma and Gangamma every now and then?" Varijamma frowned. "Yes," she said, "but it is none of your business. Why don't you go out to play?"

When I went in I saw Kamalamma, Lakshmi's mother, crying. She was a kind, affectionate person who always gave me whatever I asked for: a piece of tamarind, or a pickled mango, things I could not get from my mother. I was quite fond of her.

"What are you crying about?" I asked her. "Is it because of Lakshmi?"

She nodded. "I have enough worries as it is; and now this problem. Who will go looking for a husband for my child? Where will the money for the marriage come from?"

"But why did Lakshmi tell you people that a crow touched her?" I asked her. I went close to her and said, "Do you know, Atte, I was eating a happala the other day, a crow came and took it away. Its wings brushed my cheeks but I didn't tell anyone. I didn't want to spend three days and nights in the outer courtyard."

Kamalamma smiled through her tears. "You are going out to play, aren't you? Go and play, but don't tell anyone about what has happened, please."

There was great excitement among the boys of the hamlet that morning: the monkeys had come, after a gap of more than a week. They raided the hamlet almost every day when the schools were open because they were not afraid of women. They took eatables like happalas left in the sun to dry, and if the doors were open, they sneaked in and grabbed whatever they could lay hands on. Then they would sit on the roof in full view of the women, eating the spoils of their raid with great relish, totally unconcerned about the women's war dance with brooms and sticks in the courtyard below. Their nonchalance infuriated the women but there was nothing they could do.

They were wary of us boys because we could throw stones with a fair degree of accuracy. But though they were much bigger targets than the mangoes, it wasn't easy to hit them because they could dodge and weave out of the way of a flying missile with great agility. Among us they were afraid of only Raju who could throw a stone straight like a bullet.

Raju was not around that day and the monkeys were moving about on the roofs with confidence. When I went there I saw only Little Ramu standing quietly with a few stones heaped in front of him. Ranga and Mahabala had gone home for breakfast.

"Shhh..." said Ramu, "Don't throw stones now; pretend that you are not interested in them. Just watch and see the fun."

I knew what fun he wanted to see. I had seen it all before. On the roof of the upper storey of our house—the highest roof in the hamlet—the monkeys were usually at ease, as they felt sure that the stones hurled by me could not do them much harm. There they did things that I found fascinating. The leader of the group was a big male who sauntered around lazily. He was the boss and could have his own way with the others of the group. When he approached any monkey, male or female, they obediently turned their backsides to him for inspection. Sometimes he stopped a little short of them and pulled them by the tail to where he sat. After a quick inspection, he would push them away, except when it happened to be a female and he liked what he saw. Then he would pull her by the tail right under him and mount, not with his hind legs on the ground like a dog or a bull—the only other animals we had watched doing this sort of thing—but climbing and holding her hind legs with his hind legs, something which only monkeys are capable of. That's because all their four legs are prehensile. They have, really, four hands, not legs.

On that day I and Little Ramu had to wait for some time for the fun to begin. There were a couple of females with flaming red cheeks. Ramu said that they had used monkey-make-up to make themselves attractive to the big male. "Like your mother," I wanted to say, because she was the only one in the hamlet who used make-up. She powdered her face heavily and chewed betel leaves with lime to keep her mouth and lips red. But Ramu was unpredictable. He cursed her himself but if any of us said anything about her he would rush home and report; and she would sail out, after putting on an extra coat of powder, not to catch the culprit but to his house, to scream out abuses at the whole family, particularly the women. So I kept my trap shut.

The big monkey did not show any interest in the red-cheeked females. He was sunning himself. A plain female came and started picking lice from his fine grayish white coat. As he was well groomed she found only two or three, and promptly ate them.

Then he got up and she obediently turned her backside to him. He inspected it and got interested. He pulled her by the tail right under him and mounted.

"Now," said Ramu, with a hissing whisper, and we sprang into action. Ramu's stone missed by a mile but mine hit the male monkey right on the shoulder. He winced in pain but did not dismount. My next stone grazed his right ear, delicate and unprotected by hair, and we could see a thin red line appear on it.

He got down from his perch quickly and came towards us, bristling in anger, brows raised and mouth in a threatening pout. Little Ramu ran, but I had already picked up a thin flat stone, and hurled it at him without taking aim. The curve of that stone's trajectory deceived the monkey. He ducked right into it. The sharp stone hit him near the mouth, another unprotected area. I had done something which even Raju had failed to do till then: I had drawn blood.

There was no fear on the monkey's face even then but he turned and bounded away. The other monkeys had already scampered to the other side of the sloping roof. I hurled another stone at the retreating figure, and wonder of wonders, I scored a hit again. This time the stone hit him just below the tail. It was not a hard hit but it was certainly a blow to his dignity. He scampered away to the other side of the roof like the rest of the herd. Before Ranga, Mahabala and the other boys could come the monkeys had become mere ripples in the thick foliage of the trees behind the houses, and then they were gone. They did not come back till the end of the vacation.

Ramu was in ecstasy. "Good God, Sudhakara," he said, "There has never been anything like it, I bet; four throws and every one of them a direct hit!" Then he started giggling and said, "That last hit was the best! The big boss who examines every monkey's bum—he will have to get *his* bum examined now."

"Just a fluke," said Ranga, when he was told about the incident. "I bet Sudhakara will never hit a monkey again." His prediction proved right: I did not score another hit during the next two years. But then, the monkeys did not give me a chance. They recognized me and always gave me a wide berth thereafter. Fluke or not, I had won their lasting respect.

We sat in the shade of the mango tree in front of Mahabala's house, talking. Ranga, at fourteen, was the oldest among us. Mahabala was twelve, Raju eleven and I was nine. We were in the same class. It was the summer vacation after we appeared for the Fifth Standard examination, perhaps the last exam for the three of them. Most of the boys of the hamlet left school after the Fifth and went to work in restaurants and hotels in towns and cities over the ghats. That was how Ranga happened to be the oldest boy among us: the older ones were already working. Ramu was just six days younger than me but was in the Second. Even in that class he was the smallest. You would think he was five or six till you looked into his eyes, which were old and knowing. If anyone taunted him about his being still in the Second while I was in the Fifth, he would shake his head and say, "My fault, entirely. I didn't stand on the table and pee at the headmaster."

"Tell me, Ranga," I said, after a while, "why do crows touch only women?"

Little Ramu roared with laughter and Mahabala tittered. Ranga's face bore that broad smile for which he was famous in school. He had lost his two front teeth while playing kabaddi. Most of us had a tooth or two missing, but Ranga's toothless smile was incomparable. Our teacher, fed up of caning him every time he did not answer a question—and he could not, most of the times, because his mind went blank when a question was put to him—had devised a novel punishment for him. He was made to stand on the bench and asked to keep smiling. The moment he closed his mouth the teacher would say, "Open, sesame," and Ranga had to grin and bare the gap again.

"Oh, this Sudhakara, he's the limit," said Ramu, still laughing. "They call him Babu at home and he's really a baby; a thumb-sucking baby who knows nothing."

I lost my temper. "As if you know everything!" I said. "You tell me then, why do women sometimes sit out for three days without touching anyone, without a bath, without even combing their hair? Why do they say, if you ask, that a crow has touched them?"

"I know everything," Ramu said, backing away from me. "You are a fool to believe that a crow comes regularly to touch them. What happens is—don't tell anyone I told you—they bleed in their bums, that's what happens. They lie to us because they think we know nothing and will believe anything."

"Nonsense," I said. "He's right," said Ranga, and then with a knowing smile asked, "Who's it now that's touched by a crow? Is it Lakshmi for the first time?"

I remembered Kamalamma's words and kept quiet. Ranga laughed. "These women are crazy," he said. "They think they can keep a thing like that secret. When a girl sits out for three days like an untouchable, how can that be kept secret? They think it will be difficult to arrange a girl's marriage once it's known she's grown up. Now marriages don't take place as early as they used to. Most girls sit out at least a few times before they get married. Look at Kaveri, her marriage is next week, but she has been sitting out for at least four years."

Ramu bristled a little because Kaveri was his sister. She looked nearly as big as her mother, and in our hamlet her not getting married for such a long time was quite a scandal. But she was getting married at last and so Ramu kept quiet.

"Silly, that's what we are," said Ranga, "We don't remember that dosas have holes in every house." Dosas, when well made, invariably have holes.

Ranga had quoted a well-known Kannada proverb, and its appropriateness to what we were talking about made us all laugh. Ramu laughed the loudest.

But I was still confused. "Why," I asked, "if it happens to every girl, why should people hide it, why should it make finding a husband for the girl more difficult?"

"Because it shows that the girl is ready," said Ranga, "and the parents don't want that publicized."

"Ready for what?" I asked.

"Ready to do what the monkeys were doing a little while ago," said Ramu, laughing.

᠔᠔

Two or three months after this I had one of the most embarrassing moments of my young life. I had slept in my uncle's bed since I was one, and I must have wetted it hundreds of times, particularly till I was five. My uncle did not use a mattress; he used two or three cotton sheets on a reed mat. He had to wash them every alternate day because of me. So he devised a method for finding out when I might wet his bed. After midnight he would touch my shorts over the crotch to see if it was fuller than usual; if it was, he would lift me up and carry or drag me to the outer courtyard to pee.

My sleep was disturbed that night. I woke up some time after midnight and lay awake thinking—of what Ranga and Ramu had told me. I thought of the monkeys, of Lakshmi's unripe mangoes and of Kaveri's ripe ones. I felt strange stirrings in me.

My uncle lazily put his hand on my crotch. "Oh, God," he said, and scrambled up in a hurry. He dragged me to the outer courtyard, but fortunately it was too dark there for him to make out whether I peed or not.

Next evening I went and sat near him when he was doing his parayana. "Doddappayya," I said, "I think I'll sleep in my own bed from tonight."

"But why?" he asked me, looking startled. He had hinted, once or twice earlier, that I should learn to sleep alone, but I had said no, because I often had nightmares and woke up in a fright, and then needed his reassuring presence by my side.

"Because I am growing up," I said, "and all those boys, Ranga and Raju and even Little Ramu, they tease me and call me a baby because I don't sleep alone."

"Yes, we'll make a separate bed for you after supper," uncle said. He smiled ruefully and added, "Yes, you are growing up."

The Play

❧

With the exception of Ranga, all of us passed our Fifth Standard examination. It made no difference to Ranga that he failed or to the others—except me—that they passed, as all the three boys were to go, in a couple of months, to work in restaurants where their fathers were already employed. They were not unhappy about it, as the prospect was not bad: plenty of free snacks to eat, no teachers to harry them, and, above all, a quick ascent to adulthood. Lakshmi and Savitri were happy that they passed and did not have to study any more. But Aditi, who topped the school, was despondent because she wanted to study further but knew there was little chance of that.

Mr. Holla came to our house specially to talk to Chikkajjayya and persuade him to send Aditi to the high school or to the higher elementary school. Chikkajjayya as usual was very enthusiastic. Mr. Holla was so surprised by his response that he kept on arguing when there was no need to do so. Their conversation went on like this: "Aditi is an outstanding student, sir, she must continue her studies." "Yes, yes, she must." "I know it is not customary to educate girls but times are changing, girls must learn to stand on their own feet." "Yes, yes, they must, they must." "One can never be sure about the future, sir, if something happens a girl must not become a burden to her parents; she must be independent." "Ah, yes, anything can happen. Look at my three daughters, they have become big burdens to me." "Aditi is such a good student; she will bring credit to you." "She is good, she is good, she will bring credit to all of us." And so on.

Mr. Holla went away in a daze. Aditi of course knew that she had no chance of studying further. Chikkajjayya was like that: he enthusiastically accepted every idea. It is said that the secret of happiness lies in our ability to accept things with enthusiasm, and he was certainly one of the happiest of men. Only, if he had acted on those ideas he so readily accepted, he could have made others happy too; but actions, unfortunately, can lead to troubles and even unhappiness, and Chikkajjayya did not want any of those.

After my dependence on my grandmother and uncle decreased, Chikkajjayya became my best friend at home. I loved to talk, and had lots of interesting bits of information, collected at school or from my reading, to communicate. I could not have found a more enthusiastic listener than Chikkajjayya. As he was not very intelligent—that was evident to me even then—I could, if I had nothing interesting to say, invent things and bluff, and he would say, with his usual enthusiasm, "Ha, is that really so, how wonderful!" As this habit of mine had made others, even Lakshmi, Savitri and Aditi, take most things I said with generous pinches of salt, Chikkajjayya was an invaluable listener.

He once saw me practising *kumchet*, a way of jumping in which you have to, with every jump, hit your buttocks with your heels. "Why are you practising kumchet?" he asked.

"We are putting up a Yakshagana play, 'The Battle of Karna and Arjuna'," I said, "You know I can act and speak much better than Raju, but they have made Raju Karna, and me only Arjuna, because he can jump more kumchets than me. That's why I am practising."

In Yakshagana plays the battle scene is always stylized; the two heroes vie with each other, doing either *mandi*, where you go down on your knees and turn like a top—which neither I nor Raju could do—or jumping kumchets. Arjuna might be the hero of the *Mahabharata*, but in the episode we wanted to play he was the victorious villain and Karna the real tragic hero. I wanted to play Karna and melt the audience into tears, but with my inability to do more than a dozen kumchets at a stretch, I was handicapped.

"That is not the way to jump kumchets," said Chikkajjayya after watching me practising, "Don't come down so heavily on your feet. The heels should not touch the ground at all; land on your toes lightly, and then spring up again."

I tried that and immediately found that I could jump more easily. "You are a great coach, Ajjayya," I said, "how many kumchets could you jump when you were young?"

"Two hundred, or more. Maybe I could have done three hundred, if challenged. I always asked those who wanted to compete with me to jump first—I was the champion, you see—and I had to jump just one more kumchet than they did, to win."

"Good God," I said with awe, "two or three hundred kumchets! A world record, that was what it must have been. How many can you do now?"

"I don't know," he said, "Let's see; how old am I now? Sixty...sixty-five..."

"You are seventy-one," I said. "Gangamma told me that yesterday."

"Am I, really. How time flies! If I am that old, maybe I can't jump more than a hundred now; maybe not even a hundred."

"That's still very good," I told him; "You know Raju and Ranga think no end of themselves, but they can't jump more than fifty. Do you know, Ajjayya, we two must have a competition. But not now. I'll practise hard for a week and then we'll see. I know I can't beat you but I want to try."

"No harm in trying," Chikkajjayya agreed.

A week later we had the competition. As the challenger, I had to jump first. With great determination I did forty. The last three jumps would not have qualified as real kumchets as the heels had not struck the buttocks, but Chikkajjayya did not seem to notice it. "Forty is not bad for a beginner," he said encouragingly. He tied his *bairasa*, the knee-length loincloth, properly. "We don't want it to fall off, do we," he said, then bent his knees in style and tried to jump.

But his feet refused to leave the ground. It was as if they were stuck to the ground with glue. He tried again, and succeeded in jumping but the heels were nowhere near his buttocks. He tried a third time and then sat down, looking bewildered and lost. "I can't do it," he said, "I don't know why, Babu, but I just can't do it."

As I ran out to meet my friends—we had to rehearse our play—I felt guilty that perhaps I had brought some unhappiness to the life of one of the happiest of men. I need not have worried. By the time I came back he was his old cheerful self again.

Yakshagana is called a 'field play' because it is performed in the middle of an open field after the harvest, when the fields lie fallow waiting for the rains. Four bamboos stuck in the ground, with festoons of mango leaves, demarcate the performing square. The play is actually a long poem in a variety of metres, sung by a man called *Bhagavata*, who also talks to the characters and controls the flow of action. The characters dance or put on appropriate poses when the Bhagavata sings, and when the singing gets over they speak. But the speech is always extempore, never learnt by heart. It is called 'interpreting', and is firmly based on the verse just sung. A good actor is one who can 'interpret' the verses eloquently—by his dancing and gestures when the Bhagavata is singing and by his speech when the singing stops.

Our play had to be a parody of these plays because we were brought up on them from our infancy. We saw most of the plays staged in nearby villages. It was all free, of course. The Yakshagana troupes were attached to different temples, and the plays were sponsored by devotees as votive offerings to the God or Goddess of the temple. The performance lasted the whole night so that people from distant villages could come before nightfall and leave at dawn. We went with reed mats, spread them round the performing square and sat down for a full night's uninterrupted entertainment. Small children slept after a couple of hours, but only after obtaining a promise from the elders that they would be woken up at the arrival of the 'Bannada Vesha'. This term, which literally means 'colourful role', refers to the demon or demoness who comes at the end of the play, wearing a fantastic dress and make-up that is truly awe-inspiring.

A poor parody, that was what our play was. The elaborate dresses, crowns and other paraphernalia which are essential for a Yakshagana performance were beyond our reach. We did not even have a *chande*, the drum without which there can be no Yakshagana dance. We tried a kerosene tin but the sound was too cacophonous even for our ears. Ranga, our drummer, finally chose a large bronze pot from his house, after trying out several pots, pans and drums. We did not have a Bhagavata, as there was no one in the village who knew any Yakshagana play by heart. Ranga, when he was not beating the pot, acted as one, and sang snatches of verses from different plays, which had, of course, no relevance to the particular play we were staging.

There were not enough boys in the village to play all the roles and so we had a few guest artistes from Kone. We took all the plum roles: I was Arjuna, Râju Karna, and Mahabala Krishna. Little Ramu fought for and got the role of the Clown, who, in every Yakshagana play, is named 'Hanuma Nayka'. The boys from Kone came on the condition that the visit would be reciprocated and that we would go to their village and play bit roles while they would take the plum ones. But we all knew that such a return visit was most unlikely. Our play was staged at the fag end of the summer vacation, just before the onset of monsoon, and we were mostly from the Fifth Standard. Who knew where the boys would be, whether from Kone or Nampalli, at the end of another year?

When the play started at four, the sky was overcast and we could hear the rumblings of distant thunder. "Poor boys," said Varijamma, who had come early and was waiting for the play to begin, "they have no drums—no chande, no *maddale*—only the pot Ranga's mother cooks rice in; but who cares for that? The gods themselves are beating drums!"

Hanuma Nayka had no role in our play but we had to accommodate Little Ramu, who provided us with most of the make-up materials. His entrances were incongruous, but then Hanuma Nayka himself is an incongruous figure in the heroic world of Yakshagana. Dressed like an ordinary villager and speaking the local dialect, sometimes in its most vulgar form, while all the other characters speak highly Sanskritized bombastic Kannada in a stylized tone, he is often like a member of the audience who has strayed into the heroic world by mistake. Little Ramu wanted that role because it gave him licence to mouth obscenities in front of an audience. His remarks drew titters and giggles at first, but that only encouraged him to become more audacious. "Ayyayyo," said Varijamma, expressing the feelings of most of those present, "this Hanuma Nayka is too much. He will make the Hanuma Naykas of all field plays curl up and die of shame."

The central scene of the play, the duel between Karna and Arjuna, was a disaster. Raju had, with great difficulty, learnt a part of the dialogue by heart, but he forgot it all in his confusion when he found Arjuna extemporizing freely. The battles in Yakshagana are mostly verbal. Every time Raju found that he had no answer to my argument, he said, "Let us stop talking and start fighting." Then he would start jumping kumchets. Once in desperation he even went on his knees and tried to do mandi, but had to get up wincing with pain because the ground we played on was too hard and stony.

As great archers Karna and Arjuna had to fight with arrows, but in Yakshagana even that is done verbally, with a few dance movements. The warrior holds the arrow in his right hand, the bow in his left, dances a few steps and says, "Lo, I am shooting this arrow at you, counter it if you can." The great epic heroes did not use plain arrows. They fought with arrows powered by mantras, and each of those *astras*, as they were called, had counter astras. Raju could not remember the names of these arrows. When I shot at him 'Agneyastra', the Arrow of Fire, he shot back 'Vayavyastra', the Arrow of Wind or Air. I laughed, in the typical Yakshagana style, and said, "O Karna, you fool! You should have countered my Arrow of Fire with 'Varunastra', the Arrow of Neptune. That would have quenched the fire, but like a fool you have used the Arrow of Wind, and that can only fan the fire further. If you did not know the rudiments of archery, why, O fool, did you come to fight with Arjuna, the greatest archer in the world?" The audience clapped, as they always did at a well-delivered speech. Raju lost his head. "Now I am going to use the 'Brahmastra'," he said.

There was a howl of protest from the audience. The 'Arrow of Brahma' is the most powerful of all astras, the ultimate weapon, like a nuclear bomb. In fact many Indians believe that the nuclear bomb is nothing new, but merely 'Brahmastra' rediscovered. "You can't use 'Brahmastra' just like that," said Varijamma, getting up, "It is a terrible weapon. No one used it in the Mahabharata war!"

"How do you know that?" said Raju's mother, also getting up; "Were you there in person?"

So the argument had shifted from the playing arena to the women in the audience. When Ranga saw that he began to play the drum, and Raju and I began to jump kumchets. I saw, for the first time, a grin on Raju's face. This battle, he must have thought, he would surely win. The grin faded when we touched the twenty mark and disappeared when we reached thirty. His heels wouldn't touch the buttocks any more. He was tired after all the kumchets he had jumped earlier. He stopped at thirty-five. I went on to complete forty, amidst loud applause from the kids in the audience.

Something strange happened then. Our Hanuma Nayka, who was sauntering around the stage, suddenly dived and hid himself under the bench on which our drummer and some women were sitting. We looked up and saw Ramu's mother, in a wild fit of anger, rushing towards us brandishing a broom.

We knew the cause of that anger. In her absence Ramu had emptied the tins and jars of cosmetics in his house—powders, foundation cream and mascara—and brought them in paper and plantain leaves for our make-up. We had applied them so liberally that the first reaction of our audience was, sniff, sniff, how nice they smell!

The moment Ramu's mother was sighted, someone said, "Aha! The Bannada Vesha has come!" and a wave of laughter swept through the audience. Ramu's mother found her son quickly enough because she knew by experience that he, the little mouse that he was, always holed up under a chair or bench when frightened. Then began a chase all round the stage, as Ranga, in an inspired burst of drumming, produced on his pot the appropriate rhythm used when the demoness chases her victim.

Then the sky opened and the rain fell in torrents. We ran for shelter laughing all the way. Women of the hamlet spoke of the play, and of the entrance of the 'Bannada Vesha' at the end, for years.

Caves and Tigers

Ever since it was discovered that I knew how to read, my uncle had been bringing me books to read from his school library. That supply stopped during the summer vacation. I enjoyed my vacation—the games, the companionship, the play we put up, and, above all, the unbridled freedom to roam about the hamlet and in the woods behind—as much as the other boys did. I happily turned into an earthworm during that period but the bookworm in me lay dormant, waiting for the vacation to get over.

Uncle used to hunt for books suitable for my age at first but soon gave that up because there weren't too many children's books in Kannada then. He brought me novels and stories and found that the bigger the book, the happier I was. I read novels like *Devi Choudhurani* and *Kapala Kundala*, Kannada translations of exciting Bengali novels by Bankim Chandra Chatterjee, when I was just nine or ten. Linguistic and other difficulties did not deter me. All that I wanted was to enter the world of the novel, and I was not bothered much if I did not understand everything I saw and heard there. They say a cockroach can enter a cupboard if it finds just enough space to push its antennae in. I was like a cockroach. Once inside the novel I felt snug and happy. Words buzzed around me, many of them new, but I could mostly guess what they meant. Even when I could not, it did not matter as long as I could get the main drift of the story. To a child the world of fiction is like the real world—exciting even when not fully understood.

I did not know that this ability of mine was unusual. So I could not understand why people laughed at me and thought that I was merely pretending to read when I sat engrossed in a large novel. I found it easy, so I thought it must be universally easy. I could not appreciate how fine and penetrative were the literary antennae I then had, which helped me enter, cockroach-like, the toughest of novels.

I realized this some years later, when I was sixteen and a confirmed bookworm. I had started reading English novels a couple of years earlier. I had begun with abridged and simplified versions of the classics, but soon found that I could read with ease novels other students with linguistic ablities similar to mine wouldn't even dream of opening. In two years I had read most of

Dickens, most of Scott, all the novels of Jane Austen and a large number of novels by writers whom no one reads now, like Edgar Wallace—my father had a large collection of his works—and Pearl Buck, Mr. Mayya's favourite author.

Something unusual happened when I started reading *A Passage to India*. I was reading Forster for the first time but I had a curious feeling that I was entering a world I had seen—perhaps in a dream—before. As I went on reading I began to feel a strange kind of prescience—a kind of thrilling, exciting *déjà vu*, if I may use an oxymoron. Here was a novel I had never seen before and yet it was as if I was re-reading a long-forgotten novel, read in a prenatal existence as it were.

Then I remembered. My uncle had once brought from his school a book which *he* wanted to read. He thought it was a philosophical work because the title was *Bharata Marga*, or 'the Indian way'. He stopped reading it when he realized that it was a work of fiction, and that too a translation of an English novel.

My father was taken aback when he saw me immersed in that book. "What have you brought for Babu?" he said to my uncle, "This is no book for kids. It's a translation of a difficult English novel. And the Kannada version is tougher than the original. I should know because I tried reading it once but could not go beyond the first two pages." He shook his head, and then added, "How long will this kid go on pretending he can read everything? He's living in a dream world all the time."

That night, when I was about to fall asleep, uncle asked me, "Babu, did you really understand what you were trying to read today?" and I answered, sleepily but truthfully, "I don't know."

I remembered this when I was halfway through *A Passage to India*. After completing the novel I hunted for the Kannada translation and found an old copy in a library. My father was right: the Kannada version was almost unreadable.

And yet at the age of seven or eight I had read that novel. Perhaps I understood very little of what I read but I had undoubtedly penetrated that world; entered it—God knows how—as certainly as Adele Quested had entered the Marabar Caves.

There was one dissenting voice when I joined high school: my mother's. "Why send Babu all the way to Chandapur?" she said, as she was serving us rice. "Why not to Kantheshwar, which is nearer, and what's more, we are likely to shift there soon."

Uncle looked up. This was perhaps the first time he had heard of our shifting to Kantheshwar. He looked at grandmother but she had not heard the remark at all. She continued eating, as if eating was an activity that needed total concentration.

"Nonsense," said my father, "the school at Kantheshwar is only a higher elementary, and Babu will have to appear for the E.S.L.C. exam to pass his Eighth Standard. That is a tough exam. Babu is so unpredictable. He manages to fail in one paper at least, even when he does well in others, in every exam. If that happens in a public exam, like the E.S.L.C., he fails. In high school he is safe because the exams are school exams till the Eleventh. They won't detain him if he fails in one paper."

That silenced mother. She certainly did not want me to lose a year. But her objective was to let grandmother and uncle know that we would shift to Kantheshwar some day, and she had succeeded in that.

I looked at uncle but he was not listening to what my father said. He was looking at his mother, concern writ large on his face.

My grandmother's condition was a cause for concern. That magnificent mind of hers was breaking down. The memory, which held thousands of folk tales and every obscure episode in the epics, had begun to fail. She had lost control of her imagination and that fine line between the imaginary and the real had got blurred. She often talked of uncle as the Swami of our Matha and scolded him for not wearing saffron. Everyone took it as a joke at first, but that pretence could not be maintained for long. Not after the people of the hamlet began to notice that there was something seriously wrong.

We had four cows and five calves in our cowshed, and it was grandmother who had brought them all up. Two of the cows, Kapile and Ganga, allowed only grandmother to milk them. Ganga's month-old calf fell ill. She had loose motion but grandmother knew what medicine to give her. She prepared the medicine, a concoction made of herbs and buttermilk, poured it into a small foot-long bamboo and went looking for the calf.

A few minutes after she returned, Janakamma from the neighbouring house came shouting. She wanted to know what grandmother had fed to *their* calf, and why.

We could not believe it. Our calf was a delicate fawn-like creature, just a month old, but Janakamma's was a five months old bull calf, known and feared for his butting. How could grandmother mistake him for ours? And how did she manage to feed him the medicine? The usual practice was to stand astride a calf, lift and pry open its mouth with the slanted mouth of the bamboo, and then pour the medicine into its throat. Grandmother had done that to that butting bull calf and he had meekly swallowed the medicine!

Everyone laughed but Janakamma said, as she turned to go, "But this is no laughing matter. Nothing will happen to that calf of ours, but what about Ajji? It's she who needs some medicine. You should take care of her."

Nothing happened to Janakamma's calf but ours died the next day. After this, grandmother withdrew into her shell completely. The bewildered look that came when she first heard that she had given the medicine to the wrong calf never left her face again.

It was grandmother's condition which made it difficult for father to make up his mind about shifting residence to Kantheshwar. His practice suffered because he stayed at Nampalli. But what was to be done about grandmother? She would be totally lost at Kantheshwar. Even at Nampalli Janakamma had seen her once walking round our house aimlessly. When she saw her the third time, trudging along with a despairing lost look, she asked her what she was looking for. "I have lost my way," grandmother had said, "I can't find the door of our house." If that could happen to her at Nampalli Matha, where she had spent more than fifty years of her life, how would she fare at Kantheshwar? Then there was uncle. He certainly wouldn't want to leave Nampalli and go and stay in his younger brother's house. For father it was a real dilemma.

Something happened then which forced father to make up his mind.

I was sound asleep one night in November when a hubbub of voices, Varijamma's louder than the others, woke me up. I saw father sitting in a corner. Though it was well past midnight and rather chilly, he was wet with perspiration. He had just come home on his bicycle and on the way he had had an encounter with a tiger.

Father got up and went to have a bath. Whenever he came late, it was almost invariably because of some delivery he had to attend to, and so mother always kept some hot water ready for him. After attending to childbirth he had to take bath before he could sit down to eat.

But he did not want to eat that night. Mother, who always ate after he did, did not want to eat too, but she had to tidy up things in the kitchen before she could go upstairs. So father turned to me and said, "Will you come up, Babu, and sleep with us tonight?"

I was more than willing. An encounter with a tiger on the road was a rare event and I wanted to hear all about it.

He was quite willing to talk. After putting Savita in her bed, he told me the story.

He was coming home on his bicycle after attending to a difficult 'case' at a remote village called Vakkodi. It was past midnight. He was dead tired, but he pedalled fast, because he wanted to get home soon and rest; and also because the night was dark and the bicycle's headlight, powered by the little bottle-shaped dynamo attached to the rear wheel, gave enough light only when the machine was ridden at full speed. The mud road was narrow but he knew it well. Then he saw, right in the middle of the road, two red shining lights. He instantly knew what they were: light reflected by the eyes of a tiger.

"You know, Babu, the eyes of all animals shine in the dark. Those who go hunting at night carry powerful torches, and they can make out what animal they have encountered by the colour of the light reflected by its eyes. If the colour is a burning red, like what I saw, it has to be a tiger or an owl."

So it was a tiger and father had to take a split-second decision what to do. If he stopped his bicycle the headlight would go off and he would be in total darkness—with a tiger facing him just a few feet away! Turning back was impossible on the narrow road without slowing down, and that would put the light out. The only hope was to ride past the tiger at full speed, putting his trust in the popular belief that nocturnal creatures were so mesmerized by powerful beams of light that they would stand still and not attack.

There was another decision, even more crucial and terrible, to take. The tiger's eyes were seen at the centre of the road, where would its body be? If the beast was coming from the thick jungle on the right, its body would cover the entire right half of the narrow road; if it was going back to the jungle, it would be the left half of the road that was occupied. Which side should he swerve to while passing the tiger, the right or the left?

"I was so close to the tiger, Babu, that at the speed I was travelling I would have crossed it—or dashed against it—in less than two seconds. And yet how many thoughts came crowding in, in that brief moment! I thought of you, of Sita and Savita, and of the dispensary I was building at Kantheshwar. I thought of your uncle, and wondered how he could take care of you all, and of Amma too, if anything were to happen to me. I wondered who would come looking for my body tomorrow. Time can expand, Babu, or human thoughts can so contract that many of them can crowd into a single moment.

"At the last moment I swerved to the left. I immediately saw I had done the right thing, for I could see the tiger on my right as I passed. I could hear its low throaty growl and almost feel its breath on me. And the tiger—can you believe it Babu—raised its paw as I passed, as if it wanted to touch me. Not in anger, I thought, but out of curiosity."

My father was a man of few words. I don't think he had ever spoken to anyone at such length as he did to me that day.

We heard Amma coming up the stairs, dragging Sita along. "Go to sleep," said father, "she won't like it if she finds you still awake. She'll think you have been pestering me for details." I covered myself completely with a cotton blanket and pretended to sleep.

"Has Babu been pestering you for details?" she asked, as she sat down and gave father the glass of milk she had brought. "Tell me what happened,"

He told her the story but with such brevity and curtness that it disappointed me. Perhaps he had exhausted his words, and feelings, while telling me the story.

"But why were you so late?" she asked.

Father touched my blanket-covered head. "Are you awake?" he asked, but I pretended to be fast asleep. So he started telling mother what had happened before he met the tiger.

He had gone to Vakkodi for a difficult delivery. The husband of the woman had come running at the last moment, when he found that the baby wouldn't come out. It was a first pregnancy, and a late one. The woman was nearly thirty-five and she had conceived after praying to every deity in the district. And yet they had not got her examined, nor had they called anyone—not a midwife, not even an experienced woman—to help.

The moment father looked at the condition of the woman, he knew. There was no way he could save both the lives. In a hospital it could have been done but in that village, with no facilities for any kind of surgery, one of the two— the child or the mother—had to die. The child's head was just too big.

The woman was a strong person, both physically and mentally. She had been straining for hours, and sweating profusely, but there was no fear on her face. She heard father whisper to her husband that only one life could be saved. "Save the child," she said, "save my son. We have waited for him for years..."

Father took the husband out but the man was in no condition to decide anything. "We prayed to the Goddess of Kamala Shile and my wife became pregnant, after so many years," he whimpered, "Do what you think is right, Ayya, do whatever is right."

Time was running out and father did what he had to do; the only thing that could have saved the woman's life.

He pierced the child's head and pulled the brain out. The skull collapsed, and the head, and the body, came out easily. Craniotomy, that is what the operation is called. I learnt the word years later.

"O God! How could you do that!" For a moment I thought I had said it, but it was not I, it was mother. "Was the baby alive when you did that?" she asked.

"It was," he said. He sounded very tired. "When I pierced its head, there was a muffled yelp; then, silence."

There was silence for some time. Perhaps they were trying to sleep. Under the blanket I felt suffocated.

"But how long can this go on?" said mother. Her voice had lost its tremor and she was her old nagging self again. "You can't go on risking your life like this. You yourself say that your practice is suffering because we stay here. This house is awful. I can't call it our own, with all those daughters of Chikkajjayya prowling around. Children have to walk miles to go to school. And you don't know what kind of friends Babu has. We must shift house to Kantheshwar, we must think of our own future. We can't think, all the time, of other people."

"*Other people?*" said father, "Who are you talking of? My mother, who gave me birth and brought me up, as we are bringing up our kids? Or my brother who helped me to become a doctor? You know that my father had no earnings." His tone had a sharpness, brought on, I think, by a combination of irritation and fatigue, that silenced mother.

There was silence again. Amma's breathing became rhythmic, a sign that she had fallen asleep. But father apparently did not realize that. In a kinder tone he said, "Don't you worry, Sarasu, I know what to do. A doctor is trained to take harsh decisions." He was silent for some time, and then suddenly asked, "But where is Kamala Shile?"

When there was no reply he realized she had fallen asleep. He sighed, and fell silent.

I could have told him lots of things about Kamala Shile. Grandmother had told me fascinating stories about that temple which was in the middle of a thick jungle. The Goddess of the temple rode a tiger. Devotees were scared to go to the temple in the evenings as tigers from the surrounding forests were often seen roaming freely in the courtyard. When the River Kubja, which skirted the temple, was in spate, and the villages and the jungle got inundated, the people of the villages and the tigers of the forests took shelter on a rocky plateau above the temple, the people huddled in a corner, but not afraid, because the tigers never harmed anyone. In April, when people of the four villages surrounding the temple heard the tiger's roar close by, they took it as a signal—an invitation—and got ready for the car festival of the Goddess.

I fell asleep thinking of all this and slipped straight into vivid nightmares. In the first one I was travelling with father on his bicycle. It was pitch dark and he was pedalling like mad. Then we saw, in front of us, two luminous eyes.

It seemed to me that father was riding straight at those eyes. "Turn to the left, Appa, turn to the left," I screamed, but when he turned, the road turned too, and those two eyes remained in front of us. Then they came closer and burned brighter, and thinking that we were about to crash into them, I screamed in fear and woke up.

"What happened?" asked my father. He was still awake. He patted my head gently and I soon fell asleep. I had several dreams thereafter which I could not recollect the next morning. And then a frightening nightmare that is still etched in my memory.

This time the bicycle was stationary, on its stand, the rear wheel off the ground. We were in a thick jungle. Father was furiously turning the pedals with his hand to keep the headlight on. And those burning eyes were right in front of us. In the bright beam of light I could see clearly the head of the tiger. It was a frighteningly large head, stuck in a cave.

"Let us run, Appa," I pleaded but he went on turning the pedals. I saw, in the light, the cave trembling. A few pebbles got loose and fell. I could see that the beast had lowered its head and was pushing hard, trying to break free.

"Let us run," I said again, nearly crying, but father was too intent on examining that head to listen to me. "The head is too big," he said. "It can not come out. Take this, Babu, and pierce the centre of the head, you will find it quite soft."

He thrust a forceps-like instrument into my hand. Even in the midst of my terror I remembered the crazy story my grandmother had told me: that the centre of a tiger's cranium is so delicate that a falling gooseberry can kill it; and so tigers never sleep under gooseberry trees!

"I can't do it," I said, "I am not a doctor like you, Appa." I was whimpering now, and he said, "All right, you turn the pedals and keep the headlight on. I'll do the operation."

I started turning the pedals as fast as I could, till my hands hurt. I was so involved with my struggle that I did not notice when father moved in and pierced the head with the forceps. He moved aside but I was caught in the stream of blood that gushed out. I felt its warm wetness, and woke up.

I had wet my father's bed. I felt terribly ashamed. He was sound asleep, snoring. I could see that dawn was about to break. I quietly got up and went to Sita's bed. Before I fell asleep I said to myself, "Whatever else I may become, I am not going to be a doctor."

And I fell into dreaming again. This time I was sitting huddled with several people, only one of whom I knew: my grandmother. I tried to talk to her but it was no use. She looked totally lost. Then I saw that on the other side of the raised ground, a little away from where we were sitting, there were tigers walking about. I looked round and saw that the whole place was surrounded by water.

A cold breeze blowing from across the flooded river made me shiver. I pulled my blanket closer and tried to sleep. Then I saw, through a hole in the blanket, a tiger moving towards me. I could do nothing but pretend that I was asleep. The beast raised a paw and shook me but I refused to wake up. Then the shaking became violent.

"Wake up, you good-for-nothing," said mother, shaking me hard; "You are eleven years old, but like a small baby you have wetted your father's bed. Aren't you ashamed of yourself?"

My father laughed. He was sitting up, with his back to the wall. The sun had risen outside and a ray lighted up the wall just above his head, throwing a halo round it.

"Leave him alone," he said; "he has wetted his uncle's bed hundreds of times, but mine, never, till now. I have waited for ten years, for this."

Habba

The day after this I found Gangamma sitting with Savitri, holding her by the hair. She was performing a combing operation for lice with an old wooden comb that had lost nearly one third of its teeth. Though Savitri winced in pain when her hair was tugged and pulled, she was a willing victim. She was delighted whenever her mother found a big louse and handed it over to her. With great concentration she placed it on the nail of her left thumb, and crushed it with her right thumbnail. I watched with interest the little creatures explode and die, producing 'chit, chit' sounds.

"Yesterday was a bad day," said Gangamma. "Today is *amavasye*, the night of no moon, but the day prior to that, the fourteenth day of the dark fortnight, is more inauspicious." I knew she was referring to what had happened to father. Then she smiled and said, "A fortnight from now is *hunnime*, the full moon day. You know what's on on that day, don't you?"

"What's on?" I asked her.

She looked surprised. "Why, it's Kodi Habba, of course. You didn't know that the *habba* is only a fortnight away?"

It was my turn to be surprised. Kodi Habba, the car festival of Kantheshwar, was an awfully important annual event. People of Kantheshwar and surrounding villages looked forward to it and made preparations weeks in advance. Children collected and saved all the money they could, so that they could spend it at the festival. Men working in far away places took their annual leave and came home for the event. The day was only a fortnight away and I did not know it! It was unbelievable.

I blamed my cousins of deliberately keeping me in the dark about the festival because they did not want me to collect more money than they could. "Ha, as if we can," said Lakshmi, "You spend all your money, then pester your father and uncle and get more money than we collect."

"We didn't keep it a secret," said Aditi. "It just happened that you were away when we sat down to count our coins or make plans for the festival. Don't forget, Babu, that you are in your school most of the day, whereas we sit at home doing nothing."

I went to the neighbouring houses and found that everyone was well aware of the coming festival. It was perhaps more important to them than to us, because the men of the hamlet who worked in hotels in distant towns and cities were due to come home for the festival. Only Ramu's father was not expected as he had spent more than a month at home at the time of Kaveri's marriage in June.

We reached Kantheshwar in time for the pulling of the chariot. The image of the Lord had already been brought out and placed on the huge wooden chariot, hundreds of years old, which moved ponderously only when thousands pulled the two python-thick ropes with all their might. We all joined in, some—like me—pulling with all their might, and the others just touching the rope as a token of participation.

The chariot stopped after reaching the eastern end of the Car Street, which also happened to be the centre of the pethe. People came with offerings of coconuts and plantains to receive the Lord who had come from the sanctuary of the temple to be with them, in the market place, for a few sacred hours. The ropes were then removed and tied to the other side of the chariot so that it could be pulled back late in the afternoon to its original place in front of the temple. There was time now for meeting people, gossiping and shopping.

Uncle took me to father's dispensary. As there were no patients waiting, father came out with us and took us to his new dispensary under construction.

We had heard of the new building but had no idea how far the work had progressed. We were surprised when we saw the dispensary, gleaming with fresh paint, ready for occupation. Only the furniture had to be moved in. And behind the dispensary was the house. That too looked as if it was nearly complete but father said that more than half the work remained.

He laughed a little nervously, pointed to a room in the corner and said, "Who do you think is that room for, Babu?"

"For me," I said, and he nodded in agreement. "And the next one is for your uncle. I want him there to see that you study a bit and don't waste all your time dreaming."

"I did not know," said uncle, "that the work had progressed so much."

"The work started nearly six months ago," said father, "and has been going on by fits and starts. It's only during the last fortnight that it has picked up. There are more people working now because I want the work to get over soon." He took a deep breath, and continued, "To tell you the truth, I don't like what I am doing—building a new house, leaving Nampalli and putting you in a quandary. But what else can I do? My practice is suffering because I am not at hand when my patients need me in an emergency. And after what happened a fortnight ago…you must have seen that I come home early these days. I have stopped all night visits and that is bad for my practice. You know I have a reputation as someone who can handle difficult deliveries; but such cases, God only knows why, always come at night."

He wiped his brow and continued, "I know you don't want to leave Nampalli. I understand your attachment to the place and your devotion to Lord Krishna. But the present Swami does not care for us. He takes away all the income from here to his new Matha and spends nothing here. He has not visited our Matha during the last five years. Maintaining a mansion like that costs a fortune. Who is to pay for it? Another couple of years of neglect and the place will begin to crumble. And soon there will be no one to share the duties of the pooja with you. Chikkajjayya is past seventy, he can't go on forever. If we get out, the Swami will surely make arrangements for the daily rituals. It's his responsibility, not ours."

Father kept on talking all the way back to the dispensary. The panic that had loosened his tongue a fortnight earlier still seemed to work. At the end of it, he looked relieved and happy. Uncle, who hadn't spoken except for one interjection, seemed troubled and sad.

When we reached the dispensary, father took out his purse. "I nearly forgot why Babu has come to see me," he said, laughing. "Ah, here it is; my little contribution to your festival expenditure account."

He gave me a ten-rupee note. I thought it was a mistake. "But it's ten rupees!" I said.

"Why, is that too little?" he asked. When I shook my head, he laughed again. "Go and spend it," he said. "Kodi Habba doesn't come every day."

Even uncle felt that it was too big an amount to be spent by a boy. "Spend it if you must," he said, "but not all on yourself, Babu. Buy some things for your mother, sisters and your cousins."

He did not stay on to see how I spent the money. He went away early because he wanted to reach home before the lighting of the lamps. He was worried about grandmother. She and Chikkajjayya were the only people left behind in the hamlet.

I wish I could give a vivid description of the habba, its sights and sounds and smells, its colourful rituals, and the many quaint customs that make it a unique festival. I was first carried to it when I was a year and a half, and I attended every one thereafter till my fifteenth year. Most of my friends and I would have chosen the festival day as the most memorable day of the year. And yet the pictures of those days, when I try to recollect them, are all hazy and blurred, as if I am still looking out on the festival scene from one of those fast-rotating 'cradles' of the giant wheel I was so fond of. Those manually operated wooden contraptions, much smaller than the electrically rotated 'giant wheels' of today, were to us the ultimate source of excitement. After half a century I can just close my eyes and recollect, vividly, what I felt as a child sitting on those 'cradles': the fear in the guts as the cradles we sat on lurched and tilted, the feeling of levitation and weightlessness when we reached the top and hung there, and then the crazy 'wind in the anus' feeling as we descended.

I even remember when I used that phrase first. We were standing in front of the madly wheeling machine, with its agonized 'kree-ee-yo-o-o-o-n-n-n' sound, waiting for it to stop. I had already ridden it four or five times. Aditi was too scared to try it, Lakshmi and Savitri had one turn; they said they liked it but did not want to spend any more money, because then they would have had less to spend on ribbons, bangles and so on, than Aditi. With the ten rupees father had given me I was feeling rich and generous. So I offered to pay for one ride and they happily agreed. "But you have sat on it five times already," said Aditi, "and each time it costs you one anna. What do you get out of it?" I said that what I enjoyed most was the feeling of air entering my anus. Savitri giggled, but Lakshmi said "Isshi" in disgust. Then they both said, "Isshee, we don't want any such rides." So I saved two annas.

Little insignificant details come to mind when I think of the habba. I remember how we used to go round the chariot looking for the first unripe mangoes of the season. The festival is held in November, when the mango trees just begin to flower. Some years it comes earlier, well before the mango trees show any signs of blossoming. But somewhere, in some village, a tree would flower earlier than others, a bunch or two of tender unripe mangoes appear, and the owner of the tree, or whoever saw the bunch, would take it down carefully and bring it to Kantheshwar, to become a part of the decoration of the chariot. They say there has never been a habba, held however early, when the chariot of the Lord moved without a bunch of tender mangoes dangling from it.

But why was it that I, who did not miss a single habba till my fifteenth year, never attended another thereafter? Ranga asked me that question about ten years ago when I met him in Hyderabad where I had gone for a seminar. Finding his house was easy because Ranga had become a big man; he owned eight restaurants and a hotel in the city. When I reached his spacious bungalow I saw him sitting cross-legged on a sofa facing the door, his large tummy resting on his lap, looking like the smiling Buddha. Prosperity had changed his shape and size, but not his smile. It was as broad as ever, and the gap in the teeth as wide: he had not bothered to get it bridged.

"When did I see you last?" he asked and answered the question himself. "Thirty-five years ago, when you were in S.S.L.C., at Kodi Habba. I never miss a habba but I never met you again. I meet Raju and Mahabala and everyone else, who all come to the habba year after year, whatever their problems, but you have never turned up. Why?"

Why? I had no answer to that question. So I asked him whether the habba had changed in recent years or was the same as before.

"Yes and no," he said. "Most of the shops and stalls now are put up by outsiders. But in spite of that, the habba hasn't changed much. People still buy and eat the same candies we used to as children. Do you remember *battas*, the flat round sugar-candy, and the candy-sticks? You rarely see them these days but they come to the habba in larger quantities than before. People buy them, give them to their children and talk about the good old days. They all come, wherever they are. But not you, though you loved the habba like we all did. Why?"

A servant came with a variety of dishes. I was hungry and the homemade delicacies made my mouth water. Ranga had diabetes and could not eat sweets but urged me to try them all. He took only a plate of *vangi bhaat*, a spicy dish made of brinjals cooked in rice. He started eating with great relish but stopped abruptly because he found a long hair in it.

"My wife's hair," he said, looking at it with disgust. "No one prepares vangi bhaat like she does. You taste it and you know that it is prepared by her. Why does she have to leave one of her hairs in it to show that it is made by her?" He sent the plate back and asked for another. Then he laughed and said, "It's a miracle, the way she keeps losing hair, but does not go bald, like me."

A car came and two children, a boy and a girl in school uniforms, got down. "My last son, the eighth one," Ranga said. "The girl is my granddaughter, my eldest daughter's eldest child. They are both thirteen, and, can you believe it, they were both born on the same day, in the same hospital. You should have seen my wife's face during those days, it was a miracle she did not die of shame." He chuckled, and said, "Just think of that, mother and daughter giving birth on the same day, on adjacent beds!"

"About Kodi Habba," he continued. "Some of the changes are for the better. There are lots of cultural activities now, a full week of it. Classical dances and so on. All sponsored by us restaurant people. You would love them if you were to come. But you haven't, for so many years. Why?"

I had to give an answer and so I groped for one. "You have your roots, Ranga," I said, "and you are still a Nampalli boy. Somehow, I don't know how, I seem to have lost mine."

That may sound all right in English but in Kannada it did not make sense. Ranga laughed derisively. "You and your crazy ideas!" he said. "Human beings don't get roots. They have legs, legs which carry them where they want to go." Then he laughed again, this time good-humouredly. "Maybe what you say is true about my mother. I have never been able to persuade her to come to Hyderabad. She prefers to stay alone at Nampalli though she is nearly eighty now. Next time I go home I must take a look at her feet and see if she has grown roots."

Ranga's question troubled me, and I realized that it was a vitally important one. I knew it would continue to haunt me. You can exorcise a question like that only by finding an answer, honest and adequate. I loved the habba in my childhood and I found its memory still precious. Yet something held me back, some demon within me I could not come to terms with, and I did not visit the habba for thirty-five years. Ranga and Raju and others were uprooted from their village when they were still children, worked in some alien land and prospered; but nothing could stop them from going to the habba every year, year after year, where they met their old friends and childhood companions, bought the good old candies, ate them if they did not have diabetes, pulled the chariot, and went home to their old houses in their old village, which they maintained with care though they stayed there for only a week in a year. They contributed money for cultural programmes, helped the habba to grow, but saw to it that there was both continuity and growth. They were so simple that they could not understand what roots and alienation meant. But they had their priorities right because their hearts were in the right place. They were not confused, they did not feel lost. Whereas I, lost in the concrete jungle of Bombay, acutely conscious of my alienation, could not see that some commitment like theirs might have acted as a buffer against such feelings. Perhaps it was better to be simple minded like them.

From inside came the sound of violent quarrelling. The two kids were screaming at each other in English. "You thief, you filcher, you have opened my purse again," said the girl's voice. "That's my father's money, not your father's, you bloody bitch," said the boy's voice. Someone started an air conditioner somewhere within and the noise drowned the sound of voices, but I could still hear words like 'bastard' and 'bitch', and finally the girl's voice saying, "Fuck off."

I looked at Ranga. The broad smile on his face could only be called beatific. "Can you make out what they are saying?" he asked me. "They are quarrelling," I said. He laughed, beaming with happiness. "They always speak in English," he said. "It's always 'tis pis, tis pis' between them. They use Kannada only when they talk with us. I don't know a word of English, but these kids, they even quarrel in English! It's great, isn't it."

৵

On the day of that habba, the last one I went to from Nampalli, we started for home well after sunset. But that was no cause for concern as it was hunnime, the full moon day. The sky was clear, and I heard someone say, "If it remains cloudless like this for a few days more, we shall have plenty of mangoes and cashew apples this season." The moon was so bright that I thought one could read in its light and was surprised when I found that I could not read the handbill I had found on the road. We were all tired and fell into groups as we trudged home, most of the boys walking in front, Gangamma, Savitri, Aditi and a few other girls a hundred yards behind. Varijamma, who was terribly flatfooted, Lakshmi who was sleepwalking, a couple of women carrying sleeping babies and a few older women brought up the rear. Most of the men, and Little Ramu, had stayed behind. They would come back at midnight, after all the temple rituals were over, and the last stalls and shops closed down for the night.

I was with the boys in front. We had fun trying to read the handbill and then I wanted to show it to Aditi. So I went back to the second group but Aditi showed no interest in my discovery, and the others looked tired and morose. I threw the handbill away and waited for Varijamma and her companions. "Do you know," I said to her, "that demons and ghosts, when they want to waylay people, wait for the hindmost group? They let the others pass and then they strike!" "Go, go," said Varijamma, in a voice made hoarse by a full day's gossiping, "Don't forget that you always frighten yourself most when you try to frighten others. Then you get nightmares and wet your bed."

Feeling insulted, I ran ahead. I caught up with Gangamma and her group and started walking with them. Then I noticed that Gangamma was crying.

"Why are you crying?" I asked her but she did not reply. So I asked Savitri and she said, "My Chikkamma is dead."

At first I could not understand who she was talking about. Gangamma was the youngest of Chikkajjayya's daughters and so there was no one whom Savitri could call her Chikkamma or 'small mother'. Then I realized that she must be talking about her father's second wife.

"Good God," I said, "but how did it happen?"

"She died in childbirth," said Kamalamma. "Poor woman. She had eight pregnancies in eight years. Four miscarriages, and two children, both boys, stillborn. It was a boy again last time but it was born so weak that it survived for only a few days. So she was fed the best of food this time, almonds and fruits and plenty of milk, and someone who saw her a fortnight ago said that she looked like a queen, so plump and fair and lovely. But the child survived this time, a nice-looking boy they say, but she is no more."

I stood on the road and waited for Varijamma and her slow-moving companions. I wanted to give Varijamma the news. She hadn't apparently heard it, otherwise everyone would have been talking about it.

As I stood there waiting, a cold breeze blew from the forest and I shivered. Then a thought struck me: how did she die, this young woman?

Did the doctor who came to deliver the baby say that he could save only one life, not both? Did he find that the child, fattened in the womb with milk and almonds, had too big a head? Did Savitri's father, who had waited for a male heir for so many years, choose the child's life instead of his wife's?

I had been horrified by my father's description of how he saved the mother's life at the expense of the child's. What horrors would be revealed if this doctor were to talk of what he did to the mother to save the child?

I was so absorbed in my thoughts and so lost in horror that I did not notice when Varijamma and others reached me. I nearly screamed with fright when I suddenly heard her hoarse voice say: "Babu, do you know where you are standing and waiting for us? You are standing at the exact spot where the tiger, fifteen days ago, was waiting for your father."

Shifting Sands

By the end of April our house was ready, and we shifted to Kantheshwar in the second week of May. But a number of things happened before that, some of them totally unexpected, making me wonder whether we were on terra firma or had built our lives on shifting sands.

Within a couple of days all the men who had come for the habba left Nampalli and with them went my friends, Ranga, Mahabala and Raju, swept away suddenly into working adulthood. I could not meet them before they left because it used to get dark by the time I reached home from school, and my mother would not allow me to go out after that. So on Sunday I went out to see what the place felt like without my friends. I saw Ramu loitering about, his face looking more pinched and drawn than usual. He bristled with irritation when he saw me.

"The big high school student has come," he said; "He has grown so big that he cannot find the time to come to bid farewell to his friends." Then he took a step towards me and stood threateningly. "Why have you come now?" he asked; "In a few months you too will go away, I know. Leaving me in this hell, alone."

His vehemence shocked me. What was he talking about, I wondered. I also felt irritated. There were two little boys, both four or five years old, stark naked and with running noses, playing nearby. I pointed to them and said, "Why do you have to be alone? Why don't you go and play with boys of your own size?"

He nearly had a seizure and spat out obscenities. He even picked up a stone and threatened to hit me. I walked away disgusted. "He has gone crazy," I thought, and decided not to talk to him again.

I met him only once thereafter, and that was when he, unexpectedly, came to see me off on the day we left Nampalli. I was rather curt with him then. Months later I came to know what he had been going through but by then it was too late to make amends.

The departure of my friends was expected but not what happened the next Sunday. Perhaps Gangamma and others expected it but I was taken by surprise by the sudden arrival of Savitri's father. He was on his way back from Gokarna, a pilgrimage centre known for its facilities for funerals, after performing his wife's last rites there. He had come to collect his first wife and daughter if they were prepared to go with him.

He sat on the raised platform on which Chikkajjayya usually sat. Chikkajjayya stood in front of him, too much in awe of his rich son-in-law to sit by his side. So he called me and made me sit by him. Then he raised his voice and announced the reason for his visit. Though he appeared to be talking to his father-in-law, his raised voice and the way his eyes moved left and right, without settling on Chikkajjayya, showed that the words were meant for other ears.

"I have come," he said, "to take my wife and daughter home—if they want to come. I still don't understand why they left my house but I am not the kind of person who dwells on old questions. I say, what's past is past, let us look forward. My second wife, poor woman, is no more, but the child, a son, has survived. One without a son has no salvation, the *shastras* say. I married a second time to get a son, not for any other reason. This boy will pour Ganges water into my mouth at my last moment and he will do that for my wife too. He has no mother other than her. That is why I have come now. The child is taken care of by my sister at present but she has her family to attend to, and cannot stay at my place indefinitely. So I want to know: does my wife want to come with me now, and be a mother to the motherless child? It is for her to decide."

Chikkajjayya clearly did not know what to say. "Go, Babu," he said, "and call Gangamma." I found them all—Gangamma, Kamalamma, Varijamma and the girls—standing at the corner, just out of view, hidden by the inner temple. "Please tell my brother-in-law," said Kamalamma, "that my sister understands her duty. She will come and take care of the baby." Her brother-in-law heard her. In a rather pleasant voice—not the stiff formal tone he had used before—he said, as he opened a bundle and took out three silk sarees and a silk dress, "I brought these for my wife and daughter. I didn't bring anything for my sisters-in-law, or for my nieces, as I was not sure who were all here. My wife will no doubt make amends for that after she takes charge of my house."

I was asked to eat at Chikkajjayya's kitchen as he was still tongue-tied and someone was needed to talk with his son-in-law. I was made to sit by his side. When Gangamma came to serve rice, wearing one of the silk sarees, he smiled approvingly. But when Savitri came to serve ghee, wearing another of the sarees he had brought, he frowned. "Who is this girl?" he asked me in a whisper.

"Don't you know her?" I asked in surprise. "That's Savitri."

He gaped at her and then burst out laughing. "Good God," he said, "I did not know I'll have to leave every other work and go husband-hunting for my daughter! She is a woman now. A very good looking woman, thank God." In fact Savitri's appearance surprised everyone. A saree can make a girl look grown up but Savitri's transformation was indeed startling.

Savitri had to wear the saree brought for her mother because she could not get into the dress her father had brought for her; it was too small. Gangamma wanted Aditi to try it on but Savitri would not let her touch it. "No, no," she said, "I don't want to give it to anybody. It's too good." And Aditi, hurt by that remark, said, "I don't want anything from anybody. My old dresses are good enough for me." Then they both started quoting proverbs. Savitri said something about a poor man's pride hurting his stomach, and Aditi about a mean person's newfound riches going to his head. Lakshmi, confused and on the verge of tears—no one had ever left our house without Lakshmi shedding some—said, "You are going away, Savitri, leaving us behind. And yet you look so happy. Have you no tears for us?" But Savitri, unable to get out of the argumentative mood, said, "Why should I cry when I am feeling happy? I am not a stupid girl!" Then she made the unkindest remark of the day. "Why do you cry at my good fortune? Is it because you are jealous?"

Everyone was shocked, and Gangamma slapped Savitri, perhaps for the first time ever. Savitri burst out crying and that was a signal for Laksmi's floodgates to open. Soon they were all crying, the three girls, and then they were joined by the three women.

On the way to school next morning I told uncle about it and said, "It was silly. Savitri was mean and Aditi stupid. They have been such good friends! Why should they quarrel just when Savitri was going away?"

"It is difficult, Babu, really impossible, to say why people act the way they do. Savitri, perhaps, was thoughtless because she was too excited to think. And poor Aditi was hurt, and when you are hurt you can't think. They were both thoughtless, not mean or stupid. But no, we may never know why they quarrelled, we can only guess."

"Perhaps they quarrelled," I said, "because they did not want to cry."

Uncle stopped in his tracks and stared at me. "Did you say that, Babu?" he asked in wonder, "Did you really say that they quarrelled because they did not want to cry?"

"Did I say something silly?"

"No, no," he said. "It is not silly, it is in fact too wise an observation to come from a ten year old." He shook his head and said, "I have watched you from the day you were born, Babu, and how many times you have surprised me by your remarks! Where do those thoughts and insights come from, I wonder. And then I see you acting, and you are no better than most boys of your age. You can be thoughtless, you can get into needless quarrels, you hurt people you love. Will you ever have the maturity to act as wisely as you can talk, I wonder."

"But words," he continued, "they have their value, they are precious in their own way." He was in one of his philosophical moods when he was most instructive and most boring. I paid no attention to what he said at such moments but remembered his words years later. "Your words," he said, "seem to come from some spring within you. Keep that spring clear and clean, Babu, so that you can always think with clarity. Maybe you will write some day. Maybe your words will light up the path for others even when *you* walk in darkness." We walked in silence for some time. Then he said "You spoke the truth, Babu, though how you guessed it I don't know. People quarrel for all kinds of reasons; they prefer anger to sorrow; they would quarrel rather than cry."

"But they did cry finally, all three of them."

"That's because they are girls," he said. "Girls are nicer than boys, Babu, they are more natural. Grown up men are the worst. Some keep their anger burning, even till they burn on the funeral pyre."

The next in the series of events was totally unexpected. It happened when I was away in school. I came home that day, anxious to tell Aditi something wonderful I had learnt in school: that if you stand on the North Pole, you can't go north or east or west, you can only go south; whichever way you turn, it's south. I saw Varijamma sitting on the verandah, stooping over some flowers, trying, in the fast fading light, to weave them into a garland. She was alone. "Where is Aditi?" I shouted when I was still some distance away.

She did not look up. I went and sat by her and saw she was crying. "Why are you crying?" I asked her.

She wiped her nose with the end of her saree. That was what she did whenever she cried, because more rheum came out of her nose than tears from her eyes. "They are gone," she said, "they went away to their house."

It was difficult to draw the story from Varijamma, between her sniffs and sobs. Kamalamma's husband's elder brother had come that day. He had thrown them out eleven years earlier soon after his younger brother's death. Now he came, penitent, asking them to come home again. He blamed his wife for all that had happened earlier. She had died a month earlier, after a long illness. They had no children. It was his wife's barrenness which made her bitter and jealous, he said. She had made him quarrel with all his relatives.

He now lived alone in his house, brooding over his ill-treatment of people, particularly of his brother's family.

And Kamalamma had to go for the sake of her daughters. Who would find husbands for them and get them married off? One of the things the man said was that he had done nothing good in his life, accumulated no *punya*, and he wanted to make amends for that by doing *kanya daana*, if his sister-in-law would give him the chance. That had settled the issue.

'Punya' and 'paapa' are key words in Hindu ethics. Good deeds, prayers, pilgrimages, etc. earn you 'punya', or merit, and they are all recorded in the other world. 'Paapa' is sin, and all your sins are also recorded. The balance sheet is maintained by divine accountants called *Chitra Guptas*. *Daana*, or giving, is one of the ways of earning punya, and the best of all daanas is kanya daana, the giving of a girl in marriage to a deserving man. Kamalamma's repentant brother-in-law wanted to earn some 'punya' by shouldering the responsibility of his nieces' marriages.

So I lost my three childhood companions, Lakshmi, Aditi and Savitri, in just three days. I missed them a lot, and so did others, uncle in particular. He was very fond of Aditi. I saw him sitting for parayana one evening, without turning the leaves of the palm-leaf manuscript in front of him for a long time. He was brooding. "With those three girls gone, the house has become emptier than before," he said.

But the one who missed them most was Varijamma. She was a changed person after her sisters and nieces left. Her tongue suddenly stopped wagging and she did not always listen when others talked to her. She asked uncle to get her an exercise book, and to teach her to write 'Shree Rama' in Sanskrit. Someone had told her that if she wrote that name ten million times in Sanskrit, she would get a good husband in her next birth.

She started the exercise, wrote with extraordinary care and completed one page in three days. When she showed it to uncle he was deeply moved. "It's beautiful," he said, "it is better than my hand. It is wonderfully neat." It was indeed a neat job. She had written the divine name four times in each line and drawn fifteen lines on each page, so that counting would be easy. "How many pages I'll have to fill up to write the name ten million times?" she asked me.

I took a long time to calculate it and the answer stunned me. I ran to where she was sitting and said, "You'll need one lakh, sixty six thousand, six hundred sixty six pages!"

She was not much perturbed but wanted to know how many days it would take.

I went back to calculating. I was really shocked when I got the answer. "O God," I said to uncle, who was watching me, "Varijamma will have to write for one thousand three hundred eighty eight years."

He frowned. "She will write faster with practice," he said. "But it is not important how much she writes. She is happy that she has to write the name ten million times; she will be less happy if the goal is only a thousand. How many people do everything they want to do? It is enough if she does whatever she can, as well as she can, and with love. Enjoying every moment of it, not bothering about the final pleasure of completion—which often turns out to be empty, disappointing. Did you see how happy she was when she looked at that single page she had created?"

I did not tell Varijamma how long it might take her to complete the task. I was sorely tempted to because I had worked hard to get the answer. I hadn't enjoyed the work as I hated calculation, so all the pleasure was in the completion of the task. That had to be empty because I could not shock Varijamma with the news, not after what uncle told me.

The last of this chain of events took place in March. Uncle Janardhana, Chikkajjayya's son, unexpectedly arrived, not just with a large trunk as in previous years but with all his belongings. He had sold his restaurant in Bangalore and had come to settle down at his native place.

This was in 1947, a few months before India became independent. The British soldiers in the Bangalore Cantonment were restive. Their future was uncertain, and in many cases, bleak. Here they belonged to the ruling elite but in post-war Britain they would be nobodies. The white man did not want to put his burden down because he was scared of weightlessness.

One of these soldiers wandered into Janna uncle's restaurant one morning just before dawn, apparently from a late night party. He was not one of the 'regulars', who came to Udupi restaurants because they had developed a taste for South Indian snacks and coffee. He had come because these were the only restaurants that opened before dawn. He ordered a coffee. Perhaps he wanted black coffee; when he was served the light brown coloured South Indian coffee instead, with plenty of milk and sugar, he threw it at the waiter's face and slapped him. And when uncle intervened, he kicked him.

It is difficult to explain what a terrible insult a kick with a booted foot was in those days. To an Indian, and that too to a South Indian Brahmin, it was the ultimate insult. What made it unbearable was the fact that the soldier was a puny chap, and Janna uncle could have easily lifted and thrown him out. But you could not do that to a British soldier in the Cantonment area. Janna uncle could not swallow the insult. It stuck in his throat.

He closed the restaurant for the day, went home, took a purification bath, fasted and prayed. But he still felt unclean. He began to feel that perhaps he deserved the kick for forgetting his Brahminical duties and earning his living by selling food. So the moment he found a buyer, he sold his restaurant and started packing up.

But it was clear that he would not be living at Nampalli for long. He used to complain about the heat on his earlier visits, but this time his chief grouse was about the lack of toilet facilities. None of the houses at Nampalli had a lavatory. Everyone went, when they had to, to the woods behind the hamlet. This was tough on Janna uncle who was suffering from what doctors, who cannot diagnose stomach disorders, conveniently call 'Irritable Bowel Syndrome'. Whether you go to the lavatory once in three days or three times a day, to the doctor it is the same ailment: IBS.

Janardhana uncle's IBS, unfortunately, was of the three-times-a-day kind, and after the British kick it had become worse: he had to rush to the woods after every meal, sometimes even after a cup of coffee. So he started looking for a house with a good lavatory, or a good lavatory with a house. The search soon ended happily at Chandapur. He did not like the house he had gone to see and was about to leave with the usual "I'll let you know soon" remark, when the owner forced him to have some snacks and coffee. The irritable bowel immediately registered its protest. He had to go to the lavatory.

It was a case of love at first sight. A thing of beauty, that's what he called it. Not the kind of toilet common in Chandapur then, where your thing slid down a slope and became the topping of an already existing heap, raising a cloud of flies. It was the only one of its kind in the town. All that you had to do was to pour a bucket of water after the job was done, and *woosh, pulk*, the thing just disappeared. Squatting there in the lavatory, Janna uncle took his decision: he was going to buy that house.

He came and told us about his success in the evening, just when we were eating our supper. He also told the story to his father, who, as usual, listened with enthusiasm. "Janna says that the thing just disappeared when he poured water, where could it have gone, Babu? There must be some magic," he said to me the next morning.

So ten days before we shifted to Kantheshwar, Chikkajjayya and his family left for Chandapur. Chikkajjayya took it in his stride. He had never left Nampalli in the seventy-odd years of his existence but like a child he looked forward to the lavatory where the thing just disappeared when a bucket of water was poured. But Varijamma was inconsolable. She shed only an occasional tear but her nose ran continuously. She showed us the pages of Shri Rama's name she had already written. Her speed had increased to three pages a day but she still wrote with the same meticulous care. After they left, I sat down and calculated: the number of years needed had decreased dramatically: Varijamma had to write on for just 154 years to complete her task.

At home the next ten days were terrible. The tension mounted as father desperately tried to persuade uncle to come to Kantheshwar. "You can't live alone in this Matha, now that Chikkajjayya has left," he pleaded. "You think you have to stay here for the sake of the pooja? That's stupid. God does not need your pooja, you do it for your own sake. You can as well do it at Kantheshwar." The pleadings soon turned to accusations. "It's your pride that stops you from coming with us," he said. "You think it demeaning, don't you, to stay in your younger brother's house! Oh, how I wish I had never taken any help from you when I was studying."

I could see that uncle was terribly hurt. But the more hurt he was, the more silent he grew, and his silence incensed father. Two days before the shifting he said, "This is positively the last time I am asking you: are you coming to stay with us at Kantheshwar?" uncle, sitting in front of his parayana books, bent his head in silence. "All right," said father, "stay here if you like. I swear I'll never speak to you again." "No, no," cried uncle, looking terrified, "Don't take such an oath before God." But father, looking grim, walked away shaking his head.

It was all a mistake, a terrible misunderstanding. I think uncle had no insurmountable objection to moving to his brother's house. Reluctance there was but that was understandable. He did not want to be in the way. He must have guessed that at least one person would be more at ease, more at home, without him being around: my mother. She disliked Nampalli and was building her own nest at Kantheshwar; why should he go and spoil it for her? The sentimental reasons were also strong: Nampalli was the place he really belonged to; the place where he grew up, found happiness, and suffered; where he cremated his wife and his only child. But he was a man of love. He loved his younger brother, loved me, loved Sita and Savita, and I am sure he had genuine affection for Amma too. That pull would have brought him to Kantheshwar, frequently at first and then perhaps permanently. But father, instead of ignoring his reluctance to come, or breaching it tactfully, made a frontal attack on it. This made uncle bolster his defences till they became impregnable. Then in the heated atmosphere something happened which took them both by surprise.

I am convinced that the 'oath' was the most preposterous of mistakes. I don't know who should be blamed most for it, uncle or father. What father said was that he would never again speak to uncle about coming to Kantheshwar. He said it when uncle happened to be sitting before the temple and perhaps used the word 'swear' merely for the sake of emphasis. And when uncle, hurt and frightened by the course the quarrel was taking, mistook it for an oath before God, that mistake must have hurt father into accepting it as such: "If my brother thinks that I can take such an oath, all right, so be it." That was what he must have thought.

You hurt people you love. Uncle had said that to me a couple of months earlier. We all do, even the most mature among us. You cannot love and be thick-skinned at the same time. Wisdom and maturity might teach you to hold your tongue but what can you do if silence hurts?

When we were about to leave for Kantheshwar I saw Little Ramu standing at a distance. I decided to ignore him but uncle said, "Come, Ramu, your friend is leaving, come and talk to him." He came sheepishly and started walking with me. My reluctance to talk had nothing to do with our quarrel. He looked so dirty and dishevelled that I felt ashamed of him in my mother's presence because she used to taunt me often about the 'wonderful' friends I had.

He came with me till we reached a spot from where he could take a short cut to his house. He stopped there and said, "So you are going away. Leaving me here, in this hell."

I remembered how he had said the same thing months earlier. "Oh, come," I said, "Don't call Nampalli a hell."

"It's not Nampalli," he said. Then he looked at me and I was surprised by the smouldering anger in his eyes. In a voice which had suddenly become venomous he said, "I am going to kill her. Just you wait and see, I'll do it. One of these days I'll kill my mother."

I was shocked. The chap had really gone crazy. "Come, come," I said, pretending it was a joke. "You haven't ever killed anything bigger than a fly. How will you kill a grown up person, someone as big as your mother?"

"I'll burn her," he said. "I'll set fire to her bed when she's sleeping. I'll burn them both to death." Then he ran, taking the short cut to his house, making 'chug, chug' sounds all the way like a train so that no one would see the misery he was in.

PART III
A Tree in Kantheshwar

৪৯

Home is where one starts from. As we grow older,
The world becomes stranger, the pattern more complicated.

T.S. Eliot

Godhooli

By the time uncle came to Kantheshwar after completing his pooja at Nampalli, most of the rituals of the 'house entrance' ceremony were over. I saw him only a couple of times, once sitting quietly in a corner and then talking with one of the elderly guests. I was too busy meeting old friends, and making new ones, to pay him much attention. Lakshmi, Aditi and Janna uncle's three sons were all there. My two aunts, my father's elder sisters, who usually came only once a year to attend the death anniversary of my grandfather, had come with their children. In all the excitement of the day I did not notice when uncle quietly went away in the afternoon. At night the two aunts—the other guests had left—gave a lecture to father on what he should do to persuade uncle to leave Nampalli and come to Kantheshwar. I saw father's ears reddening—a sign that he was getting angry—but he listened to them in silence.

The house was much bigger than originally planned. The rooms we had seen under construction on the day of the habba were pretty, but none of them was suitable to be a kitchen, dining hall, storeroom, pooja room or a bathroom. So father had a long line of rooms built, beginning with a dining hall and ending with a cowshed. The cowshed nearly touched the compound wall. I heard someone say that the house would have gone on and on, like Hanuman's tail, if the compound wall hadn't come in the way or the land beyond the wall belonged to father.

The land beyond the wall was the one with the suragi tree. Father bought it after a few months but by then the house had lost its urge to grow. The cowshed remained the last room. When the house changed into a hospital years later it became the nurses' room, but was still called the cowshed.

Only four of our cattle—two cows, a heifer and a calf—were brought from Nampalli. The others were given to our tenants, a Devadiga family, with the condition that they should take proper care of them and should not sell them to strangers. This proviso was necessary because strangers used to come to villages looking for cattle, offering prices higher than usual. They offered the same price for male and female calves and this made people suspicious. Govinda Seregara, one of the tenants of the Matha, sold two calves for a hefty sum and then came to our house looking worried. "Ayya, I can't understand this," he said to uncle, "Why should anyone pay the same price for a *gudda*—a bull calf—as for a heifer which will soon become a cow and give milk? Our guddas are useless, they are good for only mounting their mothers. They don't even make good draught animals, we have to buy our bullocks from across the ghats. But those two fools, they gave me the same amount, a good fifteen rupees each, for my heifer and gudda. Why did they do that, Ayya?"

"What did they look like?" asked uncle, his brow creased with worry.

Even from Govinda's disjointed description uncle could make out that the men were outsiders, in all likelihood agents seeking cattle for some slaughterhouse. "How could you sell those calves, Govinda, those innocent things, to total strangers?" he said in anguish. Govinda was shocked. "How can anyone have the heart to kill calves like that?" he asked. Then he got up to go, shaking his head sadly. "I don't mind about that gudda so much," he said, "he butted me from behind only yesterday, and I fell down on the dung heap. But that heifer, Gauri; she was like a daughter to me..." He took a few steps and then came back. "Don't tell this to anybody, Ayya," he said, looking worried; "my wife didn't want me to give Gauri away. She hasn't eaten since yesterday. If she comes to know this I don't know what will happen to her."

It is difficult to make outsiders understand our feelings and sentiments about cows. We don't worship them, though my grandmother or uncle or mother, if you had asked them, would have said, "Yes, we do. They are sacred, because that is what the scriptures say." What we feel for them is affection, not awe or reverence. The only pets we had in our childhood were calves. The calves we loved and played with grew up into cows, gave us milk and became symbols of motherhood. Once a year we actually 'worshipped' them, on *Go Pooja* day—one among a cluster of festivals that comes around Diwali—but even that was a light-hearted ritual. We caught hold of our cows and calves, decorated them much against their will and saw to it that they did not eat, during the ceremony, the garlands we had put round their necks. Then we fed them delicacies specially prepared for the day. Older people sometimes put on an air of reverence, but it was fun all the way. The cows went back to their grazing after the ceremony got over but the calves gaily danced about, trying to get the garlands off their necks to see if they were edible. It was ceremonies and symbolic rituals like this that enriched our lives and made them meaningful. Yeats understood it well: *Ceremony is a name for the rich horn*.

Our tenants were happy to get Ganga and the two calves. Ganga was big with calf and was given on condition that the calf, if female, should be given to us after it was weaned. The two calves were male and could be put to the plough in a year or two. They did not, however, want Tunga, the oldest of the cows, and took her only as a part of the deal. They did not deliberately starve her but the scarce fodder went to feed the cattle that were productive, including the buffalo and the two bullocks they already had. Tunga was left to fend for herself by grazing. But in the month of May the earth was parched and she could not find a blade of grass. So when uncle came home late one evening, he was surprised to find a shadowy figure lurking near the cowshed. It was Tunga.

She could not lift her head when he went close to her, she had grown so weak. He gave her some water and opened the door of the empty cowshed. She went in quietly and stood in her accustomed place. He kept some rice for cooking, finished his pooja quickly and took most of what he had cooked to Tunga. She was still standing, as if she was scared that she would not be able to stand up once she lay down. He gave her the watery rice gruel he had prepared, and it was only after she had eaten it that she lifted her head and looked at him. Then she lay down.

Uncle went to Devadigas' house early next morning to get back the bottle of medicated oil grandmother had prepared for Tunga's sores. "We didn't drive her out, Ayya," said Bachchi, "she went on her own." Her husband Subraya offered to come and take Tunga back but uncle said no. "Let her be with me," he said, "now that she has come home to die."

Uncle applied the medicated oil on Tunga's open sores before he took his bath. When he came to Kantheshwar in the afternoon to meet my aunts, I could smell that oil on him from a distance. It was the awful smell of the oil which kept the flies away and that helped the sores heal up; because flies bred maggots that bored into the animal's flesh and prevented wounds from healing.

My aunts were deeply moved by Tunga's plight. They were also concerned about uncle. "How will you take care of her, alone?" they asked him. He laughed. "I don't have to take care of her," he said. "She will take care of me. She has started doing that already." Then he explained: he had been cooking a little rice only once a day, and that too because he had to offer something to God at the time of his pooja. Tunga had made him cook a second time the previous day. "I don't know how long she will live," he said. "But as long as she is there I'll have to cook twice a day. Maybe she has come to force me to do that."

Chandratte, the younger of my aunts, cursed the Devadiga family for starving Tunga but uncle said there was no point in blaming them. "Tunga gave us milk for a number of years. It is our duty to take care of her in her old age. How can we pass on that duty to someone else?" he said.

"Where is Amma?" he asked, and Nagatte said, "She is in the cowshed, in front of the manger, that is where she is most of the time. She was standing there for a long time yesterday trying to talk to Kapile. So I asked Lacchi to put a chair there. She must be there now." She wiped her eyes and said, "It's so sad. She doesn't remember any of my children. I tell her who they are but she forgets it in a few minutes, and then she asks, Nagu, who is this girl, and why are *you* combing her hair."

Uncle went in to meet grandmother. He came back after a short while, looking solemn but not unduly disturbed. "She looks the same as before," he said. "She looks lost but so did she at Nampalli. I was worried that her condition might change for the worse with this change of residence. It hasn't. I wonder whether she knows she is no longer at Nampalli. Do you know what she asked me? 'Has anyone applied that medicated oil on Tunga's sores?' she asked. I said yes, I have. I couldn't have said that if she had asked that question yesterday. Thank God Tunga has come back.

"Then she told me that the oil should be applied only once in the morning. That will keep the flies away. 'It is strong medicine,' she said, 'if you apply it more than once a day it might corrode the skin and deepen the sore.' How does she remember all that when she can't remember where she is, or even who she is, at times?"

When uncle started for home I went with him for some distance. He went to Martappayya's shop to buy two anna worth of coconut oil-cake for Tunga. "People like you should buy *seers* of oil-cake," said Martappayya. "What do I do with it?" said uncle. "There is only an old cow left at home and she is counting her days. I give her the same rice gruel I eat. But she may crave for something extra, a little something to tingle her taste buds occasionally. Like I crave for mango pickles."

"We all crave for pickles," said Martappayya smiling like a child. There was nothing childlike about the man except his smile, and that only because he had lost all his teeth. "Our taste buds become more demanding as we grow older. Because there is nothing else we can do but eat."

On the way back home after leaving uncle at the corner, from where a narrow winding lane took him towards Nampalli, I was brooding over the strange and inexplicable ways in which people lost or regained their happiness. I had seen uncle suffering in silence since the day of the habba. And it looked as if he would have to carry that burden of sorrow forever. I could not understand how the return of an old dying cow, with sores all over her body, could lighten that burden.

My aunts left for home the next day. As long as they were there I had no shortage of playmates. My cousins were excellent companions. The boys were boisterous and the girls, though quieter, were full of fun. But they were, at the same time, surprisingly obedient to their mothers. When Nagatte's strident voice called "Vasoo," Vasu, who was batting then, did not, as I would have done, pretend that he hadn't heard the call. "I'll be back in a minute," he said to us, dropped the bat and rushed in, and true to his word he was back in the batting crease within a minute. Nagatte just wanted to be sure that he was around and had not fallen into one of the two wells we had in our compound. The way my cousins could combine obedience with plenty of mischief was a revelation to me. Obedience never curtailed their freedom. I thought they were clever kids who knew how to humour their mothers while having their own way. But I now realize that their freedom was achieved, as freedom always is, through mutual trust, and love free from tension.

The day before they left—the day after uncle came smelling of grandmother's medicated oil—the sun was so hot that we decided not to play cricket in the afternoon. "Let us go and sit under the suragi tree, it is so cool there," said Malati, Chandratte's third daughter. "Yes," said another, "and Babu can tell us stories."

We sat under the tree and I told them stories. There were nine of them, five boys and four girls. If I have to choose one day in my life as being the most creative, it was that day. I began with stories I knew, the ones I had heard or read, but I wove so many new strands into them that they became entirely mine. My cousins sat spellbound. When I paused for breath, or for effect, we could hear little Meera's guttural breathing, and birdcalls, and the cawing of a crow at a distance. Once we heard another faint call, 'Vasoo', but we ignored it as if it were just another birdcall.

Then I stopped, tired out. As we got up to go home little Meera gurgled, "Whath naith tholieth I thaw thu-day!"

"Stupid," said Malati, patting her younger sister on the head, "You didn't see any stories, you heard them."

"No," said Meera obstinately, "I thaw them."

After my cousins left I made friends with a few boys of our neighbourhood. On the right side of our house lived the Shetty family, with six boys and a girl. Two of the boys were roughly my age and I soon became very intimate with them. They took me to the school ground to play cricket and ball badminton.

Sometimes we went into the woods behind the school looking for cashew apples and purple berries. The boys took me to a cashew orchard where the owners allowed us to eat as many apples as we wished on condition that the nuts would be all handed over to them. I ate so many of them the first time that I developed a sore throat that lasted for a week, and an aversion for the fruit that has lasted till now.

Late May was the time when the purple berries ripened. You could eat them for only about a week, because once the rains came they lost their sweetness. I found it strange, the way the rains could so completely wash away all the sweetness from those berries. The ripe ones were ebony black but the flesh within was purplish blue; and so was the stain they left on our clothes, particularly the pockets of our shirts and shorts.

I had learnt cycling during the vacation and wanted to go to Nampalli on a hired bicycle, which was available for two annas an hour. But I could do so only on the last Sunday of June as it rained heavily on the earlier Sundays. I got the bicycle I wanted—the only one in the shop small enough to allow my feet to touch the pedals—and set out in the afternoon.

It was a lovely ride. The rains had made the road better. It had firmed up the treacherous patches of sand on the way where I had seen even experienced riders wobble and fall. I reached Nampalli in quick time, but though the door of our house was open uncle was not in. The door of the cowshed was also open. I knew uncle kept it open so that Tunga could go out or come in when she liked. I tried to talk to her but was disappointed when I saw no signs of recognition in her dull eyes.

I went to see what Little Ramu was doing. But I found the door of his house locked with a big padlock. On my way back I saw Janakamma, Ranga's mother, at her door. "What has happened?" I asked, "Where's Little Ramu and his mother? Why is their house locked?"

"Don't talk about Ramu's mother," said Janakamma, after asking me to come in. "To talk about that woman is to dirty one's mouth." Then she went on talking about her for the next thirty minutes.

Ramu's mother, she said, was a bad woman. Everyone knew that but the extent of her depravity came to light only after Kaveri's marriage. Till then she had kept some control on herself.

The first one seen coming to her house was the goldsmith from Kantheshwar who had prepared the ornaments for Kaveri at the time of her wedding. But he came on the sly, in the afternoons, and once he realized that people knew about his visits, he stopped coming.

"She really went mad then," said Janakamma. "All sorts of men started coming, at odd hours. We got scared. The only men in our hamlet are Raju's grandfather who is seventy and your uncle who never comes out of the Matha once he comes home from school. What protection can they give us? So we made them send telegrams to our men, including Ramu's father. 'Matter serious, come immediately,' that was the message.

"In three days they came, all except Ramu's father. He came late at night, the poor chap. You know he can't walk easily, ever since his foot got caught in the rat trap he had himself set and lost all the toes of his left leg. That was when Ramu was a baby and he was worried that the rats would nibble at his child.

"He didn't know what the matter was. He had even brought a saree for his wife, poor man. He heard loud laughter in his house and went to the window to see what was going on. He saw two strangers with his wife, all naked." Janakamma stopped suddenly, put her hand over her mouth, shocked. "My God, why am I telling you all this, you are still a child, you won't understand all this wickedness."

But she did continue with the story. "Poor man, he didn't know that some of our men had already come. He thought he couldn't, in the middle of the night, knock on the doors of houses where only women were present. He couldn't do anything himself because he had seen two men and feared there might be more. So he sat on the steps of his house the whole night when all sorts of things were going on in his house.

"At dawn he went to see Raju's grandfather, found the other men and then they all went to his house. Those inside must have seen them coming for suddenly the door opened and two boys—must be of sixteen or seventeen, not more—rushed out and ran away.

"Ramu's father dragged his wife out and thrashed her with the cane which he always carries, because of his limp. He beat her black and blue but she didn't cry at all. 'Come, beat me,' she said, the shameless woman, 'Beat me with your cane, that's all you can do. What else do you have except your cane?'"

"But where was Little Ramu?" I asked, sick with worry.

"I was coming to that," said Janakamma. "After Padmanabhayya beat his wife till he was tired out, he remembered his son. 'What have you done with my son?' he shouted, 'Where is Ramu?' 'In the *panitha*,' she said."

"Oh, God!" I said, and shivered. 'Panitha' is the little unventilated cell in which paddy is stored. It is one of the most dreadful places to be locked up in. I should know because I had once, during a game of hide and seek, hid myself in our panitha. It was too good a hiding place. My cousins, unable to find me, went away, and some elder who did not know I was in latched the door from outside. When I realized what had happened there was no one within earshot. Not much sound came out of that dreadful hole anyway, even if one shouted oneself hoarse. Fortunately it dawned on me that banging the door was better than shouting. Aditi, who had sharp ears, heard the banging and told the others that a big rat was creating a racket in the panitha. So they came armed with sticks, opened the door and found me inside. The coughing and sneezing I developed then lasted for nearly a month.

"When they opened the door of the panitha," said Janakamma, "they found Little Ramu—sleeping. He is surely the strangest of boys. They thought he was unconscious, or even dead, but he was sleeping. As if he had got used to sleeping there. I suppose that awful woman locked him up there every night when she was having her fun."

Ramu's mother was driven away, with a warning that her backbone would be broken if she ever tried to come back. The house was locked up and Little Ramu was taken away by his father. "I was a fool to trust my child with that ogress," he said while leaving. "I worked day and night for her sake. Now that I have only this boy to provide for, I'll give him good education. I'll see to it that he becomes a big officer or doctor."

≫⊙

When I went back to the Matha I found uncle returning from the woods, dragging some leafy branches he had cut to spread on the floor of the cowshed. He looked so happy and at peace with the world that I did not have the heart to talk to him about Ramu.

"Tunga is better, isn't she?" I asked. "There are no sores on her body."

"Yes, she is better. But she is waiting for something. I don't know for what…" He looked thoughtful. "You know I keep the door of the shed open. The first three days she was too weak to stir out. But now she goes out every day, at dusk, at the time the cows come home. The *godhooli* time, Babu. She stands at the gate and looks out. The cows come rushing up to our open gate, then swerve to the left because they belong to our neighbours. She still keeps looking. She goes in only after the dust settles down. It is as if she is waiting. For some visitors who don't turn up."

I laughed. "But cows don't get visitors," I said. He smiled too, as if in agreement.

But we were both wrong. Tunga had visitors three days later.

Uncle came back from school that day at dusk and found Tunga at the gate. It was godhooli time. 'Go Dhooli': cow dust. Cows come home in a mad rush at that time because night comes suddenly in the tropics and they don't want to be caught outside. The dust they raise turns golden in the evening light. We regard it as the most auspicious of moments. Once in a rare while there is real golden twilight; for a minute or two sunlight gilds everything it touches. People in regions where twilight lasts a long time can never know what these moments mean to us. Their brevity makes them divine. We think they come straight from God.

It was one of those golden godhooli moments. Uncle stood with Tunga and watched the cows rushing home. The dust they raised became a golden mist and hung like a curtain. The cows turned left, as usual, but Tunga still stood there: staring, waiting, expectant.

And then uncle saw a lone cow coming through that curtain of gold, trailing a long rope: Kapile. And some distance behind her, a tiny staggering figure: grandmother.

"It was a miracle," said uncle, when I went to see him next Sunday. "Out of the golden mist they emerged, Kapile and my mother. I don't know who brought whom, but it looked as if Kapile, her tawny skin glowing like gold, was bringing mother along. In answer to the silent prayer of an old ailing cow, at the most auspicious of moments, godhooli.

"Godhooli. The best of times for a marriage. I married Sita then."

I looked at him in surprise. I had always heard of his marriage as the biggest tragedy of his life. He had lost his wife within two years and then the child had died. But what I saw, when I looked at his face, was happiness. It was as if the happy memory of those two years had touched the present moment with its golden fingers, and made it gold.

How does one understand the alchemy of happiness? Just two years of muted happiness, that was all uncle had, and at the end of it, darkness. 'Muted' because the couple could meet only late at night, after the work in the kitchen got over, and she would have left his bed well before dawn. They did not talk during the day; it was not the done thing. And there was no privacy in that large joint family. But that brief interlude of happiness somehow lighted up his life. Like the brief but golden godhooli.

Man is in love, and loves what vanishes, what more is there to say?

Memories and Dreams

I spent a good deal of time yesterday worrying about a problem I encountered while writing about the past. I had just completed the chapter, *Godhooli*. I was reasonably happy with what I had written. I thought I had recollected that scene with uncle vividly and recreated it with a fair degree of accuracy. My speech sounded all right, close enough to how I must have actually spoken in my childhood—except of course it was in Kannada, not English—but there was a nagging doubt: what about the thoughts and the feelings? I was only eleven then. Surely I could not have thought and felt what I expressed at the end of the chapter? That stuff about the alchemy of happiness, for example, or that quotation from Yeats at the end. Had I failed to demarcate clearly where my childhood thoughts ended and the adult mind took over? If I had, did that amount to a falsification of experience?

Then I remembered a film seen long ago: Bergman's *Wild Strawberries*, about an old man who is on a journey down the memory lane. While depicting his recollections, Bergman did something unusual. Instead of finding a suitable child actor to represent his protagonist, he sent the old man himself into the past, so that there was this delightfully incongruous but poignant scene of the portly old man sitting with his dashing young father! The scene threw light, I thought, on the strange paradoxical ways of human memory. It showed that memory, which takes you to your childhood days, actually prevents you from regaining your childhood; that you cannot be the child that you were *because you are caught in a cocoon of memories*. Perhaps only a knock on the head—and the consequent of loss of memory—can make you a child again!

Wild Strawberries taught me something precious. As the mind that recollects the past is your active adult mind, it is inevitable that the recollected thoughts and feelings of childhood merge and blend with thoughts and feelings roused by their recollection. But there is no need to sift and separate them, if what you want to explore is not the past that is past, but the living past that is present in the present moment.

When I came back from school that day—the day Kapile took grandmother on a visit to Tunga—I found Lacchi running around distracted. She had tethered Kapile under the suragi tree, though my mother had told her not take the cow out of our compound. "Such nice green grass has grown there round that tree," she wailed, "and like a fool I didn't realize that the ground there was softer than in our compound. But who knew that that stupid cow would pull out the peg I had tied her to, just to show her might?"

"Where is grandmother?" I asked. "Oh, she must be in her usual place," said Lacchi, and then I saw fear creeping into her face. "Oh, no," she said, "Ajji is not anywhere near the cowshed. Where is she then?"

There was panic and confusion. Grandmother had disappeared with Kapile. Father who had just come in was very upset and angry. "None of you missed her till Babu asked where she was. Why? Babu missed her because he cares for her. No one else in the house is bothered," he said. He started sending people in different directions to look for grandmother, but when I said that she might have gone towards Nampalli, he said, "Yes, yes, that's where she must have gone," and asked someone to run there.

I went to the suragi tree to investigate. The spot where the peg had been driven to the ground showed that Lacchi had done her job very badly indeed. The peg must have been driven to a depth of not more than two inches. No cow with self-respect, I thought, would have stayed on tethered to a peg like that, however green the grass at the spot might be.

I sat under the tree and started thinking about grandmother and the cow. I did not worry much. There was something in that spot which made one feel that everything was all right, nothing could ever really go wrong. Just a month's rain and the place had grown lush green, darker and less bright than the paddy fields nearby but more soothing to the eye, a cool emerald island on the edge of a bright green sea. Lacchi was right: you did not have to be a cow to see that there was no grassier spot anywhere around.

It was a place where one could sit and dream for ages. Perhaps that was what the Yakshi did. And even the Kalkutika, under her influence, seemed to have lost his irascibility and was dreaming his days away, unmindful of people like Krishnayya who were trying hard to wake him up.

I looked at the spot with interest because I needed a secluded place to dream in. I have always been a dreamer, but after joining high school I had perfected the art of deliberate dreaming. I used to go to school from Nampalli with uncle but came back home alone, and whenever there was a football or cricket match in the *maidan* on the way, I used to hang around for a while. That meant that often it was quite dark when I reached home. On the way there were a few tamarind and palmyra trees, much favoured by demons and ghosts according to popular belief. I was terribly scared of walking under them in the dark. The tall palmyra trees really looked like demons at night, and the faintest of breezes would make them mutter and murmur most ominously. So I started the habit of dreamwalking. I would deliberately start dreaming some time before entering the dreaded zone and come out of my dream only when I reached our main door. It was all so simple: I could enter the dream world as easily as I entered the world of fiction, and coming out of it was like closing a book. The next day on my way back home I would take up that dream again and continue it from where I had left off, like I would open and start reading an unfinished novel.

How I could so easily dream-walk on those narrow ridges between fields in the uncertain light of dark evenings, I don't know. Perhaps my eyes and other sensory organs were fully alert and guided my legs without interrupting my dreams.

An incident that happened during one of those dream-walks to Nampalli was so weird that I doubt if it would be believed. It was an hour after sunset but there was fairly bright moonlight. I saw, as I was walking and dreaming, a big snake crossing my path. Its leisurely movement suggested that it was a cobra because a rat snake would have been in a much greater hurry to get away from a human being. Must be a cobra, I thought, and stopped and waited for it to pass. Before entering a hole under the tamarind tree the snake turned its head, opened its hood just a little, as if it wanted me to know that it was indeed a cobra. Yes, I said to myself, it's a cobra all right, and continued walking.

When I reached our door I closed my dream and came out. Then I panicked. Fear came slithering in like a snake and I was drenched in a cold sweat. Like most village boys I was terribly scared of cobras. To us they were not just poisonous reptiles but creatures endowed with supernatural powers. Yet I had felt no fear when I nearly stepped on one because my mind was totally wrapped up in my dream. But my eyes noticed that faint movement in the dim light, and communicated it to my mind or to a part of it, which came to the conclusion that it was indeed a cobra and took appropriate steps. But that dream-wrap I had woven for myself and donned kept all fears out till I reached home and doffed it.

Even after shifting to Kantheshwar I used that dream-wrap almost every day on my way back from Chandapur. In the morning the boys from Kantheshwar went in a group because we had to reach school at the same time.

But in the evenings we came back at different times. I deliberately avoided company on my way back because I enjoyed my three-mile long lone walk, when I could dream uninterruptedly for an hour.

But a boy's day-dreams are not like the eddying dreams of an old man. They move forward towards a conclusion, and if they are left incomplete they demand, like half-read novels, that you take them up again and complete them. But dreaming, alas, is not accorded the respect and legitimacy reading gets. Even my mother, who used to grumble about my reading, did not like to disturb me when she found me immersed in a book. She had no such compunctions about breaking into my dreams. "Stop ruminating like a buffalo," she used to say, and send me on some stupid errand or other. So I needed a quiet place when I had an unfinished dream to pursue, especially on Sundays and holidays. I thought I had found that place at last.

The Suragi Tree

Grandmother and Kapile were brought back from Nampalli the next day. We never learnt how or why they went there. Lacchi kept on asking grandmother whether she took Kapile to Nampalli or was forced to go there, hanging on to Kapile's rope because she could not stop the cow. Grandmother looked more and more confused as the questioning continued. Amma finally lost her temper. "Why don't you go and ask Kapile?" she said to Lacchi, "Who knows, you might even get an answer." I wondered who she was really angry with: Lacchi or grandmother.

After the monsoon got over, I started going to the suragi tree, with a book or a dream, whenever I found the time. The place was clean: with Yakshi and Kalkutika present, it needed no 'commit no nuisance' board. And the tree itself was lovely. Most trees in forests and gardens have to compete with other trees for their share of the sky and sunlight. But my suragi, with no other tree nearby to warp its growth, had grown up in complete freedom. She had risen and spread as Nature wanted her to. She stood there in that open ground, a school-marm in a gorgeous green saree. And as she murmured her lessons, the bushes that squatted all round listened spell bound.

In the second half of February the suragi flowered. Clusters of tiny buds erupted all over the tree. They were like little glowing pink pearls at first but soon turned white, and when they blossomed a few days later, I found the very feminine fragrance heady, almost intoxicating. Honeybees and flies buzzed around the fallen flowers, and their dizzy, lurching flight suggested that they too found the fragrance intoxicating.

When the fallen flowers dried up, their fragrance changed, mellowed, and became more delicate. I don't think there is another aroma like that of dried suragi flowers. I am told that people now collect the dried petals from under the trees and sell them to joss stick makers. But in those days the fallen flowers dried where they fell, making a rich aromatic carpet under the tree, till they were washed away by the rains in June. The delicate aroma hung around the place for days.

My reading continued, though I had not yet become a confirmed bookworm. The first novel I started reading under the suragi tree—on a

Sunday morning—was *Marali Mannige*. I had heard so much about that book, though most of those who had spoken highly of the book had warned me that I would not get much out of it. "Not meant for an eleven year old," they had said, "you are sure to be bored. There is no exciting story, nothing much happens; it is just life."

But I had learnt, by experience, not to bother about what people said regarding the suitability of books for my age and taste. I did not worry what kind of books I was reading. I just read them. I found most of them interesting.

But after nearly three hours of reading under the tree that morning, when Amma sent Lacchi to see what I was doing and to call me home for lunch, I had read only about eighty pages. What slowed me down was the language, simple, earthy but evocative. I was surprised and delighted by the novel's use of simple everyday words, some of them so quaint that I had heard them spoken only by very old women of the working class, who were too old to do any work in the fields, and so came to our house at Nampalli seeking simple chores like cleaning rice. They loved to talk while working and like with most old people, their mind often went back to the past, to the distant days of their childhood. I was always an avid listener. The first few chapters of *Marali Mannige* recreated those times so vividly that I was enchanted.

I read another eighty pages in the afternoon under the suragi tree. At night father saw my excitement and smiled knowingly. "What book are you taking to bed tonight?" he asked me.

When I said "*Marali Mannige*," he was surprised. "So you have started reading books like that," he said; "When do you think you will complete it? Because I would like to go through the book, if I can find the time."

"Tonight," I said.

He raised his eyebrows and shook his head. "No, no," he said; "I don't like the way you read in bed in the dim light of that little kerosene lamp. It is bad for the eyes. You *must* stop reading by eleven. If I find you reading after twelve, you will get a thrashing."

I started reading and entered the world of the novel. The sound of the big clock outside striking eleven, and then, a little later, twelve, came to me as if from another world. I thought of father's threat vaguely, but continued reading.

At half past two someone knocked on the door. I opened the door, and he was there, my father.

"It's past two, Babu," he said; "Enough of reading, now. Go to bed."

"Yes, Appa," I said obediently, closed the door, put off the light and went to bed.

But I could not sleep. So I got up and tried to light the lamp but found that I had turned the wick so far down that that I had to open the lamp and dirty my hand with kerosene if I wanted to light it. So I brought in one of the two chimneys mother kept in the verandah and lighted it. The chimney, as usual, gave more smoke than light, but I wanted to read on for some time at least. I closed all the windows, as I was worried that father might pay me another visit.

What we call a 'chimney' in our villages is a kerosene lamp, usually made of copper, with a homemade wick of cotton rags. I don't know why it is called a chimney. Perhaps because it has no chimney—a glass tube to protect the flame—or because it belches smoke like a chimney.

I read in the light of this most primitive of kerosene lamps for some time and then dozed off to sleep—or that was what I thought.

I woke up next morning feeling groggy. I found it difficult to breathe. I thought it was still dark but when I opened the door bright sunlight hit me like a slap. I could not still breathe properly and soon found out why: both my nostrils were packed tight with soot. I opened the windows of my room, and then quietly went to the bathroom to wash my face and nostrils. My only worry was that my father or mother might find out what had happened and scold me for my carelessness.

When I opened *Marali Mannige* during the lunch break in school, I was surprised to find that I could not remember where I had left off. This had never happened before. But still I did not realize how close to death I was that night. Then I forgot the whole incident.

Nearly half a century later, when I was reading *Marali Mannige* again, the whole scene recurred. I have written about it in an earlier chapter. After the initial shock was over—when my dead father knocked on the door and told me I had read enough and asked me to go to sleep—I recollected the earlier scene and realized, for the first time, the gravity of what had happened. I remembered how the chimney, full of kerosene, had gone off on its own, apparently because there was not enough oxygen left in the room. I could have died too. I lay down and wondered where I would have gone then if I too had gone off like that chimney. Perhaps to the world of Parothi, Sarasothi, Nagaveni and Little Rama.

৯

I went to the high school at Chandapur for only three years. When I was in the Eighth Standard—called Third Form in high school—some of the people of Kantheshwar came together, collected donations, and persuaded the government to upgrade the higher elementary school into a high school. The new high school was to open with the Ninth Standard—Fourth Form—the year after, and my parents naturally wanted to enroll me there.

But my performance in the Third Form threatened to upset all plans. There was something peculiar about my intelligence, or at least my ability to pass exams. It waxed and waned in a cycle of three years. Not exactly like the moon, because though the waning was a continuous decline the recovery was sudden, like a near empty hour-glass turned upside down. I was very good when I joined school at the age of six and urinated my way into the Third Standard, but in three years the royal horse had indeed become a donkey. I was a horse again in the First Form, but by the time I appeared for the Third Form exam, I was worse than a donkey, I was a mule. I somehow lost track of what was being taught in the class. Unfortunately uncle was not there to check my slide. He was on leave for three months. Someone he knew, a distant relative some years younger than him, also a Shiromani, had been looking for a job for years. He could not get one because Sanskrit was taught in few schools. Uncle went on leave so that the man could work in the leave vacancy and gain some experience. That would have strengthened his claim for the post when uncle finally retired.

So when the result came everyone was shocked, including myself. I had hoped that I would make a last ditch effort and somehow scrape through. I suppose I was dreaming. The result came as a rude awakening. I had failed in mathematics, science and geography.

Father was furious. Mother said, more than once, that I would not have failed if her advice had been heeded and I had joined the school at Kantheshwar. "I am sure his uncle will do something," she said finally. "He is one of the senior teachers of the school, and surely the headmaster will listen to him."

"His uncle?" said father, with a mirthless laugh. "He loves his nephew all right, but he loves his principles more. If they show him his nephew's marks and ask him what to do, he will tell them to demote him to the Seventh!"

Uncle came to see Amma that day. After his quarrel with father, her attitude to him had changed. She treated him with respect and sometimes even affection. She asked him to do something to help 'poor Babu'. Then she told him what father had said: that he loved his principles more than he loved his nephew.

Uncle winced, as if he had been slapped. When he got up to go I saw he looked old and tired. "There is a meeting in the school tomorrow," he said;

"Maybe something can be done." Then he turned to me and said, "How are you today, Babu?"

"I'm all right," I said.

He asked me that question because of something that had happened a week earlier, at Nampalli, when I had had a close brush with death.

I think it was that incident which made him forget his principles for once and plead my case in the school meeting. He told them that I was joining the new high school at Kantheshwar. Should I join the Eighth or Ninth Standard, that was what they had to decide. Someone raised an objection that there were two students who had done slightly better than me but were not promoted. "No, no," said uncle. "If they are not promoted, I don't want Sudhakara to pass." So they finally decided to pass all three of us.

About that brush with death: I had gone to Nampalli in the morning that day with an anthology of short stories after telling Amma that I would not be coming home for lunch. I wanted to spend the whole day at Nampalli, reading and talking with uncle. I saw him coming out of the Matha with the copper pooja vessels. He wanted to scrub and wash them in the tank and then have his ritual bath, in preparation for his pooja. "I'm going to eat with you today," I said, and he smiled; "I'm going to help you to cook," I said and that made him laugh.

I went in, took off my shirt and shorts and wore a bairasa. I wanted to have a leisurely bath in the tank and learn to swim if possible. I remembered how Savitri had learnt it in half an hour. Lakshmi and I were the only ones in the hamlet who never learnt to swim.

But the sight of the water made me change my mind. It was the height of summer then, and the water looked thick and dark green and uninviting. I sat on the granite steps, three steps above the one where uncle was washing the utensils, and said, "I know how to swim now."

Those days I had, occasionally, a sudden and irresistible desire to tell lies. Harmless lies from which I derived no benefits. They were, I think, mere extensions of my dreams.

Uncle looked up in surprise. "Where did you learn swimming?" he asked. When I said "At the Kantheshwar temple tank," he shook his head. "That is the biggest tank anywhere around," he said. "They say it is so deep in places that those who go down don't come up at all. You should be careful."

A yellow water snake glided across the tank, holding aloft a little squeaking frog. I marvelled at its graceful undulating movement. Close to where it disappeared under some moss, I saw the head of another snake jutting out of a crevice in the sidewall of the tank.

I threw a pebble at it, and perhaps because I had not taken aim, nearly scored a hit. But the snake did not move. The pebble hit the water so close to its head that water splashed on it, but it lay there unmoved.

"It is doing *tapas*," I said to myself. Sages of yore sat or stood in some posture suitable for meditation for long periods, sometimes for years, and meditated on God or on some divine power. They stopped breathing and needed no food or water. They were so still that anthills grew round them. Indra, the king of gods, often got scared of their tapas, because he thought that their aim might be to attain his throne. He was doubly scared when tapas was done by Rakshasas, who too had unlimited powers of concentration and endurance. But unlike sages whose aim usually was to establish contact with God, the Rakshasas craved for power. Indra's throne was for them an obvious object of desire. So whenever the king of gods found anyone doing tapas for long, he tried his best to disturb and break it.

So the snake was doing tapas, I said to myself. At its successful completion, what boon would the little demon ask? Maybe it would ask for the discomfiture or even destruction of all mischievous boys who, for no reason at all, threw pebbles at its kith and kin. I smiled and then decided that I must, like Indra, break the snake's meditation.

The tank had granite steps on one side for people to walk down to the water. The other three sides were steep walls made of laterite stones, with narrow ledges every six feet or so. The snake's head was lying on a ledge close to water. I took a pebble, and walking gingerly on the ledge above, arrived at the spot from where I could drop it on that still head. I did not want to kill it— uncle would have hated it—but I wanted to break its siesta or meditation or whatever. I looked at uncle to see if he was watching me and found him busy scrubbing the vessels with tamarind. The acid in tamarind made the copper gleam like gold. A sunbeam bounced off from the vessel he was washing and caught me in the eye.

I held the pebble in front of me and very carefully dropped it. I don't know whether it hit or missed the head, because even as I dropped it I lost my balance and toppled into the tank.

The cold green water swallowed me and then I came up gasping. I saw uncle looking at me with concern. I smiled at him.

It may sound crazy, but that was what really happened. I smiled at uncle. I knew I was drowning, had already swallowed some of that murky water, but when I saw my uncle I smiled. And he turned away reassured that I knew swimming and had jumped into the tank because I wanted to swim.

But fortunately he was always a little worried, and never quite sure, of what I could or could not do. The desperate splashing he heard behind him made him turn again, and when my face bobbed up next time he could see that it had gone blue.

He dived and came to help me but he knew it was not going to be easy. He had not swum for years and did not know much about how to save drowning people. Fortunately he got hold of my hair as I was sinking again, and somehow succeeded in dragging me close to the steps, before I caught hold of him and nearly drowned him. But his feet could touch the slushy bottom of the tank by then and we were saved.

I scrambled to safety and sat huddled on one of the steps, like a rat that had just escaped drowning. He lay half in water and half on the steps, his lips moving in silent prayer. Then he looked up at me, trying to say something, but the words just would not come out. I thought he wanted to ask me why I had lied to him that I could swim and wondered what excuse I could give. But when he found his voice finally what he asked me, in anguish, was "Why did you smile when you looked at me, Babu, how could you do that at such a moment?"

Uncle came with me to Kantheshwar that evening to tell Amma about the mishap and get scolded for his negligence. But Amma did not oblige him. I watched the meeting between them with a certain amount of bafflement because there was a complete reversal of roles. In all their earlier arguments—dialogues, rather, which never developed into full-blown arguments because uncle refused to be drawn into one—I had always seen uncle relaxed, comfortably seated, and Amma standing, restless and flustered. Here it was Amma who was sitting, looking contented and totally at ease. Moni, a three months old baby then, was on her lap, his head hidden under the loose end of her saree, and she was breast-feeding him. I saw Moni's plump legs kicking in happiness. With a pang of jealousy I noted that Amma never looked more contented than when she was suckling Moni. Uncle stood in front of her looking nervous and flustered, unable to meet her eyes. "Babu nearly died today," he said. "It was all my fault. I was negligent, I should have kept an eye on him." "But he is so restless," said Amma, "it's impossible to keep an eye on him. And he isn't a small child anyway." "I shouldn't have allowed him to walk on those narrow ledges," said uncle, "no wonder he lost his balance and fell down." "Oh, he falls down every now and then," said Amma. "The other day he fell down from a cashew tree. It was lucky you were there when he fell into the tank." This continued for some time, uncle becoming more and more unhappy because Amma would not blame him. Then the feeding got over and

Moni's bald head popped out from under the loose end of Amma's saree. He burped and threw a toothless smile at uncle. Uncle nearly cried.

After breakfast next morning I went and sat under the suragi tree. I read the last story, the only one left unread in the book I had taken to Nampalli. Then I sat dreaming. There was a cool breeze blowing. It must have rained somewhere, I thought. I closed my eyes, and then suddenly began to feel I was sinking. When I opened my eyes and looked up, the sky and the sunlight seen through the thick green foliage of the suragi tree looked so startlingly like what I had seen the previous day, through the green waters of the tank, that it took some time for me to recover from the shock.

Gradually the suragi tree became the centre of my inner life. I sat under the tree with my dreams and my books so often that its green shade got associated in my mind with the world of fiction and of day-dreams. And after I fell into the Nampalli tank, and saw death, before I was rescued, as something cold and green, it somehow got associated with death too. I don't think I understood those feelings—they never crystallized into thoughts—but gradually, in the green shade of the tree, I began to feel, vaguely, that death was not something terrible but an escape into the world of imagination, of dreams and fiction.

Fires and Fireflies

It was Martappayya who told me about the darshana. I had gone to his shop to buy some *akroot*, a kind of candy he made from jaggery and left-over flours, stir-cooked for a long time and made so tough that one could chew it for hours. When it stuck to our teeth it was a problem pulling it out. There was a rumour current among children that whenever the akroots he made became too tough to be sold, Martappayya ate them himself—because he was stingy and did not want to waste anything—and that was how he lost all his teeth, without visiting a dentist. We loved akroots because they were cheap and gave us more than our money's worth of chewing: three for a *pavane*, or 192 for a rupee; though only a mad man would have bought akroots worth a rupee.

Martappayya took his own time to give his customers what they wanted but no one seemed to mind it. He had an acerbic wit that stung but titillated, and people with nothing better to do loitered around his shop. They laughed at his jokes, and when the joke was at their expense, they laughed at his language. Like almost all the shopkeepers of our place, he was a Konkani speaking man, and spoke Kannada with a strong Konkani accent. The accent in fact was so strong that he sounded as if he was parodying Konkani-Kannada rather than merely using it.

When I went there for akroots, Martappayya was lying on the bench in front of his shop. Sheena from the village of Kumri was there, waiting for him to get up. Sheena came to the pethe once a week for his grocery, which he bought at some other shop, and then came to Martappayya's for one anna worth of akroot. He wanted thirteen akroots for one anna, because there were thirteen akroot-chewing children in his house, and it took half an hour's bargaining, every time, to get that extra akroot. Martappayya always tried to convince him that he should spend an extra pavane and buy fifteen akroots, so that he could give one to his wife and eat one himself. That would make them both even more fecund—his akroots, he claimed, had that property—and soon there would be more akroot-chewing mouths in the family.

Martappayya opened one eye and looked at me. He realized that I had come for akroots and so could wait. If my mother had sent me to bring something she needed urgently, he would have got up quickly enough. Then he opened both eyes, saw Narayana Aras passing by, and got up.

Aras was a young man, working in a restaurant somewhere, who had just come home and got married. He was all decked up in a silk shirt and Manchester dhoti, and about fifteen yards behind him walked his shy, very pretty young bride. That was how couples walked in those days and you could measure how old fashioned or modern they were by the distance they kept between them. Very few were mod enough to walk side by side.

"Hoi, hoi, Narayana Aras," said Martappayya, "haven't seen you for ages. What brought you home at this time of the year, when there is no habba?" The young man had to stop. He gave a nervous, embarrassed smile.

"Who is that pretty girl?" asked Martappayya; "I don't think I have seen her before." And the man, sensing trouble, looked even more embarrassed. "My wife," he said.

"Your wife?" said Martappayya, as if in great surprise. "I didn't know you were married. How could you marry without giving us a grand dinner? I thought you big hoteliers were generous people!"

Then he looked at the girl who was standing a little away, with her face averted. "Aa ha," he said, looking very innocent with his cherubic toothless smile; "Your wife, is she? I didn't know that. You know, I lay here on this bench and found her very good. Right here on this bench, in front of my shop! Your wife, is she? I didn't know."

His remark was far from innocent. He wanted to say, presumably, that he was lying on the bench in front of his shop when he looked at Narayana Aras's wife and saw that she was good-looking. But the wrong prepositions, and accent, made it appear that he lay with the girl on the bench right there in front of the shop and found her good. And that polite apology, 'I didn't know she was your wife', made matters worse.

It is impossible to translate what Martappayya said. He made syntactical and other errors but used them with great subtlety. The result was that one could not take offence at what he said even when others laughed at the remark because one could not be certain what they laughed at: perhaps they laughed at Martappayya's language. So when Sheena's permanent grin—he had buck-teeth of such size that he could never close his mouth fully—spread from ear to ear, and the loiterers present tittered, and the bride blushed and turned away, Aras had to pretend that nothing offensive had been said. He walked away, looking very dignified and foolish.

Martappayya laughed. "He was walking like a proud cock, that hotel boy," he said, "and his ego had to be punctured. Look at the way he strutted, as if getting married was a great achievement, which no one else had done. Not even his father perhaps." He laughed again, and then, in a changed voice, said: "He will learn his lesson soon enough."

Two boys, holding a cricket bat, came for akroots. They were apparently in a hurry. Martappayya took their pavane and gave them three akroots. "Give us four," they pleaded, "so that we can share them equally."

"Go, go," said Martappayya, "Go and make a fly pregnant. That's all you are good for."

"How does one do that, Martappayya?" they asked, grinning.

"That's easily done," he said; "look at that jaggery." He pointed to an open tin of liquid jaggery over which flies were buzzing. Occasionally a fly made the fatal mistake of sitting on it and got trapped. People said that Martappayya did not mind it if the quantity of his jaggery increased with drowned flies. "Take a drop of that," said Martappayya, "put it on the tip of your thingumajig and wait. When flies come and sit on it, make them pregnant."

The boys laughed so heartily that Martappayya relented and gave them the extra akroot they wanted. Sheena too laughed. "But what if the flies are male, Ayya?" he asked.

"Don't be stupid," said Martappayya. "All flies are female."

Sheena's jaw fell in surprise. "How can that be?" he asked.

Martappayya looked at Sheena's open mouth and buck teeth with intense distaste. "Where did you do your *horakade* today?" he asked.

Horakade in Kannada means 'outside'. It was a euphemism for faeces, but had been used for so long and so frequently that it ceased to be a euphemism and came to stand for the thing itself. Sheena was clearly embarrassed by the question. "Where did I go for doing *outside*? Where can I go but to the woods behind my hut?" he asked.

"Were there any flies around? Did they sit on your *outside*?"

"Oh, yes, Ayya," said Sheena; "big flies, bigger than the ones that sit on your jaggery. And I saw that wherever they sat on my *outside*, little worms came from inside as if to meet them."

"Oh you fool!" said Martappayya, "Those worms did not come from inside your *outside*. They came from inside the flies, they are their young ones that will grow fat in your *outside* till they become full-fledged flies. It shows that all those flies that laid their young ones in your *outside* were females. Do you know who is the male, the only male?"

Sheena scratched his head and kept quiet. Martappayya's face had suddenly become grim.

He turned to me and said, "Do you remember, little doctor, the poem you studied in the Third Standard? Who says to the fly, *Come O fly, come O fly, if you are tired of your flight in the sky, Come to my bed of softest down…Come to my nest, if you need some rest?*"

"The spider," I said. That poem, written by Panje Mangesha Rao, was one of my favourites. I still think it is one of the finest children's poems in Kannada. My love for the poem got me into trouble in the Seventh Standard where we had to study the English version of the poem. When our teacher announced that the Kannada poem we had studied in the Third Standard was only a translation of the English poem we were studying, I let out an involuntary howl of protest and was thrown out of the class.

"The spider, of course," said Martappayya, looking grim, "The spider is the only male. He is the one who seduces the fly to come to his bed and then strangles her. He is the Byari, the Mapille. The long-legged spider who comes on a bicycle with baskets of fish, looking for stupid flies."

I felt very uncomfortable and so did the others. Byaris or Mapilles were Muslim men from Malabar who came to our district to trade in fish. They bought fish from the fishermen on the coast and took them inland, over long distances, on their bicycles. They left their women back at home and were always on the look out for willing women they could sleep with. Martappayya's wife had run away with one of them several years earlier.

Come O fly, come O fly…. Martappayya sang in a harsh discordant voice. "My son had to learn that poem by heart when he was in the Third Standard," he said. "Poor boy, he just could not memorize it. He read it so many times that I knew the whole poem by heart, till it began to ring in my head, but my poor boy, he could not memorize it. He failed in the Third Standard, his first failure. Now he has got used to failure."

He gave me my akroots and then said, in his normal tone: "So you are organizing a darshana of the Kalkutika."

When I said no he laughed, a dry mirthless cackle. "The same old story," he said. "Something happens in your backyard, and you are the last person to know it. No one tells you because they think you already know."

On the way back home chewing a tough akroot, I was brooding over Martappayya and his son. Narayana had failed again. He was the mildest of boys, friendly and helpful but also at times irritatingly stupid. We teased him a lot, but he bore it all with such patience that we felt guilty and soon gave it up. Only once had I seen him really angry, and that was when a boy said something insulting about his mother. He had gone berserk then, and lashed at the boy with his bag and umbrella so violently that his umbrella broke into two, and the slate in his bag into smithereens. And the boy, much bigger and stronger than him, ran away frightened. I thought of Martappayya's jokes and of the burden of sorrow he carried. I must have seen, even then, some vague connection between the kind of jokes he cracked—their cutting edge and their scatology—and what he had gone through and was going through.

When I reached home I found Krishnayya, with four others, waiting in our courtyard. He was telling Amma that they had come to invite us to the darshana of Kalkutika to be held next Friday, when father walked in from the dispensary. "What's going on here?" he asked.

I looked at Amma's face and saw there a wry smile. The moment of truth, she must have felt, had arrived. Krishnayya started stammering. "We have come," he said, "to take your permission for the darshana of the Kalkutika, to be held on Friday. People of the village have been suffering for years because we have neglected the deivas..."

"But you decided on this darshana now," said father, his ears turning a dangerous red, "only after I told you, two days ago, that I was thinking of building a fence round that plot of land, now that people seemed to have forgotten those deivas."

"No, no," said Krishnayya, "We planned it a long time ago. People are suffering, you know.... We want to ask Kalkutika what has gone wrong."

Father was furious. "By all means," he said, in a low rasping voice, "But also ask the deiva what's wrong with you the next time you catch something. Ask the Kalkutika to give you your next shot of penicillin."

Father walked away leaving Krishnayya stuttering. "Doctor was joking," he said. "But he has given his permission. 'By all means', he said, and that means we can go ahead. But if he doesn't come to the darshana, the deiva will ask, 'Where is the landlord?' What can we say then?"

"Don't worry," said Amma, "Babu will come, to represent our house."

I was, of course, interested. "Who is going to be the patri?" I asked, and was surprised when I was told it was Soora—a very old man who could not even walk steadily. How would he perform the vigourous dance of a deiva, and that too of Kalkutika?

I thought of the several darshanas I had seen, of the awesome energy and physical prowess of the patris. The most unforgettable of them was the darshana during the annual Deiva Festival held in front of the House of the Deivas, a mile away from Nampalli Matha. I think I was six then. The patri was not a young man but his energy and stamina were incredible. As the different deivas came on him, one after the other, he danced, moved about and talked in a variety of styles, each appropriate to the deiva in possession. I remember how, in the middle of the performance, he suddenly started dancing on one leg. Instead of announcing to the audience who he was, as the other deivas had done, the one in possession asked, "You recognize me, don't you?" and the audience replied, "Yes, yes, we do. You are the One Legged Bobbarya." All through the long session with Bobbarya the patri remained on one leg, shaking and shivering and dancing without once losing his balance, as if that was the easiest thing on earth to do.

So he danced on, for how long I can't say. Sweat poured from his body, and when he applied, in moments of frenzy, the lighted torch to his glistening hairy chest, it was perhaps the sweat which protected it from getting singed. If he wasn't dehydrated it was because every deiva, at the time of departure, was offered tender coconuts. The way the patri downed the water from those coconuts, five or six at a time, and then threw the empty ones around like so many decapitated heads was an awesome spectacle.

And then came the sacrifices. It was close to midnight by then, and all the women and children from our hamlet had left. My uncle, though he hated bloodshed, had to stay on as the representative of the Matha. I refused to budge without him. The place of sacrifices was some distance away from where we sat, and uncle turned his back on the scene and got into a conversation with Raju's grandfather. In his anxiety to shut himself off from the scene of bloodshed he forgot that I was present. So I quietly went and stood with a few boys of the Seregara community and watched, with horrified fascination, the slaughter of goats, sheep and cocks.

It was a gory spectacle. The patri held the centre of the stage, lighted by burning torches, a gleaming sword in his hand. I saw the sword rise and fall, and the head of a goat severed with a single blow. I was terrified but could not turn away. The animals writhed and died where they fell but the decapitated cocks ran or flew as if the loss of a mere head could not stop them. I screamed in terror when a headless rooster came running all the way to where I was standing and fell at my feet, its neck squirting blood. I ran to uncle. He saw me trembling, held me in his arms and covered my head with his shawl. "It's all right, Babu," he said, "It's almost over; we'll go home now."

But it was not all over yet. The run round the village started. The patri, or the guardian deiva of the village who possessed him, ran round the entire village to chase away all the evil spirits that could bring plague and pestilence to the village. Four men held him lest he should run away in pursuit of some evil spirit, and yet he ran at such speed that the men who went along with burning torches to light his way found it difficult to keep pace with him. We left immediately after the run started but when I looked back a minute later, the bobbing torches had already become a dancing cloud of fireflies.

On the way back home I was silent. It was uncle who did all the speaking. He was trying to explain to me things which perhaps troubled him more than they troubled me. We walked in the light of a hurricane lamp brought by Raju's grandfather and a burning torch made of coconut leaves which Subraya Devadiga carried. Our progress was slow because Raju's grandfather found walking in the ploughed-up fields difficult.

"You should have gone home with the other children," said uncle. "The sacrifice is no spectacle for kids. But there is nothing to be scared of, either. Did you get scared, Babu?"

I kept quiet. He continued, after a pause. "It's easy," he said, "to condemn the killings and bloodshed. We are Brahmins, we don't eat meat, we don't have to kill. But all those people eat meat, Babu. The rice and fruits we eat, don't we offer them to God before we eat them? We feel we have failed in our duty to Him if we don't do it. That is precisely what those people are doing, when they sacrifice chicken and goats to the deivas. Who are we to blame them?"

৯৹

The darshana of Kalkutika was about to start when I went there. I was made to sit on a bench, with Krishnayya sitting by my side. Soora had already donned the ceremonial dress and was putting on the sacred brass anklets. I saw him swaying and shivering, in tune with the pulsating music of drums and pipes. Two men held him lest the deiva, living for long in a cold stone, should get exited by its sudden possession of a warm flesh-and-blood human body and decide to run away with it. Or perhaps they held him only to support him because he did look old and frail.

But not after he was fully possessed. Buoyed up by his own movement and the hypnotic music, Soora needed no one's support. He was no longer the timid frail old man who came to my father asking for medicine for his chronic asthma. He was Kalkutika, the powerful deiva, and he danced with vigour and spoke with authority. From where did that power and authority come? Did it come from the depths of his own being, a power which he did not know how to tap at other times, or did it come, as all those present there thought, from outside, from the world of spirits? Or can one answer both these questions with an aye, and say there is no contradiction, because when you delve deep within yourself you also reach out?

"Where is the Doctor Ayya who owns this land?" asked the deiva, looking round theatrically; "Why hasn't he come? Does he think I am of no importance?"

Krishnayya looked around gloating. He had predicted that the deiva would ask that question and the deiva had. "No, no," he said, smirking, "Doctor thinks highly of you but he is busy. So he has sent his eldest son."

The patri looked at me and nodded. In spite of his grim aspect, the old man's sunken eyes held a warm sympathetic smile.

But I could not concentrate on the dialogue that followed. People asked questions and the deiva answered them, but I found nothing to interest me. The Kalkutika could make the old man dance but even he could not make him talk with clarity. Soora had only two teeth left in his mouth, and they only served to make speaking difficult. Those who asked questions apparently understood the answers but I could not. So I turned to the suragi tree. I started wondering what the Yakshi, unused to such noise, thought of all that music and dancing in her normally quiet bower.

Who was this Yakshi, I wondered. Most of the deivas of our place had familiar Dravidian names like Haiguli, Bobbarya and Panjurli. But Yakshi was a Sanskrit name, right out of the *Puranas*: Yakshas and Yakshis lived in the Himalayas, in 'Yaksha Loka'. How did my Yakshi escape from her cold Himalayan kingdom to our warm South Indian village, from the Puranic past to the present?

Someone tapped me on my shoulder. It was Krishnayya. "The deiva is speaking to you," he said.

"Does the young Ayya have any questions?" asked the deiva, with a twinkle in his eyes, and I blurted out: "Who is Yakshi? Where has she come from?"

Kalkutika smiled. "Young Ayya is interested in Yakshi," he said. Some of those present tittered and Krishnayya laughed aloud.

The patri lifted his right hand and struck a theatrical pose. It was a gesture that demanded silence. Then the index finger of his raised hand pointed to the suragi tree. He stood so motionless and steady that all the brass bells in his dress fell silent.

In the silence his words came out with surprising clarity. He spoke in a kindly voice, and it was to me that he spoke.

"The Yakshi is my sister," he said, "my adopted sister. I call her my Akka, my elder sister, because she is a devata whereas I am only a deiva.

128

"She is from the north, from the cold misty mountains. Don't ask me what brought her here, because these are questions spirits never entertain. All that I can tell you is that she hates heat and noise and so has chosen the suragi, the coolest of trees, growing in this quiet place, as her abode.

"We deivas love fragrance. Ultimate happiness, to me, lies in inhaling the delicate fragrance of the shringara flower. It is the suragi flowers for my sister. Her heart glows with happiness when the suragi tree blooms.

"She is alone, but not lonely. Birds come and build their nests in the tree, and she likes it. You sit quietly in the shade and read your big books, and she likes it. Take care of her and she will take care of you."

I told Subbanna about the darshana that evening, when we were sitting talking in the school ground after a game of cricket. The sun had set and it was getting dark. "Hey, let us go and see what your suragi tree looks like in the dark," he said. "Maybe we'll catch a glimpse of the Kalkutika and Yakshi walking about." "All right," I said, laughing.

The stars grew brighter as we walked, talking about the day's cricket match. We were so busy talking that we looked up only after we reached the spot.

There was a gasp of surprise from both of us. "Good God!" said Subbanna, in awe. "A part of the sky has fallen down."

It did look like that. All over the suragi tree and the surrounding bushes, including the one where Kalkutika kept his vigil, danced and flew a host of fireflies. As if the sky had fallen and the stars come down.

Shame

❧

The three years I spent in the high school at Kantheshwar were fairly happy years. We grew up with the school: those of us who joined Form Four in the inaugural year had the rare privilege of being students of the school's topmost class for three consecutive years. I had found the atmosphere in the high school at Chandapur, an old well-established institution, too formal and stifling. Here in the makeshift classrooms, with young and mostly inexperienced teachers, and a laboratory devoid of equipment and a library with just a handful of books, I could breathe more freely, and found the process of learning reasonably enjoyable. There were, among the teachers, a couple of killjoys, but most of the teachers were friendly, and there was this feeling, among the teachers and the taught, that we were all participating in the growth of the school.

That was perhaps why that cycle of a bright beginning followed by a three year period of decline did not recur. I made a good beginning and maintained a kind of erratic progress. I took part in most of the activities of the school: elocution, debating, sports and games. I also started writing.

The first story I wrote came to me under the suragi tree. It was based on a little comic anecdote I had heard about an old orthodox Brahmin and his obsession with 'madi' and 'mailige', the clean and the unclean. All Brahmin rituals are to be performed in a state of cleanliness, or madi; but during centuries of blind unthinking adherence to rigid ritualistic codes the term had got mixed up with the idea of untouchability, so that 'madi' came to mean a dip in a tank or a river, or pouring some water from a well on oneself, and then a strict avoidance of contact with anything considered unclean or untouchable. It did not matter if the water of the tank was dirty or the cloth the Brahmin wore, the ubiquitous bairasa, had never seen soap and was stiff with accumulated sweat and mud. It was still madi, as long as the Brahmin did not touch anything that was not madi after his bath. Even as a kid I found the whole thing ridiculous. When I was four years old I used to chase Varijamma, who made a fetish of madi, all over the place, till Amma put an end to the fun by stripping me 'clean' by pulling off my shorts; because I was unclean only as long as I wore some clothes. I did not like my three cousins—

Lakshmi, Savitri and Aditi—laughing at my nakedness, and so had to leave Varijamma alone.

My story was about an old Brahmin whose obsession with madi led him to several ridiculous actions. In the last of these he had taken his bath in a dirty pond and was waiting for his two pieces of cloth, washed in the same pond, to dry up. He was in a hurry because he was one of the priests invited to conduct an important ritual. He found a dog, considered an unclean animal, nearby and when he tried to chase it away, it trotted right under the branch of the tree he had hung his cloths on.

He was in a dilemma. Whether the dog had touched those pieces of cloth or not became a very important question. If it had, he had to wash them again and take another dip in the pond himself. He would then miss the ritual and the feast. So to clear his doubts he decided to run on all fours, like a dog, under the branch, to see if the cloths would touch him.

They did not. Then he remembered the dog's tail. And though the animal had trotted away when he chased it, it had done so showing no fear; not with its tail between its legs like a frightened dog would have but holding it aloft like a pennant! Did the tail touch the pieces of cloth?

So when the people who had arranged the ritual came to see why the learned Brahmin was late, they saw a strange sight: they saw the old man trotting on all fours like a dog, with a tail made of a leafy twig of some plant tied to his backside!

I remember how heartily I laughed as I thought up the story. I wrote it down that night. There were no problems of composition because the entire story had come to me in a flow of words. My imagination has always been strongly verbal and my head buzzing with words.

On my way to school I gave the story to Vasudeva Bhat, who was working as my father's compounder then. Vasanna, as I called him, knew very little about compounding medicine but father needed someone to sit in his dispensary when he was on his visits. He was more knowledgeable on literature, and had become my literary guru.

When I came back from school I found Vasanna sitting alone in the Dispensary reading the weekly, *Karma Veera*. "How did you like my story?" I asked him.

"Ah, your story," he said, and took out the manuscript from his pocket. He unfolded it and looked at it thoughtfully. "Not bad, that's what I think," he said, "but how can I read and judge a story when it is written so carelessly and illegibly? If you want me to evaluate it, you should write it down neatly, on only one side of the paper."

So I sat up that night and wrote the story again as neatly as I could. I gave it to Vasanna in the morning. But in the evening I found that he had taken it to his house when he went there for lunch and left it there. "Tomorrow," he said, "tomorrow I'll bring it. I think it's not bad, but I'll give you my considered opinion tomorrow."

But that tomorrow never came. I asked him several times about the story but apparently he had misplaced it. Then I forgot all about it, as I was preoccupied with my struggle to get into the school cricket team.

About a month and a half after I wrote the story, the post man came to our class, with a packet for 'N. Sudhakara Rao.' That was a real surprise because no student had ever received any mail at the school address. Rama Rao, our Kannada teacher, a man with a permanent scowl on his face, was in our class then. He took the packet himself. "What is this?" he asked with a frown, opened the packet, and found a copy of *Karma Veera*. "Why has this magazine come for you?" he asked me, and then started turning the pages. "Good God," he said, "'Madi and Mailige', *a short story by Nampalli Sudhakara Rao!* When did you send it for publication?"

There was a buzz of surprise in the class. I was myself quite taken aback. "I didn't send it," I said, "I had given it to Vasanna, I mean Vasudeva Bhat, to read. He has apparently sent it, without telling me."

Rama Rao glanced through the story quickly, frowning all the time. I hoped the ending would make him smile but it did not. "Kid's stuff," he said in a sneering tone, "they have printed it in the Children's Corner."

I was at first a little riled about the story getting published in the Children's Corner. My story was not kid's stuff. It was a satire which showed how the Brahmins, who, as religious teachers, were responsible for the social evil of untouchability, had themselves become its real victims. If Vasanna had not revealed, by my address, that I was a school boy, the editor might not have pushed my story to the Children's Corner.

So I wanted my next story to be something no one would dream of putting in the Children's Corner. This time the story did not come to me. I sought it myself, and finally decided to make Varijamma my protagonist. I changed her name to Padma because the name Varijamma did not sound romantic enough. I made her her father's only daughter, because I did not know what to do with Kamalamma and Gangamma. And by the time I had finished describing her, she bore no resemblance at all to the gossipy, plain-looking Varijamma we all laughed at.

Padma's husband disappeared soon after her wedding. He had been bitten by the ascetic bug and had agreed to the marriage only because of a promise he had given to his dying mother that he would get married. Padma's father asked several wise men, who knew how to penetrate the unknown with the help of cowrie shells, what had happened to his son-in-law, and he always got the same answer: the man was living the life of a *sanyasi* in the Himalayas.

So Padma too lived a simple life in her father's house. She did 108 pradakshinas of the village temple every Tuesday, to pray for her husband's safe return—like Gangamma. She set herself the task of writing 'Shree Rama' ten million times—giving me a chance to make use of my old calculations.

Then one day, when her father was away, a mendicant came to her door asking for alms. When she came out with the usual fistful of raw rice, he asked her if she could give him some cooked food instead, as it was past noon and he did not cook anything in the afternoons.

She served him some rice on a plantain-leaf on the outside verandah. He went to the tank and came back after washing his feet, hands and face.

When he was drying his hands and feet before sitting down to eat, she saw that he had six toes on his right foot. She was shocked. She remembered how she had seen, during her wedding ceremony—she was only eight years old then—that her husband had six toes on his right foot, and that discovery had so fascinated her that she had kept on staring at the foot. Now, after fifteen years, that right foot with six toes was the only thing she remembered of him, but she was quite certain that the mendicant was her long lost husband.

At this stage I had to stop the story because I simply did not know what my protagonist would do next. I knew what Varijamma would have done: she would have run away from the back-door and taken shelter in our neighbour's house. But Padma was not Varijamma. What would *she* do?

I made a neat copy of the incomplete story and gave it to Vasanna.

When I came back from school that afternoon, Vasanna was waiting for me. He looked quite excited. "This is a great story," he said. "This is almost like a story by A.N. Krishna Rao. I'll read the story again tonight. Then we'll decide how we should end it."

But the next day he quarrelled with my father and quit his job in a huff. He had asked for a raise but father felt he did not deserve one because he knew little about compounding medicines, and was not interested in learning either. Then he had a quarrel with *his* father, who did not want him to give up his job, and left his house, without telling anyone where he was going. And with him disappeared the manuscript of my most ambitious story.

A month and a half after this, our school decided to put together a hand-written Annual Magazine. Rama Rao was the Chief Editor. Three students with good handwriting were chosen as student editors. I was one of them.

"As you have some literary pretensions, you can write a story or two for the magazine," said Rama Rao loftily. So I wrote down one of my grandmother's stories, about a jackal and the tiger, and gave it to him. It was pure kids' stuff, but Rama Rao liked it.

But that incomplete story about Padma kept on bothering me. So I wrote it again, and again reached that dead end. I showed the incomplete story to Mr. Mayya, our new science teacher.

"A bit sentimental," he said, "but well-written. How will you end it?"

"I don't know," I said. "I'll think about it and complete it in another day or two. I want to submit it to the school magazine. Can I show it to you after I complete it, sir?"

"No," he said. "You'd better give it to Rama Rao directly."

It took me more than a week to complete the story. I tried out several endings but they all rang false. Then it struck me that there were situations when the only action possible was inaction. I remembered the Kannada proverb, *placing a lamp on a cross wall*. When a blank wall confronts you and you can't see beyond, the thing to do is to place a lamp on it.

So in my story I made Padma, after serving the man food, close the door and sit in front of the little shrine in their house, praying. For fifteen years she had prayed for her husband's return but now that he was there, she did not know what to do.

There was a gentle rap on the door but she did not open it. She continued praying.

When she went and opened the door an hour later, she found that he had properly cleaned the place where he had eaten and was gone. She sighed. "What right have I to interfere in his life, after all these years?" she said to herself: "For him the path he has chosen; for me the path that has chosen me."

I thought that the ending sounded all right. I gave the story to Rama Rao.

The next day, during the recess, the headmaster sent for me. Rama Rao was standing by his side. The headmaster looked very angry. "Did you write this story?" he asked me, pointing to the manuscript lying on his table.

"Yes, sir," I said, a little worried, wondering what objectionable thing I could have written. I saw the headmaster's hand move towards the cane on his table. *Nagara bettha* they called it, the 'cobra cane'. It really hissed and stung. "I shall give you only one chance to tell the truth," he said, "tell me from where you stole this story."

I was flabbergasted. "No, no," I said, "I wrote it myself."

"Hold your palm forward," he said.

The most terrible thing about caning in our schools was that we had to hold our hands forward, palms upward, as if we were begging for alms. When the punishment was for something minor and the caning not too hard, offering our hand for the blow was not difficult. But when the headmaster was angry and the cobra cane hissed and stung, only a hardened criminal could hold his hand steady, without flinching.

I held my hand forward. I had no experience of a real caning till then. *Swish* and *whack* came the blow, and I had to bite my lower lip hard, to prevent myself from crying out in pain. Nagara bettha had really stung.

"Come out with the truth now. Where did you steal the story from?"

I was in a real panic. I could not say anything because I was scared that if I opened my mouth I would start whimpering.

"Bring your hand forward. Keep it steady."

But my hand now suddenly developed a life and volition of its own. It refused to move forward and when I pushed it forward it sprang back at the slightest movement of the cane. I closed my eyes and somehow managed to present my palm for the next blow.

*Swish, WHACK…swish, WHACK…*the cobra cane stung twice in quick succession. I bit my lip harder, but could not prevent tears from coming out of my closed eyes.

"Open your eyes and look at this," said Rama Rao. He was holding a magazine, *Prajamata*, open in front of me. There I saw my story, 'Padma Remembers'; and below the title the words, *a short story by K. Vasudeva Bhat.*

I was horrified. "It's too late for confessions now," said Rama Rao. "Do you know what punishment you deserve? You should be paraded all round the school, and sent to every class, with a placard round your neck, stating 'I am a plagiarist, I have stolen a story. I deserve your contempt'."

Despair, that was what I felt. Before me yawned an abyss of shame. There was no chance of escape. No one would ever believe me.

Just then Mr. Mayya walked in. He felt the tension in the room, said "I'm sorry," and was about to leave, when he saw me. He saw my look of abject terror, the tears, the despair. He hesitated, and then stopped.

"What happened, sir?" he asked.

The headmaster did not say anything. Perhaps he did not like his junior questioning him. But Rama Rao could not help crowing. "Look at this," he said, holding *Prajamata* out to him, "Look at what your favourite student has done. Just a day after *Prajamata* is released, he copies a story from it and

135

submits it as his own to the school magazine! Does he think we are all illiterates here who don't even read magazines?"

Mr. Mayya looked at me with concern and then glanced at the magazine. "Oh, God," he said, and took it from Rao's hand. He read a few lines quickly and shook his head in disbelief. "But this *is* Sudhakara's story," he said. "You say *Prajamata* came out only two days ago. But he showed me this story ten days ago."

"That's impossible," said the headmaster.

"But it is true, nevertheless. He said he had written this story a month and a half earlier, but could not complete it. He is very sensitive, sir. He said he could not complete the story because he was not sure how his main character would act in that situation."

"But who is this Vasudeva Bhat?" asked the headmaster, turning to me. "How did he get hold of your story?"

My explanation, punctuated as it was with sobs, must have been quite incoherent, but he listened with patience. I told him when I had written the first incomplete version of the story and why I had given it to Vasanna. He seemed convinced I was telling the truth.

He turned to Mr. Mayya and said, "Do you know why both Rama Rao and I were so upset? We were sure that the boy had plagiarized. That seemed obvious and was bad enough. But it was his choice of the story which made us really angry. The story—the one in *Prajamata*—is quite obscene. The ending—the boy has changed it, though, or that was what we thought—is quite luridly sexy."

"How does it end, sir?" asked Mr. Mayya.

It was Rama Rao who answered that question. "It is a much better ending—better-written, I mean—than the one Sudhakara has given. The sanyasi, after the meal, enters the house. He catches hold of the woman and tries to molest her. She resists at first, and then submits. There is a lurid description of what follows. At the end of it the man says, 'When a lonely woman treats me with so much of kindness, I know what she wants.' And then he adds, 'I liked the food you gave me. Have I satisfied your hunger as well as you have satisfied mine?' She says nothing. 'Where is your husband?' he asks and she says, 'Look at the mirror, and you will find him.'"

I groaned. Rama Rao looked at me in surprise. "You think it is a bad ending?" he asked.

"It is terrible," I said. "Varijamma—I mean Padma—would have died of shame if something like that had happened."

Mr. Mayya cleared his throat. "May I say something, sir?" he said.

"Go ahead," said the headmaster, leaning back in his chair.

"Plagiarism is bad, sir. But somehow it is not so bad when a youngster indulges in it. We all know how we fall in love with a story or a poem and sometimes wish we had written it. An immature boy might imagine—dream—that he has written the story and might even pass it off as his own. It is wrong—I am not defending it—it is a crime, but a crime more likely to be committed by a boy who loves literature than by one who does not care for it. I think we should keep that in mind."

Mr. Mayya took a deep breath. Then he continued, "I am glad Sudhakara has not committed that crime. But even if he had, he should not have been punished the way he was." He stopped short, looked at the headmaster, who said nothing. "But that man," said Mr. Mayya, "the grown up man who betrayed this boy, he should not be spared. But unfortunately there is nothing we can do to him."

"Perhaps I can write to *Prajamata*," said the headmaster.

It is difficult to describe the relief I felt when I came out of the headmaster's room. I had stood tottering on the brink of an abyss of shame, but I had not fallen over. I had escaped, with nothing worse than a palm that tingled for a day. This led to a nervous, restless kind of euphoria that lasted till evening. Then a tidal wave of bitterness came sweeping in. I was angry with everyone except, of course, Mr. Mayya. The headmaster did not even have a word of regret when he discovered that he had caned an innocent boy. As for the Kannada teacher, he was the real villain of the piece. He was the one who carried the tale to the headmaster and egged him on to punish me. And the placard he talked about—my blood boiled every time I thought of it.

And then there was Vasanna. I trusted him completely and he betrayed me. And the way he ended the story hurt me even more than his betrayal. The sanyasi of his story was not the only rapist; Vasanna was guilty of the same crime. He had raped my story.

But the tide of bitterness receded after a couple of days. I read Vasanna's version of the story and found that the ending was not badly written. It was contrived, but so also was my story. And I also realized that after ending the story the way he did, Vasanna could not have published it in my name.

The incident taught me something. It made me realize that one of the most awful things in life was shame. What terrified me that day in the headmaster's room was not the caning but the threat of shame. The placard round the neck.

But shame can also trouble you, not as a big blow but as little irritations. It can be, then, even more insidious.

I realized this when my grandmother died. She was a great cook before she lost her mind. Even after she handed over the task of daily cooking to mother, she used to go to the kitchen to prepare a variety of snacks, salty and spicy like *chaklis* or sweet like *ladus*. She kept them in little tins, and though they were meant for me and my sisters, she was very fond of them herself. After we shifted to Kantheshwar she missed them badly. The kitchen was now entirely her daughter-in-law's domain. Mother prepared snacks like chaklis occasionally, but grandmother invariably overate them and then had bad stomach upsets. So mother kept whatever snacks there were on the topmost ledge in the kitchen, out of grandmother's reach. One day, when mother was in the cowshed, grandmother whose urge to eat something spicy could no longer be controlled, placed one large pot on another and tried to reach the ledge by standing on them. This was a balancing act even I could not have performed. Grandmother fell down and broke her hip bone. She was bedridden for months and then she died.

Nagatte came six days after grandmother's death but Chandratte could come only on the ninth day. All shows of mourning were over by then, though the funeral rites were on. I was playing with Vasu when I saw her approaching. She was my favourite aunt. So I ran to her smiling broadly. "Ha, Chandratte," I said, "At last you are here." Then I saw the look of pain on her face and remembered that she often had toothaches. "What's wrong, Atte?" I said, "You look as if you have a bad toothache."

Chandratte looked at me in dismay. Then I saw her ears turning red, like father's when he got angry, and remembered that she was quite touchy about her toothaches. "I have lost my mother," she said, "and you ask me what's wrong! She gave me birth and brought me up, and when she dies her favourite grandson asks me what's wrong." She started sobbing. "All through the years, month after month, I slog at my husband's house; taking care of my children, tending my in-laws, working like a slave; and dreaming of my mother's house and of visiting it once in a while to see my mother. She is dead now and you ask me if I have toothache! What do you know of a woman's need for her mother's house. Now that my mother is dead, what can I do but cry—and you talk of toothache!"

Father came out and saw Chandratte blubbering. "No, no," he said, quite distressed at the sight of her tears, "Please, don't cry here, come in, control yourself. What is the use of crying?" He took her by the hand and led her inside. He had heard, perhaps indistinctly, her last few words. So he said, with concern, "Is the tooth hurting very badly?" and poor Chandratte, to his surprise, stamped her foot in anger and burst out crying again.

I quietly sneaked away. Suddenly I felt very depressed. "Aren't you coming to play?" asked Vasu but I did not reply. I went out of the wicket gate at the back and sat down heavily under the suragi tree.

At first I tried to work up anger. All the grown ups were hypocrites, I said to myself. Nagatte came a week ago and cried a lot. The next day she was her usual smiling self. Chandratte was crying, and perhaps Nagatte would join her, but after a good cry today, they would be smiling and gossiping tomorrow.

But no, there was something wrong, not with Chandratte but with me. I *was* my grandmother's favourite grandson. She had taken care of me, fed me, told me stories. When she lay dying she recognized only me. Uncle came every day but on most of the days she did not even recognize him. Father had ceased to be her son, he had become the man who came to examine her and cause her pain, so the moment he came in she used to start whimpering. She only wanted me. "Where is Babu?" she asked, five or six times a day, and whenever I was at home I had to go and sit by her bedside, in that room which smelt of stale urine and some awful disinfectant. I hated it.

Sitting under the suragi tree, I tried to see things as they really were. This was perhaps my first serious attempt at introspection and what it revealed was not flattering. I was shocked when I realized that what I had felt at my grandmother's death was not grief but relief. How could I be so heartless, such a selfish brute? How could I forget her love, and what she had meant to me in my childhood?

I realized that at the root of my problem lay that most insidious of feelings, shame. I, who loved grandmother, had gradually grown ashamed of her. I tried to convince myself that there was cause enough to feel ashamed. The way grandmother wandered about the house with a vacant look on her face, and sometimes with not enough clothes on, was terribly embarrassing, specially when my friends were around. But a moment's reflection showed me that at Nampalli my attitude was different. We did laugh at grandmother and her absent-minded ways, but it was always good-humoured affectionate laughter. But that changed after we shifted to Kantheshwar. Vanity, that was what was wrong with me. At Nampalli I was simply the boy of the house of the Matha, but here I was the Doctor's son, with an image to maintain—or that was what I felt. Vanity made me self-conscious and paved the way for shame.

With a shock I realized that during the previous few years I had even grown ashamed of my uncle. In my first year in the high school at Chandapur I had felt a good deal of admiration for him as a teacher. He taught us well, and students loved him because he kept them entertained with stories and treated them with kindness. But things changed in the second year. He was not a strict disciplinarian like most of the other teachers. So boys who felt suffocated and bottled up in the other classes became boisterous and rowdy in his. He did not mind it but I felt embarrassed, especially when some of the boys tried to show off, in front of me, how they were not afraid of him. One of these, Shekhara Shetty, told me once that he would go and pull my uncle's *juttu*, the sacred tuft of hair Brahmins wore on their head. That was both an act of bravado and insult, like bearding a lion. The other boys dared him to do it, so he went with his exercise book to uncle's chair, stood by his side, and when uncle was busy correcting what he had written, gently fingered his tuft of hair. Uncle must have felt the touch but pretended he had not. He obviously did not mind it but I felt miserable and humiliated.

So when the time came for me to shift school, I heaved a sigh of relief. Relief! I realized how shame could sour and curdle love, like a drop of lime juice in milk. The warmer the milk, the more easily it curdled. But it was disgraceful.

I was brooding over this the next day on my way to school. When I am brooding or dreaming I can perceive things all right, but the mind takes a little longer to put together—conceptualize—what is perceived, and so I tend to stare at things without recognizing them. On that day what confronted my sight in the middle of the pethe was a big bare female breast, heavy but not sagging, jutting out of a torn blouse. It looked as if the blouse was torn purposely to let the breast out. Its twin was not visible as it was covered by the loose end of the saree. I must have stared at it stupidly for a few seconds. Then I heard a giggle. I looked up and saw the face, grimy and haggard, the hair unwashed and matted, the dull eyes full of despair. I did not recognize the woman till she giggled again and said, "Ah, Sudhakara, don't you know me," and bounced her breast.

Little Ramu's mother. I panicked and ran. I stopped only after I reached school.

"You look as if you have just seen a ghost," said Subbanna. "Not a ghost, but a mad woman," I said, laughing nervously. "It must be mad Venkata Lakshmi of the big breasts," said Nagaraja, another of my classmates; "She sleeps anywhere and with anybody. When her husband threw her out, they say she went and stayed with a fisherman, whose wife had quarrelled with him and gone away to her mother's house. But the fishwife rushed back home the moment she heard of her rival and drove the Brahmin woman out. She went mad, they say, after that and has been sleeping on the roadside, on those platforms round pipal trees, and on the outer verandahs of temples, and any man who feels the itch can go and mount her, they say." Then he looked at me and said, "Hey, they say she is from Nampalli. You know her then, don't you?"

"No, I don't," I said.

I had to do some soul searching that evening. I had not thought of Little Ramu for months. What I saw and heard that morning reminded me of the enormity of his shame and made me realize how petty my own little problems were in comparison. In fact there were no problems, I had created them with my own pettiness. A mean ungrateful creature, that was what I was. Remorse could not set right my treatment of grandmother but I decided I must go to Nampalli regularly and spend some time with my uncle

I thought of Little Ramu and said to myself, thank God he had escaped. I thought of his mother, and of her eyes dulled by despair. Since then I have seen that look of despair in the eyes of some other mentally deranged persons. I have often wondered whether they were driven to despair by their madness, or to madness by their despair.

I was wrong about Little Ramu. He had not escaped. He knew, or perhaps realized as the years rolled by, that no one could escape from a shame of that magnitude by merely running away. It was not something he could leave behind in the village because it had bitten deep into him and had become a part of his life. So he had to confront and conquer it. When he did that finally—and I heard of it, years later, from Janakamma, the person who had told me earlier of his shame—he stunned everyone by his courage and his bigness of heart. But of that, later.

Final Year in School

My final year in school was a happy one. There were no tensions at home or in school. I regularly cycled down to Nampalli to meet my uncle. He had become more taciturn after grandmother's death, but that caused no problem. Sometimes we sat together for hours without talking, he immersed in his parayana or pooja or some household work, and I in my reading; but I could see that my silent companionship meant a lot to him.

Rama Rao chose three student-editors from the Tenth Standard for our magazine, because he said that Eleventh Standard students should concentrate on their studies. But he wanted me to contribute a story or two to the magazine. "I have stopped writing stories, sir," I said.

He looked hurt and that surprised me. I did not know he cared. He called me again a few days later. "I am told you write poems now," he said. "Why don't you give a few of your poems for the magazine?" When I blushed and said that they were not worth publishing, he smiled. "That is for me to decide," he said.

My poems had got me into a mess. I had started writing them under the suragi tree, and the way the words came dancing on metrical feet took me by surprise. I did not have to hunt for rhymes; they came and presented themselves when I needed them. I used both end rhymes, which came to modern Kannada poetry from English, and the traditional *khanda prasa,* where the second syllable of each line is rhymed, with a felicity that surprised and delighted me. It was all rhyming and verbal music, nothing more; but it was heady and I felt intoxicated. I was in love with words.

Then I fell in love, perhaps because I needed a subject to write poems on. She was a rather a pretty girl, of my age, studying in the Eighth. I used to dawdle at the corner where the lane from her house joined the main road, so that I could go the short distance from there to school walking behind her. I kept a safe distance and pretended that I was walking in deep thought. But I was watching her all the time. I was hopelessly in love with those two long plaits of hers, and the single rose she invariably wore in one of them. Even more enchanting was the slight swing of her hips as she walked, and the way the plaits moved to and fro, brushing those small but plump buttocks with a rhythmic regularity that could have inspired Galileo. Her face was less attractive but I had no courage to look her in the face anyway. I was in love, madly in love, with her divine backside.

I used to show my poems to my friends and bask in the warmth of their admiration but I did not know what to do with my love poems. Finally I took Subbanna into confidence and showed them to him.

His admiration warmed the cockles of my heart. But a week later I found that every boy in school knew about the poems and some even knew a few of my lines by heart. I was harassed by little boys who, whenever I passed by, sang, with great gusto, the lines I had penned in the anguish of my love. The poor girl too was given the same treatment, for I had, very foolishly, named her in the poems. She had to stop attending school for a few days and her father lodged a complaint with my father.

I don't know what my father felt. He shouted at me and called me a shameless rascal but there was a twinkle in his eyes that suggested that he was highly amused.

That was why I blushed when Rama Rao said that he heard I wrote poems. Apparently he did not know what kind of poems they were. I was touched by his anxiety to make amends for his earlier treatment of me and decided that I must write a poem for the magazine, for his sake. I had just read 'Golgotha', a long poem in blank verse by Govinda Pai, on the crucifixion of Jesus. I started a poem on the death of the Mahatma in the same style and called it 'Another Friday'. The poem began quite splendidly but I ran out of steam at the end of two pages. A narrative poem in sonorous blank verse should go on for at least thirty or forty pages but there was nothing I could do about it. Rama Rao accepted it, saying that it showed great promise.

The very next day he called me again. He had asked the headmaster to write a message for the magazine, to be placed on the first page, but the headmaster had suggested that a poem would look better there. "Why don't you write a little poem," he asked me, "as a prologue to the magazine?"

I felt flattered. That afternoon I sat under the suragi tree and tried to compose a poem. Our magazine was called *Parimala*, meaning 'fragrance', and that became the title of my poem. 'Tried' is hardly the right word, because the poem came so easily that it was like opening a window to let the sunlight in. What I give here is a rough translation which does not capture the poem's verbal music:

> May 'Fragrance' endure.
> May it become a garland of fragrant flowers
> garnered from the school's garden.

When the leaves are yellow with age
and the flowers are dry,
may 'Fragrance' endure

and surprise the reader
like fragrance from a dried garland
of suragi flowers.

I had used khanda prasa all through the poem, and end rhymes at the end of each stanza. Mr. Rama Rao went into raptures over the poem.

That was the last poem I wrote under the suragi tree. The exam was approaching, and as ours was the school's first batch of students appearing for the dreaded S.S.L.C. exam, everyone, including the teachers, grew nervous and tense. The Prelims were over soon and then began the preparatory holidays. Three of my friends, Narayana Vaidya, Ramadas Shet and Sanjeeva Shetty, rented a room so that they could study together. I decided to join them in the evenings. Narayana said that he could not study at home because his mother 'sat on his head', exhorting him to study all the time. She even followed him to the woods, he said, when he went there in the mornings with a tumbler of water, asking him not to dawdle, but finish the job quickly, come home and study. Ramadas's father wanted his son to sit in their grocery shop and study. Not many customers came to the shop but Ramadas found it impossible to study there. Sanjeeva could not study at home because they had guests all the year round.

I had no problems. I joined my friends simply for the sake of company. I went there every night at half past eight, after supper. Sanjeeva had a big kerosene lamp with a chimney which he always kept spotlessly clean. We lay round the lamp, with our heads towards it, sometimes on our backs with pillows under our heads, or prone on the ground with the pillows under our elbows. We kept on disturbing each other with questions and problems. By half past nine Narayana's eyelids, and then his head, would become heavy with sleep. We woke him up but he protested that it was the wrong time for arduous studies. He said that according to his father, who was a well-known astrologer, the best time for study was the *brahmi* period, the period of 90 minutes before sunrise, when the human mind was most fresh and receptive. He said that his father should know, because he knew more mantras by heart than any man on earth.

So we slept by ten, after setting the alarm to ring at five a.m. Sanjeeva had an alarm clock which made a real racket, like the clanging of temple bells at pooja, but over the years he had developed the habit of getting up and silencing it with a knock on its head and then going back to bed, without opening his eyes. So we kept the alarm clock by Ramadas's bed. I shall never forget how we woke up, the first morning after we started our joint study, to the horrible sound of the clanging of the alarm clock and a piercing agonized cry from Ramadas. For Sanjeeva had crawled out of his bed the moment the clock started clanging and his knock to silence the alarm bell had landed on Ramadas's head.

But we were all too sleepy to study so early in the morning. Narayana said that according to his father the best way of getting rid of sleep and freshening oneself up was to have a cold water bath. So we trooped out to the temple tank, waking up all the sleeping dogs of the alley on the way. As my friends were all good swimmers, it was nearly six before we came out of the water. Then we felt cold and wanted to warm ourselves with hot coffee at Pai's Restaurant, which always opened at six in the morning.

We never got more than ten minutes of the blessed brahmi period to study in. We did read for an hour or two thereafter, and then felt hungry. My friends went back to the room after breakfast but I went to the suragi tree, sat in its cool shade and immersed myself in my studies from nine to noon, and then again in the afternoon. My mind worked with surprising clarity. Even things I had not understood in the class suddenly became clear. I think those twelve hours I spent everyday in the company of my friends were not wasted. I studied very little then but I came back relaxed and refreshed, ready and willing to study alone for the rest of the day.

I did well in the exam but did not know how well, till I went to collect my certificate on the day of the results. The headmaster was there, standing near the table of the clerk who was distributing them.

He took my certificate—a thin booklet—and handed it over to me personally. "This is terrific," he said, "a great performance. Honestly, I didn't know you had it in you. You stand first in our school but that is not all. I have sent a peon to Chandapur to find out what their highest is, because I think you might have outscored everyone there." He shook hands with me and then patted me on the back.

I went out of the office treading on air. I saw my friends, Sanjeeva, Narayana and Ramadas standing in a corner and rushed to them. "This is fantastic," I said, bubbling with happiness, "I can't believe I have really got these marks! Do you know what I have got in…"

Then I saw the expression on their faces. The pain and the anger. It was Sanjeeva who spoke first. He turned to Narayana and hissed, "Narayana, tell this son of a bitch to get lost, if he doesn't want me to break his teeth and give them in his hand."

"What's wrong?" I asked, badly shaken. "What have I done?"

"What's wrong, he asks, this son of a widow," said Narayana. "After spending twelve hours every day disturbing our study, he goes home and studies the whole day on the sly, and then comes again in the evening to disturb us! And he wants to know what he has done!"

"You want to know what's wrong?" said Ramadas, on the verge of tears. "We have failed, that's all. All three of us, thanks to you. We are the only three who have failed in our class...the headmaster. said we had spoiled the school's result, brought it disgrace. But what do you care, you the great scholar who has brought honour to the school?"

I walked away feeling terribly dejected. Anyone looking at me walking with my certificate would have thought that I must have failed miserably in the exam. "I wish I had failed," I said to myself, for then I could have stood in the corner with my three friends, united in misery. Then I thought that I would have gladly given my friends half my marks, for then we would have all passed. But when Mr. Aithal of the cycle shop came out of his shop to congratulate me—for the news of my success had already spread—I started feeling better. Then I began to feel that my friends were terribly unfair. How could I be blamed for their failure? I was not the one who suggested that we should bathe in the tank or the one who went on swimming till six. What business had they to heap abuses on me, and call me a son of a widow, one of the worst abuses in Kannada?

When I reached home I found Amma busy giving Moni an oil bath. Like all children I hated oil baths in my childhood. Amma had to chase me all over the house and catch me with the help of my three cousins before she could massage me with coconut oil, pour several spoonfuls of it on my head till it ran down my neck, and made me feel so sticky and uncomfortable that the final torture with hot water and soap was not unwelcome. But Moni, the little pig, loved oil baths. "Amma, I have passed," I said, but she merely said, good, go and tell your father. "I have passed in the First Class," I said, but she was so engrossed in washing off the oil on Moni's head with soap and water—so happy about his squeals of delight—that she paid me no attention. In desperation I said, "I have stood first in my school," and she said, "Oh God, Moni has dropped the soap down the drain, go and get a new one, be quick."

When father saw my marks he stood, for a long time, speechless—as if he could not believe his eyes. Then he came to where I was sitting and tousled my hair. He did not say a word, he just came and tousled my hair.

He scolded Amma for not preparing any sweets for lunch. "Your son stands first in his school, and you don't even prepare a *payasa?*" he asked. So we had green gram payasa and cream-of-wheat ladus that night.

After supper father took his easy chair out into the courtyard and sat down. I think it was the ninth night of the bright half of the month, and the courtyard was brimming with moonlight. Father wanted another cup of payasa. I, Sita and Savita sat on the raised ridge of laterite stones built round a coconut tree, eating ladus. Amma came with the payasa, tugging Moni along, who climbed on to father's lap and sat there very quietly.

Father looked happy. I had ever seen him so happy before—and I never saw him happy again. "Babu is intelligent," he said, "but he is not disciplined. He has never tried to do well in exams. Sometimes I feel dispirited, Sarasu. The life of a village doctor is a lonely one. But now I know everything will be all right. Another seven years and Babu will be here to assist me. Dr. N. Sudhakara Rao. We will make a doctor of him, Sarasu, I know we can do it."

My mouth and throat went dry. A piece of ladu got stuck in my throat and I nearly choked.

The confrontation, when it took place, was terrible. At first father refused to believe that I really did not want to become a doctor. "Go, go," he said, "It's no joke, becoming a doctor. First you study hard for the next two years, do well enough in your intermediate exam, and then we'll see how to cross the bridge when we come to it."

Then he grew angry. "What do you mean, you don't want to become a doctor? What the hell you want to do, if you don't want to be a doctor?"

I said I wanted to take up Arts. "Arts? What will you do with Arts? Become a penpusher or a school teacher? If you want to become a clerk, why should I waste my money and send you to college? Your S.S.L.C. marks are good enough to get you a clerical job. Go and get it."

I said that at fifteen I could not get a job. "Oh, you are too young, are you? But you are old enough to decide you don't want to be a doctor! Old enough to care two hoots for your father's long cherished wish. Old enough to decide what you want to study and what you want to become."

He expected me to buckle under his angry outbursts, and when I did not, he was furious. "Who's going to pay for your college education?" he shouted. "Do I pay or do you have some other father? I tell you here and now: I am not going to pay a pavane for any arts or farts. Don't I have the right to choose what I pay for?" He was so shaking with anger that I was scared he might get an apoplectic fit. Amma tried to calm him down and asked me to get lost.

He broke me. He broke me the way they break animals like horses. By the sheer force of his uncontrolled anger he bulldozed me into submission. In the process he lost my respect. I had worshipped him right from my childhood. My love for him did not cease altogether but it changed, and an acute awareness of his lack of self-control undermined my hero worship of a man who was, in my eyes till then, faultless.

I think he knew that it was but a Pyrrhic victory he had won. A couple of days after I capitulated, or at least stopped protesting and arguing back, he came to my room when I was lying in bed moping in darkness. I felt his presence darkening the door and then he shuffled in and sat down on the chair near my bed. "I want you to know," he said, in a quiet voice, "what I have gone through in life. Nobody wanted me to become a doctor. Nobody believed I could. My mother did not want her son to take up a profession where he would have to touch people of all castes and communities. Father opposed it mainly because there was no money, not even for my journey to Madras. Nagu's marriage had emptied the family's coffers, and Chandru's had landed us in debt. Annayya's marriage had not improved matters for his wife had not brought any dowry. He had just got his job. He never said no to me but every time I talked about my determination to become a doctor, his face fell; he did not know where to get the money from. Finally he gave me the money to go to Madras. I did not ask him where it came from, for I was scared that that might make me change my mind. Years later I came to know, not from Annayya but from my mother, that his wife had given him her gold bangles to sell. 'What better use can I ever have of them?' she had said, 'If they can come in handy to give my brother-in-law good education, why not sell them?' I did not even thank her.... She was not alive when I came back.

"I don't want to tell you how I survived in Madras. I humbled myself, swallowed insults, lived on one meal a day. Most of those I asked for help did not believe that I could last out the full five years. Annayya sent me whatever he could. Things eased out a little in the final years but it was tough, it was really tough."

Father took a deep breath. "Setting up practice was not much easier. I found it humiliating to sit in my dingy dispensary waiting for patients while people went to an unqualified quack from Kerala just opposite. During the first couple of months I had just one or two patients a day, and they too had come because they were fed up, waiting at the other dispensary." He sighed again and added, "I don't know how long this would have continued, if Kamalamma, the village midwife, had not come to my aid. She was attending to a difficult delivery but found, at the last minute, that she could not manage it on her own. The family doctor, from Chandapur, had gone out of station, and so she asked them to call me. The first ever call I received in my life and a tough one at that. But I was lucky, and so was the patient; both mother and child survived. Kamalamma went round the village telling people what a wonderful doctor I was, and I had no shortage of patients thereafter.

"It has been a hard struggle. Now my dream is to see my son a doctor. My practice is waiting for him. After all these years of struggle, don't I have the right to wish that my son would come and team up with me?"

I was deeply touched but did not know what to say. Then I saw a faint movement in the darkness. He was getting up. My last chance of telling him what I wanted to say. So I said, "You have struggled a lot, Appa, but you struggled to realize *your* dream. You went against your parents' wish, you struggled, you won. You could do that because it was your dream. If I too have a dream, Appa, is there anything wrong? I want to devote myself to literature; I want to read, I want to write, I want to teach...."

But he was not there listening. I heard him dash against a chair in the verandah outside. He was limping a little the next day.

I went alone to Udupi for my college admission. Father gave me the money I needed, and a letter to Professor Saralaya, H.O.D. of Physics. "He is going to do everything needed," he said. "He will fill up the form for you and sign as your guardian. You just pay the fees." When I was about to leave, he said, in a stern voice, "Remember, he will do everything. Don't interfere, don't argue with him."

Professor Saralaya was a pleasant looking man. He told me that he and my father were together at Madras, he doing his M.Sc. with Physics and father a final year medical student. "A very intense person, your father," he said. "Not an easy man to get along with, but upright and hard working." He read father's letter and laughed. "Another father-son conflict," he said; "Take it in your stride, that is the way of the world. He insists that you should take up science. There is nothing wrong with that. After completing your Inter Science, you can change over to Arts or Commerce. But you can't change from Arts to Science." He looked at my marks, and said, "Good. 90% in Maths, 85% in Science. The only trouble is you have taken General Maths, not Composite Maths. But don't worry, the Maths syllabus in Intermediate is pretty elementary."

I kept quiet because that was what my father wanted me to do and also because Professor Saralaya talked so fast that it was difficult to put a word in, even sideways. He filled up the form, signed as my guardian, and asked me to stand in the proper queue to pay the fees.

It was when I was standing in the queue that I realized what had gone wrong. My father's letter had stated—stressed repeatedly—that I should take Science and not Arts. But there were two groups in Science: Group A, where you studied Physics, Chemistry and Maths; and Group B, with Physics, Chemistry and Biology. To go for Medicine one had to take Group B, not A, but Professor Saralaya, who had certainly taken Maths in Intermediate himself, simply wrote Group A in my application form.

I had reached the Payments Counter by then. There was not much time to think. I gave my application, paid my fees and said to myself: "Good, father said I should not argue or interfere with the professor. I won't."

But it did not take long for me to realize that I had got myself into a real jam. Our school, being a new one, offered only General Mathematics, which was nothing but simple Arithmetic, whereas in Composite Maths one studied Algebra and Geometry, both important parts of the Maths syllabus in Inter Science. Professor Saralaya thought that it was all elementary but for someone like me who had no aptitude for Maths, or for the kind of abstract thinking it required, nothing could be drier or more difficult.

The first thing the Professor of Maths asked us in the class was how many of us had taken General Maths in school. Five hands went up. He flashed at us a brilliant smile and said, "If you don't understand what I teach, don't blame me. I can't possibly waste the time of my other students explaining things they already know." Then he smiled again.

After that, in all his lectures, he studiously ignored us, except for an occasional smile specially meant for us. I hated that smile.

It was a real mess I had got myself into. If I had taken Biology I would have had no problems at all. The only subjects I was interested in—English and Kannada—were compulsory for all Intermediate students. I did not much care for History or Logic or any other Arts subject. I would have found Biology at least equally interesting. And I would not have found myself in that awful Maths class, without understanding a word of what was being taught, constantly irritated by that flickering smile on the Professor's face which seemed to say, Ah, you General Maths worms, let us see how long you can endure my incomprehensible lectures.

I was not there in the class for long. Fifteen days after the lectures started, Professor Tenkillaya caught me reading a novel in the class. I was on the last bench with a copy of *Pride and Prejudice* open inside the desk. The student sitting next to me, Guru Patwardhan, woke me up. It took some time for me to come out of the novel.

"What is it you are reading?" asked the Professor. The smile was brighter than usual.

"*Pride and Prejudice*," I said.

"A good novel," he said. "I compliment you on your taste in literature; and also on your concentration, because I have been trying to catch your attention for some time now. But don't you think you would be happier reading that book elsewhere—where you are not disturbed by a boring Maths lecture—in the library, for example?"

I kept quiet. He smiled. "Are you very fond of novels?" he asked.

"Yes."

"How do you find *Pride and Prejudice?* Good?"

"Yes."

"Better than my lecture?"

"Y-yes"

"Then why do you come to the class? Is it for the sake of attendance?"

"Yes."

"Ah, you are honest. Here is an agreement between the two of us. You don't come to my class again, and I give you full attendance."

I stood with my head down. "Come, come," he said. "Don't hesitate. Go straight to the library, and don't worry about your Maths attendance."

I left the class, went to the Library and sat down in a corner, feeling terribly depressed. But then I started reading *Pride and Prejudice* and found my depression evaporating. That placid world of Jane Austen can make you forget your worries as nothing else in literature can. When Guru Patwardhan came looking for me at the end of the morning session, he was surprised to find me totally immersed in the novel, oblivious of the stir I had created in the class by accepting Professor Tenkillaya's 'agreement'.

Three of the five General Maths students changed over to Arts after this. They had all taken Maths because they did not have the requisite marks for Biology, a subject in great demand. I had the marks but in a stupid fit of contrariness had kept my trap shut when Professor Saralaya filled up my form wrongly. Now I was in an awful hole, a dead end from which I could see no escape.

There was no escape because Biology seats were full; and I could not change over to Arts without my father's permission and he did not even know that I had taken Maths! I knew there would be an explosion when the truth finally came to light.

The bubble burst during the vacation at the end of the first term. Ramesh Hebbar, the only other boy from our school to join college, had taken Maths like me and then changed over to Arts. His father told my father what I had done. The explosion was more terrible than I had anticipated. Father nearly went crazy. "What have you done, you idiot," he shouted, "why have you destroyed your own future? Just to spite me? You are not interested in Mathematics, you haven't studied Composite Maths, you knew you would fail, yet you took Maths! Why, why, why?"

"Professor Saralaya…"

"But you, why didn't you tell him you had to take Biology? Why?"

"*You* asked me not to interfere or argue with him.."

He slapped me, for the first time in my life. We were both shocked, he more than me perhaps. He must have been more hurt too. We were both thin-skinned but he was less analytical, less communicative, less verbal, than me. So his suffering and anger smouldered on, eating into him, long after I had made my hurt bearable through analysis and verbalization.

He did not talk to me for nearly two years after this. He got upset every time he saw me and could not eat when I sat next to him. Twice he got up, after only a few morsels, as if he could not swallow his food. The second time this happened Amma said to me, "Do you want to kill your father? Can't you see he can't eat when you are sitting by his side?"

"What should I do?" I said, terribly hurt.

"Come for food before him, or if you are not hungry, after he has eaten."

I felt suffocated at home. I suppose that was what he felt too, when I was present.

For the next year or so I spent most of my waking hours reading. With my speed, I must have created some kind of world record. I did not, of course, like everything I read. I found *Brothers Karamazov* deeply moving, but *Crime and Punishment* was somehow too painful. *The Possessed* was one of the very few books I returned unread. I preferred Tolstoy to Dostoevsky. I was caught in the sweep of *War and Peace* for three whole days. But the novelist I never tired of reading and re-reading was Jane Austen. *The Complete Novels of Jane Austen* was the only book I kept for full fifteen days. When the librarian, who was quite fed up of my habit of returning the books I borrowed the very next day, said, "This time I can believe you have read the book; you have, haven't you?" Guru Patwardhan laughed and said, "You should ask him how many times."

I read *Mansfield Park* and *Northanger Abbey* only once each, and *Sense and Sensibility* twice. But I don't know how many times I read the other novels, and how often I dipped into them. *Pride and Prejudice* I had read before, but I read it again now with the other novels. And as I read them together, the novels melted and merged to become one great novel, depicting a world very different from the one I knew, but thoroughly convincing and real—more real, in fact, than the world of smiling maths professors and angry overbearing fathers and insensitive mothers which I found baffling, even nightmarish. This fictional world became my home during those troubled years. The gates always opened for me. *Home is the place where, when you have to go there, they have to take you in.*

I remember how easily I could slip into that world and feel totally at home there. When experts on teaching English talk about cultural barriers, and of the need to bore our students to death with the cultural history of 18th century England before we teach them any of Jane Austen's novels, I don't know whether to laugh or cry. I needed no background information of any sort to get into Jane Austen's world. In fact, I learnt from those novels all that I now know of late 18th century England. Those gates that opened so readily for a fifteen-year-old boy from a remote Indian village, surely there is no need to break them open with the heavy hammers of 'background information' our English pundits recommend.

I failed in Maths in the final examination that year—got a zero, in fact—but as it was only a college examination, and I had passed in all the other subjects, they promoted me. At the beginning of the next academic year Guru Patwardhan—we called him Pat—said to me, "Look, Sudhakar, your problem last year was a real one. But Algebra and Geometry are over now, we have to study Trigonometry and Calculus this year. They are as new to Composite Maths students as they are to you. If you study them well, there is no reason why you can't pass in the final exam. A few additional marks you can get by studying some of the easier theorems in Algebra or Geometry. So swallow your pride and attend the Maths lectures regularly."

So I swallowed my pride and went to the Maths class. Professor Tenkillaya saw me the moment he entered the room.

"Patwardhan, who is the new student sitting next to you?" he asked.

We both stood up. Professor Tenkillaya smiled. "Please tell your friend, Mr. Patwardhan, that the old agreement still stands. And as for you, please remember, bringing outsiders to the class is an offence."

I went back to the library. That was the last I saw of Professor Tenkiliaya, except for a couple of minutes during the final exam when he came to the hall to see how his students were faring. He saw me writing furiously and was shocked. The smile momentarily disappeared from his face. But it came back, broader than ever before, when he realized what I was doing.

A month before the final exam, Pat had tried his best to teach me some theorems and a bit of Trigonometry, but found me unteachable. The evening before the day of the Maths exam he came again to my room and said, "Look, you idiot, study at least one theorem. This one is sure to come and even a blockhead can learn it. You will get six marks for it, and six is much better than zero." "Not just much better," I said, "infinitely better." That much of Maths I knew: that six divided by zero was infinity.

So he taught me the binomial theorem. What I found specially interesting about the theorem was that one could go on and on with it till the nth degree.

We were not allowed to leave the examination hall during the first thirty minutes and my problem was what to do during that period. The binomial theorem solved that problem. I remember how I attacked my answer paper straightaway and wrote faster than anyone else in the hall. It was then that Professor Tenkillaya strolled in and momentarily lost his smile. He stood irresolute for a moment, then said "Excuse me," and turned the pages of my answer paper backwards. The lost smile returned. I smiled back at him. His smile grew broader. So he went away, out of that hall and out of my life, with a smile that would have made the Cheshire cat die of envy. R.I.P.

I failed, of course. Though there was no new explosion, the tension at home was unbearable. The one year I spent at home after my failure must rank as one of the unhappiest years of my life.

The Unhappy Year

It was *one* of the unhappiest years, certainly. If it does not deserve to be called the saddest year of my life, it is only because at seventeen you don't lose hope completely. There were moments of total despair, but I recovered, saying to myself, "Everything passes, this too will pass."

At home it was terrible. Father and I avoided each other. I saw that my presence irritated and angered him. But whenever it became obvious that I was avoiding him, that hurt him even more. "My son is avoiding me," I heard him say to mother, "as if I have got the small pox."

He spoke to me only once during the year. That was the day I had to send my application for appearing in the October inter exam. He expected me to approach him for the money needed, and when I did not, he was furious. "What are you doing?" he shouted at me, storming into my room; "Don't you know today is the last day for filling up the examination form?" He snatched the book I was reading—Premchand's *Manasarovar*—and when he saw it was a Hindi book, he could not believe his eyes. "Hindi!" he said, "So you are reading Hindi novels now?"

"Not a novel," I said, "It's a collection of short stories."

I said it because I did not know what else to say but to him it must have appeared an impudent answer. He raised his hand as if to strike me, then struck himself on the forehead. "Oh God," he said, "I can't understand this. You don't care for Hindi, you didn't even appear for your Hindi paper in the S.S.L.C. exam because you said that the Madras Government had made Hindi optional. And now you sit with a big Hindi book when you should be studying for your October exam! You want to drive me crazy, that's what you want to do."

It is strange the way real life can turn into a play. Perhaps it *is* a play, and we mess up our roles only because we don't know what the play is all about. We say something unpremeditated, something even out of character, but that remark might set the tone for the rest of the scene, as if it were a piece of dialogue in a play which forces us to act according to what is written in the script. I was in dread of that encounter with father, which was inevitable once he learnt I was not going to appear for the October exam. I had no valid explanation to give for skipping it. I could not tell him the truth: that I hated Maths, and my mind went dry whenever I opened the Maths texts, and so I had gone on postponing studying Maths till it was now too late to think of appearing for the exam. But that remark about *Manasarovar*, irrelevant and therefore impertinent, somehow helped me to play my role in that difficult scene with some nonchalance. "It's no use appearing for the October exam," I said to father, "I can't study two years' syllabus of Maths in this short period. I need more time. And anyway, I can go for further studies only when the colleges re-open in June next, after the March exam results, so what does it matter whether I appear for the exams in October or in March?"

Father looked as if he might tear his hair in exasperation. Then he walked away, looking terribly dejected. I felt sorry for both of us.

I must say something about how I happened to be reading a Hindi book. It was curious. My supply of books, both in English and Kannada, had dried up. I had read all the readable books I could get hold of in our village. I needed books to read because the only other thing I could do was to dream, and my dreams often turned bitter during that year of near-despair.

Our school library was always open to me because the clerk, who acted as the librarian, was my friend. The only section of the library I had not touched was the Hindi section. As no students ever read any Hindi books—the Hindi taught in our schools was elementary—our Hindi Pandit had stocked that section with books only he could read, including everything written by his favourite author, Premchand. So on a day I was desperate for something to read, I borrowed the first volume of *Manasarovar*—the collected short stories of Premchand in several volumes—to see if I could get anything out of the book.

The going was tough at first but I persevered, for I found the stories interesting. But though I read almost all of Premchand's stories and a few novels—*Karma Bhoomi, Ranga Bhoomi* and *Gaban*—I never really got used to the Hindi script. Even when I succeeded in entering the fictional world, I found those letters crawling all over the place, like ants. They kept troubling me the way those floating specks—*muscae volitantes*—bother old people when they look at the sky.

That reading helped me in an unexpected way. A month after that scene with father Mr. Mayya, to whose house I had gone to borrow a novel, said, "Look, Sudhakara, this is no good, you can't go on postponing your study of Maths. You have to start now or else it will be too late for the March exam. I have talked to Mr. Ural, our Maths teacher, and he is prepared to help you."

I asked him what I had to pay, and he said that that was between Ural and my father. It was obvious that father, who did not want to talk to me directly, had asked Mr. Mayya to convince me that I needed tuition. I knew I needed it desperately. So I started going to Mr. Ural's house for Maths tuition. At first he was friendly and sympathetic. But it did not take long for him to be convinced that I was the biggest blockhead he had ever had the misfortune of teaching Maths to and that I had, somehow, lost whatever intelligence I might have had earlier. In the state of mind I was then in, he could have easily persuaded me that I had really become a moron, if it was not for my fairly successful attempt at reading Hindi novels. No moron, I knew, could have achieved that.

I remember one afternoon when he was so upset that he stopped the tuition abruptly after only a few minutes. "It's no use," he said. "What you need is not Maths tuition but a thorough examination of your head for premature brain decay. If I try to teach you any longer today, I'll certainly go mad. Come tomorrow."

I went from his house to the school to return a Hindi book I had borrowed. I was feeling terribly depressed. The Hindi Pandit was there, near the shelf housing Hindi books. He was a quiet man who kept himself aloof and spoke only in whispers. He looked with surprise at the novel I returned. "*Karma Bhoomi?*" he said, "Did you read this novel? You could understand it?"

"Yes. I mean—I understood it well enough to follow the story."

He asked me a few simple questions about the story of the novel, and then said, "It's incredible. You hardly know Hindi and yet you read and understand one of the toughest novels in the language. I don't know how you do it, but you *are* a genius." Then he shook his head. "But this is not the time to try your reading skills though. You should concentrate on the coming exam, shouldn't you?"

I have not read a Hindi book since then. I know the language a little better now, having lived in Bombay—where Hindi is spoken widely—all these years. But I wonder whether I can read a Premchand novel now. Perhaps I can, if I were to find myself in a situation similar to the one I found myself then in. Something like being marooned on a desert island with nothing to read but Hindi books.

The next day I did not go to Mr. Ural's house. I went to Nampalli instead. Kodi Habba was just two days away, and I wanted to see if Ranga and others had come.

I parked my bicycle in front of the Matha—my uncle had not yet come home—and found myself walking behind a young woman with an extraordinarily voluptuous behind. She had just bathed in the tank and was walking back home. Her wet saree clung to her body, revealing the contours of her magnificent dimpled buttocks. When she turned her head slightly and realized that she was being followed, that awareness galvanized her behind to vibrate and swing more vigorously than before. I felt both excited and embarrassed. I did not know whether to walk past her or walk slowly. Then she turned, looked at me and grinned. "Sudhakara," she said, "why are you walking silently like a thief?"

It was Gulabi, Raju's sister. I could not believe my eyes. She was a scrawny little girl when I knew her, a real plain Jane, always scratching her head because her hair was full of lice. She had got married six months earlier. I knew marriage changed some girls, but this metamorphosis was incredible.

"I heard you failed in college," she said, giggling. "You were so good in studies earlier. What happened? Did the girls in your college bother you much?"

"Have Ranga and Raju come?" I asked, feeling embarrassed, and she laughed. "They have all come," she said. "They won't miss Kodi Habba for anything. They left for Kantheshwar half an hour ago to meet you. They were complaining that you did not come to the last two festivals, though you were at Udupi just twenty miles away. They thought you must have been very busy with your studies!" She giggled again and asked, archly, "What were you so busy with?"

"They must have gone by the short cut," I mumbled, "I'll see if I can meet them." "What's the great hurry?" she said. "You must have come cycling. So you won't meet them on the way. Come home and have some coffee."

"No, no," I said, "I'll be late." I turned back as if in a hurry, but after I turned the corner and Gulabi was out of sight, I slowed down. Uncle had not yet come. I sat down on the outer verandah of the Matha. My head was in a whirl.

I felt my ears burning. Gulabi, the minx! Talking about my failure and its causes, as if she knew everything. She was six months younger than me and I had always treated her as a kid. Now suddenly, after her marriage, she was talking to me as if I were a kid and she a grown up woman. Then I thought of her mischievous dancing eyes and that vibrating behind, and said to myself: God, I wish I had come a few minutes earlier and gone down to the tank to wash my feet when she was still there bathing. The thought turned into a dream. I walked down the steps of the tank, deep in thought, and saw her bathing, neck deep in water, her breasts lifted up by the water's buoyancy. I turned back but she giggled and said, "Sudhakar, it's only me, Gulabi. You don't have to run away." As I stood on the last step with the water lapping against my feet, she emerged from water and stood near me, her wet saree tantalizingly transparent. "I heard you failed in college," she said, giggling. "What happened? Did the girls in college bother you much?" While trying to go up the steps she stumbled and I caught her in my arms. "Not as much as you bother me now," I said, crushing her in my arms till she cried out in pain and desire, "Not so tight, please, you are hurting me…"

"What are you dreaming of?" said uncle. I had not seen him coming. My ears began to burn again. "You look feverish," he said and felt my forehead with the back of his palm. "No, there is no fever," he said, looking relieved. "Wait a little, I'll go to the tank, wash my hands and feet and come."

I looked at his stooping figure, the faltering steps, and said to myself, "Oh, God, he looks so weak and old all of a sudden." He was only in his fifties but he looked frailer than Chikkajjayya who was some thirty years his senior.

We had a long chat that day. For the first time after my failure in the exam I opened my heart out to him. I had taken care, earlier, to keep my troubles to myself because I did not want to add to his burden of sorrows. But now it came out in a torrent—the long suppressed tale of my troubles, frustrations and anger. I knew that there was nothing he could do to help me and I was causing him needless suffering, but once I started I could not stop. And after a time I did not want to stop. I think I *wanted* to hurt him, perhaps because I was upset that he would not blame my parents in spite of my complaints; or maybe I simply wanted someone I loved to suffer with me. Poor uncle. He could do nothing but listen, his brow creased with worry and distress, except for an occasional, almost inaudible, protest when I said things like "My father hates me and can't stand the sight of me." Only once he said "Don't say that," and that was when I said that mother never ever had any love or sympathy for me. "Don't blame her," he said, "poor girl, she had had a tough beginning to her married life and perhaps still feels insecure." But he would not tell me what that 'tough beginning' was. He looked so unhappy when I asked him that question that I had to change the topic.

He tried to console me. Once I pass my Inter exam, he said, my problems would be over. "Not much chance of that," I said, "I am going to fail in Maths again."

"Why do you say that?" said uncle, his brow creased in worry again. "Mr. Ural is teaching you, isn't he? He is very good in Maths."

"Oh, he is good in Maths all right," I said in bitterness, "but he is even better in beating his student's brain into pulp. He has mastered that art."

"How—how does he do that?"

"His method is simple and effective. He begins with a problem that is just a wee bit too hard for me. A simple problem, according to him, but he forgets that I don't have any Maths background. Oh, he is hard working all right. He doesn't give up easily. Keeps on hammering my head with the problem till I start feeling dizzy. Then he gives it up in disgust and takes up another problem, saying, 'This one, I am sure even you can understand.' But I cannot, because he has already so softened my brain with his hammering that it is no longer capable of grasping even simple mathematical problems. But he doesn't give up still. He takes up another, even simpler, problem, saying, this one even a moron can understand, let's see what you do with it. But by then my brain is totally pulverized. I'm no longer just a moron, I have become an idiot. So he dismisses me but says, 'Come tomorrow!' And what frightens me is that he says it quite warmly, as if he enjoys giving me the treatment."

Uncle smiled ruefully. "Your language is as colourful as ever," he said, "but don't worry, I'll talk to Ural."

He must have done so for there was a perceptible change in Mr. Ural's method of teaching thereafter. He stuck to simple problems and I had no difficulty in following him. But he gave me the impression that he was no longer interested in teaching me. Perhaps he resented uncle's interference. Or he must have seen in my mind a self-erected barrier against Mathematics and found the task of breaking it down a challenge, and lost interest once that challenge was taken away. Or it might be, simply, that he lost interest because he could no longer derive any sadistic pleasure from pulverizing my brain. Human motivation is so complex. All that I knew was that there was less warmth in those two words—Come tomorrow—with which he invariably ended each session of teaching.

About the difficulty of understanding human motivation: how I wish I could understand my own motives better. Why did I, for example, add to uncle's burden of sorrows by talking about my troubles—knowing fully well that there was nothing he could do to help as his relationship with father was still strained? I was playing for his sympathy, yes; I wanted to unburden myself, perhaps; I needed someone to share my sufferings, maybe. But the real reason, I suspect, was something more ridiculous, even absurd: Gulabi's voluptuous behind and my erotic daydream. Uncle had caught me dreaming, and though there was not the faintest chance of his guessing the nature of my dream, he had made me feel ashamed. He had asked me what I was dreaming of and I did not want him to ask that question again. It was, I think, to hide my embarrassment that I had gone on talking, overwhelming him with my tale of sorrows. Life, they say, is a tragedy to those who feel, and a comedy to those who think. I suspect that with most people like me it is the Theatre of the Absurd.

I felt, however, less burdened after that talk. But my depression returned the next day—the day before the Habba—mainly because I could not share the excitement I saw all around. Even father exhibited some, as he was the chairman of the Festival Committee. Little Moni was the most thrilled of all and kept on chattering about the festival till he fell asleep. He wanted me to take him to the habba and sit in the 'cradles' with him. I promised him I would.

Moni used to sleep with me in the upstairs room which father had designed as his master bedroom. 'Father's Folly', that was what I called it. He had lavished every attention, and plenty of money, on the room's décor. But it could not be occupied because mother felt giddy climbing the steep staircase which led to it. Father went alone and slept there in solitary splendour for a night or two but soon gave it up, as coming down that unlighted staircase in the middle of the night was not just inconvenient, it was dangerous. Upstairs rooms with attached bathrooms were unheard of in those days.

So the room remained unoccupied till I returned after my Intermediate fiasco and needed a place to hole myself in. It gave me privacy and helped me to keep out of father's way. But I found that opulently furnished room with its massive four-poster bed, large chest of drawers and a full-length mirror with gilded frame unnervingly imposing, especially at night. So I started taking Moni up, enticing him with the promise of stories. Moni was not a demanding child. Just a minute or two of story telling and his eyes would close, and in another second or two he was sound asleep. He snored gently in his sleep and I found that a comforting sound.

At two I carried him to the balcony, and with my arms safely encircling him, I made him stand on the broad parapet wall and said, "Come, Moni, do your water-fall," and without opening his eyes he squirted water well beyond the sloping roof on to the road below. Even on nights when I forgot to take him to pee, he never wetted my bed. He was so different from what I was as a child. I sometimes think that he was born in answer to my mother's prayer for a son totally different from her elder one. As I carried him back to bed and patted him to sleep, it struck me, one night, that I had started slipping into a new role—my uncle's.

That night I lay brooding for a long time. I thought of the people I would meet, and the questions I would have to face, if I went to the Habba the next day. The most irritating would be those well-meaning people commiserating with my 'poor father'. 'Ah, how disappointed your father must be', 'Oh, how he used to look forward to your becoming a doctor' and so on. I realized that I just did not have the stomach for that kind of grilling and decided that I would stay away from Kantheshwar for the whole day.

I told my mother in the morning I would not be coming home for lunch. Then went to my room—the downstairs room father had built for me—and found, sticking out of my Trigonometry book, a ten-rupee note. My father's contribution to my festival expenses. It nearly made me cry. I pocketed it because I needed it. Then I took my bicycle and pedalled away, away from Kantheshwar, towards the beach. Moni, I hoped, would find someone else to guide him through the festival.

We have one of the loveliest beaches in the world. I did not know it then, though. I thought that all beaches were like ours. It was only in Bombay that I realized how beautiful our own beach was, compared to what I saw there. The sea is ailing in Bombay. The sand is dirty and dark, the sea and the sky a dull and sickly grey. The sand is golden in our place, the sky azure. And the sea is always wide-awake, its waves roaring like a million lions on leash.

I sat quietly for some time on the beach and then decided to have a dip in the sea. It was quite safe even for those who did not know swimming, because the land sloped very gradually and you could walk a hundred yards into the sea without the water level coming above your navel. So I kept my clothes neatly bundled on the shore, tied a bairasa round my middle and waded into the sea.

The sea was comparatively calm that day. A couple of waves passed me without breaking, and that allowed me entry into the placid waters beyond the breakers, where all that I had to do to keep my chin above water was to jump up a little when waves heaved past me. It felt great. The buoyancy I felt when I jumped and found the waves lifting me up was an exciting experience. I had never ventured that far into the sea before. The slight fear I felt added to the thrill.

I turned to the shore and found a dog sniffing my clothes. I wondered whether it would finally lift one leg and wet the bundle. As I kept watching the dog, I failed to notice that the water level was dropping rapidly where I stood. It was only when it came down to the level of my knees that I realized something was wrong, turned back and saw a giant wave about to break right over my head.

I panicked and tried to run. The next moment I found myself rolling, whether into the sea or on to the shore I did not know. My first thought was about father. "O God," I prayed, "Let me not die now, or father will think that *he* drove me to suicide."

But the sea had no intention of swallowing me that day. It rolled me onto the shore, but to show that it could have taken me if it wanted to, it took away my bairasa. I scrambled up and ran to my bundle of clothes. The dog got up and wagged its tail as if to assure me that it was only guarding my clothes; and then came and sniffed me, perhaps to ascertain that the clothes really belonged to me.

I sat huddled on the beach for a while, thoroughly shaken. It was the first week of December but it was noon and the sun was hot. There was not a soul anywhere around. I started feeling a prickly sensation all over, as the seawater evaporated leaving tiny crystals of salt all over my skin and in my hair.

Curiously, though, that feeling of deep depression which had troubled me for days was gone. I was feeling strangely elated. But I also began to feel hungry and thirsty. So I retreated to the cool shade of the coconut grove on the edge of the beach to see if someone could get me a tender coconut.

All the huts were closed. Everyone, apparently, had gone to the festival. I gave a loud 'koo hoo' call to see if anyone were around. A wizened old man came out of a low door and stood staring at me. I asked him if he could get me a tender coconut. "I might," he said, "but it will cost you a rupee."

"That's too much," I said. "Tender coconuts don't cost more than four annas."

"It's not too much," he said, pointing to a coconut tree, "when you consider that it is a very old man, with a bottle of toddy inside, who has to climb that tree."

Those were days of strict prohibition. But men, who had got used to drinks during the British Raj, found ways of getting them during the 'Gandhi Raj' too. The old man was clearly inebriated.

When I agreed to pay him the rupee he squirreled up that tree at a surprising speed. He chose a coconut, twisted it till its stem gave way and dropped it on to the sandy earth below. He waited there in his perch and said, "Do you want another? It will cost you only eight annas now."

"Six annas," I said. He dropped another coconut and slithered down the tree.

I thought I had never tasted better coconuts. The water was sweet, and the thin soft kernel even sweeter.

When I was about to leave, at four, he came to me again. "You want another coconut? It will cost you only four annas." When I laughed and said no, he said, "Only two annas."

I was surprised. "How can you afford that?" I asked.

"Why not," he said coolly, "when the tree does not belong to me?"

Four o'clock was too early to go home, though my itching skin demanded a fresh water bath. The festival would still be on. So I decided to go to Chandapur, eat a dosa in one of the restaurants and then pay a visit to Chikkajjayya. The old man on the beach had reminded me of him.

Chikkajjayya was not himself. He had slipped and fallen in the bathroom two days earlier, fracturing his left leg, and some doctor from Chandapur had put it in one of the largest plaster casts I had ever seen. Nothing I said could cheer him up, not even my description of how I nearly got drowned. "We all have to die," he said in a mournful voice, "I am sure this broken leg will be the death of me."

Varijamma had to miss the Habba because of her father. I went and sat by her as she busied herself with her task of writing Rama's name ten million times. Her mind, however, was not on the task. She was looking out of the window every now and then. "What are you looking at?" I asked. "Shh…" she said, "not so loud, Babu. Look at the verandah of the next house. Do you find a girl there?"

I did. She was a plump girl in an ankle length skirt digging her nose. "She is digging her nose," I said.

"Forget what she is doing. What does she look like, to you?"

"She looks quite fat," I said, and Varijamma nodded. "She wasn't quite so fat just a couple of months ago," she said, "She was as thin as…." Another girl, in a saree, wearing a black bead necklace which showed that she was married, joined the fat girl. Varijamma pointed to her. "That thin girl is the elder sister. The younger one was as thin as she was two months ago. Now look at her! What do you think has happened?"

"How do I know? Do you want me to go and find out what she eats?"

"No need to do that," said Varijamma, her voice dropping into a whisper. "It's not her eating that has caused her to swell. She is pregnant, though no one in the family seems to have realized that as yet. Do you know who is responsible?"

"How can I know?"

"But make a guess. You will never be able to make the right one. Make the wildest possible guess."

"Chikkajjayya."

That floored Varijamma—literally. While she had been writing the Lord's name for thousands of hours, keeping the books on the floor and crouching over them, her posture had changed from sitting to lying. It was as if she was growing from a tree into a creeper. Now she lay on the ground and laughed.

"That is a wicked joke," she said, and then added: "I'll tell you. It's her brother-in-law. The elder girl's husband. That girl is deaf and they couldn't get her a husband. So they found a poor homeless chap and made him their *mane aliya*. And this is what he has done."

Mane in Kannada means house, and *aliya*, son-in-law. Hindus *give* their daughters away in marriage. Occasionally a doting parent may not want to lose his daughter and so may look for a poor boy willing to stay in his house after marriage. Such a son-in-law is called mane aliya, the in-house son-in-law. It is not a position of any dignity and men with self-respect, even if they are poor, shun it. The in-house son-in-law—mane aliya in Kannada, *ghar jamai* in Hindi—is a figure of fun in Indian literature. Varijamma's neighbour's in-house son-in-law had gone beyond his sphere of duty and impregnated his sister-in-law.

Because I found Varijamma in a gossipy mood, I thought of leading her to a subject that was troubling me after my chat with uncle. "How old were you when my father got married?" I asked her.

"How old was I? Why, as old as your father. He is six days younger than me."

"Do you remember the wedding? Was it a grand affair?"

"Do I remember the day? How can I forget it? God, how it rained that day. And just before the wedding there was thunder and lightening. A real thunderstorm. Even Annayya got scared and started praying, 'Arjuna, Arjuna.' You know, thunderstorms are sent by Indra, the god of rain and lightning, and he relents only when you pray to his son Arjuna. We were all scared, but we were looking at Krishna to see if he showed any fear. He is brave otherwise but has always been terribly scared of thunder and lightening. But no, on that day he showed no fear at all. He was too angry and upset to feel any fear."

"Angry and upset? Why?"

"Oh, it is a long story," she said, "it's because of that girl Lacchi. She had an eye on Krishna. Whenever he was at home she used to be around. She would come to bathe in the tank and then go back home in her wet saree. Krishna used to stand on the verandah and watch, and if he was not there the shameless girl used to come right into the Matha, under the pretext of doing pradakshinas. She was only thirteen or fourteen but was quite a woman, and a very good-looking one too.

"Poor Krishna. As soon as he came back from Madras after his exams, his parents wanted him to get married. At first he said no, he did not want to marry till he settled down as a doctor. But they wanted a daughter-in-law, they needed little grandchildren to light up the house. 'Why shouldn't Annayya marry again?' he asked, but no one who had seen Annayya's suffering at the time of his wife's death, and then of his daughter's, had the heart to pressurize him.

"It was then that Krishna mentioned Lacchi's name. He didn't mind marrying her, he said. There was such an uproar because your grandmother wanted to bring Saraswati, her sister's brother-in-law's daughter, as her daughter-in-law. She did not want Lacchi, whom she thought a very forward girl.

"Lacchi's father came with a proper proposal of marriage but he foolishly let out that his daughter herself had sent him. That set your grandmother firmly against the poor girl. 'We don't want such a forward hussy,' she declared, and finally Krishna had to agree to marry the girl of her choice. But he looked so angry and morose that the guests kept on asking if he was not well."

"What happened after the marriage?"

"To Lacchi? She went wild, that was what happened. She wasn't a bad girl, Babu. She used to make garlands of suragi flowers and give them to me sometimes. They had a suragi tree behind their house. Her father had it cut off after her marriage because someone told him that the smell of suragi flowers attracted cobras. But that was some years later. Do you know what she did when Krishna got married? She ran away with a carpenter boy, that was what she did. Luckily someone recognized them when they were about to board a bus at Chandapur, frightened away the lad and brought her home. Who would marry the girl after such a scandal? Her father had to find a homeless orphan from a distant village and make him his mane aliya."

"What happened...to my parents?"

"The marriage was a grand affair in spite of the rains. A big band had come from Chandapur, though they could not compete with the thunderstorm. You know something...I haven't told this to any one, except to Akka and Gangamma, and a few others, but I'll tell you now. The bride and groom, as you know, have to garland each other, and it was garlands of suragi flowers that were used then. Garlands of *dried* suragi flowers, of course, because the marriage season comes after the season of suragi flowers is over. They were thinking of using garlands of some other flowers instead because they could not find suragi garlands, when suddenly two very pretty ones appeared from nowhere. I realized who had sent them. It is not easy to make suragi garlands that last. The flowers shrivel when they dry up, so unless you know how to knit them very tight, the garlands become loose. Only Lacchi in our hamlet knew how to make them really tight."

"But what happened...to Appa and Amma?"

"Krishna looked morose, as I said. Then he left for Madras, immediately after the wedding. He had to work in a hospital for six months. But he didn't come back even after six months. He started working with a big doctor in Madras. He wanted to learn from him everything about delivering babies because he thought that that was what a doctor had to do most of the time in our place. We laughed when we heard that. Who will call a young man when a woman is giving birth? Krishna was being stupid, we thought. But no, he was right, he is making lots of money delivering babies. The world is really becoming shameless."

I kept quiet. Varijamma had to tell her story at her own speed, in her own meandering way. But she did come to the point soon.

"He came back nearly two years after his marriage. But even then there was no talk about bringing his wife home. Your grandmother kept on pestering him, but he said that he had listened to her once, and that was once too often. Finally the girl's father brought her here and said to your grandfather, 'I am going to leave my daughter here. If you won't accept her as your daughter-in-law, she will stay here as your servant. She belongs to your family now, not mine.'

"She didn't talk to any of us. To me, never. And all because she heard me say once, to Akka, that Lacchi would have made a better wife for Krishna. She would have filled the house with laughter. I shouldn't have said that, I know, but can you believe it, Babu, she never spoke to me even once till the day we left for Chandapur.

"Krishna didn't talk to her for nearly six months. Your grandmother used to send her upstairs with a glass of milk for him, but he used to make a sign to her to leave the milk and go away. Then your grandma told her to sleep upstairs. 'If he doesn't allow you to sleep in his room, sleep in the hall,' she said. Then there was a thunderstorm one night and he allowed her to sleep in his room. I am sure *he* was the one who got scared, because *she* has never shown any fear of thunder at any time."

Varijamma smiled. "That is the end of the story, Babu. If you keep butter near a fire, it is bound to melt. Your father melted. You were born."

I got up to go. "You haven't told me," I said, "the most important point in the story. Who is this Lacchi? I never heard of any Lacchi in our hamlet. The only Lacchi I know is our servant woman at Kantheshwar."

Varijamma sat there with her mouth open. A perfect example of the condition called 'chapfallen'. "Oh, God," she said, "Didn't you really know, Babu, who was Lacchi? No one calls her Lacchi now, of course. Even in those days she didn't like being called Lacchi, and when she didn't like something she made it quite clear to everybody that she didn't. Even to her father, who had given her that pet name. So everyone called her by her full name, Venkata Lakshmi."

I sat down. My head was in a spin.

"Venkata Lakshmi?" I said, "Little Ramu's mother?"

"Yes," said Varijamma. "Little Ramu's mother." Then she added, with a faint touch of malice in her voice, "she could have so easily been your mother."

I got up and went to say goodbye to Chikkajjayya but he was sitting with his eyes closed, sound asleep. I sat watching him as Varijamma made some coffee for me. He looked like a wizened old monkey tied to a large white log of wood.

As I was leaving I said to Varijamma, "I don't understand one thing. You say Ramu's father was a mane aliya. How could he, in that case, throw his wife out? Didn't the house belong to her?"

"Nothing belongs to a woman," said Varijamma, and I could hear in her voice the sadness and resignation of all womankind. "I don't know about the law. But when a woman belongs to her husband, everything she has belongs to him. When she herself doesn't belong to herself, how can anything belong to her?"

She looked depressed and I did not know what to say. Finally I ended up saying something stupid. "But cheer up, Varijamma, you belong to yourself," I said, but that made her look even more depressed. "Who do you belong to?" I asked.

She stared at me for a moment, her face expressionless.

"To Yama," she said, "to Yama Dharmaraya."

Yama, in Hindu scriptures, is the God of Death.

Back to College

Varijamma's revelations shocked but did not hurt me. The way things affect you often depends on the mood you are in. After the drenching in the sea, after that giant breaker took away my black mood and my bairasa, I was surprisingly serene. It was as if my world had suddenly become different, where strange things could happen, like in the world of fiction. I could stand aside and watch them dispassionately like a novel reader, even when I was myself involved. It was in that mood that I viewed Varijamma's story, which turned father and mother and Lacchi into characters in a compelling novel. I thought I could understand father's frustrations and anger better now. I could understand and even sympathize with Amma's coldness, her jealous and possessive love for father, her aversion to Nampalli and her warm love for Moni, the child born after we left Nampalli. Uncle was right. She had suffered, and perhaps still felt insecure.

But sympathies are difficult to sustain when you have to *live* with people who constantly rub you the wrong way, something characters in a novel don't do. Amma said, when she was serving me rice and *saru* that evening, "Where were you the whole day, after promising Moni to take him to the festival? If you have to roam around like a stray dog, why make that promise to the child?" A little later with the curry came this: "Mr. Ural himself came to see your father today, to ask why you hadn't gone there for three days. Father is furious. If you prefer to live like a vagabond and don't want to study, why do you want to waste his hard earned money?" Then with yogurt she served this one: "Your three friends from Nampalli came three times to see if you were at home. They all looked prosperous and confident. They are your age, but they are no burden to anyone. They have come to the Habba to spend *their* hard earned money, not their father's."

But these pinpricks I could bear. The next few months were spent in a half-hearted struggle with Mathematics. But the Maths paper turned out to be tough and I messed it up badly. I was in despair: there was no way I could get more than forty-five marks out of hundred and fifty, and the minimum required for passing was fifty-three. That was what I got, finally, to my great surprise and relief. When I showed my marks to Ural and said that I had cut it very fine indeed, he laughed. "They don't fail students for just a few marks," he said. "They add some to make them pass. They call them 'grace marks'."

So I was 'graced', thank God. "Lucky chap," said Mr. Ural, with a wry smile, "no more Mathematics for you." I think he was as relieved as I was.

My passing evoked little response at home. Father was clearly relieved but he was determined not to show much interest. Amma said nothing. But at Nampalli uncle nearly cried. "It was a big crisis, Babu, the biggest of your young life," he said. He asked me to wait for the pooja, and at the end of it blessed me with a warmth he had not shown for years.

I talked to him about what I wanted to do. "The college at Udupi is going to be a degree college from this year," I said. "But they will start only B.A., and give us no options: we have to take whatever subjects they offer. But I am used to the place and it's less expensive than Mangalore. I can economize by boarding at one of the Mathas, if you can talk to them and arrange it."

"I can do that," he said. "But are you sure your father won't mind?"

"I don't think he will. His practice is not what it was. In fact it's bad, it's in the doldrums…and it's all my fault… that's what Amma and Appa think."

I nearly broke down, suddenly and without any warning, to my own and uncle's surprise. It is strange the way long suppressed sorrows, suppressed so well that you forget their very existence, suddenly come to the surface and shock you.

"What's it, Babu," said uncle, "what has gone wrong?"

It took some time for me to recover. "Most of father's patients have left him," I said, "because he is not there in the dispensary when they need him. He has suddenly developed a new interest—in farming. You know he has been buying land right and left. Quite a few of the pieces of land he has purchased are farmlands—paddy fields, mostly. Paddy farming is not profitable unless you have the expertise and the fields are in close proximity. Our fields are scattered all over the place and father knows nothing about farming. But he spends most of his time going from one field to another while his patients wait for him at the dispensary. They wait for some time and then go either to the old Ayurvedic Pandit from Kerala or to a new doctor who has just set up practice. One Dr. Acharya."

"But farming is not so bad…"

"But it's bad, the way we do it. Last harvest was the first one we brought home. Do you know how that was done? In bullock carts! Most of the paddy fell by the wayside, because bullock carts on rough tracks are so jerky that there is no further need to take the harvest to the threshing floor."

"Your mother—didn't she object to all this?"

"Not at first. She revelled in all those activities: so many people working in our courtyard, the threshing, the building of haystacks and so on. But then she realized what was happening. I was there when she asked him why he was ruining his own practice. He said...he said...he was expiating a sin. His father did not want him to become a doctor. 'He wanted me,' he said, 'to take up a small job nearby, do pooja, and farm the family lands. He wanted me to be like him. I went against his wish and broke his heart. I now realize the enormity of my crime. I can't do pooja now, but I can do some farming.' That is what he said. Amma looked at me. 'See what you have done to your father,' she seemed to say."

"Poor Babu," said uncle, and then, in a softer voice, "poor Krishna."

"You know your father," he said, after a moment's silence. "When he is upset or angry, he says things which he doesn't really mean. He knows why our father did not want him to go for medical studies. It was only because there was no money. When Krishna came back a doctor, no one was prouder of him than father. As for his newfound interest in farming—I don't think it has anything to do with you. He is a restless man and gets bored easily. He is trying out something new but he will come back to his practice soon."

Father agreed to my suggestion—that I should go to Udupi and do my B.A.—readily enough. But when I said that I would like to board at one of the Mathas, his brow darkened a little. "My practice is not as good as it was," he said, "but it is not so bad that I have to send my son for free meals." "It's not that," I said. "The food served in some of the Mathas is better than what most restaurants serve. Why waste money when good homely food is available free?"

He said nothing but I knew he was relieved. His neglect of his practice had gone on too long and he had begun to feel the pinch. Sita had grown up, she was in S.S.L.C. In another year he would have to start thinking of her marriage.

The two years I spent at Udupi, studying for my B.A., were happy tension-free years. I did not even have to ask father for money. My maternal uncle, Ramu Mawa, was a very simple person—simple to the point of being a simpleton. I have not seen anyone who irritated father more than he did. Father often lost his temper and shouted at him, and then in contrition gave him whatever he wanted—loans, mostly, and usually against his better judgement, because Ramu Mawa was notorious for his carelessness in money matters. He borrowed two thousand rupees from father to buy a piece of land, and gave it to the owner of the land without any witnesses. When the man bluntly said, two days later, that he had not received any money, Mawa was shocked but there was nothing he could do about it. He wanted to return the money to father in small installments. As he was working in one of the Mathas at Udupi, father told him that he could settle the account by giving me, every month, what I needed for my expenses. So I had money on the tap, as it were, with no one to ask me how I spent it.

So I was an Arts student at last. But I soon found that it was not all fun. We had to study a real mixed bag of subjects. Four papers of English, two of Kannada, three of Economics and one each of Politics and History. I loved English and Kannada, but the Economics papers bored me to numbness.

Of the four papers in English one was on Shakespeare. We had to study *Othello* and *As You Like It*. I found *Othello* too painful and heartless. Even its formal perfection, I thought, added to the pervasive air of cruelty: the tight well-crafted plot was as ruthlessly efficient as the plot Iago engineered to trap poor Othello and Desdemona in. I admired the play but found it suffocating.

Perhaps it was this which made me love *As You Like It,* a play which is in every respect the antithesis of *Othello.* It has practically no plot. The songs are as irrelevant as songs in a Hindi film. Events follow one another with no regard for probability: hungry lions and gilded snakes appear from nowhere when they are needed, villains change into good men when the author wants them to. After the claustrophobic experience of reading *Othello*, where the relentless logic of cause and effect held sway over every event, I found the open air world of *As You Like It,* and its sequence of improbable events, a great relief.

Professor Krishnaraju, who taught us the play, was a newcomer. A thoroughly incompetent teacher—that was what we thought—he could not even read the play well. He mumbled and mixed up his words so that we had to look at the text to keep track of what he was teaching. It was quite different when our principal was teaching *Othello*; he used to hold us spellbound with his diction and we used to forget the text and stare at him in awe. Professor Krishnaraju, who came from Bangalore, did not like Udupi. He did not like our class and he did not like *As You Like It*. He also said that he did not like teaching. He had done research on F.R. Leavis for two years, but when he found the goal, Ph.D., still distant, he decided to take up teaching. In the class he spent a good deal of time grumbling: he grumbled about the heat, the humidity, the food in our restaurants, the stupidity of his students, and, above all, the stupidity of the play he was forced to teach.

I had a continuous running battle with him all through the term. He did not mind students arguing with him, perhaps because that gave him relief from the difficult task of reading the play aloud. I was a bit hesitant to speak at first, but he was helpful whenever he found me struggling for words. But that was only in the beginning. Once I got used to speaking in English, there was no stopping me. Soon it was I who provided him the words—the names of poems or authors or whatever—he was desperately looking for in his lectures, which often turned into wild goose chases of disparate ideas. Suddenly one day, for example, he started criticizing some poets of late nineteenth century. "What's that lousy poem," he said, "where some woman...or is it an angel...has three stars and seven lilies...or is it the other way round?" He looked at me in desperation, and when I said 'The Blessed Damozel', he stared at me in amazement. He often made outrageous statements but *wanted* someone to contradict him. So my tongue wagged almost continuously during his lectures. The other students enjoyed the fun, but sometimes got fed up and said, "Shut up, Sudhakar, let sir teach."

Professor Krishnaraju complained about the total lack of realism in *As You Like It*. "Look at this awful scene," he said, while reading the one in which Orlando's rescue of his elder brother Oliver, who had earlier tried his best to get him killed, is reported; "Oliver is sleeping, and a hungry lioness is waiting to attack him when he wakes up. Where did a lioness come from, in the forest of Arden, which is nowhere near Africa? But no, that is not enough for Shakespeare. He brings in a 'green and gilded snake' that has wreathed itself round the man's neck, ready to enter 'the opening of his mouth'. Crazy, that is what the whole scene is."

"That is not fair, sir," I said, "for two reasons." I had then a strange habit, while arguing, of mentioning 'two' or 'three' reasons, even before I was sure how many reasons I actually had. Most of the times, though, the first reason itself would evoke a long argument, and the fact that I had no other reason went undetected.

"What are your reasons?"

"Shakespeare knew, I presume, that a lioness in the forest of Arden was absurd enough. Yet he introduced that snake deliberately. Why? Perhaps he wanted to make it doubly obvious to his audience that he was telling a fairy tale?"

"Not convincing and not consistent. Only the other day you were arguing with me about Shakespeare's realism."

"Oh, that was different," I said. And indeed it *was* different. Professor Krishnaraju on that day was ridiculing Orlando's poems. That was fair enough. But he also criticized Orlando for writing such rubbish and Shakespeare for his inability to find a better hero. It was fashionable, I discovered later, to belittle the romantic heroes of Shakespeare's comedies. I liked Orlando. I argued that though he wrote bad poems, he was a wonderful person. His brother had denied him proper education and there was no way he could have written good poems. Shakespeare was realistic about it. But his love for Rosalind stirred him into writing poems, and he enjoyed rhyming Rosalind's name. I found the scene, in which he ran about the forest hanging his awful poems on trees, delightful.

"It was different," I said, "because we were talking of Orlando's poems, and Shakespeare's portrait of Orlando. The story is a fairy tale but that does not mean that the characters should not be realistic. Shakespeare explores reality even in his fantasies, doesn't he? Here he shows us a spirited young man in love, making a fool of himself—though he is no fool, otherwise— trying to write poems. It is a wonderful portrait."

"What is your second reason?" said Professor Krishnaraju. For a moment I thought I was stumped. Then I realized that there *was* a second reason. I must have felt it lurking in the shadows, at the back of my mind, when I said, 'two reasons'.

I felt quite excited. "You see, sir," I said, stammering a little, "this speech of Oliver, it's so different from his usual speech…this man who spoke earlier in crude prose suddenly breaks into flowery poetry. The 'green and gilded snake' and the other details are ornaments meant to make the speech more impressive. The speech has an important dramatic purpose…"

"What purpose?"

"To make Celia fall in love. I mean, that is Shakespeare's purpose, not Oliver's. You have said that one of the incredible things about the play is the way Celia falls for Oliver. This speech is Shakespeare's justification for that. So he makes it as impressive as he can."

"Falling in love for the sake of a bombastic speech? That's silly."

"No, sir," I said. "Oliver is a repentant sinner, and innocent girls do find them attractive. And speeches, in plays, are more important than in real life…" I found this point difficult to explain. Theatre has its own kind of reality. In Yakshagana plays, for example, speech is everything; it is action, it is heroism. But I only said, "A repentant sinner who speaks beautifully, how can Celia resist him?"

"You seem to know a lot about how girls fall in love," said Professor Krishnaraju, and the class tittered. Professor Krishnaraju frowned. "I know your knowledge comes from your reading," he said. "There is nothing wrong with that. One rarely learns anything from life. What little one learns from life, one learns a bit too late."

A couple of months later I was sitting in my room feeling quite depressed. We had preparatory holidays, and the exam was just a month away. The subject I had set myself to study that day was the *Economic History of England* as part of our Economics syllabus. My depression was caused by my sense of futility of studying that subject ten years after Independence.

Then I started thinking about *As You Like It*, and Professor Krishnaraju. I wanted to tell him about some things I had discovered about the play. So I put my *Economic History of England* aside and went to college.

Professor Krishnaraju had not come to college. So I went to his rented house. I found him sitting in his front room, with the door and the windows wide open, wearing only a white *mundu*, an ankle-length piece of cloth worn in our district as a lower garment. He had a folded newspaper in his hand to fan himself with but was sitting motionless like a statue. A melting statue: he was perspiring so much that it looked as if he was melting.

"Sit down," he said and I sat down, and straightaway started telling him about my discovery. Halfway through my monologue I realized that he was listless and inattentive but I completed what I wanted to say. "Interesting," he said, without any enthusiasm, "perhaps you can write an article on it some day." Then he started fanning himself with the newspaper. "This heat is killing me," he said, "and I don't know what to do. If I fan myself, that exertion makes me sweat more. Thank God I am going away. I'll not be here next summer."

"Why, sir? You are not thinking of resigning?"

"I'm not *thinking* of resigning. I have resigned." He hesitated for a moment, and then said, rather grimly, "Why tell a lie? I was asked to resign. In fact I have been thrown out. Shown the door. Fired. Dismissed."

"But why?" I asked in shock. "Because I'm incompetent," he said. "I can't teach. I can't control my class. My class is like a weekly village market where everyone is shouting his wares. It is so noisy that the other classes are disturbed."

He looked at me with, I thought, an accusing eye. Then he saw my look of dismay and relented. "I am not blaming anyone," he said, "I know I deserve the boot. I can't get myself interested in books that have no social relevance. Why should we force you students to read Shakespeare three and a half centuries after the fellow kicked the bucket? No, no, please, don't start an argument now. I know *you* enjoy your Shakespeare. But what about the other students? And as for my classes being noisy, why shouldn't they be noisy? I don't want...I don't want, in my class, the silence...the silence..." He could not get the right phrase, and looked at me, as he had so often done in the class, for help. And I gave it to him for the last time ever. "Of the graveyard," I said.

He stared at me. "You always know what I want to say, don't you?" he said, a little grimly. "That means I am predictable. I am not half as original as I think I am." He shook his head in mock dismay. "But don't sit there with that commiserating look on your mug. Go home and study."

I went to the college library. A few of my classmates were there, reading. "Something terrible has happened," I told them, "they have asked Professor Krishnaraju to resign—because his classes were noisy—and it is all our fault. Ours was the noisiest of his classes, perhaps the only noisy one."

"What do you want us to do?" they asked me. "Let us go to the Principal," I said, "and tell him that Professor Krishnaraju was a good teacher; that he didn't lack class control, he only encouraged discussion..."

"Nonsense," they said. "He was *not* a good teacher. He was so incoherent. Half the time we did not know what the two of you were wrangling about. He has given us no notes, he has left us in the lurch. He couldn't even read a passage aloud properly. No, we are not going to tell anyone that he was a good teacher."

I went back to my room and started studying *Economic History of England*.

Those Two Years

⁂

I saw Professor Krishnaraju for the last time at the bus stand on the last day of our exam. He was sitting in a bus going to Malpe, fanning himself vigorously. I was in a hurry to go to my room and pack up but he called out to me quite cheerfully.

"This bus stand is the hottest place in Udupi," he said. "I hope I'll not melt away completely before the bus starts. How did you fare in your English papers?"

"Not too well," I said; "I couldn't complete any of them. In the Shakespeare paper there was a question on the characters of, and the roles played by, Jaques and Touchstone. A four-in-one question, really. By the time I finished answering that question and woke up, nearly two hours were over, and I had only an hour left for the remaining four questions. So I had to leave out two."

Professor Krishnaraju clicked his tongue in sympathy. "Our examination system is rotten," he said. Then he added, "I am going to Malpe, for the last time. That's one place I'll miss when I leave Udupi. None of you seem to know you have one of the loveliest beaches in the world here. I don't go to the main Malpe beach; I cross the river and go to the other side. Hidden behind the coconut trees lies a crescent shaped beach stretching on for miles. The loveliest in the world."

The bus started spluttering. I wanted to tell him something, but I did not know how to begin. The bus started moving. He put his head out of the window and said, "I want to tell you something, Sudhakar. I am not sure how much I have taught you, but I have learnt a lot from you."

The bus sped away and I stood there feeling miserable. I knew I was not likely to meet him again. All through those exam days I was living with a strong feeling of guilt: I felt I was responsible for Professor Krishnaraju's sacking. Maybe he did not *teach* me much but he certainly helped me to learn a lot. I wanted to tell him that I had learnt a lot from his lectures. But he took the words out of my mouth, and said to me what I wanted to tell *him*. I felt wretched.

It is strange, the way human memory works. When I began to recollect those two fairly happy years I had spent as an undergraduate student at Udupi, I had no idea that Professor Krishnaraju, and the play he taught, would figure so prominently in the account. *As You Like It* has remained one of my favourite plays. I may not include it among the six best or even the ten best of Shakespeare's plays, but it is the one I love most. It is a love that started with that romp in the class, and it is only now that I realize that I owe it to Professor Krishnaraju, who did not just tolerate my cheekiness but actually encouraged it. Perhaps he enjoyed it as much as I did. And I thought he was a bad teacher! I saw his many blind spots, his pet likes and dislikes; but not his integrity, and that rarest of qualities, a total absence of pedagogic ego and pretentiousness.

As a teacher I have been, in many ways, his opposite. He used to struggle for words; I have been fluent to a fault. I have a reasonably catholic taste and have made every effort to overcome my blind spots. But did I ever, in any student, kindle the kind of interest Professor Krishnaraju kindled in me for *As You Like It*, through his 'inefficient' teaching? Can one be, as a teacher, too efficient and too thorough? How did I fail—for Professor Krishnaraju appears before me and suggests that I have—did I fail because I overawed my students with my fluency and scholarship and turned them into mere listeners?

This sudden emergence of Professor Krishnaraju has taught me something: that even the past, like everything else that is temporal, is ever changing.

There is one distortion in my account of those two years I must set right. Those years were not all spent studying or attending lectures. The time we spent in the classroom was not much, and it was not of much significance either. In most of the classes we dozed off or sat daydreaming. The lecturers lectured on and then dictated notes, which some of us took down and some others, like me, pretended we did. I spent most of the time drawing sketches of the teachers. As that involved concentration and frequent glances at the teachers, they all believed that I was a conscientious student who took down their bullshit—or cowdung—with care. Someone has defined notes-giving as an activity where something is passed on from the teacher's notebook to the student's, without entering the head of either. It is true that even the most restless of teachers become quiet and tranquil when they dictate their notes. Their minds go to sleep and if you want to catch them in your sketch book, they are like sitting ducks then. Some twenty years after I passed my B.A. I found an old notebook of mine full of these sketches. They were all there, my old teachers, the sketches smudged but still recognizable. Professor Krishnaraju was not among them.

Life was outside the classroom, in the streets, in the Temple Square with its three main temples, and, for me, also in the various libraries and reading rooms. I had a group of friends, all like me free boarders at one or the other of the Mathas. We went to college and came back together. In the afternoons we haunted the Temple Square, the happy hunting ground for all those who wanted to ogle pretty girls, who came there in giggling groups, or with their mothers. The advantage of a temple was that you could look at the girls from close quarters, to your heart's content, follow them as they did their pradakshinas with a religious fervour matching theirs, and occasionally even brush against them. On festival days the temples—Krishna Matha in particular—used to be crowded, and we skillfully maneuvered ourselves in such a way that we got caught in jostling crowds of girls. We walked with our hands folded, looking straight ahead, but our minds were concentrated on our elbows, which often felt the pressure of female breasts from behind. I remember once going round the temple—a full pradakshina—with the same breast pressing against my right elbow almost continuously, till, to my growing excitement, the nipple, which could hardly be felt at first, hardened gradually and made its presence felt. I walked on without looking back or even sideways, worried that any fidgeting on my part might frighten the breast away. And when I finally managed to look back, at the end of the pradakshina, I could not make out who the girl was.

We were quite innocent, I think, and decent. We never let our ogling upset the girls. Each one of us had his favourite. My dream girl came to the Temple Square from Thenka Pethe, the southern lane, at six every afternoon with her aunt. She had delicate, chiselled features and was rather pale. She was too shy to look straight at me but whenever she felt my eyes on her she coloured, dimpled and grew vivacious, setting my heart on fire. All that I knew about her was that her name was Uma. None of us ever tried to talk to our girls, or did anything to turn our dreams into reality. But we respected one another's dreams. My friends never ogled my girl, and on days when I sat reading in my room and did not go to the Temple Square, they reported to me how Uma looked listless that day, as if she was waiting for someone.

There was another kind of skirt-chasing, less decent and more aggressive, of which I came to know during the Laksha Deepa Festival. I don't think I shall ever forget that evening. Laksha Deepa, the festival of a hundred thousand lamps, is one of the most popular events in Udupi. The Temple Square gets unusually crowded that night, the crowds hanging on till the festival ends with a spectacular display of fireworks. We were standing together that evening close to a group of girls, waiting for the fireworks to begin, when Ramesh Rao, one of my classmates, sauntered by. "Ah Sudhakar," he said, "doing your bit of sly ogling?" He looked at us with pity. "You Brahmin boys eating free food at the Mathas," he said, "You are not young men, you are girls. You don't even have the guts to look straight at women. I can tell you one thing: like all good girls, you'll lose your virginity only on your wedding beds."

He spoke quite loudly, but because of the great din made by the fireworks only I could hear him. "You are hopeless," he continued. "You look at girls as if you are scared your hard looks might hurt them. You tickle them with your glances, get excited, and go home and shake it off! Do you want to know what real aggressive skirt chasing is like? Come with me if you want to know."

Ramananda, who was standing next to me, heard the last bit of this speech. If he had heard the entire speech he would have really lost his temper. "Go, go with him," he said; "find out what the wise guy has to teach you."

Ramesh took me to Thenka Pethe, from where most of the prettier girls came to the Temple Square. He gave me a lecture on the way. "When you brush against a girl," he said, "she must *know* that you have done it deliberately, though she should not be able to *prove* it. What's the use of your touching a girl if it does not lead to something more? You can as well fondle Murali, your roommate, who is as pretty as most girls. Once a girl knows that you have deliberately touched her, you can make out from her reaction when you see her next what the signal is like: green or red. If it is green you can try to go ahead."

We stopped when we reached the end of the lane. "Let's turn back now," he said. "The fireworks will end any minute. Then the lane will be full of girls hurrying home, like cows rushing home at dusk. Make use of your hands when we wade through the herd." He saw my hands folded and laughed derisively. "Are you going to use your elbows to shield yourself from them? Then why take all this trouble? Look at my hands. Stay behind me and watch how I use them."

We met the crowd of girls halfway down the lane. Ramesh's hands were down, the palms facing forward. As we waded through the crowd, I saw his hands moving, caressing the thighs they encountered on either side, and sometimes probing the region between them. It was quick work but I got scared. Occasionally he used his middle finger to dig deep. I knew he was safe because there was no way a girl could *prove* that the touch was not accidental. They all *knew* that it was deliberate but the experience obviously was too embarrassing and humiliating for them to complain about. And if any girl complained to her parents, the first casualty would have been the little freedom *she* enjoyed.

The stupid swine, I said to myself, what bloody pleasure could he get by touching *anything* at such speed, just for a fleeting second; except the sadistic pleasure of hurting and humiliating girls and the perverse one of boasting later on that he had touched hundreds of female genitals. I felt disgusted. What really upset me was that I could, walking a few feet behind him, see what *he* could not: the expression on the faces of those girls just before and after he had done his thing. The sudden transformation was shocking. They all looked so happy and tired and relaxed, after the day's outing, before he hit them. Some who were lightly touched ignored what happened. But the faces of those who received his special attention blanched in shock at first, and then turned red in shame, disgust and anger. I got scared at the anger I saw in their eyes and decided that I had had enough. I decided to stand aside in one of the shops and let the crowd pass.

Before I could do so I saw Uma. She was just a few feet in front of me. When her eyes met mine, she blushed and dimpled. Ramesh must have seen that faint smile, a mere shadow of a smile that manifested itself only as a dimple and a sparkle in the eye, and perhaps took it as an encouragement. His hand moved and the girl doubled up in pain and shock. When she looked up, I saw her features distorted in fear and shame and her mouth open as if she was about to scream.

It was all over in a few seconds. Ramesh had moved on quickly and the group of girls with Uma went past me, Uma leaning on the girl by her side, who was anxiously asking her what happened. I moved aside and stood on the raised platform in front of one of the shops, feeling giddy and distraught.

I went back to my room. I did not tell my friends what happened. I just could not. I stopped going to the Temple Square at six and never saw Uma again. But her face haunted me for years, not the dimpled vivacious face I loved but that pale death mask, with the features distorted in fear and shame.

To Bombay

❧

I had to rush home immediately after the exams got over. Ramu Mawa had brought the news that Sita's marriage was just a week away. The groom, he told me, was a doctor, who was just about to set up practice in Bombay. His father once owned a restaurant there, which was sold after his death. All the money from the sale was spent on the marriages of the two sisters of the boy. So they expected the girl's father—my father—to provide the necessary funds for setting up a dispensary in Bombay. Ramu Mawa did not know the exact amount needed but said that it was substantial. After selling a big tract of land, which he had bought some years earlier, father still had to go for a loan. He had even asked Ramu Mawa how much of the amount he had borrowed still remained unpaid.

"How much remains?" I asked him, worried. "Nothing," he said, "not a rupee. The sixty rupees I gave you a week ago was the last installment of my loan. I have given you, during the last two years, all the two thousand rupees I borrowed."

"*Two thousand rupees!* Did I spend two thousand rupees in two years?"

"That was exactly what your father asked. In the same tone."

"But I was not even eating in restaurants. I have been eating in Shirur Matha all these days. Free meals!"

"That was precisely what your father said, in the same tone."

I felt terribly guilty. I knew where the money had gone, of course. Books. There were books on my bed, on my steel trunk, and on the table I shared with three other boys. The last one I bought was the costliest: Shakespeare's Complete Works, Oxford Standard Authors Series. Twelve of the sixty rupees Ramu Mawa had given me a week earlier had gone for that.

I was upset and angry with myself, and as often happens when one is angry and upset, my anger turned against father. "This is madness," I said, "Why should father choose a boy who demands a dowry? Is he the only boy in the world?"

Ramu Mawa sat in silence, fingering his juttu, the sacred tuft of hair at the back of his head. It was a brand new one, grown at the insistence of the Swami of the Matha he was working for. "Don't walk about with your head cropped like a Christian's if you want to work here," the Swami had said, and Mawa had to obey. The new appendage made him self-conscious and he fingered it whenever he was at a loss for words.

"I know why father has done it," I said, feeling bitter. "He wants a doctor as his son-in-law, at any cost. Because his son didn't want to become one."

Ramu Mawa looked at me in surprise. "That's precisely what your mother said," he said, "in the same tone."

When I went home I found our house crowded. Sita's was the first marriage in our family after father's. As it was vacation time for schools our close relatives like Nagatte and Chandratte had come with their full brood of children. Father looked flustered and mother harried. Money, I saw, was flowing like water.

Dr. Shreekanth Rao, my brother-in-law, turned out to be a nice, soft-spoken person. His mother looked good-natured, and that relieved our women-folk of their chief worry, that Sita, a timid girl, might get an ogress as a mother-in-law. Shreekanth's two sisters were very modern, and their bobbed hair and lipstick shocked and bewildered Varijamma, who could not take her eyes off them all through the wedding ceremony. She even asked one of them whether she had lost her hair in some illness. The young woman looked confused, especially since Varijamma's question came with several others, like how much gold she got from her mother at the time of her wedding, what salary her engineer husband got and why there was no child even after two years of marriage. Amma was furious. She could not make a scene right there but she called Varijamma aside and scolded her roundly later on. "What did I do wrong?" said Varijamma, looking hurt and confused, "I was only trying to be friends." "Oh God," said Amma in exasperation, " I think I'll be free from these daughters of Chikkajjayya only after I end up on the funeral pyre." Kamalamma started crying when she heard that, saying, God, why did I come to this wedding, I came only because I couldn't forget how I carried that little child Sita in my arms and wanted to see her as a bride; had I known that we were so unwelcome, I wouldn't have come at all. Then Lakshmi started crying because her mother was crying, and the plump little child in Lakshmi's arms started shedding tears because she saw *her* mother crying. Emotional scenes like this were not uncommon during weddings in those days. I wonder why. Maybe because in the placid low voltage lives of our women marriages were the only emotional high points.

The morning after the wedding my brother-in-law had a chat with me. "I am told you want to do your M.A. with English Literature at Madras," he said. "Why not come to Bombay? The university is not bad. The city is cosmopolitan and has one advantage over other cities. You can work and do your M.A. at the same time. In fact the majority of those doing their post-graduation in Arts or Law in Bombay are working students. Earner-learners we call them."

"I don't know," I said. "I must see my results first before I decide on anything. In fact I'm thinking of working for a while before going for post-graduation."

The results caused me a lot of anguish. Not because I got fewer marks than I expected but because I got more, and missed a Second Class in English by the narrowest of margins. After leaving out questions totalling a hundred marks, out of four hundred, I did not expect to get more than a hundred and fifty, but actually I got a hundred and ninety-five, missing a Second Class by just five marks. By just one mark, in fact, because they usually gave one percent 'grace marks' to those who missed a class by that margin. I stood first in our college but that was no consolation. The college needed an English tutor that year and I could have got that job if only I had got that one extra mark. I got fairly good marks in the other papers but that could not alleviate the disappointment of missing a Second in English so narrowly—and missing that job, which I really coveted.

It hurt. Undoubtedly the most painful and difficult period in life for most Indians is the period of transition from youth to adulthood. For girls the age of anxiety begins quite early. Parents begin to worry about their daughter's marriage when she nears the age of puberty, and the worry increases with every passing year. Girls wilt and wither in the heat of parental worry as they sit at home waiting, as eligible boys come with their family and friends to 'see' them, and then disappear because the horoscopes don't tally, or because the girl is too short or too tall or too smart or not smart enough, or because the girl's parents cannot cough up enough dough. The interviews are, at times, humiliating. In the first such interview Savita had to face she was asked by the boy's mother, who wanted to make sure that her eyesight was all right, to thread a needle. Savita tried it for a few seconds and then called our maidservant, Janaki. "Janu," she said, "This old lady wants this needle threaded. Please do it for her." But that was in her first interview. She soon learnt to curb her tongue, and spirit, though she seethed with suppressed fury all through the interviews.

For boys it is job hunting. Incapacitated by an educational system designed by Lord Macaulay to produce clerks for the British Raj, our young men can only apply for some routine white collar job and wait, for 'a favourable reply', as patiently and hopelessly as our girls wait for eligible boys. The long wait is soul-destroying. For me it lasted only six months but it was long enough to make me realize what kind of a slough of despair our jobless young men could sink into.

I got my job through my father. Some six months after my result he came to my room one evening and said, "Babu, go to Udupi tomorrow. Meet Dr. Shantharam Pai in the New Hope Insurance Office. Perhaps he will give you a job."

I was surprised. I did not expect that father would go to Udupi and meet his old friend, Dr. Pai, for my sake. "But do they have a vacancy?" I asked.

"Maybe they don't," he said, frowning a little; "but they are going to recruit some people nevertheless." He came close to me and said, "The government is planning to spring a surprise on the insurance companies soon by nationalizing them. But the companies, which have their moles in every government department, already know about it. So they are on a recruiting spree now. They want to give jobs to their kith and kin. Why not? After a month or two it will be the government that has to pay their salaries. But don't tell this to any one."

I got the job, and a very cushy job it was, with practically no work. The salary was a meagre forty rupees per month but we all knew that nationalization was imminent and with that would come better emoluments. I looked forward to nationalization for another reason: I might then be able to get a transfer to Bombay and continue my studies as an 'earner-learner'.

Nationalization came after a few months and we, working till then for a tiny insurance company, suddenly found ourselves the employees of a mammoth public sector organization, the newly formed Life Insurance Corporation of India. Udupi became the Divisional Headquarters of the Corporation. Our salaries were more than trebled. As I was on probation, I had to wait for my confirmation before I could apply for a transfer. But the moment people came to know that I wanted a transfer to Bombay, I became a person much sought after. Quite a few people from our district working in various insurance companies in that city wanted to come to Udupi through 'mutual transfer' with someone working here.

A few days before my probation period ended Sita came to Kantheshwar for her delivery. Shreekanth wanted her to stay back in Bombay but father insisted that his first grandson should see the light of day at our house. Satish came into this world on the day I got my confirmation letter. I went home to see the baby who had made me an uncle. I found him surprisingly small, with a mop of thick hair on his tiny head. He is a big-made man now and has gone partially bald.

The work at the Divisional Office at Udupi was easy, and fairly interesting. It was dreary ledger work at first but one day the superintendent of my section asked me to draft a letter. He made some changes—added a few set phrases of officialese—and sent it to the officer in charge of the section for his approval. The J.O. circled all the officialese with a red pencil and sent the letter back to the Superintendent with a note: 'Good drafting, Mr. Pai, but cut out all the flatulence.'

Mr. Pai looked troubled. He called me to his table and wanted to know what 'flatulence' meant. He was a fair plump man of fifty and turned red when I told him the word's meaning. "These young officers," he said, "they have no respect at all for experience and grey hair." He was hurt by the word because he was terribly flatulent, and often, to his extreme embarrassment, broke wind with surprising loudness. We called it the 'big bang'. Sometimes his desperate attempt to stifle the sound resulted in a series of staccato sounds, which we called 'machine gun fire'. At other times he sat tight in his seat, with a martyred expression, and then, from his chair came a prolonged sound like an old door creaking open. Even his niece, who sat next to me, found it difficult to control her laughter when this happened.

The result of that note was that Mr. Pai, from that day, entrusted the job of drafting letters entirely to me. When my drafts came back from the officer's table okayed, with no changes made, his attitude to me changed. He was an expert in routine office jobs and it was difficult to please him with such work. But he found the drafting of letters tough. So I soon found that five or six letters were all that I had to draft to make him feel that I had done a good day's work—and it took me only a couple of hours. So I could sit dreaming, right in front of him, with a half finished letter on my table and he would say, "Good, good, think well before you write, choose your words with care."

I got my transfer later than I expected: in September. Too late to enroll for M.A. that year. But in one way, it came at an opportune time. Shreekanth could not come to collect his wife and son. Father could not leave his practice, so it was I who took Sita and Satish to their home in Bombay.

Father hired a car and took us up to Harihar and from there we went by train. As our train moved away from the open sunlit platform, I stood at the door watching my father's glowing figure grow smaller and smaller, and then suddenly disappear from sight as the train took a turn.

I went into the compartment and sat with Sita. And then I remembered: in all the running around I had to do getting ready for my journey, I had totally forgotten uncle. I had not seen him for months. Neither him, nor the suragi tree.

PART IV
Bombay

భ

You are not the same people who left the station
Or who will arrive at any terminus,
While the narrowing rails slide together behind you.

T.S. Eliot

The Journey

❧

Bombay was a byword for bigness even in those days. A bustling city bursting at the seam, but still growing. Even Varijamma, who did not know where the City was, spoke of the bigness of 'Bombai'—that is how the name is pronounced in Kannada—quite often. 'Bai' in Kannada means mouth, and when Varijamma wanted to call some woman—Raju's mother, for example— a big mouth, she would say, "Oh, that woman's bai, it is a big Bom-bai."

After applying for a transfer to Bombay I made friends with a couple of young men who had come on transfer from there. I wanted to know more about the city, and they were more than willing to talk. It was evident that though they had sought and got their transfer, they all missed the excitement of life in the metropolis. "God, what a city," said Patrick Pinto, "Every day is an adventure there. You should see the babes in Bombay, boy, such big, beautiful breasts they have. And the way they flaunt them! Not like the girls here, who, the moment their teeny weeny mosquito bites turn lemon-sized, grow self-conscious and shy, and start wearing sarees so that they can cover and hide them." We were walking behind a couple of saree-clad young women on Church Road—our favourite haunt then—and Pinto, looking at them, groaned in mock-despair. "Why do women here have such narrow hips?" he asked. "How do they manage to have children, I wonder. You should see, oh boy, the big, expansive bottoms of women in Bombay! You'll go crazy." Pinto himself was small made, but that did not prevent him from admiring bigness. "Big Bombay," he said with reverence, "everything is big in Bombay. Big buildings and big bazaars. Big bosoms and big bottoms. B for Bombay. The capital letter 'B', that's what represents Bombay. Can you guess, Rao, what that letter makes me think of?"

"I can't," I said, quite overwhelmed by his description.

"Of boobs and buttocks, of course. Think of the shape of the letter, man. Doesn't it make you think of a pair of boobs or buttocks? Big round ones?"

I laughed. "Why the hell did you leave Bombay and come here, if you miss the place so much?" I asked.

That brought him down to earth all right. He looked a little sheepish. "That's a million rupee question," he said. "The fact is, Bombay is a tough city

190

to settle down in. Damn expensive for one thing. It's fine when you are young, seeking fun and excitement. But I want to get married and settle down and that's not possible in Bombay—unless I find a rich girl with a flat of her own. Even if I do, it's still tough. You have to spend hours travelling in Bombay, from your house to your place of work, and back again in the evenings, dead tired, in overcrowded buses and trains. You may enjoy even that in the beginning, especially when a gorgeous girl with big boobs comes and sits next to you in the bus. Let the traffic jam continue forever, you might feel then. But not after your home becomes important to you and you want to reach it at a reasonable hour. Do you know, Rao, there are doting fathers in Bombay who can play with their children only on weekends? Because they leave home in the mornings before their children wake up, and by the time they come back at night the children are already asleep?"

"I enjoyed my stay in Bombay," he said, after a little while. "But I think I got out at the right time. A few years more and it might have been too late."

"Why do you say that?"

"Because Bombay can become a habit. People get used to it, and not just to the good things either. They get used to the noise, the crowds, the commuting. One is on the move all the time in Bombay—not doing anything meaningful, just going to the office or going back home—but on the move. It's really awful, this perpetual motion, but once you get used to it, it gives you a sense of mobility; you feel you are going places. Quite a few men in Bombay, I think, are sustained by that delusion, and also have this lurking fear—that if they leave the city they might suddenly discover that they have been stagnating all the while."

"I have seen this happening," he said, " to so many people. People who hate the city but won't leave it. They keep on complaining about its noise, its pollution, its interminable traffic jams and so on, and advise everyone to leave the place, but they themselves stay put where they are. Some even make an occasional half-hearted attempt to leave but nothing comes of it. Oh, they have their excuses: 'If I leave Bombay now, my children's education will suffer,' or— if they are older—'How can I leave Bombay when my sons are employed here?' or, 'I am dying to get out but my wife says no.' The last one is not just an excuse, it's a fact. You know, Rao, women, even the most orthodox of them, who, you'd think, would be happier at Udupi going to the Krishna Temple every day, don't want to leave Bombay. Does that surprise you?"

It did. "There is nothing surprising about it, really," he said. "You know, we don't realize—even our women don't realize—what a load they have to carry here all the time; the whole awful burden of customs and decorum, of doing the right thing, wearing the right clothes and so on is mainly on their shoulders. They live here in perpetual dread of what others, other women specially, will say about them or their daughters. In Bombay they feel liberated, free. There are no wagging tongues there. Their neighbours don't know what their customs are and so leave them alone. Even hubbies don't interfere; they are too tired, poor things, after the day's hard work and harder commuting. If your mother, for example, were in Bombay, and decides that she's fed up of sarees, and walks out in a pair of trousers, no one would comment on it, no one would perhaps even notice it."

"That's great," I said.

"You can't guess how wonderful it must be. Why do you think girls here are not curvaceous like Bombay girls? Why don't we see those big bosoms here? Of course it's partly genetic; Punjabis and Sindhis and Gujaratis are by birth better endowed that way, I guess. Partly it might be the diet. But mainly, I think, it's the stifling atmosphere here, which stunts the growth of our girls. In Bombay girls are proud of their breasts; here they are ashamed of them, feel embarrassed by them.

"There is another reason why women like Bombay. The city has no seasons. A bitch in heat all the time, that is what she is. You know, you get some vegetables only in certain seasons here, but in Bombay you get them all the time. If you have money, man, you can buy anything there, and not everything is expensive either. It's all very convenient for housewives. For a mere ten paise you can get what they call 'green masala'—a few green chillies, a sprig of curry leaves, mint leaves, some coriander leaves and even a little piece of fresh ginger—enough for a day's cooking. Here you have to go hunting for each of these items separately and you may count yourself lucky if you find them all."

A tall lissome girl, with a very pretty face, passed us. Pinto, who was only five three, had a weakness for tall girls. "Gosh," he said, "she is graceful and lovely; sways like a coconut palm in the breeze!" and then added, with a groan, "but where are the coconuts?"

He came to my room late in the evening when I was packing up. I was to leave Udupi the next morning. "I wanted to talk to you," he said.

I finished my packing quickly. All that I had to do was to redistribute my books among the three bags I had. Earlier I had put them all in one bag and found that I could not lift it. Then I sat down in front of Pinto because he made me feel that he wanted my undivided attention.

He began hesitantly. Wanted to know if I planned to come back from Bombay immediately after finishing my M.A.. "I don't know," I said. "Perhaps I might stay on for a few years. Teach in some college there and work for my doctorate."

"That's sensible. But I wonder if you realize what teaching in a Bombay college can be like, for a good-looking young man. You will be teaching mostly Arts classes. Nearly ninety percent of the Arts students are girls. Good looking girls. There is a danger, Rao, that you might be so thrilled by the attention you get that you'll forget Kantheshwar, forget Udupi, forget your doctorate."

I laughed, but Pinto did not. I had never seen him so serious before.

"You have told me a lot about yourself," he said. "But I have been merely yapping about Bombay all the time. There's something I admire in you: the way you talk about yourself almost as if you're talking about a third person. Wish I could do that."

The current went off, but there was moonlight outside. Enough of that light percolated into the room to make us see each other's silhouettes, though we could not mark the expressions on our faces. I think Pinto liked it that way.

"I went to Bombay," he said, "fifteen years ago. I was just fourteen then. My maternal uncle, Patrick D'Souza, took me there because we had only a higher elementary school in our village and the nearest high school was ten miles away. I completed my schooling in Bombay; got a job in the insurance company my uncle was working for, and then did my B.A. as an earner-learner.

"We lived at Bandra, in a predominantly Christian locality. Life was easy. I used to play table tennis for a while in the office gym and reach home late. Uncle used to cook something and wait for me. He is a bachelor, you know, and a fantastic cook. On some days he used to come late and I had to cook something for him. He didn't want me to wait for him but I used to, because he needed help on those nights—he used to come dead drunk.

"On one such night I waited for a long time and then slept. That was February 15th, six months ago. I remember the date because it was uncle's birthday. I went home early that day with a cake. I felt guilty that I had forgotten to wish him happy birthday in the morning and so wanted to surprise him with the cake.

"When he woke me up, it was well past midnight. 'Wake up, Pat, for Chris-sake,' he said, shivering and sweating, in a kind of fright I had never seen him in before. 'Who is that horrible guy in our house, Pat, come and see him,' he said, and dragged me to the large mirror on the dressing table. 'Oh, you are in there too, thank God, but who is that awful old man standing with you?'

"I swear, Rao, that apparition in the mirror was really sickening. Uncle was a very handsome man once, but God, how he had gone to seed. He stood there framed in that mirror, so sloshed that he looked as if he were drowned in drink, so haggard and ugly that I felt like crying. He had stripped and had nothing on except a striped underwear. He looked terrible, man, he really did. Mirrors, sensible and sedate, can sometimes become cruel.

"It was uncle who started crying—something I had never seen him do before. 'Oh, Pat,' he whimpered, staring at that apparition in fear and despair. 'Is that me, Pat? Me, Patrick D'Souza, the handsomest guy in our office? What's happened to me, man, how did I grow so horrible and ugly so suddenly?'

"He sat down heavily, and I, may God forgive me for it, started laughing. I was on the verge of tears, but I found myself laughing, almost hysterically, because he had sat on the stool I had kept his birthday cake on.

"He looked at me in complete bewilderment. 'Why are you laughing?' he asked, and when I couldn't speak, he said, looking more and more confused, 'Why are you laughing, Pat, tell me why you're laughing.'

"I felt awful. I didn't know whether I was laughing or crying. 'I'm sorry,' I said, 'but you're sitting'—to my horror I found myself laughing hysterically again—'you are sitting on your birthday cake, uncle—Black Forest, your favourite—I ordered it specially for you—don't you remember, uncle, it's your fifty-second birthday today.'

"His back straightened and he spoke to me in hurt dignity—but he was still sitting on the Black Forest which I had asked the cake-maker to make with an extra dash of rum—an absurd tragi-comic figure in his striped underwear. 'There is no need,' he said, 'to remind me that I'm fifty-two. I know it.'

"We had a long talk that night, or morning I should say, because by the time we cleaned up the mess and uncle Patrick had a shower it was 3:30 a.m. He was dead sober, but softened by the experience, he opened his heart to me as he had never done before.

" 'I came here when I was twenty,' he said, sipping the strong coffee he had prepared. 'I was healthy, handsome, athletic. I played football, and the record I created in long jump at the College Meet stood for some years. Girls used to go gaga over me, boy, both in college and in the office. You know why I didn't get married, Pat? Not because I couldn't find a girl but because there were too many in love with me. I didn't want to marry one and break a dozen hearts. Sounds crazy, I know, but I have always been a softhearted fool where girls are concerned. And now suddenly I find I have grown old and ugly. It's not fair, Pat, it's not fair.

"'You know, Pat, I used to say that the greatest thing about this city was that time flew here. I used to grumble, whenever I went down to our village, that time stood still there and I was bored. Oh, God, I didn't foresee this. Time does fly here, and how. It's as if I came here only yesterday, man, and I'm already old junk. Pat, take my advice. They say that there are vacancies in the new Divisional Office at Udupi. Take the opportunity and get out of this city. Live in a small town where time moves slowly, get bored, get married, and grow old gracefully and slowly. I was thinking of applying for a transfer myself, but no, there is nothing for me there, anymore.'"

The bulb above our head flickered and came to life. I did not know what to say to Pinto. "Strange you have the same Christian name as your uncle," I said, rather lamely. "Oh, I was named after him," he said, "because he was the handsomest guy in the family and mother worshipped him. 'You should grow up like your uncle Pat,' she used to say. And really, Rao, he's a wonderful person, with a terrific sense of humour. You know, he's much in demand at Mangalorean weddings in Bombay because no one can propose a toast like him. You know what he said the morning after his birthday when I was leaving for office? He was still dressing up and was putting on the tie I had given him the previous night—he is quite a dandy still—'I have had a good time, Pat,' he said, ' but every party has to end.' Then he laughed and added: 'I learnt yesterday the hard way—no, no, the soft way, because your Black Forest was pretty soft—that you can't eat your cake and sit on it too; and I have been sitting on mine for too long.' That's my uncle Pat." Pinto sighed, looked at his watch and got up to go. "Forget what I have said, Rao," he added; "I didn't come here to warn you or anything. I talked rot because I had to get it off my chest. Bombay is a fine place, man, a city of opportunities. I'm sure you'll come back at the right time because you have your strong bonds. Like your uncle and the suragi tree. Wish you all the best."

సం

On the hard bench of the Bombay bound train I sat brooding over that conversation with Pinto with increasing uneasiness. Those strong bonds he had talked of were perhaps more fragile than we both assumed. How could I forget to go to Nampalli to see uncle before leaving for Bombay? What must he be thinking of me?

But even as I was worrying about the weakening of those old bonds, a strong new one was being formed. I had found Sita's baby quite unattractive when I first saw him. His face looked pinched, as if he was clenching it tight, like another fist. I had laughed when Sita said that he looked like his father, because Shreekanth was a handsome well-built man. But now at three months the baby had grown into a charming cherub with a divine smile. He had only one tooth, but he showed it at every opportunity. He smiled and gurgled, and kicked with his plump legs as if he was riding a bicycle. I had never carried him in my arms till then because his neck was a bit weak and Sita insisted that he should be carried only in a particular way. I was asked to hold his two feet in my left hand, slide my right palm down his pink bottom and back till his head rested on it, and only then lift him up, taking care to see that his head, a bit too heavy for his neck, was properly supported. Too much of a hassle, I had thought then. But in the train when Sita went to the toilet, or had to rummage in her bag for something or the other, I had to take care of him for long periods. Once her confidence in my ability to take care of her precious baby grew, Sita just placed him in my lap whenever she felt like it and went to gossip with a fat woman who was travelling to Bombay with her two pretty daughters. I did not mind it, especially since the two daughters came to play with Satish whenever Sita went to talk with their mother. They tickled the baby, and when he gurgled in happiness, drooled over him. I found the experience of two good-looking girls drooling over a baby lying in my lap, their pretty heads close to mine, an exciting one. Namita and Namrata. They took our address and we made plans to meet in Bombay, but nothing came of it.

At night Sita was worried that her son might fall off the bench if she went to sleep. I woke up at two and found her still sitting, dozing, with the baby in her lap. As it was no use arguing with her, I sat cross-legged on the bench, like uncle used to sit while doing his parayana, so that she could place Satish in my lap and go to sleep. I was surprised to find the baby wide-awake at such an odd hour. He wanted me to play with him but when he found that I would not oblige, he just lay there watching me, with a suggestion of a smile hovering on his face. As I patted his head gently trying to make him fall asleep, I remembered—but without any sense of guilt now—uncle and his love for me. There's more than one way, I thought, of repaying old debts.

Our train reached Bombay six hours late but there was a small reception committee waiting for us at the Dadar Station. Shreekanth's mother was there, and his two sisters, husbands in tow, had come especially for the occasion, one from Poona and the other from the even more distant Baroda. None of them could come to Kantheshwar to see Satish when he was born but they were all there to receive their VIP guest on his arrival in Bombay. Shreekanth's house at Hindu Colony was crowded, and though I knew that the two young women and their husbands were there for only a couple of days, lack of privacy made me feel uncomfortable. I needed some sleep but could not relax. So in the afternoon when Sita dozed off to sleep and the four guests sat down to a game of cards, I decided to go out for a walk.

Sunanda, the younger of Sita's sisters-in-law, instructed me how to go to Five Gardens, the only garden within walking distance. "But be careful while crossing the main road," she warned, "this is not Kantheshwar."

The road within the Colony was not crowded. At the end of it I turned to the right, as I was instructed, and suddenly found myself in the middle of a cackling drove of schoolgirls. In spite of all that Pinto had said about Bombay's bigness I must admit I was quite taken aback. The girls looked so healthy and well-fed, so well-endowed, so buoyant and full of life, that I felt angry, like Pinto, that girls in our place should be so shy and shrinking; angry with our tradition-bound society that stunted their growth. Of course it was not all just righteous indignation at a social wrong; I also felt cheated: seven or eight years of girl-watching and I had not seen bosoms like that before.

I was so overwhelmed by what I saw that I was nearly run over while crossing the main road, first by a truck, and then, on the other side of the road, by a car that came suddenly speeding from behind a double-decker bus. I said to myself that if I was not careful I might die a martyr to bosom-watching.

The pavements around the gardens were full of girls because their school was nearby and they were on their way home. I watched them with a great deal of interest. What surprised me was the way they walked, as if the whole place belonged to them. They were not bothered about people dashing against them the way girls in our villages were. With bags loaded with books strapped to their backs and equally well loaded in front, they came like trucks with headlights on. To avoid a head-on—or bosom-on—collision with one of them I hastily stepped aside and bumped into a young man. He was leaning against the railing round one of the gardens and talking with a girl on the other side.

"I'm so sorry," I said but he burst out laughing. "Oh God," he said, in mock-dismay, "look at who has come bird-watching all the way from Udupi to Bombay! When did you come here?"

It was Ramesh Rao. Though I had not forgiven him for what had happened two years earlier, I was glad to see him. "Only a few hours ago," I said. "You came here immediately after your graduation, didn't you? I heard you now have a nice job in Air India."

"Ah, yes," he said, throwing a glance at the girl in the garden. "I'll come in a minute, Jenny," he said to her and took me by the arm and led me away. The girl looked at us angrily and moved away to a pram in which a nice-looking baby was sitting quietly, sucking its thumb. The girl was awfully plain: short, dark, flat chested, and with a face full of pimples.

"Why the hell you had to talk about my job in front of that girl?" Ramesh asked me in irritation. "What's wrong?" I said, "Have you lost your job or something?"

"No," he said, "but I don't tell my girls where I'm working. I have told her I'm a student and that isn't a lie either. I'm studying Law, you know."

I was quite taken aback. "Your girl?" I said. "But she's awful-looking! Couldn't you find a better one in all Bombay?"

Ramesh looked angry. "Like one of these?" he asked, as two hefty school girls came marching. He patted the backside of one of them as they passed us. "Dirty bastard," she hissed, without turning back or slackening her speed. Ramesh laughed. "It isn't too difficult to make friends with pretty girls," he said; "But what's the use? I have had a couple of college-going girlfriends. They made me spend money like hell and I got nothing in return. One of them occasionally allowed me a dry kiss while watching movies, and the other to fondle her a bit. But what the hell, why should I pay through my nose for little intimacies?"

"But who's this Jenny?"

"You can make out what she is, can't you," said Ramesh, in irritation; "She is a servant girl; an ayah working in one of the Parsee houses here. There is a big Parsee colony around these gardens. The Parsees aren't as well-to-do as they used to be but they can't do without a retinue of servants. They prefer Christian girls because they wear skirts and speak a bit of English. So all the ayahs here are poor Christian girls from Mangalore or Goa. They are well fed but are hungry for love and sex. They see lots of things happening around them—Parsees are pretty liberated people—and that turns them on. Rosie— an ex-girlfriend of mine—told me that the old man in the house she worked in watched blue films in the afternoons when his daughter-in-law went to her office, and he didn't mind Rosie watching them too. Poor Rosie. The old man was well past eighty."

"But how do you make friends with them?"

"Pretty easy. They all speak Konkani, Christian Konkani, and you know I can speak that lingo very well. God, you should see the way they brighten up when they hear their lingo spoken by a well-dressed chap. As if the man of their dreams has come. It's all so easy, man. Easy come, easy go. That's why I go for them."

"But why do you hide from them the fact that you are working for Air India?"

"I don't hide anything. I just don't want to give them my address, that's all. I take all the precautions, but there might be trouble, perhaps not of my making. If that happens I don't want them to be able to trace me."

A rather pretty but faded-looking girl came pushing a pram near the pavement where we were standing. "Hi," said Ramesh, and spoke to her in Konkani, "What a pretty baby! Is it yours?"

"God, no," she said, giggling nervously, and touching the cheek of the infant in the pram as if for protection; "What an idea. I'm not married." Then she looked at him and asked shyly, "Are you one of us?"

What she meant was whether he was, like her, a Mangalorean Christian. But there was something in her voice, and in the way she looked up at him— she was on the road and we were standing on the pavement—which touched my heart. She looked so delicate and vulnerable that I had no curiosity left to see how Ramesh tackled her. Suddenly I felt I had had enough. "See you some other time, Ramesh," I said and turned away. "Hey, wait a minute," he shouted, "you haven't told me where you are staying," but I pretended I did not hear him.

Upset and baffled by the sudden feeling of revulsion that rose in me, I took the wrong lane on my way back, and found myself in front of the Dadar railway station. It was evening, the time the commuters came home. I was taken aback by the crowd that flowed out of the station, a faceless multitude in the gathering dusk which somehow unnerved me. I had seen crowds as big as this before, at the festivals at Kantheshwar and Udupi, but they were so different from this one: there was life and confusion there, and excitement, whereas here everything was methodical and dead. I remembered some lines from Eliot, a poet I did not much care for. Professor Krishnaraju had forced me to read *The Waste Land*, and he used to gloat over the beauty of the lines that described a crowd flowing over London Bridge: *so many, / I had not thought death had undone so many*. At that uncertain hour when streetlights were struggling to take over from the fast fading daylight, Bombay, I thought, did become an 'unreal city', like Eliot's London.

That night I lay awake for a long time, troubled by mosquitoes and my own buzzing thoughts. I was upset by Ramesh but could not understand why. I had not seen him doing anything as objectionable as what I had seen him do at Udupi but somehow I felt that he had degenerated. He was, in spite of everything, a likeable person at Udupi, but just two years' stay in Bombay, I felt, had coarsened him terribly. I then wondered why *I* should be troubled by his degeneration, even if it had really taken place and was not just a figment of my imagination, an imagination affected by lack of sleep.

Then I thought of the crowd near the station and wondered why I had found that an unnerving experience. Perhaps it was because I had lost my way and found myself unexpectedly at the station, and that crowd had aggravated my feeling of being lost. I thought of Eliot and of that line from *The Waste Land*. Just before I fell asleep I said to myself that in my dream that night I might see that crowd again; and perhaps meet Stetson, and ask him whether the corpse he had planted in his garden the previous year had begun to sprout.

I did get dreams that night but nothing so terribly literary. They were quite stupid really. I dreamed that I was in front of Nampalli Matha, in the midst of a very noisy herd of schoolgirls in uniform from that school near Five Gardens. "Oh God," I thought, "how did they come here to Nampalli following me? What will Janakamma and Raju's mother and others say? They will be shocked when they see these big bosomed girls prancing about in such short dresses!" I looked at the girls milling around, and all that I wanted was to get away from there before uncle came back from school. Then I found that one of the faces among them looked familiar. "Who's that girl with big breasts jumping about with such gay abandon?" I thought, and nearly woke up with shock when I realized who it was. It was Little Ramu's mother. She looked very happy, full of life, and she wasn't more than sixteen years old.

Bombay and Nampalli

ॐ

It did not take long for me to get used to Bombay. I joined work the very next day and found the atmosphere in the office cordial, and the work easy. Adi Irani, the chap who occupied the table next to mine, guided me in my work, introduced me to his friends and even took me to the typing section to introduce me to the girls there. "This is my harem," he said, and they tittered. "Now that this handsome chap has come, don't desert poor old Adi Irani," he said, and they laughed again.

I found Adi fascinating. I had never met anyone whose attitude to women and sex was so completely uncomplicated and amoral. He was a shortish man in his early thirties, with crew cut hair and a goatee. He wasn't good looking but claimed that girls found him irresistible. There was a rather incongruous mixture of the boyish and the manly in him which perhaps appealed to them. His figure and the crewcut head were boyish, but the face, with its cigarette-darkened thick lips and large nose, was manly; and so was the voice, a thick deep bass that could become raucous when he cracked his raunchy jokes, but soft and caressing when he wanted to talk romantic nonsense to girls. He wore tight trousers and high-heeled, narrow, pointed shoes. The crew cut, the tight trousers and high-heeled shoes were all in vogue then, but Adi somehow managed to look rather clownish by going to extremes. The trousers were skin tight and worn so low that the shirttails often came out. The crew cut was cropped so close that it made his large faun-like ears stick out. The high-heeled shoes made him walk like a goat. In fact I had never seen anyone who reminded me so strongly of a goat as Adi did.

I found the way he talked to girls, and the kind of things he said, shocking. He often made Stella De Souza, a fair complexioned innocent looking girl from the Typing Pool, turn beetroot red with his remarks; but she kept on coming to our section under the pretext that she could not decipher the hand-writing of Mr. Mhatre, our section Head. I must say that she really asked for trouble. "Adi," she said one day, "you wear your trousers so low, man, that girls in the Typing Pool always wonder how's it they don't fall off." Adi flashed a brilliant smile and said, "Don't you know, dear, that I have a peg to hang them on?" She blushed and ran away. An hour later she came back again. This time she was blushing even before anything was said—it was clear someone had asked her, or perhaps challenged her, to say something—and began hesitantly: "You know, Adi, the girls in the Typing Pool are saying...if what you say about your trousers is true, then what a strain it must be, to keep them up all the time!" Adi laughed aloud. "No, sweetheart," he said in a honeyed voice, "It's no strain at all, as long as you keep coming here every now and then."

I could not help laughing aloud. For a moment or two she could not understand what he meant and stood there looking perplexed. Then understanding dawned, and she turned vermilion. "You're crazy," she said and ran back to the Typing Pool. "You have upset her, Adi," I said, "she's certainly very angry with you." "Nonsense," he said, "Let's listen to the noise from the Pool. If she's really upset, she won't tell them what I said." But she certainly reported what he said because we soon heard squeals of delighted laughter from there. "I have tickled them," said Adi in glee, "sitting at my table here I've managed to tickle those girls sitting in front of their typewriters. I say, this is real long distance tickling."

When Miss De Souza came again a couple of hours later, she was angry—not with Adi but with me! "What do you mean by laughing at everything Adi says," she said, and I did not know what to say.

Vinayak Dongre, a boyish-looking chap who had known Adi longer than I did, was baffled by the ease with which Adi could make propositions to women. "He is quite shameless," he said, "The other day he invited Mrs. Mundkur to see *The Seven Year Itch* with him. She said she was going to see it with her husband. Do you know what he said? 'It's no fun to see a film like that with your hubby,' he said, 'see it with me, and we'll have some real fun afterwards.'"

"Wasn't she angry?" I asked.

"No, and that's what surprised me," said Dongre. "Mrs. Mundkur just laughed, called him a shameless rascal and asked him to go to hell. That was all. How does he manage to remain friendly with women even after making such propositions?"

"Why not ask him that?" I said, but Dongre shook his head. So I asked Adi how he managed to propose to women so brazenly without upsetting them.

"Maybe I am more tactful than you people," he said.

"Tactful my foot," I said. "Dongre overheard what you said to Mrs. Mundkur the other day. It was not tactful, it was crude."

"Oh, that Dongre chap was eavesdropping when I talked to Mrs. Mundkur, was he?" said Adi, "That was why she turned me down perhaps.

But what was crude about my proposal? I liked the way she looked that day, felt an urge to take her out, and asked her. She said no, and there the matter ended." He looked at me and said, "If you feel like taking a girl out, you wouldn't have the guts to ask her, would you?"

"I wouldn't," I agreed, a little shamefacedly. "Why not?" said Adi.

"For two reasons," I said—I still hadn't lost that habit—"Firstly, I'd be scared that she would be angry with me for making an indecent proposal..."

"Of course she would be angry," said Adi, looking angry himself. "If you think it's an indecent proposal and still make it, she has every right to be angry. But why is it indecent? What's wrong if you ask a girl to spend an evening out with you? Even if things happen, you aren't going to do anything that your parents or grandparents or great grandparents haven't done. Were they indecent? Don't tell me that our ancestors always did every thing within the confines of marriage. You know they didn't. Read the *Puranas*, read history, read the Bible, read anything. And remember, our parents and forefathers, unlike us, got married quite early."

"There is another reason," I said. "If the girl says no, as Mrs. Mundkur did, I would sink down into earth in shame. I would never be able to face her again."

"Nonsense, arrant nonsense," said Adi, and this time he was really angry. "What arrogance you men have, to think that a girl must always come out with you when you ask her! Doesn't she have the right to say 'no'? If you invite me for a cup of tea and I say no, do you sink down into the earth or gutter or whatever? Why can't you take a 'no' from a woman?"

"I'll tell you what is wrong with you people," he said, cooling down a little and scratching his goatee thoughtfully. "It's neither arrogance nor timidity. It's simply a case of a thoroughly wrong attitude to sex. When you ask a girl to come out with you, you aren't inviting her to have some fun, *you are asking her to commit some sin*. Shame and losing face and all that rot come into it because you think sex is sin, not fun. Which girl with self-respect will come out with you once she realizes that that's your attitude? No, Rao, it's hopeless, a no-win situation. If the girl says no, you lose face and your self-respect, and if she says yes you lose your respect for her. Any sensible girl—even if she likes you—will say no to you, though she might say yes when poor Adi Irani, who's not much to look at but is more sensible, asks her."

One thing about Adi baffled me: one of the strongest emotions among men in our society is sexual jealousy, but Adi, though a known skirt chaser and a successful one, had no enemies. Dongre was equally baffled. "Mr. Mhatre is such a puritan," he said, "but even he likes Adi a lot. I can't understand it."

We were eating fruits-in-milk with cream at Brighton Milk Bar, just a stone's throw from our office, during lunch break. Adi hadn't come with us that day; he had taken a fresh young thing who had joined our office a few days earlier to another, more fashionable, restaurant.

"Mr. Mhatre is as baffled by Adi as you are," I said. "He can't figure him out. He likes Adi because he is an excellent worker. Mhatre believes that those who spend their time and energy chasing skirts have none left for their work. So he refuses to believe that Adi is after girls."

"How can he he be so blind?"

"He is not blind, he is only a bit confused. He is right in his observation that most skirt chasers are bad workers. I am not sure how it is, but I think people, when they do things which *they* think are wrong, tend to get obsessed with their wrongdoing. The load of guilt they carry exhausts them. But Adi enjoys his sexploits. They do him no harm because he doesn't think he is doing anything wrong."

"Wrong," said Dongre, "is wrong, irrespective of what one thinks."

"Not really. Now tell me, honestly, do you think Adi is a bad chap?"

"Oh, he is all right, but..."

"Don't bring in that 'but'. Adi is all right because he does not do anything that he thinks is wrong. He is not like Puranik. You don't like Mr. Puranik, do you?"

"No chance," said Dongre with disgust. "Who can like that creep?"

Mr. Puranik was the Head of of our neighbouring Section. He was an aging Lothario, or that was what everyone thought, though in reality I don't think he was much older than Adi. He was, a few years earlier, a very good looking man and was known as a lady-killer. But he lost his looks early—went bald, developed double chin and a paunch—and started getting so worried about his loss of good looks that he lost them all the quicker. The worry gave him dark circles round his eyes and made him desperately strive for new conquests. The way he tried to ingratiate himself with every female who was sent to his Section, however plain or even ugly, was both pathetic and comic. But Dongre, who was his neighbour at the distant suburb of Kalyan, found it sickening because Mr. Puranik had a very beautiful and faithful wife whom Dongre had admired when they were in school together. Puranik, said Dongre, never invited him home because he was jealous of his wife; but the creep sometimes visited Dongre's house and tried to be friendly with his good-looking unmarried sister.

"Do you understand what is the main difference between Adi and Puranik as Lotharios?" I said. "Mr. Puranik thinks that extra-marital sex is a sin. He thinks he is doing something forbidden when he runs after those girls. That's why he looks like a creep, sly and conspiratorial, when he takes them out to lunch or tea. Adi says that he doesn't enjoy his skirt chasing anymore, he is merely doing it out of habit. Poor Puranik. If sex were just fun to him as it is to Adi he would have given up skirt chasing when he lost his looks and his plumage. After all he has a nice-looking wife waiting at home, you say. But it is difficult to give up sinning. Don't ask me why, I don't know. Maybe the sins you commit alter your identity so that you can't give them up without an identity crisis."

"You are talking in riddles," said Dongre. "But you can't convince me that a sin ceases to be a sin if your thinking changes. If I think murder is all right, does it become all right?"

"Can you think murder is all right?"

"No. But we can certainly think that sex outside marriage is no sin, if that's going to make things easier for us."

"Can you? If Adi were to ask you if he could take your sister out, because he had heard, from Puranik, that she was pretty, what would you say?"

"I would break his crew cut head, as well as Puranik's," said Dongre.

"There you are," I said, laughing. "No, Dongre, you can't change your thinking. Nor can I. Do you know what Adi would have said if he were in your place? 'Why are you asking me,' he would have said, 'go and ask my sister.'"

Dongre looked thoughtful but not convinced. "You can't change your mindset whenever you want to," I said. "You are trapped in your mind as badly as you are trapped in your body. You may pretend that you are liberated but it's no use; you will be just fooling yourself. 'There is nothing either good or bad but thinking makes it so.' Does that sound very modern? It was written three hundred and sixty years ago, by Shakespeare. Do you know who said it? A character tragically trapped in his mindset, desperately trying to break free. He couldn't, though he understood the situation well enough to make that profound statement. Poor Hamlet. He strove so hard that he finally went out of his mind."

"You talk a lot of bullshit," said Dongre as we walked back to office. "It's interesting and sounds profound but it's all illogical. If a crime is not a crime because the criminal *thinks* it's all right, we may as well close down our courts."

It was too late to enrol for M.A. that year, but when I went to the university to find out what the timings of the lectures were like, I was in for a rude shock. The English lectures were in the afternoon, from two to five. Earner-learners could take only subjects like History where evening lectures were held. This was a real blow. Adi tried to console me by saying that getting attendance was not much of a problem. I could ask the other students to enter my name in the attendance sheets passed around in the class. "So don't start worrying now," he said.

But getting attendance was not the only problem. I was really looking forward to studying literature systematically. I wanted to attend lectures and interact with the other students. I realized that there was only one job which allowed one to be a full-time student of literature: school teaching. Most schools in Bombay work in shifts, the high school section usually in the morning and the primary section in the afternoon. The morning shift would have suited me splendidly. Giving up my fairly good 'permanent' job was all right, for I had no intention of working in an office for long. A few years of that kind of work I could take, but not a life sentence. So I decided to take up school teaching, and when the schools started advertising for teachers in April, I sent a couple of applications and waited.

The first interview was a nightmare. The school, which ran an English medium morning shift and a Hindi medium afternoon shift, was housed in a ramshackle barrack. The applicants, some twenty of us, stood in a small antechamber and heard every word of the interview conducted in the next room. I did not have to wait too long for my turn. I heard two or three minutes of an interview in Hindi where only one voice, a loud one, was heard hectoring; and then the voice abruptly said 'Next', and a clerk who stood at the door called out my name.

"N. Sudhakar Rao," boomed that voice, "What's this 'N' in your name? You don't know you should give your full name when you apply for job? What you teach the istudents of this iskool if you can't write your application correctly?"

As my eyes got used to the dim interior of the room, the voice turned into a man, thickset and heavy-jowled, bald as an egg, but with bushy eyebrows and bushier whiskers that adequately compensated for the missing hair on the head. Throughout the interview he alone spoke, and the three other men present kept on nodding their heads. He fired a barrage of questions at me giving me time for only one-word answers. "So 'N' stands for your village? Why you did not give it full? You are not coming from English medium, how you teach English to English medium istudents? They are istudying English from K.G. class, they are very smart, they ispeak good English, only they are not knowing proper grammar. You are good in grammar?" This strident monologue went on for some time till he said "Next," and the clerk at the door called out, "Satyaprakash Shivnarain Dubey," and I had to get up and make way for Mr. Dubey, the next one to be interrogated.

No more interviews, I decided. But in the next day's *Times of India* there was an advertisement from a 'Prestigious English Medium Girls' School' for an English teacher, and I could not resist the temptation of 'one last try'. This time I wrote my name in full in the application: Nampalli Sudhakar Rao.

About a week after this Sita told me, when I came home in the evening, that a peon from 'that girls' school near Five Gardens' had come looking for me and had left a note. I very nearly panicked. On days when I came early from office I used to go to Five Gardens for a stroll and sometimes hang around that school's playground, watching those big girls play basketball—really a sight for sore eyes. I wondered whether anyone had complained about it to the school authorities. But the note dispelled my apprehensions: it invited me to attend an interview the next morning at ten, but added that the post was a leave vacancy for just three months.

I was thrilled. Shreekanth could not conceal his surprise or control his mirth. "You teaching in that school?" he said, laughing aloud. "God, I can imagine what will happen to hundreds of little fluttering female hearts. But that school never takes any male teachers if women are available, how come they have called you for an interview?" Sita was worried about my taking up a temporary job for three months and then becoming jobless. "We will worry about it after I am offered the job," I said, "Let me first attend the interview."

I don't think I'll ever forget that interview. In the morning Shreekanth was after me, urging me to dress up well. "Dress to kill," he said and offered me his wedding suit, but I said that to wear that woollen suit in Bombay's sweltering summer was to dress to die, not kill. He made me wear a tie, though. He tied the knot himself, stepped back to take a proper look and yelled in delight. "Gosh," he said, "You are handsome, man, that's what you are. I didn't know a mere tie could bring about such a transformation." He dragged me to the full-length mirror in their bedroom and made me look at myself.

I must say that I was surprised. As a kid I was nice-looking but somewhere around my thirteenth year I had started shooting up and become terribly skinny and gawky. I became acutely conscious of my lack of good looks, and my aunts and other relatives, whenever they visited us, made me more self-conscious by talking about how good-looking I was as a child, and how terribly I had changed for the worse. Now I suddenly realized that I *was* handsome. The eight months I had spent in Bombay had brought about a few changes. I had grown fairer—not uncommon among South Indians when they move northwards—and my form had filled up. But more than anything else, it was the look in the eyes that had transformed my appearance. There was a new sparkle, brought about, perhaps, by the fact that I had become, in Bombay, less inward looking: I spent less time reading and dreaming because there was more to look at in big Bombay.

I don't know how the tie worked. But it did work. I slouched less and carried myself better when I wore it. I think it propped up my sagging self-confidence the way a brassiere supports a woman's sagging breasts.

When I reached the school I found girls all over the place. Must be their recess time. I got a proper share of attention this time. A little girl near the gate gave me a wolf whistle and the bigger girls nearby laughed aloud. "Smart boy," said another little one, and a bigger one said, "Gosh, look at him blushing." "Shireen, look who's coming," shouted someone and a fair girl standing near the main entrance turned and stared at me with such longing in her large eyes that it was clear that she was putting on an act. They ignored men outside the premises of the school, but within its protective precincts they indulged in a bit of Adam-teasing.

I saw just two women waiting for the interview in the vestibule. Apparently the school had not called all the applicants at the same time. It was all so orderly, so different from what I had witnessed in the other school.

When I was called in for the interview, however, there was utter confusion. "How, what, who are you, I mean, what's your name?" said a thin tall woman, staring at me from over a pair of gold-rimmed spectacles. The two women sitting on either side of her looked even more surprised.

"I'm Sudhakar Rao," I said, quite taken aback by the confusion my entrance had caused. "N. Sudhakar Rao."

"But who's Nampalli?" said the thin woman, "Whose name is that?"

"That's my village," I said.

The plump woman sitting on the thin one's right turned red and started shaking. She was desperately trying not to laugh. I realized that her control would give way any minute and then she would really burst. Throughout the interview I was waiting for that catastrophe.

"There has been a mistake," said the thin woman, calm and composed now. "The custom here is to write one's personal name first, and then the name of one's father or husband, and finally the surname; so we thought...please sit down, what's your father's name?"

"Dr. Krishna Rao," I said.

"You should have written your name as Sudhakar Krishna Rao, you see. But you wrote Nampalli Sudhakar Rao, and we naturally thought that you were a girl and your first name was Nampalli. That's why we called you for the interview."

"The custom in our place is to write one's village name first," I said, feeling quite dejected and a little angry. "And I'm sorry, but I don't think there is any girl in this world named Nampalli."

"How are we to know that?" said the thin woman. "There are all kinds of names, particularly among you Southies, I mean, South Indians. The person who has gone on leave is a South Indian like you. Shreevalli R. Raman. Her first name, Shreevalli, doesn't sound too different from Nampalli."

"Her sister is our student," said the short, phlegmatic woman with thick glasses sitting on the thin woman's left. "Her name is Alameruvalli."

"It's all a mistake," said the thin woman, looking a little impatient, "and we are terribly sorry about it. Ours being a girls' school, we naturally prefer women teachers, and don't usually call men for interviews; certainly not untrained men."

I got up to go. The fat woman finally opened her mouth. "Shreevalli," she said, "who has gone on maternity leave, was such a good dancer. *Bharata Natyam*, you know, South Indian women are so good at it. She taught English, but also choreographed our dances. Very graceful, you know." She waved her fat arms, trying to imitate the hand movements in Bharata Natyam. "We thought.. We thought.." She now suddenly lost her control on that laughter which had been threatening to break out ever since I entered the room, and instead of speaking, started quacking, "We thought...you would turn out to be a graceful South Indian beauty...who'd teach our girls Bharata Natyam!" She burst out laughing, and again tried that awful imitation of the hand movements of Bharata Natyam; and managed to look like a fat quacking duck desperately trying to take off.

"If you want to teach English in an English medium school in Bombay," said the short woman, "you must do something about your accent. You do speak reasonably well but like many South Indians you say 'yen' for 'en'." Then with a straight face she imitated my accent: 'Aiyam yen Sudhakar Rao.'"

That was the proverbial last straw. I went out of the room with burning ears. The girls had all disappeared into their classrooms, except for the girl they called Shireen, but she looked sad and morose. Apparently she had been sent out of her class for some misdemeanour.

At supper that evening I made Shreekanth nearly choke on his food by telling him about the interview, turning the whole thing into a comic anecdote. But somehow I could not tell him about 'en' and 'yen'. I was angry but I also felt upset and ashamed. For a few days I even toyed with the idea of changing my name to 'Sudhakar Krishna Rao', and asked Mr. Puranik, who was a Law graduate, how to go about it. He gave me a long lecture on how I should first announce my intention in the Government Gazette, etc., but halfway through his monologue I lost interest and stopped listening.

But I had felt strongly, after so many years, that insidious feeling, shame. Once again I was ashamed of something I loved: this time it was Nampalli, my village.

A Student of Literature

✦

Adi was right. It was not too difficult to get adequate attendance at the university while continuing to work for L.I.C. I even managed to attend most of the lectures I wanted to. I had one month's 'Earned Leave' to my credit, took half of it at the beginning of the term and attended all the lectures during that fortnight religiously. We also had fifteen days' Casual Leave per year and we could take them all as half-days if we wanted to. So during those two years I made use of my thirty days' C.L. to get sixty free afternoons, something Mr. Mhatre found really puzzling. People rarely took half-day Casual Leaves because the toughest part of office going, in Bombay, was commuting, not warming a chair for six and a half hours. Mr. Mhatre had no objection to what I did, though, because taking all my C.L. as half days meant that there was no day I was absent from office. On some days I worked a little longer in the morning and took my lunch break late, so that I could attend the first lecture and then rush back to office. It was all quite hectic, but I was happy. For the first and only time in my life I had an overriding sense of purpose and was doing something I had always wanted to do.

I think I attended as many lectures as I would have if I were a full time non-working student. Most of the lectures, however, were really bad. The professors came, as visiting faculty, from different colleges. I don't know who selected them or why they chose to come. Perhaps they came because they lacked something, either in their paper qualifications or in their self-esteem. But it was clear that there was no real motivation.

The one who took the cake for sheer incompetence was Professor Totani, who lectured to us on Shakespeare. In his first lecture he told us that he had taught our seniors 'Mayor for Mayor' the previous year and had derived great 'player' from it, and was going to teach us *Henry IV Part One*, a play in which there was a very fat man called Falstaff. Then he opened his copy of the play, in which there was a picture of the fat knight, and took it round the class to show one and all how fat Falstaff really was. "See how fat he is," he said, grinning like a child, and we all nodded in silent agreement.

Strangely enough no one laughed, no one even wanted to know what play it was that he called 'Mayor for Mayor.' I knew why *I* could not laugh: My great ambition in life was to teach English literature in a college or university; and here was someone who had reached that goal, and God, what a sorry figure he cut. His incompetence made a mockery of my ambition. Even his appearance was pathetic. He looked like a scarecrow but a harmless one that would not scare a sparrow. He wore a cotton suit that had never been pressed, and the same tie, all the time. A small shrunken man, he gave one the impression that he had been washed with his suit on, dried in the sun, and then sent out into the world to lecture on Shakespeare. And lecture on Shakespeare he did, year after year, with great aplomb. Perhaps the M.A. classes were the only ones that tolerated him.

The other lectures were only marginally better. Some were informative but they gave us information we could ourselves easily gather from books. There was no interaction at all between students and teachers. If a teacher threw a question at the class, no one picked it up even if half the class knew the answer. The professors came, lectured, and went away. We sat reading or dreaming. They did not disturb us and we did not trouble them.

But somehow it did not matter one bit to me that the lectures were mostly insipid. I was happy to be there in the class, whatever the quality of the lecture. I was on a high most of the time because I was, at last, a student of literature, and only literature, and had to study no other subject—no maths, no science, no economic history of England. What did it matter if the lectures were dull?

There were occasional and unexpected gains. Professor Mathews, who lectured on modern poetry, one day wrote on the black board a few lines from Hopkins —the first few lines of 'The Windhover'—and read them aloud. Suddenly there was electricity in the air. I had not read Hopkins before. The only poem of his I had come across, in an anthology, was 'Inversnaid', and I had found it perversely obscure. Professor Mathews' interpretation of the lines and his comments on Hopkins were fairly simplistic, but for a few minutes the air around me crackled and a few lines of unexpected beauty came to life. The magical moment did not last long but its effect was lasting. In fact I think it marked a turning point in my career as a student of literature. I was, till then, not much interested in poetry. It was fiction I cared for most. I had even managed to read a fair amount of poetry as fiction: I read the first two books of *Paradise Lost* with interest, skipped through the next, found the fourth book fascinating, and then after skipping through the next four books with the kind of perseverance inveterate novel readers develop, found my reward in Book IX which made great reading. Byron's *Don Juan* was another of my favourite poems. I was fond of poetry in Kannada but I don't think I read lyric poetry in English with much interest or insight till I discovered Hopkins.

I found Hopkins intoxicating. For days I could talk on nothing but Hopkins. I even tried to read 'The Wreck of the Deutschland' to Adi and was shocked when the last line of the first stanza tickled his fancy in an unexpected way. When I read what Hopkins says to God, "Over again I feel thy finger and find thee," Adi laughed aloud. "God fingering the old priest?" he said, "What an image!"

I had forgotten what Hopkins meant to me and how intensely I loved his poems, till I received a visitor from the past about a year ago. I was sitting alone in college, in our Department Room on the fifth floor. The other teachers had gone to their classes. Someone stood at the open door and asked me if he could meet Professor Rao.

I asked him to come in. He was a frail old man and was breathing hard because he had come walking up the stairs. The lift, he said, was not working. I told him that there was another lift working at the other corner of the building, and that information made him look sadder.

He peered at me and smiled. "You don't recognize me, do you?" he said; "Not surprising. We met thirty-five years ago, in a friend's room. I have changed a lot, I know. You look the same, almost."

"Do you recognize me?" he asked again, and I had to admit that I did not. "Your face looks familiar," I said, prevaricating a little, "but I can't place you."

"I'm Narayana Murthy," he said, and that did not ring any bell either. "It's all right," he added, "I didn't expect you to remember me after all these years. We met for a couple of hours in your friend's room. He had called me specially to meet you. You were doing your M.A. with English literature then, and working in L.I.C. 'The fellow talks a lot of bookish nonsense sometimes,' your friend said, 'but you are fond of books. Come and meet him, you might find his talk interesting.' That was how I met you."

I could not still place him. He took out, from his bag, a book and placed it on the table. It was Hopkins' *Collected Poems*. "I was on my way to the British Council Library to return this book," he said. "I heard, some years ago, that you're working in this college. I thought—because your college is on the way —I might meet you for a few minutes." He patted the book on the table. "Does this book remind you of anything?"

It did not. I shook my head. "I was very fond of poetry," he said; "I still am. But I was working as an accountant in a bank then, and there was little time to read. And I needed guidance. At that time I had read only Shelley and Wordsworth. I asked you which poet you liked best, and you started talking about Hopkins. God, how you talked."

213

He looked at me with something close to awe. "You recited lines from 'The Windhover', from 'God's Grandeur', and some of the last sonnets. You talked of Hopkins' love for the word 'dappled'; you also said something about 'inscape' and explained that term to me with a great deal of patience. And I think you were not more than twenty then. You looked younger, very boyish."

He shook his head, as if he still found it difficult to believe that a twenty-year-old could be so knowledgeable. "There was a glow about you," he said, "a kind of passionate intensity. I was so impressed because everything you said was yours, not from some book. I mean, they might have come from books, they must have, but you had made them your own; because you gave the impression that you did not speak from memory, you spoke from your heart."

What could I say to that? His words certainly came from his heart. We sat silently for a moment, and then I said, "What are you doing now, Mr. Murthy?"

"I'm a retired person now," he said. "I retired as the General Manager of the Corporation Bank. A fairly successful career, but now it's all over. I had a good academic record, you know, B. Com, and then Law, and I also passed a few banking examinations. That helped me in my career, though I was never considered a very dynamic officer. But what I loved most was literature, especially poetry. Couldn't find the time to read all that I wanted to read when I was working. Now that I have retired, I have started reading a bit."

He hesitated a little and then said, "Will you read for me a few poems of Hopkins? I'd love to hear you reading some of those old favourites of yours again."

I felt embarrassed. I had not read Hopkins for years. My passionate love for his poems had lasted only a few months, and it never got renewed because I had no occasion to teach him. The University of Bombay—its Department of English—could not make up its mind whether Hopkins belonged to the 19th century or to the 20th, and in which of the two papers he should be placed. So he was never prescribed. And I could not remember, at that moment, which of his poems were my favourites. So I asked Mr. Murthy what *he* wanted me to read.

"Read 'The Windhover'," he said, without hesitation.

I read that poem and made a mess of it. For some inexplicable reason I was nervous. Perhaps I tried too hard to emote, to read with feeling. Mr. Murthy looked a little disappointed. "Read 'Pied Beauty', please," he said.

Once I started reading 'Pied Beauty', it all came back: the extraordinary intensity of Hopkins' poems and the excitement I had felt when I first read them thirty-five years earlier. Mr. Murthy looked deeply touched. "Read 'God's Grandeur'," he said, and after that he wanted me to read a few of the dark sonnets.

So I read 'I Wake and Feel the Fell of Dark', and was surprised by the strong feelings the poem aroused. Then I began to read 'Thou Art Indeed Just, Lord', and halfway through the poem realized that something was happening to me. When I came to those moving last lines, my voice broke down: "...*Birds build*—" I read, nearly choking, "*but not I build; no, but strain, / Time's eunuch, and not breed one work that wakes. / Mine, O thou lord of life, send my roots rain."*

Mr. Murthy sat speechless for some time. "I remember—so clearly—how you recited some of these lines," he said. "You said that Hopkins wrote two kinds of poems: exciting nature poems celebrating the beauty of God's creation, and the terrible last sonnets describing his feeling of spiritual desolation. And you said that you found both these sets of poems deeply moving, but when you read them together they became simply overwhelming. I can see now what you meant."

I did not know what to say. How could I tell him that I had absolutely no recollection of ever having met him, and he was, to me, a total stranger? We sat in silence for some time.

He got up to go, took his book and put it in his bag. "I am glad that I came," he said. "I was worried, you know. People change, and one shouldn't try to go back to the past. But you haven't changed much, at least as a student of literature."

I went with him to the lift to show where it was and also to see that the liftman took him down, because outsiders were not allowed to use the elevator to go down. On the way he asked, "You still don't remember me?"

"To be honest, no," I said. "In fact I still don't know in whose room we met."

"Oh God," he said, "Didn't I tell you where we met? It was in your friend Ramesh Rao's room, at Santa Cruz. Ramesh Rao of Air India. You remember him, don't you?"

It was my turn to be surprised. When had I gone to Ramesh's place?

"You came there on a Sunday," said Mr. Murthy. "You two were very close to each other, I thought. You are not in touch with him these days?"

"No," I said, "in fact I think I met him only once, during the last thirty-five years. That was about fifteen years ago, when he came with his daughter seeking admission for her in our college. I couldn't help him. The girl didn't have enough marks, admission for such cases was solely in the hands of the

Principal, and I didn't want to go to the old man because he was angry with me for refusing to edit the college magazine. I had done that thankless job for nearly twenty years, you see, and I was fed up."

The lift took a long time to come up. "He was very upset because I didn't help him," I said. "His daughter was surprisingly fair. Looked like a Parsee, I thought. So I asked him, when he was leaving, when he had got married, and he said it was none of my business."

"God, didn't you know how he got married?"

The lift came up and I entered it with him. I wanted to know more about Ramesh, and about his marriage.

"It was a sad affair," said Mr. Murthy. "I hope it's all right, my talking to you about it. I don't like to gossip, you see. It's not a well kept secret, anyway. Everyone in our neighbourhood knows about it. She was a Catholic girl, one who was working as an ayah. Jenny Crasto, that was her name. I don't know how they became intimate, but she was in trouble, and your friend got caught because the Parsee gentleman in whose house she was working happened to be a top ranking officer in Air India. Ramesh had to marry her; he would have lost his job, and taken to court perhaps, otherwise. But he came to know, after the child was born, that he was not the one who had got the girl into trouble. It was that Parsee officer, Keki Mistry. Ramesh came to my house dead drunk one evening—he is almost an alcoholic now—and cried and said that 'Cuckoo Mistry' had turned his house into a crow's nest. Poor chap. He had no one to turn to for help or guidance. He's not yet reconciled to the whole thing, though he loves his daughter; loves her more than he loves his own son, born two years later."

"Where is his mother now?"

"She died soon after his marriage. Ramesh doesn't go to Udupi these days. He says he has nobody there."

It was in the evening that day that I remembered why I had gone to Ramesh's room at Santa Cruz thirty-five years earlier, and how violently we had quarrelled at the end of my visit. I could not remember Mr. Murthy at all. Nor could I remember talking about Hopkins.

Ramesh had somehow found my address and come to see me on a Sunday about a year after I went to Bombay. Then he started coming frequently. He had a way with women and children, and both Sita and little Satish grew quite fond of him. He always came with some gift for Satish. I don't know whether I was jealous, but I certainly got worried. I thought I should warn Sita that he was not the spotless lamb he appeared to be.

But Sita was not the sort of person who would take hints. "What's wrong with him," she said, "he's a nice chap." So I told her about his ayah chasing. She was shocked but wouldn't believe it. "No, no, you're exaggerating," she said.

I then told her something which I couldn't even tell my friends at Udupi: What I had seen him doing at Thenka pethe. I suppose I *had* to tell it to someone some day. All my old anger and distress came out and made his deed appear darker than it perhaps was. So much depends on the way things are narrated. I was aware, even as I was telling Sita about the incident, that the whole thing would have become just a joke if I were to tell someone like Adi about it. Sita was suitably shocked. "What wretches you have for friends," she said. "If he comes calling I'll shut the door on his face. You tell him he shouldn't come here."

I was in a fix. So I rang up Ramesh on Saturday and told him that I would be coming to his place the next day. I must have met Mr. Murthy there.

The quarrel took place at the bus stop when Ramesh came to see me off. I told him on the way that I would visit him again next Sunday. "No," he said, "I'll come to your place. I want to see Satish, I miss him a great deal."

We had reached the bus stop by then. "Don't come home," I said. "If you want to see me let's meet at Five Gardens." I hesitated a bit and then added, "My sister doesn't want you to come home."

"But why?" he asked in shock, and I had to tell him. "She has come to know what you go to Five Gardens for, what you do there."

"She has come to know—*what*? What did you tell her, you creep? What rot did you tell her?"

"I told her only the truth, about the ayahs," I said; "She is my sister and I have every right to warn her."

He was livid with rage. His neck bulged, as if the blood vessels might burst. I thought he was going to hit me. "You bastard, what have you done," he said, raging. "I looked on Sita as my sister, you creep. I have no other sister and you know that. How could you think that I'd look at her—my own sister —the way I look at those girls!"

I did not see him again for nearly twenty years. Even when he came to see me for his daughter's admission, I did not recollect the quarrel. It was as if I had deleted, deliberately, the whole unpleasant incident from my memory. But it burst into view again that evening as if a searchlight had suddenly been turned on, on a spot long in darkness. The enormity of my betrayal hit me hard. Was I, in some way, at least partly responsible for what had happened to him? Did my betrayal push him to greater indiscretion?

What sins one has to expiate, God, I said to myself, as I lay awake for a long time that night. Our thoughtless deeds, and even words, hurt people, sometimes they damage and maim them. We go on with our lives as if nothing had happened. When we realize, years later, what had happened, and it is too late to make restitution, our deeds become dead albatrosses round our necks.

But I was happy and carefree during those days, and soon forgot the quarrel with Ramesh. Life was full of excitement. The hours spent in the office were not too tedious, but I lived for those hours spent with the other English literature students—in classes, in the university library, and in the canteens of colleges where the lectures were held. The majority of my classmates came from good English medium schools and spoke English much better than I did. If that did not give me an inferiority complex, it was because of Subhash Salvi, one of my classmates. An intense person, Subhash had worked extra hard to acquire a near perfect British accent, so that the confidence the accent gave helped him to overcome a tendency to stammer. He was the one who helped me to get rid of that 'South Indian' accent the school ma'am at the Five Gardens School had laughed at.

My passionate involvement with Hopkins lasted only a few months. Frost succeeded him and then Wilfred Owen. Finally I discovered Yeats.

I read the poems of Yeats in *The Faber Book of Modern Verse*, one of our prescribed texts, with excitement and also a strange kind of dissatisfaction. A dissatisfaction that made me crave for more. So I borrowed *The Collected Poems of W.B. Yeats* from the British Council Library, bought a 200-page notebook, and set out to make a small anthology of my favourite Yeats poems.

I read all the poems of Yeats in sequence so that I could choose the ones I liked best and take them down. It was no cursory reading. I read every line with care because I had to decide whether I wanted it in my anthology. But I was not unduly concerned with the 'meaning' of the poems. If I liked a poem, I was prepared to wait for the poem to give out its meaning at its own sweet time. So I took down some poems I could not fully comprehend because they moved me and I intuitively recognized the presence in them of the genuine stuff of poetry. As I copied those poems with their fascinating core of mystery, I recollected some lines—from Kingsley Amis, I think—that described love at first sight as *"a stellar entrant thrown/ Clear on psyche's radar screen/ Recognized before known."* For about a month I was in continual touch with one of the most exciting minds of our century. It was strange, the way this dead Irish poet came alive in my mind. And that act of copying down those poems in *my* hand, in *my* notebook, that too was important. It was an act of love, of acquisition, through which I made those poems my own.

I was fairly confident, at first, that I would do well in the exam. But the craze for 'reference work' among the students, the way they referred to innumerable critical books and took down copious notes from them, began to trouble me. They grumbled when there were many books to refer to, but they also complained when there were no critical works to read. "There is hardly anything on Stendhal," complained a horsey Parsee girl—Stendhal's *Scarlet and Black* was one of the novels prescribed in the Form paper— "What are we going to read? The critical works are all in French, and that gives a terribly unfair advantage to those who know French!" "Why not concentrate on the novel?" I asked, and they looked at me as if I had come from another planet. "There is an essay on *Scarlet and Black* in Maugham's *Ten Novels and Their Authors*," I said, mainly to placate them, and immediately pens flashed out of purses and pockets. "Somerset Maugham?" *Scribble, scribble.* "What's the name of the book, you said?" *Scribble scribble.* Finally I too caught the fever and began to feel that I had gathered very little notes compared to what the other students had accumulated. So I approached a doctor who specialized in medical certificates, and got from him, for five rupees, a certificate stating that I suffered from general debility and neurasthenia and needed complete rest for two months. With the help of that I got from my office two months' medical leave without pay. I collected quite a bit of critical material but did not know what to do with it. The notes were of some use to Subhash Salvi finally, who found, just a fortnight before the exams, that his own notebooks were missing. His cousin, a school dropout, had sold them to a roadside vendor, who used those scholarly pages to make paper cones to sell monkey-nuts in.

A week before our exams started news came that Moni's *Upanayana* or 'thread ceremony', the ritual in which he would be given his sacred thread that would make him a full-fledged Brahmin, was to be held on the day I had my Criticism paper. Sita said that we must all go or else father would be very upset. It took all her husband's persuasive powers to make her realize that my exam, on which my whole career depended, was more important than my presence at a ritual where I had no role to play. Finally no one from Bombay attended the function because Shreekanth's mother fell ill the day before Sita and little Satish were to leave.

I did badly in the very first paper but the other papers were all right. Sita's mother-in-law recovered and went to Poona for a few days. Sita went with Satish to Kantheshwar a week after my exams got over, the boy's first visit to his place of birth. She wanted me to go with them. But I told her that I had absented myself from office too long and did not want to lose my job before I was sure of getting another. That first paper had shaken my confidence and I was no longer certain that I had done well enough in the exam to get the post of a lecturer in English.

But the results, when they came, were not disappointing. I passed in the Second Class. So did Subhash, in spite of the scare caused by his last minute loss of notes. There were no First Classes. No one ever got a First Class in English M.A. then. Fifteen of the hundred and twenty students who appeared for the exam passed in the Second Class and that was considered a very good result.

The results were announced on Saturday, 19th of June, my birthday, and Yeats's. My friends and I spent that weekend trying to find out which colleges had vacancies in their English departments. There was no time to lose because the colleges were re-opening, after the summer vacation, on Monday, June 21.

Sita and Satish came back early in the morning on Monday. I could not talk with them because I had to rush to a nearby college where they had a vacancy in the English Department. I did not have to borrow a tie from Shreekanth this time. After that interview in the girls' school I had been buying one tie every month.

I met Professor Vanjpe, the Head of the English Department of the college—a very dignified man with well-groomed white hair that gleamed like platinum —as he was coming out of the Staff Room. He was also the Vice-Principal, and looked harried. "Yes, yes," he said, "we do have a vacancy." He took my mark list from me and looked at it. Students were milling around, and a peon came and said to him, in Marathi, that students of Inter Arts wanted to know where they should go for their lectures. "Yes, yes," he said, "send them to the Gymkhana Hall." The peon started herding the milling crowd to the Hall above the Staff Room. The professor turned to me. "But where is your mark list?" he asked me. "It's in your hand, sir," I said. "Ah, yes," he said, and looked at it again. The peon came once more and said, "Who's to take their class, sir, they say they have English Prose."

The H.O.D. looked at the mark list and at a book he had in his hand. Then he smiled at me. "Go to the class and take it," he said, thrusting the book into my hand. "You can give your application afterwards."

The English Lecturer

❧

The Gymkhana Hall, a long narrow room, was on the second floor. It was not meant to be a lecture room. The Intermediate Arts Class had actually two divisions, but as the students did not as yet know which division they belonged to, they were all there in that hall, creating a racket. The hall was so vast that even in pin drop silence my voice would not have reached the last benches, but the noise that crowd of nearly two hundred and fifty students made in that narrow reverberating hall had to be heard to be believed. They were Second Year students, who had come back to college after resting their vocal chords during the long summer vacation of nearly three months. They knew that I was a new teacher, and as I stood trembling there on the platform at one end of the room, they really let themselves go.

I was not prepared for that ordeal by noise. I should have just stood there and waited for the storm to subside. But like a fool I kept on trying to speak and make myself heard above that roar. As the Niagara of noise that greeted me at first changed into a stormy sea, with the roars coming in waves, I tried desperately, during those momentary lulls between waves, to reach their ears. "If you don't want to hear me," I pleaded, "if you won't listen…how can I teach you…how can anyone teach you…"

The roars continued and so did my hopeless efforts to be heard. A boy sitting in one of the middle rows got up and shouted, "We can't hear you, sir, we just can't hear you." "What can I do?" I shouted back, "I can't speak any louder."

Now the word 'louder' is a bit tricky, because it can sound like the vulgar Hindi word meaning 'a big male organ'. So the boys on the last benches took it up as a chant. "Loudah, loudah, loudah," they shouted, as some of the girls on the front benches covered their faces with their hands, and some started giggling.

In despair I looked at the book Professor Vanjpe had thrust into my hands: *Selected English Prose and Verse, for Intermediate Arts.* I held up the book and shouted, "Do you have this book?" and the roar rose higher than before: "N-O-O-O-O." It was a stupid question. I should have remembered that it was their first lecture and it took time for students to buy their textbooks.

The waves of roars, and my struggle to be heard, continued all through that interminable period. When only a few minutes were left for the bell to ring, the noise subsided a little. I heard my voice, unrecognizably hoarse, saying, "When you come to the class next, please bring your textbook. And please read..." I opened the book and found Hawthorne's short story 'Mrs. Bullfrog' there. "Please read the story 'Mrs. Bullfrog'," I said. "We'll take that up for study next time."

I don't know from where I got the crazy idea that one could ask one's students to read an extract and come to the class prepared. It does not work even in classes where students have opted for English literature and so are better motivated. To ask Inter Arts students in the Compulsory English class to do that was rank stupidity. But I found myself repeating, "Read 'Mrs. Bullfrog' before you come to the class next time."

Someone from one of the last benches stood up and said something. The class was comparatively quiet then and he spoke loudly, but with all the shouting I had done, and my voice reverberating in my head, I could not hear him. I thought he wanted to know what story I had asked them to read. So I said, "Mrs. Bullfrog."

The roar that emanated from the class shook the windowpanes. The young man's question was an expected one. In all that noise and turmoil I had forgotten to introduce myself to the class and so he had asked me what my name was. And I had replied, 'Mrs. Bullfrog.' The roar that greeted this reply rose like a huge wave, like that giant wave from the Arabian Sea that had, several years earlier, nearly drowned me and taken away my loincloth.

Professor Vanjpe greeted me with a broad smile when I went, drenched in perspiration, to meet him after the lecture. "One lecture is enough for today," he said, "you can begin in right earnest tomorrow. First write your application and give it to Mr. Kale, the superintendent, in the office. Ask him to put your name in the Staff Muster. Come in the morning before seven tomorrow." He smiled again, and said consolingly, "The morning students are all earner-learners. They are responsible and sedate, not boisterous like the day students."

After giving my application I went to the L.I.C. office by train. As it was noon, the compartment was not crowded. So I sat down and wrote two applications: one, a note for half-day's Casual Leave—it was the first time I took half day off in the morning—and the second, my letter of resignation. I wanted them to relieve me immediately and take one month's salary in lieu of one month's notice.

Mr. Mhatre was shocked when I told him why I wanted to resign in such a hurry. He was fond of me and had been concerned about my health when I took leave on medical grounds. Now when he realized that I was perfectly all right during that period and was busy studying for my exam, he was naturally upset. He was hurt I had not taken him into confidence.

But his anger and irritation were nothing compared to what Sita felt when I went home in the evening with the wonderful news that I was no longer plain Mr. Rao but had become Professor Rao. I was taken aback by her reaction. I had expected her to feel happy that I had at last achieved my goal. "How could you," she said, sounding very much like mother, "how could you throw away a job *father* had got for you without telling him? Can't you see what he will feel when he finds that you have taken such an important step without consulting him?"

"Where was the time?" I said, "The college needed someone immediately, and if I hadn't taken up the job, they might have found someone else."

"There is always time when you want to do something," she said. "How many times have you written to him since you came here? Just one short letter to tell him we reached Bombay safely, that was all. In two and a half years! Even that was written after I reminded you several times."

Her nagging continued even when we sat down to eat. "You don't think it's necessary to keep him informed about anything," she said. "You didn't write to him when you joined M.A., or went on long leave. Not a word about how you fared in the exam! He was so upset!"

"But you went there after my exam. You could have told him how I fared."

"That's not the same thing as *your* writing to him. He was so worried. Worried and upset. 'To your brother I'm a supernumerary already,' he said to me, 'he thinks I'm no longer alive.' The way he said it, I felt like crying."

She went on and on till Shreekanth, who was taken aback by this newfound ability of his wife's to nag, intervened. "Why don't you let the chap eat in peace?" he said; "This is an important day for him. He has achieved what he wanted to achieve, and you know things have not been easy. But instead of congratulating him, you are nagging! This is not fair." Then he added, laughing, "As for myself, I must thank God your brother is around. Otherwise you might start nagging *me*."

Sita was upset. "I don't nag," she said, "have I ever nagged you at any time? But I'm worried how Appa will take it. There is a new college coming up at Chandapur. Appa is on the College Committee and he is looking forward to Anna coming there as a Lecturer. He has already talked to people about it.

He will be terribly upset when he comes to know that his son has taken up a job here without speaking a word to him."

This was news to me, and not welcome news either. Why did I feel, when I heard about the new college at Chandapur, a sudden stab of fear?

Sita was right about one thing. She was not the nagging type. She had always been a girl of few words. Perhaps women grew more like their mothers as they grew older, I said to myself. I remembered some wise guy saying that even in case of love at first sight, one should take a second look—at the girl's mother.

But it was not that, really. I realized that it was her concern for father that made her take up the cudgels for him in a way which made her sound more like mother than herself. There was something in him—some tragic quality, a predisposition to intense suffering perhaps—which pulled at the heartstrings of women of all ages. Grandmother, for example, was never much bothered about uncle's feelings, but was always concerned about what her Krishna felt. Mother of course sprang to his defence at the slightest provocation. Some twelve years after this incident little Suneeta, Sita's daughter, who was just eight then, and had just come back from a fortnight's visit to Kantheshwar, told me with flashing eyes what a wretch I was not to have gone home for years to see her grandfather. I still remember the shock with which I saw in the child's eyes, and heard in her voice, my mother whom I had not seen for eleven years.

I felt sorry for Sita. She was sitting alone at the table, and eating so slowly that it was clear that her mind was not on what she was doing. She always insisted on serving us food first, before she sat down to eat. Shreekanth's sisters used to laugh at her for being so old fashioned but it was no use. She firmly believed that food tasted better when served by loving hands and that her husband, who worked so hard, deserved that luxury. So I went and sat by her and said that I would serve her. "No, Anna, you go and talk to your brother-in-law," she said. "I am so sorry, I did not even congratulate you."

"Did you meet Doddappayya?" I asked.

"Oh, God," she said, "That was the first thing I wanted to tell you. I couldn't meet him for fifteen days. He had stopped coming to Kantheshwar because he's badly suffering from *vaata*—what do you call it, osteo-arthritis?—in both his knees, and can hardly walk. I wanted to take Satish to see him, and do you know, it was Satish who reminded me that we should go there. 'I want to see Doddappayya,' he said, 'I want to lie down in his lap and listen to stories, like Mawa did.' When did you tell him that?"

"But somehow I could not go. Then Doddappayya himself came one afternoon, walking with great difficulty, and I felt so bad, Anna, he looked so tired and old. I think it was the pain in the knees that made him look so haggard. Satish made him sit cross-legged and lay down in his lap. He asked him to tell him a story like he used to tell you. Uncle could not tell him anything coherent. He was too moved. 'Babu still remembers me, does he,' he said with moist eyes.

"He sat there talking with me, with the boy in his lap, gently rocking his left knee on which the boy's head was resting—do you remember how he used to put us to sleep when we were kids?—and Satish fell asleep! It's impossible to make him sleep in the afternoons but he fell asleep that day in uncle's lap.

"But when I lifted up the child I realized that uncle was in agony. He couldn't straighten his legs. He is the kind of person who will always hide his suffering, but that day the pain was so much he couldn't help showing it. I asked him to wait till Appa came back—he had gone to Chandapur for some work—but he wouldn't wait. 'No, no, I'm all right,' he said, 'I'll walk slowly, I'll feel better by and by.' I really cried when I saw him walking, he was in such obvious pain."

Sita wiped her eyes with the loose end of her saree and then looked at me straight. "You don't feel like going home even to see him?" she asked.

Satish came to sleep with me that night. "So you have met Doddappayya," I said to him, "What did you think of him?" He lay quiet, for a few moments, as if he was thinking. Then he said, simply, "He is very very old."

Satish soon fell asleep. He was tired after the twenty-four hour bus journey. But I lay awake for a long time, brooding. I thought, with an aching heart, of uncle living alone in that crumbling old house at Nampalli. Then I recollected what Sita said about the new college at Chandapur and the stab of fear I had felt at the news. I realized that I had found in the news a threat—a threat to my new life of burgeoning happiness as a teacher of English in Bombay, a life I had been looking forward to for so long. I was certain I would be happy here once I got used to teaching. Happy and free. It was my freedom that was threatened. The strong bond of love between my father and me was a source of happiness and security in my childhood, but after that terrible conflict which was never completely resolved it was felt as a *bond*, as something that *bound* me and restricted my freedom. And now it threatened to become a tentacle that could reach out and drag me back; a lasso that could be thrown at me, in Bombay, all the way from Kantheshwar.

I began to review the day's events and felt quite excited at the ease with which I had got the job I yearned for. Go and take the class, said Professor

Vanjpe, and I went and took the class! It was that easy. Then I felt my ears burning as I remembered that awful lecture, and wondered how I would face that class again, and whether they would call me Mrs. Bullfrog, now that I had given that as my name! I thought of Mr. Mhatre's hurt feelings, and Sita's nagging, and wondered why nothing ever happened to me that pleased everyone.

My first year of teaching was both nerve-racking and exciting. While preparing the final timetable, a week after the lectures began, Professor Vanjpe offered to give me mostly morning classes. He raised his eyebrows in surprise when I said that I preferred day classes. I told him that I found it difficult to get up early to take classes beginning from seven a.m., but the real reason was that I found the morning classes awfully drab. The students were all working people, earnest and dull, who had made it clear to me, in the few classes I took, that they were interested in nothing that had no direct bearing on their examination. And there was no colour in those classes, no pretty girls, only a few sleepy-looking working women who looked at me with lacklustre eyes, or glasses. In one of the classes I even found an obviously pregnant married woman sitting on the front bench, listening to my lecture attentively but at the same time busily knitting.

But the day classes were colourful, noisy and exciting. That Inter Arts class was divided, and Professor Vanjpe gave me Division A, which had its full quota of a hundred and fifty students, mostly from Marathi medium schools. Division B, with only a hundred students, most of them coming from English medium schools, would have been easier to manage, but the H.O.D. perhaps wanted to make me realize that I had chosen ill when I opted for day classes. That class gave me hell almost throughout the year. They had gained a kind of ascendancy over me during that first lecture and were not prepared to let it go. I had three lectures a week with them and at the end of each of these lectures I was a near nervous wreck. God, how I dreaded those lectures.

Then suddenly one day in mid-January, a couple of months before the end of the second term, a strange thing happened. I entered the class with my heart pounding as usual but found the class absolutely silent. As my lecture, and the silence, continued, I became more and more nervous. Finally I could not bear the suspense any longer. I threw down the book on the table and shouted, "What's wrong with you today, why are you so silent?" They kept silent for a few seconds more and then broke into loud cheering. It was crazy and inexplicable but it was great fun teaching that class thereafter.

Soon there was a girl in my life. Not the kind of girl I was dreaming of, I must admit. Teachers can't choose because they can't chase; at least I was not the type. I had to wait till someone made advances. Someone did, soon enough.

I could go home from college either by bus or walking. To catch a bus I had to walk for nearly fifteen minutes to the bus stop, and I could, in the same time, go the other way and cross the long pedestrian bridge spanning the Central and Western Railway lines, and then walk for another fifteen minutes to reach home. As the waiting period at the bus stop was uncertain, I often walked home, crossing that narrow and dreary bridge which was, for some reason I could not find out, called the Monkey Bridge. I was trudging along that bridge one day when I found a girl walking ahead of me, and realized that it was Usha Barve from the Inter Arts Additional English class. She was a sprightly girl with sparkling eyes, someone I liked, but I slowed down because I was tired and in no mood to get into a conversation. But she too slowed down, turned back and smiled. "God, how slow you are," she said, "I have been walking slowly so that you would catch up, but it looks like you don't want to go home today."

That was how it all started. We often crossed that bridge together. As the bridge was narrow, we were pushed close to each other whenever groups of people went past us. Our hands sometimes touched, and then one day her fingers closed on mine, and we walked, to the end of the bridge, hand in hand.

Usha was no beauty queen but she was smart and intelligent. We often sat in a tiny restaurant at the foot of the bridge and had some soft drinks before we went home. Her parents were abroad—her father had been sent on a deputation to the Bahamas by the Reserve Bank of India—and she was staying with her maternal uncle who was the H.O.D. of Mathematics in a Bombay College. I liked her but was not sure whether I was in love. Usha must have found me a little backward. She sometimes talked about movies she wanted to see, and must have been disappointed that I did not jump at the chance and offer to take her to them. Instead of that I gave her a lecture on how much I disliked Hindi films, and how I had taken a vow not to see any after being dragged to three of them in one week by a friend at Udupi.

She agreed that Hindi films were stupid. "It's time I start studying seriously, anyway," she said, "the Inter Arts exam is only a month and a half away. But on the last day of the exam I want to see a film with you. A film of your choice, but please, don't choose a good one. I don't want you to get engrossed in the film and forget poor me sitting by your side."

I really looked forward to that movie and booked two balcony tickets at Metro well in advance. But on the day of the movie the postman knocked at our door early in the morning, before sunrise, with a telegram from father. It said, *Mother serious, come home immediately.*

The Crisis

❧

The journey by bus was plain hell. Train tickets were all booked months in advance and the buses were also full. Shreekanth rang up several people but there were no empty seats in any bus. He was told that I could be accommodated only if I was prepared to sit in the gangway on a stool, and I said yes, I was.

I packed a few clothes in a hurry, promised Sita that I would give her a trunk call or send a telegram immediately after reaching Kantheshwar, and left. But when I reached the place from where the bus was to start, I found there were ten persons in all whom they had agreed to 'accommodate' in the gangway, and they had only four stools. So I was given an empty kerosene tin to sit on. The 'cleaner' of the bus, who also acted as a conductor, folded a thick dirty Turkish towel and placed it on the tin. He assured me that it would protect my bum even if the tin gave way.

So I sat on that wobbly tin, hanging on grimly to the pillar it was placed next to, for nearly twenty-six hours. The bus took at least a couple of hours longer than it should have because the driver skirted a few large towns on the way lest he should be stopped by the Road Traffic Police for taking extra passengers. So I reached home at noon, sleepless and dead tired, my backside battered and bruised, my whole body aching. The physical torture I endured had however numbed me and taken my mind away from my worries and anguish. What had happened to Amma? The word 'serious' was never used in a telegram in India unless the person referred to was actually dying, and Amma was only forty-two.

The first person I saw when I entered our courtyard was Amma. She came out from the kitchen to throw some rubbish away and she looked perfectly healthy.

"Amma," I said in utter bewilderment, "you are all right?"

She looked at me in surprise. "Oh, you have come at last," she said, in her usual cold tone, "You must be hungry. Go to the bathroom and have your bath, food is ready. You can eat and then go to sleep."

"But you are all right, Amma? Nothing the matter with you?"

She knitted her brows in impatience. "Of course I'm all right," she said.

"Then why did father send a telegram saying you were serious?"

"I, serious? Nonsense," she said, turning to go back to the kitchen, "You'd better read the telegram carefully again."

I felt angry but was so tired and sleepy that my anger could not reach the boiling point. I dropped my bag right there in the courtyard, took a towel from my sling bag and wearily dragged myself to the bathroom.

The bathroom door was latched from inside. When I knocked, it slowly creaked ajar, and a strange-looking head peeped out. It was a turbaned head with a round face, and a big red pimple on its snub nose made it look grotesque.

"Anna," said that face, giggling. "So you got a telegram saying mother's serious? Appa sent a wire to you all right but what he wrote was 'matter serious.' But who can read his handwriting? Certainly not the Post Office people. They must have read it as 'mother serious' and telegraphed you accordingly."

"But what is this 'matter' that's so serious that I had to leave everything and rush home?"

"Matrimonial matter," she said, and shut the door. When she came out after a minute I was surprised to find that she had grown quite plump. She was much taller than Sita and now she looked really big made. "I've grown awfully fat, haven't I, Anna?" she said. "It's those interviews. Every time a boy comes to look at me and says no, I put on a couple of kilos in relief."

I don't know how I had my bath, or what I ate, or when I slept. Appa woke me up at five. "You were groaning in your sleep," he said with concern and touched my forehead. "It's time to get up, anyway. If you sleep any more you'll get no sleep at night. Go and wash your face. I want to introduce you to somebody."

The somebody happened to be Mr. Madhav Rao, the richest landlord of our village. "Meet my son," said father, sounding excited and proud, "you have seen him before, of course. But he has really grown handsome, hasn't he?"

"Youth," said Mr. Madhav Rao, smiling. He gave me a limp hand to shake. "I remember you when you were his age. You were very handsome too."

After they left I asked Savita what was brewing. "Barter," she said. "Madhav Rao has a son and two daughters. The son is an engineer. The elder daughter is four years my junior, she is just sixteen. The idea is to tie her round your neck and tie that engineer round mine, in a barter deal beneficial to both parties."

"Tie him round *your* neck?" I asked. "Yes," she said, with a touch of disgust in her voice. "He is at least two inches shorter than me."

I went to the pethe and met there, of all the people, Shreesha, a cousin, from another branch of our family, who was with me in college at Udupi and later worked with me at the Divisional Office of L.I.C. He was waiting for a bus. "What brought you to Kantheshwar?" I said.

Shreesha said that he had come to pay a visit to Nampalli. He was thinking of getting married, but had come across some problems. He was told by an astrologer that he should worship the God of his ancestors and that would remove the obstacles in his path. So he had gone to Nampalli and after offering his prayers there, was now on his way back to Udupi.

I asked him if he had met my uncle at Nampalli. "Yes, I met him," he said, looking serious. "And I tell you, if *you* want to meet him you'd better go there soon. I don't know how he has managed to survive so long all alone in that ghost house. But he won't much longer, unless someone takes care of him."

"I'll go there tonight," I said.

"I'm at Belgaum, now," said Shreesha, "at the Branch Office of L.I.C. Belgaum is a lovely city. Excellent weather, and it's on your way to Bombay. Why don't you be my guest for a few days on your way back? You will like the place, the weather and the people. There are four families there, all related to us. Very hospitable warm people. When I first went there and could not find a place to stay in, I was told I could stay in a room in one of the cinema theatres belonging to them. Then I found a place but they would not let me go."

The sun had just set when I started for Nampalli. It was the fourteenth day of the bright half of the month, and the familiar road on which I had travelled so often as a young boy was brightly lit by moonlight. I marvelled at the brightness of the moon. In Bombay the moon is dead. It is only a dull pale disc no one takes any notice of. I had once asked my students, while teaching *A Midsummer Nights Dream*, when it was that they had last seen the moon. There was no immediate answer. Then I told them that the previous night had been a full moon night, but admitted that I had myself noticed that accidentally.

I was happy to find uncle looking much better than I had anticipated. He was very weak and moved about with some difficulty, but there was an unusual glow about him, a halo of happiness that shone in the light of the lantern he lit.

He prepared a little rice porridge for me, and after food we sat and talked. I did all the talking. Halfway through my long rambling discourse on my life in Bombay, my reading and my teaching, I began to feel that he was not listening.

I mean he was *listening*, listening with his whole being, drinking in every sound I made, but he was not paying any attention to what I was trying to convey. It was like listening to music, perhaps, where the more intensely you listen, the less attention you pay to the meaning of the words of the song; because the meaning is in the music, not in the words, the meaning *is* the music. I had this curious feeling that for him the years had slipped away and he was listening again to the meaningless prattle of the child he had brought up and loved.

I don't know when I fell asleep but I slept like a log. It was father who woke me up. "What are you doing here?" he said. "I told Madhav Rao we would be coming to his house to see his daughter at eight, and here you are, still asleep."

Uncle had already had his bath and was doing his morning *japa*. I looked at him and saw that the glow I had seen the previous night had died out. He looked frail and very ill.

I went out, picked up a fallen mango leaf, carefully tore one side of it, and then folded that blade and used it to brush my teeth. The other side I used as a tongue cleaner. That was how people brushed their teeth in our villages and they never had any dental problems.

I took my time brushing, and I had to think hard. Father apparently had made up his mind about my marriage and once his mind was made up it was like set concrete. A conflict, a head-on collision, was inevitable. Better to get it over with, I said to myself. So as soon as my brushing got over I told him that I had no intention of getting married so soon. I wanted to do my Ph.D. and would think of marriage only after another four years.

As I expected, there was an explosion. "What do you mean, so soon?" he shouted, "You are not a kid, you are nearly twenty-five! No one is going to stop you from doing your Ph.D. after you get married. You are just being contrary, you oppose everything we suggest, you have always done it."

It was as yet an explosion under control but I got worried. I looked at uncle and saw in his eyes the same abject terror I had seen in them during his quarrel with father fourteen years earlier. Oh, God, I said to myself, this time he would not be able to take it. Father saw where I was looking, turned angrily and looked at uncle—for the first time that morning. He had avoided looking at him till then.

Father nearly choked. I am convinced that the two persons he loved most in life were his brother and myself. Of course he loved his wife and his other children, but there was something special, something sacred almost, in his attachment to his elder brother and eldest son. The tragedy of his life was that both these attachments failed him.

He saw, for the first time perhaps, how ill his brother looked. He turned his face in dismay and said, in a hoarse voice, "Let's go now. They would be waiting for us at Madhav Rao's house. It will be bad if we don't go. We can think about other things afterwards."

"Go with him, Babu," said uncle in a pleading voice. Then he directly addressed father, for the first time, I think, after their quarrel. "Krishna," he said, "today is Chitra Poornima, the day when Lord Hanuman was born. It's Hanuman Jayanti. I thought last night, when Babu suddenly appeared, how wonderful it would be to light a few lamps to the Lord in the evening today. I don't have the strength to perform a regular Ranga Pooja now. Just a few lamps and a simple pooja so that I can pray for Babu's wellbeing. Will you send him in the evening, please?"

"Yes," said father in a hardly audible voice.

Uncle got up with a great deal of difficulty. "I went out in the morning and brought some milk to make coffee for Babu. Let him drink a little milk, please."

He sat in front of me when I was drinking the milk. In a strange gesture that troubled me for years, he held his two hands loosely in front of him as he watched me drinking. Like an anxious grownup kneeling in front of a baby who is just learning to toddle, his hands ready to catch the little thing if it slips or stumbles.

Father had come in his car, a second hand one bought two years earlier. From the car I looked back at uncle standing near the door, looking so frail, so different from the uncle I knew that I felt like crying. That glow I had seen the previous night, caused by my coming, was like the glow of a dying lamp, I thought.

I *must* come back to Nampalli in the evening, I said to myself. Father was talking all the time on the way but I was too absorbed with my worries about uncle to pay attention to what he was saying. I must come with oil and cotton wicks and whatever else was required for the Ranga Pooja. If I help uncle, he might be able to do a regular Ranga Pooja, and that might give him confidence and set him on the road to recovery.

…owned half the land in our village, and some fields even in neighbouring villages, Father was saying. *And after his death Madhav Rao, the elder son, got most of the land, because his younger brother, a spendthrift, preferred hard cash. Madhav has since then bought all the land from the brother, and made some new purchases too, so that he is now a much bigger landlord than his father was.*

Father's mind was obviously made up, I thought, but I should not panic. If life at Kantheshwar became difficult after the inevitable conflict, why not come and stay for a few days at Nampalli? I could take care of uncle, nurse him back to health. That would be the right thing to do. I might not be good at household chores but my presence might help him, like the coming of the old cow Tunga did years ago.

...two bungalows at Chandapur, one each for his two daughters, I heard father saying. *They have been given on rent now, but you can take one after your marriage, it's so close to the new college. If you don't want to stay with us, if you want your independence, you can stay there with your wife, we don't mind.*

The 'interview' was brief. The girl came in with a tray full of snacks, kept it on the teapoy and disappeared. She was just a plain-looking kid, short and mouse-like. Madhav Rao asked me whether I wanted to talk with her and I said, no.

Father left me alone till lunch. Amma was with him when he came to talk with me. I thought bitterly that they must have had a conference and drawn their battle plans. I now think Amma came with father to see that he did not explode in anger the way he had done earlier, when he first came to know that I had taken Maths instead of Biology. He had nearly had an apoplectic fit then. He was now eight years older and suffered from hypertension, so Amma was naturally worried about the effect of the conflict on his health.

Father did not flare up even once during the hour-long argument. It looked as if he was ready for a protracted battle. He pleaded, coaxed, threatened and argued by turns. "You have to think about your future, not just about your present inclinations," he said. "You have chosen, in your career, to follow Saraswati, the Goddess of Learning, not Lakshmi, the Goddess of Wealth. Now Lakshmi, on her own, is knocking at your door. If you shut the door against her, she will never come near your doorstep again." Amma added her bit of wisdom. "If you feel reluctant to get married, don't you worry about it. Men rarely make willing bridegrooms. They all fight shy, as you are doing, but after marriage they can't live a day without their wives." I looked at Appa to see what his reaction to this was but he wasn't listening. He was too busy pushing me against the wall.

That ordeal, apparently, was only the first session. "We'll talk again after dinner," said father loftily, "I'm sure you'll think about the whole thing and come to the conclusion that this is the arrangement that best ensures your future happiness." "Of course he will," said Amma; "he is not such a fool that he can't see we only want his happiness." Appa got up and then sat down again. "Your best friend Subbanna," he said, "got married a month ago. Got two lakhs dowry. His father Mr. Ramanna Shetty fixed the match without even consulting him. The boy was in Bangalore then and came to see the girl only after everything was settled. I asked the father if he was not worried that his son might not agree to the marriage. 'What nonsense,' he said, 'who has given him the right to say 'no'? Marriage is no kids' play; it's a serious thing, a linking up of two families. It's to be decided by the elders of the household, not the kids.'" Appa got up to go, gave me a nervous smile, and added: "We are not so old fashioned, that's why we are consulting you. But there is sense in what he said. Marriage is no kids' play."

They went out of my room, and then father came back again, alone, looking apprehensive and nervous. "You are going to say yes to the proposal, aren't you, Babu?" he said. I felt miserable, but what could I do but tell him the truth? I shook my head and said, "no."

I went to Subbanna Shetty's house. It was four and he was sitting alone near the open door, fanning himself. "Ah, the poet-professor has come," he said, grinning happily, and then gave me a sympathetic hearing. "Let's walk up to Chandapur," he said. "There's a new restaurant that has come up, which serves good dosas. On the way we can talk."

He did most of the talking on the way. "It's easy to say that I too faced a similar problem," he said, "but that wouldn't be the whole truth. You must have heard that I got married a month ago. Father didn't think it necessary to consult me before deciding on the marriage. But that's our custom and I was prepared for it. We Shetties, being the landowner class, are quite feudal, you know, and we see to it that through judicious alliances our landed properties keep on increasing. So I was quite prepared for it all along. I had my flings and affairs, but I always told the girls that marriage was out of the question. My father, I told them, would come with a double barrel gun if he heard that I was thinking of marrying without his consent. You know, that made things easy. My affairs were happy because we kept them simple and down to earth.

"Our community is unique, you know. Two things, which hold us together, are that we are rich, and matrilineal. Property is inherited from the mother's side. But we are not matriarchal, it is the men who are in the drivers' seat. I inherit my maternal uncle's property even when he has children. My children will get their mother's property, managed by her brothers. What will happen to my children if I marry outside my community? They will not get my property because it will go to my sisters' children, nor will they get their mother's. It's not easy to say you'll sacrifice your property for the sake of love or whatever, when the property in question is more than you can ever hope to earn in your lifetime.

" So I had no choice and that's really a blessing. You, poor chap, you have to choose. You belong to two worlds, you are neither here nor there."

We were walking on the road. We heard a car coming from behind and stepped aside. The car honked and stopped a few feet ahead of us. Father looked out and called Subbanna. "You tell this idiot son of mine what's good for him," he said, as soon as Subbanna neared the car. "You have been a good son to your parents, but this he-buffalo thinks he must oppose every wish of his parents'. Bring him to his senses." I moved away, to be out of earshot, but father was really screaming.

"This is the last straw," I said to Subbanna, after the car sped away, backfiring and raising a cloud of dust. "I am going back to Bombay."

I found at Chandapur that tickets to Bombay were available easily as the buses were going to Bombay half empty, to come back from there over-loaded. So I bought a ticket in a bus that was to leave Chandapur at seven p.m. that day.

"So you are running away," said Subbanna and I said yes, I was. What else could I do?

I thought of my plan to go and stay with uncle at Nampalli and nurse him back to health. That would have been noble and heroic. But I was no hero, I just wanted to run away. If father could stop his car and urge Subbanna to persuade me to marry, what was there to prevent him from coming to Nampalli and pressurizing his brother to do so? No, the only safe thing was to run away.

Packing my bag took only a few minutes because I had not really unpacked it. Savita came in and stood there, silently crying. I couldn't see Moni anywhere around. "Will you please tell Appa and Amma I'm going?" I said.

"No, no, I can't," she said.

"You just tell Amma I'm packing," I said; "I don't want to spring it on them too suddenly, that's all."

Amma looked grimmer than ever when I went to see her. She also looked, suddenly, frail, almost brittle. "You haven't told him yet, have you?" she said. "He is lying down in our room with a bad headache. Wait outside."

She went in, and came out after a couple of minutes, looking even grimmer. "If you are determined to go, go," she hissed.

I bent down and touched the ground with my forehead. That's how we do our obeisance to our elders in the south when we take leave of them. We don't, like North Indians, touch their feet, because our elders are often in madi and we don't want our touch to pollute them. South Indian Brahmins, I think, touch each other less than any other community in the world.

When I was getting up I saw father standing just beyond the doorway. I could not see his expression because he was standing in the comparative darkness of that low-ceilinged room. He spoke in such a low voice that I had to strain my ears to catch what he was saying.

"Go away, get lost," he said. "But bear this in mind before you go: you are not going to come back. You have no home now, no parents. I'll tell the world I have only one son and two daughters." Then his voice rose, suddenly, and he shouted in English, "Get lost, don't show your face to me again. I disown you, I disinherit you. You'll not get even a square inch of land that belongs to me."

That was how I left home. I did not go back for fourteen years.

PART V
In the Wilderness

৶৯

People change, and smile; but the agony abides.

T.S. Eliot

An Indian Summer

ॐ

There was a surprise in that bus to Bombay. Shreesha. He had boarded the bus at Udupi and was on his way to Belgaum. He was shocked to find me getting into the bus. "You came from Bombay only yesterday," he said. "What's wrong?"

"Let me settle down first." I said. I got a window seat on the right and Shreesha sat next to me. The bus was half empty. It started even as the sun set on our left and a bright ruddy moon rose on the right. I watched the moon racing our bus, darting between trees, sometimes bounding clear over the trees like a ball and then dipping and hiding behind a hillock that suddenly rose from nowhere.

Shreesha was waiting for my explanation but I did not know how to begin. The moon's hide-and-seek game was a ruse. When he came out from behind that hillock, he had left the bus far behind and gone ahead. The breeze became cooler. We had turned to the right and were climbing the Ghats. The valley on our right began to overflow with moonlight. "Today is Chitra Poornima," I said. "The day Hanuman was born. Do you know why he is so important to us Maadhwas?"

"No, I don't," said Shreesha; "I know very little about these things. My parents are the most—what shall I call them, 'areligious'? I mean, they spend money on religious rites and rituals, but are not bothered about their significance. Forget about the significance of Hanuman, do you know when I first heard the full story of *The Ramayana*, and from whom?" He waited for a moment, and when I did not respond, he said, "From you, fifteen years ago, at Nampalli."

"No," I said, surprised.

Shreesha laughed again. He had a very pleasant laughter, something that began as a gurgle and then broadened out. You could not help liking the chap once you heard him laughing.

"Yesterday's visit to Nampalli was only my second," he said. "The first one was fifteen years ago, when my grandfather died and the funeral rites were performed at Nampalli. I was then at Nampalli for ten days.I don't think you recollect me, but I remember how well you told us stories. The last night we spent there was a bright moonlit one. We sat in a semicircle in the courtyard and you told us the story of *The Ramayana*, the entire story, from the childhood of Rama when he cried for the moon and someone satisfied him by giving him a mirror, to the final slaying of Ravana. It was great."

This was news indeed. "We were in college and then in L.I.C. together," I said, accusingly, "and you didn't remind me of this even once."

"We moved in different circles," he said, simply. "You were about to tell me something about Hanuman. What's it?"

I could not remember why I had started talking about Hanuman. Then I thought of uncle, and of how he must be waiting for me at Nampalli. I felt uneasy and sad. "Ours is a religion of devotion, of *Bhakti*," I said, "and that's what makes Hanuman so important. Because he is the supreme example of devotion. My uncle believes that we can't, by ourselves, reach God. Our Bhakti is not strong enough. But if we pray to Hanuman, and through him to God, *his* great devotion can lift us up and help us to reach our goal." I saw Shreesha looking at me curiously. "No, I have not suddenly become religious," I said, "I'm saying this because my uncle...who is very ill...is waiting at Nampalli now...to do pooja to Hanuman, and for me to join him..." I nearly broke down.

Shreesha patted my left hand. "Tell me what happened," he said.

So I told him about the telegram and the conflict with father; of uncle's desire to light a few lamps to Hanuman and do his pooja that night, on the sacred Chitra Poornima day; and my promise to him that I would be there. "And here I am," I said, "running away to Bombay, when uncle, who's sick and dying, is waiting for me. I'm a coward, Shreesha, I have no moral courage at all."

"We are all cowards," said Shreesha, "in certain circumstances."

We sat quietly for some time. Then Shreesha said, "But why did you object to this proposal even before you saw the girl? Are you in love with someone?"

"Not really," I said. "Yes, I'm rather fond of a girl in Bombay. We were to see a movie together on the day I got my father's telegram. God knows how long she waited at the bus stop where I had asked her to come. But I'm not sure I'm really in love, or if she would make a good wife. My objection was to the way everything was about to be decided, with no importance at all given to my wishes. It's my life, and my marriage. Do I have no say in the matter?"

"It's wonderful to be in love," said Shreesha with some hesitation. "You find that your life is just dragging on, everything is routine and dull, and then you fall in love, and everything is transformed. Life becomes meaningful and joyous."

It was evident that Shreesha was in love and was dying to tell me about it. A little prodding and he started talking about the girl he was in love with. Sumati, that was her name. She was the eldest daughter of Narayana Upadhya, who was running a small restaurant at Belgaum. He was not doing too well; in fact he was the poorest among our relatives there. "He looks so worried all the time when you see him outside," said Shreesha. "But when you see him at home, in his small rented house, surrounded by his family, by his wife and seven daughters, he is a different person. He looks so happy and contented.

"My parents are against the match because the family is poor. But what does it matter, Sudhakar, we Brahmins don't have a dowry system like the Shetties have. I think their main objection is that I have chosen the girl myself without consulting them first. But the biggest hurdle is my grandmother, my mother's mother. She stays with us—my mother is her only child—and has a big say in the running of the family because it is run on her money. My father has lost twice as much as he has earned through his business, you know. She is dead set against Sumati because Sumati's mother's mother and she were cousins. There was some rivalry—God knows what—a long time ago, and my grandmother hasn't forgotten it. 'I don't want Meenakshi's grand-daughter in my house,' she says, though poor Meenakshiamma died several years ago. It's all so crazy."

"The whole world is crazy," I said.

The moon was running with the bus again. He floated well above the trees now and had lost his ruddiness. I said to Shreesha, "Look at the way the moon is coming with us, running all the way. I feel like telling him, don't come with me to Bombay. The pollution and the artificial lights there will get at you and make you a pale shadow of what you are. Better stay here among the trees and the hills."

"You can easily stop the moon," said Shreesha. "Get down at Belgaum and stay with me for a few days. The moon will stay with us."

We reached Belgaum at dawn. I had by then almost decided that I would stay with Shreesha for a few days. What would I do in Bombay during the long vacation, I thought. I did not tell Shreesha about it till the very last minute. But that pleasantly nippy breeze which greeted us when we got down at Belgaum settled the issue. Bombay, I knew, would be sizzling at that time of the year.

Shreesha took me to the house of Narayana Upadhya in the evening. We stopped for a few minutes at a little restaurant on the way. Shreesha introduced me to a stocky sad looking man in his late forties, sitting at the counter, who brightened up when he saw us.

"Dr. Krishna Rao's son?" said Mr. Upadhya, "We are related then. Let's see how. My uncle, my father's elder brother, married your grandfather's sister. That's a fairly close relationship." He told us that he would close the restaurant and come home within an hour. "Very little business," he said, "most of my customers are college students and it's vacation now."

I don't get used to people easily. Everyone thinks I am a friendly chap, one who can talk readily with strangers. But the fact is that I talk too much because I am ill at ease. In Mr. Upadhya's house I found I could sit back and relax. It was amazing how those warm, simple people could so easily make me feel at home. Transparent goodness and genuine warmth, that was what I found there.

A petite girl of fourteen or fifteen opened the door for us. "This is Sunanda, Narayana uncle's second daughter," said Shreesha. "She is in the tenth standard now. If she passes she will go to S.S.C. in June."

Sunanda smiled. "I'm the stupid one of the family," she said to me. "Everyone expects me to fail in every exam, but somehow I have managed to pass, so far." She made us sit on the sofa and went in to call her mother.

They all came, one by one, the smiling mother and the very pretty daughters, including the last one, a chubby one-year-old baby who was actually called 'Chubby', a short form of her name 'Sabita', in the arms of nine-year-old Surekha. The girls sat on the ground and smiled when Shreesha introduced them. Mrs. Upadhya, a plump woman of extraordinary charm, sat on a chair. She smiled, and then shook her head in a kind of gentle dismay when her daughters were introduced. "All six of them here. I tell them not to come together when guests come—some might find it upsetting—but no, I can't stop them." Eighteen-year-old Sumati came a little later, from outside, with her father. She had just started working for a bank. I noticed that she did not smile as readily as the others did. Her father did not want to sit on the chair next to his wife's. "I'm tired of sitting on a chair the whole day," he said, and sat on the ground with his daughters.

No wonder Shreesha was in love, I said to myself. It had to be Sumati because she was of the right age, but no susceptible young man, I thought, could help falling in love with this entire family.

We ate at nine and left their house at ten. The food was excellent. The moon, not perceptibly different from the one we had brought with us the previous night, had already climbed over the rooftops. "Wonderful family," I said, "and lovely dinner. But when was it prepared? They were sitting with us all the time."

Shreesha laughed. "That used to mystify me too," he said. "You didn't notice that the girls—the two older ones—frequently got up and went in for a minute or two? They were taking care of the cooking that was going on inside in the kitchen, started by their mother before she came out to meet us. It's incredible, I know, but that is how things are managed there."

"Incredible efficiency," I agreed.

We went there the next evening too, and Radha Atte—Mrs. Upadhya—said, when we were eating, "Shreesha, your Lakshmi Atte must be be very angry with you because you haven't taken your guest there for two days. I won't be surprised if you get a show cause notice and an invitation tomorrow."

The invitation came in the morning when Shreesha was getting ready to go to office and I for a stroll in the camp area. A rather shortish boy of about eight swept in like a little whirlwind. "Amma wants you two to come home tonight for dinner," he said, and then caught hold of an imported bottle of perfume, one of Shreesha's treasures, and started spraying it all around.

Shreesha snatched the bottle from him and pushed him out of the room. "Wait outside, we'll come in a minute," he said. "Why, you have to change your underwear?" said the boy. "None of your business," said Shreesha.

The boy disappeared and then reappeared in a minute looking quite excited. "Shreesha, come and look what's there in your bathroom," he said. Shreesha ignored him but I went with him to see what he had to show. "Look there, inside the bathroom; something cold and nasty," he said. When I went in and stood at the centre of the bathroom looking down, he quickly turned the cold shower on.

"Wasn't it cold and nasty?" he asked me, as I came out of the bathroom shivering.

When we went to his house in the evening, however, the boy was sitting very quiet, in a corner. "He is damned scared of his mother," said Shreesha laughing.

Laksmi Atte—Mrs. Lakshmi Acharya—was plump to the point of fatness. I found that there was not a single person —man, woman or child— among our Belgaum relations who looked emaciated and frail like my mother or uncle, or thin like me. They all ate well, perhaps because they had guests all the year round. And they all looked happy, as plump people usually do. Laksmi Atte stood talking with us for only a few minutes and told me how I was related to her. The relationship was too complicated for my comprehension. Then she looked at her son sitting in the corner and said, "Did Suri trouble you in any way when he came to your room? He is so mischievous." "Not at all," said I, "he was all right." Suresh, called Suri, winked at me.

Mrs. Acharya went back to the kitchen. "She is not like Sumati's mother," said Shreesha in my ear; "She is a terrific cook and is proud of her cooking. She doesn't trust her daughters with it. If you like the food you'd better tell her that you liked it, otherwise she'll keep worrying that something has gone wrong."

A plump girl of ten, with large eyes that stared at you, came and stood in front of me. "I am Premu," she said. "I'm the fourth daughter, and the fifth child, of the family. After me there's only that monkey who's sitting in the corner. Now, on behalf of all my brothers and sisters, father and mother, I want to ask you: You came to Belgaum three days ago; you went to Surekha's house on two successive evenings. Why didn't you come here?"

"Ask Shreesha," I said, laughing. "I went with him."

"Shreesha has his reasons to go there," she said.

"What reasons?"

"Don't pretend you know nothing," she said, opening her wide-open eyes even wider, "Everyone knows he's in love."

I looked at Shreesha. He had told me only the previous day that Sumati was very particular that no one should know about their love. "I trust you," she had said, "but what if your parents put their foot down and you succumb to their pressure? If people come to know we want to marry, and if the marriage does not take place, nothing will happen to you but I'll be ruined. I and my family." She was right. One of the most awful things about our society is the way it treats premarital love—not sex but love—as a stigma, a stain on the girl's character. Shreesha looked quite disconcerted. To hide his confusion he said, "All right, I'll bring him here everyday. But what if he falls in love with you?"

"With me? Fat chance he'll have if he falls for me. I'm not going to marry any Babu from Bombay."

She was using a common phrase, 'Bombay ka Babu', but Shreesha, who was upset by the realization that his love affair had become—through his own carelessness no doubt—common knowledge, stupidly asked her, "How did you come to know that his pet name is Babu?" Premu screamed in delight. "Oh, is that your name?" she said to me. "That's wonderful. We'll all call you Babu now onwards. Hello Babu, little Babu, how are you?" The word 'Babu' means a gentleman in most North Indian languages but in Kannada it means a baby.

They all called me Babu from then onwards. Even Shreesha, once he realized that I did not mind it. "That's what I used to call you," he said, "fifteen years ago at Nampalli."

Those thirteen days I spent at Belgaum were among the happiest in my life. The Cantonment area of the city, I think, is one of the most beautiful places I have seen. It is cool, clean and green, and I just loved to stroll there with the kids when Shreesha was in his office. We all went for a picnic on a Sunday, I remember. I can't recollect the name of the place. It was some ten miles away from Belgaum; there was a river, a dam and some gardens, and there was happiness.

It was an oasis of happiness that I found at Belgaum. Those wonderful people, only distantly related to me, but so warm and friendly, so ready to share their happiness with someone—me, a poor disinherited chap—whom they did not know well at all, what made them tick, I wondered. How did they achieve that luminous happiness that brightened up a few days of someone so close to despair?

But all happiness is ephemeral, fragile. I realized that a few days later at the house of Narayana uncle. I was sitting alone with Mrs. Upadhya. The children were inside doing something or the other. Shreesha sneaked in to have a word or two with Sumati who was in the kitchen. I saw a cloud coming over Mrs. Upadhya's face, which was usually so calm and serene.

Surekha, who was reading a book of stories I had given her the previous day, came out to ask me the meaning of a difficult word. She had, like the other Upadhya children, impeccable manners. The right amount of playfulness and politeness. By asking me the meaning of that word she was showing me that she was reading and appreciating my little gift. I was touched. After she went in I said, "What lovely children you have, Radha Atte."

She smiled a little wanly. "They are nice," she said, "but they are growing up."

"Of course they are growing up. They should, shouldn't they."

She shook her head as if she was trying to shake off some worries. "Seven daughters," she said. "Sumati is eighteen. We have to think of her marriage now. And then six more marriages. How will we manage?"

"They are all pretty and you have brought them up well. You won't have to go hunting for grooms, boys will come and ask for their hands."

She smiled, perhaps at me for talking like an elderly person. "Do you know how much a marriage costs for the girl's parents, even if there is no dowry and no demand of any sort from the boy's side? Some gold for the girl, some silver vessels—*madhu parka*—for the boy, and the expense of a feast for a couple of hundred people. Clothes for near relations." She shook her head again. "Where will the money come from? The earnings from the restaurant are not much. We live reasonably well but from hand to mouth. There are no savings."

She was glancing at the inner door while talking. Obvously she did not want anyone to hear what she was saying. She had to get it off her chest, somehow, and in me, a comparative stranger who was sympathetic, she found the right listener.

"I have tried to skimp and save," she said, "but it's no use. You have seen your uncle's nature,"—she was referring to her husband—"he is an easy going affectionate person, generous to a fault. He works hard, though he is by nature lazy, and comes home tired. He wants to be happy with his children, eat well and see them eat well. He is proud of their good looks and loves to see them well dressed. No one complained when I tried to economize—not even my children—but I found he was sad when his daughters could not get what they wanted. Then I realized that with all my skimping I was not saving enough. I have given it up now. I still see nothing is wasted, but I don't deny my husband or my children anything. The bubble will burst some day, but let us be happy now."

"But the wedding expenses can be reduced, can't they?" I said. "Madhu parka, for example, that ornate set of silver vessels for the bridegroom. He is supposed to use them to do his pooja and japa, but the silver vessels lie idle, locked up in a cupboard. Why waste money on them? Or the gold ornaments for the girl..."

She shook her head. "You don't understand," she said. "We can't break the customs and the traditions. If we break them, what are we left with? The ceremonies will have to be performed in the traditional way or they cease to be ceremonies. And your uncle—he will die of shame if people laugh at him for being niggardly at the time of his daughter's wedding. No, there is no way out."

For the first time in Belgaum I could not sleep well that night. Shreesha was sleeping peacefully, and then he started snoring. A couple of mosquitoes buzzed near my ear and kept me awake. Where did they come from, suddenly?

I was badly disturbed by what I had heard from Mrs. Upadhya. It hurt me as if it were a personal sorrow. I had seen what I thought was perfect happiness in their house, and had drawn from that well some happiness for myself at a time I needed to be assured that happiness was real and attainable. Then I found that their little house of happiness was built on quicksand. Mrs. Upadhya was right; there was no way out. Even if Shreesha succeeded in persuading his parents not to demand anything, the Upadhyas, worried about their likely displeasure and about what people would say, would spend more than they could afford. The money would come from loans, loans that could never be repaid because there would be new ones every three years. It was hopeless.

The next day, a Friday, I was depressed. It was my last night at Belgaum. I had already booked my train ticket to Bombay by Saturday's Mahalaksmi Express. The dinner that evening was at Ranganatha Upadhya's house. He was the richest of our Belgaum relatives. It was understood that any visitor to Belgaum related to the four families had to have his farewell dinner there. Perhaps the custom started because Mr. Upadhya's wife Bharati was an expert in preparing *shamige*, a kind of rice noodle which was usually prepared and served to a guest only on the eve of his departure.

The food was excellent that night. Some of the kids from the other houses —Sunanda, Surekha, Premu and Suri—had also come. There were a couple of other guests. Ranganatha uncle told one of them, who had come that day from Udupi, that the shamige was in Sudhakar Rao's honour. He said that to assure the guest that he was welcome to more dinners, but I felt honoured all the same.

After dinner the elderly people sat inside preparing and chewing *paan*, betel leaves smeared with lime and wrapped round areca nuts. No adult meal was considered complete without paan, though youngsters were discouraged from chewing it. The preparation of paan was itself a ritual. Sitting round a large brass plate filled with accessories like betel leaves, a little silver pot filled with lime, areca nuts and an ornate nutcracker, the elders went about this task at leisure, talking all the time. Both the chewing of paan and the talking were leisurely deliberate activities, quite different from drinking, which was, of course, unheard of in our families. While alcohol loosened one's tongue and led to loose talk, paan thickened it and produced deliberate, considered and wise talk. They kept the thick red liquid the chewing produced in their mouth for a long period, sucking it slowly. If they used tobacco, however, they had to spit it out finally.

The younger people and the children sat outside on the large verandah, talking. I think Shreesha and I were the oldest among them. Suddenly Premu, who was laughing and joking till then, looked as if she might start crying. "Don't go away tomorrow, Babu," she said, her large eyes moist, "where's the hurry? You still have a month-and-a-half's vacation left. What are you going to do in Bombay?"

"Yes," said Surekha, "what are you going to do there?"

What was I going to do in Bombay, in summer? Why shouldn't I stay on with these lovely people for another month? I was about to say yes, I'll postpone my journey, when Pranesha Acharya, the guest from Udupi, came out. He was chewing paan with tobacco, and his mouth was filled with its pungent juice which he wanted to spit under the coconut tree. I think he wanted to delay the spitting as long as possible, and so stood in front of us with his chin thrust forward so that the red liquid would not spill out. He looked at Shreesha.

"Sheesha," he said, speaking with difficulty, "you belong do Namballi fambily?"

"Yes," said Shreesha.

"Death in the fambily," said the man, "Soodaka over. Vaikunda Samaaradhane doday." Then he made a sign for us to wait, and went to spit out the paan juice.

Shreesha looked at me with apprehension in his eyes. Vaikuntha Samaaradhane was the feast that was held on the thirteenth day after a death, to celebrate the ascension of the soul to Vaikuntha, the abode of Lord Vishnu. The period of mourning, the polluted *soothaka* period, would be over then. But whose death was the man talking about?

Pranesha Acharya came back after spitting that blood red liquid. Shreesha and I waited, too scared to ask him who had died. "Perhaps you don't know the deceased well," he said to Shreesha, "He's from another branch of your family. He died at Nampalli Matha. A saintly man, Narasimhayya, a great Sanskrit scholar. He was living alone in that Matha, it seems. When he died..."

He went again to spit some areca nut pieces he had found in his mouth. "It was a great death," he said, when he came back. "He died on Chitra Poornima day. He had done his pooja of Lord Krishna and of Lord Hanuman. He lighted two lines of lamps in front of Hanuman. And then he prostrated himself before the Lord to pray, and while praying to the Lord, he died.

"Fortunately some women and children of the hamlet came in to make their obeisance to God, because it was Hanuman Jayanti, otherwise the body might have lain where it was too long. They saw him prostrate before Lord Hanuman and thought he was praying. Then they started doing some pradakshinas of the inner temple. You have seen Nampalli Matha, haven't you? A very beautiful edifice. The temple of Lord Krishna is right at the centre of the main structure, and opposite to that is the little shrine of Hanuman.

"When the women, after four or five pradakshinas, found that Narasimhayya was still lying in the same position, they realized what had happened. Then of course the news spread around. But what a wonderful way to die, I say. To die praying to Lord Hanuman, on Hanuman Jayanti day! You know why we call Hanuman Mukhya Praana? Praana is the soul, or consciousness; it is air, the breath that keeps us alive. Lord Hanuman, who is called Mukhya Praana, is the Lord of all praana. He is the one who has the ability to purify our souls when they finally escape from our earthly bodies, free them from the ever turning wheel of birth and death, cleanse them of all dross so that they can stand before Lord Vishnu and attain union with Him. Only Lord Mukhya Praana can do that. So what a great death it was!"

I sat stunned. Shreesha patted my hand, and kept on saying, be brave, be brave. But Little Suri, who had been sitting quietly for too long, because he was mortally scared of Ranganatha uncle, felt that Pranesha Acharya had given a good speech and deserved to be applauded. So he started clapping.

From Red Brick to Plate Glass

Our train reached Bombay four hours late, at noon. After a fortnight in Belgaum, Bombay felt like a furnace.

I shifted residence to the college hostel after duly quarrelling with Sita. The quarrel was needless and avoidable. We were both tensed up I suppose. She had come from Kantheshwar just the previous evening with her husband and son, after attending uncle's funeral rites. As it was to be a short trip, Shreekanth had hired a car. They had reached Kantheshwar early in the morning on the Dharmodhaka day—the tenth day when all close relatives were supposed to take a ritual dip in the tank—and had left the place immediately after the Vaikuntha Samaraadhane.

My absence at the funeral was a big scandal, Sita said. "Father could have forgiven you everything but this. Uncle regarded you as his son. You should have set fire to his funeral pyre and performed the last rites. That was your right and duty. The whole pethe had seen you that day, and they all knew that you had come only the previous day. 'Where's your son,' people kept on asking father and finally he told them—do you know what he said?—He said that there had been two deaths in the family. He had lost both his brother and his son. 'Please don't ask me any more questions,' he said. If you have a heart you can guess what he must have felt when he said that. But do you have a heart?

"Oh, how desperately father tried to find and contact you so that you would come at least on the Dharmodhaka day! But you had just disappeared. Some of Doddappayya's former students came and took the ritual dip, saying they were like his sons. Some even came from distant places. But the one person he really loved and regarded as his heir, he had just disappeared!"

In her distress Sita said some harsh things and I, terribly hurt and angry, spoke harshly too. Finally I walked out saying I did not want to see her face again. I shifted to the hostel the same day, before Shreekanth came back from his dispensary. The quarrel and the pain it caused were all needless and avoidable but I was not myself that day. I had already decided to leave their place but I could have done so in a friendlier way.

Perhaps the one who was hurt more than either Sita or myself by the quarrel was little Satish. He loved us both and he stood there, when I was leaving, with such a look of bafflement and distress on his face that I nearly broke down. I decided I should stay away from their place till Satish forgot me. I had no business to befriend the child and then break his heart. But Shreekanth rang me up a week later and told me that the child had had high fever for three days soon after I left. "Nothing serious, but you know how he wants you when he has fever," he said. "The fever has come down, but if you come and meet him he might feel better."

"I'll come straightaway," I said.

It was something strange, the way Satish needed me whenever he had fever. He used to get very high temperature, particularly at night. "Some children are like that," Shreekanth used to say, but Sita was always on tenterhooks at such times, especially since Satish used to become delirious and wake up from his dreams shivering in fright. On one such night she had asked him whether he wanted to sleep with his uncle, and when he said yes she had brought him to me saying, "Let him sleep for some time with you, Anna, I'll come and take him later." But he had spent the whole night with me, holding me tight when he felt scared, and there was no question of taking him away. I could not, of course, get a wink of sleep, with that hot little body clinging to me. The child came to believe, from that day onwards, that only his uncle could keep his fears at bay when he had high fever.

Satish was alone at home when I went there. Sita had just gone out to buy some vegetables. He looked worried and anxious but not very ill. "Amma has prepared some *malpuri*, I'll give that to you," he said. I went to the toilet, and when I came out I found him right at the door, holding up a plate full of malpuris. His mother always kept the sweets she prepared on a ledge above the kitchen platform. The little chap had lugged a stool from the hall to the kitchen, scrambled on to the kitchen platform and got those sweets down, because he was worried that I might leave without eating them.

I carried him, with the plate of malpuris, to the hall. We sat on a sofa munching the sweets. I had to feed him because he was holding my left hand with both his hands, as though he was scared that I might just disappear. "Are you going to see Amma's face?" he asked me anxiously, and for some time I could not understand the question. Then I hugged him and said, "Let's see what her face looks like." He looked worried till his mother came home and made me a cup of tea.

I went to their house every afternoon during the vacation thereafter, and took Satish out for walks, either to the Five Gardens or to Dadar Circle, where we went to an Irani restaurant and shared a Coke. Satish loved to drink Coca-

Cola with a pinch of salt in it. He burped quite loudly after the drink, and looked around to see if anyone had noticed him burping. The louder the burp, the happier he was.

Once college started I met him less frequently. I had no problems with any of my classes that year, but was a little tense just before entering a class—any class—and that made teaching an adventure. It did not become a routine for me for a very long time. I liked our college, its lovely red brick buildings and its old world charm. It was considered a rather unfashionable college but I felt at home there.

I met Usha on most of the days and occasionally walked with her across the Monkey Bridge. She had taken Psychology for B.A. As her compulsory English lectures were taken by others, I was no longer one of her teachers. Whenever I went with her across the bridge we sat in that old restaurant for some time. We talked about marriage, and she said that she was going to talk with her parents only after she completed her graduation. I had a feeling that her ardour was cooling off a little now that she no longer saw me on the dais lecturing.

The year passed quickly and soon only a month was left for the vacation. Principal Joshi, who rarely left his cabin during college hours, sent for me one day. I went to his cabin wondering whether the call had anything to do with what Professor Vanjpe had hinted a few days earlier: that he might recommend to the Managing Committee that I should be made a Life Member of the Society that ran the college. That would have been a terrific honour indeed.

Principal Joshi looked nervous, as usual. He had a small turtle-like head and a longish neck, and always wore a suit that was too large for him. He gave one the impression that if frightened, his head and neck would shoot back and disappear into his suit. "Can I ask you a few personal questions?" he said, and began to question me about where I came from, what was my father doing and so on.

When he started asking me about the property we owned, I began to feel that the questioning was becoming too personal. Principal Joshi realized that too, and almost blushed in embarrassment. "I'm sorry, but someone I know is interested in you, personally. That's why the questions."

"Interested in me? But why?"

"It's a marriage proposal. From a Maharastrian family."

I was taken aback. "But I am not interested," I said. "Firstly, I don't want to get married now. Secondly, when I decide to marry, the sensible thing would be to marry a girl with a similar background as mine, wouldn't it be?—I mean, a girl who speaks my language and cooks the kind of food I am used to. And about property, sir. We have very little ancestral property. My father has acquired some, but he is a strict man and will cut me off without a square inch of land if I marry outside the community or against his will."

Principal Joshi looked deflated. "I'll tell them that," he said.

I thought I got out of a difficult situation rather well. I told Usha about it that afternoon, as we sat in that little restaurant sipping soft drinks. "Who can it be," she wondered. "Must be the parents of Sulabha Deshpande. She is crazy about you. You don't know her?"

"No," I said.

"I'm glad you don't. If you did, you might have found it difficult to say no to the proposal. She is very good looking and her parents are fabulously rich."

"What class is she in?"

"I am not going to tell you that," she said archly.

Those of us who had completed two years of probation had to apply for confirmation. I handed over my application to Professor Vanjpe, who smiled mysteriously and said that he might make some special recommendations in my case. He was a real absent-minded professor and had forgotten that he had already told me what his recommendation would be.

The college exams, including Usha's Junior B.A. exam, got over. We were to meet only after the vacation as she was going to the Bahamas for a month. So I decided that I would go to Belgaum and stay with Shreesha.

Then it came, a real bolt from the blue: a letter from the principal stating that my application for confirmation had been turned down. I was totally unprepared for the blow. I rushed to Professor Vanjpe's house, as he was ill and had not come to college for three days. "There must have been some mistake, Sudhakar," he said, "I'll come to college tomorrow and find out what has happened."

When I went to meet him the next day, however, his face was a mask. "Sorry, Professor Rao, I cannot help you," he said. He was not even prepared to disclose the reason for the decision. The principal was equally non-communicative. Every time I asked him a question, he looked as if he would withdraw into his closely buttoned suit, like a turtle. "If I am not confirmed I'll have to resign," I said, and his response was, "Yes, yes, we understand that."

So I submitted my resignation and suddenly found myself adrift, lost, without a home and without a job, in a city where I still felt a stranger. I knew that it would not be too difficult to get a job as there were vacancies in several colleges, but I felt a sense of insecurity then that has dogged me ever since.

I landed a job finally, just a week before the end of the vacation, in one of the better known colleges in the heart of the city. It took me, however, a fairly long time to get used to the new college. The multistoried building looked more like an office building than that of a college. I thought I had drifted from a Redbrick college to a plate glass one, except that it was not plate glass but ordinary glass—of rather poor quality.

It was some six months later that I came to know why my application for confirmation had been turned down in my previous college. I met Professor Vanjpe at a party and we had a long chat. "I felt so bad I couldn't tell you what had happened," he said, "in fact I did not know the whole story then."

He made a long story of it, with an elaborate introduction, quite characteristic of English teachers. "Principal Joshi was a brilliant student," he said, "He was two years my senior in college at Poona. He won the University Gold Medal in Economics, went on a scholarship to the London School of Economics, where he was a student of John Maynard Keynes."

"His closest friend there was one Mr. Barve. They both came and joined our college in Poona after completing their studies in the London School. Professor Joshi became a Life Member and stayed on, but Mr. Barve, who was more ambitious, left teaching and joined the Reserve Bank of India as an Officer. From there he went to the United Nations on a deputation, and is now in the Bahamas, I am told.

"His daughter is a student of ours. Usha Barve, a nice girl." Professor Vanjpe looked at me but I kept quiet. "It seems Mrs. Barve received some letters from two of her close friends residing at Matunga near the foot of the Monkey Bridge. She was informed that her daughter was having a very serious affair with a young professor. One of the friends had seen her walking hand in hand with the chap in public. The other had seen her with him in a dark corner of a restaurant sitting for hours. Mrs. Barve was warned that if she did not take care, her daughter would soon elope with the man.

"Mrs. Barve panicked. You know what mothers are like. I know Usha; she is a sensible girl, and has a head on her shoulders, but to her mother she is still a child. So she wanted to rush back to India but her husband stopped her. He rang up some people and got it confirmed that the affair was real, not just idle gossip. Then he asked his old friend Principal Joshi to find out about the young man and what his intentions were."

"Oh, God," I said.

Professor Vanjpe smiled. "Life is full of ironies," he said. That was one of his favourite statements, but as he used it too often, it did not mean anything much.

"Principal Joshi called you and talked with you," said Professor Vanjpe. "Poor chap, he is not used to this kind of dealing. You gave him the impression that you were not interested in marriage and was only flirting with the girl. He reported the matter to his friend, who berated him roundly for tolerating such a teacher in his college. So the Managing Committee, which met to decide who among the teachers who had completed two years of teaching should be confirmed, was informed that the principal himself had talked to you about a girl you were having an affair with, and had been bluntly told that you had no intention of marrying the girl. The girl's name was, of course, not revealed. Under the circumstances you can't blame the committee for the decision they took, can you?"

"I suppose I can't," I said. I was feeling a little giddy.

The Managing Committee's decision was unexceptionable, under the circumstances, but there was certainly something wrong with the circumstances themselves, and in the mindset of people that made the circumstances what they were. At least two of the committee members knew that I was going steady with Usha. If Principal Joshi had mentioned her name they would have known what had happened. Why don't we realize that a little more openness in matters relating to girls and love affairs would save us from awful misunderstandings?

But there was no point in worrying about what was past and beyond recall, I said to myself. Professor Vanjpe asked me how I was getting along in my new college, and I said "Quite well." "That's good," said Professor Vanjpe. "All's well that ends well...I suppose you are still going steady with Usha Barve."

"No," I said, "We have drifted apart."

Professor Vanjpe shook his head sadly. "Life is full of ironies," he said.

My new college was cosmopolitan, with the students coming from varied backgrounds. They were more sophisticated than my earlier students and the girls more glamorous. They took to me because I had gathered a fair amount of surface sophistication, spoke with an accent even that school ma'am from the Five Gardens School would have found unobjectionable and was always well dressed. But deep down I disliked sophistication. I think I was caught between two worlds, like Subbanna said I was, and my attitude to most things was ambivalent. For example, those were days when mini skirts were coming into vogue, and quite a few girls in my new college went for it in a big way. I found it exciting to lecture to those rows and rows of pretty legs, especially in gallery classes; but at the same time I missed those demure saree clad girls of my former college.

I changed a lot during the next few years. The English Department was the glamour department of the college. Professor Joshi, the H.O.D., and I were the only men; the others were all women, wives of rich businessmen or of high-ranking officers. They were not career women and the salary they got was mere pocket money to them. They spent twice as much on their clothes and make up, and on dinner parties they gave in their lavishly furnished apartments frequently. I learnt to drink, and eat meat, in these parties. I developed a taste for beer and for good scotch, but I was never happy eating meat. Two of those who gave frequent parties were Parsees, and they could not fully understand the Brahmin taboo about eating meat. The main dish in their parties was invariably *dhansak*, a thick spicy lentil preparation with muton or chicken. If you said you were a vegetarian, they would remove the meat and give you only the gravy. It was difficult to explain to them that to an orthodox Brahmin the mere touch of meat made the dish unholy and 'non-vegetarian'. Professor Joshi simply told them that he was a 'strict vegetarian' and then ate whatever was offered. He got nicely inebriated on a glass or two of shandy and was in no condition to worry about the food thereafter. But I was, and then decided that the only way out, for me, was to become omnivorous.

I never liked the taste of meat, though. I think I changed my food habits because I wanted to conform and not be the odd man out in parties and dinners, and also to break free from my Brahminical past. That bond hurt because it constantly reminded me of my frayed and inadequately severed relationship with my parents.

I stayed as a paying guest with a Maharastrian family, at Shivaji Park, Dadar, and boarded out in restaurants for some years. They were, in retrospect, happy years. I often went to Sita's house, which was just a kilometre away. She gave me information about my parents, but I usually listened without comments. "They have found someone for Savita finally," she said one evening, "and the marriage is likely to take place in May." I quietly went away in May to Mahabaleshwar, a very beautiful hill station, and spent fifteen days there. By the time I returned the marriage was over. I was both relieved and hurt when I found that no one had bothered to send me an invitation.

Sita's second child, a daughter, was born in Bombay. Father came to see the child—his one and only visit to Bombay—but he stayed on for just two days. I did not go to meet him. When Sita asked him whether he wanted to see me he turned his face away, and so she did not call me.

I was happy and busy with my teaching and my friendships. I read a lot of poetry, attended poetry reading sessions, watched a number of good films and plays, sometimes with my students. Our college was close to the City Centre, which also happened to be the hub of cultural activities; and Dadar, where I stayed, was close enough to the city. Bombay had a throbbing cultural life then. I can't say when that pulse began to fail, but fail it did, gradually, as the city became more and more commercialized.

The only two letters I received from Kantheshwar during those years were from Moni. The first one was written when he passed his Pre-University exam and got admission in a medical college at Hubli. The letter was brief and the handwriting as illegible as father's. As he wrote just before leaving for Hubli, and did not give his Hubli address anywhere in the letter, it was clear he did not expect me to write a reply. The language was coldly formal but I thought I could feel, in the letter, an undercurrent of excitement. Sita said that he had worked really hard for his Pre-University exam because he had set his heart on becoming a doctor. I felt happy that he had done well, and not a little relieved that a hurt I had caused to father was perhaps alleviated by the success of his younger son. But there was also a slight feeling of regret, a kind of ache, which I could not fully understand. The second letter came five years later, after Moni passed his M.B.B.S. exam. He did not, again, give his address. I think I understood that feeling of regret better this time. I was, of course, happy at his success. I loved him too well to feel any jealousy. But there was a vague feeling of doubt and uncertainty, a kind of apprehension, about my own future: while Moni's life would now merge and flow with the family stream, strong and steady, I, who had left the main stream, what was in store for me? Where was I heading, into which desert would my meandering life flow, where would it finally dry up?

It flowed pleasantly enough, for the time being. I had a couple of mild love affairs, but I think I was over-cautious and rather reluctant to fall in love. Once smitten, twice shy. My age was one of my problems. I was thirty-four but looked much younger. I could not help being a little vain about my boyish good looks but it also put me into embarrassing situations where I had to tell girls to come to their senses because I was ten years older than they thought I was.

Then I met Farida, a petite Parsee girl, who became a good friend. I was teaching a poem—Gray's *Elegy*, I think—to her class one day but found the students more than usually apathetic. I can fight active hostility but indifference makes me feel helpless. I had this pet theory then that the main cause of student apathy was the addiction of students to Hindi films. So I put down the poem I was teaching and started speaking about student apathy and Hindi films. I knew, of course, that the moment I started talking about Hindi films the interest of the students would be roused, even if my remarks on the movies were not complimentary.

My main objection to these so called 'masala films', I told my students, was that they were almost invariably mindless. The filmmakers did not even bother to tell a good story because they did not want to tax the brains of their audience with a new story every time. The same one was repeated, with minor variations, with plenty of songs and dances that had nothing to do with the narrative, so that the audience could watch the movie in a state of mindless stupor. Secondly, in recognition of the state of mind of their audience, they deliberately made the movies awfully loud. When anything was said or done that the audience should not miss, they introduced loud background music to wake them up.

"There is another thing," I said. "These films are thoroughly escapist. The hero, for example, is simply incredible. He can dance, sing with the voice of the best playback singer, fight with ten people at the same time and so on. Where can you find such a person? There is a very real danger here. These thoroughly unrealistic films can make you feel that real life, in comparison, is dull and boring. So to escape from your boredom you go to these films but there is no escape, there is only a trap. The more you watch these films, the more bored you are with life, and so you spend more and more time watching them."

I warmed up to my subject and continued. "Your teacher, poor chap, has no chance at all because teaching and learning can take place only when the students are actively involved. He cannot teach you when you sit in front of him in a stupor, as if you're watching a Hindi film. He cannot bring a trumpet or something to the class and use loud background music to wake you up every time he makes an important statement!" I made an imitation of Hindi film background music, and the students roared with laughter. As I came out of the class, after a rather diverting lecture, I wondered whether I had given the students exactly what they wanted: entertainment.

One student who was disturbed by the lecture was Farida, who watched a lot of Hindi films because she thought she was in love with an actor who was, then, the rage among Hindi film viewers. She came to see me after the lecture, looking upset. "They are not all bad," she said, "some movies are good, especially the ones where He has acted."

"Who is this 'he'?"

"Rajesh Khanna," she said, in a tremulous voice.

I had heard of Rajesh Khanna and of his immense popularity among girls. I had seen him only in a couple of trailers and thought that he looked rather stupid and affected. I found it funny that thousands of women of all ages, from six to sixty, should imagine themselves in love with him. But I could not openly laugh at Farida who was sensitive to the point of being fragile. So I tried to explain to her that she could not see how stupid the films she watched were only because she had not seen any good films she could compare them with.

I talked to her about Satyajit Ray and Mrinal Sen. Then I said, "Why don't you go to Akashvani Theatre and see *Vamsha Vriksha*, a Kannada film they are showing now? It may not be a great film but it's a good one. It's a faithful and honest rendition of a good Kannada novel. It will certainly make you realize what's wrong with most Hindi films."

"But I don't know Kannada," she said, "If you come with me and explain to me what happens in the movie, perhaps I can appreciate it."

So I went to *Vamsha Vriksha* with her. We saw quite a few good movies together thereafter. I found her perceptive and sensitive—though she still clung to her infatuation for Rajesh Khanna as if it was something she needed, as a protection against falling in love perhaps. As for me it was only after I had seen three films with her that I realized that I had broken what was to me a cultural barrier, so to speak. In our district a grown-up male and female did not go to the theatre together unless they were husband and wife. But here in Bombay I could do so with a girl who was just a student and a friend, without feeling that I was doing anything unusual or romantic. There was no misunderstanding even from her parents. When we went to evening shows, it was either her mother or father who came to the theatre, at the end of the show, to take her home.

The academic year ended, as it always did, with a flurry of extra lectures, farewell parties, invigilations at the college exams and long tedious hours of evaluation of answer papers. Then the three-month-long summer vacation neatly cut off the year, so that it fell on top of a mouldering heap of several such years—nine, to be exact—and I was left sitting in my room brooding over the past and worrying about the future. It is strange how a teacher's life is broken into separate years by these vacations. A new academic year means new students, new classes, new texts; and a new timetable and a different schedule of working hours. Perhaps I felt this discontinuity more than most other teachers because I was unmarried and homeless. I had only college life, not the continuity of family life most of the others enjoyed, or suffered. There was also another reason: The reopening of college after the vacation coincided with my birthday, and so I was reminded, every year, that I was getting on in years.

I spent a good deal of time, during that vacation, in introspection. I would be thirty-five when the college reopened. It was high time I settled down. I found myself in a rather strange situation: there were some nice single girls of my age teaching in the college but I somehow found them intimidating. Most of the girls I found attractive were young, and if I did not make up my mind about marriage soon, I might reach a stage when I might make a fool of myself and fall for someone less than half my age. Cradle snatching, that's what I would be accused of. Hindu society had become finicky about age difference in marriage: the girl should never be older than the boy, even by a day; the right age difference was between four to six years. More than ten or less than two years of difference would make many eyebrows rise, and Hindu society feared raised eyebrows more than any other Indian community. I remembered how, when I was teaching *Emma*, the majority of my students found it difficult to accept Emma's marriage with Mr. Knightley because of the difference in age, and even more so because of their relationship, that Mr. Knightley was Emma's *elder* sister's husband's *elder* brother. They were surprised that no one in the novel—not even Emma's elder sister or father—had any objection to the marriage.

So I started thinking of Farida. I was not in love with her, it was true, but I was fond of her. I believed that fondness and affection were more important prerequisites for a happy marriage than love. As Parsees were the most westernized of Indian communities, the difference in age might not matter, especially since her parents seemed to like me. As for her infatuation for the actor, I was sure it would disappear the moment she felt certain that there was no need to keep our relationship Platonic.

During the previous seven or eight years I had received, through Shreekanth, several marriage proposals from parents of girls of my community staying in Bombay. I had told him plainly that I was not interested in an arranged marriage. "An arranged marriage," I said, "means my parents will have to take part in the ceremony. I don't want to trouble my father any more. I have caused him enough anguish already. To him I am out of sight, and hopefully, out of mind, and let me remain that way." Shreekanth said something about *he* talking to father, but I said, "no, I've made up my mind. I'll marry only if I fall in love, and it will be a civil marriage. I'm fed up of ceremonies."

That was another reason why I thought of Farida as the right choice for me. A marriage with a girl from another community would make my break with my family irrevocable and set me free. Asking her about marriage was no problem, because a 'no' from her was not likely to hurt my ego much. I would be disappointed, yes, but there was such genuine affection and ease in our relationship that there would be no bruised ego, and we could perhaps still remain friends. It struck me that this was the kind of relationship I had been looking for all along in my life, after the bitter experience of strong possessive love.

But things did not turn out the way I anticipated. When Farida came to see me three days after the college reopened, I was in no position to ask her anything. I had already been highjacked.

Love

❧

I noticed her almost immediately after entering the class. It was a compulsory English class with Junior B.A., my first lecture of the year. More than half the students in the class were familiar faces, students I had taught in Inter Arts the previous year. But there were some new faces, students who had come from other colleges for the sake of certain subjects we offered. She was one of them.

I think I felt her eyes on me before I looked at her. She was a stunner. She had eyes so large that when she opened them wide you could see the whites both above and below the pupils. This made one feel that she was staring hard at you even when she was merely looking. I noticed that the pupils were honey brown.

I looked at her a couple of times, and every time our eyes tangled, I could feel the voltage in her stare rising. She had eyes like Goddess Durga's, I said to myself. I tried not to look at her because she made me forget my words. The last time our eyes met, just before the lecture ended, she opened her eyes really wide, and I discerned a faint trace of a rather feline smile on her small mouth. She certainly knew the power of her eyes.

Three girls from the class—Nita, Shabnam and Olivia—came to our Department Room to see me after their last lecture, and she was with them. Shabnam and Olivia were earlier toying with the idea of taking up English literature for B.A., but they had changed their mind because of Nita, who was determined to take Psychology. They did not want to lose Nita's company, they said. The new girl with her Gioconda smile hovered just behind them, but she was not introduced as I was in a hurry to go to the college office.

I saw her the next day outside college when I was on my way to the bus stop after the lectures. The bus I wanted to catch did not come for some time and I saw the queue growing behind me. After a few minutes I saw Nita, Olivia and the newcomer at the end of the queue.

When the bus arrived, I went, as usual, to the upper deck. I had often seen Nita and Olivia travelling in that bus but they always sat in the lower deck as they had only a short journey to make. This time they came up and sat in the seat in front of me. I moved closer to the window so that the new girl could sit next to me.

Nita, who was not very talkative normally—Shabnam was the chatterbox among them—kept up a continuous stream of chatter till she and Olivia got down near Metro. "Sorry, sir," she said, "that I lured away two of your prospective students. Ollie and Shab were thinking of taking Literature but they were neither of them very keen, really. It's only because of your teaching that they toyed with the idea. There is too much to read in Literature and none of us are good readers. We read our Mills and Boon all right but not heavy stuff like Shakespeare. Then the crowd, sir, is very good in Psychology. More than half the students come from other colleges, which don't offer Psychology Major like we do."

"There is no crowd at all in English," I said, unable to prevent a slight note of bitterness creeping into my voice; "Only six have taken Literature this year."

"We are so sorry," said Olivia. They got up as their stop was approaching. "But even that small group of six," said Nita, her expression suddenly hardening, "would have been one too many for me. With that creep around."

The venom in her voice shocked me. "Who are you talking about?" I said.

"Farida," said Nita. Olivia looked embarrassed. "Please take care of our new friend, sir," she said as they were going down.

I did not know what to think. I was under the impression that Farida, with her childlike innocence, was universally liked. She certainly was, by the boys. Nita's intense dislike for her was both surprising and disturbing.

But I was in no mood to brood over the problem, with that gorgeous girl siting next to me. "Your friends are strange people," I said to her, "They haven't even told me your name."

"I'm Dakshayini," she said, "Dakshayini Thakur. My friends call me Dakshi."

"Are you a Maharashtrian?" I asked her.

She laughed. "You said in the class yesterday," she said, "that you could make out which part of the country a person came from, from the way he or she spoke. Can't you guess where I come from?"

"I made no such claim," I protested. "All that I said was that English was spoken in such a wide variety of ways in India that there's perhaps no such thing as Indian English; I mean, we have Gujarati English, Marathi English, Bengali English, and so on, not Indian English; and that one could *guess* where a person came from by the way he spoke English. But I am no Professor Higgins. All that I can guess about you from your accent is…" I looked at her and saw her grinning. "You are in all probability brought up in a city, like Bombay; that you come from an English medium school, but not a very good one."

She was upset by the last bit of my remark. Perhaps I said it because I was irked by her grin. I liked the way anger made her eyes brighter. Slight anger, or pretended anger, is attractive because it's one of those things people— especially women—practise in front of mirrors. Real uncontrolled anger is always ugly.

It was only a couple of months later that I came to know that my guess was surprisingly accurate. She was in fact a student of that awful school where I had gone for my first interview. Had I joined that school I might have taught her when she was in the third or fourth standard. I sometimes wish that I had. My whole life would have changed then perhaps. If I had seen her as a kid of eight or nine, and taught her, there was no way I could have fallen for her, however gorgeous a creature she had later grown up into.

It was good that I did not enter the guessing game, because she came from a small community I hadn't even heard of. "I'm a Pahadi," she said.

Pahadi means 'of the hills'. "You are not from one of the hill tribes?" I asked and that made her bristle with anger again. "We are no tribals," she said loftily, "We think we are pretty high among the hierarchy of communities, because we come from the high hills of the north."

"All communities think so," I said dryly, "even if they come from the low plains of the south. Even the tribals are very proud people. Why shouldn't they be? They have their own rich heritage." She kept quiet.

"Dakshi," I said, musingly, "from the cold misty mountains of the north."

"I usually get down at the next stop," I said, as our bus approached my stop. "I eat in a restaurant here before I go to my room. Why don't you join me for lunch? Great Panjab, where I'm going to, is pretty good. You get the best tandoori roti and paneer bhurji in town here."

I did not expect her to come, of course. The alacrity with which she jumped up took me by surprise. A couple of months later, when I teased her by telling her how I had asked her to lunch with me on that day merely out of politeness, without expecting her to come, and was quite taken aback when she did, she cried out in anguish. "Don't remind me of that, please," she said, "Whenever I think of what happened that day I feel like—you know how Sita asked Mother Earth to open up and swallow her, in *The Ramayana*? I feel like that!"

"Why did you come then?" I asked her. "It was all Nita's doing," she said, "she had brain-washed me so." She had met Nita and her group when she first came to our college seeking admission. Nita had helped and guided her. "She is really a nice girl," said Dakshi. They had become good friends. Then the classes started, she saw me in the class and fell in love. "I had to tell it to somebody," she said, "I would have burst otherwise." So she confided it to her new friends. They encouraged her, and started planning to bring the two of us together. They told her about my routine and brought her to the bus stop at the time I usually went home. Nita had taken it on herself to help and guide her again. She sent Shabnam away so that only three of them would be there. It was planned that Nita and Olivia would sit together so that Dakshi could sit with me. "Keep talking to him, after we get down, or at least answer his questions," Nita had said, "keep him engaged in conversation, otherwise he might open a book and start reading. He eats out, you know, so he might get down to lunch in some restaurant on the way. If he asks you to give him company don't act shy, jump at the chance. You may not get another for some time."

"I was not myself then," said Dakshi. "I had joined this new college and had just fallen in love. I didn't know what I was doing."

"But why did Nita and her friends take such interest in *your* affair?"

"I don't know. But yesterday Nita said something that showed—well, I'm not sure what it showed, but I think it was not just a simple desire to help a friend. 'I'm so glad,' she said, 'that someone from our group got Professor Rao finally; and not that pale faced wax doll.' You know whom she meant: Farida."

I was quite shaken by that revelation. I knew something about Nita which I could not tell Dakshi. Two years earlier, when she was in First Year Arts, Nita had fainted in my class. When I mentioned it in the Department Room Miss De Souza, who was working as a tutor in our department, had smiled wryly and said, "Another conquest, Rao, the girl's in love with you."

"How can you jump to a conclusion like that?" I had asked.

What I learnt then was this. One of Miss De Souza's friends worked as a counsellor in the school where Nita was a student. Nita had a problem when she was in the eighth standard. Three or four times she had fallen unconscious in her Hindi class. Miss De Souza's friend had taken her and her parents to a psychiatrist. It was discovered then that the kid had a crush on her Hindi teacher. Once she was made aware of that and properly counselled, she was all right.

"There must have been a recurrence of the problem in your class," said Miss De Souza. "But this time she will know immediately what has happened. She is a smart girl. I don't think she will fall unconscious in your class again. By the way, don't tell this to anybody. It's unethical to reveal secrets like this."

I was badly shaken by Dakshi's revelation. Nita was just a kid—a frail girl who looked hardly fifteen. That this mere slip of a girl could manipulate and make a grown up person, her teacher, fall in love with a girl of *her* choice was not only humiliating, it was somehow frightening. I had left home because I did not want anyone—not even my father—to influence my marital choice, and here I was, manipulated by a kid, breaking off one relationship she did not like and falling into another *she* chose for me!

On that day I knew nothing of all this and led Dakshi rather self-consciously into Great Panjab. Jagjit Singh, the manager, was a good friend of mine, and his eyes nearly popped out when he looked at the girl by my side. Dakshi had a kind of beauty which made people turn and stare, the kind Hindi films had made popular. It struck me that it was wasted on me, a South Indian, but I could not help feeling flattered.

Panjabi food is eaten with one's fingers, not with knives and forks. There are certain rules which are strictly observed when Hindus eat with their fingers; and the strictest of them is that you *always* eat with your right hand, never with your left. I could not therefore contain my surprise when I found Dakshi eating with her left hand. "Good God," I said, "You eat with your left hand?" "I do," she said. "But the left hand is supposed to be unclean," I said. She laughed and said, "It's my right hand that's unclean."

I think it was then that I fell in love. Here was this beauty who looked as if she had just stepped out of a fashion magazine, eating tandoori rotis and paneer bhurji with her left hand, and telling me, while eating, that her right hand was unclean! How could I, who loved incongruity, resist her after that?

Most Indians will understand what I have written here but a foreigner might need some explanation. The all important question is: who am I writing this for? For myself, yes, but I can't talk to myself all the time. If I think of an audience, it has to be all those who read English—including people who don't readily understand Indian customs and mindsets. I clarify this because Indians writing in English are often criticized (by Indians, of course) for pandering to foreigners by describing, in needless detail, things which everyone (meaning every Indian) understands. But customs and mindsets are not as simple as we think they are. We get *used* to things, and then our minds, like all *used* things, get desensitized. We take too many things for granted. It's only when we try to explain them, in an alien language, to a partly alien audience, that we realize that they are—like everything else in life—tangled and complicated. Perhaps that's why I have opted to write in English.

We Hindus believe that water is the only cleanser, the only purifier. So we can never understand or accept the use of toilet paper. When I was a small kid, I had often heard my elders talking with incomprehension about this Western habit. To them it was another instance of the white man's lack of cleanliness. Janna uncle, who was the only person from our village to have seen white men at close quarters, defended them by claiming that they did not defecate messily like we did but dropped clean round pellets, like goats. Things have not changed even today. Very few Indians, however westernized, use toilet paper.

I was myself taken aback when Satish told me that his American friends found our habit as surprising as we found theirs. "How can you touch the *thing* with your fingers?" was the question he encountered. "How would you answer that question, Mawa?" he asked. I could not answer it then, because Sita, who was at the table eating her supper, flared up. "Can't you two, uncle and nephew, find some less disgusting topic to discuss when I am eating my food?" she said.

So here is my answer. We are brainwashed, right from childhood, into believing that only water can clean properly. We are also trained to do the job as cleanly as possible. Till the child is two or three years old it is the mother who does the cleaning. And then he is taught to clean his bum—*always with the left hand*—when the mother pours water. After this difficult task is mastered, the child is taught how to pour water from a tumbler with his right hand while washing himself with his left. When the task is properly performed, the fingers of the left hand clean and are cleansed at the same time in that stream of water. But it is a bit messy at times and that is why the left hand is considered unclean.

So I was surprised and delighted when Dakshi told me, *while eating*, that her right hand was unclean, not her left. I found her attitude robust and healthy. I was glad that she was not finicky about such matters like most girls.

When we were waiting for Dakshi's bus after lunch she said, a bit hesitantly, "You said something strange today, something I did not understand."

"What did I say?"

"You said—it was not *what* you said that was strange, but *how* you said it —you said: 'Dakshi; from the cold misty mountains of the North.' As if you were quoting someone.." Her bus came then and she hurriedly got in, saying, "Don't forget, we'll meet tomorrow at the same bus stop, at the same time."

My head was in a whirl. God, what a girl. Just one day's acquaintance and it was as if I had known her for years. Then I started thinking about that remark of mine that she found strange. It did sound like a quotation. Perhaps I was quoting a line from a long-forgotten but once-loved poem.

It was after a couple of months that I realized whom I was quoting when I said, 'from the cold misty mountains'. I was with Dakshi the whole afternoon that day, first in a restaurant and then watching an awful Hindi film in a bug-infested theatre. I was in a disturbed state of mind because I had heard from Sita, the previous night, that father was very ill. In the evening, when I was taking Dakshi to Chembur by bus, she suddenly turned to me in irritation. "This is too much," she said, "not once or twice, but four times today you have called me 'Yakshi'. How can you forget my name? And who *is* Yakshi?"

It was then that I remembered Kalkutika's words.

৯৹

I met Farida for the first time after the vacation the next day. She had not come to college on the two previous days. She came up to the Department Room, after the classes, to meet me. I was surprised by her appearance. Normally she did not bother much about the way she dressed. But on that day she wore a saree—the first time I had seen her in one—and had used make up: mascara, and eye shadow, and a faint suggestion of lipstick. My heart sank when it struck me that she too might have brooded over our relationship during the vacation the way I had, and perhaps had arrived at the same conclusion. Oh, God, I said to myself, this was the last person in the world I wanted to hurt; but if my guess was right, I was not just going to hurt her, I might break her heart.

She smiled at me and said, "They are going to show *Aparajito* at the Akashvani tomorrow. Shall I get two tickets for the afternoon show?" *Aparajito* is the second part of Satyajit Ray's 'Apu trilogy'. We had seen *Pather Panchali*, the first part, and *Apur Sansar*, the third, together. I had of course seen all the three films alone much earlier.

I could see, from her expression, that she had no doubts at all that I would say yes. "This is bad," I said to myself, "This is a terrible mess we have got into. The sooner we get out of it the better it is for both of us." So I told her that as I had already seen the film, I had no desire to see it again.

"That's all right," she said with a smile; "You had seen *Pather Panchali* four times and *Apur Sansar* twice before you saw them with me. So you can certainly see *Aparajito* again, for my sake."

Her confidence shook me. She was basically a diffident person and if she felt so confident about me, it must be because of my behaviour. I felt sick. I also felt my anger rising. I was angry with myself, but I was also angry with her for forcing me to hurt her.

"I'm sorry," I said, "I don't want to see the film again. Please leave me alone."

I must have sounded harsher than I meant to. She stood there, the colour totally drained out from her face, as if I had slapped her. I felt terrible. I went back into the Department Room and sat down, feeling like a wretch. When I got up and went to the door a few minutes later, she was gone.

She was in the class the next day. I had to take the English Special class five times a week that year, and there were only fifteen students: six from Junior B.A. and nine from Senior. There was no way we could have avoided each other. She never missed a class during those two years. I don't think she ever complained to anybody, but I could feel in the class a certain antagonism, something I had not experienced before. Perhaps some of them thought that I had betrayed her, and I myself felt that I had. The antagonism did not last long, mainly because she distanced herself from the other students and lost their sympathy by showing them that she did not care for it. I wonder whether she did it out of pride, or deliberately to save me from their dislike. She knew how much I depended on student response. She was quite capable, I think, of that kind of generosity.

A Troubled Relationship

I was very excited and happy with Dakshi for about a month and a half. We spent hours together everyday, after the lectures, and I usually went with her to Chembur and then came back alone. That was a pretty tiring bus journey, but I was young and in love. The only problem was that she was crazy about Hindi films and thought that my objections to them were stupid, the result of a South Indian's irrational prejudice against Hindi. "It's our national language, Proffie," she said, "and it's a shame, the way you speak it. Maybe some of the movies are stupid, but so what? If they teach you to speak Hindi better, that would be wonderful." She called me 'Proffie'— her own short form of Professor—because she said that my name, Sudhakar, was an impossible one: it could no be shortened and could not be spoken lovingly.

She was a tyrant. Despite my protests she dragged me to two Hindi films during those early days of our love. The first one was a tragedy. She had already seen it once, she told me, when she was in school, and had cried so much that her handkerchief was fully wet. She wanted to see it again with me, so that she could cry over my shoulder. But I found the movie so melodramatic and absurd that I kept on laughing all through the show, and though she protested at first, she could not help seeing the absurdity of some of the scenes herself and joined in my laughter, much to the irritation of the other viewers. At the end of it all, however, she was quite upset. "I wanted to have a good cry," she said, "and you spoiled it all. You don't deserve to see a good tragedy. I wanted to see *Anand* with you next week but now I don't think I should. That's a great film, Proffie, the greatest film ever made. That's the film in which Rajesh Khanna dies. The first time I saw it I cried so much in the theatre; and then at night, when we were dining, I suddenly remembered the film and burst out crying. Papa was furious and said that I had gone mad. You'll like Papa when you meet him. That's when I can muster enough courage to take you to see him, of course."

She dragged me to a 'comedy film' next and it turned out to be one of the most pathetic movies I had ever seen. Slapstick without style and taste can be a real drag. "No more Hindi movies," I told her, "and certainly no more comedies. I'd rather see a tragedy that makes me laugh, than a comedy that makes me cry."

But we were happy together, and wandered around, hand in hand, in some of the unlikeliest spots in Bombay, including some of the messiest vegetable markets, and tiny restaurants tucked away in remote corners. She was a great bargainer, and once even took me to Chor Bazaar—which means either 'Market of Thieves' or 'Market of Stolen Goods'—to buy something worth four rupees because the thing cost five rupees elsewhere. As there was no bus to that market from where we started, we spent twenty rupees on taxi. She often took me to the Dadar vegetable market, renowned for its stench of rotting vegetables, because she swore that vegetables were cheaper there than in most other markets. She had a way of bargaining with the vegetable sellers that was quite novel. If they said that cabbages were five rupees a kilo, she would argue and ask them to reduce it to four rupees; the argument would continue for some time, and if they still stuck to their original price, she would then say, all right, let it be five rupees, but give me one and a quarter kilos for the amount. For some reason I could not understand, they invariably agreed. So she usually bought *savva* (one and a quarter) kilos of most vegetables. I did not like to enter the market but Dakshi wanted me by her side, especially when she wore a mini, though I had strict instructions not to interfere with her bargaining. She was a big made girl—quite a woman—and when she wore a mini she looked voluptuous. The usual sales cry of the vegetable sellers, '*taaja maal, taaja maal*', ('fresh stuff, Fresh stuff') would increase in volume when she went in alone, to the accompaniment of loud laughter, and sniggering from saree clad housewives who came to the market to buy vegetables. That did not happen when she was escorted by a man.

The little restaurants were *my* discoveries. During a dozen years of eating out I had discovered a fairly large number of obscure restaurants that served good food: home made dosas, home made Chinese food, and so on. I loved the way Dakshi relished all kinds of food.

For about a month and a half we happily roamed Bombay, and then the bubble burst. One day I found her unusually excited. "On Wednesdays you have only two early morning lectures, don't you," she said, as we boarded the bus to Dadar. "Next Wednesday I am going to bunk my lectures. We'll spend the whole day together. I've planned everything, Proffie. Breakfast at ten, at Sathkar. Then we'll go to Minerva for the 11 o'clock show. Then a leisurely lunch at Great Panjab, and a 4 o'clock show—another Hindi Film!—at Broadway. Then we'll have dosas in Jyoti, your favourite restaurant at Dadar. How do you like it?"

"Impossible," I said, "I can't survive two Hindi films on one day."

"Oh, God," she said, looking both hurt and angry, "*you* are impossible. What kind of a lover are you, Proffie? You throw a wet blanket on all my plans, and say 'impossible' straightaway, without even asking me what's the occasion!"

"What's the big occasion?" I asked.

"It's my birthday," she said.

My heart sank. For some time I could not make out why, and then I realized that the moment of truth had at last arrived.

For one and a half months in my happiness I had totally ignored a vitally important problem: the difference in age between the two of us. I don't know why the question did not bother me. I think it was partly because Dakshi looked quite womanly. Those who saw us together often took us for a well-matched married couple. Once at Dadar Dakshi had just boarded a bus and I was about to follow her, when she saw one of her aunts already seated inside. She hastily asked me not to get in and the bus immediately started. Dakshi told me the next day about the very embarrassing scene that took place in the bus when a woman there thought that the bus had started before I, whom she mistook for Dakshi's husband, could get in. She shouted at the conductor and proclaimed that he had rung the bell before everyone could board the bus. "This poor woman," she said, pointing to Dakshi, "her poor husband is left behind. He was about to get in, poor chap, but the conductor rang the bell and the bus started." It was fortunate that the conductor, like all hard pressed bus Conductors in Bombay, ignored the woman, and Dakshi's aunt, an absent-minded woman sitting immersed in her own thoughts, did not notice the hullabaloo.

So I sat quietly without asking Dakshi how old she would be next Wednesday. But she mentioned it herself. "It's an all important birthday for me, Proffie," she said. "After Wednesday next I'm no longer a minor. It's my eighteenth birthday."

That was a blow, one for which I was unprepared. She was even younger than Farida. My fear had come true. I had fallen in love with someone half my age.

I knew that the situation was hopeless. She came from a small North Indian community with its own rigid social norms, and even without this age difference she would have found it difficult to persuade her parents that she had made the right choice. Now it was impossible.

I shook my head in dismay. "It's impossible, Dakshi," I said. For a moment she thought I was referring to the impossibility of watching two Hindi Films and bristled in anger, but then she saw the despair in my eyes, and said, "What's it, Proffie, what's the trouble?"

"How old do you think I am?"

For the first time in those one and a half months I saw fear in her eyes. "Are you," she said, "are you...thirty?"

It was getting worse and worse. She did not ask me how old I was, she asked me whether I was thirty. The troubled tone in which she asked that question said it all. She was worried—scared—that I might be *thirty*. And I was thirty-five.

"I am thirty-five," I said.

A muffled cry of despair escaped from her. Then she turned her face away and sat huddled in her seat, silently crying, and I said to myself, Oh God, she is just a child. "It's all my fault, Dakshi," I said, "I am the only one to blame. I should have foreseen this, I should have. You don't look the kid you are, but I should have realized that a girl in Junior B.A. can't be much older than nineteen or twenty. For forty-five days we have been seeing each other and I couldn't tell you how old I am. I deserve to be hanged."

We got down at Dadar because she had to buy vegetables. It was drizzling but she had become dry eyed. "You don't come into the market today," she said, frowning, "this drizzle can make the place terribly slushy." The rain became heavier as I waited for her outside the market. She came back in ten minutes, loaded with vegetables. I had never seen her looking so weighed down. But when I asked her to give me her bag she said no, she wanted to carry her load herself.

At the bus stop she saw me looking at her right temple. "What's it?" she said.

"Nothing," I said. "Yesterday I saw a white hair just above your right ear. It's gone today."

She smiled, for the first time that day, but it was a tired smile. "I plucked it out yesterday," she said. "I shouldn't have. It runs in our family: we go grey quite early. You have such glossy black hair, Proffie. If my hair turns grey completely in another ten years—and yours remains unchanged—perhaps my Papa will say yes then and we can get married."

"Perhaps," I said.

By the time the bus came the rain had become a downpour. "Don't come to Chembur with me today," she said, as she pushed her way into the bus, "Go home before you catch cold. I'll not see you for a couple of days, perhaps. I need to take stock of what has happened."

Dakshi did not come to college the next day. I thought I caught a glimpse of her outside my class the day after, but she did not come to meet me and I did not see her at the bus stop. So it was all over, I thought, good that it ended before it was too late. Being young and resilient, she would recover soon. But for myself I was not sure that it was not already too late. I felt an emptiness within me that was strangely unnerving.

The day after that was Saturday. I went to the bus stop a bit late. I did not expect to see her but she was there, right at the head of the queue. My heart skipped a beat. She was looking the other way and for a moment I felt that the wisest thing to do was to sneak away quietly from there. I knew how she adored her parents. She would never have the heart to walk out on them and marry against their wish, and there was little chance of *their* agreeing to the match. I had suffered hell during the two previous days and was feeling a little better that day. I did not want to start it all over again. But I could not just leave her there and walk away. I had to talk to her and make her see that it was better for both of us that we ended the whole thing before it was too late.

Then she saw me and gestured to me to go and join her at the head of the queue. "Why are you so late today," she said, "God, I was scared that you might have gone by some other bus. There is so much to do. I have asked Sakina, who stays close to Minerva, to get us two tickets for the 11 o'clock show on Wednesday. But you'll have to go and get the Broadway tickets yourself, Proffie, it's close to Great Panjab…Why are you staring at me?"

She looked beautiful. She wore an off-white silk saree with a broad vermilion border, and the bigger-than-usual vermilion mark on her forehead made her look like—like a goddess, I said to myself. There was a certain restlessness about her that made her eyes sparkle. What could I do? I knew that I had to make her see reason, but I was hopelessly in love, incapable of any reasoning myself. We boarded the first bus that came and sat so close together that some of the people in the bus could not help staring at us.

"Where were you for two days?" I said.

She sobered down immediately. "I was not well," she said. "I came to college yesterday, but went away, after a couple of lectures, to my old college. I wanted to talk to Daisy, my best friend there; I wanted to tell her about you, Proffie, about you and me, and our problems. I wanted to ask her what she thought of them.

"She has seen you already. She came to our college once specially to look at you. 'Well, he's handsome,' she had said then, 'and you make a nice couple.' So I told her about the—the difference in age. I told her you're—thirty-two."

"But I'm thirty-five!"

"So what," she said, tossing her head, "Can't I give you, considering how handsome you are, a discount of three years?" Then she giggled a little nervously

273

and said, "But do you know what Daisy said? She said, 'it's all right, Dakshi. I wouldn't bother about my fiancé's age unless he is more than thirty-five. Thirty-five; that's where I would draw the line.' I felt so happy and grateful that I kissed her right there in front of the college. 'Keep all this for your Professor,' she said."

"It's *not* all right," I said, shaking my head. "It's all wrong. Why did you tell your friend that I was thirty-two? It's because you can't face the truth. Why did you choose Daisy to confide in? Because you thought she was the likeliest among your friends to say it was all right. Being a Parsee—or is she a Christian?—You rightly thought that she would be less particular about age differences than others. But ultimately what Daisy thinks does not matter at all. It's what *you* think, and feel, that matters. You and your parents. You told me a few days ago that you would never do anything that would make them unhappy..."

I stopped because I saw her silently crying. I felt helpless. I took her hand in mine and said, "Look, I'm not going to talk to you in this vein ever again. I think it's hopeless, but I hope I'm wrong. The best time to break off, I think, is now, before it's too late, but perhaps it's already too late, I don't know. I leave it to you Dakshi. You can convince your parents, or decide to marry me against their wishes, or you can pick and choose your own time to break off this relationship. I leave it to you. And you need not worry about me. I'll never blackmail you emotionally by making a mess of own my life because you have ditched me. I'll try to live my life as well as I can, whatever the circumstances."

True to my word, I never again talked to her about breaking off. Twice she stopped meeting me and stayed away for a few days, but she came back and the affair continued. We went 'steady', as they say, for nearly four and a half years, till she completed her M.A. with Philosophy and the family shifted to Delhi. It was a troubled relationship all along. We were happy at times but a sense of insecurity undermined our happiness. It often made her jealous and possessive, and me short-tempered. Quiet happiness, the state of mind I treasure above all, was something I could never experience during our long futile courtship.

One exceptionally awful day I must describe here. Satish's S.S.C. exam was going on. When only his last paper was left, there was an emergency. Sita rang me up and asked me if I could stay in their house and take care of him for a couple of days, as she and Shreekanth had to rush to Poona. Her mother-in-law had had a heart attack there.

So I shifted to their house at Hindu Colony. Satish's last paper went off well but he came back home with high fever. This was quite typical of the chap.

He was always outwardly calm but often worried himself to sickness during exams. I think he worked too hard and kept his tiredness at bay till the exam got over, but it took its toll the moment he relaxed.

I prepared some rice gruel for him that night, which he ate with difficulty. Next morning I gave him a light breakfast of bread and milk, prepared a little gruel for his lunch, and left for college after telling him that I would come back early in the afternoon and take care of him.

I had work in college that day till two. I had not seen Dakshi for a few days but at twelve she peeped in at the Department Room and called me out. "Thank God you're in," she said, "I have been desperately trying to ring you up for two days. Your landlord said that you had gone to stay at your sister's place. We are going to a movie at 4 o'clock. Don't say no, it's an important occasion, and the tickets are already booked. Meet me at the bus stop at quarter past two, please." Before I could open my mouth she had disappeared, leaving me no chance to say no.

It was in the bus—not our usual one but one that took us to a seedy cinema house in Central Bombay—that she told me what the important occasion was. "You would never guess it, I'm sure," she said, "even if I were to give you a dozen chances." But I was in no mood to enter into a guessing game. "You know, Proffie," she said, "The day after you took me to Great Panjab for the first time, Nita and my other friends grilled me about it—they were dying to know what had happened, you know. They were quite thrilled at the turn of events. 'It's a great beginning,' said Shabnam, 'and we are all so glad. But you are very fond of Hindi films, aren't you? If you are dreaming of watching your favourite films with him you will be disappointed. He doesn't like them at all. He only watches arty-farty films, the kind they show at Akashvani.' And Nita, who was unusually silent that day, said, 'Yes, that's where he used to go, with that wax faced doll Farida.' That upset me all right and I told them that I would never see any art films with you, and I was sure I'd be able to take you along when I wanted to see my favourite Hindi films. They didn't believe me then. God, you should have seen their faces today, when I told them—Can you guess, at least now, what's the special occasion, Proffie?"

I kept quiet. I had a sinking feeling, a kind of premonition that I was going to hear something that would upset me badly.

"My friends were really surprised—when I told them that today the two of us were going to see our fiftieth Hindi film together. Mind you, that's without taking into account the dozen English films we have seen. I have a kept a record of all the Hindi films we have seen together, Proffie. We have known each other for less than two years and yet we have had a fifty-film partnership! It's great, isn't it."

I felt awful. I also felt a strange kind of loneliness—because there was no way I could make Dakshi understand why I felt so bad. Cinema was important to me, not as mere entertainment but as a vibrant contemporary art form. I loved good films the way I loved good poetry or good fiction. I still do. Good taste to me is important, a part of my morality. I believe that people with good taste have a duty to ensure that good art prevails, and it can prevail only if they refuse to patronize bad art. And yet I had grown so weak in my love that I had allowed this girl to drag me to not one or two but fifty bad films. I had wasted nearly a hundred and fifty hours watching mindless entertainment. How could I grow so weak?

Dakshi was prattling on. "Do you know what Nita said? 'It's unbelievable,' she said, 'You have really enslaved him, haven't you?' I laughed and said…"

That was even better. I had become the laughing stock of my students. "What's the name of the movie we are going to see now?" I asked.

"Why this curiosity, suddenly?"

"I just wanted to know the name of the very last Hindi film I'll ever see in my life."

We had a quarrel right in the bus. It was a miracle we controlled ourselves well enough to enter the cinema hall together. I found myself seething with anger.

The auditorium was pitch dark. Darkness brought her close to me and we stood clinging to each other in the aisle, till the usher guided us to our seats. Once the thin beam of light of his torch moved away, we were in complete darkness again.

Darkness has a way of erasing, for the moment, even the bitterest of quarrels. She was in my arms in that dark auditorium, and we kissed.

I heard—or felt—a faint murmur spreading like a ripple from where we sat, as if I had dropped a pebble into a placid pool of water; and I thought—or imagined—that I heard someone whispering, some distance away, 'Professor Rao.' A couple of minutes later I realized what had happened. That auditorium was *not* totally dark. Because we had entered it, hurriedly, from the blazing sunlight outside, we could see nothing and thought we were in total darkness. But the others in the auditorium, whose eyes were already accustomed to the dim light within, had seen us entering, and kissing. It was equally obvious that some of my students were present and that startled whisper had come from one of them.

I felt my ears burning. Smooching in a public place is not just considered indecent in India, it is unlawful. One could even be arrested for it. Dakshi must have felt equally embarrassed but her reaction was quite different from mine. The embarrassment gave her a kind of euphoria and she kept on prattling—in a low voice, of course—giving me a running commentary on the film that drove me nearly crazy. "That's Amitabh Bacchan, Proffie," she said, as if I hadn't seen that tall gangling actor in half a dozen movies already. "He's so handsome, isn't he. And his voice, it's just great! How well he speaks Hindi, Proffie, you must learn to speak Hindi like him…" I asked her to shut up but it was no use. Four people came to beat up the hero and she said, "They have no chance, those hoodlums, look at the way Amitabh will bash them up, Proffie, just look." It was her embarrassment, I am sure, which made her talk in that puerile fashion, but I could not bear it any more. "I have had enough of the movie and your commentary," I said, getting up, "I'll wait outside, till the movie ends." She tried to stop me but I went out and threw myself on a sofa in the lobby, feeling utterly dejected.

I thought she would watch the film to the end to teach me a lesson, but she came out in ten minutes. One look at her face and I realized that something had gone seriously wrong. She looked not just angry but devastated—angry and frightened and lost. She did not look at me. She stared straight ahead and said, "I'm getting out from here. This is not a good place. If you don't want to give me your company I'll go alone."

I followed her to the bus stop, and when a bus to Sion came finally, into the bus. Never once did she look at me either at the stop or in the bus. She went and sat with a woman so that I had to sit separately.

It was half past six when we reached Sion. It was peak hour traffic then, and there was a long winding queue for the bus to Chembur. We stood for some time at the end of the queue. I looked at Dakshi's face and saw that her anger had given way to a look of utter misery. "I'm hungry, Dakshi," I said, "I haven't had anything since morning. Can we go and have some snacks and coffee?"

It was in the restaurant that I learnt what had happened in the auditorium of that theatre, which made her come out looking so terribly upset. Some ten minutes after I left my seat, a man had come and occupied it. He had apparently seen us smooching, and then I had left; and that made him draw his own conclusions. "How much did that man offer you?" he asked Dakshi, "I'll give you fifty." It was so unexpected that Dakshi did not understand him at first. "I beg your pardon," she said, and he said, "All right, if you speak English in such style, I'll make it sixty." Then he tried to lay hands on her, and she screamed and rushed out.

"How could you leave me alone in a place like that, Proffie," said Dakshi, holding back her tears with difficulty. "It was not like we were in Metro or Regal. It was a bad theatre, in a disreputable part of the city. And you left me alone, and walked out simply because you didn't like the movie! How could you do that?"

What could I say to that? I could have said that if the theatre was a bad one, and the locality disreputable, what were we doing there, in the first place, but that would have been heartless. The fault was mine, I had no doubts at all about that. I should have put my foot down right at the beginning and refused to go to the movie. But after going there it was my duty to stay with her till the end. I was full of remorse but I did not know how to express it. Before I could say anything another of that day's humiliating chain of events took place.

We had ordered for masala dosas, a kind of stuffed pancakes, which took a long time to come. We were sitting up in the balcony, in full view of the manager at the counter below. He was eyeing us with suspicion, perhaps because Dakshi looked as if she might burst out crying any minute. Maybe he thought that we were a couple who might make a scene and upset the decent crowd who came there to eat. So the waiter, when he came to our table with the dosas we had ordered, brought the manager's message that we should not sit there for too long.

This was a totally unwarranted insult I could not bear. I pushed the dosas aside, asked the waiter for the bill, paid it and got up. Dakshi, lost in her own misery, hadn't heard what the waiter said and looked at me in wonder. "Let's get out from here," I said, "This is not a good place, either."

At the bus stop the queue had turned into a milling crowd. Someone said that a train had derailed on Central Railway, and the railway commuters had all come out on the roads. "It's my life," I said to myself, "It's my life that's derailed."

After a long wait, we managed to push our way into an overcrowded bus. Dakshi was always better at this than me. Once inside the bus I tried to move up the aisle to reach her, but found her desperately pushing forward, till she reached the front seat. "Didi," she cried out in ecstasy, as a big made woman seated there looked up. Didi, her elder sister. After a couple of stops Dakshi got the seat next to her and never once did she look behind thereafter to see where I was.

I got down at Chembur. The two sisters got down together busily chatting and moved away, arms interlocked, without a glance at me. I stood there alone feeling stupid and miserable. I knew that Dakshi could not have introduced me to her sister. She was a twenty-eight year old unmarried woman totally devoted to her father, who called her his 'right hand man'. She was dead set against our love. But I felt neglected nevertheless. Dakshi was herself a big made broad-hipped girl but her sister was enormous. As I watched them from behind sailing away, arm-in-arm, their broad hips touching one another, I became acutely conscious of my own smallness and insignificance.

I crossed over to the other side of the road and started my long wait for a bus.

I finally got a bus to Dadar and sat brooding over the day's events, and the mess I had made of my life. I thought I would take a cab from Dadar to go to my room at Shivaji Park. It was only when I was about get down that I remembered that it was not to Shivaji Park that I had to go; there was somebody waiting for me, at my sister's place, hungry and ailing: my nephew Satish.

He looked tired and sleepy when he opened the door. "Did you eat anything?" I asked him. "There was nothing to eat," he said; "I finished the gruel at noon."

I touched his forehead and saw that he still had fever. "I'll make some rice gruel," I said, "I haven't eaten anything myself throughout the day." It was close to midnight when we sat down to eat. Neither of us liked rice gruel but it tasted all right that night. Satish ate better than he did the previous night and I thought that was a good sign.

When I was about to fall asleep, I heard Satish groaning. I found him half-awake, perspiring profusely. His bed was wet, and the thin muslin shirt he wore was dripping. I remembered how he used to sweat like that in his childhood when fever left him, and how I or Sita used to sit by his side and towel him. So I sat wiping his sweat with a towel, and patting his head, till his groans changed to happy cat-like purrs, and then to gentle snoring. As he fell asleep I saw on his face, again, after several years, the same smile I used to see in his childhood—when fever left him, and someone he loved, his mother or uncle, sat by his side.

For the first time that day I felt like crying. "I have failed," I found myself saying, in my fatigue and despair, "I have failed your love." Then I realized that I was not saying that to Satish, who was sleeping. I was saying it to my uncle.

There was no repetition of that awful day ever again. Dakshi was more restrained thereafter and I was more careful. Her exam was approaching and that Amitabh Bachchan film was in fact the last film she wanted to see during that academic year. I wish I had realized that then.

She got a high Second Class in B.A. and then enrolled for M.A. with Philosophy. As she was no longer a student of our college, we met less frequently than before. It was nearly six months after the Bacchan film that she wanted to see a Hindi film again. She was so circumspect and apologetic about it that she made me feel, once again, very unhappy about my earlier behaviour.

"It's not a bad film, Proffie," she said, "it's in fact a very good one. Do you know why I want to see it? It's because Papa asked me yesterday if I had seen it, and how it was."

"Your Papa? But you have always said that he is not interested in movies, and knows nothing about them."

"That's true," said Dakshi. "That's in fact the only grouse Mama has with him, because she would like to see a Hindi movie once in a while, but he is not interested. But this film is special, Proffie. Papa has read the novel and loves it, so he wanted to know what the film was like."

"What film are you talking about?"

"*Bhuvan Shome.*"

I started laughing. Mrinal Sen's *Bhuvan Shome* was a film I badly wanted to see. I was in fact on the verge of asking her whether she would like to see it but was worried that she might dismiss it as 'arty-farty'.

So *Bhuvan Shome* was the fifty-first Hindi film we saw together. Dakshi found the film delightful. There was nothing wrong with her taste, really. She simply refused to discriminate when it came to watching films—like most people of her age. So one should perhaps call the trouble between us 'generation gap'.

Her three elder sisters got married, one after the other, when she was doing her M.A.. The grooms were all from Delhi, and as most of their relatives were in that city, the marriages took place there. Her elder brother, the fourth child of her parents, was in I.I.T., Kharagpur. Dakshi's father had spent all his working years in Bombay and so had some attachment to the city, but he had retired ten years earlier and there was no reason for him to stay on. So five months after Dakshi passed her M.A. the family sold their Chembur flat and shifted to Delhi.

Dakshi was terribly upset at the time of parting. As for me, I had long realized that our affair had reached a dead end and was leading us nowhere.

There was no chance of her parents agreeing to our marriage. She had twice broached the subject with her father but he had reacted so violently to my age and South Indian origin that Dakshi had to accept that there was no point in talking to him again, at least in the near future. I had my doubts too. I loved her, of course, and would miss her badly. But that night at Dadar, sitting by Satish, I had realized that there was something even more important than love: one's freedom to do the right thing. I was not sure that marriage with a strong person like Dakshi would leave my freedom intact. What had hurt my love for Dakshi most was not that she was at times overbearing, and dragged me to films I did not want to see, but that she prevented me from taking care of my nephew when he needed my care. I knew that it was not her fault—I had not told her that Satish was ill—but though I could forgive her, I could not forgive myself. Why did I allow her to sweep me off my feet like that? It meant that our relationship was something I could not handle.

So when the Thakur family shifted to Delhi I accepted it as something that had to happen. In Delhi Dakshi might be able to think clearly and decide what to do. I could, in the mean time, live my life the way I wanted to, and see what difference her absence would make to it.

We wrote to each other regularly. She wrote two or three letters a week, and if I did not reply every letter, immediately, she used to panic and dash off another letter. So I, who had written only a couple of letters in my entire life till then, became an expert letter writer. Had I thought of writing a novel then I would have used, like Richardson, the epistolary form.

I could blame Dakshi for one thing though—she had prevented me from visiting Kantheshwar for four years. A couple of months after I met her I had heard, from Sita, that father was very ill. Sita felt that he wanted to see me. I decided to go home in the summer vacation but Dakshi panicked when I mentioned it to her. She knew what had happened during my earlier visit and was scared that pressure might be brought on me again to get married. So for four years she kept me away from home.

In April I wrote to her that I was planning to go home to see my ailing father. Her reply was all about how it was my fiftieth letter to her and how much she loved and treasured my letters and read them often. But she wrote nothing about my decision to go home. Apparently she felt she had lost her right to stop me.

Home Again

So I went home in May, fourteen years after I had left the place in despair. I did not know that I was away for so many years—time does fly in Bombay, as Patrick Pinto's uncle had found out several years earlier. The sun had not risen when I reached Kantheshwar. I was some fifteen feet from our main door when I saw Amma coming out. She recognized me immediately. "Stop where you are," she screamed, "don't enter the house."

I stood in disbelief. I had not expected this kind of welcome. She saw my bewilderment and said, in a quieter tone, "Don't you know you have come home after fourteen years? You should not enter the house through the main door, you should pass through the cowshed first."

The cowshed housed a buffalo, a cow and a calf. The buffalo ignored me but the cow and the calf looked startled. They had apparently not seen a well-dressed man walking on that floor, covered with dung, with his shoes on.

"It's not I who has kept count of the number of years you were away," said Amma, as I sat in front of her in the kitchen, sipping coffee. "It's your Appa. He got Sita's letter five days ago. 'Rama is coming back home,' he said to me. 'Which Rama?' I said. Sometimes I don't understand his talk these days. 'Our Rama,' he said, 'who has spent fourteen years in the wilderness.' Then he said…"

Amma started crying quietly. I had never seen her cry before. "What did he say," I said, finding it difficult to speak in a normal voice.

She waited for some time. Then she said, without looking at me, "He said, 'Rama will be surprised …to find Dasharatha still alive…though he's dying.' That's how he talks these days."

Amma wiped her eyes with her *seragu* and told me how Sita had brought the news, four years earlier, that I was coming home in May. "Your Appa was quite excited," she said. "Then May passed, and you did not turn up. One day he suddenly said, 'Babu won't come for another four years.' 'Why do you say that?' I asked. 'Because his banishment to the forest is for fourteen years,' he said. That was when he first referred to *The Ramayana* and he has been referring to it ever since. Not continuously, because he talks very little these days. A few days later he said, 'This Dasharatha did not have to die when

Rama went away. Why should he? He is a bogus Dasharatha, not the real one who loved Rama more than his life. The real one died of a broken heart, all alone, at Nampalli, praying to Lord Hanuman to take care of his Rama.' He keeps everything bottled up within him, Babu. What's really eating his innards is not so much your going away, as his brother's death. He once had severe heartburn. Do you know what he said? He said that the fire he lit to cremate his brother was still burning inside."

I kept quiet. What could I say? The parallels to *The Ramayana* were striking. In that epic Dasharatha, the father of Rama, had died of a broken heart when Rama was banished to the forest for fourteen years. I realized that my homecoming was not going to be a picnic. Old wounds were still bleeding; even mine.

I was thoroughly shaken by father's appearance when I met him. He still walked erect, but every step was taken with deliberate effort. He had not grown thinner—in fact he looked a little puffed up—but he appeared to be in constant pain. My efforts to have a heart to heart chat with him failed. He was always a reticent man but now he had become more laconic than ever. Sometimes he got up when I was talking to him, murmuring "I'm not well," and slipped back into his bedroom.

What upset Amma most was the way father's anguish was affecting his other relationships. "He was so happy when Moni came as a doctor and started practising with him. 'I have not two but four hands now,' he used to say. He thought highly of Moni and said he was learning some new things from him. But everything changed after Sita brought the news you were coming in May and you did not come. One day he came home quite depressed. Some patient who came when Moni was out on a visit did not want to be treated by him, and told him that he was 'waiting for Dr. Moni.' 'I have become superfluous now,' he said. It was then that he said that Moni was Bharata, who had taken over Rama's kingdom. 'Who am I then,' I asked, and he said that I was Kaikeyi!"

That afternoon I sat for a long time under the suragi tree, brooding. I was trying to figure out how father's mind was working. Moni had become a highly successful doctor. He was there to assist father when he needed assistance, and now he had taken over his practice because father, with his ill health, could not carry on. I was sure father was happy about Moni's success. But pain over his elder son's abdication remained, and in his illness that pain perhaps outweighed his happiness at his younger son's success.

But calling Amma Kaikeyi—Rama's stepmother, who wanted him banished to the forest, and her son Bharata crowned in his place—that was outrageous and enigmatic. I had a grouse all through my childhood that my mother did not love me as much as she loved Moni. Perhaps I was not wrong. But I did not know that father had perceived the problem. Did he perhaps feel that his wife's neglect of her eldest child had led to his alienation?

Human mind is a labyrinth, I said to myself. My father was not an articulate man but he was a man of strong feelings. God knows what thoughts and feelings troubled him and made him talk in a way that Amma could not understand.

I stayed at Kantheshwar for just twenty days. I spent most of the time reading in the upstairs bedroom. Moni had a fairly large collection of Kannada and English novels. Among them I found eight books by a new writer: K. Vasudeva Bhat.

I was surprised. I read the novels with a good deal of curiosity. They were shapeless and repetitious, but there was flow and a kind of crude vigour. The same characters appeared under different names in the different novels. That was perhaps inevitable considering that Vasanna had written nearly thirty novels in the preceding fifteen years. His first book, I found, was *Padma Remembers and Other Stories*. Moni did not have a copy of that work.

Some fifteen years earlier an enterprising publisher had started what he called 'Kannada Pocket Books.' The books were no different from the other books in appearance—most Kannada books were, and still are, paperbacks—but he printed five thousand copies instead of the usual one thousand, and priced the books low. A four-hundred-page novel would have cost four rupees then but he could price it Rs. 1.50 because he printed more copies, and that attracted a large number of buyers. The first edition of the first novel published was sold out in a matter of days. The great novel boom was on. Publishers went hunting for new authors. It was then that Vasanna and a host of other writers appeared on the scene.

"How come you have so many books by Vasudeva Bhat?" I asked Moni. "He gave them to me," said Moni, quite proudly. "He had come to our college to inaugurate our Kannada Association, of which I was the secretary then. I told him I was Dr. Krishna Rao's son and he was delighted. He told me he had seen me as an infant. He came to my room in the evening and gave me copies of a dozen of his novels. He asked me a lot of questions about life in a medical college. When he came here a couple of months ago he was again very inquisitive. Wanted to know how women react when they have to show their private parts to a young male doctor, and so on. 'You are sitting on a gold mine,' he said to me; 'why don't you write, Mohan. I'll see to it that your novels are published.'

"Did he ever mention my name?" I asked. "Oh, yes," said Moni, "He asked me what you were doing and whether you had written anything. 'Not that I know of,' I said. 'It's a pity,' he said, 'because he showed some promise when he was a kid. But not all people, alas, can keep the celestial fire burning.' He is a nice person, Anna. Not proud and jealous like other established writers."

Two days before the day of my departure Appa spoke to me on his own. "You must be bored here," he said. "No, no," I said, "I'm at home, and I have lots of books to read. What more can I ask for?"

"Then why are you leaving so early?" he said. "You have been here for eighteen days. Fourteen years of absence—to be compensated by just twenty days?"

"I'll make it forty before the year is out," I said. "I'll come back in October, Appa, during the Diwali vacation."

"I hope I'll be alive then," he said. He sat brooding for some time and then looked at me. "I want you to make a promise," he said. "Please remember the full moon day of the month of *Mesha*. When you go back to Bombay find out from a *purohit* when that day comes. That's the day your uncle's *Shraddha* is to be performed. I have been doing it all these years, but now, I don't know…You'll have to do it from next year, Babu. He had no other son but you."

"He died on Chitra Poornima," I said.

"Some years the day comes on Chitra Poornima, some years it comes a month later, on the next full moon day," said father, suddenly sounding very tired. "It's all so confusing because we follow the solar calendar. I don't understand how it is calculated but a competent purohit will tell you when's the day. You just remember, *Poornima in the month of Mesha.*"

It was this talk which made me feel that I must pay a visit to Nampalli. I asked Moni the next day whether there was anyone at Nampalli Matha to do pooja. He was busy in the dispensary, which was full of patients, most of whom, I noted, were young women. "Ah, yes," he said, with that childlike smile which showed why he was so popular. "There is one Mr. Acharya, a very devout man."

So I bought two coconuts and some plantains in the market and went to Nampalli in the afternoon. Memories haunted me all the way, vague, confused memories of a childhood spent at Nampalli thirty years earlier, and of the night I had spent in the Matha on the eve of Chitra Poornima fourteen years ago.

Nampalli Matha looked, not like the ghost house it was when uncle stayed there alone, but the same as in my childhood. I found a couple of little children playing hide and seek around the vrindavanas, under the old gooseberry tree, as I used to with Lakshmi, Aditi and Savitri thirty-five years earlier. A slightly older girl sat on the verandah holding a little baby in her arms. I asked her whether Mr. Acharya was at home.

She turned her head to the door and screamed, "Amma, someone has come asking for Appayya." She had to scream twice, before a hoarse female voice was heard, from deep within the Matha, saying, "Yes, yes, I'm coming."

A tall gaunt woman came to the door. It was difficult to say how old she was because her hair was covered with some fine white powder. Her saree and hands were also covered with it. She was evidently preparing happalas, which involved the use of fine powdered rice. She peered at me and said, "What do you want?"

I took out the coconuts and plantains from my bag. "At what time is the pooja at night performed?" I asked. "I want these to be offered to God then."

"He has gone to Chandapur," she said. "He might come late, maybe after eight. The pooja will be after nine then."

"I can't wait that long," I said. I took out a ten rupee note and kept it on the coconuts. "Please tell your husband to do tonight's pooja in my name."

"Babu," she said, sending a shiver down my spine. It was as if the call had come from the cavernous depths of my past. A boy of about eleven or twelve appeared, and she said to him, "Babu, take down this gentleman's name and *nakshatra*, tonight's pooja is to be in his name."

Nakshatra means star. We are all identified by the star we are born under, especially when we perform any religious rites. "This pooja or rite is performed for the benefit of so and so, born under such and such a star," the priest announces at the start of the pooja. Only then is one assured of the benefits of it.

The woman stood there staring at me and frowning, when her son Babu took down my name and nakshatra. When I said, "Sudhakar Rao, Vishakha Nakshatra," a muffled cry escaped from her. She gaped at me and said, "Oh God, it's Babu! Babu, Babu, Babu, where have you come from?"

I recognized her then. She was unrecognizable, really, but something in the way she pronounced my name, some forgotten gesture or mannerism, which she must have shed with the passage of years but which came back now, when she saw me, her childhood companion, helped me to see in that plain aging woman the proud beautiful girl who had left Nampalli, stars in her eyes, some thirty years earlier. "Savitri?" I said, in utter disbelief, "You are Savitri, aren't you?"

It was Savitri all right. She called me inside and made a cup of coffee for me. The children came and sat round me and I felt bad that I had brought nothing for them. Apart from the five I had seen already, there were two other girls who were busy preparing happalas. It was a scene from the past, from my childhood. Savitri said that her eldest daughter was married and had a one-year-old son. "I am now a grandmother," she said. Her second son was away working in a restaurant.

"Are you wondering, Babu, how I came to be here? I'll tell you the story, but you must stay with us tonight. My husband has heard of you and would love to meet you. He knows that you were the only brother I knew in my childhood."

I told her that I *had* to go home because I was leaving for Bombay the next day and father would be worried if I did not reach home soon. "But wait till your brother-in-law comes," she said and I agreed.

Savitri's story was a long one. Sometimes she was so deeply moved that she became incoherent but such moments were rare. She was always a lucid speaker, unlike Lakshmi.

She was very happy at her father's place for some years. "You haven't seen the place, Babu," she said, "It's a palace, not a house." She lived like a princess. Her mother doted upon the little motherless child put into her care and Savitri herself was very fond of her brother. Troubles started when she grew up and her father started looking for a son-in-law. There was a well-to-do man in the village, not as rich as her father but quite powerful. His only son, Nagesh, was a good-looking Lothario who had set his eyes on Savitri. A marriage proposal came from them but Savitri's father turned it down. "Your son has no character," he told the man, "I hear he has affairs with some girls among your tenants." Father and son took that as an insult and became his mortal enemies.

They spread all kinds of rumours about Savitri, that she had had several affairs with boys, including Nagesh. When a marriage was almost fixed, Nagesh himself went and met the family of the groom and asked them why they wanted 'second hand goods'. Savitri's father did not know what to do. Finally he found a boy from a very poor family who was studying Sanskrit and priesthood in one of the Mathas at Udupi. "I don't want a rich son-in-law," he said, "I have enough money as it is." He wanted a *good* boy who would do the pooja at their family shrine and help him to take care of his property till his son grew up.

The enmity continued even after Savitri's marriage. 'Nagesh' means the king of cobras, and the young man proved to be a poisonous creature with a long memory. Savitri's younger brother grew up into a thoroughly spoilt child. "It wasn't his fault, perhaps," said Savitri, "Amma doted on him and spoilt him. She would never let father punish him, whatever his offence." By the time Manohar, Savitri's brother, was twelve, her father had fallen ill and lost all control over his son. Then they realized that Nagesh had been cultivating the boy's friendship ever since he was ten, and had him completely under his influence. "It's terrible, Babu," said Savitri in a horrified whisper, "Can you believe it, Manu started going to a brothel with that wretch when he was just twelve!" The agreement between the two was that Nagesh would finance him till he came into possession of his wealth and then he would repay Nagesh with interest.

Savitri's father died when Manohar was fourteen, and there was no stopping him thereafter. Her husband could do nothing, the boy even threatening to beat him up with hired ruffians. "My husband is such a saintly man," said Savitri, "He felt helpless." All the things in the house—silver articles, gold ornaments and even wall clocks and so on—were sold by the boy even when he was a minor, and once he came to majority all the lands and other immovable properties were disposed off. It was then that Savitri's husband met the Swami and decided to take up the pooja of Nampalli Matha.

"My husband is happy," said Savitri. "We are poor, he says, but we are free."

"Where is Gangamma?" I said.

"Amma died about ten years ago," said Savitri, "We had shifted to Nampalli two years earlier. My brother was twenty, and had sold everything except the house by then. But oh Babu, the way he cried when Amma died, the way he was inconsolable! He hadn't cried at all when father died and we all thought that he was heartless. But he had a heart all right and it broke when Amma died. But what is the use? He sold the house for a pittance, within a month of Amma's death, to the same Nagesh Hebbar. That man has become very powerful now. Have you heard of him? He is the local M.L.A. now, a big leader of the Congress party. He has thrown Manu out and Manu goes about telling people that he is going to take revenge. But what can he do to that man? A poor man's anger hurts his own stomach, as they say.

"I met him last year, most unexpectedly. Raja Rao—your friend Raju, who is a rich hotelier now—wanted some religious rites performed because his horoscope showed that he was passing through a dangerous period. He had *Kuja Rahu Sandhi*, and my husband, who is a good astrologer, told him what poojas, homas, and japas had to be performed to propitiate the planets. The rites were performed here, with my husband as the main priest. But the day was an auspicious one, there were lots of marriages all around and it was impossible to get cooks to prepare the feast. So Raja Rao had to call a team of cooks all the way from Udupi. I was shocked to find that one of the team was Manohar.

"I recognized him immediately though he has changed a lot and has a bushy beard now. I did not talk to him because I was not sure he wanted me to. I watched him working. He knows his job, Babu, God knows where he learnt to cook, but he is quite an expert. He went away after the feast, not with the other cooks, but alone. A few minutes after he left, Gayatri came in—she is the one who is holding the baby—and gave me thirty rupees. She said the bearded Mawa had given it to her. I asked the head cook about him and he said that Manohar was not a regular member of their team but they called him whenever they needed extra hands. 'How much did you pay him?' I asked, and he said, 'Thirty rupees.'"

Savitri was silent for a moment. "He did not even keep a rupee for his bus fare. Gave everything he had to his niece whom he had never seen before. He was always like that, recklessly generous. Why do good people fall into evil ways and ruin themselves, Babu. He was such a lovely child, such a lovable boy."

Savitri's husband came from Chandapur then, carrying on his head a heavy load of vegetables. He looked younger than Savitri. He was apparently more at peace with the world and had accepted his changed fortunes better.

"Please stay for the pooja," he said. "If you *have* to go home tonight, I and Babu will come with you, after the pooja, till you reach the main road."

But he did not have to take that trouble. Appa sent Moni on his motorcycle to see what had happened to me. I am scared of pillion riding but that night I was so full of concern for Savitri's fate that before I realized I was on a wobbly bike on a treacherous road we had reached Kantheshwar. Fate plays strange tricks on people. Laksmi or Aditi would have been at home at Nampalli Matha, but Fate chose Savitri to be the unhappy mistress of that crumbling mansion. I thought of Professor Vanjpe and his hackneyed statement, 'Life is full of ironies.'

Next day I left for Bombay. There was no moon in the sky when I left. It was the dark half of the month.

Dakshi and Delhi

When a teacher like me speaks of a year he does not usually refer to the calendar year beginning with January, or of the Financial Year, or of the Hindu Year beginning with Yugadi, which comes in April. He speaks of the academic year beginning around June 20. The year which followed my visit home after fourteen years was surely the darkest year of my life.

My landlady died on the last day of June. She had met with an accident thirteen years earlier when she was on the pillion of her husband's scooter. A taxi had hit them from behind and sped away. She was unconscious but there were no outward signs of any injury. Her husband had only superficial wounds and cuts, but he was bleeding profusely and so received more attention than she did initially. It was after she regained consciousness in the hospital that they discovered that she had a serious spinal injury and had become paraplegic.

They had some financial problems then. They had bought a new house, the wife lost her job because she was immobilized after the accident, the compensation for the accident took a long time to come and there were medical expenses. That was why they decided to take a paying guest. They gave me the hall, which was their best room, because it had a separate entrance. I liked the place and they liked me. So I stayed on there for thirteen years though initially they had wanted to rent out that room for only a year or two.

The doctors had ruled out surgery in the case of my landlady but there was hope that there might be a spontaneous recovery. She clung to that hope for thirteen years. She did not allow her husband to bring a wheelchair because she said that she was going to walk some day. Finally in the first week of June that year he brought a wheelchair home. She sat on it only once. Something gave way then, her desire to live snapped, and by the end of the month she was dead.

I admired both my landlady and her husband a great deal. They were simple people but I found something heroic in the way they faced adversity. They were strongly attached to each other till the end. On some nights when I came home late I used to hear loud laughter from their room. They used to sit up late playing rummy. The wife was a better player and used to win money from her husband and then lend it to him with heavy interest.

Her husband was inconsolable at her death. He started drinking heavily but stopped it after a few days. Fifteen days after his bereavement he came with a group of people to my room. There were three women, one in her late thirties and the other two younger, and two men, on this or that side of thirty. My landlord introduced the older woman as Miss Pahadkar and then left all the talking to her. He had to, because she was one of the most loquacious persons I had ever come across. She told me that she was the elder sister of the two young men, one a doctor and the other an engineer, and that she had brought them up after the early death of their parents. The two young women were the wives of the young men.

I found Miss Pahadkar bossy and loud, the others—including Nana, my landlord—treating her with great deference. She declared that my room was the best in the house and without it the house was incomplete. "How old are you?" she asked me, and when I told her my age, she said, "You are the same age as me, why are you not married still?"

Nana came to see me an hour after they left. He smelt a little of country liquor—he must have visited the illicit liquor bar behind the bus stop after seeing off his guests. "I wanted to tell you something," he said hesitantly.

"I can guess what it is," I said, smiling. "You are thinking of getting married."

"How did you guess," he said, but there was no surprise in his voice. "Yes, I'm thinking of getting married. I know people will laugh at me, and some might even call me heartless, to marry so soon after Kusum's death." Then he became quite agitated. "Why others," he said, "my own sister-in-law said yesterday that I was a heartless scoundrel and had been waiting for Kusum's death. She went away with her bag and baggage to her brother's house." The sister-in-law referred to was Kusum-tai's elder sister who had taken care of the family all those years.

"No one understands what I feel," he said, "no one cares, not even my children. I was a good husband to my wife, wasn't I, professor? But I can't live alone. I was so lonely after Kusum's death that I started drinking heavily. Do they want me to become a drunkard rather than get married? What do they want?"

I asked him to calm down and gave him a glass of water. He sat quietly for some time and then said, "I wanted to tell you another thing…"

"I know," I said. "This house is incomplete without this room, and so I must look for accommodation elsewhere."

"How did you guess?" he said, and there was real surprise in his voice this time. "But there is no hurry. I'm getting married after a fortnight but you can stay here till you find a suitable place. You have stayed here with us, after all, for thirteen years. We didn't need the money after a year, when we got the compensation, but Kusum said no, we should not send him away. But now... I'm really sorry."

"No need to feel sorry," I said, "Kusum-tai needed no privacy in the house because the children were hers. But they are now grown up, and your new wife, even if she looks on them as her own, will certainly need some privacy, a separate room for just the two of you. She has every right to demand it."

"You are so understanding," said Nana, for the first time that day breaking into a smile. "But there is no hurry, take your own time." Then he sat back and relaxed, and started talking about the 'greatness' of the woman he was going to marry. She had refused to marry all these years, he said, because she had to take care of the family and educate her two brothers. It was only after they were well settled that she thought of her own marriage. "A great lady," said Nana. "She understands everything. 'I have made my brothers what they are —a doctor and an engineer,' she says, 'but I will not depend on them to take care of me in my old age. I must have my own house and family, for that. Then only their love will continue for me.' What do you say, professor, she is great, isn't she?"

I agreed that she was, just as I had agreed earlier, on more than one occasion, that his wife Kusum-tai was a "great lady." I was a little disappointed that the man, whose support and treatment of his bed-ridden wife for such a long period was so admirable that I thought it was little short of heroic, was now in such an unseemly hurry to get married. That drama of getting drunk to show he was broken hearted, and then its sudden stoppage as soon as he found a woman—that was not just unheroic, it was ridiculous. But I was wrong. What I had admired was not some out-of-this-world heroism but something more precious, the heroism of ordinary people. That such people were also capable of appearing ludicrous at times should cause no surprise or disappointment.

I was upset, however, that I had to leave that place which had been, for thirteen years, my home. It was close to Sita's house and fairly close to my college. But I decided that I should go away before Nana got married. One of my friends, who had lost his wife soon after marriage and had made up his mind not to marry again, was staying alone in the distant suburban township of Borivli. I rang him up and asked him if I could come and stay with him, and he readily agreed. So a week after Miss Pahadkar's visit to my room I shifted to Borivli.

This made a big difference to my lifestyle. I became now a commuter totally dependent on trains. From my Shivaji Park room I could go to college either by bus or by train, but I preferred buses because I felt that train-travelling was dehumanizing. To sit in that mechanical caterpillar bound to the tracks, with no freedom to swerve even if it wanted to, was to lose, at least partially, one's own freedom of movement. One became, like the driver, just a part of the train. I also missed the controlling presence, sometimes abrasive but always efficient, of that live wire, the bus conductor. For sheer efficiency and energy the Bombay bus conductor is hard to beat. He is there at the door to let you in, or stop you from entering; or give you a tongue-lashing if you break the queue. And the way he moves around the crowded aisle distributing tickets, collecting money, giving small change and detecting people who don't buy tickets is nothing short of miraculous.

Dakshi's letters had become erratic. She would write every alternate day for some time, and then stop writing for days. The changing moods of her letters disturbed me. Sometimes she wrote as if she had no care in the world, but at other times the letters were so lachrymose that I saw telltale signs of her mood in some of the blotched words and letters. There was nothing I could do to help her. Then in September a new tone, and theme, entered the missives. She was desperate to see me. "I haven't met you for nearly a year," she wrote, "when are we going to see each other?" In the next letter the tone was more urgent: "Can't you come and meet me in the Diwali vacation, Proffie? I have begun to despair." In the next one the question had turned into an imperative. "Please come Proffie, if I see you once, again, that might give me strength to live on for some more time."

So I left for Delhi as soon as the vacation started. "I'm coming on one condition," I wrote to her, "I *must* meet your father this time." I also wrote to a former colleague who had left teaching some years earlier to join the Indian Administrative Service, and was stationed at Delhi then. There was a long-standing invitation from him to go to Delhi and be his guest.

Dakshi came to the station with a cousin of hers, her only confidante in Delhi. She had telephoned my friend Sirdeshpande and told him that she would bring me to his office. I saw that she had grown thinner and her large eyes looked larger than before. Her cousin, who must have been of her age but looked younger, stared at me through thick glasses with unconcealed curiosity.

Sirdeshpande, who did not know Dakshi, was quite impressed by her. "Why the hell have you been dragging your feet all these years, man?" he said. "I would have eloped with her long ago."

"That's not so easy," I said, "She worships her parents and they are dead set against this marriage. Because of the big difference in age."

"What do you mean by 'big'? How old are you now?"

"I'm forty."

That shook him a little, I think, though he tried not to show it. He must have thought that I was around thirty-five. In India we think of forty as the beginning of old age. That's why so many people—even men—remain thirty-nine for years. Presbyopia begins at forty. The most commonly used Indian word for reading glasses is 'chalees', which means, simply, 'forty'.

"But why are *you* so concerned with age difference?" said Sirdeshpande. "If *she* thinks it's all right, it's all right. She is not a kid, she can decide for herself."

"She was almost a kid when she fell in love," I said. "And how can I be not concerned? I am concerned—and worried—about her happiness. No, no, don't misunderstand me, I'm not being selfless. You can call it enlightened self-interest if you like. How can *I* be happy if *she* is unhappy with me?"

"Oh, God," said Sirdeshpande. "You know what you are, Rao? You are a coward, that's what you are. A coward with a hyperactive conscience." Then he smiled ruefully, and said, "Sorry, for the harsh words, but I must tell you what my secretary said after you two left, yesterday. 'God, what a lovely couple,' she said, 'they look as if they are made for each other. And so much in love with each other too!' She is very romantic, but do you know, when the two of you are together you do look like a dream couple. It will be sad if nothing comes out of all this."

I was in Delhi for fifteen days. Dakshi met me every day except one. I did not ask her how she managed it. She asked me once whether I could not stay for a few days more as the Diwali vacation was for four weeks, but when I said that I had promised my father that I would spend the whole vacation with him and so must go home for at least a week, she was silenced. "I'm sorry, Proffie," she said. I did not ask her when she was going to take me to meet her father. What was the point? If there was any possibility of such a meeting, Dakshi would have spoken to me about it herself. It was evident that she had not told her parents that I was in Delhi. She would not have found it easy to come out and meet me if she had.

The weather in Delhi was lovely. We moved around the city, did a bit of shopping, and spent hours in a cozy bookshop, browsing. The first day I bought a cookery book for her, and the next a book I had been thinking of buying for years: *The Collected Poems of W.B. Yeats*. We also watched a couple of films. It became clear to me soon that Dakshi had called me to Delhi so that we could be together for some time—for the last time perhaps. Why spoil that by insisting on meeting her father if nothing but pain would come out of the meeting?

During all our meetings Dakshi was dry-eyed, except once, and that was when we were watching a Hindi film. The setting was Bombay and the protagonist of the movie was in a desperate hurry to reach home. It was his first wedding anniversary and he knew his wife would be furious if he was late, but he was hopelessly caught in the usual peak-hour traffic jam of Bombay. It was a comic scene and the Delhi audience laughed, some saying audibly, "Ah, look at Bombay…that is Bombay." It was then that Dakshi clung to me and cried as if her heart was breaking. "Oh, Proffie," she said, "how I miss it all, how I miss it!"

She did not cry at the station when she came there, with her cousin, to bid me farewell. It was her cousin who cried and cried, till her thick glasses became foggy and she could not see where I was.

I stood at the door for a long time, even after those waving figures on the platform went out of sight. Then I went to my seat, opened my bag and took out Yeats' Collected Poems. I opened the book and started reading, at random:

> *Does the imagination dwell the most*
> *Upon a woman won or woman lost?*
> *If on the lost, admit you turned aside*
> *From a great labyrinth out of pride,*
> *Cowardice, some silly over-subtle thought*
> *Or anything called conscience once;*
> *And that if memory recur, the sun's*
> *Under eclipse and the day blotted out.*

I sighed. *Cowardice, conscience; some silly over-subtle thought.* Sirdeshpande would have concurred with the diagnosis. But pride? Perhaps it was a kind of perverse pride that made me insist that Dakshi should not be unhappy with me. What happens if I stress the last two words? 'Dakshi should not be unhappy *with me*.' That's pride all right. And Yeats, I thought, had every right to chide me with those words. He had the courage to make a fool of himself in love. He had proposed to his old love, Maud Gonne, when he was fifty-two, and when she said no, he had proposed, the very next day, to the girl he was really in love with, Maud Gonne's seventeen year old daughter, Iseult.

Then he had married a twenty-two year old girl, and it was a very happy marriage. George Hyde Lees was one year younger than Dakshi when she married Yeats, who was then fifty-two. My head started aching. Some day when I look back at my life I might feel that *the sun was under eclipse and the day blotted out.* But in the mean time all that I felt was an overwhelming feeling of weariness.

I reached Borivli, after two days of travelling, at 9 p.m. I went to a restaurant near the station and had Chinese fried rice and two bottles of beer. I never took more than one bottle usually, but on that day I felt that I needed two.

I was perhaps a little tipsy when I reached my room. Rajanna, in whose house I stayed, opened the door, and looked at me with pity. "Thank God you're here," he said. "Why did you leave no forwarding address when you left for Delhi?"

"Why, what's happened?"

"There are two telegrams waiting for you, both from your brother Moni. The first one came just two days after you left for Delhi. The second one came a week ago." He gave me the two telegrams, both open. The first one read 'Father serious, come immediately.' The second one said, 'Father expired last night.'

"What are you going to do now?" said Rajanna.

"Sleep," I said. "Tomorrow—tomorrow I'll go home by the morning bus. But right now I just want to sleep."

The Funeral

❧

I reached home in time for the final phase of the funeral rites. There were some accusations, scolding and tears, but the days of weeping were already over. "I'm told he waited for you," said Chandratte, "waited till your vacation started, but when he saw that you did not turn up, he died." "It's like you're in New York, not Bombay," said Nagatte, shaking her head. Her son Vasu, an electronics engineer, was in New York, but he had come home in three days when his father had a paralytic stroke. But they scolded me, I must say, with pity, not anger.

Cremation has a finality about it which burial does not have. There was no grave I could visit with flowers. Father was gone, leaving nothing behind; he had merged with the five elements—earth, air, water, fire and *akasha*, or space. Twelve days after his death a hastily prepared portrait, made by the drawing teacher of our school, arrived. He had enlarged an old photograph and touched it with paint. It was of poor craftsmanship but I withheld my comments when I saw that all the women liked it, and Amma sat in front of it, in a trance, for a long time. That portrait and a few fading group photographs were all that we were left with, to remember a man who was so important to all of us when he lived.

The way money was spent during the rituals was mind boggling. Janna uncle was in charge. He went round the house hunting for things that could be given to Brahmins as *daana*. Savita came to me and said, "Anna, someone has to stop Janna uncle. Yesterday he saw that huge brass lamp worth thousands — they don't make brass lamps like that any more—it's a precious heirloom, Anna—and his eyes began to gleam. 'That's a wonderful lamp to give to a Brahmin as daana,' he said, 'such a lamp given as daana to a good Brahmin will light up the departed soul's path to heaven.' And Amma of course readily agreed to give it away. So many things, Anna, things our family treasured, are all given away. And the amount of money given as dakshina to the Brahmins, it's just too much. Janna uncle holds the bowl filled with money, takes whatever he thinks is right, and hands it over to Moni. Moni has to give it to the Brahmin. The Brahmins of course are all happy and shower blessings on us and on Janna uncle. 'Generous Janardhana Rao,' that's what they call him."

"Why don't you talk to Moni about it?" I said.

"I did, yesterday. 'Tell Anna,' he said, 'now that he has come home at last, let him take charge.' He thinks it's difficult for him to be strict because he has to live and work in this place, but *you* need not bother much about people's feelings."

I shook my head and said, "I'll talk to Moni, I can't do anything on my own."

But I could not talk to Moni till the rituals were over. I found him sullen and laconic. The Brahmins went away happy and contented; and so did Janna uncle, whose reputation for generosity remained untarnished. Amma thanked him profusely for managing everything so well. To be honest, there was nothing devious in the way he spent our money. He had, after all, spent his own hard earned money equally lavishly and become a pauper, to earn that sobriquet, 'Generous Janardhana Rao'.

The night after the Vaikuntha Samaradhane Moni and I went up to the upstairs bedroom to sleep there. It was then that I asked Moni something which was bothering me. I knew we had spent too much but most of it had come from the house. I wanted to know how much of hard cash had been spent, and what my share was. Moni smiled, for the first time after my coming. "If you don't mind my asking you—what's your bank balance like?" he asked.

"I'm not quite sure," I said, "I think there must be five or six thousand."

"Is that all?" said Moni. "You have been working for nearly twenty years! Can you guess how much I have saved, during the last five and a half years?" He waited for a few seconds, but when I did not hazard a guess, he said: "It is nearly a hundred times as much as what you have saved."

He saw my astonishment and changed his tone. "Of course I had no expenses and Appa allowed me to keep all my earnings to myself. You pay income tax because you are a salaried person, but the taxman's hands are not so long that they can reach doctors in remote villages." He looked at me to see whether I was jealous—he is quite suspicious, my brother—and then added, "And anyway, there's no need to worry about the expenses. Your friend Subbanna Shetty wanted to buy a small piece of land from us. Father agreed to sell it to him for ten thousand rupees. Now of course the consent of all of you—Amma, you, Sita and Savita—will be required. If you agree we can sell the land and that will take care of the 'hard cash' part of the expenses."

I felt relieved. That bank balance was there because I had started saving a bit, with a definite end in view. I wanted to book a small flat. I did not want to remain a paying guest forever.

"There is something else I wanted to discuss with you," said Moni. I was glad that he had started talking freely again. "You know Appa has left no will. That means all five of us—Amma, and we four—share the property. Not equally, of course, because girls get a smaller share of ancestral property; we'll have to find out the rules from a good lawyer." Moni looked at me, saw me frowning, and said hastily, "No, no, I'm not talking of partitioning the property right now. But I have a problem. I want you to listen to me with patience."

"I'm listening."

Moni took a deep breath and began. It looked like he was going to give a long speech. "You know Appa was a great doctor," he said, "and even greater as a man. He could have made plenty of money but he did not go for that. He hardly earned one fourth of what he could have earned. But he earned people's love and good will instead. He served the people of this place for more than forty years. I have a dream, Anna. We must build a memorial for father. And the right memorial for him would be a hospital built in his name."

"A hospital? In this village?"

"Why not? Kantheshwar is not what it was twenty years ago. It's changing fast; our entire district is changing. There is plenty of money in circulation. There are no industries in our district, and the land is no good for agriculture, but people go out, earn money and bring it here to spend. Do you remember your childhood friends, Ranga Rao and Raja Rao and Mahabala Rao of Nampalli? Ah, you look surprised that I know them; they were your friends before I was born, weren't they? But who doesn't know them now? They are millionaires, all of them. They went as hotel boys, but they now own restaurants and hotels all over South India. They come to our dispensary flashing their diamond rings, and ask me where is Sudhakar now. There are hundreds of such people now, who go out and make money and bring it here to spend. So land has become costly, because it's in demand, and labour is costly because there is no poverty here any more. That's how agriculture has become unprofitable. The only industry that can do well here is the service industry—hospitals, for example. You know about Manipal, don't you? When Madhav Pai wanted to build a medical college and a hospital there, in that wilderness, people laughed at him. But now that place has become one of the best-known educational and medical centres in the country. People come there for treatment from other districts, and even neighbouring states!"

Moni paused for breath. He had rattled on at such speed that I simply sat gaping at him. He saw my stunned look and blushed. "I'm sorry if I sounded like I was giving a speech," he said.

"But you haven't told me yet what's the problem."

"The problem is—well, I want to build a hospital in memory of Appa. It's going to be difficult but not impossible. I have saved some money, as I told you. Some amount can come from banks as loans. And people, especially the shop-owners and businessmen of our pethe, will support the effort whole-heartedly. Father was their family physician and they loved him. There is so much of good will for him that it would be stupid not to make use of it. Once they hear that a hospital is going to be built at Kantheshwar in his memory, by his son, people will, on their own, come forward to help. But the cost will escalate if I try to buy land for the project. And where will I get prime land as suitable as ours? Our house is too large and not suitable to be a residence. But it will make, with some alterations, a good hospital. My plan is to build a nice cozy house in the next plot of land—the one with the suragi tree—and then convert this house into a hospital."

I stared at Moni. It took some time for me to realize the full implications of his dream, or plan. He wanted to convert our house into a hospital—in father's memory, of course, but it would belong to *him*, naturally. He would build a house on the other plot of land, the only other piece of prime land we owned, and naturally it would be *his* house. "You said you had a dream, Moni," I said, "and now you talk of your plan. What is it, a dream or a plan?"

"What's the difference?" he said. "I don't have idle dreams. When I dream, I plan."

"You haven't yet told me what the problem is."

"I'm sure you have guessed what it is. It's your consent—yours, Sita's and Savita's. I can't build anything on our land without your consent. Not just your oral consent, but a proper agreement." He hesitated a bit and then said, "I'll have to sink hundreds of thousands into this project. I'll have to go for loans. I can't ask you to become partners because I know you don't have that kind of money or the expertise. I don't want to put all my money into the project, get into debt, and then be told that the hospital belongs to the family and not to me."

He is deep, I thought. *He knows that none of us can offer to become partners in his project, and he is taking advantage of that*. Moni watched me and perhaps read my thoughts. "I'm not asking you," he said, "to give this house and the land as a gift to me. I want it as my share. There is plenty of other property which can be shared among you. I know this land is prime property and the other lands we have are mostly agricultural lands. But we can have a proper valuation of all the properties at the time of partition. If it's found then that I have got more than what is legally due to me, I'll pay ready cash for it. If the partition takes place before I have cleared all my debts, and I'm short of funds, I may ask you for time and pay in installments, but pay I will."

But a 'proper valuation' of the property—how is it to be done? The actual price of land is never shown in full during sale because of high taxation. In all land deals in India 'black' or unaccounted money plays a big role. But I kept these thoughts to myself. What right had I to doubt Moni's integrity? If we made an agreement with Moni on the lines suggested by him, it's true we would be putting ourselves at his mercy, but why should we not trust him? "Have you talked to Sita and Savita about it?" I asked.

"I have," he said. "Sita is very supportive, but Savita, she thinks I want to swallow all Appa's property. She has become very selfish, Anna. Her husband is not doing well in business. That has made her selfish and greedy."

"Don't use those words," I said, suddenly losing my temper. Perhaps I was angry because I had learnt from Sita, just a day earlier, about the difficulties Savita was facing. Her husband, a man of many talents, had messed up his business in Bangalore by quarreling with his partners. "If you think of her as selfish and greedy, why shouldn't she think that *you* are selfish and greedy? You want this house and land, and the next plot of land too. You want an agreement on your terms. Aren't you selfish?"

Moni's brow darkened in anger. "It's as I suspected," he said. "You are against me. You belong to Savita's party."

That did it, and I had to laugh. He might have become a big man now, full of ambitions, but he was still the child I knew, who often used to quarrel with Savita and ask me and Sita whether we belonged his 'party' or Savita's. "No, no, Moni," I said, "Why do you think of parties and camps? If there are two parties, you can't go ahead with your project. If Savita has some objections to your project, sit with her and try to find out what the problems are. Learn to trust her if you want her to trust you. Don't force her to go against you."

"Why don't you talk to her and make her see reason?" said Moni, and I said, "No, you have to do the talking yourself."

Moni sat brooding for some time. Then he said, "Anna, do you think I am selfish?" "I do," I said, and his face fell. He did not look angry this time, he looked sad and upset. "You are selfish," I said, "but you are not mean. You want to be the sole owner of this house, this land and the adjacent one too. That's selfishness all right. But there is no meanness in this, because you want to make this place a better one than it is. You don't want to see this property fragmented. And once your dream comes true, I'm sure the doors of your house will remain open for all of us: Sita and Savita and me. You want to play Appa, don't you?"

Moni smiled. After he switched off the light I said, "But why are you in such a hurry? Father's funeral is just over. Why not wait for things to settle down?."

"No," said Moni. "You don't know how much the people here loved Appa. You should have seen the way all the shops in the pethe downed their shutters when he died. But people have short memories. If I start building the hospital now I'll get their full support. If I delay, other feelings, like jealousy, will creep in."

This chap will succeed, I said to myself. He can dream like an idealist but can also be practical and down to earth. As for myself, I have got it all wrong. My dreams are spoilt by cynicism and when it comes to acting, I become hopelessly idealistic. *Conscience, and silly over-subtle thoughts*—they won't stop Moni from achieving his goal.

"Have you talked to Amma about your project?" I asked. "I don't think she will agree to leave this house. This has been her home all these years, the only home she has known after her marriage. She never felt at home at Nampalli."

"That's no problem," said Moni. "She has already said yes. I told her about this idea a couple of months ago. Father was very ill then and a nurse was coming to tend him. 'It's all right,' she said, 'this house is already a hospital.' She has changed a lot, ever since she heard that father was terminally ill. She agrees to everything now, never says no. She said that *you* might have some objection."

"I? Why should I have any objection?"

"I don't know," said Moni, yawning loudly, a childhood habit he hadn't outgrown. "She thought you might not like some of the things I was planning to do. I want to shift that Kalkutika stone to one corner of the plot. Then I might fence off that corner. What's wrong with that? I don't want people to have the run of our garden." I heard Moni yawning again. "All right Anna, go to sleep now. You won't get much sleep tomorrow as you will be spending the whole night in your bus to Bombay. Good night."

There was silence for some time. Then I heard Moni's bed creaking; perhaps he was turning on his side. "Ah, yes, there is another thing," he said, "I also want to get rid of that other nuisance. I want to cut down the suragi tree."

Orphaned

❧

My bus was to leave Chandapur late in the afternoon. So after lunch the next day I went to Amma's room to sit with her for some time. The room looked bare, like her forehead; all the furniture had been removed at the time of the funeral rites. I found her sitting in a dark corner of the room, on the ground, looking frail and small, as if she had shrunk to half her size. She had an open book on her lap and a large pair of spectacles on her small nose but she wasn't reading. Varijamma sprawled in the centre, the only part of the room that received some light from the open door, bending over an exercise book. Her kumkum looked bigger than usual. She was busy writing 'Shree Rama' in Sanskrit script.

"Look at Varijamma," said Amma, "She is older than me but she can read and write without spectacles even in dim light. I am trying to read *Vishnu Sahasra Nama,* but even with these glasses I cannot."

I sat with Amma for more than an hour. She rambled on in a manner so different from her usual style of talking that I felt bewildered. "Poor Varijamma," she said, "they are not treating her well, particularly your Janna uncle's last daughter-in-law. So she comes here and sometimes she goes to Nampalli. But she can't stay in one place. She has wheels in her feet, Babu, she loves to move about. She is all bent now, and when she goes up or down an incline she has to walk sideways, like a crab, but she thinks nothing of walking all the way to Nampalli. I told her this morning, you stay here, we two old women will sit together, you writing the Lord's name and I reading *Vishnu Sahasra Nama,* 'The Thousand Names of Vishnu', but no, she wants to go to Nampalli tomorrow because Savitri has called her. Then she will go back to Janna uncle's house to be ill-treated and chided by that young woman, because she insists that she has a right to stay there."

"Why shouldn't I?" said Varijamma. "It's my father's house, not that virago's." Even while writing the Lord's name with great concentration—she never ever made a mistake—she always had her ears open to what was being said.

Amma talked about Nampalli, about the early days of her marriage, the support and advice she received from grandmother—"she was a real mother to this motherless girl," she said—and about uncle and his love for his brother's family. There was no trace of rancour in her recollections. There was only love, a blanket of affection that covered even Varijamma, her *bete noire* at one time.

How she had changed, I thought. I found the way she spoke about uncle most astonishing. "We were all orphaned when he left us," she said. "Your father had not taken his parents' death so badly, but his brother's death broke his heart. I was scared, Babu, scared something would happen to him, because he could not even cry for the first few days. He was desperately trying to find where you were. Then on the *dharmodaka* day, when all our relations, near and distant, even Aditi and Lakshmi, and Kamalamma who was ailing herself, and some former students of your uncle who were not related to us at all, when they all came but we did not know where you were, that night your father broke down. 'I promised you, Annayya,' he cried out, 'I promised you I would send Babu to you in the evening that day, but I drove him away. I drove him away when you needed him most.' Oh, how he cried, Babu, how he cried."

We sat silent for some time, both of us dry-eyed. My mind was in turmoil. What had happened to Amma, I wondered. It was as if her ego, and all the petty jealousies bred by her sense of insecurity, had been burnt out on father's funeral pyre. But curiously there was no remorse either. She was at least partially responsible for uncle's decision not to come to Kantheshwar, and she had kept herself aloof and repulsed all overtures of friendship from 'Chikkajjayya's daughters', but she seemed to feel no regret. It was as if she had gone beyond all petty feelings including remorse.

My own reaction to this change was ambivalent. She had lost all those things I disliked in her—her irascibility, her aloofness and the frequent show of petty-mindedness—but I was not happy. That perpetual frown on her face had been replaced by a sad smile, but I missed the frown, and found the smile somehow vacuous. But at the same time I was aware that if she had not changed I could not have sat talking with her for so long.

"What's happened to Ramu Mawa?" I said. "He didn't come to the funeral."

"Didn't he come, really?" said Amma, with just a touch of surprise in her voice. "Strange, I didn't notice it. This is what happens, Babu. People get forgotten, even near and dear ones. Ramu got married eleven years ago when he was forty. His father-in-law is a rich landlord in Kasargod. The girl is his only daughter, but she is lame in one leg, you know, and he wanted a mane aliya. It was a good match for Ramu because you know what he is like: rather slow and innocent. I went to the marriage with Moni and Savita; your father had stopped going to all such ceremonies. I invited the couple home and they came here for a visit. But that girl is very proud, Babu. She did not like the way we treated her husband. Ramu is my younger brother, isn't he? He has always been a bit slow, and I'm used to talking to him a bit roughly. But she did not like it. Ramu came only once thereafter, alone, for Savita's wedding, and he said that his wife did not want him to go to a place where he was not treated with respect."

Amma sat musing for a moment with that sad smile flickering on her face. "I don't know, Babu," she said, "which is more important, respect or love. But I wonder why Ramu did not come to the funeral. He looked up to his brother-in-law as if he were a God. Maybe Moni forgot to send him a letter. But look, Babu, what is strange is not that he did not come, but that I did not notice that he hadn't come. He was my only brother, a child I had taken care of when my mother died, and I was only ten then. And yet I did not miss him." She shook her head sadly and said, "Will you please tell Moni to find out if Ramu's name is in the list of people who were invited? If it's not there, he must include it now and keep that list carefully. It would be sad if my own brother is not invited to my funeral."

I got up reluctantly, because I had to pack up my things. "I'll be home again by the end of April," I said; "I'll spend then at least two months here."

She smiled. "Come soon," she said. "This is your place. You must not wander about in an alien land as if you have no place of your own. Come home, even if I am not alive."

"You *will* be alive," I said. "There is nothing wrong with you and you are only—fifty-seven? You are too young to think of death."

But when I came home in May she was not alive. I had booked my ticket for the 1st of May, but Rajanna told me that it might be a bit risky to travel on that day. May 1st is Maharashtra Day, the day when the State of Maharashtra was formed. There was a long-standing border dispute between Maharashtra and Karnataka about Belgaum, which Shiv Sena, the militant Maharashtrian party, wanted to rake up that year at the time of Maharashtra Day. There were rumours that buses from Bombay to Mangalore could become targets of mob violence. So I postponed my journey by three days. Amma died on the 2nd. When I reached home on the 5th, she had already been cremated.

I was terribly upset, even more upset than when father died. Upset and angry. During those five months in Bombay I had often thought of Amma and of her transformation. Her smile troubled me. I have called it 'vacuous' because there was no obvious reason for the smile. Perhaps she smiled simply because there were no reasons to frown: neither any worries or fears or anxieties, nor expectations of any kind. She was a woman of strong likes and dislikes earlier, but it looked like she disliked no one after father's death. Even her love had changed and become diluted into a kind of general benevolence that covered everyone, from me and Moni to even Varijamma. And when she recollected the past, she remembered only pleasant moments, moments of happiness and love, her memory acting like a sieve and keeping out all unhappy and unpleasant events. One of the things she told me during that hour long talk was about Kamalamma, and how she had come to her father's house with just a handbag, and two whimpering children, one-year-old Aditi and Lakshmi who was three. That was some six months before I was born. "I loved that child Aditi," Amma said, "She was such a quiet little beauty. I was disappointed when you were born because I wanted a girl like that." This was a real surprise to me because I could not remember any signs of an attachment between Amma and Aditi. All that I remembered was that she did not dislike Kamalamma and Aditi as violently as she disliked Varijamma. Where had she kept that love hidden all these years?

All through the uncomfortable journey from Bombay to Kantheshwar I was brooding over this transformation. This woman who loved so fiercely, and jealously guarded her little world centred round father, resenting all intrusions by others—by even those who loved her husband—how changed she was after father's death! I wanted to sit with her and help her to recollect the past. I wanted to know her better—now that the hard crust she hid behind all these years had crumbled—so that I could understand myself better. But when I reached home I found that she was already gone. I felt cheated.

Amma's last rites were on a much smaller scale than father's. The expenditure was perhaps one fourth of what was spent earlier. Savita's husband was in charge. Obviously Moni and he were on very good terms. Janna uncle came every day but he was sidelined. I did not like the way Savita's husband mentioned more than once, in the presence of Janna uncle, that because *he* was in charge the expenses had come down drastically.

I felt within me a simmering discontent and found myself complaining and grumbling oftener than usual. "Why didn't you write to me that Amma's condition had deteriorated? I might have come a few days earlier," I said to Moni.

"There was nothing seriously wrong with her," he said. "She had minor problems like diabetes and hypertension, but they were all under control. It was just that she lost her will to live."

I was unhappy that many who knew Amma—Aditi and Lakshmi, for example, who had attended father's funeral earlier—did not come this time. No doubt they had much fonder memories of uncle and father. I wanted to tell Aditi what Amma had said about her. Then on the last day, the day of the Vaikuntha Samaradhane, I realized that even Ramu Mawa had not come.

"Did you send Ramu Mawa an invitation?" I asked Moni. "We must have," he said. "I gave the list to Ganesh and asked him to send the printed cards to every one." I checked up with Ganesh, Moni's Man Friday, who acted as his compounder, clerk and errand boy, and found that Ramu Mawa's name and address were not in the list.

I was terribly upset. I talked to Moni but his nonchalance infuriated me. It was not his fault, perhaps, because I could not recollect whether I had told him about Amma's instruction. "Even if you have," said Moni, "where do I get his address from? He has not been in touch with us for years."

The day after the Vaikuntha Samaradhane Savita's husband brought to me, soon after breakfast, a document to be signed. It was the agreement Moni had spoken of. I saw Sita and Savita had already signed it, and so put my signature without reading. "You should never sign a document without reading it," said Savita's husband. "If *you* have approved of it, that's good enough for me," I said.

At noon that day I went to the plot of land Moni wanted to build his house on—my first visit to the place after Amma's death. The place, where I had spent thousands of hours dreaming and reading, looked totally unfamiliar. All the bushes had been cut and the ground levelled. An imposing compound wall had sprung up, except on the southern side, where a pile of granite blocks showed that a wall would soon be erected. There was a newly built little shrine, not more than four feet high, with two little domes, at the southern end. Kalkutika, apparently, had been shifted there. At the centre of the ground stood the suragi tree, looking smaller than before, a forlorn green figure under the blazing sun.

The heat of the noonday sun was unbearable. There was no breeze where I stood but a whiff of breeze must have brushed past the suragi standing in that wide open space, for her leaves rippled suddenly as if to beckon me. For a moment I thought of going there and sitting in that shade, to see if I could find my way into the green world of my childhood dreams again. But in that forbidding white expanse of heat that shade looked all too inadequate. I turned back, feeling a strange mixture of nostalgia and nausea.

That night I asked Moni how far his project had progressed. "I have applied for the bank loan," he said, "and it will be sanctioned. I have built the compound wall for that other plot. I have shifted the Kalkutika to a small shrine. But that suragi tree is causing problems. No one is ready to cut the tree. The tree harbours a Naga Yakshi, they say, a snake goddess, and they are all too scared to touch it. This kind of superstition is so irritating, really. Do you believe in these deivas, Yakshi and Kalkutika and so on?"

"I don't know. Long ago I asked Amma whether the deivas really existed. She said that that they existed because people believed in them."

I don't think he understood what Amma meant, or what I thought she meant. "But I don't believe in them," he said. "So how do I get rid of the tree?"

"Why don't you cut it yourself?"

He looked at me in surprise. "Don't be crazy," he said. "You know this place. If I start cutting that blessed tree a crowd will collect in no time—to watch the fun and laugh at me. A doctor is not expected to do this kind of work."

But I think the idea took root in his mind. In the meantime I began to feel restless and bored. Savita and her family left for Bangalore by the night bus the day I signed the agreement. Shreekanth and Suneeta had left on the day of the Samaradhane itself. Satish had not come because he had no vacation then. He was a First Year student at I.I.T., Bombay. Sita stayed behind because she wanted to set Moni's house in order. She wanted to teach Ratnamma, a lazy woman Moni had appointed as a cook, how to manage things better, but she found the woman intractable and argumentative. So when I told her that I was going back to Bombay she said, "Book my ticket Anna, I'll come with you."

The day prior to our departure Moni came home at four looking terribly flustered. "That Sheena should be flogged," he said. "I gave him hundred rupees to cut the tree. I saw him and his brother starting the work and then came back to my dispensary. In five minutes the idiots came running. Sheena said that he had seen a big yellow cobra hanging from one of the branches of the tree. 'Did *you* see it?' I asked his brother. He hadn't, naturally, because he was sober, whereas Sheena was stinking of country liquor. I went with them to the tree and there was of course no cobra in sight. 'Why the hell did you drink so early in the day?' I asked Sheena. 'I needed courage, Ayya, I needed something warm inside me to give me courage to cut that sacred tree,' he said."

"What are you going to do now?" I said. "I think I'll have to cut the tree myself," he said. "There seems to be no other option. We'll have to cut it ourselves." He looked at me pleadingly and said, "Will you help me out, Anna? I can't go there alone and start cutting the tree. I'll look ridiculous. But if the two of us do it, it would be fun, a good morning's exercise. Will you come, please?"

"But I'm leaving tomorrow," I said. "You are leaving by the evening bus, aren't you?" he said. "We can do it in the morning, immediately after breakfast. And I am sure of one thing, Anna. Once we start cutting the tree, the others will come. We won't have to do all the work ourselves. Will you come, Anna?"

"Let's see tomorrow," I said, and he took it as a consent. "Aye," he said, in triumph, raising a clenched fist.

My head was in a whirl all that afternoon. I could not decide whether I should tell Moni that I hadn't actually agreed to the felling of the tree. I spent a restless night. I was sleepless most of the time, and then fell into a state where I was not sure whether I was dreaming or awake. My dreams were like snippets, and in one of them I found myself eating in our kitchen, with Amma asking me, while serving saru, why I had made that promise to Moni if I did not want to fulfill it. Then I found myself chased by a huge tidal wave, unable to run. When I woke up finally, it was rather late in the morning and I had a splitting headache.

Moni was already up and about. He had brought from somewhere two axes. When I said that I was not feeling well, he laughed. "What you need is exercise," he said. "Once you start cutting the tree and sweat a little, you'll feel better."

I find it difficult to remember or describe the events of the next few hours with any degree of clarity or coherence. When I try to recollect them, my memory gets blurred and I see a haze, as if I am still bedazzled by the blazing sun of that awful day. We started cutting the tree at quarter to eleven. The tree's shade lay a few feet to the west of where we stood, giving us no protection from the heat. The dark shade moved slowly towards us as we kept on chipping at the tree. Neither Moni nor I had ever wielded an axe before. Moni's first blow could have ended in tragedy; the axe bounced off the tree, slipped from his loose grip and missed my right foot by a whisker. "God, I nearly chopped off your leg," said Moni.

I was soon thoroughly exhausted but continued as if I could not stop. The only thing I wanted, at that moment, was to finish it off and get it over with. The way we went about it, we were not just killing the tree, we were inflicting slow torture on it. In my misery I remembered a long forgotten incident from the dim past of my childhood, when I was not more than two or three years old. Someone had given me a *peetle*, a little air-gun made from a small piece of bamboo. A berry that grew on a tree on our hedge was to be used as a bullet. With my shirt pocket bulging with those berries, I started moving about, a hunter looking for game. Aditi ran away and hid herself, and Savitri threatened to beat me up with a stick if I aimed my gun at her. So I went out and saw, on our outer verandah, a lovely black-and-brown caterpillar. I decided to shoot down that woolly creature.

My first few shots missed it, and that roused my hunter's instincts. The fourth shot hit the mark and I was delighted. The delight turned into anguish when I saw the creature writhing in pain. I wanted to finish it off and end its suffering, but somehow I could not think of doing it in any other way than by shooting it with my little peetle. When it would not die even after half a dozen hits, I lost my head and began to howl in misery, till Savitri, who came out to see what had happened, threw the caterpillar away and took me inside.

That long-forgotten misery rose and surfaced again, after nearly four decades, and merged with the feelings of the moment. Every time my axe made a cut in the suragi's bark I could feel the tree writhing in pain like that caterpillar. I looked at Moni, but he was swinging his axe with evident enjoyment. I realized that it was, for him, a good morning's exercise, nothing more. I looked at the group that had collected near the gate. I saw someone detaching himself from that group and coming towards us. It was Ganesh. "Let me try my hand, sir," he said and took the axe from me, and I tottered back in relief, and sat down on the western edge of the shade, the other side of which was now touching the tree.

Someone else came forward and took Moni's axe. By noon the work was almost over. A breeze blew suddenly, the tree made a creaking sound and we all moved away from the tree and waited.

But no, the tree was not ready to fall yet. "This shaven widow of a tree," said Sheena, "it will not fall down till I give it a blow." He was standing with his brother, holding a rope tied to the tree, so that they could pull it in the right direction when it was about to fall. He left the rope, walked up to the tree and picked up one of the axes. He gave a well-directed blow, and then another.

Suddenly, without any warning, the tree fell. Shankara, Sheena's brother, yelled and pulled at the rope with all his might, desperately, but the tree fell in the other direction. As it lay writhing on the ground, raising a cloud of dust, we realized, to our horror, that Sheena had disappeared under it.

It was then that we heard that cry. It was an unearthly screech, a scream of anguish, a sound that could have come from no human being. I don't think I have ever heard a sound quite like that. In that blinding noonday blaze we could see nothing. The crowd stood petrified for a moment and then rushed forward to see what had happened to Sheena.

But Sheena was all right. Quick though the tree's fall was, he was quicker, and had scampered away like a rabbit. He had escaped from the falling trunk which would have otherwise crushed him to death, but the branches, the thin ends of the branches fortunately, had caught him. People pulled him out, bruised and badly shaken, moaning in pain. "It was all right, cutting the tree," he moaned, "because I was paid for it and was doing only my duty, but I had no business to curse the tree. That was why I was whipped." He touched himself all over, winced in pain, and said, "God, I have never been whipped like this since my father died."

"But the way you screamed, you idiot, you frightened us all," said Moni in irritation. "You screamed like a pig that's being scalded."

"It wasn't Sheena, Ayya," said Shankara, who was standing a little away trembling. "Sheena cannot scream like that. It was something in the tree, Ayya. I saw something white—like a flash of light—circle the tree and then fly away."

"It must be the snake, Ayya," said Sheena, now looking terrified. "Nonsense," said Moni. "A snake that flies? It must be some bird that had built its nest in the tree. Its cry and your scream must have combined to produce that awful sound." He gave Sheena a cursory examination to see if he was hurt, and said, "All right, keep the full amount I have given you; drink well tonight so that you will see not just snakes that fly but birds that crawl tomorrow. But you must do your work first. Now that the snake has flown away, you can chop and cart the tree away. And see to it that the roots are dug out and the ground levelled."

He was in high spirits. "Come home and have some sherbet," he said to the people who had collected there but they said no, and moved away. "Let's go home, Anna," he said and turned and looked at me. "God, you don't look all right," he said with concern. He touched my forehead. "No, there is no fever. For a moment I was worried that you might have had a sun-stroke."

At home he took my blood pressure but did not tell me what the reading was. "Can't you postpone your journey by a couple of days?" he asked. "There is nothing wrong but a bit of rest will do you a world of good."

I shook my head. Sita was quite concerned about my health but she too did not like the idea of postponing the journey. "He will be all right," she said. "I'm there to take care of him, aren't I? But one thing, Anna, you are not going to Borivli till you are all right. You are going to get a proper check up from your brother-in-law and stay with us for a couple of days."

"I'll give you a tranquilizer," said Moni. "Take a light meal and take some rest. A proper siesta, and you will be ready for the journey."

I took the tablet Moni gave me, and tried to sleep. It was strange, the way dreams troubled me even during that short nap. I dreamt that I was sitting under the suragi tree, feeling terribly unhappy because the shade was not green but a dark gray. Then the tree fell and I heard someone trapped under it screaming in anguish. Then I saw Sheena rising from among the branches, flapping large white wings and flying round and round. Oh God, it's not Sheena, it's an albatross, I thought. Then I found myself wandering in a hot dusty bowl of a place, and realized I had lost my way. There were no trees, not a blade of grass, but I found a scarecrow, a tattered coat upon a stick, right in the middle of the place. On closer inspection it turned out to be Professor Totani. I told him I had lost my way, and he said, *yonder all before us lie deserts of vast eternity,* and I woke up.

It was half past four. Sita had already packed my bag. Ratnamma brought for me a poisonous looking brew, which she called tea. In spite of all Sita's instructions she insisted that tea could only be prepared by boiling tea leaves for at least half an hour, thickening the resulting brew with plenty of milk and sweetening it with three spoons of sugar for each cup.

When I was putting my shoes on, the drawing teacher of the school, looking very important and carrying a large parcel wrapped in brown paper under his arm, arrived. He had been our photographer ever since the opening of the high school and had prepared the portrait of my father earlier. Now he brought with him the one he had prepared of mother.

"You can take this as my humble gift in memory of a great soul," he said, smiling. "I hunted among all the old negatives I had and finally found one, of an old group photograph, where every other figure had disappeared because of fungus except your mother. In fact, if I remember rightly, it was a faulty negative and no photograph was ever printed of it. You have a surprise in store for you." Then he unwrapped the portrait and held it up for us to look at.

It was an amazing picture. Technically it was no better than his earlier portrait of father, but there was life in it, and we saw a woman of strange beauty standing there. It was not the Amma we knew, though the features were hers. She looked young, shy and vulnerable, not like Amma as she was but as she could have been if she were happier, if she hadn't had to harden herself because of her problems.

"God, look at the flowers," said Sita. Amma had never shown any great fondness for flowers, but in the portrait her head was covered with garlands of them. It was like *jalli,* a kind of flower decoration covering the entire head— usually of white jasmine—given to a woman when she is pregnant for the first time.

The drawing teacher smiled, delighted by our reaction. "Can you guess what flowers they are?" he asked.

Sita went close to the picture. "It's not jasmine," she said. She studied the picture carefully. "I know what they are," she said, finally. "You have made it difficult to recognize them, sir, by touching them up rather heavily, but I know them. They were my favourite flowers once. Suragi flowers."

PART VI
Adrift

෨

We had the experience but missed the meaning,
And approach to the meaning restores the experience
In a different form...

T.S. Eliot

Letters from Dakshi

❧

I could not sleep in the bus till four in the morning. At six Sita woke me up. "Every one is getting down," she said, "I think this is where we get our morning tea." Several Bombay-bound buses were already there. The hotel we stopped at had two or three toilets with inadequate water supply and nearly three hundred people from the buses, who urgently needed to use the facilities, had messed up the place so badly that I turned back from the door itself, feeling sick. I wanted to warn Sita but she had already entered the Ladies' Room. She came out in a hurry looking blue in the face. "Shall we have a cup of coffee or tea?" I asked, but Sita said that she would puke if she took anything before she could forget what she had just seen. "This place is hell," she said. We brushed our teeth, washed our faces in the basin outside the restaurant and went back to the bus.

There was only an old man sitting in the bus. "What's this shitty place called?" I asked him. "It's Belgaum," he said.

Sita smiled wryly. "Is this your Belgaum?" she said. "I heard you tell your brother-in-law once that the place is a paradise on earth."

I gave Sita the window seat because I was scared that she might remember what she had seen and throw up. "What can the place do?" I said. What could it do, really. The whole system was bad, and stinking, like those toilets. The hotel owners bribed the drivers to stop their buses at their hotels, so that they could make easy money by serving the travellers sub-standard stuff at exorbitant prices. The local people, who could have become their regular customers, shunned these hotels because they were dirty and sub-standard. So the hotels *had* to bribe the bus people, and so on. Wherever you find a mess you find a vicious circle. But it hurt me that I got the reply 'Belgaum' when I asked what the shitty place was.

People started boarding the bus. "The mind is its own place, and in itself can make a heaven of hell, a hell of heaven," I said.

"What's that?" said Sita. We always talked in Kannada—though Sita understood English well enough—but I had spoken that last sentence in English.

"It's a quotation from *Paradise Lost*," I said. Sita laughed. "How was paradise lost?" she asked.

"By the desecration of a sacred tree."

Sita looked at me, troubled, and shook her head. "I thought it was because Adam ate an apple," she said. "Didn't God throw him out of paradise because He had asked him not to eat apples from a tree, and Adam ate them?"

"That's the story," I said. "But you make God sound like an old fashioned doctor like father, who ordered his patient not to eat apples, and when the poor chap broke the regimen, threw him out of his hospital."

Sita smiled. "Thank God you are joking. So you are all right now. You hardly spoke a word after the tree was cut yesterday, and that got me worried."

"I joke even when I am not all right," I said.

Sita started looking out of the window. My mind was in a turmoil and my head buzzing with words, words that came from all kinds of sources. Perhaps because I had already quoted from one of Satan's speeches in *Paradise Lost*, words came from another, and I spoke them aloud: "Which way I fly is hell; myself am hell."

Sita turned to me with concern. "Stop it, please," she said. The bus started, and for some time we sat silent. Then she said, "Why are you making such a big issue out of something so simple, the mere cutting of a tree?"

"One can put the same question to God, why make such a big issue of something so simple, the mere eating of apples."

"Did God ask you not to cut the tree, like he asked Adam not to eat the apple?"

"Devaru did not, but a deiva did," I said.

"What do you mean?"

So I told her about the darshana of the Kalkutika. It was strange, the way I could remember every detail of an event that had taken place thirty years earlier. I told her what the Kalkutika had said about Yakshi and her love for the suragi tree, and his final words addressed to me: "Take care of her, and she will take care of you."

Sita was really disturbed. "Oh, Anna, don't you know that these darshanas are held to fool gullible villagers? How could *you* believe in something so stupid?"

"It's not a question of belief," I said. "It's the impression made that matters. The darshana must have made a deep impression on my mind, or else I would not have remembered every detail of it after thirty years. An impression of this sort is like a scar, or a tattoo; you can't rub it off. You have to live with it."

I hesitated, not sure Sita would understand what I was trying to tell her. "There is something else," I said. "Something I realized only after the tree was cut. I can say I loved that tree but love is not the right word." I shook my head. "You don't know, Sita, how many hours I used to spend under that tree, reading or dreaming. Sometimes I just sat there and waited. Birds came and sang, and sometimes words, words for the poems I wanted to write, whole lines and stanzas sometimes; and at times they were words I did not use because I loved the music they made in my mind and was worried that the music might disappear if I wrote them down on paper. Sometimes I waited— for nothing. I don't know whether I should tell you all this. It may sound crazy to you, but I really got a thrill out of sitting there and waiting, waiting with my whole being. I felt there, in that shade, in that tree, the presence of someone or something that loved me and wanted me there. Yakshi? I don't know. I had this vague feeling that if I waited patiently and receptively, and with love, something wonderful would happen some day. The tree became a part of me. It was also a home. I don't know, I still don't know, what I have lost."

We were silent for a long time thereafter. Sita kept on looking out of the window as if she was fascinated by the changing landscape outside. Then she turned to me and I saw that her eyes were red. "There is something *I* want to tell you," she said. "I don't know whether I should. While talking about Yakshi you mispronounced that name twice. You didn't say Yakshi, you said Dakshi."

She turned to the window again and started looking at the scene outside with greater concentration than before. "A mere slip of the tongue, that's all," I said rather lamely. But I was troubled nevertheless. Sita had met Dakshi once, and she had not liked her. Not because she found anything wrong with the girl but because she thought she was doing no good to me or to herself, by carrying on an affair so obviously doomed to failure.

By noon I had developed a severe headache. By three the discomfort was almost unbearable. We were approaching Sion. The bus we were travelling by was bound for Borivli. At Sion it would take a U-turn and start going northwards. To go to Dadar we had to get down at Sion and take a taxi but I did not want to go to Sita's place. I desperately wanted to go to my room and lie down.

Sita, who was dozing, woke up and looked out. "We are nearing Sion, aren't we?" she said. Then she turned to me. "I'm glad of one thing, Anna, that you spoke freely today. When things bother you, you must not keep them bottled up inside. You must speak freely and get them out of your system."

"I know, I know," I said. I hesitated for a moment and then said, "I'm sorry, Sita, but if I don't get down at Sion, if I go straight to Borivli, is it all right? Can you go to Dadar by taxi on your own?"

"No," she said, quite firmly. "You know what the taxi drivers here are like. And why have you changed your mind? You promised to come and stay with us. Today is Sunday, Satish will be there. You haven't met him for a long time."

I had made no such promise. Why did people take my silence as consent? Moni had done the same thing about the cutting of the tree. I *must* be more firm and learn to say no.

"I have a bad headache," I said, "and am feeling acute discomfort. You know me, Sita. When I am unwell, I don't like company, not even of people I love. Right now I just want to be left alone. I'll come and meet you when I'm all right."

"But what's the trouble? Is it your blood pressure? Shouldn't you come home and get a check up from your brother-in-law?"

"No," I said, "I don't think it's BP, I think it has something to do with what you said—about getting things out of one's system—not keeping things bottled up. The headache is because of what happened—or did not happen—in the morning."

"What do you mean?"

"Did I tell you what happened when I went to Guntakal? How I kept things bottled up for a full week, when I found that the hotel I stayed in had no toilet facilities, and I was expected to go and squat—with hundreds of others—in the open ground under the Railway Bridge?"

"Several times," said Sita, wrinkling her nose in disgust.

"You exaggerate, as usual," I said. "But anyway, that ability to keep things comfortably bottled up for days, I have completely lost it now. Just one morning's failure to evacuate, and my stomach frets and fumes. And the fumes go straight to my head and I get a severe headache. So what I want now is to go to my room, take some analgesic with a big glass of Eno's fruit salt and lie down."

We reached Sion and were pleasantly surprised to find Satish at the stop. As an I.I.T student he had to stay on in the campus but came home every weekend. He missed us, I think, and came to the stop so that he could see us a bit early. I told him I would meet him next Saturday, got back into the bus after they got into a taxi, and proceeded to Borivli.

In my room I found two letters from Dakshi. The Delhi post marks showed that they were both posted on the same day: 2nd May, the day I lost my mother. I did not open the letters immediately. I took a big glass of water, put two spoons of fruit salt into it, and after the fizz died out, put an aspirin in my mouth and started sipping the drink. It tasted good. The bitterness would come finally, with the last sip. Then I opened the letters.

After my return from Delhi I had received only one letter from Dakshi. One letter in six months from someone who used to write practically every alternate day. I received that letter a month after I came back from Kantheshwar, after attending father's funeral. Perhaps I should have written to her about father's death. I did not, for two reasons: firstly, I had got used to a correspondence where every letter I wrote was in reply to one of hers. My letters were more than mere replies, they were much longer than the ones she wrote, but I always wrote *after* I received a letter from her, not before. Maybe I did not want to break the symmetry of the chain. As I had written to her just before leaving for Delhi, it was her turn to write.

But at the Delhi station she had said, "Please write to me when you reach Bombay, I'll be waiting for your letter." In Bombay I found those two telegrams waiting for me. I had to rush home for father's last rites, and when I came back I was in no mood to write letters.

The letter I received from Dakshi a month after I came back from Kantheshwar was a bitter one. It was written in pain, anger and self-pity. There she was, in Delhi, fighting a battle all alone, refusing to succumb to pressure from her parents and relatives that she should agree to marry some boy of *their* choice; and here was I in Bombay, taking things easy, and having a nice time with my female admirers perhaps, not finding time to write a simple letter to her stating I had reached Bombay safe and sound. She did not know, of course, what I had gone through, but the letter upset me. I had this feeling that Dakshi was in some ways responsible for what happened to father. She had kept me away from home for four years when he was very ill and then she had called me to Delhi, with that despairing letter I could not ignore, making me break my promise to father that I would spend my Diwali vacation at home. This was the second reason why I did not write to Dakshi about my bereavement: I was worried that my letter might make her feel that I blamed her for what had happened. But now I *had* to write a reply to her letter—and mention the fact that I could not keep my promise to father, and could not be by his bedside when he was dying, because I was in Delhi then. The letter must have hurt her badly. There was no reply from her.

I first opened the envelope which looked badly crumpled and immediately found out why it looked so old. The letter was started on February 1, three months before it was posted. Clearly it was not an easy letter for her to write. Something of her anguish could be seen in the blotches, words struck off or rewritten, and the several emendations. God knows how many times she had drafted and redrafted the letter, but it was still not coherent.

She wrote about her anguish at my bereavement. She blamed herself for what had happened. She should not have called me to Delhi when she did not have the courage to introduce me to her father. But what could she do? Her father had had a mild heart attack a fortnight before my Delhi visit, and so she had to be careful. She had already called me to Delhi and desperately wanted to see me. "I was scared," she wrote, "that you might ask me to take you to father. Thank you, Proffie, you did not. How did you guess I was helpless?"

"It's all so hopeless," she wrote. "I don't even know whether I should really post this letter. What is the use of keeping up this correspondence? But then I can't live without your letters. Oh Proffie, what should I do?"

Apparently she decided against posting the letter. Then why had she posted it now, after nearly three months? And why the new letter?

I was nervous and apprehensive when I opened the next envelope. The first half of the letter was more like a note than a letter. Dakshi was usually very formal and methodical in her way of writing. But this time there was just the date, 1st May, on top. Then this note:

"Yesterday I had a long chat with father. He was not feeling well, and thought he was not going to live much longer. He made me cry, the way he said it. He said that he had only one desire left: to see me well settled, married to a boy he could trust. There were a few boys he had met and liked: well-educated boys from good families. 'Will you trust me to choose a suitable boy for you?' he asked. 'Or you can choose one from among the boys we all approve of. If you say yes I'll be able to die in peace.'

"I said that I wanted a little time. 'How long?' he said, 'I have been waiting for years now.' 'Just a few hours,' I said, 'I'll tell you by evening.'

"All my three sisters came home in the afternoon. They wanted to talk to me, but I said no, let me make up my mind first, and then I'll talk to you. Didi was very keen to give a lecture, but I was not prepared to listen.

"I brooded over my problem till I thought my head would burst. Then I decided. What good is our love doing to us or to our family? Perhaps it was responsible for your father's death, and my father's heart attack. Perhaps you are already fed up. Why haven't you written a reply to my earlier letter? It's three months since I wrote it. No, I have no stamina left to fight this battle. So I went to father and told him that I trusted him and was prepared to marry the boy of his choice, without asking any questions.

"Then I came back to my room and started writing this. Sulakshana, my second sister, came and knocked on the door. She was scared that I might do something desperate. I told her I was merely writing a letter—my last one—to you, and she started crying. She is a softhearted girl. She once came to our college to see you, but went away without meeting you because she was scared that at the time of the final showdown with father he might think that she had encouraged me. It is strange how fear and love coexist in our family. We are scared of father because we worship him.

"So it's all over now. This is the last letter you will receive from me. Please take care of yourself. Please take care of your mother. Go and meet her often. I know your heart is in your village, not in Bombay. That is another reason why our love was doomed to fail. What do I, 'Dakshi, from the misty mountains of the north,' do in your South Indian village? Do you remember when you called me that?"

But that was not the end of the letter. There was a postscript, written in a hand almost illegible. "It's a mess, Proffie, I'm betrayed," she wrote, "and there is nothing I can do about it, nothing at all. Didi came to my room after I completed the letter. I had folded it and was about to put it into an envelope. She asked me what I was writing, and I told her it was my last letter to you. I gave the letter to her and said, 'Will you post it for me please.' She took it from me and suddenly started crying. I had never seen her crying in my life. I had to console her. 'It's all right,' I said, 'don't worry about me, I'll be all right.' 'I have done something terrible,' she said. Then she told me that the letter I had written to you three months earlier, and given to Neetu, my cousin, to post, it was never posted. She had seen it with Neetu and taken it away. She had threatened Neetu that she would tell Papa and that was why Neetu, my only friend here, had been avoiding me for months. Oh, Proffie, what do I do. I now know that you did not write a reply to my letter because you had not received it. Not because you don't care. But what can I do now? I can't go to father now and tell him I have changed my mind. That would break his heart. And what is the use, what's the use of any resistance any more, when I know we can't marry, there's no way we can come together. You knew that long ago, and wrote it in my autograph book, remember?

"Didi took out the poor letter from her bag—it was all crumpled—and tried to give it to me. I did not take it. I told her I would add a postscript to my second letter and give it to her so that she could post both of them. 'Can you still trust me?' she asked. 'If I don't trust you whom can I trust,' I said, and she started crying again.

The rest of the postscript was in a much better hand. She had written it the next morning.

"*The sun hasn't risen yet. Didi is sound asleep in my room. I must complete this letter before she wakes up and give it to her to post.*

"*But what is there to write? Except to say I'm sorry, sorry, sorry, but even if I go on writing sorry for hours it will not lessen my sorrow, or the injury I have caused you. This is my last letter, Proffie. What will you do with these two letters and with the eighty-one earlier letters I wrote—if you have kept any of them? Please destroy them. I'll have to destroy your letters too. I have three autographs of yours in my autograph book. The first one I'll keep; it's fairly harmless. I remember how I asked you to draw something, and you said only schoolgirls drew pictures in each other's autograph books. When I insisted that you should, you carelessly started doodling with a ball pen. 'You are spoiling my autograph book,' I screamed. But then your doodle turned into a very beautiful tree, and you wrote under it, 'May you be like a green laurel, rooted to one dear perpetual place.' The other two I love but I can't keep them, and I don't want to destroy them, so I have carefully cut them from my book and I'm sending them to you. Please take care of yourself, Proffie, for the sake of all those who love you.*"

That was all. I sat looking at the letters for a long time, unable to think clearly. Perhaps I was too tired, after the long journey. How many miles I had travelled, what awful distance I had covered, in the last twenty-five days. The funeral, and then the cutting of the suragi tree—and now the letters, telling me of the snapping of the last tie that bound me.

I felt a surge of pity for Dakshi. Poor girl, she did not know how to accept defeat. Perhaps I could bear my disappointments more easily because my devotion—to anything—was less single-minded than hers was. But she was young, she would recover. She would perhaps realize that the decision she had taken—under duress though it might be—was the right one after all; she might begin to feel that her attachment to her well-knit family was more real, more solid and longer lasting, than her romantic love for a man she did not fully understand.

But what anguish she had to go through, in the mean time. I could not help feeling that it was all my fault. Five years earlier, moved by her tears, I had taken the easy way out and left all decision-making to her. I had told her that she could convince her parents, *or* marry me against their wishes, *or* pick and choose her own time to break off our relationship. "I leave it to you," I had said, in a show of great magnanimity. But was it really magnanimity or weakness?

What I had in reality done was to pass on the onus, the terrible burden, of decision-making to the poor girl, without realizing that she would be torn between her loyalty to her parents and her love for me.

I sat looking at the two pink pages torn from Dakshi's autograph books enclosed with the letter. I recollected the days when I had written them. How different the situations were on those two days! The first one was written when Dakshi came with Nita, Shabnam and Olivia at the end of the academic year when they were in Senior B.A. They were all in high spirits. "We'll come and collect our autograph books after the next lecture," she had said, and then added, "but mind you, you must draw something real nice, no doodling this time." I saw an ad in the newspaper lying on the table, showing a young mother breast-feeding a baby. My sketching is amateurish—I have no bold strokes—but I can sometimes make use of that weakness, and working with small strokes produce sketches that look like woodcuts. So I sketched that breast-feeding mother in Dakshi's book and wrote: *May you be always happy—and may I have a share in that happiness.* Dakshi blushed when she saw it, but showed it to her friends who had come to collect their books. "How sweet," I heard them say as they stood outside the Department Room giggling, "how sweet and naughty."

The second one was written the day before Dakshi left Bombay. She was in the Department Room when I came back from my last lecture of the day. There were some snacks and sandwiches and empty soft drink bottles on the table. Her face looked drawn, as if she hadn't slept well. "Professor Joshi has given me a farewell party," she said.

She had already collected the autographs of the other English teachers present there. So she asked me to write something, said she would meet me in the Library and went down. She must have felt a bit uncomfortable in the Department Room, though most of my colleagues were quite fond of her.

There were some coloured felt-tipped pens on the table. "Your girl insisted on my sketching something," said Professor Joshi, laughing a little nervously. He showed me what he had drawn, a badly sketched scene of the sun rising between two brown hills. "How is it?" he asked me, "Is it very bad? I haven't drawn anything since I left school, you know." "It's very sexy," I said. "What do you mean?" he said in bafflement. "What I see here," I said, "is a very suggestive picture of a pair of pointed female breasts and a bristling red porcupine nestling between them." The other English teachers in the room started laughing, and Professor Joshi, a virgin bachelor of fifty, turned beetroot red. "What has that poor innocent girl done to deserve a chap like you?" he said.

I did not know what to draw. I was feeling depressed and was in no mood to sketch anything elaborate. In Bombay the sun does not rise among hills, he rises among ugly tall buildings. Nobody watches him rising. But sunset is something we all watch. Professor Joshi's house at Shivaji Park was close to the beach and I often used to go there with him to see the sun set. So because I could not think of anything else to draw, I drew some blue undulating waves of the sea in the top left hand corner of the page, and above them an orange sun. Then I drew two parallel lines across the page so that I could write something—some quotation—in the bottom right hand corner. I think it was those parallel lines that brought to my mind some lines from Marvell, and I wrote them down:

> *As line so Loves oblique may well*
> *Themselves in every angle greet;*
> *But ours so truly parallel*
> *Though infinite can never meet.*

Professor Joshi stood behind me and looked at what I was doing. He could not of course read what I had written because of his bifocals, but he could see what I had sketched. "Why the setting sun?" he said, "What is the symbolic significance?" I think he was a bit riled by my description of his sketch as 'sexy' and 'suggestive'.

"The orange sun we see at the time of sunset is only an image," I said, a little impatiently. "I have told that to you several times, during our walks on the beach, haven't I? That's why we can look at it, and why there are no rays." I looked at the picture I had drawn, sighed and said, "This is not the setting sun, Professor Joshi, it is not real. It's only an image—an image of the sun that has already set."

Rajanna

"Brush your teeth and come for the cup that cheers," said Rajanna, as soon as I woke up the next the morning. "I think we must have a chat," he said, when I sat down with a cup of tea. "You looked so sleepy last night when you opened the door that I did not want to talk with you then."

"I had had two sleeping pills," I said.

He looked concerned. "Are you all right now? Have you recovered from—the journey, and what you had to go through at your place?"

I was about to say I was all right, then realized that that would be a big lie. I did *not* feel all right. But what was the point of telling him—or anyone—the truth about what I felt? There was no way I could make him understand the situation, without giving him a detailed account of my whole life. My mother's death and the break off with Dakshi—they had both hurt me. They were both expected, of course, but their impact was made stronger by a sense of guilt I could not shake off. I had woken up that morning with some words ringing in my head: *you have only yourself to blame.* It was strange the way that line kept on troubling me till I remembered where it came from—from a poem by Stephen Spender. But those feelings of guilt were nothing compared to what I felt when I thought of how I had participated in the killing of the tree I loved. How could I explain that to Rajanna, or to anyone?

"You have had a tough time," said Rajanna, shaking his head. "Within the span of six months you lost both your parents, and they weren't very old people either. Then these letters from Delhi. Is it all over between the two of you?"

I looked at the chap in surprise. The previous night I had gone out and had a couple of bottles of beer, and when that increased my headache instead of helping me, I had taken two sleeping pills and gone to bed. In my misery I had forgotten the letters and left them open on the table. Had Rajanna read them?

He had. "You had kept those two letters open on the table. That meant that you were terribly upset. I got worried. I wanted to find out what had happened and so I glanced through the letters..." He looked at me, held his hand up and said, "Before you say anything, try to understand me. I am not a Westerner with an exaggerated respect for people's privacy. I am a nosy Indian, very concerned about my friend's problems. I read the letters, and then kept myself awake the whole of last night—because I was worried you might do something rash. Now tell me, did I do something terribly wrong in glancing through the letters?"

What could I say to that? "You did," I said, but my tone had no anger in it. "Even if you feel you have some right to intrude into my privacy—because you care—what about the other person's privacy? You had no right to read that girl's letters. By reading them you have turned my act of forgetfulness—leaving those letters open on the table—into one of criminal negligence."

"But I don't know her," he said, looking a little hurt. "My reading of her letters will do her no harm."

I kept quiet. He sat silent for some time and then said, "Perhaps you are right. Maybe I had no right to read those letters. But the fact is…it's really a question of attitudes, not morality. You are much more westernized than I am. How long have we been living together in this house? Ten months? But you have never shown any curiosity about—about my wife's death." He shook his head, and added, "At first I was happy about it. You know I sold my flat at Sion and came to Borivli because I was fed up of people's sympathy—and questions. When you came to stay with me but showed no curiosity about my tragedy, I was happy at first and then began to feel—irritated and hurt. I started thinking that you did not care.

"About a month ago I was on the verge of talking to you, on my own, about the tragedy. That was when Mr. Amin came for tea on a Sunday, and you two had an argument about the different ways girls were brought up, here and in our place. Some Gujarati girl from our building—I think it was Hansa—was standing near our door and having a long distance conversation with her friend on the fourth floor, in a shrill high pitched voice. What an awful voice that girl has, really. You said that if a girl were found screaming like that in our place her mother would have skinned her alive. Amin agreed. He started eulogizing our girls, saying how wonderfully feminine and soft-spoken they were compared to girls in Bombay.

"You changed your tune then. You started arguing that the way they stifled a girl's growth in our place was cruel; as cruel as the old Chinese custom of binding a girl-child's feet to prevent them from growing big. Mr. Amin was quite taken aback by your sudden turnabout and did not know what to say.

"It was then that I wanted to talk to you about my wife's death."

Rajanna got up and went for his bath. He had to reach his office at Colaba by half past ten, which meant he had to leave home by half past eight. I could take things easy and dawdle as I still had twenty-five days of vacation left. I prepared some breakfast—scrambled eggs and toast—for the two of us.

It was when we were about to sit down for breakfast that he asked me, "Do you know anything about—how my wife died?"

"I heard that she was killed," I said.

Rajanna sat quietly, looking at the scrambled eggs on the plate. "It's not easy to talk about what happened," he said.

He narrated the events calmly enough. It was only his hands that betrayed how difficult it was for him to talk. When I gave him a glass of water at the end of his narration—because he looked like he needed some—his hand was trembling so much that he found it difficult to keep the water from spilling.

He told me that he had married four years earlier, when he was thirty-four. The girl was his neighbour in his village. "It wasn't what you would call a love marriage," he said.

He had come to Bombay when he was eighteen, after passing S.S.L.C., because his father refused to give him money to go to college. His father was his grandfather's only son and had inherited a lot of wealth. He was a big show off and was always surrounded by a group of toadies, on whom he spent money lavishly. He wasted his inheritance by never learning to live within his means, and finally could not spare any money to pay for Rajanna's college education. "What do you want a degree for? Haven't I lived a good life without even going to high school?" he said. So Rajanna quarrelled with him and came to Bombay, worked as a peon in an office and did his B.A. as a working student. Whenever he went home—"I went home only to meet my poor mother, who was treated like dirt by her husband," said Rajanna—he made it a point to incense his father by openly telling everyone that he was working as a peon in Bombay.

He became a clerk in the same office after his graduation, and then did his L.L.B. He got a good job as an officer in another company. His father, now quite proud of his son, started looking for a rich girl who would bring him a dowry, but Rajanna shocked him by telling him that he wanted to marry the girl next door, the daughter of a chap who used to hang around Rajanna's father, doing odd jobs. "Poor girl, " said Rajanna. "She had lost her mother when she was just twelve. Whenever I went home, I used to watch, with admiration, the way that frail girl took care of her little brother and her good-for-nothing father. The way she managed to do all the household chores, take her brother to school and then attend high school herself, with no help from her father, was just miraculous."

There was a big quarrel between father and son. Rajanna was determined to marry the girl, but the girl's father was too scared of Rajanna's father to agree to the marriage. It was only after he died, four years later, and the girl shifted to her maternal uncle's house in another village, that Rajanna could marry her. His parents did not even come to the marriage.

He brought his wife to Bombay six months after marriage, when he managed to buy a small flat at Sion with the help of a loan from his company. As he had little money left, he bought some old pieces of furniture from his office when they were put up for sale. He was very happy with his wife. "Gentle and soft-spoken, affectionate and understanding—she had every quality I had wished for in my wife," said Rajanna. "I had made the right choice, Rao, of that I was convinced."

The only problem was that she felt lonely when he was in his office. She was too diffident and shy to speak to her neighbours—because she did not know Hindi well enough. So even after staying in Bombay for six months she had no friends.

Some workers had come to Rajanna's office to repair the wicker chairs there. As Rajanna had the same kind of chairs, needing urgent repair, he asked the contractor if he could send someone to his house for the job. The man agreed to send two of his boys the same afternoon. So Rajanna telephoned home and told his wife about it.

When he reached home at eight—his usual time—his wife was not there on the balcony looking out for him. She did not come to open the door when he rang the bell. He had to open the latch with his key, and when he entered the house he found that she had been murdered.

"It was awful, Rao," said Rajanna, "an absolutely messy job. Those boys did not know how to kill. She had been throttled, hit with something blunt, stabbed repeatedly with a screwdriver. She had struggled, she had fought back though she was so frail. Why didn't anyone come to her help in that crowded building?

"Nobody did because she did not shout for help. She kept on calling 'Gurkha, Gurkha,' and people who heard her thought that she was calling our watchman, a Nepali Gurkha boy, for some work. She was dying, my poor wife, but she did not know how to scream for help.

"That was how she died, my soft-spoken wife. She died because she could not scream. She had been told, right from her childhood, that decent girls did not raise their voice. All of us admired her for being so gentle and soft-spoken, so full of feminine grace—all, including her poor husband who could not guess that she might one day die a martyr to those qualities."

As he was leaving—in a bit of a hurry, because he was getting late—Rajanna said, "You understand, Rao, why I am telling you all this. I'm sure this talk will help me—though right now I might not look as if it has done me much good—and if *you* can talk to me freely about your problems, perhaps it will help you too."

Over the next few days we had long chats about Rajanna's tragedy and my own more complex problems. Rajanna's was a simple tragedy. He loved his wife and losing her was like losing a limb—an irreparable loss. But there was no feeling of guilt, no self-reproach. Someone else in his place—someone with a hyperactive conscience like myself—might have blamed himself for sending those furniture-repairers home without taking proper precautions. But Rajanna was realistic. How could anyone have guessed that something so gruesome could happen in a crowded building in broad daylight? It was an accident, a terrible but rare misfortune. No one was to blame but Fate. That was what he thought, at first.

Then he found that there *was* someone to blame—his father. Six months after his wife's death he left for home because his younger brother was getting married. He had to get down from the Bombay-Mangalore bus at Mulky and take a rickshaw to go to his village. The rickshaw driver was a stupid-looking young man with a perpetual grin on his face. He was from Rajanna's village. "I am Somanna Poojari's son," he said, grinning broadly. Somanna was one of the hangers-on who were always with Rajanna's father.

"You lost your wife?" he asked Rajanna, with a big grin, as he took the rickety rickshaw on a bone-rattling drive on the narrow road. "We all knew something was going to happen because your father was against your marriage. He is a very powerful man, your father. They say the deiva Rahu listens to everything he says, because he has arranged so many darshanas, and offers the deiva so many coconuts and cocks every year. They say he asked the deiva to break his son's marriage and make his son come back to him. Now see the power of the deiva, your wife is dead, and you are on your way home!"

Rajanna asked the lad to stop the rickshaw. He questioned him about the veracity of what he had said and how he came to know of it. "It's no secret," said the driver, "Your father keeps nothing secret. Even if he has to commit a murder he will do it openly, he is that kind of man. The whole village knows about it."

Rajanna forced the driver to turn the rickshaw back. "I'll be skinned alive if your father comes to know about this," said the lad, the grin vanishing from his face, but he had to take the rickshaw back to Mulky. A couple of hours later Rajanna was on his way back to Bombay by one of the afternoon buses.

He sent to his father a short letter. "When an evil prayer is made to a deiva, he grants you only half your wish," he wrote. "Your daughter-in-law is dead, but as far as you are concerned, so is your son. You will never see him again."

"Those two boys were soon caught and they are both in jail now," said Rajanna to me. "But the real murderer, my father, walks free."

"That's silly," I said. "You know your father did not kill your wife. Maybe he prayed for her death, in his anger and frustration, but if he had a chance to kill her himself, do you think he would have done it? There is always more violence in our thoughts and speech than in our actions, thank God."

But Rajanna did not agree. "My father *wanted* my wife killed and he *got* her killed," he said. "His was not an idle prayer. When he asked Rahu, the fiercest of deivas, to break my marriage, it was like he was hiring an assassin."

It took some time for me to realize that Rajanna's belief in deivas was quite different from mine. He belonged to the caste of toddy-tappers, which also performed the pooja and darshanas of deivas, and so was called the 'Poojari' caste. "You Brahmins don't really believe in deivas," said Rajanna, "because you worship the higher gods, and God. You may come to watch a darshana or the pooja of a deiva condescendingly, but you think they are for lower castes, not for you. We too believe in God but the deivas are closer to us; because we can approach them directly, whereas we can approach God only through you."

"But what you say about your father still does not make sense," I said. "No one can be certain that the deivas exist; or if they exist, they would do one's bidding and work as hired assassins—and kill someone staying hundreds of miles away! Think of someone whose belief in God is total, for example. Can such a person ever seriously think that he can kill anyone by just praying to God?"

"God is far away," said Rajanna, sounding a little sad; "and when I say that, I am not talking of physical distance. You cannot approach Him with your mundane wishes, you cannot sway Him, even you Brahmins who think you have direct access to Him because you know the divine language, Sanskrit. But the deivas are different. They are all around us, living in stones and trees; and they are passionate creatures like us, though incorporeal, and they can get passionately involved with those who believe in them and worship them. And my father, a firm believer in Rahu, is *convinced* that if he appeals to the deiva his work will be done. So when he prayed to Rahu to get rid of my wife, he took aim with a gun which *he believed* was loaded, and pulled the trigger. To that extent he is guilty."

I found the strength of Rajanna's belief in deivas simply staggering, considering he was such a well-educated man. A graduate in Economics and in Law, he had also kept terms for M.A. with Philosophy though he could not find the time for studying and appearing for the exam. My own belief—if I can call it that—appeared to be something fanciful and romantic in comparison with his. But he could not, on his part, understand my anguish at the cutting of the suragi tree. "I agree it's bad to dis-house a deiva," he said, shaking his head sagely, "but it can be set right easily. You can build a little shrine for Yakshi and arrange for the offering of a coconut once a month. Which deiva wouldn't prefer a permanent home and regular worship to living in a tree?"

There was no way I could make him understand my feeling that the Yakshi I believed in was the spirit of the tree I loved, and that in participating in the cutting of that tree I had done violence to my love. "That's all fanciful," he said. "Your idea of a deiva is terribly westernized. You think of her as a kind of nymph living in a tree? That's silly."

He could not understand what I felt about some of my other problems either. He was quite shocked when I told him that I had felt, among other feelings, a sense of relief when I read Dakshi's letters. "Relief?" he said, in a tone of utter disbelief, "You loved that girl, Rao, I know you still love her. I didn't tell you this, but I saw you with her several times—at Dadar, at Sion, three or four times at Flora Fountain. You didn't notice me because you had eyes only for her. It was clear that you two were very much in love. And now you want me to believe that you felt *relieved* when you lost her?"

The number of people, by the way, who have told me, or my acquaintances, that they had seen me with Dakshi at this or that place is phenomenal. Sita, for example, used to hear practically every alternate day that someone or the other had seen us together. "I am fed up," she said to me once, "Is there any place in Bombay the two of you have not been seen together?" We must have been—I don't know how—the most conspicuous couple roaming about in Bombay then.

I tried to explain to Rajanna that love, even genuine love, can become a burden but he thought that I was merely putting on a brave front, and trying to hide a broken heart. But the truth was different. What did I actually feel, when I read those letters? An overwhelming sense of pity for Dakshi and her suffering at first, and then a painful and persistent feeling of guilt that it was my own weakness and indecision that brought matters to such a crisis. There was a feeling of loss, of emptiness, but along with that there was, deep down, an almost surreptitious feeling of relief. At first it was simply relief that I did not have to answer those long letters. I had always found letter-writing a painful task because I could never quite reconcile my penchant for precision with my feeling that a letter should be spontaneous, and so often rewrote letters because I found the language either too studied, or too casual. So when I realized that it was all over, after writing nearly four hundred pages of letters to Dakshi in the course of a few months, I said to myself, Oh God, at last I don't have to write any more letters.

But the writing of letters was only one of the pressures. There were others. I realized that I had grown tired—emotionally fagged out—of that long drawn out, uncertain, high voltage love. I wanted peace and quiet, and freedom to live my life my own way, reading and dreaming. I needed love, but of a quieter kind, where I could feel at home and find rest. I wondered why all my relationships had gone sour, and all emotional bonds finally hurt by becoming too tight and stifling. I loved my father but the relationship became suffocating. No doubt it was because he was so overbearing and demanding, but why did I go and fall in love with a girl who was, in her own way, almost equally overbearing and demanding? My fight with father had caused such pain to both of us that I felt burnt out. And that made me reluctant to oppose Dakshi when she dragged me to all those Hindi films. If I had shown some resistance right at the outset—refused to do things I did not want to do—our relationship might have gone on splendidly. But I allowed it to become a bond, a burden, and though I continued to love her, just as I continued to love father, my loss of freedom rankled. So when the relationship ended finally I felt grief, yes, but also—faintly but unmistakably—relief.

Rajanna listened patiently one evening to my rambling and not very coherent talk about love and freedom—I had even quoted Chesterton who, while talking of 'Free Verse', had said that it was, like 'Free Love', a contradiction in terms, meaning that if you were free, you were not in love, and if you were in love you were not free—and then said, "All right, now you aren't in love with any one, you feel free. But the question is—are you happy? Does freedom bring happiness?"

I found it difficult to answer that question. I needed my freedom, yes. It was perhaps more important to me than to most people because I had tasted it right from my childhood. My mother's neglect had given me a certain independence which children tied to their mothers with uncut umbilical chords rarely experience. Then my freedom was threatened—by my father's possessive love—and I had to fight for it. I won the battle but at a terrible cost. I would carry the scars of it forever. One of the costs I had to pay, perhaps, was that I would always find it difficult to strike a balance between my need for independence and my need for love. After the death of my father and mother, and the cutting of the suragi tree, when the break with Dakshi came, it meant the snapping of the last bond that tied me. I was free at last. But did that make me happy? I valued my freedom, certainly, but with almost all my bonds gone, perhaps I had begun to feel—lost. As if I had lost my moorings and was adrift.

Little Ramu

Moni certainly knew where *he* was going. He was not adrift. Six months after mother's death he started, with great fanfare, the 'Dr. Nampalli Krishna Rao and Saraswati Rao Memorial Hospital' at Kantheshwar. He stayed in the upstairs bedroom and converted the house into a hospital. Hectic construction activity, he wrote to me, was going on: his bungalow, in the plot where the suragi once stood, and a new wing for the hospital, adjacent to the old building, were both expected to be ready by April. I was quite taken aback by the letterhead of the hospital on which Moni had written his letter: the name of the hospital, printed in big block letters, under a big round emblem with the letters 'N.K.R. & S.R.M. HOSPITAL', covered nearly half the page. Moni certainly liked to do things in a big way.

I could not go to the opening of the hospital, but I went in April to the opening of the new wing, and the *Griha Pravesha*, the 'house-entering' ceremony. They were on consecutive days, the hospital function at noon on the tenth and the Griha Pravesha in the evening of eleventh. Before leaving for Kantheshwar I found from an almanac that the next day, April 12, was Chitra Poornima.

The opening ceremony of the hospital's new wing was a grand affair. All the local bigwigs were there, but I sneaked away from the meeting because Moni wanted me to give a speech. I wandered around the new wing, and then the old one—my home for many years—and realized with surprise that the house my father built as a home had become a hospital with very few alterations. I pushed open the door of what was once my room and peeped in. I had to turn away hastily when a massively pregnant woman lying in a bed there stared back at me.

There was dinner after the function in a specially erected pavilion between the two wings. Moni went around inviting people to the Griha Pravesha next day. He called it a 'house-warming' ceremony, but when I stepped inside the house in the afternoon I realized that the house needed no warming, it was hot like hell. The old architectural style of our district, with sloped tiled roofs and wooden ceilings, is suited to our weather, but Moni had gone for the western style cement-concrete 'bungalow' which was then coming into vogue. The house looked impressive but the heat was incredible. Moni had kept the roof flat because he wanted to construct another floor some years later. As there was not a single tree in the compound, the house grew warmer as the day progressed and in the afternoon the torrid sweltering heat became unbearable. And it was only the first half of April.

I looked around and saw that a large area in front of the bungalow had been cemented, and beyond it the land, blanched by the pitiless sun, blazed in the afternoon like desert sand. I remembered with an ache, with 'a longing like despair', how green the place was some years earlier, under the suragi tree. Just a few minutes spent inside the house convinced me that I would not like to spend a night under that flat roof. I had come with the intention of staying for a week, but I went out and bought a bus ticket for Bombay for April 13.

Savitri's husband had come as one of the purohits for the double function. I asked him if he could arrange for a Ranga Pooja on the twelfth, as it was Chitra Poornima and Hanuman Jayanti. "My uncle died on that day sixteen years ago," I said. "Is it his shraddha?" he asked, and I said, "no, he died in the solar month of Mesha, so it will come a month later this year." He agreed to make all the arrangements for the pooja. I told him I would come in the afternoon so that I could personally invite the people of the hamlet.

I slept that night and the next one in my father's upstairs bedroom. Quite a few guests followed me because they found the new house too warm. Then on the twelfth I went walking to Nampalli at half past four in the afternoon. Moni was to bring Chandratte, her daughter and a few others—who had come for the Griha Pravesha—by car later in the evening.

All along the way I was brooding over that Chitra Poornima sixteen years earlier. Uncle wanted to light a few lamps to Lord Hanuman that evening. God knows how long he waited for me. I should have gone to Nampalli, even after that bitter quarrel with father. I could have helped him to do the pooja and perhaps nursed him back to health. I would have at least been with him at the time of his death, and it struck me, with a stab of pain, that had he been granted one last wish, he might well have asked that his Babu should be with him when he breathed his last. I was a coward, I said to myself, and then felt that it wasn't cowardice, it was something much worse. Father could not have stopped me from going to Nampalli. It was I who ran away, not out of fear but out of a meanness of spirit. I, a pampered and spoilt brat, did not have the stomach to stay with and nurse a dying old man, a man who had given me the purest and most undemanding love anyone could ever hope to get.

I went by the short cut that took one to the hamlet first, and then to the Matha, because I wanted to finish the task of inviting people to the Ranga

Pooja first. The first house I reached was the farthest from the Matha. As expected it was locked, and so was the next one. The one next to that was Little Ramu's and I was taken by surprise when I found the door open, the courtyard clean and well swept. Sound of pleasant laughter came floating from within. Had Ramu or his father sold the house, or given it to some family to take care of?

I stood at the gate, hesitant. A pretty girl of about ten came out laughing and stood on the steps looking back. She turned and looked at me, smiled and went back into the house. I thought I discerned in her a faint resemblance to Kaveri.

A shortish, plump but pleasant-looking woman came out. The girl came with her and I noticed that though not more than ten or eleven, she was already an inch taller than her mother. A sweet-looking boy, with a striking resemblance to the woman, stood behind them.

"Whom do you want?" said the woman. When I said "Little Ramu," she smiled and the two kids laughed aloud. The woman had an extraordinarily sweet smile, which lit up her face and made it beautiful. "It's his house all right," she said, "but he is not at home. And he isn't a little one now, he is above six feet tall."

"Six feet two inches," said the boy.

I stood tongue-tied. "I am his wife," said the woman, "and these two are our children. May I know who you are?"

"I'm Sudhakar, one of your husband's childhood friends," I said.

"You are Sudhakara uncle?" said the boy, jumping down from the steps and coming to the gate. "Pappa so often speaks about you. Pappa can't tell stories, you know. Whenever I pester him for stories, he begins one and then gets stuck; then he says, I wish my friend Sudhakara were here, he was such a great one for telling stories. You will tell me a story today?"

"Let uncle come in first," said the girl. "He is still standing at the gate and you have started pestering him for stories!"

"Please come in," said the woman, and the boy took hold of my hand. "I'm in a bit of a hurry," I said, "I came to invite you all to a Ranga Pooja at the Matha. I have to go to the other houses to invite the people there."

But I went in, nevertheless. "There is plenty of time," said Ramu's wife. "It's only five now. Please wait, I'll make you a cup of coffee." She went in, and the boy said, "When are you going to tell me a story?"

"After an hour," I said, "when you come to the Matha. The pooja is after seven, I think, but if you come early I can tell you stories."

"I'll come right now with you," he said.

"No," said his sister. "Uncle has to go to all the houses, meet people and invite them. Then he may have some work in the Matha. You'll be in the way. Didn't he say 'after an hour'? We'll both go together at six." Then she smiled at me and said, "I also love to listen to stories."

Their mother came out with a cup of coffee. "My husband would have been so happy to see you," she said, "but he had to leave for Hubli suddenly. A message came through the Chandapur Police Station last night." She saw my look of surprise and smiled. "My husband is in the police, you know. He is the District Superintendent of Police at Hubli. Belongs to the 1962 I.P.S. batch."

I could not believe my ears. Little Ramu a police officer, after getting selected for the I.P.S., one of the toughest competitive exams in the country. It was incredible.

I was so tongue-tied that the kids must have started wondering whether I was really capable of telling stories. So I asked, "Do you come to Nampalli often?"

"For the last six years we have been coming here once a year. We come at the end of May and stay for about a fortnight. My husband loves the rains here. 'When the first rains come I want to be in my village to receive them,' he says. This year we came early because he suddenly got this urge to perform his Mother's shraddha here, in this house where she was born and grew up. The shraddha was yesterday. I wish you could have come."

"His *mother's* shraddha?"

She saw the look of utter bafflement on my face, and coloured a little. "It looks like you are out of touch with what has been happening here," she said.

I got up to go. "Please come to the pooja, all of you," I said, and to the children I added, "Come at six, if you want to listen to stories."

The door of Ranga's house was slightly ajar. When I pushed it, it opened with an awful creaking sound. The door, I thought, had developed a natural burglar alarm. Janakamma came out of the kitchen and I saw that she had not changed much since I met her thirty years earlier. She had only shrunk a bit and become smaller, but the features were the same and the hair was still pitch dark.

She could not recognize me at first. "I'm Sudhakara," I said, "Ranga's friend, Sudhakara." "Ah, yes," she said, "the boy from the house of the Matha." Then came a string of questions. "When did you come? Where is your wife? How many children do you have?" But without waiting for my answers, she wanted to go back to the kitchen to make me a cup of coffee.

"Please don't," I said, "I just had coffee at Ramu's house. Ramu was not in, but I met his wife and children. His wife said—that they performed Ramu's mother's shraddha yesterday."

Janakamma sat down. "Sit down, Sudhakara," she said. "That woman,"—she used that word, this time, not in contempt but in a kind of awe—"That woman, Venkatalakshmi, whatever sins she might have committed in this life, she must have accumulated plenty of punya in her previous birth. How else could she have got a son like that!"

"Do you remember, Janakamma, when I met you last?" I said. "That was about thirty years ago. I came here to meet Ramu. His house was locked. You told me how his mother was driven out and Ramu was taken away by his father."

"Of course I remember," she said. "It was such a terrible thing. Who could have foretold then that things would end this way?"

Janakamma told me that Ramu's father came to the village just once to make some arrangements for the leasing out of their agricultural land. He said that Ramu was working very hard and doing well in his studies. As Mahabala worked in the same town, Davangere, news came regularly about Ramu's progress; how he passed his B.A., went to Dharwar to do his M.A., and how he finally passed some big examination and was about to become a police officer.

Padmanabhayya died soon after Ramu got his job. Two months after his death, Ramu came to Nampalli, his first visit after he left the place.

"He stood in front of me and I could not recognize him," said Janakamma. "He had grown so tall, taller than anyone in our village. Very thin he was—he has put on some weight now, after his marriage, and looks better—but he stood straight like an areca palm. 'Do you recognize me, Janakamma? I am Ramu,' he said.

"'Which Ramu?' I asked, and he said, 'Venkatalakshmi's son.'

"I asked him to sit down, and made him a cup of coffee. 'You are the same age as my daughter Sushila,' I said, 'so you must be twenty-six now. I hear you have become a big officer. You have lost both your parents; it's time you get married now and build a home for yourself.'

"'I have lost my father but my mother is still alive, isn't she,' he said.

"Then he told me that he had come with two purposes in mind. He wanted to get married, but before that he wanted to find his mother. 'Do you know how and where I can find her?' he asked me.

"'What do you want to do when you find her?' I asked, and he said, simply, 'I want to take care of her.'

"I was stunned, Sudhakara. I thought he did not know what hell she had sunk into. So I told him not to be stupid. 'You are a big officer now,' I said, 'any man will be happy to give you his daughter. But not if you bring that woman home.'

"'I don't care,' he said, 'She is my mother and I must look after her.'

"'You don't know her condition now,' I said. 'She is beyond help, beyond redemption. She has been on the streets for years. She used to live with all kinds of men, but they all used her and threw her out. She went completely mad, and has been sleeping wherever she could, eating whatever she could find, and they say now only beggars and lepers and such men who can't find any other woman go to her, and she never says no to anyone.' Then I looked at Ramu and saw that his face was like stone. 'I'm sorry,' I said. 'I know I have hurt you badly, but I must tell you the truth.' Then the strangest of things happened: I found myself crying. I don't usually cry. We women cry so much in our younger days that we are left with no tears, in our old age. I thought I was crying for Ramu, but no, it was not for Ramu, it was, for the first time in my life, for his poor mother. For I suddenly remembered Venkatalakshmi as she was when I first came as a bride to this village. She was such a sweet little child then."

Janakamma wiped her eyes with the loose end of her saree and continued. Ramu was quite determined to find his mother, she said. She quoted his words because they had made a deep impression on her mind. "Nothing can alter the fact that I am her son," he had said. "The question is, do I let her rot on the roads, or do I take care of her. Should I be the son of a woman who dies uncared for, or of one who dies a decent death, whatever her past might have been."

He told her that he could not come earlier because his father would not have liked it. "I was helpless then," he said, "but now I think I have the strength to do what I should do: try to take my mother out of the hell she has sunk into. I don't know if I can save her, Janakamma, but unless I try to, I can't save my own soul."

Janakamma told him about Putta, the youngest son of Bachchi and Subraya Devadiga. The Devadigas had become quite well to do in recent years, and their last son, pampered by his parents, had become a loafer. A school dropout, he spent all his time moving about on his new bicycle. He was the one who had last seen Ramu's mother lying stark naked under a pipal tree somewhere near Kota.

Ramu took the lad in his jeep and found his mother. "She was naked, and stinking like rotting flesh, Amma," reported Putta to Janakamma when he came back, "and she was not fully conscious. But Ramu Ayya paid money to some women living in a hut nearby, got her washed and clothed, and took her to Manipal, to the big hospital there. He paid me twenty rupees."

A week after this Janakamma's brother came to see her. He had a pretty daughter, a graduate, but she was quite tall and in India boys have a hang up about marrying girls who aren't shorter than they are. So he was looking for a tall boy, and when Ramu came in he was highly impressed by the young man. Once the introductions were over he told him about his daughter and broached the subject of marriage. But when he came to know that Ramu had found his mother, taken her to Manipal and got her admitted there, and that he intended to take her home after she recovered, he developed cold feet. "How can that be?" he said. "People know who she is, of course, but no one is bothered now. She has gone beyond the pale of gossip and is just a mad woman to the world. Why do you want to create a problem for yourself by taking her home, after all these years?"

"Ramu said nothing," said Janakamma, "but his face was like stone again. My brother is a sensible man. He had married late, and married a stupid woman, and that has taught him wisdom. 'I understand your feelings,' he said to Ramu, 'I respect them. But yours is not a wise decision. When a woman loses her mind, she has lost herself. The road is the most anonymous of places. A mad woman on the road has no identity. She is no longer anyone's mother. If you take her away from the road that has become her home, will she be happy? If you try to give her back her lost identity, will she be able to bear the burden?'

"Ramu shook his head. 'I understand your point,' he said, 'and also your motive. You think I'll make a good son-in-law for you, but not if I take my fallen mother home.' He saw the look of pain on my brother's face, and softened his tone. 'Please don't get upset,' he said. 'I know there is truth in what you say but we all tend to see the facet of truth that is convenient to us. That is human nature.'

"My brother was silenced. Then Ramu said, 'I have had only one burning desire all these years, to stand on my own feet and try to help that poor woman to stand up again. I am not going to renege now. But I have learnt something from what you have said. I will see to it that in my effort to save her I don't cause her pain.' Then he looked at my brother and added, 'I want to marry a girl who would like to share with me the care of a suffering woman. But once I am assured of her willingness, I'll take care to see that the task does not become a burden to her.'

"'When will you come to see my daughter,' asked my brother, and Ramu said 'Right now.' My brother panicked. 'No,' he said, 'I can't take you home to see my daughter without first informing my wife. She will need hours, to prepare things to eat, and deck her daughter and herself up. She will be mad at me if I take you just like that.' But Ramu was firm. 'I don't much care for food,' he said, 'and as for your daughter, I would like to see what she looks like in her everyday attire. I have myself just come from Manipal, and haven't had a good night's sleep for the last one week. Your daughter should see what a police officer looks like after a few sleepless nights.'

"So we three went to my brother's house at Tekkatte in Ramu's jeep. I had to go because they both insisted that I should. As a group of three is considered inauspicious, we took a little girl from the next house with us.

"Seema, my niece, was at the door. She was in a crumpled housecoat. My brother introduced her to Ramu. She is a very pretty girl, and the way they looked at each other, I felt they would say yes to marriage.

"But things went wrong thereafter. My brother's wife was very upset when she came to know that Ramu had seen her daughter in a simple housecoat with no make-up on. And the interview was a disaster. Seema became upset and nervous because her mother was upset, and the moment Ramu told her that he wanted to take care of his mother, she screamed in protest. 'No, no,' she said, 'I can't stay in the same house as that woman.'

"When we came out of the house, we saw Poornima coming out of the cowshed. She is my youngest sister's daughter. Poor thing, she lost her mother when she was just six months old and then her father married again, and her stepmother treated her very badly. So my brother brought her to his house, and though she was not ill-treated here, she was not treated like a daughter of the family either. She was in Seema's class and they passed S.S.L.C. together with roughly the same marks. Seema went to college but not Poornima.

"I still feel like laughing when I think of what she looked like at that moment. Her feet and hands were covered with cowdung, and she had hitched her housecoat up because she was cleaning the floor of the cowshed. There were marks of cow-dung on her face too. She forgot all that and broke into a broad smile when she saw me—she has always been very fond of me, poor thing. You must have seen her smile; she is rather plain-looking otherwise, but when she smiles she becomes beautiful.

" 'This is my niece, my youngest sister's only daughter, Poornima,' I said to Ramu. Poornima looked at Ramu. 'You have seen the house next to ours at Nampalli, always locked, haven't you?' I said to her, 'Ramu is the boy of that house. He has passed some exam and has become a big police officer now.'

"Poornima looked embarrassed. She could not even drop the hem of her dress, which she had hitched up, because both her hands were covered with cowdung. 'I'll wash my hands and feet and come,' she said to me, but Ramu said, 'just wait for a minute, please.' I looked at him in surprise and found him smiling for the first time. He must have caught it from Poornima.

"'I just want to tell you something, and it won't take long,' he said to Poornima. 'I'm the son of Venkatalakshmi. Have you heard of her?' She looked at him with wonder, and nodded. 'I could not come here till I got a job. I came a week ago and found my mother on the road, dying. I have taken her to Manipal and put her in the hospital there. They say she might recover in a month or two. When she does, I want to take her home and take care of her. She has gone through hell and so it may not be easy. I am looking for a wife— someone who is willing to share with me the task of taking care of that suffering soul.'

"I saw Poornima looking at him with sympathy, understanding and— reverence. She had forgotten what a sight she was with all that cowdung, and her housecoat hitched up above the knee. Ramu smiled again. 'Can you help me to take care of her?' he asked, and for the first time there was a faint note of pleading in his voice. 'I'll see to it, of course, that you are in no way harassed.'

"She blushed, poor thing. Then she said 'Yes' in a scarcely audible voice and ran away to wash her hands and feet.

"That was how Ramu found his wife," said Janakamma. She sighed and then added, "The marriage was a simple affair. Venkatalakshmi recovered, and as soon as she was well enough to be taken home, Ramu and Poornima came and took her to Hubli. But she hardly spoke a word, they say, as long as she lived. She was always a little scared of Ramu, so he left her to his wife's care, and she grew very fond of her daughter-in-law. She was also fond of Padma—Ramu's daughter—and she died seven years ago, just before Prashant was born."

"There's a Ranga Pooja at the Matha this evening," I said, getting up. "I came to invite you to the pooja." "Ah, yes," she said. "Today is Hanuman Jayanti, isn't it. How many years ago was it—fifteen years?—that your uncle died on that day, all alone in the Matha?"

Janakamma shook her head. "Your uncle was a saint, a man whose heart was full of love and affection. He had such a nice wife—Sita was her name— such a lovely person she was. She was my age and I was very fond of her. He lost her. He loved the child, but she too was taken away from him. He loved his brother, and he really loved you, Sudhakara. But when he died he was all alone, whereas Venkatalakshmi, who never cared for anyone but herself, died at home, surrounded by her family. It's not fair."

I stood speechless. "I had gone to the Matha that day to do Pradakshinas," said Janakamma, "and I was one of those who saw him lying prostrate before Lord Hanuman. I'll never forget that sight." She looked at me with pity. "Don't feel too bad," she added, "no one can undo the past. I don't go to Ranga Poojas these days because I can't see clearly at night. But I'll come tonight."

The door burst open and little Prashant dashed in, followed by Padma. "You are still here, uncle?" he said in surprise, "It's nearly six and we two are on our way to the Matha! We came to tell Grandma that Amma will take her to the Matha at seven." He turned to Janakamma and said, "Don't worry about not being able to see at night, we have a police torch so bright that it will turn night into day."

The kids came with me to the other houses, to invite people, and we reached the Matha in less than five minutes. Prashant called a couple of other kids to come and listen to stories and at the Matha Savitri's younger children joined in. So when I started telling stories I had at first an audience of seven, and then it grew to more than a dozen as the women of the village started coming with their children, the women doing pradakshinas and the children gravitating to the spot where I sat surrounded by my young audience. Moni brought a few of his guests at half past six in his car—because Chandratte and her daughter Malati wanted to spend some time in the house where they were born—and then went away saying he would come back at half past seven. Malati came with her daughter and joined our group. Even Savitri came and stood nearby for some time, till she was called away by her husband for some work.

It was as if I was in a trance that evening. Stories from the past, the ones I had heard from my grandmother, uncle and others in my childhood, together with the ones I had myself concocted and narrated, they came crowding back, from the dark nooks and corners of that old house where they had waited, breathless, for decades. They wanted me to breathe life into them again and narrate them to those children hungry for stories. I was only dimly aware of what was happening outside our magic circle. Women doing pradakshinas slowed down when they neared us. Chandratte came and sat nearby, and I even noticed the sad look on her face and wondered vaguely why she was unhappy. Savitri's husband delayed the start of the pooja, not, I think, because

I was busy telling stories but because Moni had not come. Moni, as the family doctor, was more important to him than I was. The session of story telling continued for nearly two hours.

It ended at eight, when Moni came and the Ranga Pooja started. I don't know who got more out of that session and regretted its termination more, I or the children. "When will you come again and tell us stories," asked Prashant several times. As I was leaving for Bombay the next day I could only say that perhaps we would meet again next year.

But I never met them again. They had given me their address at Hubli and I had promised to write to them, but days passed and I did not write; and then I began to feel that it was too late to write.

Years later I heard that Prashant died, at the age of eleven, in a jeep accident. His father was at the wheel then. When I heard this news it was already five years old, and there was no point in probing old wounds by writing to the parents. The news shook me as if it were a personal bereavement, but it cured me of a little tinge of envy I had unknowingly harboured till then. Poor Ramu, how much he had suffered in his life. If he still got more out of life than I did, he deserved it. *He* did not flinch from suffering.

Moni's car was overloaded on the way back. The bout of remorse and depression I had felt earlier in the afternoon had disappeared after the story-telling session and the pooja, and I was in high spirits. I was surprised to find Chandratte on the verge of tears.

"What's wrong," I said, "You have toothache again?" She did not realize I was joking. "How can I have toothache when I have no teeth?" she said. "You know I am wearing dentures now."

"It's Annayya," she said, a little later. "Three women—not one or two but three—told me this evening how they had seen Annayya lying prostrate before God, dead, sixteen years ago. First it was one who made a nice story out of it. Then came another, and when she started telling the same story again, the first one, instead of telling her that the story had already been told, joined her with great enthusiasm. Just after their duet got over came Janakamma. I was fed up, Babu. So I got up and came and joined your group.

"I watched you telling those kids stories and felt like crying. That little boy who was listening with his ears and eyes and mouth all open, who kept on moving closer to you and finally ended up sitting on your lap, such a sweet kid he is; and I thought: if Babu had married, he would have had a son like that. Then my mind went back to the past and I thought of my childhood, and of how we used to sit at the same spot, listening to stories, sixty years ago. There were more children in our house then than in your childhood, Babu. Some of the stories we heard then were so much like the ones you narrated today that I said to myself, stories don't die, they don't grow old like us. And do you know who used to tell us stories? It was Annayya. He was such a fine teller of stories. Like you."

Another Play

❧

The morning after I reached Bombay I heard, when I was taking my bath, someone knocking at our door. At first it was gentle hesitant tapping, but soon it changed into loud insistent banging. "Wait a moment, I'm taking my bath," I shouted, but the banging continued. So without even drying myself up properly, I wrapped a towel round myself and rushed to the door. When I opened it I found a bunch of kids of our building there, led by one of the most talkative persons I have ever come across, seven-year-old Prachi Pradhan.

Prachi opened her mouth the moment I opened the door. "Uncle," she said, "we are going to celebrate Maharashtra Day, you know, we children only are going to arrange everything; we are going to have a party and after that we are going to put up a play, a small play but we children only are going to put it up."

Prachi's fluency was mind boggling. She spoke with the same fluency in three languages, Marathi, Hindi and English, and she could also speak in Gujarati. With me she always spoke in English because she had a very poor opinion of my Hindi.

"But Maharashtra Day is still sixteen days away," I said, "there's surely time enough for me to go in, dry myself up, and put on some decent clothes?"

"Ah, yes," she said, grinning, "You look quite comic in this towel."

I came back quickly, and because I wanted to pack them off soon I said, "So you want me to donate some money for the programme, right?"

"Wrong," said Prachi. "We are going to collect money from each house, not each person, so we are going to ask Poojari uncle only, because he is the owner of the flat, no? We are going to collect twenty rupees from each house and..".

"Wow, that's a lot of money," I said. We had sixty flats in our building, and twelve hundred rupees was a big sum, to be managed by these kids.

"It's not a lot of money," said Prachi, "in fact it's not going to be enough, because so many people will come to the party, uncle, this boy Gattu, you know how many people are there in his house? His father and his two uncles, and his mother and two aunts, and his sister and kid brother and seven cousins, and his grandfather and grandmother; there are seventeen people in the house! No, sorry, eighteen people, because I'm so stupid, I left *him* out! You know, uncle, why Chintu, Gattu's younger brother, does his number two behind your flat every morning? Because there is always a long line of people waiting in the mornings in front of their bathroom door, and Chintu can't wait, you know, he always has to do it urgently. Of course the men from his house won't come to the party, because they are working in the city market, but the three aunties and the ten children will come, and I'm telling you they won't give one paisa more than twenty rupees! And we must give all those who come at least one slice of cake each, and some snacks and wafers and sherbet, you know how much it will cost! Of course we are going to make sherbet at home only, my mummy and Rohan's mummy will make it, so it will be free, but more than half the money will go for eats only, and what do we do for the stage? How much money will a stage cost, uncle? And..".

"But why do you need a stage?"

"To put up the play!" said Prachi. "Oh, you uncle, how can we put up a play without a stage? The play, you know, is as important as the party! And..."

I had discovered that the only way one could say something while Prachi was speaking was by cutting in when she stopped for breath, and she always did that after the word 'and'. Perhaps that was her way of reserving her right to speak some more. I asked them where they wanted to organize the party, and when they said that it was in the garden behind our building, I suggested that they could put up a play right there in the garden, without a stage.

The building I stayed in then had four wings, and there were four small gardens behind. The one behind C wing was the biggest, and that was where they wanted to have the party. We went to the garden and I showed them how they could keep all the chairs at one end of the garden, facing the building, and the play could be put up, after the party, without a built up stage, in front of the people occupying those chairs. The back entrances of the B, C, and D wings could be used for the actors to enter and exit from the playing arena.

They were quite thrilled once they understood how it could be done. "That's only why we came to you, uncle," said Prachi, "You have to help us to put up the play. You must select a play, and you must only direct it. And you must only choose the actors, because otherwise you know we are going to fight, and..".

"Let's not select a play, let's write it," I said. "But who will write it, uncle?" said Shailesh, in Hindi, "Will you write it for us?"

"Not I," I said, "We'll write it together. First we'll think of a story, choose the actors to play the roles, and then the actors will write their own dialogues. Those of you who can't write well will only speak the words, and someone will write them down for you—with some changes of course. You'll then find it easy to learn the dialogues by heart because they are mostly *your* words."

"But what story, uncle, what story," they said, all of them excited and involved now, and poor Prachi somehow lost her role as their spokesperson.

I looked at Prachi and said, "Let's choose the story—of the talkative princess."

They laughed. "I'll have to play that role," said Prachi, shaking her head, "no one else is half as talkative as I am, no? But who is going to be the hero, uncle? Who is going to be the prince?"

I looked around and saw Jatin Darji, a badly dressed boy with expressive eyes and a thick mop of unkempt hair, standing at the back. He reminded me of little Apu in *Pather Panchali*. "What about Jatin?" I said, "Shall he be our hero?"

There was a howl of protest from everyone present. The main objection was to his appearance, because he came from a poor family of tailors and was always badly dressed. "How can we make him a *prince?*" said someone. "He can't speak a word of English," said Prachi, "he is going to a Gujarati medium school, and there also, you know, he does not go everyday because his mother wants him to sit at home and sew buttons. You can't teach him to speak in English in fifteen *years*, uncle, and we have fifteen days only to put up the play!"

I saw Jatin looking down at the ground. "But why should he speak in English?" I said. "We talk in different languages in this colony, don't we? So let's have a play in two or three languages. Jatin will be our hero but he will not be a prince. He will be, well, he'll be a poor tailor boy, who, at the end of the play, becomes a king. So let him speak in Hindi, and that too our own variety of Bombay Hindi."

So we cooked up a story right there, standing in that enclosed place behind C wing which had only a couple of withered shrubs to justify the use of the word 'garden'. Jatin, I told them, was a tailor boy. He could not go to school everyday because he had to sew buttons on dresses and do all kinds of odd jobs. Flies troubled him when he was working and so he spent a lot of time swatting them. Then one day he did something fantastic. He killed seven flies with one blow!

Jatin had always wanted to get away from it all, and seek his fortune in the wide world. The killing of seven flies with one blow gave him courage. So he told his mother that he would go to some city, make his fortune and come back a rich man. Then he left his village and soon reached a dense forest.

"But how are we going to have a forest here, uncle, if we don't have a stage, and don't have sceneries," said Prachi.

"We don't need backdrops—what you call 'sceneries'," I said. "We'll have some boys, wearing masks, as scene-shifters. Do you have any masks?"

"I have twenty," said Sanjay.

"You know, uncle," said Prachi, quite excited, "this boy Sanjay, his happy birthday was a month ago, and his father brought twenty masks to be given to all the kids who came to the party, you know, but this fellow did not give them only, he kept them all for himself, such a *kanjoos* he is!"

Kanjoos is a rather strong word meaning 'stingy person'. Prachi's fluency in English came from two admirable qualities. One was her ability to anticipate moments when she might be stuck for words and avoid them by using some stock words like 'only' and 'you know'. The other was her very effective use of Indian words. When she used words like 'kanjoos' she stressed the word in such a way that she made her audience feel that the English equivalent would have been a poor substitute.

"If he gives us the masks for the play, you can't call him kanjoos," I said. Then I explained to them how the scene-shifters would sit motionless at the back, and when a scene got over, they would quietly move in and change it right in front of the audience. They would take away the stool Jatin was sitting and working on, and replace it with a few potted plants, and that would show the audience that the scene had shifted from Darji's house to a forest. Later they would remove the plants and bring in a throne and a few chairs, and the jungle would change into the throne room of a palace.

The boy was frightened in the forest, I continued, and to give himself courage he kept on saying, 'I'm not scared, I am a brave tailor boy, with one blow I can kill seven flies!' But when he was saying it the third time, when he had just said 'with one blow I can kill seven...' he saw, in front of him, a Rakshas! He was so frightened that he screamed 'Rakshas' instead of 'flies'. So what he actually said was—here I paused, and the kids, picking up the clue, said in chorus, "With one blow I can kill seven...Rakshas!"

"And the Rakshas can be Rakshit only," said Prachi, delighted by the turn of the story. Rakshit Mehta was the fattest boy of the group. At eleven he already weighed sixty-five kilos. All the kids called him 'Rakshas' and he, a good-natured boy, did not mind it. In fact he enjoyed the nickname, and loved to bare his teeth and try to frighten little boys, saying, "I am a Rakshas, I love to eat little children, ha, ha, ha."

Rakshit had a strong Gujarati accent and we decided that he should speak in that kind of Hindi with Jatin, and he and his wife should speak to each other in Gujarati. The kids were amused by the idea that Gujarati in our play was the language of the Rakshasas. We decided to make the Rakshas a bit of a moron, and that thrilled Rakshit, a brilliant student who always stood first in his class. In our story the Rakshas believed what he heard—that the boy could kill him with one blow—and so fell at his feet and promised to give him plenty of gold and diamonds and also a stolen princess, if his life was spared. Jatin was delighted. He knew that the king had announced that anyone who rescued his daughter would get one quarter of his kingdom.

"That's where I, Prachi Pradhan the talkative princess, enter the play," said Prachi, clapping her hands, and Rakshit clapped his hands too and said, "And that's where the dialogue in the play comes to an end. Because once Prachi enters the scene there can be no dialogue, there can only be a long speech."

Prachi frowned. "That will not happen," I said, "because the Rakshas in our story, unable to bear the Princess's incessant talking, had taken away her voice and kept it in a small bottle. When he gave Jatin a bag filled with gold and diamonds, together with the Princess, he also gave him that bottle, with a suitable warning..."

"Don't open this bottle," said Rakshit in a rough guttural voice, meant to be the voice of a Rakshas, "till you have packed your ears with loads of cotton-wool."

Everyone laughed, except Prachi. "That's not fair," she said, "if the princess is going to be a dumb one, why choose me for the role? Anyone can play it. And..."

"The Princess is not going to be dumb all through the play," I said, and continued with the story. "When Jatin returned her to her father, the king was shocked to find that his daughter had gone dumb. So he announced that anyone who made her talk again would get another quarter of his kingdom. So Jatin opened the bottle, and the Princess started speaking. She hadn't spoken for months, you see, so it was like a dam bursting, and she spoke incessantly and fast, *blah blah blah blah, blah blah blah blah...*"

All the kids—except Prachi—took it up, and went on and on saying *blah blah blah blah* till Prachi, who looked quite baffled at first, suddenly and unexpectedly started crying.

It's strange how even little kids wear masks, put on brave fronts, and hide their touchiness. Poor Prachi. I hugged her and said, "No, no, dear, they were not laughing at you, they were merely demonstrating how that last scene would be delightfully funny, the most effective one in the play; the princess spoke at such speed, and there was such a flood of words, that the king and the queen and all the courtiers had to hastily cover their ears and run for shelter. The audience will really enjoy that scene, Prachi, but it's going to be the most difficult scene to enact, and only you can act that role, no one else can, no one else will be able even to learn that long speech by heart..."

Prachi stepped back and looked at me. "Even you are like me, uncle," she said with a faint smile, "you can also, like me, go *blah blah blah*."

I did not have to do much work for the play. Prachi's mother got interested in it, and suggested that as the performance was in celebration of Maharashtra Day, Marathi should not be left out of the play. So it was decided that the royal family—including the princess—should speak in Marathi, not English. Prachi's Marathi was as fluent as her English was, but it was also syntactically more correct. Her mother wrote down the Marathi speeches, Shailesh's aunt and Rakshit's elder sister came forward to transcribe the Hindi and Gujarati speeches; gradually they took over the direction of the play and I very happily became a mere 'consultant'.

The play went off reasonably well. Rakshit was a great success but poor Prachi messed up her all-important long speech at the end of the play by suddenly and unexpectedly becoming nervous. But the real scene-stealer was Jatin. He moved around with such grace, and spoke so well, that even those three women directing the play, who had earlier expressed grave doubts about my choice of that boy as the hero, had to admit that he was the real star of the evening.

The day after the play was a Sunday, and Satish came to see me in the afternoon. His mother was worried, he said, about my health, as I had not called on them for days. We had tea, and then we went out for a stroll.

Satish was taken aback by the amount of attention I received on the way. "Good afternoon, uncle," came from a dozen kids, and quite a few came up to me to say that the play was terrific. A two-year-old boy, whom I did not know, came running to me, touched my hand, just said "uncle" shyly and ran away. An old woman stopped me and said in Gujarati, "uncle, please tell Rakshit not to skip his breakfast. Boys of his age must eat well, shouldn't they, uncle?"

Satish started laughing. "Here I am," he said, "quite hesitant to call you 'Mawa' because you look too young to be an uncle. That Sudha auntie, you know, keeps on asking Amma if you are really her *elder* brother, as if she can't still believe it, though Amma herself looks quite young for her age. And here, you have become an uncle even to old women!"

"Perhaps that is the role I'm destined to play," I said. "Maybe there is some old debt to be repaid."

"What do you mean?" said Satish.

"I don't know," I said. "I had a wonderful uncle, Satish. His was the greatest love I received. I don't think I was a good nephew to him. Perhaps the only way I can repay the debt I owe is by becoming a good uncle myself."

No, that did not sound all right. I shook my head and said, "I think I have got it all wrong. I'm not trying to be a good uncle to repay any old debts. I play the role because I relish playing it. Perhaps that's the only role I can play well. Maybe we can only give what we have received."

Trapped

I don't know when exactly I started feeling that I had lost my roots. It was a feeling that grew slowly, I think, over the years. Perhaps it all began with the cutting of the suragi tree, but that might just be my fancy. It was not that I was never happy after that event. I was happy that evening telling stories at Nampalli Matha, but even at that moment, surrounded by those wide-eyed kids, I was aware—though only faintly—that somehow I did not belong. I was an outsider who had come to entertain those kids, like a travelling circus. I was happy again cooking up that play with the kids at Borivli, and I loved my teaching, especially my lectures on Yeats to M.A. students. But there was always a sense of incompleteness, of alienation, even of futility.

I enjoyed my M.A. lectures. I gave no bibliography and asked the students not to read any critical works till they had read the poems. My job, I told them, was to introduce them to Yeats' poems, in a chronological order, so that we would be able to trace Yeats' extraordinary development as a poet. "If nothing else," I said, "we'll at least enjoy ourselves in the class. We shall not waste our time on dry theories and vague generalities, we'll spend it reading and discussing some of the finest poems written in this century."

It worked, for some time. I think I even succeeded in infecting some of the students with the excitement I felt for Yeats' poetry. During the first few lectures my classes were packed. Then it began to dawn on the students that I was only a visiting lecturer, not an examiner; my way of teaching might be interesting but it was not going to be of much use to them in the examination. M.A. syllabus was an impressive one, with a large number of texts, but as the number of questions students had to answer were fewer than the texts prescribed, they could 'drop' some and concentrate on the others. My students soon decided to drop Yeats.

But they came to the class nevertheless, not as many as at first but quite a few, and though I was hurt that they had decided against studying Yeats for the exam, I still enjoyed my teaching. In the second or third year a few students complained that though they understood poems like 'Byzantium' when I was explaining them, they found the meaning slippery and elusive when they tried to read them on their own. Could I recommend an essay that gave a straightforward interpretation of the Byzantium poems, they asked, and I found that I could not.

So I wrote an essay on the two Byzantium poems, in the summer vacation, so that I could show it to my next batch of students. But that year the university changed its syllabus. M.A. students had to study two major poets, Yeats and Eliot, in their Modern Period paper. The Head of the Department of English at the University retired that year and the new H.O.D. happened to be someone who had done his Ph.D. on W.H. Auden. So Yeats was 'dropped' and replaced by Auden, and my M.A. lectures came to an end.

I found that essay among some old papers a few months ago and read it with increasing bafflement. There was, in it, a kind of painful intensity that I could not at first understand. Then I realized what had happened. While writing the essay I had seen, for the first time, the connection between Yeats' 'Byzantium' and Andrew Marvell's magnificent poem, 'The Garden'. The discovery thrilled me, and the connection got, in my essay, more than its due share of attention. I saw all the important elements of 'Byzantium' in 'The Garden'. And Marvell's evocative description of the creative process taking place in the green shade of a tree somehow got connected in my mind with the hours I had spent in my childhood, dreaming and reading and creating, in the green shade of my suragi tree. So I wrote that essay in a kind of aching excitement—which I could not then understand—because I had, at the back my mind, my own lost Byzantium.

I did not try to get the essay published. I had written it, with a good deal of effort, for my M.A. students—who did not exist! I felt again a disheartening sense of futility. The whole exercise, it seemed to me, was emblematic of my life.

The cutting of the suragi tree made one important difference to my life. I did not want to go home. Staying in Moni's new house somehow became repugnant. I went to Kantheshwar just once, to attend Moni's wedding. He had chosen wisely and well. I had met the girl, a gynaecologist, the first doctor Moni had recruited when he opened his hospital, on my previous visit to Kantheshwar. She was a neat and very efficient person, delicate-looking but with surprising reserves of energy. When Moni introduced her to me—on the day of his Griha Pravesha—she was on her way to the operation theatre to perform a complicated Caesarian section. When she came back after the operation she showed no signs of fatigue, mental or physical. When she was standing there talking to us, a ward boy came and said that a woman in labour pains had just been wheeled in. She smiled at us and went back to the labour ward without a word of complaint. "A girl of amazing energy and poise," I said to Moni, and he smiled with great complacency.

I stayed at Kantheshwar for only three days. The marriage was held in a hall but the house was crowded and unbearably hot. The upstairs bedroom of our old house had become the hospital's dumping room where all the broken down equipment, etc., were kept. I spent one night there, against Moni's advice. I could not sleep a wink because rats had taken over the place and were moving around freely. I could not enjoy meeting my aunts and cousins because everyone seemed bent on asking me, repeatedly, one question: why I was not getting married. "You know what people are saying about Babu?" whispered Varijamma to someone, and I heard it because her rasping whisper was always as audible as a shout. "They say he has a mistress in Bombay, that's why he is not getting married. Why is he otherwise so keen to go back to Bombay, when it's summer vacation still?"

A couple of hours before I was to leave for Bombay I had a strange and unnerving encounter. Feeling restless, troubled by a feeling of despondency I could not shake off, I went out for a stroll and found myself in front of Martappayya's shop. I saw the old man dozing, as usual, on the bench in front of his shop. It was only after I passed the shop that I realized that there was something inexplicable in that scene—Martappayya did not look a day older than he did in my childhood! I turned back to talk to him. He opened his eyes, looked at me and smiled. It was the same toothless smile I had seen so often in my childhood. But the old man was not Martappayya, it was my friend, Narayana.

I was shocked and deeply disturbed. How old was Narayana? Forty-six, at the most, but with all his teeth gone, and his head bald as an egg, he looked exactly like what his father did in my childhood, the ultimate symbol of decrepit impotent old age. I was so upset that I had to exercise great self-control not to express my shock at his appearance, or blurt out that I had mistaken him for his father.

Narayana smiled. It was an uninhibited smile that displayed childlike joy, and the loss of all thirty-two teeth.

How did he lose them? I did not have to ask that question, he told me himself. He used to get sudden bouts of headache right from his childhood, he said. They became more frequent and unbearably intense during his father's last illness: after his father fell down in the bathroom, broke his hipbone and became bedridden. He was told by a doctor that the headaches were due to his bad teeth. It was suggested that he should get them all out and wear dentures.

"I got them all out," said Narayana, "but the headaches continued. And I could not wear dentures either because they hurt too much. Then they said that the headaches were because of some nerve in my head, and an operation had to be done. So I got operated at Manipal, and after they shaved my head for the operation, my hair did not come back properly. I had left my father in the care of one of his cousins who came from Sirsi for fifteen days. 'Fifteen days is all that I can spare,' she had said, 'If I don't go back in fifteen days, my daughter-in-law has threatened not to take me back.' When I came back from the hospital my father took one look at me and groaned, 'Oh God, I can't even die now, my son has become me.' He died a month after my operation." Narayana shook his head sadly. "I don't get headaches now. Some people say that my headaches would have gone on their own after my father's death. You think they are right? It's true that I could not bear to look at him, the way he was troubled by flies."

"Troubled by flies?"

"Yes. He was bedridden for a long time you see. He got bedsores. Flies came and sat on them, bit into them and bred maggots. I used to keep a boy to drive them away, paying him two rupees a day, but the flies were so persistent, they kept on troubling him and drove him mad. And the way he cursed them, and kept on cursing them till his last breath, it was terrible."

I stood silent. I did not know what to say. Narayana smiled like a child. "I'm so glad to see you," he said, "shall I go in and make you a cup of tea? My house is just behind the shop, you know, so it's no trouble. No customers come at this time. In fact not many customers come to our shop these days. People go to big shops now. Children eat chocolates and chewing gum, very few buy akroots."

In spite of my protest he went in to make some tea. I sat on the bench and looked at the shop. The place looked more untidy than in Martappayya's time, with cobwebs in every nook and corner. I saw a big spider sitting in a web, and was struck by a fancy—I hated myself for it—that it was Martappayya reincarnated as a spider watching over his shop, and patiently waiting for flies.

৯

There was a reason—or excuse—for going back to Bombay in a hurry. A flat I had booked at Dahisar two years earlier was ready for occupation and I wanted to shift to it. Shreekanth had bullied me into buying that flat, constructed by one of his patients. I told him that my bank balance was only six or seven thousand, and there was no way I could collect forty-seven thousand rupees, the price of the flat. Shreekanth said that that was no problem as he had already talked to Moni about it. "He rings me up frequently, and I have told him that he should give you some amount now and adjust it to what's due to you as your share of the family property. He has agreed. The down payment to be made at the time of booking is only eleven thousand and I'll get it from Moni. The rest of the amount is to be paid in installments, as the work progresses."

I had no problems paying the installments. Our salaries got revised and I got some arrears at the right time. When the flat was ready, the purohit who guided me through three shraddhas a year—father's, mother's and uncle's—chose an auspicious day for me to enter the new house. "You don't want to perform any *Vasthu Shanti?*" he asked me, and I said that I was bankrupt after paying all the installments. The belief is that at the time of construction of houses wrong things happen, evil enters the unfinished houses and waits for people, and it has to be exorcised through complicated rituals collectively called Vasthu Shanti. "Do at least this much," he said, "take a coconut and wave it clockwise in front of the door, and in every nook and corner of the house. Then take it to a corner of your building's compound and smash it to bits on the ground." I did that and then thought of how Moni had spent nearly twenty thousand rupees for his Griha Pravesha whereas mine cost me less than a rupee.

I felt lonely in my new flat. I missed my little friends of Borivli and some of my former neighbours. It was strange, how I did not even know how close I was to them. The Sheth family, for example, my next-door neighbours. Professor Sheth taught Electrical Engineering in a Polytechnic. His wife was a simple anxiety-ridden housewife, always worried about her daily chores and her children's school grades. They were not well-to-do but lived reasonably well, balancing their budget with care. There was a certain basic simplicity about them which, I am afraid, I learnt to appreciate rather late. They were the first family in our wing to buy a television set. As a result their tiny one-room-and-kitchen flat was crowded with people, especially when there was an interesting programme or a cricket match going on. People came to ask the score and stayed on to watch the match. "I'm sure you regret buying your TV," I said to Professor Sheth once, "you have no privacy left now." He did not like that remark. "Why should I regret it?" he said with a frown, "I am not an Englishman who thinks that his house is his castle. I am an Indian, I like people to come to my house." Whenever there was an interesting or popular TV programme, the husband or the wife would come out and call people home.

Mrs. Sheth took special pride in serving us tea when we were watching TV, though she herself was kept so busy in the kitchen that she rarely got the chance to watch any programme. We were a noisy audience, especially when we were watching a cricket match. Whenever there was a sudden uproar in her living room, Amitaben—Mrs. Sheth—would come from the kitchen, asking, with great anxiety, "What happened? Who got out?" and hang around for a while and then rush back to the kitchen saying, "Oh God, I clean forgot, I have kept something on the stove and it's getting burnt".

A week after I shifted to Dahisar I found myself, in the afternoon, in a mood of deep dejection. I came out on to my living room balcony and found some boys below talking loudly. Their voices grew louder when they saw me on the balcony, and that increased my despondency. I had quarrelled with them a few hours earlier because they were playing cricket below my bedroom balcony, at two in the afternoon, and God, the racket they kicked up was unbelievable. Normally I would have just asked them to quieten down a bit but I was angry because they had broken one of my window panes the previous day and were not prepared to tell me who had hit the ball up. So I went down and stopped them from playing, and then felt miserable. Now when I saw them looking askance at me, and talking more loudly than necessary as a challenge to me perhaps, my misery increased.

Then I saw Mr. and Mrs. Sheth entering our compound. It was a pleasant but real surprise. We were good neighbours but had nothing much in common, and I really did not expect them to pay me a visit. I was very glad to see them, though. "Both our kids have gone to their uncle's house for two days," said Professor Sheth, "so my wife said, let's go and see how Rao is getting along in his new house. So we are here." "You will have to cook some rice and your typical South Indian curry for us, because we are going to stay for supper," said Amitaben.

I did not have to cook much though, because they had brought lots of things with them—theplas and dhoklas and other Gujarati delicacies—and at nine we sat down and started eating. It was a lovely meal, the first elaborate dinner I had in my new flat. After food I wanted to go out and bring some paan for them but Navinbhai—Professor Sheth—said no, we'll sit down and chat.

Amitaben looked sad. Perhaps there was always an aura of sadness about her, but I had not noticed it earlier because she was always too busy, flustered and worried. But when we sat down talking after dinner on a dhurrie I had spread on the ground, she looked more relaxed than I had ever seen her look. Then I noticed that little cloud of sadness hovering about her face.

"You look sad, Amitaben," I said.

Her husband laughed. "Shall I tell him why we thought of paying him a visit today?" he asked his wife.

A sad smile flickered on her face but she said nothing. "It's my wife's birthday today," said Professor Sheth, "and she is always sad on her birthdays. It's a joke in the family. Heena, my daughter, always says, 'If Mummy looks sad, it must be her happy birthday.' So this morning I said to her, the kids are not at home and it's your birthday, so cook something light for lunch, let's go in the evening to some restaurant for supper. But she said, 'No, I'll cook something special, let's take it to Rao's house in the evening and eat with him. Maybe he feels lonely there and hasn't made friends with his new neighbours yet.' So we came here."

This was so unexpected that all that I could say was "Thanks." I don't cry easily, but on that day I felt, somehow, I was close to it. It was incredible that this couple, whose friendship I had never properly valued, should have thought of me and decided to spend their precious evening—on Amitaben's birthday—with me. Then I tried to laugh it off. "In Bombay people cannot use the word 'birthday' without the word 'happy'," I said, "then how is it you are sad, Amitaben?"

"I don't know," she said, "I have always felt sad and lonely on my birthdays." Her husband looked at her. She placed her hand on his, which was resting on the dhurrie, looked at him and said, "We have each other and we have our children. But they are growing up, and we are growing old." She sighed, looked at me and added, "Today, maybe because they were not there, I began to feel a strange kind of loneliness. You know I lost my mother when I was three, and was brought up by my father. I was always a lonely child. I did not know my birthday till, at the time of my marriage, they looked up my horoscope and said that it was 22nd May. Even now the only one who remembers it is my husband. I was saying to myself, this morning, after he reminded me that it was my birthday: we are all lonely creatures in this world. Then I thought of you. You make friends easily, Sudhakarbhai, and soon you will have plenty of friends here, but right now, I thought, you must be lonely. So we came here, instead of going to a restaurant and eating our food surrounded by strangers. We didn't trouble you, did we, forcing you to cook something for us?"

৯

I was, at first, not too unhappy in my new flat. It was my own house, my den, where I could throw things around or keep them in their proper place as I wished. I never knew, till then, the pride and pleasure of owning a house. I made elaborate plans for its interior decoration, but they were all 'future plans', because I had just money enough to buy the barest minimum furniture—a divan which also served as a bed, a writing table, and one chair.

But that contentment did not last. My flat was not bad but the situation of our building was. It lay next to a slum and our land had been used by the people there, for generations, to defecate. Maybe they found it difficult to reconcile themselves to the loss of their open-air latrine. Faeces wrapped in newspapers were often thrown into our compound. I wondered at the malice that made those people take the trouble of making neat parcels of their excrement only to harass us.

It was only some years later that I discovered the truth: that there was no special trouble taken and no malice involved. A man used to come to my house, once a month, to buy old newspapers. When I went to his little make-shift tin-roofed shop to collect the money one day, I saw a man from one of the nearby slums there. "How much?" asked the shopkeeper, and he said, "half a kilo." Our man weighed and gave him half a kilo of neatly folded old copies of *Times of India*. As I was under the impression that all the old newspapers purchased from us went for recycling or for making paper bags, I asked the man what he was buying those papers for. He merely grinned and looked at the shopkeeper. "Arre, Saab," said the shopkeeper, after the man left, "these people have no latrines in their houses. There are some public toilets behind their building. The men and women queue up there but the children can't. So they buy newspapers, and make the kids squat on them. Then they throw the parcels away." He saw my look of shock, and laughed. "This is Bombay, Saab," he said, "where half the people do not know how the other half defecate."

I had to laugh. "You are quite a philosopher," I said. "He is," said a man standing there. "Even foreigners come to listen to him."

"Don't take Trivedi Saab seriously," said the shopkeeper. "It's true that a foreigner—he was from Australia—came once. He asked me questions and then he wanted to take down what I said. "Please don't do that," I said. "Why not," he said, "you speak words of wisdom." I said that even words of wisdom were only words. Wisdom cannot be passed on, except at some blessed moments perhaps. If the written word can give one wisdom, why go beyond the *Bhagavad Gita*?"

I shook my head. "I have been living in Bombay for so long…. Yet I did not know about people buying old newspapers in kilos for a purpose like this."

"No one can say that he knows this city," said the shopkeeper. "You have heard of fourteen *lokas*—worlds—mentioned in our scriptures? They are all here in Bombay, and all kinds of people live in them. Meet our Trivedi Saab, he is in the same profession as you are. He is one of my regular customers."

"I teach Sanskrit in a high school," said the man, as he paid for his quarter kilo of old newspapers. "I did my M.A. from Benares Hindu University."

৯

Those malodorous missiles thrown in from the slum did not trouble me much. They were a nuisance to people staying on the ground floor, in flats adjacent to the slum. My flat was on the first floor on the other side of the building. Here the problem was that the slum dwellers, who had no access to any public toilets then, skirted our building and came to defecate in the open ground outside our building. They chose spots hidden from the road, but they totally ignored us, so that we got, from our upstairs windows, a ringside view of things. I still remember—vividly—the special lunch I prepared for myself on my first birthday in the new flat. I cleared my writing table, placed my lunch—rice, curry, curds, and sweet porridge of vermicelli—neatly on it, and sat down on the only chair I had, feeling happy and contented. Then I looked out of the window. I saw a woman sitting on a pile of stones, with her back to our building. Even before I realized what was happening, she lifted her saree, raised her buttocks, and defecated. I saw a long piece of faeces come out and hang, like an elephant's proboscis, for an inordinately long time before it fell. I took my lunch back to the kitchen. I used to boast I had a strong stomach but that sight hit me when I was totally unprepared for the blow.

For the next three months I tried desperately to sell my flat so that I could buy one in a better locality. I had to hurry because prices of flats were going up everywhere. After running around for three months I found a buyer and rang up our builder. The deal had to go through him because our co-operative society, which would finally own the building, had not yet been formed. "Good, good," said Mr. Shah, "What are you getting for the flat?" "Eighty-five thousand," I said. "Good," he said, "But I suppose you know we charge thirty percent for all such deals. So you will have to pay us twenty-five thousand five hundred rupees."

I nearly choked. I tried to bargain with him through Shreekanth but it was no use. Had I known about that thirty percent, I would not have tried so desperately to sell the flat. It was not that I merely regretted the wasted effort to find a suitable buyer. The last minute failure generated a kind of despair. I began to feel that I was trapped in Bombay—like a fly in Martappayya's liquid jaggery.

Bursts, Blasts and Accidents

❧

I called Bombay, in an earlier chapter, a bustling city bursting at the seam. Around the time I booked my flat at Dahisar, the city actually burst. It burst noiselessly and flowed into ugly, unplanned, overcrowded townships. The flow was mainly along the Western and Central Railway lines, the two veins of Bombay, which had both already gone varicose. I was a part of that flow. That large shapeless building with ninety-eight flats, one of which I proudly owned, was one of the early symptoms that the city had finally burst. The building had risen like a sore on a ground where people of Dahisar village had defecated in peace for years. Ours was at first the only high rise building there but not for long. Soon there was a rash of new multistoried buildings rising all around, blocking the view and turning the place into a concrete jungle.

One of the consequences of this city-burst was that travelling by suburban trains became a real nightmare. I don't think there is another ordeal quite like it anywhere else in the world. I did not usually have to travel during peak hours. I had early morning lectures and was free by noon. But soon it became almost impossible to get into a train at Dahisar even around 7 a.m. As the trains, coming from Virar, got overcrowded long before they reached our station, those who wanted to board them had to hang outside the door, sometimes with just one foot on the footboard. I tried that just once. My knees grew weak and started shaking violently within a couple of minutes. I desperately wanted to get down but could not because right up to Dadar, a distance of more than twenty kilometres, all the platforms our train stopped at came on the other side of the train. "This is terrible," I said to a frail white-haired old man who was hanging on as precariously as I was, "Once you catch the train you are trapped. You can't let go—because all the platforms come on the other side." "We're lucky that they do," he said. "otherwise we would be pushed out in every station by people getting down—and have to scramble back with those trying to get in." "But aren't you scared," I said, "that you might slip and fall to your death some day?" "If you are scared," he said, gritting his teeth, "you can't survive in Bombay."

The Virar trains, which people staying beyond Borivli have to depend on, must be the most crowded trains in the world, and the commuters the hardiest.

From Churchgate to Borivli there are several tracks and the frequency of trains is not bad. But beyond Borivli there are only two tracks used by both long-distance and suburban trains. As the population of distant townships exploded after the city-burst, overcrowding in Virar trains became mind-boggling. If you want to study the limits of human endurance, look at the people of Bombay's suburbs like Vasai and Virar, how they spend four hours or more every day packed tight in trains in the sweltering heat of Bombay and still somehow find the energy to work.

But the strain sometimes showed, especially in the evenings when they were on their way back home. Those who wanted to go to Bandra and Andheri from Churchgate soon learnt not to take the Virar trains during peak hours. "Why have you got into this train," they were asked, by people who angrily blocked their way when they tried to get down at their station, "when there are so many other trains going up to Borivli? We have no option, we *have* to travel in these hells on wheels. You want to share our fate? Then come with us and see our world!" So the chap, tired out after a day's hard work in his office, desperate to get down at Andheri and then stand in one of those serpentine queues to catch the bus that would take him home at last, had to go all the way to Dahisar or Mira Road—and then wait for a train to go back to Andheri.

They were not bad, the Vasai and Virar crowds, but sometimes they showed that the iron had entered their soul. It had to, for how else could they get the strength to survive their daily ordeal? Miss Lele, one of my neighbours working in a bank near Churchgate, had this unnerving experience. She was there on the platform when the Virar train came and so got a good seat, next to the window, in the ladies' compartment. A fat middle-aged Gujarati woman came and sat next to her. Obviously she was not a regular commuter. After the train passed Dadar she said, "Please tell me, baby, when Andheri comes."

"But this is a Virar train," said Miss Lele, "People may not allow you to get down at Andheri." "Why won't they?" said the woman haughtily, "There's a scheduled stop at Andheri, isn't there."

But she was not allowed to go even close to the door. Women blocked her way, angry women who had to travel in that awfully crowded train for another hour or so, tired leg-weary women who had worked the whole day in some office and were standing, while this fat woman was sitting comfortably, occupying the space of two. Taken aback by the hostility she encountered, she panicked and tried to force her way through them, but they poked her with their umbrellas and pushed her back. Her haughtiness melted away. "I'm not used to travelling by train," she pleaded with them, "please let me get down.

My daughter is coming to Andheri station to take me to her house, I'll be lost if I miss her." But it was no use. They would have allowed her to get down at Borivli, perhaps, but by then she had become a whimpering nervous wreck incapable of getting down on her own. Miss Lele helped her to get down at Dahisar. She was on her feet in the crowded compartment, propped up by the pressure of the crowd, but the moment she got down she collapsed on the platform. Some people helped her to get into a train going back but she did not reach Andheri alive. She died on the way.

The woman who was mainly responsible for preventing her from getting down at Andheri was arrested the next day. She was a schoolteacher, with two young children, living at Vasai village, a few kilometres away from Vasai station. Someone who spent more than four hours commuting in those hells on wheels, six days a week, in addition to the hours spent working. I don't know at what time she left for school in the mornings, leaving her two young kids at home, and when she reached home in the evenings.

The iron that enters your soul. Someone asked me once how many times I had had my pocket picked in trains, and I said, "Half a dozen times at least." "Any time in the Virar trains?" he asked. "Never," I said. "Perhaps the trains are too crowded even for pickpockets."

He laughed. "Pickpockets are in their elements in crowded compartments," he said, "though they prefer sudden crowding of their own creation to an already overcrowded compartment. But they never dare to enter a crowded Virar train."

He told me why. "Pickpockets are sometimes caught in trains," he said, "where it is not easy to make a getaway. They are usually roughed up and then handed over to the Railway Police. But they have their arrangements with the police. They are back in business the very next day, with an admonition not to get caught so easily. But if a pickpocket is caught red-handed in a Virar train his fate is sealed. You know the Virar crowd. They don't hand him over to the police, or beat him up. They joke with him, and sometimes even give him things to eat. And then when the train is thundering over the Vasai Bridge, they pick him up, swing him and throw him out into the creek below. You have seen the Vasai Creek, haven't you? It's so deep that the man, or boy—some of the pickpockets are quite young—would be dead well before he hits the water."

જી

What turned my last few years in Bombay into a real nightmare were a couple of unusual events. Bombay had always been a comparatively peaceful city, but it went mad a few days after the demolition of Babri Masjid. The city had some riots earlier, when a few shops and restaurants were stoned and even burnt, but there was little loss of life. But this time it was different. We first heard of some Mathadi workers—men working on daily wages in the docks—getting killed. The modus operandi was simple. The unsuspecting victim would be approached by a figure clad in a burqa—the black cloak Muslim women use to cover themselves from head to foot when they go out—and suddenly a knife would flash out from under the burqa, the man would be stabbed, and the burqa-clad figure—a man no doubt—would disappear among a crowd of burqa-clad women.

Then the riots spread and the city went mad. From my house I could hear, during the nights, the sound of police firing, like that of fire-crackers in Diwali. Those who lived in our neighbouring slum organized themselves into groups of vigilantes, and sometimes at night they raised alarms, perhaps only to frighten and wake us up because we did not join them in their vigil. I felt helpless and exposed. My balcony door was so weak that anyone could break it with a kick, and to clamber on to my first floor balcony was the easiest thing on earth. The kids of our building used to do that often whenever I was out and their ball fell into my balcony. The riot made me realize that we middle-class Indians were the most helpless unarmed creatures in the world. I had nothing to defend myself with except my kitchen knife, and that implement did not even cut vegetables properly.

So I desperately tried to get my two balconies covered with iron grilles. By the time I found someone and the work was done, the riots were over. But the grilles remained. I had covered my windows with grilled boxes a few years earlier to protect the panes from the cricket-crazy kids of our building. Now with all my windows and balconies covered with grilles, I felt like a trapped animal in a cage.

And then came the blasts. I don't think the people of Bombay can ever forget that Black Friday when thirteen RDX laden cars exploded in some of the most crowded localities of the city. The locations were carefully chosen. One of the car bombs exploded in the parking space under the multistoried Bombay Stock Exchange Building. If that massive edifice had caved in, it would have been a disaster of an unprecedented magnitude. Another exploded near the Air India Building. But these buildings proved to be stronger than expected. The windowpanes and everything breakable got shattered, several people died and innumerable were injured, but the structures of the large buildings targeted withstood the blasts.

It was the kind of terror Bombay was just not prepared for. The blasts shook Bombay, the most unflappable of cities, as nothing else had done before. There was fear in the air, and when people talked about the awesome power of RDX—of how people in the vicinity of the blasts just disappeared, leaving no trace, etherized by the heat—they did so not with that perverse enjoyment people often show while describing something gruesome, but with reluctance and in whispers.

I had gone back to Dahisar on that day an hour before the bombs burst. I heard the gory details, and a couple of eyewitness accounts, over the next few days. I went on commuting between Dahisar and Churchgate and avoided going to the sites of the blasts. I did not want to see anything that would further aggravate my growing feeling that life was becoming unreal and nightmarish.

A week after that Friday I had to go to see Miss Jamuna Chandnani who was injured in the blasts. She used to work in our college office and had retired but whenever there was some extra work, like conducting exams, the principal called her and she came and managed things with surprising efficiency. White-haired, pale and very frail, always dressed in a white saree, she shuffled about the Staff Room like a ghost from the past. I had thought of her as a nice old woman of limited intelligence, till one day she came with a copy of the previous day's *Times of India,* and a broad smile on her face. "Nice writing," she said, pointing to an article of mine that had appeared in the magazine section. One of my former students had got his first book of poems published a few months earlier, wanted me to write a review article, and then had taken the article himself to the newspaper. I did not know that it was published till Miss Chandnani showed it to me. What surprised me was that she had not only seen the article but read it with insight. She even quoted a line from one of the poems I had discussed in the article, and said, with a blush, "Nice line." I had no idea she cared for poetry.

Perhaps that was why I went along with some colleagues when they decided to go and see her. She was in a hospital close to her house at Worli. The blast that took place nearby was perhaps not meant for that place. The car with RDX was apparently on its way to Shivaji Park and had stopped at the traffic junction. The men in the car must have seen that a blast there and then would cause maximum damage, as hundreds of vehicles, including crowded double-decker buses, were standing fender to fender waiting for the green signal. They must have set the timer on the bomb and slipped out.

The devastation was horrifying. Every vehicle on the road in that junction exploded in the intense heat generated by the bomb so that it was impossible to say which one of them was the original car bomb. The blast created a big crater in the road. The upper decks of two double-decker buses, full of school children going home after the morning session, were blown away. The shops and restaurants on one side of the road were reduced to rubble. The low lying slum on the other side escaped with less damage, though burning pieces of the wreckage rained on it and a couple of huts caught fire. Ramadas Pande, our peon, who stayed in that slum, was on leave on that day because there was some religious function in his house. He had just come out of his hut when the road exploded. A wave of heat hit him and blew him off his feet. When he tried to get up, he was hit on the head by a boot which came down from the sky. It was a small boot, a schoolboy's perhaps, but it was heavy—because there was a severed foot in it.

Miss Chandnani, who lived alone in a first floor flat a little away from the scene of the holocaust, was watching TV when the explosion took place. She had kept the window closed to keep out the road noises so that she could watch her favourite serial in peace. That window, like the other windows of all the buildings in the vicinity, turned into a bomb and burst. "When I saw her two days ago," said Miss Khilani, our Sociology lecturer, with a shudder, "they had already removed forty-two pieces of glass from her body. Doctors think there are still some more."

"The latest score is forty-nine," said Miss Chandnani, as we stood round her bed. "It will cross the half century mark I think." She looked very frail and weak, but excited, with a smile flickering on her face.

I sat by her bedside when the other teachers went to see some other injured person whom they knew. "You are a brave girl, Miss Chandnani," I said, and she smiled at the word 'girl'. "I was worried," I added, "that your nerves might have been shattered by the blast, but no, thank God, you are in high spirits, almost—as if what happened was an adventure."

There was something wrong with the tone of that remark, perhaps. The smile left Miss Chandnani's face and she suddenly looked very old and haggard. She kept her eyes closed for some time. When she opened them she did not look at me. She went on staring at a calendar on the wall. The calendar, which advertised some baby food, carried the picture of a very pretty infant.

"I was excited," she said, "because you people came to see me. Life is so— drab, you see. No one comes to see me these days. Nothing is happening. It's as if I no longer exist....Some months ago I had to go to a dentist, for a root canal treatment. He started working on my tooth without giving me any local anaesthetic. 'Aren't you giving me the usual injection?' I asked him. He said that my teeth wouldn't hurt me any more because they had all become non-vital. That's me, I said to myself. I am not dead, but I have become non-vital. Things don't hurt anymore.

"Perhaps I became non-vital," she said, after a pause, "a long time ago. When we fled Sind and came here as refugees. I was just twenty-four. You may not believe it, but I was a very pretty girl then. My sister, two years my senior, was good-looking too, but she was rather stern and did not smile easily. Not like me. I don't know whether I was in some ways responsible for her sternness. So a couple of eligible bachelors who came to see her said that they preferred the younger sister. That was how both our marriages were delayed.

"Then came the partition and we had to flee our home, leaving everything behind. The first few years in Bombay were awful. My sister, who had done her M.A., finally got a job as a lecturer in Hindi. I had not appeared for my B.A. exam, as Father had this feeling that it was my sister's high qualification which made it difficult to find a suitable husband for her. I was not very keen on studies either because all that I wanted was to get married, settle down and raise a large family. So I had to hunt for odd clerical jobs.

"It's forty-five years since we left Sind. Nothing has happened in my life, except bereavements. First my father's death, then mother's, and then, ten years ago, my sister's. No excitement, only work, and more work, but even that got over when I retired. Then something happened at last—this bomb blast. The biggest and most awful excitement of my life in forty-five years, since we fled Sind, fear gnawing at our hearts."

She looked at me, as if what she said answered my remark about her 'high spirits.' I kept quiet. In the presence of the awesome emptiness of her life, my own little personal problems appeared petty and insignificant.

Miss Chandnani closed her eyes. "The last forty-five years," she said, "they aren't real. I keep thinking that it's all a bad dream and I'll wake up and find that I'm still the same bright-eyed Jamuni that I was." She opened her eyes and stared blankly at the ceiling. "I did wake up, finally, five days ago. And found myself in this hospital bed, with more than fifty glass pieces embedded in my body."

৯৯

Then there were the accidents. They made me acutely conscious of my own insignificance. I could be crushed to death one day but the city, I realized, would roll on unconcerned.

One of them took place at midnight, on the eve of Shreekanth's sixtieth birthday. *Shashtyabdhi Poorthi*, the completing of sixty years of one's life, is an important event in a Hindu's life. His children, grandchildren and other relatives come together and organize the festivities and religious rites, making him the central figure, treating him as if he were a bridegroom again. So I had to be there, though my visits to Sita's house had become rare after I shifted to Dahisar. The on-the-eve rituals, held in a public hall at Sion, got over rather late, and by the time we had our dinner it was half past eleven. I promised Sita that I would be back early next morning and left for Dahisar.

I found, when I reached Dadar Station at midnight, that there were no Virar trains for another half an hour. So I took a Borivli train, and from Borivli took a rickshaw to Dahisar. The driver was a very young chap and was either inebriated or in a desperate hurry to go home. He tore down the invitingly empty road as if he—or the three-wheeler—had gone berserk, and when a drunken man trying to cross the road suddenly came lurching in front, lost control of the vehicle and went and rammed into a stationary van parked on the pavement. The impact was so great that the rickshaw broke the back of the van and entered it. That was how it did not topple, and was left standing on its two rear wheels. I got out of it with a bleeding head, and asked the people who suddenly emerged from nowhere—footpath dwellers, no doubt, woken up by the explosive sound of the accident—if there was a doctor nearby. They pointed to a signboard that showed that there was a small hospital right opposite.

I spent two days in that dingy hospital. The doctor in charge stitched the wound on my head, examined my chest because I complained of pain and difficulty in breathing, gave me heavy doses of antibiotics and analgesics and asked me to go to sleep. "Can you give me some sleeping pills?" I asked him and he said no, people under observation for head injuries should not be given soporifics.

The room I got was just a cubicle, with two beds almost touching one another. There was no one on the other bed and that was a relief. But an hour after I went to bed there was a commotion and a sick young man was brought in, supported by a couple of grim-looking men and a sobbing woman. The doctor was with them. They made the lad lie down on the bed next to mine.

"What's wrong with him?" I asked.

"Oh, you are still awake, are you," said the doctor. "Maybe we'll give you a soporific after all." He made a sign to the nurse who was standing at the door because there was no space for her in the cubicle, and a few minutes later I was given some tablets powdered and mixed with water. Perhaps they did not want me to know how much I had been drugged.

I came to know the next morning why the doctor had changed his mind about soporifics. The chap who shared my cubicle was suffering from tuberculosis, and had had a serious bout of coughing and hemorrhage the previous night. I realized this when he had another bout in the morning.

I had never seen anything quite like that before. The patient was very young—not more than twenty—and before the bleeding started he did not look too ill either. Drugged and only half-awake, I watched in horror the lad cough and cough, and blood, mixed with saliva, gurgle out of his mouth, as a thick froth at first and then a gushing flow. The old woman sitting by his side started wailing, an animal-like cry that haunted me for days. Even the doctor looked flustered. He and a nurse desperately tried to raise the upper part of the bed so that the poor chap could sit up instead of lying down, and when the spring mechanism failed the doctor started shouting at the nurse as if she was personally responsible for it. Then he turned to me. "Will you please get up," he said, and when I did, he tried my bed and found that the mechanism worked. So the patient was shifted to my bed, and I stood unsteadily near the only window in the room and looked out on to the road; where I saw, as if in a dream, a small group of people looking with interest at a shattered rickshaw jutting out of the back of a van.

"What are you doing there," said the doctor, "Come and lie down. Relax." I turned back and saw that they had succeeded in stopping the patient's flow of blood. The young man reclined on my bed, eyes closed, looking deathly pale. "Go to bed, come on," said the doctor impatiently, and I realized that he expected me to go and lie down in the bed vacated by the lad. "Come on," he said again, and I looked at him in dismay. "You are not even going to change the sheet?" I said.

I had to stay on in that hole for two days and nights. The patient with the hemorrhage was shifted to the Intensive Care Unit later in the day. The doctor wanted me to stay for a couple of days more because a head injury like mine needed to be 'observed'. He even tried to blackmail me by saying that my accident was a 'police case' and he had taken a risk in not reporting the matter. "I took you in in the middle of the night," he said, "and now you want to walk out on me." I realized that hospitals like that wanted to hold on to their patients as long as they could. Finally I had to give him a piece of my mind about the way he managed his hospital, putting patients with infectious diseases and accident victims in the same cubicle, before he reluctantly agreed to 'discharge' me.

The other accident was even stranger. It took place when I was fifty-eight. It was this accident, I think, which made me realize that I could never be at home in Bombay, and feel—after a lapse of fourteen years—that I must go home to Kantheshwar, if only to see whether the place was home still.

I had started going to Borivli to catch my train in the mornings because Dahisar had become impossible. The problem at Borivli was that I had to go to the terribly congested eastern side of the station. The narrow road that runs along the station was made narrower by the long line of tourist taxis parked on one side and the State Transport buses on the other, forcing pedestrians to walk on the middle of the road. Whenever a large vehicle came, pedestrians had to scurry out of the way or hastily fall into single file so that they could walk on in that dangerously narrow space between the oncoming vehicle and the stationary one parked on the side.

Sometimes there was not enough space for that, and that was how I got caught between a BEST bus that came roaring in, and an ST bus parked on my right. A couple of people who were in front of me jumped ahead, beyond the rear side of the parked bus, to safety, and those behind ran back. The oncoming bus hit me and made me turn like a top. If it had come even a little further forward, it would have brushed the parked bus, and I would have been crushed to pulp.

Even at that moment I did not scream or shout. That old reluctance of mine to shout for help was in evidence again. Instead I heard a shrill female voice scream, "Stop the bus, someone is getting crushed to death," and the bus came to a grinding halt. The conductor looked out, saw me blackened by the grime from the two buses but still on my feet, and grinned. "Are you hit?" he said, and as I moved out of that death trap the bus started and moved away. It was only when I went back to pick up my bag that I realized that my right shoulder had given way.

"You are lucky," said a man selling newspapers, "You can go home and change your clothes and you will be all right. Yesterday a woman lost her ear at the same spot. You know, her whole left ear was ripped off and got stuck to a piece of metal on the side of the bus!" He shook his head as if he still could not believe what he had seen. "A whole ear, with a gold earring in it," he said. "Everyday someone or the other is hit. It is a miracle no one has been killed so far, not on the spot anyway. You would have been, today, if that fat woman hadn't stood in front of the bus and screamed at the driver asking him to stop. She saved your life."

"Where is she?" I said, looking around.

"She's gone," he said, laughing. "She must be in her train by now. No one has time in Bombay, not even to look at someone whose life one might have saved."

"But why isn't anyone complaining if this is happening every day?" I said, as I stood there trembling. "Who has the time to complain?" he said. "Are you going to complain, now that you are hit? No, you'll go home, change your clothes, and rush back to catch the next train. No one has the time to complain, or to listen to complaints, in this city and you know it."

He was right. I did not complain. But I did not rush back to catch the next train either. I went with a doctor friend of mine to the nearby Municipal Hospital to get my shoulder treated. After my earlier accident I had realized that Government and Municipal Hospitals were better than most private ones, especially if you knew someone who could smuggle you in without lengthy admission rituals.

After X-rays I was taken to the visiting specialist. He was a simple-looking man but the kind of awe the other orthopedic surgeons, his juniors, showed in his presence had to be seen to be believed. I stood in a corner. The great man did not deign to look at me. He only examined the X-rays and pronounced his judgement. "AC joint subluxation," he said. "An immediate operation to repair the torn ligaments might set it right but not advisable at his age. How old is he?"

"I'm fifty-eight," I said.

He still did not look at me. "See what I mean?" he said to the other doctors. "If it were a young sportsman who wanted to play, say, tennis, yes, surgery would have been advisable. Not in this case. Immobilization for eight weeks, and he will be all right. Some deformity will remain, of course."

"But I want to play tennis," I said, "after my retirement." The younger doctors looked at me in surprise. I was myself taken aback because I did not know, till then, that I had this desire. "There's no time for playing in Bombay," I added, "with all the commuting, and pressure of work.... So I have been dreaming—of spending my retired life in a small town, playing tennis.." There was a tennis club at Chandapur, I remembered. Perhaps some of our dreams run in our subconscious minds.

The specialist still did not look at me. He looked at the X-rays again. "He can, if he wants, learn to play with his left hand," he said.

৯৹

All through this work I have let recollections come to me. They came, bringing in their wake, at times, little forgotten details that turned the writing into an exploration full of surprises. But the last two chapters have been different. Here I *knew* what I was going to write. I wanted to describe how I found life in Bombay, during the last fifteen years, a nightmare. I knew what facts I wanted to make use of: the shifting of residence, the daily torture of travelling in overcrowded trains, the riots, the bomb-blasts, and the accidents that undermined my health and made me feel lost and insecure. Instead of letting my recollections dictate their own story, I tried to marshal my facts to show that the years were awful. And forgot—how could I, really—that I survived because I found, in the midst of all my troubles, kindness and sympathy, companionship, affection and love. How could I write so many pages on this period without saying a word about those wonderful kids, Bubbu, Urmi, and Harshad? It was they and their love that sustained me during those troubled years, and saved me from despair.

Bubbu and Urmi

❧

I still remember how I first saw Bubbu and Urmi on a bright sunlit morning a year after I shifted to Dahisar. Their family had come to occupy the flat below mine the previous evening, but I had not seen them as I had come home, from a party at Rajanna's house, late at night.

In the morning I went and stood in my living room balcony and looked down at a fascinating scene. A girl of five or six, long legged and with long plaits, was awkwardly riding a tricycle. She was fair, and her hair had a touch of gold in it—something unusual in India—and gleamed whenever she rode into sunlight. Behind her, on the rear seat of the tricycle, sat a one-year-old girl, dark and morose, her head clean-shaven. The older girl was riding the tricycle warily, because round and round them went Pappu on *his* tricycle, fast and furious. Pappu, a two-and-a-half year old dynamo, stayed on the ground floor. He and his four-year-old sister Preeti were frequent visitors to my house.

"Careful, Pappu," I said, "don't dash against them." The girl stopped her cycle, looked up and smiled. "He is trying to show off," she said. The little one behind did not look up. She stared straight ahead of her as if she did not want to look at anyone.

I thought that the older kid had one of the brightest smiles I had ever seen. "What's your name?" I asked. "Bubbu," she said, and flashed that smile again. "That's my pet name," she said, "my real name is Malavika. Malavika Doshi."

"Who is the little teddy bear behind you? What's her name?"

"It's my sister Urmi," she said, laughing aloud. "You called her a bear, uncle? You should have seen her before her head was shaved! She really looked like a bear cub. Everyone calls her a *richdi*." *Richdi* in Gujarati means a female bear.

Bubbu got down from her tricycle. "Can I come up, to your house?" she asked.

"You certainly can," I said. "Please bring that teddy bear too."

But the little bear did not want to come up. She did not even want to get down from the tricycle. Bubbu came up and I was surprised by the way her presence lighted up my living room. She was no great beauty. She was fair, but her skin did not have the healthy glow most good-looking children have; it was a bit blotchy, like that of sun-tanned Westerners. But what a smile she had. It had sparkle and effervescence. She smiled, dimpled and laughed, and looked at everything in my house with such curiosity, asked me if she could open my fridge, touched the ice cubes inside the freezer, asked me if I would give her ice cubes to eat, then laughed and said, no, if she ate ice cubes she got tonsils, that I was left wondering whether she had come, like Pippa, only to dispel the gloom I was then in.

She was at my place only for a few minutes on that first visit of hers. She made a quick survey of the house and announced that my house was much nicer than theirs. "It's much airier. You have two balconies, but we have none, because we are on the ground floor." Then she went to the living room balcony, looked down, and said, "Oh, God, Urmi is still sitting on the tricycle. Look at her mouth, she looks like she is going to cry, I'd better go down."

But it was Urmi who fascinated me. With her fluffy head and large coal-black eyes she looked so different from Bubbu that it was difficult to believe that the two were sisters. The contrast was even more striking in their nature. Bubbu was effusive, Urmi reticent to the point of being glum. Bubbu smiled and laughed easily, Urmi could not even cry readily. She was so shy and withdrawn that she made me think of some wild creature—like a koala bear— that had somehow strayed into our world. It was her bewildered look, I think, that touched my heart. Her mouth had a permanent downward curve that made her look pensive even when she was happy. That curve would become more acute when she felt unhappy, and then the eyes would start glistening, but she rarely cried aloud. It was this curve that Bubbu noticed from my balcony when she said that Urmi looked like she was going to cry.

Urmi had a strange kind of reticence. Though she was only one year and three months old, she talked, like her sister, with great clarity and precision— Pappu's mother, who had a hard time trying to understand her son, often talked about her clarity of speech with admiration and envy. But that was only when she wanted to speak. When she did not feel like talking, she fell silent for hours. It was strange, the way this reticence of hers often went unnoticed. I myself did not notice it, till it was *brought* to my notice by an unusual event in a restaurant at Borivli when Urmi was three years old.

We had become such good friends by then that she was with me wherever I went in the afternoons. We had gone to Borivli that day, and after I made my purchases we went to an Udupi restaurant. We must have spent nearly an hour in the restaurant that day. At the end of it, when we were about to get up and leave, a woman sitting on a nearby table came to us. She patted Urmi on the cheeks, and in a voice full of compassion said to me, "Such a lovely child, poor thing. Such expressive eyes! What a pity she can't speak."

Both Urmi and I stared at her, I in surprise and Urmi with that curious amused look which often made me wonder what she was thinking of. The woman suddenly looked confused. "The child is a deaf-mute, isn't she?" she said.

On the way back home in the bus I was wondering how I did not notice that Urmi, during that one hour we spent in that restaurant, had not opened her mouth even once—except to eat. The impression I had was that we had had a quiet, relaxed chat. Obviously I had done all the talking and Urmi had been merely listening. There was something special about the way she listened, though. She listened with her whole being. And she could use small gestures—like a nod or a little shake of the head—so eloquently that there was no need to speak.

But it took a long time for us to become friends. Six months in fact. I tried to talk with her a couple of times, but gave it up when I saw that she did not like it. I have always respected a child's right to choose her friends.

During the Diwali vacation that year I went, with Professor Joshi, to Mahabaleshwar, a lovely hill station on the Western Ghats. Professor Joshi, who believed that it was his duty to send greeting cards to everyone he knew, took me shopping for cards a week before Diwali. When I saw him buying thirty cards I felt I should buy at least a few. I bought a couple of them for Satish and Suneeta, and three cards suitable for children, which I sent to Bubbu, Pappu and Preeti.

We came back to Bombay just two days before the vacation ended. I reached Dahisar rather late in the evening, and peeped in at Bubbu's house on my way up, for their door, as usual, was wide open. Bubbu's grandmother—we all called her Ba—was comfortably ensconced in an easy chair, as she usually was at that time of the night. She gave me an infant-like smile—because she had already kept her dentures away for the night—and said, "Ah, uncle, so you have come back. If you haven't had your food, we can fix up something for you." Thanks to Bubbu and her friends, I had become a Universal uncle again, as I was at Borivli.

"It was a nice card you sent me," said Bubbu. "God," said Ba, "what troubles we had because of the card. The way Urmi cried and cried when the postman came with the cards and she found that there were none for her—it was as if her heart was broken. 'Uncle has sent cards,' she said, 'to everyone else—to Bubbu and Preeti and Pappu—but not to me.' We tried to tell her that the postman might have mislaid her card, or might bring it the next day, but she wouldn't stop crying. 'I know,' she said, 'I know uncle hasn't sent me a card. I know it.'"

I looked at Urmi. She was sitting in a corner, looking straight ahead. The downward curve of her mouth was more acute than usual. I was about to ask her how she expected me to send her a card when she hadn't ever spoken to me, but realized that that would be unkind. So I simply said that I was terribly sorry. "I've brought some things for you," I said. "They are all in my bag. You two come up, please, we'll open the bag and see what's there in it." Then I said, "Urmi, you go and ask Pappu and Preeti to come too."

They came up—Bubbu, Pappu Preeti and Urmi—in fifteen minutes. We opened the bag together. There was excitement, because I pretended that I did not remember what was inside the bag, so everything we found there was a discovery. And I found that Urmi, once she relaxed and unwound, was as full of life as Bubbu. After they got what they wanted—*chikkies*, sweets made of nuts in melted sugar Mahabaleshwar is famous for—I was surprised to find that she was, of them all, the most reluctant to go home.

She came up the next morning, and was disappointed when she saw me getting ready to go out. "You are going out?" she said. I told her I was going to my sister's place at Dadar. "Do you want to come?" I asked her, and she said "Yes."

"You can come only if your Mummy and Ba say yes," I said. "Go and ask them. But if they say no, you shouldn't start crying. All right?"

I did not think they would send her with me. They did not know me well enough. But when I went down I was surprised to find Urmi dressed up and waiting at her door, with a little handkerchief pinned to her lapel, all ready to go.

"She has promised that she won't ask you to carry her even if she feels tired," said her mother. "She always keeps her promise once she gives it. When will you be coming back?"

"In the afternoon," I said. "But if we go to Five Gardens or the beach, we might be delayed a little."

I was not quite sure how Urmi would behave at my sister's place. I was taking a risk, I thought, because a child like that might suddenly feel that she would like to go home. Home was a two hour journey away, and what if she became impatient and started crying? I was also not sure how she would take to my people. It had taken such a long time for her to get used to me; how will she react to all those strangers, who did not speak Gujarati?

But Urmi had no problem getting along with my people. I think I had overlooked one important factor: I was a total stranger when I tried to talk to her. But once she accepted me as her uncle, my people were no longer strangers to her. It was her uncle's sister and nephew and niece and brother-in-law she was going to meet; and she wanted to meet them and was prepared to like them.

Satish had not come home that day. Suneeta, who was in Second Year PUC then, was delighted by Urmi. "God, Mawa, where did you get this one from," she said. What tickled her funny bone was Urmi's hairstyle. As her hair was too short for plaits or ponytails, her mother had made two tufts on the top of her head that made her look cute but comic. "What are these?" said Suneeta, touching those tufts. "Are they a rabbit's ears, or are they horns?"

"They are horns," said Urmi, staring back at her with her large dark eyes.

That made Suneeta's day. She laughed as only she could. I got worried that Urmi, who carried an unusually large load of self-respect for one so young, might get upset but she did not. She stared at Suneeta with curiosity and amusement.

She got along splendidly with Shreekanth too. As his dispensary was closed on Sunday afternoons, he was in an expansive mood when he came home for lunch. He tried his Gujarati on her—though she spoke Hindi quite well—and put a cushion on her chair to raise its height when we sat down to eat. He sat in front of her and watched her eat with great interest. Urmi, who was not used to eating at a table, dropped a piece of vegetable from the curry on to the collar of her dress; and when she tugged at the dress, the piece of vegetable, instead of coming out, went inside. "What happened?" said Shreekanth in Gujarati, pretending to be mystified. "God, where did that vegetable piece go?"

There was a momentary look of bafflement on Urmi's face. Then she recovered her poise and said, looking Shreekanth straight in the eyes, "*Peth ma gayo.*"

I had never seen Shreekanth roar with laughter the way he did then. It was easy to see where Suneeta had got her laughter from. *Peth ma gayo* means 'went into the stomach', and Shreekanth was delighted by the answer.

Sita was the only one who did not seem to like my bringing the little child all the way from Dahisar. She was, as usual, worried. "How did her people send her with you?" she said, "Do they know you well?"

"Not really," I said. "I have talked to her parents only a couple of times. They know me only through Urmi's elder sister, who is a good friend of mine."

"How old is this sister?"

"Six and a half."

"Oh God," said Sita.

"It's all right, there's nothing to worry," said Shreekanth. "Your brother as usual is exaggerating a little. The child's people have been his neighbours for over six months—staying right under him. They apparently know him well enough to trust him. And one thing about Gujaratis. They love their children, like we all do, but they also respect them and their judgement. That's a rare quality."

Half an hour after dinner Urmi came and whispered to me that she wanted to go to the toilet. "For number two," she said. "Do you know how to wash yourself?" I asked. She looked a little uncertain. "If I pour water, can you manage to wash yourself," I asked, and got a more confident 'yes' as a reply.

When we came back from the toilet I saw a strange array of expressions on the faces of my relatives. Suneeta found it difficult to control her laughter, Shreekanth was mildly amused. Sita looked quite shocked. "How have you suddenly become so domesticated, Anna," she said. "This is something your brother-in-law has not done for his own children even once. How could you do it for a total stranger?"

"This child is not a stranger," I said. "If she were, she wouldn't have come with me to your place." "If I haven't ever washed our children's behinds," said Shreekanth, musing, "it's because I was never allowed to. Sita believes that it's a woman's inalienable right to wash infantine behinds. I didn't want to question that and be considered an MCP." That last remark was made looking at Suneeta. MCP, or Male Chauvinist Pig, was an overworked term in Suneeta's vocabulary. "When I get married," she said loftily, "—if I ever get married—it will be with an understanding that the guy will wash the kids' behinds."

"But it's nearing three," said Sita. "When are you taking the kid back home? Don't forget it gets dark early these days."

"Come on," I said, "I can't take her home straight after food. I'm thinking of going to the Five Gardens or to the Shivaji Park beach first."

"I'm free this afternoon," said Shreekanth. "My patients are all fine, there are no visits to be made, thank God. Let's all go to Juhu beach. I can drop you two at Andheri station on the way back."

So we all went in Shreekanth's car to Juhu, Bombay's premier beach, which is so crowded on Sundays that you can only see people, not the sand. Urmi had never seen the sea before. She was scared of the water at first, but once Suneeta dragged her into knee deep water, she just loved it.

Sita was fretting all the time. "It's already half past five," she said. "You'll need at least an hour to reach home from Andheri Station, don't you? It's time we start." Even Shreekanth thought it was time to start for home, but Urmi was very reluctant to leave the place. "The sun goes down into the sea, doesn't he uncle?" she said, "How does he go? I want to see it, just this once, please."

She looked so excited and happy that I wondered whether she was the same morose bear cub I had seen six months earlier. I did not have the heart to say no to her. "There is a bus-stand nearby," I said to Shreekanth. "It's the starting point for some of the buses, so getting a bus should be no problem. You go home please, we'll wait for some time for the sun to set and then we'll leave."

"You have gone crazy," said Sita, shaking her head. "I'm sure you'll find, when you go home, that the child's parents have complained to the police that she is kidnapped."

Urmi and I left the beach soon after the sun set. At the bus stand she wanted to go by a double decker bus. The bus going to Andheri Station was a single decker, but there was a double decker going to Goregaon Station. As that was a station between Andheri and Borivli, I thought it was all right to take that bus.

But the route was a circuitous one, and by the time we reached Goregaon it was close to eight. There was a nice restaurant near the station where I often used to eat on my way back from college. "Shall we eat something here?" I asked Urmi. "Yes," she said, "I am very hungry."

I introduced Urmi to Prasad Shetty, the owner of the restaurant, a good friend of mine. He shook hands with her solemnly. It was amazing, the way Urmi took everything in her stride that day. Where did all her shyness go, I wondered.

That restaurant served beer and Prasad asked the waiter to get me my favourite brand. "Not today," I said, "not with this little lady around." "Have a gimlet then," he said, "it's a good aperitif, and gin doesn't smell, you know."

When Urmi saw my drink—the clear sparkling gin and lime with soda in a delicate long stemmed wineglass, with a cherry floating in it—she wanted one for herself too. Prasad laughed, and got her a drink that looked exactly like mine, but of course with no gin in it. She stirred the drink, like she had seen me do, with great concentration and then started sipping it. "It's nice," she said. As we were sitting in what could be called the lobby of the restaurant—our table was opposite Prasad's counter—people entering the place and leaving it had a good look at this child sipping with aplomb what looked like a gimlet.

Some looked amused, some amazed, some shocked. "I wish we had a hidden camera here," said Prasad, grinning. "God, the look on the mug of some of these people!"

When we were about to finish our meal Prasad said, "Bad news, Professor, there has been a derailment near Malad, and train services are suspended. You'll have to go by bus." He looked down from the window behind him at the bus-stand below, and said, "You are going by 204, aren't you? There is a long line already, and it's growing every minute. You'd better hurry up."

We left the restaurant in a hurry and joined the queue for bus 204. It was so long that I calculated that we might get the seventh or eighth bus. How long would that take? Anywhere between an hour and a half to two and a half hours, depending on the frequency of the buses. My heart sank. It was already past nine. The long bus journey on that circuitous route would take at least an hour, *after we got the bus*. It would be well past midnight by the time we reached home.

Sita was right. Urmi's parents must be terribly worried. If they hadn't already gone to the police with a complaint, they must be contemplating doing so now.

Sick with worry, I looked at the child but felt a little relieved when I saw her looking happy and carefree. She knew there would be a long wait but she was not bothered. She trusted her uncle to take her home. She had had a happy day and she was not going to spoil it by worrying about some delay in reaching home.

God, what a child, I said to myself. Another child of her age, in her place, might have started crying long before. I could imagine the scene all right: the child crying, *I want my mummy, I want to go home, why aren't you taking me home*, and people looking at me with suspicion because they could see that we were not related, for we spoke Hindi, Bombay's lingua franca, whereas the child obviously was a Gujarati. But Urmi, God bless her, was in high spirits. She would stand quietly holding my hand for some time, then leave it and try to play hopscotch on the pavement, her attempt so delightfully clumsy— because she did not know how to hop on one leg—that I could not help laughing in spite of my worries.

After an hour and a half of waiting in the queue, I saw that Urmi was getting tired and feeling sleepy. But she did not complain even then. When I saw finally that she was too sleepy to stand, I lifted her up. "No uncle, Mummy has told me not to ask you to carry me," she said, with her eyes half closed, then put her head on my shoulder and fell asleep.

During the long bus journey, with the child sleeping with her head on my lap, I was wondering: where do these relationships begin. The child had not spoken to me till the previous day. But here she was in a crowded bus, at midnight, sound asleep with her head on my lap, with not a care in the world. Not worried that she was far from home because she trusted me completely. How did I deserve this trust, I who had messed up all my relationships—with my mother, father, uncle, with friends like Ramesh, with Farida and Dakshi. As I gently patted her tufted sleeping head, I felt within me a gush of love and tenderness, something I had not felt for years—not since Satish grew up. I also felt something which Urmi, who is grown up now, would not understand if she were to read this book. I felt an overwhelming feeling of gratitude.

My worries got the better of these feelings as we approached Dahisar. Urmi's people. They must be worried and even if Sita's apprehensions were proved false and the matter not reported to the police, they must be surely waiting anxiously for us at the gate of the building. How would I face this reception committee?

But there was no reception committee waiting for us when we reached our building at quarter past one. There was no one at the gate except the building's watchman, who was sound asleep on a chair, snoring loudly. There were no lights on at Urmi's place. Apparently her people were asleep. When I rang their bell Ba, whose bed was near the main door, opened it. "Urmi has come," she announced. "We got worried when we heard that trains were not running. We thought Urmi might become impatient and give you trouble. Did she trouble you much?"

"Not a bit," I said, not knowing what to say, "she was wonderful." All the explanations I was rehearsing on the way suddenly became unnecessary. I felt within me that warm surge of gratitude again. I wanted to tell them how grateful I was for their trust, but that must wait, because quarter past one at night was hardly the time for getting emotionally eloquent. From inside their house I heard Urmi's voice, loud and excited, telling someone—her mother probably—how she saw, that evening, the red sun sink into the sea. "Like a ball," she said, "like a big red ball, it floated on the water for some time—then it sank!"

Gratitude. I don't think we realize what an important role it plays in love. There is a feeling that it is something you owe and hence a burden. I had this notion that gratitude was incompatible with love, perhaps because of the bitter experience of a colleague of mine. She had married a man much older than her because he had helped her and her mother when they were struggling, after her father deserted his family. She had married him against her mother's advice, out of gratitude, and pity for his loneliness, though there was no love. The marriage was a disaster. "Marry for anything, Rao," she said to me once, in a moment of bitterness, "for love, for affection, for money. But don't ever marry out of gratitude."

The word gratitude—'*kritajnata*'—took on a new meaning for me when I heard a short speech in Sanskrit made by an elderly Swami of one of the eight Mathas of Udupi in a school at Dahisar. The school had invited the Swami to come and bless its students who were about to appear for their S.S.C. exam. I attended that function because I had met the saintly old man ten years earlier and somehow could not forget his eyes. It was when I met him again in the school that I realized why those eyes, brimming with love and compassion, had haunted me for so long: they had a striking resemblance to the eyes of my uncle.

The Swami spoke in Sanskrit because he did not know any of the languages the students of the school understood—English, Hindi, Marathi or Gujarati. The junior Swami of the Matha who had come with him, a young man who could speak Hindi and English with great fluency, translated his words into English. I found his speech, full of rhetorical flourishes, rather irritating, and listened only to the senior Swami's words in Sanskrit. That was the language I had heard, as a child, lying in my uncle's lap. When the English translation was going on, I looked into the old man's eyes and thought of my uncle.

He spoke with simplicity, not just of words but of thought. "What is the worst of sins," he asked, and when I was wondering whether he was referring to one of the five cardinal sins Hinduism spoke of, the first being the killing of a Brahmin—as if the killing of others did not matter so much—he surprised me by saying, "Ingratitude." "What is the greatest of virtues?" he asked, and said, "Gratitude." "When I, a stranger, do something for you," he said, "you feel grateful. That's good. But when someone close to you—your father or mother—when *they* do something for you, do you feel grateful? Do you say 'thank you' to them?"

"You don't say 'thanks' to your mother," said the old Swami, "though she showers her love on you, because you have stopped feeling grateful. You can no longer see with what love she attends to your needs—because you have got accustomed to it. You take everything she does for you, and her love, for granted. Custom is a terrible thing. It makes us insensitive, and takes away all the beauty from this world, and from relationships."

He paused for a while, and then started talking in a softer tone. "Next time someone near to you does something for you," he said, "try to see the love behind that act. Then you'll feel grateful. Say 'thanks' out of that gratitude, not out of politeness, and see what happens to your relationship. Gratitude is the greatest of virtues because it is the core of all love. Love cannot survive without it."

The Swami leaned forward now, anxious to reach out to the young students. "There is someone," he said, "someone even closer to you than your mother. God. He has given us everything, hasn't He? Is there anything in this world that has not come from Him?" He smiled, and I saw his eyes brimming with love, like uncle's. But there was, in them, a light uncle's eyes did not have. The light of inner peace. Something uncle strove for but could not achieve.

"This world is beautiful," he said. "and God has created it. But do we feel grateful? Do we say 'thank you' to Him? Do we pray? Not as a daily routine, not as a duty or a habit, but with our hearts brimming with love and gratitude?"

He shook his head a little sadly. "We don't," he said, "because we are blinded by custom and fail to see the beauty of the world. If only we can look at the world with the unclouded eyes of a child, we shall see its beauty, see that everything is good. Then our hearts will be filled with love and gratitude, and we shall pray."

I was deeply moved. "I have never heard a better speech in my life," I said to Mr. Acharya, the Chairman of the School Committee. "Yes," he said, "He is a brilliant speaker. Incredible fluency in English. He is even better in Kannada, you know, you must hear him once." I realized he was talking of the junior Swami.

"Wisdom cannot be passed on except at some blessed moments." So said that man who bought and sold old newspapers. I suppose I heard the Swami's speech at one such blessed moment. Perhaps the speech made such an impact on me because I had this curious feeling that it was uncle I was listening to. Of all the people in my life he was perhaps the only one who understood the meaning of gratitude and its relationship to love. I remembered how a little child crawling on to his lap when he was doing his parayana had made him feel so grateful that he had thought that God had already blessed him. That child, alas, messed up his personal relationships—including the one with his uncle—because he could not see, for years, how necessary a true feeling of gratitude was to sustain love.

I have spoken to people about that speech several times, calling it the simplest and most convincing exposition of *Bhakti Marga*—the path of devotion—I have ever heard. But it is only now, when I am writing about those difficult years, and about Urmi and Harshad and their love, that I understand the significance of what the Swami said. Those were days when I felt lonelier than ever before. My inner life had gone dry. My dreams had mostly grown bitter. Then suddenly I found myself one evening with a child at the beach, watching the child looking, with wide-eyed wonder, at the sun sinking in the sea. Then the bus ride, on the upper deck of a double decker bus, on the front seat, the wind screaming in our hair, the tedious bus-ride turning—after how many years?—into a joy ride. The restaurant at Goregaon, the sight of Urmi sipping that soft drink as if it were a gimlet. Then that long bus ride home, at midnight, with that little child sleeping with her head on my lap, totally at ease, at home, not missing her parents even at that late hour because she loved and trusted me. It was a miracle. What I felt then was an overwhelming feeling of gratitude, to the child who trusted me, and to—to whoever it was that made miracles happen in this world.

Urmi became my close companion. She waited for me to come back from college and spent the rest of the day with me. At first I used to make some efforts to entertain her—by telling her stories, for example—but that was a bit of a strain, and I soon found that it was not necessary. For though Urmi loved my stories, she did not mind being left to herself. When I was busy with my work, she sat in a corner with her dolls and talked to them. All that she wanted was to be with me.

It was strange, the way she took charge of my house. Whenever I misplaced something and could not find it I just had to tap on the floor with a stick. In a minute she would be there at the door, asking me what I wanted. I don't know how, but she always knew where I had misplaced my keys or purse or whatever I was looking for. When my friends came looking for me and I was not at home, people of the building directed them to her. "Ask that child," they used to say, "She'll know where he has gone and when he will be back."

It is impossible to say how much I depended on her during those difficult years when I was dogged by ill-health. The heavy doses of analgesics I was given at the time of my rickshaw accident obviously damaged my digestive system and gave me severe gastritis. The worst thing about my gastritis was that it was so severe that it became silent. I mean, I never knew when I had a bad attack—because I did not feel the usual burning sensation, as my gastro-intestinal tract was *always* inflamed—till I felt giddy and had awful nights full of maddeningly vivid nightmares. I was so upset by those dreams that I sometimes spent half the night sitting up, too disturbed to sleep. "It's not good to sleep alone in a house when you are in such a state," said Ba, "If you want, one of my sons can come and sleep in your house." "I'm going to sleep in uncle's house," announced Urmi. "I'm going to take care of him."

She did. For the next few months her thin little mattress was kept in my house. Every night she spread it on the floor near my bed and slept. She was not yet eight then, but what a comfort her presence was when I woke up in the middle of the night disturbed by nightmares. She had such large eyes that they were not fully closed even when she slept. Whenever I woke up from a bad dream, I used to sit up for a while looking at that serene face, the half closed eyes making it look like that of the meditating Buddha. One night, I remember, I had a most awful dream. I dreamt that I was cutting a tree and then found to my horror that it was not a tree but the legs of a woman tied to a stake I was hacking at. I panicked. There were people around but they all obviously thought that I was cutting a tree. I felt that they would realize the truth the moment I stopped hacking. But my axe became heavy and I could not lift it. I woke up feeling miserable, and there she was, my Urmi, looking a picture of tranquility in her sleep. "She isn't asleep," I thought, looking at those half-closed eyes. "Urmi," I said, and her eyes opened at once. "Yes, uncle?" she said, getting up.

I felt bad that I had woken up the child. "I just wanted to see if you were asleep," I said. "Go back to sleep, please."

"But why are *you* up uncle? Got bad dreams? Got scared?"

"Not really," I said. In fact my dreams were rarely frightening. They were vivid and disturbing. The worst thing about them was that in almost every one of them I found myself in a state of intense misery. The events were usually simple: I found myself, for example, feeling confused and lost, wandering about in a strange place which I vaguely remembered, as if I had been there decades earlier. But it had changed, all the old landmarks were gone and I was lost. With the realization that I was lost would come a feeling of utter misery. In another dream I was at my door, trying to open it with my key, when the door suddenly opened; and the people inside, all strangers, looked at me with suspicion. I backed out hastily, realizing that it was not my home. I came out and found that it was not my building. It was not my world, I was lost, I did not know where I was. I was a fairly happy person in my everyday life—or at least I could keep my unhappiness at bay with a variety of interests—but in my dreams I lost control of my feelings. The kind of intense misery I felt in them was at times unbearable. As the dreams were as vivid as any real experience, and more intense, the unhappiness I felt was intense and real too.

It spilled on to my everyday life and undermined my normal ability to be happy.

"Go to sleep, Urmi, I'm all right," I said, and she smiled, lay down again, closed her eyes halfway, and fell asleep.

Waking her up in the morning was no problem too. On most days I had to leave for college early and had to wake her up before her normal waking time. But I just had to call her name once, and the eyes, now fully closed, would open almost instantly. She never ever showed any reluctance to get up.

Her mother found it difficult to believe this. "Are you really talking of *Urmi?*" she said, looking quite surprised. "God, it is so difficult to wake her up at home. I even have to throw cold water on her face sometimes."

I suppose Urmi came to my house determined not to give me any trouble. But can a child's determination help her to change her sleeping pattern so dramatically? All that I know is that it did, in Urmi's case. I can only marvel at the strength of her determination, and of her love. It was another minor miracle, something to be grateful about.

Harshad

❧

Harshad came into this world when Urmi was five and a half. Ba gave me the news, beaming with happiness. "The child was born at half past two," she said. "We were all praying for a boy, and it's a boy, thank God. Both mother and son are all right. I am so happy, uncle, I have got a grandson at last."

"Good," I said, "congratulations." I did not show much enthusiasm because I did not approve of this craze for male children. But Ba would not let me go so easily. "When Manoj comes home I'll send you some sweets," she said. Manoj was Urmi's father. "The baby is nice-looking," she said. "Fair, like Bubbu. Not dark, like this one." 'This one' referred to Urmi, who was sitting in a corner silently, her face inscrutable.

I ignored Harshad for nearly eleven months, because I was worried that Urmi might feel neglected because of this new arrival in her family. Her uncle at least should remain faithful to her. But the little chap somehow took a great fancy for me from the day he started recognizing people. It was strange, and inexplicable, how this infant in arms should show such a marked preference for someone who did not seem to care for him. He gurgled and cooed whenever he saw me, but I continued to ignore him.

He was a strange child, unusually silent. "What kind of a baby have the Doshis got," said Mr. Pawar, better known as Pappu's Papa in the building, in mock-disgust one day. "A baby that doesn't cry! Never heard of one before." He shook his head, and added, "Look at my son. He was quite capable of raising any roof with his bawling when he was a baby, and he can still do that, except that we are, thankfully, on the ground floor of a multistoried building."

Harshad changed as he grew up and more than made up for that earlier abstention from crying. His bawling was soon almost as famous in our building as mine was, fifty years earlier, at Nampalli. But as a child he was silent and thoughtful, looking at the world as if he found everything a bit incomprehensible.

I remember the first time I took him to my house. He was eleven months old then. Their door was as usual open, and I stopped there for a while on my way up. Harshad was standing—he had just learnt to stand—and when he saw me he started smiling and tapping the floor with his right leg. His smile was like Bubbu's, but a bit vacuous, lacking sparkle. "Look, he is dancing," said Ba, "he is always so happy to see you. I think he wants you to take him out."

So I held out my hands to him, and he dropped to his knees instantly and came scampering on all fours like a happy little puppy. There was an anxious look on his face—as if he was not sure, till I lifted him up, if he would be accepted. He was surprisingly light. Once I lifted him up I knew that my resistance to him was a thing of the past. There was something strange, and touching, about the way he put his right arm on my shoulder, like a friend, and looked anxiously at my face. I took him up to my house, but though he looked at some of the things there with interest, it was me he was watching most of the time.

This happened on a Saturday night. At nine next morning I was preparing my breakfast when I heard someone or something scratching at my door. Satish, when he was a kid, had a tomcat that used to disappear for days, and then come and scratch at the door, asking to be let in. The sound reminded me of that cat. I opened the door and found, to my surprise, little Harshad there, alone. I took him in wondering who had brought him up and left him at my door.

Ten minutes later, when Harshad was happily gulping down little pieces of bun dipped in milk I was feeding him, I heard Bubbu calling out his name. She looked up when I took him to the balcony and exclaimed, "Oh, he is there in uncle's house! Why didn't you tell us, uncle, that you were taking him up? We have been looking for him everywhere!"

"I didn't bring him up," I said, "I found him at my door." It was soon clear that no one had brought him up. He had come on his own, climbing the stairs on all fours. That was how he came into my life, unbidden, scratching at my door like a cat, asking to be let in. I had to let him in.

He started coming up every day, sneaking out of his house the moment he found the door open. He would crawl up the stairs, sit in front of my door and scratch and push for a long time. When the door would not open—when I was not in—he would start crying, for though he could ascend the steps on his hands and knees, he was not cat enough to go down the stairs that way. He had to sit there till someone came up, saying, "God, Harshad has gone up to uncle's house again," and carried him down.

The intensity of his love for me was something that never ceased to surprise me. It surprised others too. I remember the day he came back, with his people, from Surat after being away for ten days. He was one year and some months old then, and could run about and talk with a slight lisp. 'Hacchi', that was how he pronounced his own name. He saw me standing with a friend of mine—he must have been on the look out for me—when their rickshaw entered the gate. If his mother had not held him tight he would have jumped down from the moving vehicle. The moment the rickshaw stopped, he slipped out and came running to me. "I've thum, Unthle, I, Hacchi," he said, panting with excitement and anxiety, as if he was scared that I might not recognize him. When I took my own time to lift him up—I was busy explaining something to my friend Mr. Soni—he grew impatient and tried to climb up to my arms. It was only after he found his perch on my left arm that he relaxed. "I, Hacchi," he said, happily patting his chest, "I've thum." Then he touched my cheek gently and said, "Unthle." After ten days of absence he had come home to his uncle at last.

"God, the child really loves you," said Soni, shaking his head.

It was not that Harshad loved me more than Urmi did when she was his age. He was simply more demonstrative. The Doshi family had gone to Nashik five years earlier when Urmi was three. They were to stay there for a fortnight but they came back in five days. "This girl Urmi," said Ba, "she made our life hell. She kept on crying, 'I want to go back, I want uncle.' So we had to come back." But when I asked Urmi why they had come back early, her face became a mask. When I repeated my question she said, "It was too cold there."

Even Sita was impressed by Harshad's strong attachment to me. Her first reaction when I took him to their place was, O God, Anna has brought another child too young to travel without its mother. Harshad, she thought, looked even more likely to start crying for his mother than my earlier protégé. But then she saw how attached he was to me, and said, "Poor child, maybe he doesn't get enough love at home." I laughed. "He is the apple of his grandmother's eye," I said, "and his parents just adore him. Being the only boy in the family he is everyone's favourite."

Sita looked pensive. She had changed a lot, after Satish went to the USA for his doctorate, and Suneeta to Baroda to do her MSc. "Just lift up the child and see what you feel," I said to her. She did so, a bit hesitantly, and when he put his right arm on her shoulder, as was his wont, and looked at her face, she was deeply moved. "He's sweet," she said, "He is really sweet." She put him down and wiped her eyes. She was obviously thinking of Satish who had been away in the USA for nearly three years. "Satish is a big chap now," she said, "capable of taking care of himself anywhere in the world, I suppose. Then why am I worried, Anna? Why do I see him, whenever I think of him, not as the moustached young man he is but as the child he was when he was no bigger than this boy?"

Unlike Urmi at his age, Harshad had to be fed. It was fun feeding him. He was always ready for the food when it reached his mouth and sucked it in with a little sound. Sita smiled as I fed the child and the morsels went in plop, plop. She shook her head and said, "How do you explain this relationship, Anna? Doesn't it make you believe in rebirth?"

I laughed. "Who do you think this little chap was in his previous birth?" I said.

Sita hesitated. "Don't laugh at me," she said, " but there's something about this child—the way he looks at you—which makes me think of uncle."

"Nonsense," I said and laughed aloud, and little Harshad clapped his hands and laughed too, as he often did when he saw others laughing. I fed him a few more morsels, and as they went in plop, plop, I said, "Just look at the way this kid is eating. How can you see anything in common between him and uncle?"

"How do we know what uncle was like in his childhood?" said Sita. "Even in his old age there was one thing about him. He did not hanker for anything, it was true, but when he ate he relished his food. When I met him for the last time, I gave him some malpuris I had prepared for Satish. He ate them with relish. 'I'm glad, Doddappayya,' I said, 'that you still enjoy eating sweets.' He smiled. 'It's a sin not to relish good food,' he said. 'It's ingratitude.'"

When I was in that awful hospital after the rickshaw accident, it was Harshad's people who took care of my needs. His mother brought him along with my lunch and he sat on my bed and watched me eat. He looked a little uncertain at first—because that head injury must have altered my appearance a bit—and touched me gingerly as if to make sure that I was, really, his uncle. Something in the way he looked at me—the love and concern in his eyes—reminded me of the night on the eve of Chitra Poornima I had spent at Nampalli with uncle. Harshad had light gray eyes, like Bubbu. No one in our family had eyes like that, but uncle's eyes had got clouded and turned greyish when he was around fifty—an early onset of *arcus senilis* I think—so that when little Harshad looked at me with worry and concern, for a moment I thought I was looking into the eyes of my uncle.

Hacchi had remarkable resilience. I realized this when I took him to Borivli once, after securing a promise from him that he would not ask me to carry him. We walked up to Dahisar Station that day and took a train because Harshad preferred a train to a bus. Everything was all right, the little chap even walking up and down the steep stairs of the Borivli Railway over-bridge, telling me proudly that he was now a big boy and there was no need to carry him.

It was when we were on our way back, after making our purchases at Borivli, that terror overtook us. On entering the Borivli Station I saw that it was more crowded than usual. I thought that we would cross the over-bridge and go to The eastern side of the station, from where plenty of buses were available to go home. So we went up the bridge, and then suddenly it happened: a crowd-burst. A long-distance passenger train from the north had just disgorged its human cargo on platform five, and those people were streaming up the bridge, following red-shirted Porters carrying loads of luggage on their heads. There were waiting trains on two platforms. When two crowded trains arrived almost simultaneously from the south the sea of humanity in the station suddenly turned turbulent and stormy, like a narrow cove hit by an unusually high tide.

The pressure of that turbulence was felt at its most severe on the narrow over-bridge, built some thirty years earlier when the population of Borivli was not even five percent of what it had since become. In panic I tried to go back but found that the tide was moving in the opposite direction. Little Harshad felt suffocated and started screaming. I lifted him up—and found in front of me a hefty porter loaded with bags. There was panic on his face, for he too had been taken by surprise by the sudden crowd-burst. One of the bags he was carrying fell on our head and Harshad started screaming in pain and terror.

I moved with the current, for there was nothing else I could have done. I prayed that I would not lose my footing and fall down and be trampled to death. I cursed myself for bringing little Harshad into that crowded station. I must keep my balance at any cost, I said to myself, I must not fall down, I *must* be on my feet. I shouted at the crowd, for I saw that the stampede was caused not just because there were too many people around but because everyone was in a mad hurry, to catch this train or that train, or simply to escape from the stampede. "Take it easy," I shouted, "Take it easy please," but it was like shouting at the wind, or the waves of the sea.

The movement of that human current became uncertain at the centre of the bridge. The crowd swayed this way and that, and then the current turned left and tumbled down the steep staircase to platform four. I had to go with it. I held Harshad tight in my arms and concentrated on keeping myself afloat. I noticed, in horror, that not once did my feet touch the stairs as we went down.

Then as we touched down on platform four, the crowd suddenly thinned out. It was as if there never was a crowd-burst. Only the look of bewilderment on the faces of people huddled under the bridge on the adjacent platform—people with families, and loads of luggage, who had got down from that long-distance train—told its own tale. I put Harshad down, felt his head and found a little lump just above his forehead. He was whimpering.

We heard a train coming from behind us, from the south. Harshad looked back and asked, "Our thain, Unthle?"

When I said yes, he screamed in a sudden and unexpected burst of excitement: "Our thain's thum, Unthle? Leth's lun, leth's thatch ith!"

We ran hand in hand to the place where the first class compartment would stop. I lifted him up when the train stopped, and we got in. The train was not crowded. I stood leaning against the compartment wall, cuddling the child, now safe in my arms. His cheeks were wet with tears, but there was a look of triumph in his eyes. "Our thain!" he said, "We goth our thain!" Only the tremor in his voice betrayed the terror he had just gone through.

I was deeply moved by the child's resilience. "Babu," I said, "you belong to Bombay. You are brave, you can survive in this city. Your uncle cannot. He will have to run away from here some day." Harshad could not understand what I was mumbling but he responded to the tone. He took my face in both his hands, patted my cheeks and then kissed me. It was a gesture of love—and gratitude.

%

Four years after the rickshaw accident I decided to go and spend a month in a well known hospital of naturopathy near Bangalore, to see if they could do something to set right my impaired digestive system. Harshad was inconsolable when he learnt I was going away for more than a month. "I'll come with you," he said, "Why can't you take me with you?" His face fell when I told him that I was going to stay in a hospital, where a kid like him would not be allowed to stay. "But I am unwell too," he said, "I can also get treatment there."

"What is wrong with you?" I said, laughing.

"I don't know," he said, "but I am not well. Sometimes I can't see clearly."

I thought he was bluffing. I spent five weeks in Bangalore, four of them in the Hospital. The treatment did me little good but the place was lovely. Then I spent a few days with a friend whose wife cooked divinely. God, I could appreciate that, because in that hospital of naturopathy they had practically starved me.

There I got a letter from Urmi, in Hindi. As her handwriting, like that of most Gujaratis, was awfully illegible, it took me an hour to read that one page letter.

It was mainly about Harshad. He was not eating well, she wrote, and had grown weaker. Some of the boys of the building had discovered that he lost his temper if they said anything against me, and so they teased him, and he fought with them and came home badly beaten. Something was wrong with his eyes, and he would soon get spectacles, and the specialist had said that if his eyesight did not improve with exercise and the wearing of glasses, an operation might become necessary.

I went back to Bombay as soon as I got a train ticket.

Harshad was playing behind the building but the moment he heard I had come he came running to my house. I found that he looked weak and tense. "Sorry, Hacchi," I said, "I haven't brought you any gifts, because I came back from Bangalore in a hurry." "That's all right," he said, came and hugged me. I held him in my arms and felt, with a pang, how thin he had grown in just five weeks. I kept on patting him—because I did not know what to say—till I could feel his tense body relaxing a little. "What's it, Babu," I said, "What's wrong?"

I had never seen Harshad cry in sorrow before. He often cried—bawled in fact—when he was angry or upset but when he was sad, his small face would become smaller but he would not cry. But oh, how he cried that day. I felt his thin little frame shaking with sobs as sorrows pent up for days rose to the surface. "Nanu beats me up," he sobbed, "he calls *you* a spoilsport—because you tell them not to play cricket at noon—and then he beats me up when I object—and Mummy scolds *me* for fighting with the boys—and Bubbu kicks me if I get up even a bit late because she says she has to sweep and swab the floor—and Urmi..."

"It's all right now," I said, wiping his tears, "I have come back now." Then I looked into his eyes and saw something I had rarely seen in them before: fear.

"You look scared, Babu. Why are you scared?"

He held me tight and shivered. Then he looked at me and said, "They are going to operate on my eyes, uncle, aren't they? I'm so scared."

It was not too difficult to assuage his fears and reassure him that the right glasses and exercise would set things right. He was basically of a sunny disposition, like Bubbu, and it was a combination of misfortunes—my absence no doubt the worst among them—that had got him down.

It turned out that there was no need for an operation. He soon got a pair of thick glasses. He had a small round face—like Bubbu, who had grown tall and was called a lollypop by the boys of our building—and the glasses, too heavy for his small nose, looked not just comic but grotesque. But he accepted them with resignation and wore them all the time, because he had been told that an operation might become necessary otherwise. The other boys laughed at his thick glasses and called him an owl, but he took that in his stride.

It was Harshad's weak eyesight, I realized, that had set him apart from other children. Even that feeling Sita and I had—that there was something of uncle in the way he looked—was no doubt due to his weak vision, to the way he *strained* hard to see. I had found his smile a bit vacuous, and the way he anxiously looked at people touching, but I could not put two and two together. An early discovery might have led to a quicker and easier recovery, but that was not to be.

When I got crushed between two buses and had to spend nearly two months at home with my right arm tied to my body, I came to depend on Harshad a lot. He was eight then, had got used to his specs, and his vision was improving. As soon as he came back from school he used to come running up to my house. He brought his food up and we ate together. What the specialist had said about learning to play tennis with my left hand appealed to him greatly. "You must try, uncle, to play with your left hand," he said, "there's nothing like trying." I had given him, two years earlier, a table tennis bat, asking him to practise playing against the wall. I thought it might improve his vision and his eye-and-hand coordination. He brought it up now and suggested that we should have competitions to see who could keep the ball at play longer, hitting it against the wall, he with his right hand and I with my left. After a couple of days I started winning and that made him extremely happy.

It was after he went down to play cricket with his friends—after playing with me for nearly an hour one day—that it struck me what a selfish brute I had always been compared to this child. He did not like it when I could not keep that ball longer at play than him. He was happy only when I started winning. But I, I had always played for a win when I played chess or any other game with him. What kind of a mean streak was this that made me hate to lose even to people I loved?

I realized that at the root of my problem there was an old failure. I played some games well when I was a boy, and was very impressive when we were just practising. But the moment we started a serious game I became nervous, my game went to pieces, and I lost to boys who did not play half as well as I did. This made me at times a laughing stock among the boys. That hurt and rankled, making me, forever, a bad loser. Did it cause a permanent psychological disability, a handicap that came in the way of happy personal relationships? A little boy of eight had to teach me, when I was nearing sixty, that there was joy in losing to someone you loved. If only I had learnt that years earlier.

After Thirty-seven Years

❧

It was after the last accident that I decided that I should go home during the summer vacation. Another fourteen years had elapsed since I last went to Kantheshwar. There would be no one now to tell me that I should enter the house through the cowshed, no one to worry himself sick about my second banishment. But I had to find out if I still had a home. Bombay had become impossible.

But when I mentioned this to Harshad, he looked devastated. "No, no," he said, "you can't go leaving me here. I'll come with you."

"What will you do there?" I said. "You don't know Kannada or English, and no one speaks Gujarati or Hindi there. You won't be able to speak to anyone. What will you do if someone speaks to you in Kannada or English?"

"I'll just smile," he said.

"You have a sweet smile, but you can't smile all the time," I said. "No, Babu, I can't take you with me this time. I'll have to go and see what the situation is like there. I'm going home after fourteen years, see?"

Immediately after Harshad went down, Urmi came up. "What happened, uncle?" she asked.

"Why, what happened?"

"Harshad came down with his face so small. He has gone out to play but I know he is terribly upset."

Urmi's relationship with Harshad was a strange one. They had frequent fights but when Harshad was sad and his face grew small it was Urmi who always noticed it first. She disliked his tantrums but his quiet sadness touched her heart.

I told her about my decision to go home during the vacation. "I haven't gone home for fourteen years," I said. "I must go this year and see my people. I am tired of Bombay, Urmi. In two years I'll retire. What do I do in this crowded city, after that. So I must go to my village and find out if there is still a place for me there. I must go alone, I cannot take Harshad along. Can you explain this to him?"

Urmi stared at me, her large eyes inscrutable. "I'll talk to him," she said.

But it was impossible to console Harshad. It was only a question of making him accept the inevitable, that was all. "I can't take you with me this year," I said. "But next vacation I certainly will. If I can't take you, I'll not myself go."

"But what about the year after that?" he said. "I know you are going to leave Bombay after you retire. What will happen to me then?"

"What can happen to you. I'll build a nice house there, a little bungalow with a little garden round it. You can come and stay with me."

For a moment his face brightened, and then it grew smaller and darker than before. "How can I come and stay with you when I have to go to school here?" he wailed. "It's all Mummy's fault. Why did she put me in a Gujarati medium school? If I were in English medium like Guddi and Teenu, I could have joined some English medium school at your place and stayed with you."

Guddi and Teenu were Harshad's cousins—daughters of his father's younger brother. Their parents had put them in an English medium school. That was the new trend among middle class Gujaratis, and Gujarati medium schools were closing down all over Bombay.

Harshad wanted to come with me to the airport to bid me farewell. So I asked Pappu to come along so that he could take him back home. Pappu's coming was a great help because I would have had problems with my luggage otherwise: my right shoulder was still weak and sore. Urmi decided to join us at the last minute.

The parting was painful, as expected. I was feeling awful, troubled by some vague dread, some kind of apprehension which I could not understand. Urmi saw that I did not look all right. "You should not cry at the airport," she said to Harshad. "Uncle will feel bad if you do. He has to go home to see his people. He'll come back in a month's time and then we'll all go to Mahabaleshwar."

When we got down from the taxi at the airport, Harshad took out from his pocket a chocolate bar and gave it to me. "What's this for?" I said.

"It's not for you," he said, "It's for Ashu."

For a moment I could not recollect who was Ashu. Then I remembered how I had tried to explain to him, a few days earlier, that I *had* to go home because I wanted to meet my nephew Ashu. "He is my only brother's only son," I had said. "I am his uncle, like I am yours. He is ten, two years older than you, but we haven't even seen each other. Shouldn't I go to see him?" Harshad had nodded, silently, and then said, in a hardly audible voice, "but I want to meet him too."

That chocolate was nearly the last straw. Suddenly I felt I did not want to go, leaving these kids I loved, leaving Harshad whose face looked smaller and sadder than ever before. What am I going 'home' for? Home is where there are people who love you, where you feel wanted. But there was no time to brood over things. It was my first flight and I was anxious to be inside the airport before the stipulated reporting time. I bid them a hurried goodbye, told them to go home straight and went in. I was feeling so upset and confused that I could not control my trolley and it got entangled with that of another.

"I'm sorry," said two voices simultaneously, mine and the other's. The man, a well built young chap in a blue blazer, laughed aloud. "You seem to be in a deuced hurry," he said, "which flight is yours?"

"The one to Mangalore," I said.

"There is no need for any hurry," he said, "the flight is more than an hour away. I'm also going by that flight. Came early because I had nothing else to do. I'm going to check in my luggage first so that I can wander around freely."

"This is my first flight," I said, "so I'm feeling a bit lost. I'm Rao, Sudhakar Rao. I hope you won't mind guiding me about the procedures here."

"Sure, sure," he said, "I'm Satish Shetty." Then he looked over his shoulder and burst out laughing. "Isn't that the most comic sight imaginable?" he said.

I looked back and saw a strange sight. Harshad. He had moved away from the entrance because the place had become crowded and he could not see me from there. He had moved a few feet away from the door and was trying to look through the wall of thick plate-glass by pressing his face hard against it. His little nose and mouth were flattened by the pressure and the round spectacles on top of that flattened nose made the picture supremely comic—except that to me, who was aware of the agonized effort of the child to have a last look at his uncle, it was not comic, it was heartrending.

I waved to him but he could not see me. Perhaps the light inside was not enough. Or may be he was crying.

"Can I go out for a few minutes after checking in my luggage?" I asked Mr. Shetty. "Is there time enough for that?"

"There certainly is," he said. "The call for security check is another half an hour away. Even when it's given you may take your own time. What's gained by being at the head of the queue?"

I hurried to the luggage counter. There was no queue there but the fat chap in front of me happened to be a man returning from Kuwait. He had loads of luggage and kept on arguing about the charges he was asked to pay for excess luggage. I fumed and fretted but there was nothing I could do. When my turn came at last, after fifteen long minutes, I checked in my bag and rushed to the entrance. But the kids had already left.

⁊⊱

My first flight turned out to be a thoroughly unpleasant one. Something went wrong with the air pressure inside the plane and my ears started aching like hell. It was the kind of pain that could drive one mad. Plugging the ears with cotton wool did not help. When I got down at Mangalore finally and removed the cotton wool, I was shocked to find air rushing out of my left ear with a hissing sound. A twenty-year-old injury to the eardrum, which I thought had healed up completely, had obviously left a puncture.

Moni had sent his car to the airport. I found his house, as I had found it fourteen years earlier, unbearably hot. The few plants in the compound looked withered. The heat made it impossible for me to rest or relax. So in the afternoon I went out for a stroll to the school playground, after a lapse of thirty-seven years. I know I wrote "more than twenty years" in an earlier chapter but that only shows how unreliable my sense of the passage of time then was. Now that I have started reviewing my life in a chronological sequence I know when exactly I had last visited that old haunt of mine. It was thirty-seven years earlier, the evening before I left for Bombay with Sita and little Satish.

I have already written about that stroll. In the school and its playground I was looking at a world that belonged to me once. But though it still looked the same, it was not mine anymore. I had lost it through default. My nightmares had at last caught up with me. What I felt then was precisely what the dreams had presaged. The misery was the same, except that there was now no hope of waking up. I was lost, homeless, dispossessed.

Then at night I found something I had lost years ago: an old copy of *Marali Mannige*. I have already written about that experience: how I started reading that novel and found its ivory gates opening at once, onto a world where I was again at home; how I read the book uncritically, as I had done when I read it for the first time at the age of eleven; how the book opened the clogged springs of my feelings, and gave me back, momentarily, my emotional youth; and how I gave myself up to the flow of the story and read on.

At half past two someone knocked on the door. I opened the door, and he was there, my father.

"It's past two, Babu," he said, "enough of reading, now. Go to bed."

"Yes, Appa," I said obediently, put off the light and went to bed.

399

A few minutes later, when I was on the edge of sleep, I got up with a start, goose pimples all over my body.

My father at the door? Twenty years after his death?

What door had he knocked on, O God, what door had I opened?

PART VII
Yakshi

૪ૐ

Old men ought to be explorers.

T.S. Eliot

Heat and Fever

❧

I woke up the next morning feeling feverish. A dull headache made thinking difficult. "Breakfast is ready, Doddappayya," said Ashu, peeping into my room. I called him in and gave him the pen set I had brought for him and the chocolate Harshad had given. I tried to tell him about Harshad but he did not seem to be interested. I knew that it was only shyness that made him appear cold and distant but I could not help feeling hurt.

Moni was already at the breakfast table. "I'm sorry," said his cheerful voice from behind the newspaper, "I could not wait for you. I have to be in the hospital by half past nine, you know." His wife Malini was bringing from the kitchen, one by one, hot dosas prepared by their new cook Yashodamma. "Your brother has nice table manners," she said smiling pleasantly. "At breakfast guests can only look at the back of a newspaper, not his face." "But this chap is not my guest," said Moni, "he is my Anna."

He put down the newspaper, grinned and then looked at me quizzically. "After coming home, Anna, have you begun to feel that you are sliding back into your childhood?" he asked.

"Why do you say that?"

"Because when I knocked at your door at half past two last night and asked you to go to sleep, you said, 'Yes, Appa.'"

I was taken aback. So it was Moni, not a visitation from the other world. I shook my head. I could have sworn it was Appa. He had a curious habit. He used to go to bed wearing a 'mundu' and at night it invariably used to come off. If he had to get up at night he could never find that piece of cloth in the dark and so used to come out of his bedroom wrapping round his middle anything he could lay hands on, like a bedsheet or a blanket. I could have sworn that whoever came to see me the previous night had a flowery bedsheet round his middle.

"What were you wearing when you came to see me?" I asked.

Moni grinned and looked at his wife. "Was he wearing some bedsheet or blanket?" she asked. "He does that all the time."

"He is growing more and more like father," I said.

Both Moni and his wife were already dressed up. Perhaps I had delayed them by getting up late. I was feeling feverish but I did not want to talk about it then and delay them further. My hand went to the left side of my neck to check my temperature and found there a couple of newly erupted boils.

"I am sliding back into adolescence, I think," I said, "I have started getting pimples again."

Moni had finished his breakfast. He got up, came closer and looked at the eruptions. Then with his left hand he felt my forehead. "You have fever," he said. "It's childhood you have slid back into, not adolescence. These are not pimples. I think it's chicken pox. You never had chicken pox in your childhood?"

"No," I said. "You don't know what it was like at Nampalli. A totally sheltered life. When there was chicken pox or measles in the hamlet I was not allowed to go to the other houses, and those kids were not allowed to come to ours. But you really think it's chicken pox? At my age?"

"It can come at any age," he said. He called his wife to have a look at the eruptions. She looked at them, nodded, but did not say anything.

"Take rest and relax," said Moni. "Malini will come home at twelve thirty, and I'll come at one. If you want anything in the meantime, ask Yashodamma. Don't worry about your illness, we are here to take care of you."

"I'm not worried about chicken pox," I said. "It's only a minor ailment, I know. Half a dozen kids in our building had it a fortnight ago and they were running around the place all the time. They did not even seem to need bed rest."

Moni stared at me and shook his head. "It's different with grownups," he said.

By noon my fever had risen and I began to feel acute discomfort. The heat in that concrete bungalow rose all through the day, but the fever prevented me from sweating. I felt I was on fire.

In the evening Moni had to go, with his wife and son, to see his mother-in-law at a remote village near Haladi. "We'll leave Ashu with his grandmother for a few days," said Malini, apologetically. "My sister has come from Bangalore with her two kids, and he is very fond of them. It's school vacation time, and let them have a long picnic there." She looked at my face and perhaps saw there some disappointment. "I'm sorry you'll be alone at home, but the thing is..." she hesitated a bit and then said, "Grown up people don't usually get chicken pox, but when they do it can be rather severe. And it can look quite bad. We are not worried about Ashu getting the infection, but he might be frightened by the sight of a grown up person with chicken pox. To be honest, it can be frightening."

"In fact," said Moni, "you should not look at yourself in the mirror when you have chicken pox. That's the usual advice given." He also gave me the 'usual medicine' for the disease. "Take rest and have some light food. Go to bed, don't wait for us. We might come late; once we go there we can't leave without eating."

Normally I worry so much about my health that you can call me a hypochondriac. But somehow I was not worried that day. Chicken pox, I still thought, was a minor disease. If I were to tell Harshad that I had chicken pox and was worried, he would have laughed. Many of his friends had the ailment recently and he himself had had it a year earlier. When I look back at the events of my life I find it curious that on both the occasions I was told by my father, late at night, to stop reading my favourite novel—once in person when I was reading it for the first time at the age of eleven and again forty-seven years later, through Moni—I was close to death, but did not know it; and I, who worried myself to death when I had some minor problem like sore throat, was not worried at all.

I was concerned, however, about the trouble and worry I was causing Moni and his wife. When they came home late at night I wanted to reassure them that everything was all right. "I think mine is only a mild attack," I said, "I have got only a few eruptions."

Moni smiled and shook his head. "Chicken pox does not erupt all at one go like smallpox," he said. "It comes in crops."

It did come in crops. There were more eruptions the next day, and by the evening of the third day my whole body was covered with little red boils that looked surprisingly like—like suragi buds! But still I was not worried. I looked at my arms and legs and trunk, and said to myself: *And now in age I bud again.*

That evening I had a visitor. At the exact moment when the sun set behind the hospital, Narayana Shanubhag stood at our door. For a moment it looked like I had another visitation from the other world because he looked an exact copy of Martappayya. He had a small bottle, wrapped in a piece of newspaper, in his hand. "I heard you had come and fallen ill," he said hesitantly, "I had this medicine lying with me, and I thought it might be of some use to you."

"Please come in," I said, and he came and sat down on the edge of one of the ornate chairs in the hall, looking very uncomfortable. "This is *Paripattadi Kadha*," he said, giving me the bottle in his hand. "This is the only ayurvedic medicine for chicken pox and measles but it's not available here. It's very useful because it reduces the body heat."

"You need not have taken the trouble," I said. "My brother is treating me."

Narayana moved forward, now sitting on the very edge of the chair. "That's what I was worried about," he said. "English medicine is no good for chicken pox. These doctors know they have no specific medicine for the disease, but still they give strong tablets that increase the body heat. *Ushna*, body heat, that's what makes chicken pox so dangerous. So don't take all those tablets please."

For the first time during that illness I got worried. Sunlight had by then faded away totally, but bright moonlight flowed in from the eastern window and lit up parts of the room. The chair next to the one Narayana was sitting on was bathed in that cool light, and his proximity to that light made him visible as a faint shadowy figure. Bending forward and whispering in a conspiratorial tone, Narayana looked and sounded so much like his father that I could not shake off the feeling, for the next few days, that it was really Martappayya who had come to see me.

"Is it true that there is no smallpox in the world now?" he asked.

When I said it was totally eradicated, he shook his head. "Chicken pox, like smallpox, comes from Devi," he said. "Maybe the goddess is angry now because scientists have destroyed one of her weapons. That's why perhaps chicken pox has now become as deadly as smallpox, when grown up people get it. Two of my cousins, both in their early fifties, got chicken pox two years ago. God, it was terrible. One of them took English medicine. I don't want to tell you, in your present condition, what happened to him. After seeing his fate I went to Karwar and got a few bottles of Paripattadi Kadha for my other cousin. He survived."

Yashodamma came in and switched on the light. Narayana took that as a signal that it was time for him to go. He got up and peered at me in the bright light that had driven the moonlight out. "God, you have got it really bad, worse than my cousins," he said. "It's only the third day, isn't it? Didn't the first boils come on Friday? See, chicken pox always starts on Fridays because that's the day sacred to Devi." He turned to go and said, "I'll come again, in two days, to cheer you up."

I threw away the tablets Moni had given me. The fever rose that night and I started getting strange dreams. They were not like my usual nightmares. The strange thing was that I was never quite sure whether I was awake or asleep when I was dreaming. In the middle of a dream I could say to myself, "That's enough now, I'm going to open my eyes and get out of this nightmare," and I *could* open my eyes and get out of it. But the nightmare world waited for me. The moment I closed my eyes I slid back into it even before I was fully asleep.

Next day there was a new problem. Yashodamma decided to go on leave. She pretended at first that it was because there was some important ceremony at her husband's place near Udupi, which she had just recollected. But when Malini cross-examined her she blurted out the truth. She was scared, she said, to be alone in the house with someone who had smallpox. She was not prepared to believe it was only chicken pox. She had seen chicken pox, and when she was a kid she had seen smallpox, and she knew what was what. Malini threatened not to take her back if she walked out at that juncture but she was adamant. "My job is not more important than my life," she said. She took her bag, which she had already kept packed, shed a few tears that came without warning like sudden showers on a hot humid day, and went away even as the sun was about to set.

Malini looked terribly upset. "I came home for a few minutes to get something and to see how you are," she said "There is a woman in labour pains waiting in the hospital. I have to rush back, and this mad woman has already delayed me. But don't you worry about anything please. Your brother or I will try to come home early. I'm so sorry, we shouldn't leave you alone in this state."

"Don't worry about me," I said, "I'm used to being alone."

I did not mind being alone. After Malini left I removed the towel I had thrown over my shoulder in her presence, stood in front of the full-length mirror and looked at myself. I looked awful. There was not a single square inch of skin left uncovered by those red angry eruptions. Where was the place for the next crop, I wondered, and what would happen if these buds opened into flowers. I did not blame Yashodamma for running away and I was glad Ashu was at his grandmother's place. It was good that I was alone in the house.

I had to plan my daily routine for the next few days, I said to myself, I should not leave it to Moni. I should keep myself away from him and Malini, especially when they were eating, or at night. They were both doctors and knew that a severe attack of chicken pox was only just as infectious as a mild attack. But they were also sensitive human beings and I should spare them, as far as possible, the awesome sight I had become. So that night when Moni came—he came late because he had gone to the Rotary Club—I called him and said, "Look, I know what a sight I am now. I don't want to sit at your table for breakfast or dinner and spoil your appetite. I can't eat the same food anyway. I can take absolutely no spices because my entire gastro-intestinal tract, from the mouth downward, is on fire. All that I can have is plain rice gruel. You can keep that ready somewhere so that I can eat when I feel like it. Your house is quite large. So I want you to turn my room into a kind of isolation ward…No, no, please, I'm not upset or anything, it's not for your sake that I want this arrangement. It's for my own sake. With all these eruptions I feel discomfort while wearing clothes, but I feel uncomfortable if I am not properly clothed in your presence…You are my own people, my own family, I know, I know I should not worry about what I wear and so on, but I have been away for so long…I want to be isolated because *I* need privacy."

Moni looked at me in dismay. "You have high fever and you are raving," he said. He turned and looked at his wife. I saw that her eyes were moist and she looked, for the first time, tired. "You can keep your door closed," she said, "But don't latch it from inside please, you may need help sometimes. The other doors will remain open. Don't hesitate to come out and sit with us when you need company. You'll need company, even if you are used to being alone. I think you can't even read now?"

She was right. I could not read because I could not wear my specs. My nose was completely covered with eruptions.

"You should not be alone in the house," continued Malini. "Some person is needed here, now that even Yashodamma is gone. We'll send one of our nurses here tomorrow. She is a trained nurse, so don't worry about your privacy please."

"But whom can we send?" said Moni, looking worried now. "The only efficient one is Jyothi, but Dr. Shenoy will throw up tantrums if she is taken away from him. Mary and Gayatri are irresponsible. The others—they are used to working together, and it will be a problem persuading any of them to work here."

"I have already asked that new woman," said Malini, "the one who joined the hospital yesterday. She hasn't got any fixed duty as yet and she is more than willing to work here. You remember which department she said she had worked in, in her previous hospital at Hubli? The Infectious Diseases Ward." She looked at me and added hesitantly, "But there is a problem, and I am a little worried…"

"What is the problem?" I said, but Malini looked perplexed. "I'm worried but I don't know why," she said. "Anyway, we'll talk about it after supper."

"Did you find anything strange when you interviewed that woman?" said Malini to Moni, after supper got over. "Nothing strange," he said. "She had no papers, except a recommendation letter from a doctor working as an Honorary in the hospital she was last in. She said that she had worked for sixteen years in hospitals, four years at Miraj and twelve at Hubli. She looked quite young, though. She said that she had left the Hubli hospital because she could not get along with the Matron there. You know Anna, we don't insist on paper qualifications because it's impossible to get qualified nurses here. We can't afford to give them government salary. So we take those who come and if we find that they don't know their job, we try to teach them. I asked this woman some questions about chicken pox and measles because she said that she had worked in the Infectious Diseases section, and God, she seemed to know more about those ailments than I did. It was not all bookish knowledge either. I was really impressed. I asked her when she could join, and she said, 'right now, if you'd let me stay in the hospital.' So she was appointed straightaway. No, I didn't find anything strange—except for the fact that she had come with her bag, as if she was certain she would get the job. She seemed to be a very confident person."

"Her confidence," said Malini, "it's almost like arrogance." She turned to me and said, "You know I had to rush to the hospital this evening because there was someone in labour pains. The patient is my brother's wife's cousin. She was very keen on a normal delivery. It's her first pregnancy and she wanted to savour labour pain, she said, because it was an important part of the experience of motherhood. But at the last moment it became obvious that a Caesarian was necessary. I am usually well organized but today everything went wrong. Our regular anesthetist was not available. Our surgeon was out of town. Even Leela, the nurse who always assists me, was on leave. My husband, when I called for him, was not in his room. 'Must have gone to the Rotary Club,' someone said." Malini's voice had a sharp edge that made Moni squirm a little. "So I called this new woman, but she said she did not want to work in the delivery section! I was furious, and wanted to give her a piece of my mind, but I only said, 'Come and help me now, let's see where you want to work later on.'

"I was nervous and upset, and when the baby was taken out found that it was not crying properly. I had my hands full and so I handed it over to the nurse, forgetting that it was not Leela. Leela would have known what to do. Then I realized my mistake and looked up to see what the new woman was doing.

"She was perfect. The way she handled that child and made it cry, the sureness and delicacy of her touch, it was amazing. No paediatrician could have done a better job.

"After the operation I wanted to talk to her but found she had disappeared. Gayatri said that she had gone to the nurses' room—to have a bath! 'She is a pukka Brahmin, ma'am,' she said, giggling, 'she wants a shower because she has assisted in a delivery.' Again I wanted to scold her when she came but I remembered that we needed someone here. So I told her about you and how we needed someone to work here."

"Did she agree?" asked Moni.

"Agree? She jumped at the offer. It was as if she knew it was coming and was waiting for it. That's what has got me worried."

"Why worry about it?" said Moni, a little absentmindedly, trying to pluck a hair from his nose.

"Why worry?" said Malini, a little impatiently. "There is so much to worry about. Who is this woman? We know nothing about her antecedents. Why is she so anxious to work in the house? Can we leave this stranger in charge here?"

Moni looked worried now. "What do we do then?" he said. "Maybe I'll have to send one of the boys of the hospital here, every now and then, to keep an eye on her and see what's happening. When is she coming?"

"Tomorrow. I had to ask you first whether the arrangement's all right." Malini looked at me and said, "Maybe I have become needlessly suspicious. Maybe she wants to come here because she thinks she is some kind of a specialist in infectious diseases. One thing is certain: she will be happier staying here, because she does not look like someone who can get along with the other sisters."

Moni yawned and said, "I think I'll take, first thing in the morning, whatever jewellery is in the house and put it in our bank locker. It's lying empty as it is."

I could feel my fever rising and wanted to rest. So I got up to go to my room, then turned and asked Malini, "What's the woman's name?"

"Lakshmi," she said.

I shivered and felt dizzy. It must be the rising fever or perhaps I had got up too suddenly. It was only after I lay down in my bed that I realized the cause of that sudden shiver down the spine I had felt. My hearing had stuttered a little. Before I heard 'Lakshmi,' the part of the brain that responded to auditory nerves had registered a different word: for a brief second I thought I heard the word, Yakshi.

Stories

❦

The fever rose that night higher than before. I put the thermometer under my tongue, and waited. The previous day it was 103 degrees, but at night it had risen to 105. That day at noon it was 104. As the fever invariably rose at night I wondered what the thermometer would show. As I was peering at it by holding my specs in front of my eyes, Moni walked in. "Let's see what it says," he said, smiling, and took it from my hand. "Oh, God," he said, looking shocked. "What's happening? Have you been taking the tablets I gave you? Where are they?"

I made a show of looking for them and said, "I don't know, I must have misplaced them." He shook his head in anger and dismay and walked away. I could hear him noisily rummaging in some cupboard in his room and grumbling that he could never find anything that he wanted when he wanted it. After three minutes he was back in my room with a small strip of tablets. "Paracetamol," he said, "for fever." He took out two tablets and made me swallow them. "I could not find any antibiotics. We'll get them tomorrow," he said.

"No antibiotics, please," I said. "All antibiotics and analgesics give me severe stomatitis, gastritis and so on. With my GI tract already on fire, I am scared. What good will antibiotics do, any way, in the case of chicken pox, a viral infection?"

Moni struck his forehead with his hand in anger and frustration, like father would have done in a similar situation. He was becoming more and more like father, I thought. That was surprising because everyone used to say, in our childhood, that I was like father and he resembled mother. I suppose volition and deliberate choice influence our growth as much as genetic traits do. While looking at myself in the mirror I have sometimes been surprised by a subtle but growing resemblance to uncle.

"It's easy to treat illiterate villagers," Moni said, sounding very exasperated. "They follow a doctor's instructions faithfully. But you so called intellectuals with your four-anna worth of medical knowledge can drive a doctor crazy. The antibiotics are not for your viral infection. They are given to prevent secondary infections. You don't want to get pneumonia and such complications, do you?"

410

I closed my eyes after Moni left, and was immediately sucked into a maelstrom of confused dreams. With an effort I opened my eyes and the dreams reluctantly withdrew, murmuring like receding waves. But I knew they were waiting for me. They had moved closer than on the previous nights, to the very edge of my consciousness. Were they preparing for an invasion? If they succeeded in invading my conscious mind, what would they turn into? Hallucinations?

The bedroom Moni had given me had two concrete rafters perfectly parallel to each other. Lying down on my bed I could not help looking at them. When I opened my eyes to escape from the dreams, I found that the rafters had gone crooked and were no longer parallel. At first I could straighten them and bring them back to their parallel position fairly quickly, by merely looking at them, but as the night progressed I found that this ability of mine to straighten things out seemed to decrease gradually. I had to stare at the rafters, concentrate on them and force them to become parallel. My fever, I realized, was affecting my perception.

I found something else happening to my mind which I found, at first, fascinating. My mind is always buzzing with words, especially when I wake up from dreams. But now I found something strange about the torrent of words and thoughts that flowed and cascaded in my brain—they did not seem to belong to me. Whose thoughts were they? I tried to understand what they conveyed but found them strange and incomprehensible. I found the whole phenomenon fascinating, till it struck me that perhaps the thoughts belonged to minds that had lost their bodies, minds of dead people, which were looking for some unguarded living brain they could penetrate and flow in. I got scared. I remembered frightening stories I had heard in my childhood of people becoming possessed. I must repel these alien invaders, I thought, I must repossess my brain. The only way of doing that was to think actively so that my own words and thoughts filled my brain, leaving no space for others' thoughts. But what should I think about?

Creative writing was perhaps the answer. I should write a short story, I thought. I had tried writing stories earlier but had given up the attempt in disgust, because my stories somehow became too sentimental. Then I remembered Mohan Sawant, one of my classmates at M.A. He was from a Marathi medium school, and had just started writing poems and short stories in Marathi then. Subhash Salvi thought highly of him and said that he was genuinely creative. The chap reminded me of a frog, somehow. When we had our discussions he was silent like a frog in summer but one could see that he was absorbing everything that was said. When he thought we were talking nonsense one could discern a wry ironic look on his face, but when something interesting was said, he would puff up a little, his face expressionless, like a frog that had just swallowed a fly. "He is a great listener," said Subhash once, "like you are an inveterate talker. He listens to you in particular with great interest. The little anecdotes you narrate are all stored in his brain. There they fuse and mutate, and are often twisted out of shape; he has a genuinely creative warp, that guy, and can weave a surrealistic nightmare out of your harmless anecdotes."

So I thought: why should I not become Mohan Sawant for the sake of creativity—put on his mask—and look at some of the interesting little incongruities I noticed in life with *his* squint? Nagatte, for example. I used to laugh at her craze for injections. Whenever she came to our place and had fever or even a bad cold, she wanted an injection. She used to feel disappointed when she was given the usual mixture and tablets, and used to say, "These medicines take a long time to work. Give me an injection, Krishna, I shall be all right then."

What would Sawant have made of this craze? He would perhaps see a connection between it and her libido and turn her into a sexually dissatisfied woman with an incestuous attraction for her doctor brother. Nagatte, with her very manly husband whom she adored, and her brood of well-adjusted children, just did not fill the bill. So I decided to create another woman in her place: a puritan, one who had separated, almost immediately after her marriage, from her libidinous husband because she found he had had premarital affairs. She stayed with her brother, a doctor. Her prudishness, I thought, would add to the irony of the situation, and make her craze for injections a natural outcome of her suppressed sexuality. I saw that puritanism itself—her fear of sex—as a concomitant of her suppressed incestuous love for her brother. As I tried to look at that psychological labyrinth through Mohan Sawant's eyes, I got quite excited. This was going to be some story, I said to myself. I decided to use the 'innocent eye technique', and make the woman's ten-year-old nephew—the doctor's son—the narrator of the story. I wanted to show how the boy was himself dragged into that whirlpool of passions, as his aunt saw in him an image of her brother and grew passionately attached to him. Her petting and caressing roused in him libidinous urges that troubled and baffled him.

I decided to call the story *The Death of an Aunt*. "My aunt died fifteen days ago," that was how the story began. The narrator recollects how his aunt

412

had managed their household ever since she left her husband and came to live in their house, pushing her timid sister-in-law—the boy's mother—to the background. The boy worshipped her because she was an attractive person, unlike his mouse-like mother. But he could not understand her, especially her craze for injections. He remembers how he was once shocked and nonplussed by her almost hysterical expression of jealousy when his mother fell ill and had to be given daily injections by his father. Finally he broods over the strange events at the time of her death. He was woken up at midnight to pour Ganges water into the dying woman's mouth because she had no son of her own. But she was not ready for it, she was struggling, desperately trying to say something. It was the boy's mother who finally put her ear close to her mouth, listened attentively, and announced, "She wants an injection. She thinks an injection can save her still."

The boy's father unexpectedly lost his temper at this, but his wife pacified him. "A dying person's last wish is sacred," she said. "It has to be respected. Use plain distilled water, if you like, but give her an injection." When the injection was about to be given, the dying woman moved, with a great effort, trying to turn on her side. It was clear that she wanted the injection to be given to her buttock.

She died when the injection was being given, a faint smile on her face. One of the things that baffles the boy is the change that comes over his mother after his aunt's death. She was, earlier, a reticent woman but now she becomes loquacious, and when people come calling, she waxes eloquent about the virtues of her sister-in-law. A few days after the aunt's death, news comes that her husband too had died in a remote village, alone and uncared-for. The boy's mother finds in this another instance of her sister-in-law's greatness. "What a pious person she was," she says, to a neighbour, "so deeply religious. And God gave her what she wanted: death before she lost her *mangalya*. It's every woman's wish, isn't it, not to lose her mangalya, to die when her husband is still alive. My sister-in-law hated her husband, it's true, but she valued her mangalya, as all virtuous women should. She was never seen without *kumkum*, the vermilion dot on her forehead always as big and perfectly rounded as a four-anna coin. It's sad, though," she says, crying bitterly now, "it's so sad that we could not pour Ganges water into her mouth at the time of death. She died when my husband was giving her an injection of distilled water. Such a devout person, but it's so sad…that she died when she was being given, instead of Ganga jal, distilled water…and that too to her buttock."

I was amazed by the way the story just flowed in my head. It was as if I was reading a story, not writing it. I needed, of course, the simplest of words because my narrator was only a boy of ten. But the right words came on their own and the rhythm was exactly right all through. It struck me that my mind had not worked with such creative energy and clarity since I stopped sitting under the suragi tree, dreaming up stories and poems, forty-five years earlier.

After completing the story I fell asleep. Dreams did not trouble me as much as they had done earlier, and those alien thoughts left me alone. I don't know whether it was the cathartic effect of steady concentrated creativity, or the result of my fever coming down because of those tablets Moni had forced me to swallow, but I slept reasonably well.

After waking up the next morning I stood for a long time in front of the mirror looking at myself in horrified fascination. Another crop of eruptions had come, and because there was no space left for them, they had unceremoniously pushed the earlier ones up and sat snugly under them. My face looked swollen, the face of an ogre. No make up artist, I thought, could have created a more fiendish face for a horror movie.

My creativity too erupted—like chicken pox. I wrote three more stories— in my head—in the next few days. That first story had removed whatever mental block I had had and released my creative energies. There was now no need to put on Mohan Sawant's mask. Stories and poems vaguely thought of years ago, and either never written or left incomplete, now came back demanding my attention. Sometimes they merged together, producing exciting amalgamations. Some lines from a poem I had started years earlier and left incomplete because it was, really, an impossible one to write, now appeared before me and said, we were not too bad, why don't you turn us into a story at least. It was a long poem on Bombay, narrated by a foulmouthed illiterate slum dweller. Someone writing in Marathi or Hindi could have perhaps carried it off, but there was no way I could have translated the slum dweller's pungent abusive language, a mixture of Hindi and Marathi, into English. I got some fun out of the writing, that was all.

The only part of the poem that had come off well was where the man's language suddenly lost its pungent abusiveness, became bare and poignant, because he was telling the tragic story of a lad who had come from his village to the city looking for a job. The lad was lonely, and the narrator, though touched by his air of vulnerability and innocence, kept himself aloof from him. One hot afternoon the boys of the slum, whose afternoon entertainment mainly came from peeping through chinks in the walls to see what was going on inside the huts, found the lad in a compromising position with a girl of six. It was possible that the precocious little girl, who had been seen playing this sort of game before with other children, was herself the seducer. But the lad was no child, he was eighteen. So he was beaten up, locked up in the hut and the police were called. It was quite a scene in front of the hut, with boys jeering and laughing, the girl's mother, a virago known for her army of lovers, shouting at the top of her voice, and the boy's widowed aunt, who had just come back from work, standing in a corner shedding silent tears. By the time the police came it was dark. They had to break the door open—the boy had latched himself in. The hut was in darkness because he had closed all the windows. "I went in first," says the narrator,

> And fumbled with the switches
> And put the lights on, after
> The fan. And I found him dancing.
> He had hanged himself to the fan.

This episode was based on a brief newspaper report that had somehow drawn my attention. The report was terse—just a couple of sentences—and I think it was the brevity of the report and its casual language that moved me to write. Such a Himalayan shame driving a young lad to suicide and all that it got was a few cold words. I tried to write the poem in a slum-dweller's pungent abusive language so that it would set off this little poignant story told tersely and in simple words. I wanted its brevity and casualness to shock my readers the way the newspaper report had shocked me. But the poem did not work and I left it incomplete.

This story came back now with another one which I had not even thought of as material for writing. It was something a student of mine had told me a long time ago. She was worked up—almost hysterical—and badly needed a sympathetic listener. Perhaps she chose to tell it to me because she had often seen me at Shivaji Park, close to the scene of the incidents she wanted to talk about.

The part of the beach where Professor Joshi and I went for our evening walks was always crowded. To the south of it there was the Hindu crematorium. Beyond the crematorium there was a lonely stretch of beach to which only lovers who desperately wanted privacy dared to go. I had heard that it was a dangerous spot, but I did not know how dangerous till Priya told me her story.

Behind that beach lay a large housing colony with a tall fortress-like compound wall. Priya's family had moved in to that colony a few days before she told me her story. Her building was close to the beach, and from the bedroom of her third floor flat Priya could see happenings that nearly drove her crazy.

There was a slum next to the colony. A gang of young men lived there, hoodlums who seemed to be idling their time away during the day, but at night they became active and prowled that dark stretch of the beach like shadows, looking for victims. When they found some lonely couple—poor souls who had come there perhaps because there was no space in their crowded homes for any sort of intimacy—they would surround them, bash up the man and make him run and then gang rape the woman. "It's awful," said Priya, "and yesterday I thought I would go mad. I saw this girl—someone I know though only as an acquaintance—going there with her fiancé. The sun had just set then. I desperately wanted to warn them—they were from King's Circle and apparently did not know how dangerous it was—but there was no way I could have done so without risking my own safety. The poor boy tried to fight when they came but he did not know how to, and they beat him up so badly that he had to crawl away from there on all fours —he could hardly walk. And the way that poor girl kept on screaming right up to the end, it was terrible. I ran to my parents crying and my Daddy wanted to go out with his walking stick, but Mummy stopped him. When we came out of our flat and talked to our neighbours, they said, 'This goes on almost every evening and there is nothing we can do. If you ring up the police it's no use; those goons will come to know who has telephoned, because they are into all kinds of illegal activities like smuggling and making illicit liquor, and are employed by someone who pays the police regular weekly hush money. They don't trouble our girls or us now because they know it's dangerous, but if we cross their path who knows what will happen? Leave them alone, please.'"

Both these stories—one a little item in a newspaper and the other a sickening story narrated by a girl close to hysteria—moved me greatly, but I knew that you could not create an enduring work of literature out of an experience, or a piece of reality, simply because you found it moving. But when the two stories came together, now, after a lapse of more than twenty years, their fusion created something—in my mind—which I thought was explosive.

I now turned my narrator into a young man belonging to this gang. I made him a chaste man, not a rapist, and he was with the gang only because he could not get any other job after he dropped out of college. He had gone to college on a sports scholarship—he was an excellent pugilist and swimmer— but he had to drop out after failing in Intermediate Arts twice. The gang needed a strong man and a fearless swimmer like him, as their main earnings came from unloading smuggled goods, on dark nights, from boats that anchored a long way off from shore. Anthony Silveira filled the bill.

I decided to make both my main characters Goans, because a Goan's love for his native village is something extraordinary. If you want to see what real nostalgia is, talk to a Goan abroad about his village. I made my narrator a Christian because Goan Christians are usually excellent sportsmen. I made the lad a Hindu. He had just come from Goa, was home-sick and was looking for people he could talk in Konkani with, but Anthony, my narrator, had spurned his advances, because he was wary of the fragility of his own toughness, a toughness he needed to survive in that world of violence.

But he watched the boy with interest and sympathy. He was troubled by the boy's loneliness, and when he saw something building up between him and a sixteen-year-old girl next door—sly glances and shy smiles—he was, for a time, happy. But he knew the boy stood no chance. His love was soon noticed by the boys of the gang. One of them, who had an eye on the girl and was waiting for her to grow up, said to the others, "She has ripened, man, she's ready." The boys of the gang did not do anything violent in their slum, but this boy was naturally aggressive in his advances. And the girl, tired of the other boy's backwardness perhaps, succumbed to the mixture of fear and desire gangsters often seem to rouse in girls.

Anthony saw, with his own eyes, the lad's heart breaking. He was walking on the beach one afternoon when he heard Naresh Thali, the Goan boy, calling out his name. He turned back and saw him running awkwardly on the sand, smiling. Then he stopped abruptly, forgot Anthony and stared in utter disbelief at a couple—his girl and the boy from the gang—in an intimate embrace on the beach. Anthony looked with pity at the boy's shocked, stupefied expression and walked away. There was nothing he could do.

Some days after this, the tragic incident took place. No one was quite sure what exactly the little boys had seen. Perhaps it was just an innocent affectionate hug, from a lonely young lad who missed his village and his people, was nursing a broken heart and was desperate for some love and affection. Perhaps it was only the girl's reputation that made the boys conclude that the two were up to some mischief. But Thali was dragged out of the hut and pushed around, mainly by the boys of the gang. Something broke inside Anthony when he came and heard what had happened. It was he who bashed up the boy, and he knew, even as he broke the boy's jaw with a right hook, that the look on the boy's face—a look of utter disbelief turning into shocked stupefied horror—would haunt him forever.

This story took longer to 'write' than the earlier one. That was because I had to construct and shape this story whereas the earlier one had come riding on a flow of words. It was when I was lying in my room and brooding over my story—I had reached the halfway stage—that I heard a gentle rap on the main door. It was the time of sunset, the time of arrivals and departures. Yashodamma had departed with tears at that time the previous evening and Narayana had come with his toothless smile the day before. Who had come now?

The gentle rapping was repeated, and I knew then that it was Moni. He did not usually ring the bell because he was worried about disturbing me suddenly in case I was resting. So I went to the door without bothering to throw a towel on my shoulders, my chest bare—if one can call an area totally covered with thick layers of chicken pox eruptions 'bare'—and opened the door.

But it was not Moni. A tall woman stood just beyond the doorstep. My first feeling was one of concern for her. I had opened the door suddenly, and I knew what I looked like. She might faint and fall down, or run for her life, I thought, but nothing of that sort happened. She stood her ground and stared at me. As the sun was setting behind her I could not make out the expression on her face. All that I could see was that her broad forehead had an unusually big mark of kumkum.

I stood nonplussed because for a moment I thought that she looked strikingly like Dakshi when she had come, years ago, in an off-white silk saree with a red border, and a big kumkum to match, to re-conquer my heart. "Who are you?" I said, in my confusion, and then felt that perhaps I sounded rather rude.

Then I realized who she was. The new nurse, of course. The white saree was her uniform. "You are Lakshmi, aren't you?" I said, but she continued to stare at me.

I could not blame her. I stood on the threshold, facing west, in the refulgent light of the setting sun. Perhaps she had not seen a case of chicken pox like mine in all her years in the Infectious Diseases Department. "Come in," I said, turning my back on her. As I switched on the lights and moved towards my room, I could feel her eyes on my back, where chicken pox had woven a rich red carpet of blisters. "Why is she staring at me?" I said to myself, and wondered if I had said something wrong. I don't know why, but I had this feeling that perhaps my speech had stuttered, like my hearing had the previous night. Did I say Lakshmi, or did my tongue slip, and say—Dakshi? Or Yakshi, perhaps?

Lakshmi

❧

When Lakshmi came to my room, she had changed her dress. In her faded green cotton saree she looked quite plain and I wondered how I could have seen any resemblance between her and Dakshi. She came in quietly and placed her palm on my forehead to feel my temperature. She did it so naturally—without any hesitation or repugnance—that I was surprised. Not many people would have touched that blister-covered spot with such nonchalance.

"There is some rice gruel for you in the kitchen," said Lakshmi, "I'll warm it up for you when you feel like eating. What time do you eat?"

"At eight or half past eight," I said, and she quietly went away. I was a little surprised by her offer to warm the food. Malini came from a very orthodox family but it was Moni who was rigidly orthodox and did not want anyone other than a Brahmin to work in his kitchen. Perhaps the woman was a Brahmin.

Half an hour after I had my rice gruel she came in to my room to give me my medicines. She saw immediately that I was reluctant to take the tablets. "It looks like you don't want the tablets," she said.

"What good can these antibiotics do to a viral disease?" I said. "And as for the fever, I have a feeling that it's making me creative. I have already written a short story—in my head—and am busy writing another now. I have not been creative like this since…"

"Since when?"

"Since I used to sit under a tree and dream, and think up stories and poems. That was a long time ago." I closed my eyes and felt a sudden surge of nostalgia. "I feel like crying when I think of that tree," I said.

That sounded terribly sentimental. I opened my eyes, feeling ashamed. The woman was standing just above me, with a couple of tablets in one hand and a glass of water in the other. I was surprised by the strange gleam in her large eyes. I was wrong, I said to myself. She did resemble Dakshi.

"So you don't want to take the tablets?" she said. "How can I say that?" said I, closing my eyes again because I felt tired. "Moni wants me to take them, so I'll have to take them."

"You don't have to do anything *you* don't want to do," she said. Her tone had a surprising sharpness about it and her voice a new resonance. I think I heard that resonance because my eyes were closed. One's hearing becomes more sensitive when one's eyes are not working. "It's time," she added, "you learnt to say 'no'."

"If I don't take the medicine because I don't want to, what happens? How do I explain that to Moni? What if the fever rises?"

"Let the fever rise," said she, her voice resonant and firm now, with a swing in its rhythm that made it almost hypnotic. "If it rises beyond what your body can bear, a cold compress can be applied. Who says fever is always bad? Maybe your body and soul need the fever. Maybe there's a fever raging within you; maybe it should come to the surface now and burn itself out."

I kept my eyes closed. "It's so difficult to say no," I said. "I should know, because I said 'no' once and we all had to suffer—those I loved and myself. No, I don't think I was wrong in saying 'no' then; I *had* to say 'no'. But I could have said 'no' keeping my cool, without feeling hurt. I could have then come home every year, after Appa cooled off. I know that it was because I ruined my life, and Appa's, by saying 'no' then, that I developed this fear of saying 'no'. So I couldn't say 'no' when I had to say 'no', when Moni asked me to...."

God, what a speech. It sounded like I was using too many 'no's' as if to make up for that one awful failure to say 'no' sixteen years earlier. Then I was struck by the impropriety of speaking to this stranger so freely. No, I should not allow her to tell me what I should or should not do. I must put her in her place, ask her how she, a nurse, could advice me to go against a doctor's orders. But when I opened my eyes I found she had disappeared. When did she go?

I looked up at the ceiling and found that the rafters had gone crooked again. Was I dreaming when I had my eyes closed? To this day I don't know whether I really heard the woman say what I thought she said, or I was dreaming.

The fever rose that night. Perhaps the most painful dream I had that night was one in which I saw myself wandering in what was obviously a hill station. I did not know which hill station it was, or how I had landed up there. I was walking down a slope when I heard a scream behind me. I looked back and found a wheelchair with a woman rushing down the slope straight at me. I stepped aside hastily and looked at the woman, and saw that it was Dakshi. My shock must have put a brake on the speed of my dream, because suddenly everything was in slow motion. The wind lifted her saree and I saw why she was on a wheelchair: both her legs were amputated at the ankle. She looked at me, but there was no recognition in those large panic-stricken eyes. "Dakshi, Dakshi," I screamed in terror and agony, and desperately tried to stop the chair. But it was too late. The wheelchair sped down the slope and then tumbled, in agonizing slow motion again, into a precipice at the end of that incline. I tried to run but found I could not. It started raining suddenly and I got wet and the road became unmanageably slippery. I woke up in an agony of despair.

I opened my eyes and felt, for a moment, that I was still in my dream. My forehead was wet with that rain, and she was there, my Dakshi, sitting by my bedside and looking at me. "Dakshi, Dakshi," I said, sick with anxiety, "You are all right?" "What happened?" she said, and I saw that it was Lakshmi, who was changing the cold compress she had placed on my forehead.

"The fever is coming down now," she said. "You'll not be troubled by nightmares any more. Go to sleep." She removed the compress, felt my forehead and then my neck, the forehead with her palm and the neck with the back of her hand, and then went away. It was amazing, the way she moved about silently, like a shadow or a cat, her feet making no shuffling sound and her saree no rustle.

I was wide-awake now, but my head was buzzing with words. To preempt those alien thoughts from besieging my brain, I started 'writing' the story I had left incomplete. I had spent a good part of the day brooding over a problem: Was Naresh Thali guilty of the crime he was accused of? Or was it all a terrible misunderstanding? If he was guilty, do I have to describe how his innocence crumbled at the betrayal he faced and the evil he saw all around him?

Suddenly—in the quietness of that night—it became clear to me that the questions were irrelevant. Whatever the boy had done, he was a victim, not a culprit. I saw, however, that the questions would haunt Anthony all through his life. That was the cross he would have to carry.

Once I realized that the problem did not exist, the last portion of the story just flowed. But the flow was turbulent, not smooth like that of the first story. Anthony was not an articulate man and his fury and sense of betrayal when he heard what the lad had done had to be expressed in a confused medley of expletives. His description of how he bashed up the boy, using his fists forgetting that he had no gloves on; of how he heard the sickening crunching sound of the boy's jaw breaking, and felt a shooting pain that showed that he had fractured his own right fist; of how he saw, in the boy's eyes, that look of horror and betrayal and despair; and finally his anguished feeling that he was bashing up the wrong person, that he should really turn his fury against those boys jeering at Thali, and those smug-faced people watching the fun—all this came out in a surprising flow of words. I knew of course that if I were to try to write all that down on paper I would have problems. You tend to gloss over little verbal uncertainties when you write in your head, but when you actually sit down to write they become major hurdles. But I was nevertheless surprised by the flow of the story. The words and the rhythm sounded and felt just right.

The last two paragraphs of the story came out with power. When the police came, Anthony was asked to break open the door because he was the strong man around. He was the one who entered that hut first, and fumbled with the switches, with his left hand, and put on the fan first and then the light. And heard the fan groaning as it struggled to revolve, and saw the boy dancing. Saw him turning and turning in a widening circle, his limp arms lifted up by the movement, looking as if he were crucified.

I decided to call the story 'The Cross'.

It was when I was lying with my mind blank after completing the story that I felt a strange tingling sensation in my palms. It was like my palms were being pricked by dozens of tiny pins. "Lakshmi," I called, softly, because I did not want to wake her up if she was sleeping. I was not sure whether she was within earshot but if she was, and awake, I wanted to ask her what was happening to me.

She was by my bedside almost immediately. Where was she waiting all the time, I wondered. "I'm sorry if I woke you up," I said, "but something is happening to my hands. Please put the lights on, I want to see what's happening."

In the bright light that flooded the room I looked at my palms, and was taken aback. I saw tiny red spots all over the palms, and even as I stared at them in surprise, a couple of new ones appeared with a prickling sensation that was only mildly painful. "What's happening to my hands?" I asked.

She took both my hands in hers and looked at the palms. "The last of the eruptions," she said. She stared at my palms—as if she were a palmist and was reading them—with unconcealed interest.

I sighed and closed my eyes. "Even the palms are covered now," I said. "I can't even clap my hands and squash the mosquitoes that come and hum near my ears."

"They are beautiful," she said, in a voice that took on a new resonance the moment my eyes were closed. "These dots will turn into little eruptions and tomorrow they will look like suragi buds. Then they will darken and dry up and fall, and the tree will soon forget the agony of flowering."

What was she saying, I wondered. I opened my eyes and saw that she had already left. The rafters had gone crooked again. I was dreaming.

The next two days were terrible. For the first time during my illness I panicked. Somehow it got into my head that Yashodamma was right, what I had got was smallpox, not chicken pox, and everyone was trying to hide it from me. I asked Moni, Malini and the nurse repeatedly not to hide the truth from me.

Moni and Malini looked worried. Moni came to my room several times and made me swallow all kinds of medicines. He even gave me a couple of spoons of Paripattadi Kadha, Narayana's gift. "If you think it will do you good, better take it," he said, "I don't think it can do you any harm." When he was not around at medicine time, Malini gave them to me. I don't think they mistrusted the nurse but they wanted to be sure that I got my medicines at the proper time. As for me, I was too scared to care what I swallowed. I just wanted to get well. When they were around Lakshmi stayed quietly in the background.

My panic was all the greater because it had come suddenly, without warning. And it had come rather late—on the sixth day of my illness. Moni had said, only the previous day, that I was one of the bravest and least troublesome of patients. I am afraid I spoilt it all on the sixth and seventh days. But curiously I was less afraid when I was alone, after Moni and Malini left for the hospital. I suppose it was because we are acting all the time, playing our roles even in the most tragic or happy or frightening of moments. To play our roles with gusto we need an audience.

What helped me to relax—or at least saved me from collapsing mentally—was my propensity for watching. I watched with interest the strange things that were happening to me. The mirror drew me like a lamp draws a moth, and I went again and again to it; and if I did not get singed by the awful spectacle I saw there, it was because the eruptions had come not all at once but in crops. I had watched them coming, and watched myself grow hideous gradually, so that I had time to get used to my hideousness. I realized, during this illness, that with time we could get used to everything, and even develop a morbid liking for our own monstrosity.

I am sure it was the watching that saved me. That day for example I watched those red spots on my palm turning into suragi buds with a great deal of fascination. I even watched my mind working—the way fever affected it, and the way I could keep my hallucinations at bay by thinking creatively. In Hindu philosophy they call this kind of watching *Saakshi Bhava*, the attitude of a witness. That is supposed to be a big thing, because it refers to a state of mind you develop in which you can watch everything that happens to you, and to those you love, with the attitude of a witness; take every experience—even death—as an experience and nothing more. Being a witness does not mean that you have to be passive and inactive. You act, but your actions, they say, will be more incisive and just when you practise Saakshi Bhava because your experiences, however terrible, cannot confuse and confound you once you learn to watch them. I don't know. I wonder if I will ever be able to practise Saakshi Bhava when someone I love is suffering. But during my chicken pox I realized that it was not an impossible ideal but an attitude that could help one to face one's problems, and live one's life, better.

That day I noticed something—in spite of my panic, which is the chief wrecker of Saakshi Bhava—which showed how my perception of what people looked like had drastically changed. When Malini was ready to go to the hospital I saw, for the first time, how beautiful she was. I had thought of her as a pleasant but rather homely looking person, but now I noticed that she had a lovely complexion, a skin that had the glow of a rose petal. She did not use any make up and she surely did not need to. Then Moni came in to give me my medicine. He had just had his bath, and unlike Malini he had powdered his face a little—most South Indian men do—but God, how his skin glowed. My brother, I thought, in spite of his receding forehead, was a real handsome chap.

But the biggest surprise came in the evening. It was the time of sunset and I was resting. I had just started 'writing' another story, because my head was in a real whirl that evening, and I was worried what would happen later at night when the fever rose. "Someone has come to see you," said Lakshmi's voice, "shall I send him in to your room?" "No," I said, "I'll come to the hall."

It was Narayana. He had come, as he had promised, to cheer me up. Lakshmi had put the lights on and he was sitting on the edge of a chair, blinking. His eyes nearly popped out when he saw me coming out of my room. "Oh God," he said, "oh, God." I sat in front of him on a sofa and watched him as he tried to keep his eyes away from me. His hands trembled every time he looked at me. It was clear he was terrified of my appearance.

"Oh, God," he said, "you look really bad. Even your eyes are infected. How red they have become! Take care of them please. I didn't tell you last time—I didn't want to tell you—that of my two cousins who got chicken pox last year, the one who survived, poor chap, he lost his eyesight." Then he looked crestfallen, realizing that he should not have given me that bit of information. "I didn't want to frighten you," he said, "There is nothing to worry, but be careful."

But I was not listening. I was looking at him in wonder. I had always thought of him as a good-natured person but a rather poor specimen of humanity. In his school days he was always badly dressed and untidy—quite dirty in fact—and had grown up into a clumsy diffident man. But now I noticed, for the first time, that there was, in his appearance, one redeeming feature: the chap had an excellent complexion, a skin that was smooth and fair like a young child's. With his bald pate and hesitant toothless smile, Narayana looked like a chubby baby.

"You look really nice today, Narayana," I said, in genuine admiration. "Why is it that I never noticed that you had such a lovely complexion?"

Narayana blushed, a phenomenon that could never have happened to his father. "Why, what..." he said, looking bewildered, "why do you say that?"

That blush made him look even more like a baby than before. "You look absolutely fresh and nice," I said. "If a woman fond of children were to meet you on the way, I'm sure she would want to pinch your cheek."

Narayana looked really worried and frightened now. "I must go now," he said, pleadingly. "I came here leaving my shop open, you know, it's time I go back."

"But you have just come," I said, "to cheer me up. Stay for some time."

But I knew that he was almost scared out of his wits by my appearance, and there was no point in forcing him to stay. So I got up to go back to my room, but he thought—I don't know what he thought, really; maybe he thought that I had got up to stop him physically, or pinch his cheek, perhaps. He scrambled up to his feet in a hurry. "I'll come after two days," he said, gathered his mundu up so that it wouldn't trip him if he had to run, and hurriedly left the place.

I went back to my room and stood in front of the large mirror there. I looked awful, an absolute ogre, but the sight did not frighten me because I had got used to it. I understood why I had found the complexion of Malini and Moni—and even Narayana!—so splendid and lovely. My norms and perception of beauty had changed because of what *I* looked like. I thought of the story, 'The Beauty and the Beast'. The girl in that story might have been a plain-looking one, but the Beast could not help finding her beautiful. Poor Beast.

Malini got worried when she saw my eyes that evening. She rang up Moni, and he brought along his physician, Dr. Shenoy, and their visiting ophthalmologist, Dr. Kamath. Dr. Kamath examined my eyes with care. "I don't think there will be any eruptions," he said. "It's conjunctivitis, which usually comes with severe attacks of chicken pox. Nothing to worry if the ointments and drops are applied at regular intervals."

"Do people lose their eyesight due to chicken pox?" I asked.

Dr. Kamath looked at Moni. "You had better tell him all that he wants to know," said Moni, sounding a little tired. "He knows quite a bit—enough to worry himself to death, with his half-knowledge. So better to load him with information so that there are no doubts and uncertainties left."

"There have been some such cases," said Dr. Kamath, nodding his head, "but they have been rare, and usually due to carelessness. The danger of eruptions in the eyes, affecting the cornea, is real in smallpox, but in chicken pox it's very rare indeed. It's true even conjunctivitis can cause damage if left untreated. In severe cases of chicken pox the patient might become comatose; then his conjunctivitis might not get proper treatment—and he might lose his eyes."

"Is my chicken pox severe enough for that?" I asked, and Dr. Kamath glanced at Moni. "Yours is one of the most severe cases of chicken pox I have seen," he said. "But you seem to be someone whom no chicken pox can drive comatose. You are surprisingly alert. I think you'll need a real knock on the head to go into a coma."

A little later, after Lakshmi had put some drops into my eyes and I had to keep them closed, I said, "You probably have seen more chicken pox cases than all these doctors. You think there is some danger for my eyes?"

"There is no danger," she said. I felt that hypnotic quality in her voice again. "The eyes turn red and burn in most chicken pox cases because the goddess who causes the disease is called Raktakshi, the goddess of bloodshot eyes. But there is nothing to fear. She is not after people's eyes, like her sister was."

This was not the way a nurse should talk, I thought. But scratch a nurse, and you would find a superstitious village woman. I opened my eyes and looked at her. Got scared for a moment, because she looked distorted, a larger than life figure, no doubt because of the drops in my eyes. I felt a little irritated by all this talk about the goddess with bloodshot eyes and so on. "I never saw you during the day," I said, "except when you came in for a few seconds to make me drink some water. Were you hiding in some dark corner of the house?"

"I was hiding in the blaze of the sun, not in some dark corner," she said. "You are not the only one ailing here. Not the only one who has to be given water to drink. Look at the plants, the way they are wilting under the hot sun.

426

There is no one to give them water, no tree to shade them when the sun is too hot. I was in the garden the whole day, watering and tending them. Was the place always like this—a wide expanse of heat with no greenery but some withered or wilting plants?"

I had closed my eyes by the time she was half way through her speech. I thought vaguely that some of her words sounded like mine, not hers. Then I thought of that spot as it was, years ago, when I was in my teens. "It was so green then," I said, "it was so green..."

The Seventh Day

The seventh day was the most awful. I did not know what my temperature was because I did not ask anyone. I was too scared about my eyes to worry about anything else. They were itching and burning and oozing. When Lakshmi came in and woke me up so that she could put some drops into my eyes, I got worried about the fact that she *had to wake me up*. I did not usually fall asleep in the forenoons. Was I passing into a coma? I asked her if I was, but she only shook her head and went away, after wiping the excess of drops from round my eyes with a wad of cotton. It struck me then that I had never heard her speak during the day. She spent most of her time in the garden, and when she came in, she was silent and remote. It was only during the night that she spoke to me freely.

I was dozing when Moni came in to see me. "How are you feeling, Anna?" he asked. "I'm worried," I said. "Why am I feeling so drowsy? I'm scared I am going into a coma." "Oh, Anna, Anna," he said, and his voice sounded as if he might start crying. "Stop worrying please. Just relax and rest. We are here to take care of you, aren't we? You have been having high fever for the last seven days and you haven't slept well in the night perhaps. It's but natural that you feel drowsy. You are going to be all right, there is nothing to worry please."

I felt repentant. Why am I troubling poor Moni with my fears? "I'm so sorry," I said, "I'm terribly sorry—that I'm causing you so much of trouble. I am a nuisance, aren't I?" That was the wrong thing to say, and it was said in the wrong tone. Moni looked really hurt. Even to my ear what I said sounded lachrymose, and I wondered if there were some drops of tear mixed with what was oozing out of my eyes. The fever and my fear had finally made me maudlin.

That evening I sat on my bed and prayed. I prayed to uncle. Years ago, when I was doing my M.A., Mr. Puranik at the L.I.C. Office had read my hand. I had shown him my palm just for the fun of it, because everyone believed that he was a hoax and pretended that he knew palmistry only to hold the hands of pretty girls. He was holding the hand of a very pretty girl called Sulekha Sule during lunch break, and whispering things to her—which he pretended he read in her palm—that made her blush. She looked embarrassed and a couple of chaps sitting nearby eating their lunch packets had broad grins on their faces. "You have seen her hand long enough, Mr. Puranik," I said, "why don't you have a look at mine?"

"Yes," said Miss Sule, withdrawing her hand. "Let's hear what you see in Rao's hand, how many hearts *he* is going to break."

Puranik took my hand rather reluctantly, but once he started studying my palm he got interested. "This is an unusual hand," he said, "a hand of an artist; but of one who will probably achieve nothing much, because he is content to live with his dreams. You will dream your life away, young man."

I was taken aback by that remark, which I thought was quite perceptive. "In dreams begin responsibility," I said, quoting Yeats rather lamely.

"I don't know what that means," he said, "but I see few signs of responsibility in this hand." He did not let go of my hand but continued to study it. "Look at all these lines, some so faint that they can only be studied through a magnifying glass. It's a very complex hand. The hand of a sensitive person full of doubts and anxieties. Look at the life line. Too many lines crossing it, and there are a couple of islands too. You have had some brushes with death, a couple of them close calls, and you'll have a few more. To tell you frankly, you wouldn't have been alive now, if you did not have this thin line running parallel to your life line.

"A life supporting line, that's what it is," he said, tracing it with his forefinger. "Do you have some elderly relative—father or grandfather—who is deeply religious, and who loves you?"

"Yes," I said.

"Is he someone who spends a lot of time in prayers and poojas and so on?"

"Half his day," I said, thinking of uncle. "If you count silent prayers, perhaps all his waking hours."

"He does it all for your sake," said Mr. Puranik, with conviction, nodding his head, "and it's his prayers that have kept you going."

I sat silent. I had not thought of my uncle for months, but at that moment I saw him before me—living all alone in that large crumbling mansion and praying for the welfare of a nephew who had had no time to meet him even once before leaving for Bombay. The image troubled me and I was full of remorse. "What happens, Mr. Puranik," I said, in a bantering tone put on to hide my chagrin, "what happens when he is no more? Will the life supporting system fail then?"

Mr. Puranik released my hand. "This is the wrong subject for joking," he said, looking at me with distaste. "Love does not die. Prayers don't lose their efficacy because the person who prayed is no more. You'll have his blessing all your life, though whether you deserve it or not, I leave it to you to decide."

I left him saying "Thanks," feeling humbled. My mortification was partly because of the realization that I, who prided myself on my discernment, had gone so completely wrong in my assessment of the man. I thought that he was just a silly aging Lothario. The man had unsuspected depths. He certainly knew his palmistry and was genuinely interested in it. When he was reading my palm one of Miss Sule's friends, a rather pretty girl, was waiting for her turn. But he was so engrossed in my hand that he did not even look at her. I also felt a twinge of remorse that I had spoken lightly about the time uncle would be no more—Hindus consider it inauspicious to talk about a living person's death—while *he* was all the time praying for my welfare. I had no doubts at all that Puranik's reading of my palm was accurate.

This happened just a few days before I resigned from L.I.C. I never met Mr. Puranik again. I wanted to meet him and know him better, but could not find the time. I had this feeling that he continued to play the role of a Casanova out of habit, or used it as a mask, perhaps. Some people *want* to be misunderstood.

So in that evening of fear and fever I sat on my bed and prayed. *You saved my life with your prayers when I was a child*, I said to uncle, *you saved me when I was drowning. Your prayers must have protected me when I had all those accidents. I turn to you now, because I don't know what else to do. I can't pray to God. I don't know how to.*

Then I lay down, closed my eyes and thought: what right had I, I who ran away when uncle needed my help and was dying, to disturb his peace more than thirty years after his death? No, I did not deserve his help. Then I thought of Frost's line: *something you somehow haven't to deserve.* Uncle's love was my home, what other home had I but love? But I must pray to God directly, I thought, I must pray for my uncle's soul too. So in a feverish kind of desperation I tried to pray.

I thought of Lord Krishna and Hanuman, the deities uncle worshipped with such devotion. Especially of Hanuman: Mukhya Prana, the Lord of the breath of life. I tried to remember some of the prayers uncle had taught me when I was a child, but could not recollect any of them. So trying to visualize that two-foot-tall image of Hanuman uncle worshipped with such devotion for years—not with awe but with love and affection, as if the monkey-faced god were another child, like me—I said, *My uncle used to say: when we pray to God through you, our prayers reach Him sooner. Because God loves you, His greatest devotee. What can I do but pray to you through someone who loved*

you, my uncle? But if he is at rest, let not my troubles disturb his peace...But
save me, not because I deserve to live but because I am not fit to die. And what
will happen, if I were to die now, to those two children in Bombay who call me
uncle and love me as I should have loved uncle, but perhaps did not? It was a
rambling prayer, if a prayer at all it was. The words sound childish when I
recollect them now: the words, not of an urbane and sophisticated man, but of
a confused and frightened child. But perhaps the monkey-faced god did not
much care for sophistication.

Then I dozed off to sleep. I had vague fragmentary dreams, one
meaningless snippet fading into another, and I think I was woken up twice,
once by a rather unpleasant clip of a dream, and the second time by Lakshmi
who wanted to put some eye-drops into my eyes. I wanted to ask her
something—I don't remember what—but I had to keep my eyes closed
because of the drops and I slid back into sleep without asking my question.

I had, then, one of the strangest of dreams. I should perhaps call it a
frightening one because when I try to recollect it—I can only recollect it
vaguely—I still get goose flesh. But I felt no fear at all when I was actually
viewing the dream—as if I belonged to that eerie world and was at home in it.

I found myself walking aimlessly on a hill, dull green with scruffy grass
and small thorny bushes, but with no trees. A meandering path went up the
hill, and a strange crowd was wandering among the bushes. It looked like a
fair or a weekly market in some remote tribal region inhabited by *adivasis*—
aborigines. I thought the people were adivasis because all the people—men,
women and children—wore beads. They hardly wore any clothes but were
covered with beads—necklaces, armbands, headbands, waistbands, bangles,
all made of beads, beads of different colours, red, white, yellow, brown, black
and blue-black. I saw the orange sun just above the horizon, almost touching
the hill, and as time passed I found it strange that it did not move at all, but
stood still like the arctic sun; except that even the arctic sun moved, whereas
this one gave the impression that it had stood motionless for eons. The men,
women and children moved without any sound, busily but aimlessly, and I was
surprised that they took no notice of me, the only non-tribal present there. I
watched the scene in fascination.

Then I saw something that shook me with excitement. Something so
strange and eerie that I was sure no one had ever seen anything like it in his
life. I must write about it, I said to myself, and include it in the story about my
chicken pox experiences I was planning so that people would sit up and take
notice and say, God, what an experience, and what a story.

A murmur rose then among the hills, but it did not come from the people. *There is a stranger among us*, said the murmur, *someone who wants to go away from here and write about our world.* It was the wind perhaps, though I could not feel it, and the leaves of the bushes and the blades of grass showed no signs of its presence. But it made the people—men, women and children aimlessly wandering about the bushes—shake and shiver as if they were made of paper. *We must stop him*, said the murmur, *he must not be allowed to get away.* The people shook and fluttered even more violently, and some even doubled up and fell. What was happening, I wondered.

It grew gloomier, and I felt someone close to me saying in my ear, *Go, Babu, go up the hillock, go to the top, and don't loiter here.* I felt some kind of pressure—whether physical or mental or even moral, I don't know—which forced me to ascend the hillock, against my will. Against my volition because I felt lazy, and was happy and restful where I was. The hillock was not steep but my limbs felt heavy and it was a torture going up. But that gentle pressure was on, all the time, urging me to go up till I reached the summit.

There was no path going down on the other side, but there were no bushes to impede one's descent either. *Go down now, Babu, go down quickly, and may God protect you*, I heard the voice say, as I started my descent. *What about you?* I said, but my voice was lost in the wind that rushed up as I went down, for there was a cool wind on the other side, a wind that blew on my skin and played in my hair. I felt so light and buoyant that it was like I was floating down, not running.

I woke up and found myself in my bed, but that feeling of lightness and buoyancy continued. My God, I said to myself, why was I feeling so light, almost weightless? I thought of the Ancient Mariner who, after a terrifying nightmarish experience, fell asleep finally, and then woke up feeling so light that he thought that he had died in his sleep.

I lay in bed quietly, experiencing that strange sensation of lightness. Then I felt the presence of someone in the room. "Lakshmi?" I said, and she came forward, as if she had materialized from nowhere.

"It's strange," I said, "I'm feeling so light—as if I am floating. What has happened to me?"

She placed her hand lightly on my forehead. "Your fever is gone," she said. "It was weighing you down all these days, but now it's gone. You are safe now."

"I have just come out," I said, "from one of the strangest of dreams. What I saw there—what I experienced—was something incredible, fascinating. I wanted to write about it in the story on chicken pox I am planning, but they did not want me to. *Stop him*, they said, *he must not be allowed to get away..*"

Lakshmi's hand was still on my forehead. "Go to sleep," she said, "go to sleep and forget your dreams."

When I was about to fall asleep, I heard the clock in the hall strike one. Like a warning. "Is it one o'clock?" I said, opening my eyes with an effort.

"It's half past twelve," she said.

I slept, a peaceful dreamless sleep. When I woke up I heard the clock strike one again. It must be one o'clock now, I said to myself. I turned on my side and found the moonlight outside as bright as sunlight at noon. I was wide awake—and thought that I should give Moni the good news that my fever was gone.

I walked up to his bedroom door and softly called out his name. "Yes, Anna," came his reply. I remembered what a heavy sleeper he was in his childhood. With all the worries of managing a hospital the poor chap had perhaps become a light sleeper. He came to the door and looked at me.

"My fever is gone," I said, "and I'm feeling so light, it's really incredible. I feel like—like what Sindbad must have felt after the old man fell off his shoulders."

Moni laughed and then yawned. "Good," he said, "and it's good that you came and told me. I wasn't asleep. I couldn't sleep—because I was worried about you. Now it's all right. We can all sleep without worries now. Good night, Sindbad."

I looked out of the window at the brilliant moonlight outside. "Look at the moonlight outside, Moni," I said, "It's like noon almost. Is it Hunnime today?"

Then something struck me. "What month is it today, Moni?" I asked, quite anxiously, "I mean, I know it's April, but what month is it in the solar calendar?"

"How do I know?" he said, and then added, "Ah, yes, four days ago it was Yugadi, our New Year. We didn't celebrate it ...Does that tell you anything?"

"It does," I said. "It tells me that it's the month of Mesha now, the first month of the solar year. Can you tell me if it's Poornima—*hunnime*—today? Even that calendar on your wall might give you that bit of information."

Moni went to the calendar and peered at it. He needed reading glasses but like most people in their late forties he was reluctant to use them and had not learnt to keep them handy. "Yes, it's Poornima," he said, finally, "and it's also written here—Hanuman Jayanti, and Chitra Poornima."

The Road to Recovery

I did not go to my room after Moni went back to bed. I sat in the dimly lit hall, brooding over the strange coincidence. So it was Chitra Poornima, Hanuman Jayanti and also the Full Moon day in the month of Mesha. The day my uncle died at Nampalli thirty-two years ago. The day of his shraddha, which I had been performing in Bombay since father's death. Whenever Chitra Poornima came in the month of Meena and not Mesha, and I had to perform the shraddha a month later, on the next Full Moon day, I used to feel that something was wrong. My uncle died on the day Hanuman was born, an unalterable fact, and I was unhappy about the confusion created by following the solar calendar. But this year the day had come in Mesha. So it was the day of uncle's death, the day of his shraddha, whichever calendar one followed.

I don't know whether uncle responded to my ritual offerings when I performed his shraddha. But on that day when I forgot to perform it, and did not even know that it was the day, but prayed to him in desperation, I was sure he heard me. I felt his presence near me, like I used to when I was a child. How did I suddenly think of him and pray to him that day? Maybe it was a coincidence, but if it was, it was the kind of coincidence that gave meaning and pattern to life.

I sighed and got up but did not feel like going back to my room. I looked through the large window at the moonlight outside. I had not stepped out of the house for a week because I knew what a sight I was. It was safe now, at midnight, and so I decided to go out and stand in the portico for a while.

When I went to the door I was surprised to find that it stood ajar. Had someone gone out? I opened the door a little wider and looked out.

I saw her at once. Lakshmi. She was standing on the spot where the suragi tree once stood, a radiant figure in a white saree in the effulgence of moonlight. I saw her raising both her hands up, in a gesture of wild abandon, as if she was trying to reach out to the sky. Her arms must have brushed against her hair then, which she always wore in a bun; the bun got untied, and the hair, seeking freedom like her, tumbled and cascaded down her shoulders, reaching almost to the back of her knees. I don't think I had ever seen hair of that length and

434

richness before. For a moment I stood entranced, in awe almost, and then quietly went back to my room.

I lay down and thought of the strange happenings of the day. The extraordinary coincidence of my praying to uncle on the day of his death, without knowing it was the day of his death, and to Hanuman on the day of his birth, without knowing it was Hanuman Jayanti; of my being close to death on the day uncle had died. Then I thought of that strange dream. Why did I dream that I was among Adivasis? Why did they, dressed only in beads, take no notice of me? Then that eerie sight I saw—that strange experience— but what did I actually see? What was it that made me feel that no one had ever seen anything like it before and that if I wrote about it people would sit up and take notice? What was it that I saw? God, what was it?

Whatever it was, it was gone, it had got clean out of my mind leaving no trace. I was sure I remembered it clearly when I came out of that dream. I was about to tell it to Lakshmi—but she had stopped me, perhaps thinking that I was raving and needed rest. *Go to sleep and forget your dream*, she had said, and I had fallen asleep and forgotten it.

I sighed and closed my eyes. No use trying to recollect what was so totally lost. Maybe there was nothing to recollect. What I had seen and experienced was perhaps something unsubstantial and intangible, something that would disintegrate and disappear in the daylight world of the conscious mind. If I did not rack my brain trying to recollect it, perhaps it might come back to me on its own some day. I relaxed and fell asleep.

The road to recovery was painfully slow. That sudden, almost miraculous, release from fever had made me feel that my recovery would be quick. I thought I would be all right in three or four days. When that did not happen, I fretted and chafed, feeling even more miserable than I was during the days of high fever. My eyes became worse the next day, causing real concern, and Dr. Kamath had to come for another visit. They were all right after a couple of days, but the eruptions took their own time to ripen, dry up and fall.

Those were awfully tedious days, the days I spent in Moni's house after the fever left. I could not step out of the house because of my ghastly appearance. The first week was the worst. I could not read, I was asked not to watch TV, and there was no one to talk with. In the second week I could place my glasses gingerly on my nose and read a bit. Then I picked up my habit of daydreaming again. Often I sat near the window looking out at the garden where Lakshmi was busy working.

That place in front of the house soon became a real garden. The plants began to look up, and grew greener. New plants were added every day. No one knew where Lakshmi brought them from. Malini grumbled that she had brought some wild herbs no one ever planted in a garden. "What is wrong with wild plants?" said Lakshmi to Malini, "These plants grow wild because they belong to this place. They are tough, they will survive even if they are not taken care of. A garden must look natural. There is nothing wrong if it looks a little wild."

The tone in which she said this was firm, almost sharp. No wonder Malini thought that she was arrogant.

It was a pleasure to watch her working in the garden. Most people, when they have to work for long hours under the hot sun, work mechanically, walking like somnambulists. But this woman loved her work and loved the plants; and I had a strong feeling that the plants loved her. Sitting near the window under a whirring fan that brought no relief from the heat, I watched her moving briskly among the plants, bareheaded and barefooted even at noon, first watering them with a hose and then attending to each plant with loving care.

She worked alone. Moni sent Nagappa, who had some experience of gardening, to work with her one day. He came with a big pair of shears, but was sent packing by Lakshmi within an hour of his arrival. "It was impossible to work with that nurse Amma," he said to me a few days later. "I just started trimming a plant, and maybe I chopped a little more than was necessary, but the way she flared up, that Amma, I got really scared. She did not shout at me Ayya, but her anger was like fire. She acted like I had hurt her child, not just trimmed a plant." But he admitted that she was a good gardener and had a way with plants. "If she had let me work with her I might have learnt something from her, and she from me, but for that she must let me work with her, no?" he said, shaking his head.

After working in the garden Lakshmi always went to the spot where the suragi tree once stood and washed her feet there using plenty of water. Maybe her tired feet, scalded by the hot earth, needed that water therapy. As she lifted her saree a little to wash her feet, I usually got up and went back to my room. I watched her because there was nothing else to do but I did not want any misunderstanding.

But one thing was clear: she was not going to stay for long at Kantheshwar. Malini was usually very tolerant, but Lakshmi somehow managed to get under her skin. "She is competent, I know," said Malini to me one day, "and she puts her heart into whatever work she does. But her arrogance, what does one do about it?"

There was a confrontation between the two a few days later, the day before I was to take my first bath after chicken pox. It was about working in the hospital. They had left Lakshmi at home to take care of me even though I did not, after my fever came down and my eyes became all right, need a nurse. But this could not go on indefinitely. When Leela was absent one day Malini needed someone in the obstetric ward. She sent a ward boy to call Lakshmi, who was then working in the garden. "Malini Amma wants you to put on your white saree and come to the hospital immediately," he said to her. "Where do I have to work?" she asked. When he said "in the delivery section," she turned her back on him. "Tell Dr. Malini that I can't come now because I am taking care of the plants," she said.

When the ward boy came back again after five minutes, Lakshmi was in another corner of the garden, and I could not hear what they said to each other. I saw Lakshmi walking to the hospital after ten minutes, still in the faded green saree she wore while working in the house or in the garden.

I wondered about the confrontation and its outcome. Lakshmi came back after half an hour and quietly continued with her work in the garden, now close to where I was sitting. I tried to read her face but it was as usual inscrutable. Perhaps there was a faint suggestion of something akin to amusement.

She took a lot of time with the plants that day, and when the work got over, spent more time than usual washing her feet. Then she went to the room where she had kept her small bag. She came out with her bag in five minutes.

That was the first time she spoke to me during the day. "You will have your first bath tomorrow," she said. "I have kept some neem leaves in the kitchen. Ask someone to boil them and use that water to take bath in. Don't rub yourself too hard. Most of the scabs will fall off tomorrow but if a few don't, let them be. They will fall off in a couple of days. The scabs will leave marks on your face and they will remain for a month or two. They will go sooner if you apply turmeric powder, mixed with the cream of curds, to your face every night."

"Does all this mean—you are leaving right now?"

"I am," she said. She looked out of the open door at the garden. "The garden is looking up now. The plants will miss me but I have to go." Then she turned to me and said, "You are all right now. You may not want to go out for a while. You will have plenty of time on your hands. Why don't you spend some time—when you are here—taking care of the plants?"

"I will," I said.

"Tend them with love," she said. "Talk to them sometimes. Young plants are like little children. Lovable."

I got up. It was difficult to ask her but I felt I had to. "Can I," I said, "can I pay you some money?"

"Pay me? For what?"

"For all that you have done for me. Something given in gratitude. As I am much older than you, let me say, with love and affection."

"Much older than me?" she said. I thought I saw a faint trace of a wry smile on her usually expressionless face.

I gave her some money and she thrust the notes into her bag. "No one has the right to refuse what's given in love and gratitude," she said.

I watched her walk up to the gate, open it and walk out. She did not have to close it. Someone came in as she went out, and closed the gate. Yashodamma.

I was glad to see her. "Welcome, Yashodamma," I said, quite expansively. She took one look at me, dropped her bag and nearly collapsed. For a moment I could not understand why because while interacting with Lakshmi, Moni or Malini I was never made conscious of the fact that my appearance was still awful. Yashodamma, who had run away in mortal dread twenty-four days earlier, apparently did not expect to see me with my armour of scabs still on. Poor woman. I withdrew into the hall and said, "It's all right, I have recovered now. I'll be taking my bath tomorrow." She came trembling into the house, scurried into the kitchen and closed the door.

The telephone rang and it was Moni. "Anna, where's Lakshmi?" he said.

"She has just left, with her bag," I said.

"Oh, God," he said, "Did you check her bag?"

"Check her bag? Why should I do that?"

"Because she might have stolen something," he said. He sounded, as usual, a little confused. "She had an argument with Malini an hour ago. Malini wanted her to work in the obstetric ward, but she bluntly refused. 'In that case we cannot keep you here,' said Malini. 'I'm prepared to quit,' she said. Malini did not want to have a showdown in front of the other staff members. So she said, 'Go and see Dr. Rao.' The woman came to me and said that she wanted to quit. 'You cannot quit like that,' I said. 'If you quit now you will get no salary. You have not worked for a full month.' 'That is all right,' she said. 'Then you can quit, right now,' I said in irritation and she walked away.

"I have just come to know that it was Malini who asked her to quit—she did not mean it of course, she only spoke in anger—and the woman took that

438

as an affront. But why did she go without her salary? She could have claimed her salary because *we* had asked her to quit. I wonder if she wanted to get away when we were both busy in the hospital and so took this chance—she *must* be, in that case, what Malini at first thought she might be: a thief. God knows what she has taken away. I am going to ring up the police and complain."

"Don't do that," I said, rather sharply. "What will you tell the police? Will you tell them that you dismissed a nurse without giving her her salary, and she went away quietly? And so you suspect that she must be a thief, though you don't know what she has stolen? They will laugh at you. That would be all right—but something worse can happen. Because you are a big shot and that woman is helpless, the police might arrest her. You know how our police treat a helpless woman when there is a complaint against her? Do you want that to happen?"

Shut up and get out, said Moni's voice on the phone. Then it said, "Sorry, Anna, that was not meant for you. I was shouting at Laxman here who has been pestering me for some advance. *So you have started drinking again, and that's why you need money now, right?* Sorry, Anna, I'll come there in a few minutes. Are you alone?"

"No," I said, "that paragon of virtue, the woman you would never suspect of thieving, she has come back. Yashodamma is here."

"Good," said Moni's voice, sounding tired. "Malini is very busy this evening and she will be glad if she won't have to cook when she gets home."

"I'm not too sure that Yashodamma is in a condition to cook," I said. "She took one look at me and collapsed. She is hiding in the kitchen now. You'd better bring some sedatives for her when you come."

Back to Bombay

❧

That night I heard Moni rummaging, for a long time, among the cupboards and chest of drawers in his room, trying to find out if any thing was missing. Malini was with him in the search for a short time, but she soon gave it up. "It was only a suspicion," she said, "and if nothing is missing, good, the woman was no thief." But Moni's suspicion, once roused, was not so easily laid to rest. When Yashodamma came to know what was suspected, she got so excited that she almost lost her fear of me. She did her bit of rummaging in the kitchen and other rooms and announced that two spoons were missing. I said that there were three—and not just two—in my room. After a while she came out and said that she was certain that a new broom was stolen. There were three when she left and now there were only two. "That's fine," I said to Moni. "The woman is not just a thief, she is a witch. She has apparently gone from here riding a broom. Though how anyone, even a witch, can ride an Indian broom, which has no stick attached to it, I don't know." "You are joking, Anna," said Moni, looking hurt. "Our problem is that both of us are so busy in the hospital and spend so little time in the house that if something is lost or stolen, we are not likely to miss it for days."

"Good," I said, "if you don't miss something then you haven't lost it."

"That's true in a way," said Malini to me. "But this woman, she's a mystery, isn't she? What do you think of her?"

"I don't know," I said. "She is mysterious but so are most people, when you really try to know them. The only thing I feel sure about is that she is not a thief."

"How can you be so sure?" said Moni. He was a bit like Amma. Very persistent in his suspicions and prejudices. "I still feel I should have complained. I could have asked the police to find her and search her bag—without harassing her."

"I can guess what they would have found," I said. Suddenly I felt tired and irritable. What upset me most was the way Yashodamma was still busy moving around the house trying to find out what was lost. "They will find a few clothes," I said. "Not too many, because I have seen her wearing only two sarees—a white one and a faded green one—during the last three weeks. And some money. Not much, I guess, but not less than a hundred and fifty rupees. That was what I gave her when she was leaving. I feel awful when I think of that. A hundred and fifty rupees for taking care of a very sick man—who looked a horror—for three weeks. And for turning a barren piece of land into a garden."

I spent a lot of time in the garden during the next few days. I watered the plants before breakfast, and again in the afternoon, just before sunset. After breakfast I walked among the plants inspecting and tending them—or pretending to tend them rather, because I knew very little about gardening. The house shaded the place till half past ten, and then the blazing sun drove me inside. I was forced to stay inside till five, by which time the concrete ceiling of the house would get so heated up that it would be more sultry inside than outside.

I tried to talk to the plants but I don't think they listened to me. I did not know what to say to them, or, for that matter, what kind of tending they needed. The second afternoon Moni sent Nagappa to work in the garden, and from him I learnt a few things about gardening. But I also had my say on the matter: he was quite taken aback when I told him to go slow with his trimming and pruning. "Little plants are like little children," I said, "You should be as careful when you trim them as you would be when you pare a child's nails." He stared at me and said, "That nurse Amma, before going, has put her hand on your head."

After working in the garden I went and stood at the spot where Lakshmi used to stand, and washed my feet, like her, making use of the garden hose. That was the place where the suragi tree once stood, and I used to spend hours reading and dreaming. But the entire landscape had changed so completely— with the bungalow, the new hospital building, and between the two a new road buzzing with traffic—that it was difficult to visualize that earlier scene, or even to believe that it was the same place.

After a couple of days of this routine I noticed that though I used plenty of water to wash my feet, it disappeared into the ground fairly quickly. The cement work there was of poor quality and there were a couple of big cracks. The water was obviously seeping into them. I remembered how I had noted earlier, with some surprise, that there was no visible puddle at that spot after Lakshmi washed her feet using an inordinate amount of water. Now I understood why.

Four days after I took bath I received a letter from Urmi and Harshad. As they both wrote a very bad hand, and Harshad's Gujarati letters intruded into his Hindi writing, I had a tough time reading the missive. But I was deeply moved. Even the poor quality of the writing touched my heart: only kids who really hated writing could write so badly, and the fact that they had covered nearly five pages with their awful writing showed how much they cared.

Harshad had drawn a couple of pictures in his part of the letter. One of them was of a man with a tie. It was obvious he had tried to sketch me because he had written below it the words, 'My beloved uncle'. But the sketch was so bad that he had struck off the word 'uncle' and replaced it by the word 'Ogre'. He had, however, forgotten to strike off the words 'My beloved', and so there it was, a strange drawing, with an even stranger caption, 'My beloved Ogre.' Poor chap. He did not know that chicken pox had turned me, for a few days, into an ogre much more awful-looking than the one he had sketched.

I wrote a reply that very night. My first letter in Hindi. I illustrated my letter with a few drawings—and realized immediately why Harshad had drawn those pictures. He must have found, like I did, sketching easier than writing.

I wrote about my illness, trying to turn the whole sequence of events into an interesting story. "It was lucky, Hachchi, that I did not bring you with me this time," I wrote. "What would you have done here, with me bed-ridden? And I looked, in the worst days of chicken pox, so terrible that you would have really got frightened." I drew a colourful portrait of myself in the full flowering of chicken pox, but could not make it half as dreadful as I had actually looked. But that badly sketched self-portrait gave me a shock all right. I realized that with all those blisters covering me from head to feet, I looked strikingly like those Adivasis, covered in beads, seen in my dream. Obviously they took no notice of me because I was one of them.

I made Lakshmi appear a figure of mystery. She came when I needed someone to take care of me, I wrote. She knew more about chicken pox than even doctors did. Where did she come from? She went away after I recovered. Where did she go? Was she a thief who came to steal things? But the only thing found missing was a broom. Or was she a good *pari*—a fairy—who came to save me? Or was she a witch who came to kill me but flew away riding a broom when she could not? Or was she just a good nurse, who came, luckily for me, at the right time?

It was when I was about to complete the letter that I had a sudden and irresistible urge to go back to Bombay. I wanted to sit with Urmi and Harshad and talk to them—not just write letters in Hindi, a language I hardly knew how to write in. My earlier decision to stay on in Kantheshwar till the end of

May just evaporated. "I am coming back to Bombay next week," I wrote. "Today is Monday. Next Monday I shall come. Urmi, my keys are kept in your house. Ask Shanta, my servant woman, to come that morning; and open the door for her so that she can clean the house. Harshad and Urmi, be prepared: your uncle's face looks different now. It has grown dark, like a sky full of rain clouds."

Moni and Malini were upset when I told them about my decision in the evening. "It's so sad," said Malini, "that you came here for a holiday but fell ill on the very first day. There was no fun, no parties, no outings. We could not even do simple things for you like preparing your favourite dish now and then. If you stay for a month more...perhaps we can all go for a proper outing, maybe to a hill station like Ooty."

That talk of going to a hill station reminded me of what Urmi had said to Harshad about going to Mahabaleshwar together. I should, I said to myself, try to get a room in our College Holiday Home at Mahabaleshwar for a few days and take the kids there. "There is a promise made that has to be kept," I mumbled to Malini and Moni. Urmi had not made that remark as a promise— she had merely said it to divert Harshad's attention and to assuage his grief— but somehow it became, all of a sudden, a promise, not Urmi's but mine. "I'll try to come here during the next Diwali vacation," I said. "If I can't come then, I'll surely come in May." "We'll make it impossible for you not to come in May," said Moni, "we're planning to perform Ashu's thread ceremony then."

On the day I was to leave for Bombay I got up a bit early so that I could water the garden for the last time. I made another attempt to talk to the plants. I wanted to tell them that I was going away. I had a strange feeling that day that they too wanted to talk to me, and if I stayed there for some more days tending them, I might be able to fine-tune my inner ear to their wave length and hear their voices.

It was when I was washing my feet after watering the plants that I noticed it. It was something so unexpected that it sent a shiver of anticipation down my back. I saw—or thought I saw—something green in one of the cracks in the cement floor. It was not the big crack into which most of the water I used disappeared, but the slightly smaller one next to it; and what I saw was not just moss. I felt that something green but more alive than moss—a little sprig of some plant perhaps—was slowly pushing its way through that crack towards the light of day. I felt a strange kind of nervousness that made me shy away from examining the spot more closely. I thought then that it was because of Yashodamma who kept a close watch on me whenever I went to the garden.

She had reported to Malini that I had gone crazy after my fever and started talking to plants, and Malini had told her to mind her own business. I was sure that she was, at that moment, hiding behind the curtain of the hall's front window spying on me. On a sudden impulse I gaily waved at the curtain, and was mildly amused when that produced a frantic, telltale movement of the curtain.

Moni was keen on driving me to the airport himself. But he found himself so busy that morning that he had to send me with his chauffeur. "I'll write to you, Anna," he said, while bidding me farewell, and when he saw me smiling, added, "No, I mean it. I know I'm very lazy when it comes to writing letters—I'm like my brother, ha, ha—but this time I'm going to write a really long letter—in my awful doctor's handwriting—so that you'll have to spend hours reading it."

On the way to the airport I found myself brooding over what I had seen that morning. But what had I actually seen? What did those leaves—if they were leaves—look like? I realized that my reluctance to examine that crack more closely was not because of Yashodamma, but due to some inexplicable fear. But fear of what? Was I scared of the unexpected, of a turn of events that might change the course of my life, or of disappointment? That sprig pushing its way through that crack—if it was a sprig—was it of some nondescript creeper, or an old tree, buried for seventeen years, resurfacing again?

The journey to Bombay was unexpectedly pleasant. I tightly plugged my ears with cotton wool, and waited, in dread, for the headache to begin. But the air pressure within the plane remained normal and the puncture in my eardrum was not tested again. The only unpleasant thing, during the entire journey, was what happened outside the airport, when three rickshaw drivers, to my surprise, refused to come to Dahisar. I knew they did not, after waiting at the airport queue for a long time, like to go to nearby places, but Dahisar was a long distance away. When the fourth one in the line agreed to come, I asked him, in irritation, "What's happening, brother? Isn't Dahisar distant enough for those drivers?"

He laughed. He was a dignified man with a pepper-and-salt beard, and a pleasant laughter. "It's not the distance, surely," he said. "Maybe those chaps were worried that they wouldn't easily get fares to come back to town; or perhaps they saw that you were a Bombay man, with only a small suitcase, and thought they wouldn't be able to fleece you by charging you extra for luggage and so on." He was a Muslim and spoke chaste Hindustani with an Urdu accent. No language in the world sounds better than Hindi—or Hindustani—when a middle aged Muslim with an Urdu accent speaks it.

I kept up a conversation with him because I liked the way he talked. "You are from Lucknow, I suppose," I said, and he laughed and said that he was from a village near that city all right. "You are a South Indian, of course," he said, "and you went to your village for a holiday, and got a bad attack of chicken pox there?"

"I took it from Bombay," I said. Guessing that I was a South Indian was as easy as guessing that I had just recovered from chicken pox. My Hindi was as strongly marked—or marred—by a South Indian accent as my face was by chicken pox.

We talked about a variety of things including politics, especially the politics of his state, U.P. I found him knowledgeable and his views balanced. Then he asked me, when we were nearing Dahisar, the first personal question. "Have you left your family in your village and come back alone?" he said.

I told him that I was a bachelor and lived alone. We had just stopped at a traffic signal then. He looked back in surprise—bachelorhood is very rare among Muslims—and then turned to the road again. He asked me a few questions, like whether I cooked my own food or ate out, and stayed as a paying guest or had my own flat. *We come into this world alone,* he said, after a while, *and we leave it alone.* It sounded like he was quoting an Urdu couplet. Perhaps he was. Urdu is an extraordinary language. Even trite statements sound profound when made in its sonorous couplets.

He talked about himself. He had lost his wife a year earlier and lived alone. He had seven children—three daughters and four sons—but they were living their own lives in different places. Two sons were in Dubai, one in Delhi and one in Meerut. They wrote to him occasionally but that was all. He had no desire to go and be a nuisance to them. "We are alone in this world," he said, in a matter-of-fact tone, "wife or no wife, children or no children, we are ultimately alone."

The rickshaw entered our compound. Some of the children playing near the gate saw me and shouted, *Hey, uncle has come!* We moved slowly because of the kids, and a couple of them came running alongside, and a little boy scrambled on to the rickshaw. *Harshad, Harshad, your uncle has come,* someone shouted. When the rickshaw stopped in front of our wing, Urmi came out and took my bag. Ba came out with a broad welcoming smile and said, "Ah, uncle, so you have come. But you look so different. Such marks on your face!

Must be a severe attack of chicken pox." Harshad came running from behind the building, looking all excited. I went up to my flat surrounded by kids.

Urmi, who opened the balcony door after a couple of minutes, looked down and said, "uncle, you have not paid the rickshaw driver I think. He is still waiting." So I went down to ask him if I had not paid him. "You have," he said, very gravely, "more than you think you have." Then he smiled, a little sadly, bid me goodbye and started his rickshaw. A couple of boys got into the rickshaw saying, give us a lift till the gate, uncle, and when he said yes, more children got in, and the rickshaw got loaded with squealing kids. "Your friends," he said, looking at me and shaking his head, "you are not alone." He took them up to the gate, and after they got down, drove away.

Harshad just would not leave me that evening. He came with me wherever I went. I ate at his place that evening, and then he came up to sleep in my house. Just before going to bed he said, "uncle, I have been thinking…"

"Thinking of what?"

"About that woman who nursed you. Did she have long hair?"

"Very long," I said. "It came well below her knees."

"That's what I thought," he said. " Now I know. She *was* a pari. A pari who came to save you."

He soon fell asleep. I remembered how I had told him, some years earlier, a story about a fairy who lived in a tree overhanging a deep pond, and saved drowning people by dropping her long plaits down to them. They all thought that it was some creeper hanging from the tree that saved them, except for a young man who, even while struggling to save himself, happened to look up and catch a glimpse of her. He fell in love with her. As she materialized on that tree only when someone was drowning, he had to fall into that pond again and again so that he could see her. Finally he grew so weak that he could not pull himself out of the pond even with the help of her long tresses, and got drowned.

I went with Harshad and Urmi to Mahabaleshwar in the last week of May, and spent five happy days there. Rooms in our Holiday Home were always booked well in advance but someone, fortunately for us, had cancelled his booking at the last minute.

There was a letter waiting for me in Bombay when we came back. Moni had kept his promise. The first few paragraphs of his longish letter seemed to be dictated by Malini. They wanted me to go back to Kantheshwar and stay with them after my retirement. That was the place I belonged to and they were my people. My illness had made them realize—and it must have made me too realize—that we must stay together and take care of one another. They had lived all these years with no elder to guide them and were looking forward to my staying with them as a member of the family.

Moni was planning to add an upper story to his bungalow. "I am sending you a plan of the proposed construction, for your approval," he wrote. "That's because it will be built for you; we want you to come and stay there after your retirement. You will find two staircases in the plan, one from within our house, and the other from outside. We would like you to use the inside one and live with us as a member of the family, but if your privacy and independence are important to you, you may decide to use the other staircase. You will also find that the plan includes a small kitchen. We want you to board with us but if you want to cook your own food, the kitchen is provided for."

The rest of the letter was a rambling account of some of his future plans. He wanted to make his hospital a well-equipped modern one, was planning to start an air-conditioned Intensive Care Unit, buy some new 'state of the art' equipment for pathological and other investigations, was modernizing his OT, and so on.

I read the later part of the letter with diminishing interest as I knew little about all those equipment he wanted to buy for his hospital. I was so tired after the long bus journey that I almost missed the postscript scribbled on the last page.

It read: *That suragi tree has come up again. I don't know whether it is a shoot of that old tree that gave us so much of trouble, or a new one planted by that busybody, Lakshmi, who nursed you in your illness. But whatever, there is a little sapling of suragi in the exact spot where the old one stood. I am going to get it cut and the whole place properly cemented again.*

Resurrection

I sat stunned, unable to gauge the full impact of that blow for a few minutes. It was a blow, but not, I realized, totally unanticipated. Throughout that month in Bombay, and even at Mahabaleshwar, I had felt, in the midst of my happiness, a vague apprehension, a strange mixture of excitement and dread. It had started in Moni's garden—when I noticed that green thing in the crack in the floor and felt that it might be the suragi resurfacing again. I was too scared to take a second look. I thought I was scared of being disappointed, but I now realized that what I really dreaded was the repetition of that nightmare, the recurrence of that trauma, the suragi re-emerging only to be cut down again. I had to stop it, at any cost. The tree should survive. Its resurrection was a miracle, and though miracles could be ignored, they should not be undone.

I should stop Moni before it was too late. Was it already too late? The letter was dated 'Fifteenth of May', and it was already the first of June! But Moni wrote his letters in installments—like I did before Dakshi came into my life—and took his own time completing them. When did he complete this one? When did he write that postscript? I should write to him immediately, there was no time to lose.

I sat down to write and realized that it was not going to be easy. Though a quiet soft-spoken chap, Moni had his own kind of obstinacy. I had to be tactful and firm. The problem was how to make him see that my concern for the tree was not just a whim based on some superstitious belief, but something rooted in my past, bound with memories I needed for my survival. No, it was not going to be easy.

So I wrote: *I know you might think I am crazy when I tell you: don't cut that suragi tree again. But please don't, Moni. It's a plea. I cannot explain how important that tree was to me in my childhood. I sat in its shade and read and dreamed. I wrote my first stories and poems there. I loved that tree. I regard the cutting of the tree as the biggest mistake of my life, a crime, a tragedy. I don't want a recurrence of that tragedy.*

I used, without any compunction, a bit of emotional blackmail. I knew how much he loved Amma. *Don't think I am being superstitious,* I wrote. *I don't believe in deivas like Yakshi and Kalkutika, but I have learnt to respect other people's beliefs. Amma strongly believed in them. Father could never make her agree to the cutting of the tree. If she did not object to it finally, after father's death, it was because she had sunk into a state of mind when she could not have objected to anything. If you had asked her if you could chop off her limbs, she would have said, with that sad smile of hers, 'Why not, please go ahead.'*

That was cruelly worded but I was in no mood to change it. Then I wrote: *I don't know whether I have the right—the legal right—to stop you from cutting that tree. Even if I have, I don't want to use it. But I must make one thing, about myself, clear. It is important that you understand this: I am not sure where I belong, or if I belong anywhere. I don't know whether I should stay on in Bombay after my retirement or come to Kantheshwar. Can I be at home there? I don't know. That suragi tree might make all the difference. Don't ask me why because I have no adequate explanation. I can only say this: the cutting of the tree was a wrong, a crime; and its resurrection is to me like a sign—of a wrong set right, a sin forgiven. I need a sign like that before I can come home. If that tree is cut again, it will mean that my exile is for life.*

It was well past midnight by the time I completed the letter. The night was warm and sticky. As I tried to sleep, I heard low rumblings in the east. The monsoon was still some days away but pre-monsoon clouds had already arrived.

I posted the letter at dawn when I went out to buy some milk. It was cloudy and threatening to rain. I felt restless and uneasy. So on the way back I decided to go to a telephone booth and ring Moni up.

I must have woken him up. He sounded both sleepy and surprised. "Anna?" he said, "How come you suddenly thought of ringing me up?"

"It's about that tree," I said, "please don't cut it again."

"What tree?" he said, in obvious bewilderment. "What are you talking about?"

"The suragi tree," I said. "I got your letter last evening. In your postscript you wrote about the suragi tree emerging again."

"Oh God," he said. He was silent for a moment. "There is no tree. There's only a sprig, I am told, barely visible through a crack. Yashodamma mentioned it when I was just about to complete that letter. I haven't even seen it."

"It's all right then," I said, relieved that the sprig was still intact. "I just wanted to tell you, please don't cut it."

"Why shouldn't I?" he said, and I heard a touch of cold in his voice that got me worried. "No, Moni," I said, "I spent hours last night writing a letter to you and explaining why that tree should be spared. I have just posted that letter. Will you please spare the tree till you receive my letter and read it? Will you promise that?"

There was silence for a moment and then I heard him yawning. A reassuring sound. "All right, Anna," he said. "Don't worry about that tree. It will not be cut without your permission. But how are you feeling? Are you all right?"

"I'm all right," I said, so relieved that I felt like singing. "I came back from Mahabaleshwar only yesterday after spending five very happy days there. It's a lovely place, Moni, you must all come there for a few days, as my guests. And wait for my letter, please, read it and try to understand what I feel."

When I came out of the booth it started drizzling. The first showers of the year. I used to love them in my childhood but here in Bombay they came washing down all the soot and dirt in the air and left indelible marks on your clothes. So I waited for the drizzle to subside, and then walked home with a light heart.

It started raining quite heavily after I reached home. That wonderful warm smell—the aroma the parched earth emits when the first showers drench it—came wafting in, and with it came that line from Herbert I had recollected a few weeks earlier: *And now in age I bud again*. But this time I remembered the entire stanza:

> *And now in age I bud again,*
> *After so many deaths I live and write;*
> *I once more smell the dew and rain,*
> *And relish versing: O my only light,*
> *It cannot be*
> *That I am he*
> *On whom thy tempests fell at night.*

I must write, I said to myself. Some years earlier Satish had brought a typewriter for me from America. He had met one of my former students who had told him that I was one of the few genuinely creative persons she had come across. "God, the way he could bring a poem to life in the class, and set our nerves tingling!" she had said. "But why doesn't he write? Why is he wasting his life, spending all his creative energies in lecturing to insensitive students?" So Satish had bought that typewriter. "I want you to write, Mawa," he said.

"Why are you wasting your creativity?" "I'm not wasting it," I said, "Nothing is wasted that is used. What's wrong if one's lectures are creative?" "But lectures are just air," he said, "impermanent." "So is music," I said, "specially Indian music, which is not written down. Why did all those great singers of the past devote their lives to music when there were no facilities even to record what they sang?" Satish shook his head. "Are you telling me" he said, "that you have, in the classroom, the kind of artistic freedom a musician has? Can you sing your song without bothering about the need to prepare your students for the exam and so on?" "Everything has its limitations," I had said then. "All freedom is circumscribed. And I have my own limitations too. The fact that I put my heart and soul into my lectures—and achieve creativity sometimes— does not necessarily mean that I can also write. No, Satish, I have tried writing and have failed. By my own standards. And another thing. When I lecture I only waste my breath, which is expendable. Why should I waste precious paper by writing and publishing something worthless?"

That was what I had thought all along, but on that day I felt a strong urge that I should write. An inner voice said, you must write now. That smell from the parched earth drinking in rain demanded it. Those lines from Herbert said: You must bud again, you must live and write.

The urge was so strong that I took my typewriter out and sat in front of it.

But what should I write? At first I thought of one of those stories I had written in my head during the chicken pox attack. But no, there was no fun, no surprise or excitement in copying stories already composed. I did not want to become a mere scribe, a typist. The urge was to write something new, to create, to explore.

As I sat relaxed and expectant, I saw a vision. It was hazy and shimmering, like a submarine scene seen by a scuba diver. I saw a tree, and in its shade a boy reading. Then I saw the boy hacking the tree with a hatchet. I watched that scene, cold and remote, without anguish, and realized that this was what I should write on: the story of that tree and of the boy who loved it.

From outside came the confused noise of children laughing and shouting. A rain dance was going on near my balcony and I could clearly discern Harshad's excited screams of delight among the medley of sounds. For a moment I thought of going to the balcony to look at the fun but decided against it. I wanted to begin my story straightaway.

I wondered what kind of a story it would turn out to be. What I had in mind was a short story but I knew that stories had their own pattern of growth, and though one could try to shape them by judicious trimming, one could never completely control their growth. Perhaps mine would grow into a novel. A novel in which I could review the events of my life, and examine, with honesty, their causes and hidden sources. If I could do that, and turn myself into the reader of my own life, perhaps then that corrosive feeling of self-pity would change to compassion; and I could, like Yeats, "measure the lot; forgive myself the lot!"

I was so immersed in my brooding that I did not notice when Harshad walked in.

The rain had stopped. Someone had towelled him dry and he looked fresh and clean. He stood near me, shivered a little and said: "What are you typing, uncle?"

"I am writing a story," I said.

"Wow," he said, "Is it going to be a long story? What is it about?"

"I don't know," I said. "Maybe it will be a short story. Or perhaps it will grow long and become a novel. It will be about a boy and a tree. A suragi tree. I am going to tell my own story, Harshad."

"Your story, uncle?" he said, quite excited. "Will you be writing about me?"

"I don't think so," I said and he looked disappointed. But there was no way, I said to myself, just no way I could know right then who or what would enter the story, or how long it would grow and what shape it would ultimately take. Little Harshad had no place in the story I envisioned but visions that bred stories were dynamic, not static. Maybe he would come crawling up the stairs and scratch on the door of the story, and it would open to let him in.

So I put the Caps Lock on, and with Harshad looking over my shoulder and spelling out the words, I typed the title: THE SURAGI TREE.